MILES IN LOVE

Lois McMaster Bujold

Baen Books by Lois McMaster Bujold

MILES IN LOVE

Lois McMaster Bujold

MILES IN LOVE

This is a work of fiction. All the characters and events portrayed in this book are fictional, and any resemblance to real people or incidents is purely coincidental.

Komarr copyright © 1998, *A Civil Campaign* copyright © 1999, *Winterfair Gifts* copyright © 2006; all by Lois McMaster Bujold

All rights reserved, including the right to reproduce this book or portions thereof in any form

A Baen Book

Baen Publishing Enterprises
P.O. Box 1403
Riverdale, NY 10471
www.baen.com

ISBN 10: 1-4165-5522-6
ISBN 13: 978-1-4165-5522-3

Cover art by Alan Pollack

First Baen hardcover printing, February 2008

Distributed by Simon & Schuster
1230 Avenue of the Americas
New York, NY 10020

Library of Congress Cataloging-in-Publication Data:

Printed in the United States of America

10 9 8 7 6 5 4 3 2 1

DEDICATION

For Jane, Charlotte,
Georgette, and Dorothy—
long may they rule.

CONTENTS

Komarr

Chapter One

The last gleaming sliver of Komarr's true-sun melted out of sight beyond the low hills on the western horizon. Lagging behind it in the vault of the heavens, the reflected fire of the solar mirror sprang out in brilliant contrast to the darkening, purple-tinged blue. When Ekaterin had first viewed the hexagonal soletta-array from downside on Komarr's surface, she'd immediately imagined it as a grand Winterfair ornament, hung in the sky like a snowflake made of stars, benign and consoling. She leaned now on her balcony overlooking Serifosa Dome's central city park, and gravely studied the lopsided spray of light through the glassy arc overhead. It sparkled deceptively in contrast to the too-dark sky. Three of the six disks of the star-flake shone not at all, and the central seventh was occluded and dull.

Ancient Earthmen, she had read, had taken alterations in the clockwork procession of their heavens—comets, novae, shooting stars—for disturbing omens, premonitions of disasters natural or political; the very word, *disaster*, embedded the astrological source of the concept. The collision two weeks ago of an out-of-control inner-system ore freighter with the insolation mirror that supplemented Komarr's solar energy was surely most literally a disaster, instantly so for the half-dozen Komarran members of the soletta's station-keeping crew who had been killed. But it seemed to be playing out in slow motion thereafter; it had so far barely affected the sealed arcologies that housed the planet's population. Below her, in the park, a crew of workers was arranging supplemental lighting on high girders. Similar stopgap measures in the city's food-producing greenhouses must be nearly complete, to spare them and this equipment to such an ornamental task. No, she reminded herself; no vegetation in the dome was merely ornamental. Each added its bit to the biological reservoir that ultimately supported life here. The gardens in the domes would live, cared for by their human symbiotes.

Outside the arcologies, in the fragile plantations that labored to bio-transform a world, it was another question altogether. She knew the math, discussed nightly at her dinner table for two weeks, of the percentage loss of insolation at the equator. Days gone winter-cloudy—except that they were planetwide, and going on and on, until when? When would repairs be complete? When would they *start*, for that matter? As sabotage, if it had been sabotage, the destruction was inexplicable; as half-sabotage, doubly inexplicable. *Will they try again?* If it was a *they* at all, ghastly malice and not mere ghastly accident.

She sighed, and turned away from the view, and switched on the spotlights she'd put up to supplement her own tiny balcony garden. Some of the Barrayaran plants she'd started were particularly touchy about their illumination. She checked the light with a meter, and shifted two boxes of deerslayer vine closer to the source, and set the timers. She moved about, checking soil temperature and moisture with sensitive and practiced fingers, watering sparingly where needed. Briefly, she considered moving her old bonsai'd skellytum indoors, to provide it with more controlled conditions, but it was all indoors here on Komarr, really. She hadn't felt wind in her hair for nearly a year. She felt an odd twinge of identification with the transplanted ecology outside, slowly starving for light and heat, suffocating in a toxic atmosphere . . . *Stupid. Stop it. We're lucky to be here.*

"Ekaterin!" Her husband's inquiring bellow echoed, muffled, inside the residence tower.

She poked her head through the door to the kitchen. "I'm on the balcony."

"Well, come down here!"

She set her gardening tools in the box seat, closed the lid, sealed the transparent doors behind her, and hurried across the room into the hall and down the circular staircase. Tien was standing impatiently beside the double doors from their apartment to the building's corridor, a comm link in his hand.

"Your uncle just called. He's landed at the shuttleport. I'll get him."

"I'll get Nikolai, and go with you."

"Don't bother, I'm just going to meet him at the West Station locks. He said to tell you, he's bringing a guest. Another Auditor, some sort of assistant to him, it sounded like. But he said not to worry, they'll both take pot luck. He seemed to imagine we'd feed them in the kitchen or something. Eh! *Two* Imperial Auditors. Why ever did you have to invite him, anyway?"

She stared at him in dismay. "How can my Uncle Vorthys come to Komarr and not see us? Besides, you can't say your department isn't affected by what he's investigating. Naturally he wants to see it. I thought you liked him."

He slapped his hand arhythmically on his thigh. "Back when he was just the old weird Professor, sure. Eccentric Uncle Vorthys, the Vor tech. This Imperial appointment of his took the whole family by surprise. I can't imagine what favors he called in to get it."

Is that your only idea of how men advance? But she did not speak the weary thought aloud. "Of all political appointments, surely Imperial Auditor is the least likely to be gained that way," she murmured.

"Naïve Kat." He smiled shortly, and hugged her around the shoulders. "No one gets something for nothing in Vorbarr Sultana. Except, perhaps, your uncle's assistant, whom I gather is closely related to *the* Vorkosigan. He apparently got his appointment for breathing. Incredibly young for the job, if he's the one I heard about who was sworn in at Winterfair. A lightweight, I presume, although all your Uncle Vorthys said was that he was sensitive about his height and not to mention it. At least some part of this mess promises to be a show."

He tucked his comm link away in his tunic pocket. His hand was shaking slightly. Ekaterin grasped his wrist and turned it over. The tremula increased. She raised her eyes, dark with worry, in silent question to his.

"No, dammit!" He jerked his arm away. "It's not starting. I'm just a little tense. And tired. And hungry, so see if you can't pull together a decent meal by the time we're back. Your uncle may have prole tastes, but I can't imagine they're shared by a Vorbarr Sultana lordling." He thrust his hands into his trouser pockets and looked away from her unhappy frown.

"You're older now than your brother was then."

"Variable onset, remember? We'll go soon. I promise."

"Tien . . . I wish you'd give up this galactic treatment plan. They have medical facilities here on Komarr that are almost as good as, as Beta Colony or anywhere. I thought, when you won this post here, that you would. Forget the secrecy, just go openly for help. Or go discreetly, if you insist. But don't wait any longer!"

"They're not discreet enough. My career is finally on course, finally paying off. I have no desire to be publicly branded a mutant *now.*"

If I don't care, what does it matter what anyone else thinks? She hesitated. "Is that why you don't want to see Uncle Vorthys? Tien, he's the least likely of my relatives—or yours, for that matter—to care if your disease is genetic or not. He will care about you, and about Nikolai."

"I have it under control," he insisted. "Don't you dare betray me to your uncle, this close to the real payoff. I have it under control. You'll see."

"Just don't . . . take your brother's way out. Promise me!" The lightflyer accident that hadn't been quite an accident: that had ushered in these years of chronic, subclinical nightmare waiting and watching. . . .

"I have no intention of doing anything like that. It's all planned. I'll finish out this year's appointment, then we'll take a long overdue galactic vacation, you and me and Nikolai. And it will all be fixed, and no one will ever know. If *you* don't lose your head and panic at the last minute!" He grasped her hand, and grimaced an unfelt smile, and strode out the doors.

Wait and I'll fix it. Trust me. That's what you said the last time. And the time before that, and the time before that. . . . Who is betrayed? Tien, you're running out of time, can't you see it?

She turned for her kitchen, mentally revising her planned family dinner to include a Vor lord from the Imperial capital. White wine? Her limited experience of the breed suggested that if you could get them sufficiently sloshed, it wouldn't matter what you fed them. She put another of her precious imported-from-home bottles in to chill. No . . . make that two more bottles.

She added another place to the table on the balcony off the kitchen that they routinely used for a dining room, sorry now she'd not engaged a servitor for the evening. But human servants on Komarr were so expensive. And she'd wanted this bubble of domestic privacy with Uncle Vorthys. Even the staid official newsvid reps were badgering everyone involved in the investigation; the arrival of not one but two Imperial Auditors on-site in Komarr orbit had not calmed the fever of speculation, but only redirected it. When she'd first spoken with him shortly after his arrival on-site, on a distance-delayed channel that defeated any attempt at long conversation, normally-patient Uncle Vorthys's description of the public briefings into which he'd been roped had been notably irritated. He'd hinted he would be glad to escape them. Since his years of teaching must have inured him to stupid questions, Ekaterin wondered if the true source of his irritation was that he couldn't answer them.

But mostly, she had to admit, she just wanted to recapture the flavor of a happier past, greedily for herself. She'd lived with Aunt and Uncle Vorthys for two years after her mother had died, attending the Imperial University under their casual supervision. Life with the Professor and the Professora had somehow been less constrained, and constraining, than in her father's conservative Vor household in the South Continent frontier town of her birth; perhaps because they'd treated her as the adult she aspired to be, rather than the child she had been. She'd felt, a bit guiltily, closer to them than to her real parent. For a while, any future had seemed possible.

Then she'd chosen Etienne Vorsoisson, or he had chosen her . . . *You were pleased enough at the time.* She'd said *Yes* to the marriage arrangements her father's Baba had offered, with all good will. *You didn't know. Tien didn't know. Vorzohn's Dystrophy. Nobody's fault.*

Nine-year-old Nikolai bounded into the kitchen. "I'm hungry, Mama. Can I have a piece of that cake?"

She intercepted fast-moving fingers attempting to sample frosting. "You can have a glass of fruit juice."

"Aw . . ." But he accepted the proffered substitute, cannily offered in one of the good wineglasses lined up waiting. He gulped it down, bobbing about as he drank. Excited, or was he picking up parental nerves? *Stop projecting,* she told herself. The boy had spent the last two hours in his room, tinkering intently with his models; he was due to shake out the knots.

"Do you remember Uncle Vorthys?" she asked him. "It's been three years since we visited him."

"Sure." He finished swallowing his snack. "He took me to his laboratory. I thought it would be beakers and bubbly things, but it was all big machines and concrete. Smelled funny, kind of dusty and sharp."

"From the welders and the ozone, that's right," she said, impressed with his recall. She rescued the glass. "Hold out your hand. I want to see how much you have left to grow. Puppies with big paws are supposed to grow up to be big dogs, you know." He held up his hand to hers, and they met, palm to palm. His fingers were within two centimeters of being as long as her own. "Oh, my."

He flashed her a self-conscious, satisfied grin, and stared briefly down at his feet, wriggling them in speculation. His right big toe poked through a new hole in his new sock.

His child-light hair was darkening; it might yet become as brown as hers. He was chest-high to her, though she could have sworn he had been only hip-high about fifteen minutes ago. His eyes were brown like his Da's. His grubby hand—where did he find so much dirt in this dome?—was as steady as his eyes were clear and guileless. *No tremula.*

The early symptoms of Vorzohn's Dystrophy were deceptive, mimicking half a dozen other diseases, and could strike any time from puberty to middle age. *But not today, not Nikolai.*

Not yet.

Sounds from the apartment's entryway, and low-pitched masculine voices, drew them out of her kitchen. Nikolai shot ahead of her. When she arrived behind him, he was already being half picked up by the stout, white-haired man who seemed to fill the space. "Oof!" He stopped short of swinging Nikolai around. "You've grown, Nikki!"

Uncle Vorthys hadn't changed, despite his awe-inspiring new title: same grand nose and big ears, same rumpled, oversized tunic and trousers that always looked slept-in, same deep laugh. He deposited his great-nephew on the flagstones, spared a hug for his niece, which was firmly returned, and bent and felt in his valise. "Something here for you, Nikki, I do believe . . ." Nikolai bounced around him; Ekaterin retreated temporarily to wait her turn.

Tien was shouldering through the door with baggage. Only then did she notice the man standing apart, smiling distantly, watching this homey scene.

She swallowed startlement. He was barely taller than nine-year-old Nikolai, but unmistakably not a child. He had a large head set on a short neck, and a faintly hunched stance; the rest of him looked lean but solid. He wore tunic and trousers in a subtle gray, the tunic open on a fine white shirt, and polished half-boots. His clothing was entirely without the pseudo-military ornamentation usually affected by the high Vor, but the perfection of the fit—it had to be hand-tailored, to fit that odd body—hinted a price Ekaterin didn't dare to estimate.

She was uncertain of his age; not much older than herself, perhaps? There was no gray in the dark hair, but laugh-lines around his eyes, and pain-lines around his mouth, scored his winter-pale skin. He moved stiffly, setting down his valise, wheeling to watch Nikolai monopolize his great-uncle, but did not otherwise appear very crippled. He was not a figure who blended in, but his air was notably unobtrusive. Socially uncomfortable? Ekaterin was recalled abruptly to her duties as a daughter of the Vor.

She advanced to him. "Welcome to my household . . ." ack, Tien hadn't mentioned his *name* " . . . my Lord Auditor."

He held out his hand and captured hers in a perfectly ordinary, businesslike grasp. "Miles Vorkosigan." His hand was dry and warm, smaller than her own, but bluntly masculine; clean nails. "And you, Madame?"

"Oh! Ekaterin Vorsoisson."

He released her hand without kissing it, to her relief. She stared briefly at the top of his head, level with her collarbone, realized he would be speaking to her cleavage, and stepped back a little. He looked up at her, still smiling slightly.

Nikolai was already dragging Uncle Vorthys's larger bag toward the guest room, proudly showing off his strength. Tien properly followed his senior guest. Ekaterin made a rapid recalculation. She couldn't possibly put this Vorkosigan fellow up in Nikolai's room; the child's bed would be such an embarrassingly good fit. Invite an Imperial Auditor to sleep on her living room couch? Hardly. She gestured him to follow her down the opposite hallway, into her planting-room-cum-office. One whole side was given over to a workbench and shelving, crammed with supplies; cascading lighting arrays climbing the corners nourished tender new plantings, in a riotous variety of Earth greens and Barrayaran red-browns. A large open area on the floor fronted a fine wide window.

"We haven't much space," she apologized. "I'm afraid even Barrayaran administrators here must accept what's assigned to them. I'll order in a grav-bed for you, I'm sure they'll have it delivered before dinner's over. But at least the room's private. My uncle snores so magnificently. . . . The bath's just down the hall to the right."

"It's fine," he assured her. He stepped to the window and stared out over the domed park. The lights in the encircling buildings gleaming warmly in the luminous twilight of the half-eclipsed mirror.

"I know it's not what you're used to."

One corner of his mouth twitched up. "I once slept for six weeks on bare dirt. With ten thousand extremely grubby Marilacans, many of whom snored. I assure you, it's just fine."

She smiled in return, not at all certain what to make of this joke, if it was a joke. She left him to arrange his things as he saw fit, and scurried to call the rental company and finish setting up dinner.

They all rendezvoused, despite her best intentions for a more formal service, in her kitchen, where the little Auditor foiled her expectations again by only allowing her to pour him half a glass of wine. "I started today with seven hours in a pressure suit. I'd be asleep with my face in my plate before dessert." His gray eyes glinted.

She herded them all out to the table on the balcony and presented the mildly spicy stew based on vat-protein that she'd correctly guessed her uncle would like. By the time she handed round the bread and wine, she'd at last caught up enough to finally have a word with her uncle herself.

"What's happening now with your investigation? How long can you stay?"

"Not much more than what you've heard on the news, I'm afraid," he replied. "We can only take this downside break while the probable-cause crews finish collecting the pieces. We're still missing some fairly important ones. The freighter's tow was fully loaded, and had a tremendous mass. When the engines blew, bits of all sizes vectored off in every possible direction and speed. We desperately want any parts of its control systems we can find. They should have most of it retrieved in three more days, if we're lucky."

"So was it deliberate sabotage?" Tien asked.

Uncle Vorthys shrugged. "With the pilot dead, it's going to be very hard to prove. It might have been a suicide mission. The crews have found no sign yet of military or chemical explosives."

"Explosives would have been redundant," murmured Vorkosigan.

"The spinning freighter hit the mirror array at the worst possible angle, edge-on," Uncle Vorthys continued. "Half the damage was done by parts of the mirror itself. With that much momentum imparted to it by the assorted collisions, it just ripped itself apart."

"If all that result was planned, it had to have been a truly amazing calculation," Vorkosigan said dryly. "It's the one thing which inclines me to the belief it might have been a true accident."

Ekaterin watched her husband, watching the little Auditor covertly, and read the silent disturbed judgment, *Mutant!* in his eyes. What was Tien going to make of the man, who openly bore, without apparent apology or even self-consciousness, such stigmata of abnormality?

Tien turned to Vorkosigan, his gaze curious. "I can see why Emperor Gregor dispatched the Professor, the Empire's foremost authority on failure analysis and all that. What's, um, your part in this, Lord Auditor Vorkosigan?"

Vorkosigan's smile twisted. "I have some experience with space installations." He leaned back, and jerked up his chin, and smoothed the odd flash of irony from his face. "In fact, as far as the probable-cause investigation goes, I'm merely along for the ride. This is the first really interesting problem to come along since I took oath as an Auditor three months ago. I wanted to watch how it was done. With his Komarran marriage coming up, Gregor is vitally interested in any possible political repercussions from this accident. Now would be a very awkward time for a serious downturn in Barrayar-Komarr relations. But whether accident or sabotage, the damage to the mirror impinges quite directly on the Terraforming Project. I understand your Serifosa Sector is fairly representative?"

"Indeed. I'll take you both on a tour tomorrow," Tien promised. "I'm having a full technical report prepared for you by my Komarran assistants, with all the numbers. But the most important number is still pure speculation. How fast is the mirror going to be repaired?"

Vorkosigan grimaced and held out a small hand, palm-up. "How fast depends in part on how much money the Imperium is willing to spend. And that's where things become very political indeed. With parts of Barrayar itself still undergoing active terraforming, and with the planet of Sergyar drawing off immigrants from both the worlds damned near as fast as they can board ship, some members of the government are wondering openly why we are spending so much Imperial treasure dinking with such a marginal world as Komarr."

Ekaterin could not tell from his measured tone whether he agreed with those members or not. Startled, she said, "The terraforming of Komarr was going on for three centuries before we conquered it. We can hardly stop *now.*"

"So are we throwing good money after bad?" Vorkosigan shrugged, declining to answer his own question. "There's a second layer of thinking, a purely military one. Restricting the population to the domes makes Komarr more militarily vulnerable. Why give the citizenry of a conquered world extra territory in which to fall back and regroup? This line of thought makes the interesting assumption that three hundred or so years from *now,* when the terraforming is at last complete, the populations of Komarr and Barrayar will still not have assimilated each other. If they did, then they would be *our* domes, and we certainly wouldn't want them to be vulnerable, eh?"

He paused for a bite of bread and stew, washed down by wine, then went on, "Since assimilation is Gregor's avowed policy, and he's putting his Imperial person where his policy is . . . the question of motivation for sabotage becomes, er, complex. Could the saboteurs have been isolationist Barrayarans? Komarran extremists? Either, hoping to publicly throw the blame on the other? How emotionally attached is the average Komarran-in-the-dome to a goal whom none now living will ever survive to see realized, or would they rather save the money today? Sabotage versus accident makes no engineering difference, but does make a profound political one." He and Uncle Vorthys exchanged a wry look.

"So I watch, and listen, and wait," Vorkosigan concluded. He turned to Tien. "And how do you like Komarr, Administrator Vorsoisson?"

Tien grinned, and shrugged. "It's all right except for the Komarrans. I've found them a damned touchy bunch."

Vorkosigan's brows twitched up. "Have they no sense of humor?"

Ekaterin glanced up warily, wincing at that dry edge in his drawling voice, but apparently it slipped past Tien, who only snorted. "They're divided about equally between the greedy and the surly. Cheating Barrayarans is considered a patriotic duty."

Vorkosigan raised his empty wineglass to Ekaterin. "And you, Madame Vorsoisson?"

She refilled it to the top before he could stop her, cautious of her reply. If her uncle was the technical expert in this Auditorial duo, did that leave Vorkosigan as the . . . political one? Who was really the senior member of the team? Had Tien caught any of the subtle flashing implications in the little lord's speech? "It hasn't been easy to make Komarran friends. Nikolai goes to a Barrayaran school. And I have no work as such."

"A Vor lady hardly needs to work." Tien smiled.

"Nor a Vor lord," added Vorkosigan, almost under his breath, "yet here we are . . ."

"That depends on your ability to choose the right parents," said Tien, a touch sourly. He glanced across at Vorkosigan. "Relieve my curiosity. *Are* you related to the former Lord Regent?"

"My father," Vorkosigan replied, with quelling brevity. He did not smile.

"Then you are *the* Lord Vorkosigan, the Count's heir."

"That follows, yes."

Vorkosigan was getting unnervingly dry, now. Ekaterin blurted, "Your upbringing must have been terribly difficult."

"He managed," Vorkosigan murmured.

"I meant for you!"

"Ah." His brief smile returned, and flicked out again.

The conversation was going dreadfully awry, Ekaterin could feel it; she hardly dared open her mouth on an attempt to redirect it. Tien stepped in, or stepped in it: "Was your father the great Admiral reconciled that you couldn't have a military career?"

"My grandfather the great General was more set on it."

"I was a ten-years man myself, the usual. In Administration, very dull. Trust me, you didn't miss much." Tien waved a kindly, dismissive hand. "But not every Vor has to be a soldier these days, eh, Professor Vorthys? You're living proof."

"I believe Captain Vorkosigan served, um, thirteen years, was it, Miles? In Imperial Security. Galactic operations. Did you find it dull?"

Vorkosigan's smile upon the Professor grew genuine, for an instant of time. "Not nearly dull enough." He jerked up his chin, evidently a habitual nervous tic. For the first time Ekaterin noticed the fine white scars on either side of his short neck.

Ekaterin fled to the kitchen, to serve the dessert and give the blighted conversation time to recover. When she came out again, things had eased, or at least, Nikolai had stopped being so supernaturally good, i.e., quiet, and had struck up a negotiation with his great-uncle for after-dinner attention in the form of a round of his current favorite game. This carried them through till the rental company arrived at the front door with the grav-bed, and the great engineer went off with the whole male mob to oversee its installation. Ekaterin turned gratefully to the soothing routine of cleaning up.

Tien returned to report success and the Vor lord suitably settled.

"Tien, were you watching that fellow closely?" asked Ekaterin. "A mutie, a mutie *Vor*, yet he carried on as if nothing were the least out of the ordinary. If he can . . ." she trailed off hopefully, leaving the *surely you can* for Tien to conclude.

Tien frowned. "Don't start that again. It's obvious he doesn't think the rules apply to him. He's Aral Vorkosigan's *son*, for God's sake. Practically the Emperor's foster brother. No wonder he got this cushy Imperial appointment."

"I don't think so, Tien. Were you listening to him at all?" *All those undercurrents* . . . "I think . . . I think he's the Emperor's hatchet man, sent to judge the whole Terraforming Project. Powerful . . . maybe dangerous."

Tien shook his head. "His father was powerful and dangerous. He's just privileged. Damned high Vor twit. Don't worry about him. Your uncle will take him away soon enough."

"I'm not worried about *him*."

Tien's face darkened. "I'm getting so tired of this! You argue with everything I say, you practically insult my intelligence in front of your so-noble relative—"

"I didn't!" *Did I?* She began a confused mental review of her evening's remarks. What in the world had she said, to set him on edge like this—

"Just because you're the great Auditor's niece doesn't make *you* anybody, girl! This is disloyalty, that's what it is."

"No—no, I'm sorry—"

But he was already stalking out. There would be a cold silence between them tonight. She almost ran after him, to beg his forgiveness. He was under a lot of pressure at work, it was very ill-timed of her to push for a resolution to his medical dilemma now. . . .

But she was abruptly too weary to try anymore. She finished putting away the last of the food, and took the leftover half bottle of wine and a glass out onto the balcony. She turned off the cheery colored plant lights and just sat in the dim reflected illumination from the sealed Komarran city. The crippled star-flake of the insolation mirror had almost reached the western horizon, following the true-sun into night as the planet turned.

A white shape moved silently in the kitchen, briefly startling her. But it was only the mutie lord, who had shed his elegant gray tunic and, apparently, his boots. He stuck his head through the unsealed doors. "Hello?"

"Hello, Lord Vorkosigan. I'm just out here watching the mirror set. Would you, um, care for some more wine . . . ? Here, I'll get you a glass—"

"No, don't get up, Madame Vorsoisson. I'll fetch it." His pale smile winked out of the shadows at her. A few muted clinks came from within, then he trod silently onto the balcony. She poured, good hostess, generously into the glass he set beside her own, then he took it up again and went to the railing to study what could be seen of the sky past the girders of the dome.

"It's the best aspect of this location," she said. "This bit of western view." The mirror-array was magnified by the atmosphere close to the horizon, but its normal evening color-effects in the wispy clouds were dimmed by its damage. "Mirror-set's usually much prettier than this." She sipped her wine, cool and sweet on her tongue, and felt herself finally starting to become a little furry in the brain. Furry was good. Soothing.

"I can see that it must be," he agreed, still staring out. He drank deeply. Had he switched, then, from resisting sleep through alcohol to pursuing it?

"This horizon is so crowded and cluttered, compared to home. I'm afraid I find these sealed arcologies a touch claustrophobic."

"And where is home, for you?" He turned to watch her.

"South Continent. Vandeville."

"So you grew up around terraforming."

"The Komarrans would say, that wasn't terraforming, that was just *soil conditioning*." He chuckled along with her, at her deadpan rendition of Komarran techno-snobbery. She continued, "They're right, of course. It wasn't as though we had to start by spending half a millennium altering an entire planet's atmosphere. The only thing that made it hard for us, back in the Time of Isolation, was trying to do it with practically no technology. Still . . . I loved the open spaces at home. I miss that wide sky, horizon to horizon."

"That's true in any city, domed or not. So you're a country girl?"

"In part. Though I liked Vorbarr Sultana when I was at university. It had other kinds of horizons."

"Did you study botany? I noticed the library rack on the wall of your plant room. Impressive."

"No. It's just a hobby."

"Oh? I could have mistaken it for a passion. Or a profession."

"No. I didn't know what I wanted, then."

"Do you know now?"

She laughed a little, uneasily. When she didn't answer, he merely smiled, and strolled along the balcony examining her plantings. He stopped before the skellytum, squatting in its pot like some bright red alien Buddha, tendrils raised in a pose of placid supplication. "I have to ask," he said plaintively, "what *is* this thing?"

"It's a bonsai'd skellytum."

"Really! *That's* a—I didn't know you could do that to a skellytum. They're usually five meters tall. And a really ugly brown."

"I had a great aunt, on my father's side, who loved gardening. I used to help her when I was a girl. She was very much a crusty old frontier woman, *very* Vor—she'd come to the South Continent right after the Cetagandan War. Survived a succession of husbands, survived . . . well, everything. I inherited the skellytum from her. It's the only plant I brought to Komarr from Barrayar. It's over seventy years old."

"Good God."

"It's the complete tree, fully functional."

"And—ha!—short."

She was afraid for a moment that she'd inadvertently offended him, but apparently not. He finished his inspection, and returned to the railing, and his wine. He stared out again at the western horizon, and the sinking mirror, his brows lowering.

He had a presence which, by ignoring his elusive physical peculiarities himself, defied the observer to dare comment. But the little lord had had all his life to adjust to his condition. Not like the hideous surprise Tien had found among his late brother's papers, and subsequently confirmed for himself and Nikolai through carefully secret testing. *You can get tested anonymously,* she had argued. *But I can't get treated anonymously,* he had countered.

Since coming to Komarr, she'd been so close to defying custom, law, and her lord-and-husband's orders, and unilaterally taking his son and heir for treatment. Would the Komarran doctors know a Vor mother was not her son's legal guardian? Maybe she could pretend the genetic defect had come from her, not from Tien? But the geneticists, if they were any good, would surely figure out the truth.

After a while, she said elliptically, "A Vor man's first loyalty is supposed to be to his Emperor, but a Vor woman's first loyalty is supposed to be to her husband."

"Historically and legally, that's so." His voice was amused, or bemused, as he turned again to watch her. "This was not always to her disadvantage. When he was executed for treason, she was presumed to be only following orders, and got off. Actually, I wonder if the underlying practical reason was that an underpopulated world just couldn't spare her labor."

"Haven't you ever found that oddly asymmetrical?"

"But simpler for her. Most women usually only had one husband at a time, but the Vor were all too frequently presented with a choice of emperors, and where was your loyalty then? Bad guesses could be lethal. Though when my grandfather General Piotr—and his army— abandoned Mad Emperor Yuri for Emperor Ezar, it was lethal for Yuri. Good for Barrayar, though."

She sipped again. From where she sat, he was silhouetted against the darkening dome, shadowed, enigmatic. "Indeed. Is your passion politics, then?"

"God, no! I don't think so."

"History?"

"Only in passing." He hesitated. "It used to be the military."

"Used to be?"

"Used to be," he repeated firmly.

"And now?"

It was his turn to not answer. He stared down at his glass, tilting it to make the last of the wine swirl about. He finally said, "In Barrayaran political theory, it all connects. The ordinary subjects are loyal to their Counts, the Counts are loyal to the Emperor, and the Emperor, presumably, is loyal to the whole Imperium, the body of the Empire in the form of all its, er, bodies. Here I find it grows a trifle abstract for my taste; how can he be answerable to all, yet not answerable to each? And so we arrive back at square one." He drained his glass. "How do we be true to one another?"

I don't know anymore. . . .

Silence fell, as they both watched the last glint of mirror slip behind the hills. A pale glow in the sky still haloed its passing for a minute or two longer.

"Well. I'm afraid I'm getting rather drunk." He did not seem that drunk to her, but he rolled his glass between his hands and pushed off from the balcony rail against which he'd been leaning. "Goodnight, Madame Vorsoisson."

"Goodnight, Lord Vorkosigan. Sleep well."

He carried his glass in with him and vanished into the darkened apartment.

Chapter Two

Miles floundered from a dream of his hostess's hair which, if not exactly erotic, was embarrassingly sensual. Unbound from the severe style she'd favored yesterday, it had revealed itself a rich dark brown with amber highlights, a mass of silk flowing coolly through his stubby hands—he presumed they were his hands, it had been his dream, after all. *I woke up too soon. Rats.* At least the vision had not been tinged with any of the gory grotesqueries of his occasional nightmares, from which he came awake cold and damp, with heart racing. He was warm and comfortable, in the silly elaborate grav-bed she had insisted on producing for him.

It wasn't Madame Vorsoisson's fault that she happened to belong to a certain physical type that set off old resonances in Miles's memory. Some men harbored obsessions about much stranger things . . . his own fixation, he had long ago ruefully recognized, was on long cool brunettes with expressions of quiet reserve and warm alto voices. True, on a world where people altered their faces and bodies almost as casually as they altered their wardrobes, there was nothing in the least unusual about her beauty. Till one remembered she wasn't from here, and realized her ivory-skinned features were almost certainly untouched by modification. . . . Had she recognized his idiot-babble, last night on her balcony, as suppressed sexual panic? Had that odd remark about a Vor woman's duties been an oblique warning to him to back off? But he hadn't been *on*, he didn't think. Was he that transparent?

Miles had realized within five minutes of his arrival that he should probably not have let the genial and expansive Vorthys bully him into accompanying him downside, but the man seemed constitutionally incapable of not sharing a treat. That the pleasures of this family reunion might not be equally enjoyed by an awkward outsider—or the family into which he'd been thrust—had clearly never occurred to the Professor.

Miles sighed envy of his host. Administrator Vorsoisson seemed to have achieved a perfect little Vor clan. Of course, he'd had the wit to start a decade ago. The arrival of galactic sex-selection technologies had resulted in a shortage of female births on Barrayar. This dearth of women had reached its lowest ebb in Miles's generation, though parents seemed to be coming back to their senses now. Still, every Vor woman Miles knew close to his own age was already married, and had been for years. Was he going to have to wait another twenty years for his own bride?

If necessary. No lusting after married women, boy. You're an Imperial Auditor now. The nine Imperial Auditors were expected to be models of rectitude and respectability. He could not recall ever hearing of any kind of sex scandal touching one of Emperor Gregor's handpicked agent-observers. *Of course not. All the rest of the Auditors are eighty years old and have been married for fifty of 'em.* He snorted. Besides, she probably thought he was a mutant, though thankfully she'd been too polite to say so. To his face.

So find out if she has a sister, eh?

He wallowed out of the grav-bed's indolence-inducing clutches and sat up, forcing his mind to switch gears. At a conservative guess, a couple hundred thousand words of new data on the soletta accident and its consequences would be incoming this shift. He would, he decided, start with a cold shower.

No comfortable ship-knits today. After selecting among the three new formal civilian suits he'd packed along from Barrayar—in shades of gray, gray, and gray—Miles combed his damp hair neatly and sauntered out to Madame Vorsoisson's kitchen, from which voices and the perfume of coffee wafted. There he found Nikolai munching Barrayaran-style groats and milk, Administrator Vorsoisson fully dressed and apparently on the verge of leaving, and

Professor Vorthys, still in pajamas, sorting through a new array of data disks and frowning. A glass of pink fruit juice sat untasted at his elbow. He looked up and said, "Ah, good morning, Miles. Glad you're up," seconded by Vorsoisson's polite, "Good morning, Lord Vorkosigan. I trust you slept well?"

"Fine, thanks. What's up, Professor?"

"Your comm link arrived from ImpSec's local office." Vorthys pointed to the device beside his plate. "I notice they didn't send *me* one."

Miles grimaced. "Your father was not so famous in the Komarran conquest."

"True," agreed Vorthys. "The old gentleman fell in that odd generation between the wars, too young to fight the Cetagandans, too old to aggress on the poor Komarrans. This lack of military opportunity was a source of great personal regret to him, we children were given to understand."

Miles strapped the comm link onto his left wrist. It represented a compromise between himself and ImpSec Serifosa, which would otherwise be responsible for his health here. ImpSec had wanted to err on the side of caution and surround him with an inconvenient mob of bodyguards. Miles had ventured to test his Imperial Auditor's authority by ordering them to stay out of his hair; to his delight, it had worked. But the link gave him a straight line to ImpSec, and tracked his location—he tried not to feel like an experimental animal released into the wild. "And what are those?" He nodded to the data disks.

Vorthys spread the disks like a bad hand of cards. "The morning courier also brought us recordings of last night's haul of new bits. And something especially for you, since you kindly volunteered to take over the review of the medical end of things. A new preliminary autopsy."

"They finally found the pilot?" Miles relieved him of the disks.

Vorthys grimaced. "Parts of her."

Madame Vorsoisson entered from the balcony in time to hear this. "Oh, dear." She was dressed as yesterday in Komarran-style street wear in dull earthy tones: loose trousers, blouse, and long vest, muffling whatever figure she possessed. She would have been brilliant in red, or breathtaking in pale blue, with those blue eyes . . . her hair this morning was soberly tied back again, rather to Miles's relief. It would have been unnerving to think he was developing some form of precognition as a result of his late injuries, along with his damned seizures.

Miles nodded good morning to her and carefully returned his attention to Vorthys. "I must have been sleeping well. I didn't hear the courier come in. You've reviewed them already?"

"Just a glance."

"What parts of the pilot did they find?" asked Nikolai, interested.

"Never you mind, young man," said his great-uncle firmly.

"Thank you," murmured Madame Vorsoisson to him.

"That makes the last body, though. Good," said Miles. "It's so distressing for the relatives when they lose one altogether. When I was—" He cut off the rest, *When I was a covert ops fleet commander, we'd move the heavens to try and get the bodies of our casualties back to their people.* That chapter of his life was closed, now.

Madame Vorsoisson, splendid woman, handed him black coffee. She then inquired what her guests would like for breakfast; Miles maneuvered Vorthys into answering first, and volunteered for groats along with him. As she bustled around serving, and mopping up after Nikolai, Administrator Vorsoisson said, "My department's presentation will be ready for you this afternoon, Auditor Vorthys. This morning Ekaterin wondered if you would like to see Nikolai's school. And after the presentation, perhaps there will be time for a flyover of some of our projects."

"Sounds like a fine itinerary." Professor Vorthys smiled at Nikolai. In all the hustle of their hurried departure from Barrayar, he—or perhaps the Professora—had not forgotten a gift for his great-nephew. *I should have brought something for the kid,* Miles decided belatedly. *Surest way to please a mother.* "Ah, Miles . . .?"

Miles tapped the stack of data disks beside his bowl. "I suspect I'll have enough to occupy myself here this morning. Madame Vorsoisson, I noticed a comconsole in your workroom; may I use it?"

"Certainly, Lord Vorkosigan."

With a polite murmur about getting things in order for them at his department, Vorsoisson took his leave, and the breakfast party broke up shortly thereafter, each to their assorted destinations. Miles, new disks in hand, returned to Madame Vorsoisson's workroom/guest room.

He paused before seating himself at her comconsole, to stare out the sealed window at the park, and the transparent dome arcing over it to let in the free solar energy. Komarr's wan sun was not directly visible, risen to the east behind this apartment block, but the line of its morning light crept across the far edge of the park. The damaged insolation mirror, following it, had not yet risen over the horizon to double the shadows it cast.

So does this mean seven thousand years bad luck?

He sighed, darkened the window's polarization—scarcely necessary—seated himself at the comconsole, and began feeding it data disks. A couple of dozen good-sized new pieces of wreckage had been retrieved overnight; he ran the vids of them turning in space as the salvage ships approached. Theory was, if you could find every fragment, take precise recordings of all their spins and trajectories, and then run them backward, you could end up with a computer-generated picture of the very moment of the disaster, and so diagnose its cause. Real life never worked out quite that neatly, alas, but every little bit helped. ImpSec Komarr was still canvassing the orbital transfer stations for any casual vid-carrying tourists who might have been panning that section of space at the time of the whatever-and-collision. Futilely by now, Miles feared; usually, such people came forward immediately, excited and wanting to be helpful.

Vorthys and the probable-cause crew were now of the opinion that the ore tow had already been in more than one piece at the moment it had struck the mirror, a speculation which had not yet been released to the general public. So had the evidence-destroying explosion of the engines been cause or consequence of that catastrophe? And at what point had those tortured fragments of metal and plastic acquired some of their more interesting distortions?

Miles reran, for the twentieth time that week, the computer's track of the freighter's course prior to the collision, and contemplated its anomalies. The ship had carried only its pilot, on a routine—indeed, dead boring—slow run in from the asteroid mining belt to an orbital refinery. The engines had not been supposed to be thrusting at the time of the accident; acceleration had been completed and deceleration was not yet due to begin. The tow ship had been running about five hours ahead of schedule, but only because it had departed early, not because it had boosted hotter than usual. It had been coasting off-course by about six percent, within normal parameters and not yet ready for course correction, though the pilot might have been amusing herself trying to achieve more precision with some unscheduled microboosting. Even with the minor course correction due, the tow ship's route had been several hundred comfortable kilometers from the soletta array, in fact farther away than if it had been precisely on course.

What the course variation *had* done was take the freighter's track almost directly across one of Komarr's unused wormhole jump points. Komarr local space was unusually rich in active jump points, a fact of strategic and historic consequence; one of the jumps was Barrayar's only gateway to the wormhole nexus. It was for control of the jump points, not for possession of the chilly planet, that Barrayar's invasion fleet had poured through here thirty-five years ago. As long as the Imperium's military held that high ground, its interest in Komarr's downside population and their problems was, at best, mild.

This jump point, however, supported neither traffic nor trade nor strategic threat. Explorations through it had dead-ended either in deep interstellar space, or close to stars that did not support either habitable planets or economically recoverable system resources. Nobody jumped out through there; nobody *should* have jumped in through there. The immediate vision of some unmotivated pirate-villain popping out of the wormhole, potting the innocent ore freighter—by some weapon that left no traces, mind you—and popping back in again was currently unsupported by any evidence whatsoever, though the area had been scoured for it. It was the news media's current favorite scenario. But none of the five-space trails generated by ships taking wormhole jumps had been detected, either.

The five-space anomaly of the jump point was not even observable by ordinary means from three-space; it should not, just sitting there, have affected the freighter in any way even if the ship had passed directly across its central vortex. The freighter was a dedicated inner-system ship, and lacked Necklin rods and jump capacity. Still . . . the jump point was there. Nothing else was.

Miles rubbed his neck and turned to the new autopsy report. Gruesome, as always. The pilot had been a Komarran woman in her mid-fifties. Call it Barrayaran sexism, but female corpses always bothered Miles more. Death was such a malicious destroyer of dignity. Had he looked that disordered and exposed when he'd gone down to the sniper's fire? The pilot's body showed the usual progression: smashed, decompressed, irradiated, and frozen, all quite typical of deep-space impact accidents. One arm torn off, somewhere in the initial crunch rather than later, judging from the close-up vids of the freezing-effects of liquids lost at the stump. It had been a quick death, anyway. Miles knew better than to add, *Almost painless.* No traces of illicit drugs or alcohol had been found in her frozen tissues.

The Komarran medical examiner, along with his six final reports, included a message wanting to know if he had Miles's permission to release the bodies of the six members of the mirror's station-keeping crew back to their waiting families. Good God, hadn't that been done yet? As an Imperial Auditor, he wasn't supposed to be running this investigation, just observing and reporting on it. He did not desire his mere presence to freeze anyone's initiative. He fired off the permission immediately, right from Madame Vorsoisson's comconsole.

He started working his way through the six reports. They were more detailed than the prelims he'd already seen, but contained no surprises. By this time, he wanted a surprise, something, anything beyond *Spaceship blows up for no reason, kills seven.* Not to mention the astronomical property damage bill. With three reports assimilated, and his bland breakfast becoming a regret in his stomach, he backed out for a short period of mental recovery.

Idly, while waiting for the queasiness to pass, he sorted through Madame Vorsoisson's data files. The one titled *Virtual Gardens* sounded pleasant. Perhaps she wouldn't mind if he took a virtual stroll through them. *The Water Garden* enticed him. He called it up on the holovid plate before him.

It was, as he had guessed, a landscape design program. One could view it from any distance or angle, from a miniature-looking total overview to a blown-up detailed inspection of a particular planting; one could program a stroll through its paths at any given eye level. He chose his own, at ahem-mumble-something under five feet. The individual plants grew according to realistic programs taking into account light, water, gravitation, trace nutrients, and even attacks by programmed pests. This garden was about a third filled, with tentative arrangements of grasses, violets, sedges, water lilies, and horsetails; it was currently suffering an outbreak of algae. The colors and shapes stopped abruptly at the unfinished edges, as if an invasion from some alien gray geometric universe were gobbling it all up.

His curiosity piqued, in best approved ImpSec style he dropped to the program's underlayer and checked for activity levels. The busiest recently, he discovered, was one labeled *The Barrayaran Garden.* He popped back up to the display level, selected his own eye-height again, and entered it.

It was not a garden of pretty Earth-plants set on some suitably famous site on Barrayar; it was a garden made up entirely and exclusively of native species, something he would not have guessed possible, let alone lovely. He'd always considered their uniform red-brown hues and stubby forms boring at best. The only Barrayaran vegetation he could identify and name offhand was that to which he was violently allergic. But Madame Vorsoisson had somehow used shape and texture to create a sepia-toned serenity. Rocks and running water framed the various plants—there was a low carmine mass of love-lies-itching, forming a border for a billowing blond stand of razor-grass, which, he had once been assured, botanically was not a grass. Nobody argued about the razor part, he'd noticed. Judging from the common names, the lost Barrayaran colonists had not loved their new xenobotany: damnweed, henbloat, goatbane . . . *It's beautiful. How did she make it beautiful?* He'd never seen anything like it. Maybe that kind of artist's eye was something you just had to be born with, like perfect pitch, which he also lacked.

In the Imperial capital of Vorbarr Sultana, there was a small and dull green park at the end of the block beside Vorkosigan House, on a site where another old mansion had been torn down. The little park had been leveled with more of an eye to security concerns for the neighboring Lord Regent than any aesthetic plan. Would it not be splendid, to replace it with a larger version of this glorious subtlety, and give the city-dwellers a taste of their own planetary heritage? Even if it would—he checked—take fifteen years to grow to this mature climax. . . .

The virtual garden program was supposed to help prevent time-consuming and costly design mistakes. But when all the garden you could have was what you could pack in your luggage, he supposed it could be a hobby in its own right. It was certainly neater, tidier, and easier than the real thing. So . . . why did he guess she found it approximately as satisfying as looking at a holovid of dinner instead of eating it?

Or maybe she's just homesick. Regretfully, he closed down the display.

In pure trained habit, he next called up her financial program, for a little quick analysis. It turned out to be her household account. She ran her home on a quite tight budget, given what Administrator Vorsoisson's salary ought to be, Miles thought; her biweekly allowance was rather stingy. She didn't spend nearly as much on her botanical hobbies as the results suggested she must. Other hobbies, other vices? The money trail was always the most revealing of people's true pursuits; ImpSec hired the Imperium's best accountants to find ingenious ways to hide their own activities, for that very reason. She spent damn little on clothes, except for Nikolai's. He'd heard parents of his acquaintance complain about the cost of dressing their children, but surely this was extraordinary . . . wait, that wasn't a clothing expenditure. Funds squeezed here, here, and there were all being funneled into a dedicated little private account labeled "Nikolai's Medical." Why? As dependents of a Barrayaran bureaucrat on Komarr, weren't the Vorsoissons' medical expenses covered by the Imperium?

He called up the account. A year's worth of savings from her household budget did not make a very impressive pile, but the pattern of contributions was steady to the point of being compulsive. Puzzled, he backed out again and called up the whole program list. Clues?

One file, down at the end of the list, had no name. He called it up immediately. It turned out to be the only thing on her comconsole which required a password for entry. Interesting.

Her comconsole program was the simplest and cheapest commercial type. ImpSec cadets dissected files like this as a class warmup exercise. A touch of homesickness of his own twinged through him. He dropped to the underlayer and had its password choked out in about five minutes. *Vorzohn's Dystrophy?* Well, *that* wasn't a mnemonic he would have guessed offhand.

His reflexes overtook his growing unease. He had the file open simultaneously with belated second thoughts, *You're not in ImpSec anymore, you know. Should you be doing this?*

The file proved to contain a medical course's worth of articles, culled from every imaginable Barrayaran and galactic source, on the topic of one of Barrayar's rarer and more obscure home-grown genetic disorders. Vorzohn's Dystrophy had arisen during the Time of Isolation, principally, as its name suggested, among the Vor caste, but had not been medically identified as a mutation until the return of galactic medicine. For one thing, it lacked the sort of exterior markers that would have caused, well, *him* for example, to have had his throat cut at birth. It was an adult-onset disease, beginning with a bewildering variety of physical debilitations and ending with mental collapse and death. In the harsher world of Barrayar's past, carriers frequently met their deaths from other causes after bearing or engendering children, but before the syndrome manifested itself. Enough madness ran in enough families—*including some of my dear Vorrutyer ancestors*—from other causes that late onset was frequently identified as something else anyway. Thoroughly nasty.

But it's treatable now, isn't it?

Yes, albeit expensively; that went with the rare part, no economies of scale. Miles scanned rapidly down the articles. Symptoms were manageable with a variety of costly biochemical concoctions to flush out and replace the distorted molecules; retrogenetic true cures were available at a higher price. Well, almost true cures: any progeny would still have to be screened for it, preferably at the time of fertilization and before being popped into the uterine replicator for gestation.

Hadn't young Nikolai been gestated in a uterine replicator? Good God, Vorsoisson surely hadn't insisted his wife—and child—go through the dangers of old-fashioned body-gestation, had he? Only a few of the most conservative Old Vor families still held out for the old ways, a custom upon which Miles's own mother had vented the most violently acerbic criticism he'd ever heard from her lips. *And she should know.*

So what the hell is going on here? He sat back, mouth tight. If, as the files suggested, Nikolai was known or suspected to carry Vorzohn's Dystrophy, one or both of his parents must also. How long had they known?

He suddenly realized what he should have noticed before, in the initial illusion of smug marital bliss which Vorsoisson managed to project. That was always the hardest part, seeing the absent pieces. About three more children were missing, that was what. Some little sisters for Nikolai, please, folks? But no. *So they've known at least since shortly after their son was born.* What a personal nightmare. *But is he the carrier, or is she?* He hoped it wasn't Madame

Vorsoisson; horrible to think of that serene beauty crumbling under the onslaught of such internal disruption. . . .

I don't want to know all this.

His idle curiosity was justly punished. This idiot snooping was surely not proper behavior for an Imperial Auditor, however much it had been inculcated in an ImpSec covert ops agent. Former agent. Where was all that shiny new Auditor's probity now? He might as well have been sniffing in her underwear drawer. *I can't leave you alone for a damn minute, can I, boy?*

He'd chafed for years under military regulations, till he'd come to a job with no written regs at all. His sense of having died and gone to heaven had lasted about five minutes. An Imperial Auditor was the Emperor's Voice, his eyes and ears and sometimes hands, a lovely job description till you stopped to wonder just what the hell that poetic metaphor was supposed to *mean.*

So was it a useful test to ask himself, *Can I imagine Gregor doing this or that thing?* Gregor's apparent Imperial sternness hid an almost painful personal shyness. The mind boggled. All right, should the question instead be, *Could I imagine Gregor in his office as Emperor doing this?* Just what acts, wrong for a private individual, were yet lawful for an Imperial Auditor carrying out his duties? Lots, according to the precedents he'd been reading. So was the real rule, "Ad lib till you make a mistake, and then we'll destroy you"? Miles wasn't sure he liked that one at all.

And even in his ImpSec days, slicing through someone's private files had been a treatment reserved for enemies, or at least suspects. Well, and prospective recruits. And neutrals in whose territory you expected to be operating. And . . . and . . . he snorted self-derision. Gregor at least had better manners than ImpSec.

Thoroughly embarrassed, he closed the files, erased all tracks of his entry, and called up the next autopsy report. He studied what telltales he could glean from the bodily fragmentation. Death had a temperature, and it was damned cold. He paused to turn up the workroom's thermostat a few degrees before continuing.

Chapter Three

Ekaterin hadn't realized how much a visit from an Imperial Auditor would fluster the staff of Nikolai's school. But the Professor, a long-time educator himself, quickly made them understand this wasn't an official inspection, and produced all the right phrases to put them at their ease. Still, she and Uncle Vorthys didn't linger as long as Tien had suggested to her.

To burn a bit more time, she took him on a short tour of Serifosa Dome's best spots: the prettiest gardens, the highest observation platforms, looking out across the sere Komarran landscape beyond the sealed urban sprawl. Serifosa was the capital of this planetary Sector—she still had to make an effort not to think of it as a Barrayaran-style District. Barrayaran District boundaries were more organic, higgly-piggly territories following rivers, mountain ranges, and ragged lines where Counts' armies had lost historic battles. Komarran Sectors were neat geometric slices equitably dividing the globe. Though the so-called domes, really thousands of inter-connected structures of all shapes, had lost their early geometries centuries ago, as they were built outward in random and unmatching spurts of architectural improvement.

Somewhat belatedly, she realized she ought to be dragging the engineer emeritus through the deepest utility tunnels, and the power and atmosphere cycling plants. But by then it was time for lunch. Her guided tour fetched up near her favorite restaurant, pseudo-outdoors with tables spilling out into a landscaped park under the glassed-in sky. The damaged soletta-array was now visible, creeping along the ecliptic, veiled today by thin high clouds as if ashamedly hiding its deformations.

The enormous power of the Emperor's Voice conferred upon an Auditor hadn't changed her uncle much, Ekaterin was pleased to note; he still retained his enthusiasm for splendid desserts, and, under her guidance, constructed his menu choices from the sweets course backwards. She couldn't quite say "hadn't changed him at all"; he seemed to have acquired more social caution, pausing for more than just technical calculations before he spoke. But it wasn't as if he could entirely ignore other people's new and exaggerated reactions to him.

They put in their orders, and she followed her uncle's gaze upward as he briefly studied the soletta from this angle. She said, "There's not really a danger of the Imperium abandoning the soletta project, is there? We'll have to at least repair it. I mean . . . it looks so unbalanced like that."

"In fact, it is unbalanced at present. Solar wind. They'll have to do something about that shortly," he replied. "*I* should certainly not like to see it abandoned. It was the greatest engineering achievement of the Komarrans' colonial ancestors, apart from the domes themselves. People at their best. If it was sabotage . . . well, that was certainly people at their worst. Vandalism, just senseless vandalism."

An artist describing the defacement of some great historic painting could hardly have been more vehement. Ekaterin said, "I've heard older Komarrans talk about how they felt when Admiral Vorkosigan's invasion forces took over the mirror, practically the first thing. I can't think that it had much tactical value, at the high speed at which the space battles went, but it certainly had a huge psychological impact. It was almost as if we had captured their sun itself. I think returning it to Komarran civilian control in the last few years was a very good political move. I hope this doesn't mess that up."

"It's hard to say." That new caution, again.

"There was talk of opening its observation platform to tourism again. Though now I imagine they're relieved they hadn't yet."

"They still have plenty of VIP tours. I took one myself, when I was here several years ago teaching a short course at Solstice University. Fortunately, there were no visitors aboard on the day of the collision.

But it should be open to the public, to be seen and to educate. Do it up right, with maybe a museum on-site explaining how it was first built. It's a great work. Odd to think that its principal practical use is to make swamps."

"Swamps make breathable air. Eventually." She smiled. In her uncle's mind the pure engineering aesthetic clearly overshadowed the messy biological end view.

"Next you'll be defending the rats. There really are rats here, I understand?"

"Oh, yes, the dome tunnels have rats. And hamsters, and gerbils. All the children capture them for pets, which is likely where they came from in the first place, come to think of it. I do think the black-and-white rats are cute. The animal-control exterminators have to work in dead secret from their younger relatives. And we have roaches, of course, who doesn't? And—over in Equinox—wild cockatoos. A couple of pairs of them escaped, or were let loose, several decades ago. They now have these big rainbow-colored birds all over the place, and people *will* feed them. The sanitation crews wanted to get rid of them, but the Dome shareholders voted them down."

The waitress delivered their salads and iced tea, and there was a short break in the conversation while her uncle appreciated the fresh spinach, mangoes and onions, and candied pecans. She'd guessed the candied pecans would please him. The market-garden hydroponics production in Serifosa was among Komarr's best.

She used the break to redirect the conversation toward her greatest current curiosity. "Your colleague Lord Vorkosigan—did he really have a thirteen-year career in Imperial Security?" *Or were you just irritated by Tien?*

"Three years in the Imperial Military Academy, a decade in ImpSec, to be precise."

"How did he ever get in, past the physicals?"

"Nepotism, I believe. Of a sort. To give him credit, it seems to have been an advantage he used sparingly thereafter. I had the fascinating experience of reading his entire classified military record, when Gregor asked me and my fellow Auditors to review Vorkosigan's candidacy, before he made the appointment."

She subsided in slight disappointment. "Classified. In that case, I suppose you can't tell me anything about it."

"Well," he grinned around a mouthful of salad, "there was the Dagoola IV episode. You must have heard of it, that giant breakout from the Cetagandan prisoner of war camp that the Marilacans made a few years ago?"

She recalled it only dimly. She'd been heads-down in motherhood, about that time, and scarcely paid attention to news, especially any so remote as galactic news. But she nodded encouragement for him to go on.

"It's all old history now. I understand from Vorkosigan that the Marilacans are engaged in producing a holovid drama on the subject. *The Greatest Escape*, or something like that, they're calling it. They tried to hire him—or actually, his cover identity—to be a technical consultant on the script, an opportunity he has regretfully declined. But for ImpSec to retain security classification upon a series of events that the Marilacans are simultaneously dramatizing planetwide strikes me as a bit rigid, even for ImpSec. In any case, Vorkosigan was the Barrayaran agent behind that breakout."

"I didn't even know we *had* an agent behind that."

"He was our man on-site."

So that odd joke about snoring Marilacans . . . hadn't been. Quite. "If he was so good, why did he quit?"

"Hm." Her uncle applied himself to mopping up the last of his salad dressing with his multigrain roll, before replying. "I can only give you an edited version of that. He didn't quit voluntarily. He was very badly injured—to the point of requiring cryo-freezing—a couple of years ago. Both the original injury and the cryo-freeze did him a lot of damage, some of it permanent. He was forced to take a medical discharge, which he—hm!—did not handle well. It's not my place to discuss those details."

"If he was injured badly enough to need cryo-freeze, he was dead!" she said, startled.

"Technically, I suppose so. 'Alive' and 'dead' are not such neat categories as they used to be in the Time of Isolation."

So, her uncle was in possession of just the sort of medical information about Vorkosigan's mutations she most wanted to know, if he had paid any attention to it. Military physicals were thorough.

"So rather than let all that training and experience go to waste," Uncle Vorthys went on, "Gregor found a job for Vorkosigan on the civilian side. Most Auditorial duties are not too physically onerous . . . though I confess, it's been useful to have someone younger and thinner than myself to send out-station for those long inspections in a pressure suit. I'm afraid I've abused his endurance a bit, but he's proved very observant."

"So he really is your assistant?"

"By no means. What fool said that? All Auditors are coequal. Seniority is only good for getting one stuck with certain administrative chores, on the rare occasions when we act as a group. Vorkosigan, being a well-brought-up young man, is polite to my white hairs, but he's an independent Auditor in his own right, and goes just where he pleases. At present it pleases him to study my methods. I shall certainly take the opportunity to study his.

"Our Imperial charge doesn't come with a manual, you see. It was once proposed the Auditors create one for themselves, but they—wisely, I think—concluded it would do more harm than good. Instead, we just have our archives of Imperial reports; precedents, without rules. Lately, several of us more recent appointees have been trying to read a few old reports each week, and then meet for dinner to discuss the cases and analyze how they were handled. Fascinating. And delicious. Vorkosigan has the most extraordinary cook."

"But this *is* his first assignment, isn't it? And . . . he was designated just like that, on the Emperor's whim."

"He had a temporary appointment as a Ninth Auditor first. A very difficult assignment, inside ImpSec itself. Not my kind of thing at all."

She was not *totally* oblivious to the news. "Oh, dear. Did he have anything to do with why ImpSec changed chiefs twice last winter?"

"I so much prefer engineering investigations," her uncle observed mildly.

Their vat-chicken salad sandwiches arrived, while Ekaterin absorbed this deflection. What kind of reassurance was she seeking, after all? Vorkosigan disturbed her, she had to admit, with his cool smile and warm eyes, and she couldn't say why. He did tend to the sardonic. Surely she was not subconsciously prejudiced against mutants, when Nikolai himself . . . *In the Time of Isolation, if such a one as Vorkosigan had been born to me, it would have been my maternal duty to the genome to cut his infant throat.*

Nikki, happily, would have escaped my cleansing. For a while.

The Time of Isolation is over forever. Thank God.

"I gather you like Vorkosigan," she began once again to angle for the kind of information she sought.

"So does your aunt. The Professora and I had him to dinner a few times, last winter, which is where Vorkosigan came up with the notion of the discussion meetings, come to think of it. I know he's rather quiet at first—cautious, I think—but he can be very witty, once you get him going."

"*Does he amuse you?*" *Amusing* had certainly not been her first impression.

He swallowed another bite of sandwich, and glanced up again at the white irregular blur in the clouds now marking the position of the soletta. "I taught engineering for thirty years. It had its drudgeries. But each year, I had the pleasure of finding in my classes a few of the best and brightest, who made it all worthwhile." He sipped spiced tea and spoke more slowly. "But much less often— every five or ten years at most—a true genius would turn up among my students, and the pleasure became a privilege, to be treasured for life."

"You think he's a genius?" she said, raising her eyebrows. *The high Vor twit?*

"I don't know him quite well enough, yet. But I suspect so, a part of the time."

"Can you be a genius part of the time?"

"All the geniuses I ever met were so just part of the time. To qualify, you only have to be great once, you know. Once when it matters. Ah, dessert. My, this is splendid!" He applied himself happily to a large chocolate confection with whipped cream and more pecans.

She wanted personal data, but she kept getting career synopses. She would have to take a more embarrassingly direct path. While arranging her first spoonful of her spiced apple tart and ice cream, she finally worked up her nerve to ask, "Is he married?"

"No."

"That surprises me." Or did it? "He's high Vor, heavens, the highest—he'll be a District Count someday, won't he? He's wealthy, or so I would assume, he has an important position . . ." She trailed off. What did she want to say? *What's wrong with him that he hasn't acquired his own lady by now? What kind of genetic damage made him like that, and was it from his mother or his father? Is he impotent, is he sterile, what does he really look like under those expensive clothes? Is he hiding more serious deformities? Is he homosexual? Would it be safe to leave Nikolai alone with him?* She couldn't say *any* of that, and her oblique hints weren't eliciting anything even close to the answers she sought. Drat it, she wouldn't have had this kind of trouble getting the pertinent information if she'd been talking to the *Professora.*

"He's been out of the Empire most of the past decade," he said, as if that explained something.

"Does he have siblings?" *Normal brothers or sisters?*

"No."

That's a bad sign.

"Oh, I take that back," Uncle Vorthys added. "Not in the usual sense, I should say. He has a clone. Doesn't look like him, though."

"That—if he's a—I don't understand."

"You'll have to get Vorkosigan to explain it to you, if you're curious. It's complicated even by his standards. I haven't met the fellow myself yet." Around a mouthful of chocolate and cream, he added, "Speaking of siblings, were you planning any more for Nikolai? Your family is going to be very stretched out, if you wait much longer."

She smiled in panic. Dare she tell him? Tien's accusation of betrayal seared her memory, but she was so tired, exhausted, sick to death of the stupid secrecy. If only her aunt were here . . .

She was dully conscious of her contraceptive implant, the one bit of galactic techno-culture Tien had embraced without question. It gave her a galactic's sterility without a galactic's freedom. Modern women gladly traded the deadly lottery of fertility for the certainties of health and result that came with the use of the uterine replicator, but Tien's obsession with concealment had barred her from that reward too. Even if he was somatically cured, his germ-cells would not be, and any progeny would still have to be genetically screened. Did he mean to cut off all future children? When she'd tried to discuss the issue, he'd put her off with an airy, *First things first;* when she'd persisted, he'd become angry, accusing her of nagging and selfishness. That was always effective at shutting her up.

She skittered sideways to her uncle's question. "We've moved around so much. I kept waiting for things to get settled with Tien's career."

"He does seem to have been rather, ah, restless." He raised his eyebrows at her, inviting . . . what?

"I . . . won't pretend that hasn't been difficult." That was true enough. Thirteen different jobs in a decade. Was this normal for a rising bureaucrat? Tien said it was a necessity, no bosses ever promoted from within or raised a former subordinate above them; you had to go around to move up. "We've moved eight times. I've abandoned six gardens, so far. The last two relocations, I just didn't plant anything except in pots. And then I had to leave most of the pots, when we came here."

Maybe Tien would stay with this Komarran post. How could he ever garner the rewards of promotion and seniority, the status he hungered for, if he never stuck with one thing long enough to earn any? His first few postings, she'd had to agree with him, had been mediocre; she'd had no problem understanding why he wanted to move on quickly. A young couple's early life was supposed to be unsettled, as they stretched into their new lives as adults. Well, as she'd stretched into hers; she'd been only twenty, after all. Tien had been thirty when they'd married. . . .

He'd started every new job with a burst of enthusiasm, working hard, or at least, very long hours. Surely no one could work harder. Then the enthusiasm dwindled, and the complaints began, of too much work, too little reward, offered too slowly. Lazy coworkers, smarmy bosses. At least, so he said. That had become her secret danger signal, when Tien began offering sly sexual slander of his superiors; it meant the job was about to end, again. A new one would be found . . . though it seemed to take longer and longer to find a new one, these days. And his enthusiasm would flame up again, and the cycle would begin anew. But her hypersensitized ear had picked up no bad signs so far in this job, and they'd been here nearly a year already. Maybe Tien had finally found his—what had Vorkosigan called it? His passion. This was the best posting he'd ever achieved; perhaps things were finally starting to break into good fortune, for a change. If she just stuck it out long enough, it would get better, virtue would be rewarded. And . . . with this Vorzohn's Dystrophy thing hanging over them, Tien had good reason for impatience. His time was not unlimited.

And yours is? She blinked that thought away.

"Your aunt was not sure if things were working out happily for you. Do you dislike Komarr?"

"Oh, I like Komarr just fine," she said quickly. "I admit, I've been a little homesick, but that's not the same thing as not liking being here."

"She did think you would seize the opportunity to place Nikki in a Komarran school, for the, as she would say, cultural experience. Not that his school we saw this morning isn't very nice, of course, which I shall report back for her reassurance, I promise."

"I was tempted. But being a Barrayaran, an off-worlder, in a Komarran classroom might have been difficult for Nikki. You know how kids can gang up on anyone who's different, at that age. Tien thought this private school would be much better. A lot of the high Vor families in the sector send their children there. He thought Nikki could make good connections."

"I did not have the impression that Nikki was socially ambitious." His dryness was mitigated by a slight twinkle.

How was she to respond to that? Defend a choice she did not herself agree with? Admit she thought Tien wrong? If she once began complaining about Tien, she wasn't sure she could stop before her most fearful worries began to pour out. And people complaining about their spouses always looked and sounded so ugly. "Well, connections for me, at least." Not that she had been able to muster the energy to pursue them as assiduously as Tien thought she ought.

"Ah. It's good you're making friends."

"Yes, well . . . yes." She scraped at the last of the apple syrup on her plate.

When she looked up, she noticed a good-looking young Komarran man who had stopped by the outer gate to the restaurant's patio and was staring at her. After a moment, he entered and approached their table. "Madame Vorsoisson?" he said uncertainly.

"Yes?" she said warily.

"Oh, good, I thought I recognized you. My name is Andro Farr. We met at the Winterfair reception for the Serifosa terraforming employees a few months ago, do you remember?"

Dimly. "Oh, yes. You were somebody's guest . . . ?"

"Yes. Marie Trogir. She's an engineering tech in the Waste Heat Management department. Or she was. . . . Do you know her? I mean, has she ever talked with you?"

"No, not really." Ekaterin had met the young Komarran woman perhaps three times, at carefully choreographed Project events. She had usually been too conscious of herself as a representative of Tien, of the need to cordially meet and greet everyone, to get into any very intimate conversations. "Had she intended to talk to me?"

The young man slumped in disappointment. "I don't know. I thought you might have been friends, or at least acquaintances. I've talked to all her friends I can find."

"Um . . . oh?" Ekaterin was not at all sure she wished to encourage this conversation.

Farr seemed to sense her wariness; he flushed slightly. "Excuse me. I seem to have found myself in a rather painful domestic situation, and I don't know why. It took me by surprise. But . . . but you see . . . about six weeks ago, Marie told me she was going out of town on a field project for her department, and would be back in about five weeks, but she wasn't sure exactly. She didn't give me any comconsole codes to reach her, she said she'd probably not be able to call, and not to worry."

"Do you, um, live with her?"

"Yes. Anyway, time went by, and time went by, and I didn't hear . . . I finally called her department head, Administrator Soudha. He was vague. In fact, I think he gave me a run-around. So I went down there in person and asked around. When I finally pinned him, *he* said," Farr swallowed, "she'd resigned abruptly six weeks ago and left. So had her engineering boss, Radovas, the one she'd said she was going on the field project with. Soudha seemed to think they'd . . . left together. It makes no sense."

The idea of running away from a relationship and leaving no forwarding address made perfect sense to Ekaterin, but it was hardly her place to say so. Who knew what profound dissatisfactions Farr had failed to detect in his lady? "I'm sorry. I know nothing about this. Tien never mentioned it."

"I'm sorry to bother you, Madame." He hesitated, balanced upon turning away.

"Have you talked to Madame Radovas?" Ekaterin asked tentatively.

"I tried. She refused to talk with me."

That, too, was understandable, if her middle-aged husband had run off with a younger and prettier woman.

"Have you filed a missing person report with Dome Security?" Uncle Vorthys inquired. Ekaterin realized she hadn't introduced him and, on reflection, decided to leave it that way.

"I wasn't sure. I think I'm about to."

"Mm," said Ekaterin. Did she really want to encourage the fellow to persecute this girl? She had apparently got away clean. Had she chosen this cruel method of ending their relationship because she was a twit, or because he was a monster? There was no way to tell from the outside. You could never tell what secret burdens anyone carried, concealed by their bright smiles.

"She left all her things. She left her cats. I don't know what to do with them," he said rather piteously.

Ekaterin had heard of desperate women leaving everything up to and including their children, but Uncle Vorthys put in, "That does seem odd. I'd go to Security if I were you, if only to put your mind at ease. You can always apologize later, if necessary."

"I . . . I think I might. Good day, Madame Vorsoisson. Sir." He ran his hands through his hair, and let himself back out the little fake wrought-iron gate to the park.

"Perhaps we ought to be getting back," Ekaterin suggested as the young man turned out of sight. "Should we take Lord Vorkosigan some lunch? They'll make up a carry-out."

"I'm not sure he notices missing meals, when he's wound up in a problem, but it does seem only fair."

"Do you know what he likes?"

"Anything, I would imagine."

"Does he have any food allergies?"

"Not as far as I know."

She made a hasty selection of a suitably balanced and nutritious meal, hoping that the prettily-arranged vegetables wouldn't end up in the waste disposer. With males, you never knew. When the order was delivered, they took their leave, and Ekaterin led the way to the nearest bubble-car station to get back to her own dome section. She still had no clear idea how Vorkosigan had so successfully handled his mutant-status on their mutagen-scarred homeworld, except, perhaps, by pursuing most of his career off it. Was that likely to be any help to Nikolai?

Chapter Four

Etienne Vorsoisson's bureaucratic domain occupied two floors partway up a sealed tower otherwise devoted to local Serifosa Dome government offices. The tower, on the edge of the dome-sprawl, was not housed inside any other atmosphere-containing structure. Miles eyed the glass-roofed atrium with disfavor as they ascended a curving escalator within it. He swore his ear detected a faint, far off whistle of air escaping some less-than-tight seal. "So what happens if somebody lobs a rock through a window?" he murmured to the Professor, a step behind him.

"Not much," Vorthys murmured back. "It would vent a pretty noticeable draft, but the pressure differential just isn't that great."

"True." Serifosa Dome was not really like a space installation, despite occasional misleading similarities of architecture. They made the air in here *from* the air out there, for the most part. Vent shafts spotted all over the dome complex sucked in Komarr's free volatiles, filtered out the excess carbon dioxide and some trace nasties, passed the nitrogen through unaltered, and concentrated the oxygen to a humanly-bearable mix. The *percentage* of oxygen in Komarr's raw atmosphere was still too low to support a large mammal without the technological aid of a breath mask, but the absolute *amount* remained a vast reservoir compared to the volume of even the most extensive dome complexes. "As long as their power system keeps running."

They stepped from the escalator and followed Vorsoisson into a corridor branching off the central atrium. The sight of a case of emergency breath masks affixed to a wall next to a fire extinguisher reassured Miles slightly, in passing, that the Komarrans here were not completely oblivious to their routine hazards. Though the case looked suspiciously dusty; had it ever been used since it had been installed, however many years ago? Or checked? If this were a military inspection, Miles could amuse himself by stopping the party right now, and tearing the case apart to determine if the masks' power and reservoir levels still fell within spec. As an Imperial Auditor, he could also do so, of course, or take any other action which struck his fancy. When a younger man, his besetting sin had been his impulsiveness. In the dark doubts of night, Miles sometimes wondered if Emperor Gregor had quite thought through his most recent Auditorial appointment. Power was supposed to corrupt, but this felt more like being a kid turned loose in a candy store. *Control yourself, boy.*

The mask case fell behind without incident. Vorsoisson, as tour guide, continued to point out the offices of his various subordinate departments, without, however, inviting his visitors inside. Not that there was that much to see in these administrative headquarters. The real interest, and the real work, lay outside the domes altogether, in experimental stations and plots and pockets of biota all over Serifosa Sector. All Miles would find in these bland rooms were . . . comconsoles. And Komarrans, of course, lots of Komarrans.

"This way, my lords." Vorsoisson shepherded them into a comfortably spacious room featuring a large round holovid projection table. The place looked, and smelled, like every other conference chamber Miles had ever been in for military and security briefings and debriefings during his truncated career. *More of the same. I predict my greatest challenge this afternoon will be to stay awake.* A half a dozen men and women sat waiting, nervously fingering recording pads and vid disks, and a couple more scurried in behind the two Auditors with murmured apologies. Vorsoisson indicated seats set aside for the visitors, at his right and left hand. With a brief general smile of greeting, Miles settled in.

"Lord Auditor Vorthys, Lord Vorkosigan, may I present the department heads of the Serifosa branch of the Komarr Terraforming Project." Vorsoisson went round the table, naming each attendee and their department, which under the three basic branches of Accounting, Operations, and Research included such evocative titles as Carbon Draw-down, Hydrology, Greenhouse Gases, Tests Plots, Waste Heat Management, and Microbial Reclassification. Native-born Komarrans, every one; Vorsoisson was the only Barrayaran expatriate among them. Vorsoisson remained standing and turned to one of the newcomers. "My lords, may I also present Ser Venier, my administrative assistant. Vennie has organized a general presentation for you, after which my staff will be happy to answer any further questions."

Vorsoisson sat down. Venier nodded to each Auditor and murmured something inaudible. He was a slight man, shorter than Vorsoisson, with intent brown eyes and an unfortunate weak chin which, together with his nervous air, lent him the look of a slightly manic rabbit. He took the holovid control podium, and rubbed his hands together, and stacked and restacked his pile of data disks before selecting one, then putting it back down. He cleared his throat and found his voice. "My lords. It was suggested I start with an historical overview." He nodded to each of them again, his glance lingering for a moment on Miles. He inserted a disk in his machine, and started an attractive, i.e., artistically enhanced, view of Komarr spinning over the vid plate. "The early explorers of the wormhole nexus found Komarr a likely candidate for possible terraforming. Our almost point-nine-standard gravity and abundant native supply of gaseous nitrogen, the inert buffer gas of choice, and of sufficient water-ice, made it an immensely easier problem to tackle than such classic cold dry planets as, say, Mars."

They had indeed been early explorers, Miles reflected, to arrive and settle before more salubrious worlds were found to render such ambitious projects economically uninteresting, at least if you didn't already live there. But . . . then there were the wormholes.

"On the debit side," Venier continued, "the concentration of atmospheric CO_2 was high enough to be toxic to humans, yet insolation was so inadequate that no greenhouse effect, runaway or otherwise, captured the heat needed to maintain liquid water. Komarr was therefore a lifeless world, cold and dark. The earliest calculations suggested more water would be needed, and a few so-called low-impact cometary crashes were arranged, hence we can thank our ancestors for our southern crater lakes." A colorful, though out-of-scale, sprinkle of lights dusted the lower hemisphere of the planet-image, resolving into a string of blue blobs. "But the growing demand topside for cometary water and volatiles for the orbital and wormhole stations soon put a stop to *that*. And the early downside settlers' fears of poorly controlled trajectories, of course."

Demonstrated fears, as Miles recalled his Komarran history. He stole a glance at Vorthys. The Professor appeared perfectly content with Venier's class lecture.

"In fact," Venier went on, "later explorations showed the water-ice tied up in the polar caps to be thicker than at first suspected, if not so abundant as on Earth. And so the drive for heat and light began."

Miles sympathized with the early Komarrans. He loathed arctic cold and dark with a concentrated passion.

"Our ancestors built the first insolation mirror, succeeded a generation later by another design." A holovid model, again out of scale, appeared to the side, and melted into a second one. "A century later, this was in turn succeeded by the design we see today." The seven-disk hexagon appeared, and danced attendance on the Komarr globe. "Insolation at the equator was boosted enough to allow liquid water and the beginnings of a biota to draw down the carbon and release much-needed O_2. Over the following decades, a full-spectrum mixture of artificial greenhouse gases was manufactured and released into the upper atmosphere to help trap the new energy." Venier moved his hand; four of the seven disks winked out. "Then came the accident." All the Komarrans around the table stared glumly at the crippled array.

"There was mention of a cooling projection? With figures?" Vorthys prodded gently.

"Yes, my Lord Auditor." Venier slid a disk across the polished surface toward the Professor. "Administrator Vorsoisson said you were an engineer, so I left in all the calculations."

The Waste Heat Management fellow, Soudha, also an engineer, winced and bit his thumb at this innocent ignorance of Vorthys's stature in his field. Vorthys merely said, "Thank you. I appreciate that."

So where's my copy? Miles did not ask aloud. "And can you please summarize your conclusions for us nonengineers, Ser Venier?"

"Certainly, Lord Auditor . . . Vorkosigan. Serious damage to our biota in the northernmost and southernmost latitudes, not just in Serifosa Sector but planetwide, will begin after one season. For every year after that, we lose more ground; by the end of five years, the destructive cooling curve rises rapidly towards catastrophe. It took twenty years to build the original soletta array. I pray that it will not take that many to repair it." On the vid model, white polar caps crept like pale tumors over the globe.

Vorthys glanced at Soudha. "And so other sources of heat suddenly take on new importance, at least for a stopgap."

Soudha, a big, square-handed man in his late forties, sat back and smiled a bit grimly. He, too, cleared his throat before beginning. "It was hoped, early on in the terraforming, that the waste heat from our growing arcologies would contribute significantly to planetary warming. Over time, this proved optimistic. A planet with an activating hydrology is a huge thermal buffering system, what with the heat of liquefaction load locked up in all that ice. At present— before the accident—it was felt the best use of waste heat was in the creation of microclimates around the domes, to be reservoirs for the next wave of higher biota."

"It sounds like insanity to an engineer to say, 'We need to waste more energy in heat loss,'" agreed Vorthys, "but I suppose here it's true. What's the feasibility of dedicating some number of fusion reactors to pure heat production?"

"Boiling the seas cup by cup?" Soudha grimaced. "*Possible*, sure, and I'd love to see some more done with that technique for small-area development in Serifosa Sector. Economical—no. Per degree of planetary warming, it's even more costly than repairing—or enlarging—the soletta array, something for which we've been petitioning the Imperium for years. Without success. And if you've built a reactor, you might as well use it to run a dome while you're at it. The heat will arrive outside eventually just the same." He slid data disks across to both Vorthys and Miles this time. "Here's our current departmental status report." He glanced across at one of his colleagues. "We're all anxious to move on to higher plant forms in our lifetimes, but at present the greatest, if not success, at least activity remains on the microbial level. Philip?"

The man who had been introduced as the head of Microbial Reclassification smiled, not entirely gratefully, at Soudha, and turned to the Auditors. "Well, yes. Bacteria are booming. Both our deliberate inoculations, and wild genera. Over the years, every Earth type has been imported, or at any rate, has arrived and escaped. Unfortunately, microbial life has a tendency to adapt to its environment more swiftly than the environment has adapted to us. My department has its hands full, keeping up with the mutations.

More light and heat are needed, as always. And, bluntly, my lords, more funding. Although our microflora grow fast, they also die fast, rereleasing their carbon compounds. We need to advance to higher organisms, to sequester the excess carbon for the millennial time-frames required. Perhaps you could address this, Liz?" He nodded toward a pleasantly plump middle-aged lady who had been named head of Carbon Draw-down.

She smiled happily, by which Miles deduced her department's responsibilities were going well this year. "Yes, my lords. We've a number of higher forms of vegetation coming along both in major test plots, and undergoing genetic development or improvement. By far our greatest success is with the cold- and carbon-dioxide-hardy peat bogs. They do require liquid water, and as always, would do *better* at higher temperatures. Ideally, they should be sited in subduction zones, for *really* long-term carbon sequestration, but Serifosa Sector lacks these. So we've chosen low-lying areas which will, as water is released from the poles, eventually be covered with lakes and small seas, locking the captured carbon down under a sedimentary cap. Properly set up, the process will run entirely automatically, without further human intervention. If we could just get the funding to double or triple the area of our plantations in the next few years . . . well, here are my projections." Vorthys collected another data disk. "We've started several test plots of larger plants, to follow atop the bogs. These larger organisms are of course infinitely more controllable than the rapidly mutating microflora. They are ready to scale up to wider plantations right now. But they are even more severely threatened by the reduction in heat and light from the soletta. We really *must* have a reliable estimate of how long it will take to effect repairs in space before we dare continue our planting plans."

She gazed longingly at Vorthys, but he merely said, "Thank you, Madame."

"We plan a flyover of the peat plantations later this afternoon," Vorsoisson told her. She settled back, temporarily content.

And so it continued around the table: more than Miles had ever wanted to know about Komarran terraforming, interspersed with oblique, and not so oblique, pleas for increased Imperial funding. And heat and light. *Power corrupts, but we want energy.* Only Accounting and Waste Heat Management had managed to arrive at the meeting with duplicate copies of their pertinent reports for

Miles. He stifled an impulse to point this out to somebody. Did he really *want* another several hundred thousand words of bedtime reading? His newer scars were starting to twinge by the time everyone had had their say, without even yesterday's excuse of the physical stresses of buzzing around wreckage in a pressure suit. He rose from his chair much more stiffly than he had intended; Vorthys made a gesture of a helping hand to his elbow, but at Miles's frown and tiny head shake, suppressed it. He didn't really need a drink, he just wanted one.

"Ah, Administrator Soudha," Vorthys said, as the Waste Heat department head stepped past them toward the door. "A word, please?"

Soudha stopped, and smiled faintly. "My Lord Auditor?"

"Was there some special reason you could not help that young fellow, Farr, find his missing lady?"

Soudha hesitated. "I beg your pardon?"

"The fellow who was looking for your former employee, Marie Trogir, I believe he said her name was. Was there some reason you could not help him?"

"Oh, him. Her. Well, uh . . . that was a difficult thing, there." Soudha looked around, but the room had emptied, except for Vorsoisson and Venier waiting to convey their high-ranking guests on the next leg of their tour.

"I recommended he file a missing person complaint with Dome Security. They may be making inquiries of you."

"I . . . don't think I'll be able to help them any more than I could help Farr. I'm afraid I really don't know where she is. She left, you see. Very suddenly, only a day's notice. It put a hole in my staffing at what has proved to be a difficult time. I wasn't too pleased."

"So Farr said. I just thought it was odd about the cats. One of my daughters keeps cats. Dreadful little parasites, but she's very fond of them."

"Cats?" said Soudha, looking increasingly mystified.

"Trogir apparently left her cats in the keeping of Farr."

Soudha blinked, but said, "I've always considered it out of line to intrude on my subordinate's personal lives. Men or pets, it was Trogir's business, not mine. As long as they're kept off project time. I . . . was there anything else?"

"Not really," said Vorthys.

"Then if you will excuse me, my Lord Auditor." Soudha smiled again, and ducked away.

"What was that all about?" Miles asked Vorthys as they turned down the corridor in the opposite direction.

Vorsoisson answered. "A minor office scandal, unfortunately. One of Soudha's techs—female—ran off with one of his engineers, male. Completely blindsided him, apparently. He's fairly embarrassed about it. However did you run across it?"

"Young Farr accosted Ekaterin in a restaurant," said Vorthys.

"He really has been a pest." Vorsoisson sighed. "I don't blame Soudha for avoiding him."

"I always thought Komarrans were more casual about such things," said Miles. "In the galactic style and all that. Not as casual as the Betans, but still. It sounds like a Barrayaran backcountry elopement." *Without, surely, the need to avoid backcountry social pressures, such as homicidal relatives out to defend the clan honor.*

Vorsoisson shrugged. "The cultural contamination between the worlds can't run one way all the time, I suppose."

The little party continued to the underground garage, where the aircar Vorsoisson had requisitioned was not in evidence. "Wait here, Venier." Swearing under his breath, Vorsoisson went off to see what had happened to it; Vorthys accompanied him.

The opportunity to interview a Komarran in apparently-casual mode was not to be missed. What kind of Komarran was Venier? Miles turned to him, only to find him speaking first: "Is this your first visit to Komarr, Lord Vorkosigan?"

"By no means. I've passed through the topside stations many times. I haven't got downside too often, I admit. This is the first time I've been to Serifosa."

"Have you ever visited Solstice?"

The planetary capital. "Of course."

Venier stared at the middle distance, past the concrete pillars and dim lighting, and smiled faintly. "Have you ever visited the Massacre Shrine there?"

A cheeky damned Komarran, that's what kind. The Solstice Massacre was infamous as the ugliest incident of the Barrayaran conquest. The two hundred Komarran Counselors, the then-ruling senate, had surrendered on terms—and subsequently been gunned down in a gymnasium by Barrayaran security forces. The political consequences had run a short range from dire to disastrous. Miles's smile became a little fixed. "Of course. How could I not?"

"All Barrayarans should make that pilgrimage. In my opinion."

"I went with a close friend. To help him burn a death offering for his aunt."

"A relative of a Martyr is a friend of yours?" Venier's eyes widened in a moment of genuine surprise, in what otherwise felt to Miles to be a highly choreographed conversation. How long had Venier been rehearsing his lines in his head, itching for a chance to try them out?

"Yes." Miles let his gaze become more directly challenging.

Venier apparently felt the weight of it, because he shifted uneasily, and said, "As you are your father's son, I'm just a little surprised, is all."

By what, that I have any Komarran friends? "Especially as I am my father's son, you should not be."

Venier's brows tweaked up. "Well . . . there is a theory that the massacre was ordered by Emperor Ezar without the knowledge of Admiral Vorkosigan. Ezar was certainly ruthless enough."

"Ruthless enough, yes. Stupid enough, never. It was the Barrayaran expedition's chief Political Officer's own bright idea, for which my father made him pay with his life, not that that did much good for anyone after the fact. Leaving aside every moral consideration, the massacre was a supremely stupid act. My father has been accused of many things, but stupidity has never, I believe, been one of them." His voice was growing dangerously clipped.

"We'll never know the whole truth, I suppose," said Venier.

Was that supposed to be a concession? "You can be told the whole truth all day long, but if you won't believe it, then no, I don't suppose you ever will know it." He bared his teeth in a non-smile. *No, keep control; why let this Komarran git see he's scored you off?*

The doors of a nearby elevator opened, and Venier abruptly dropped from Miles's attention as Madame Vorsoisson and Nikolai exited. She was wearing the same dull dun outfit she'd sported that morning, and carried a large pile of heavy jackets over her arm. She waved her hand around the jackets and stepped swiftly over to them. "Am I very late?" she asked a bit breathlessly. "Good afternoon, Venier."

Suppressing the first idiocy that came to his lips, which was, *Any time is a good one for you, milady,* Miles managed a, "Well, good afternoon, Madame Vorsoisson, Nikolai. I wasn't expecting you. Are you to accompany us?" *I hope?* "You husband has just gone off to fetch an aircar."

"Yes, Uncle Vorthys suggested it would be educational for Nikolai. And I haven't had much chance to see outside the domes myself. I jumped at the invitation." She smiled, and pushed back a strand of dark hair escaping its confinement, and almost dropped her bundle. "I wasn't sure if we were to land anywhere and get outside on foot, but I brought jackets for everyone just in case."

A large two-compartment sealed aircar hissed around the corner and sighed to the pavement beside them. The front canopy opened, and Vorsoisson clambered out, and greeted his wife and son. The Professor watched from the front seat with some amusement as the question of how to distribute six passengers among the two compartments was taken over by Nikolai, who wanted to sit both by his great-uncle and by his Da.

"Perhaps Venier could fly us today?" Madame Vorsoisson suggested diffidently.

Vorsoisson gave her an oddly black look. "I'm perfectly capable."

Her lips moved, but she uttered no audible protest.

Take your pick, my Lord Auditor, Miles thought to himself. *Would you rather be chauffeured by a man just possibly suffering the first symptoms of Vorzohn's Dystrophy, or by a Komarran, ah, patriot, with a car full of tempting Barrayaran Vor targets?* "I have no preference," he murmured truthfully.

"I brought coats—" Madame Vorsoisson handed them out. She and her husband and Nikolai had their own; a spare of her husband's did not quite meet around the Professor's middle.

The heavily padded jacket she handed Miles had been hers, he could tell immediately by the scent of her, lingering in the lining. He concealed a deep inhalation as he shrugged it on. "Thank you, that will do very well."

Vorsoisson dove into the rear compartment and came up with a double handful of breath masks, which he distributed. Both he and Venier had their own, with their names engraved on the cheekpieces; the others were all labeled "Visitor": one large, two medium, one small.

Madame Vorsoisson hung hers over her arm, and bent to adjust Nikolai's, and check its power and oxygen levels.

"I already checked it," Vorsoisson told her. His voice hinted a suppressed snarl. "You don't have to do it again."

"Oh, sorry," she said. But Miles, running through his own check in drilled habit, noticed she finished inspecting it before turning to adjust her own mask. Vorsoisson noticed too, and frowned.

After a few more moments of Betan-style debate, the group sorted themselves out with Vorsoisson, his son, and the Professor in the front compartment, and Miles, Madame Vorsoisson, and Venier in the rear. Miles was uncertain whether to be glad or sorry with his lot in seatmates. He felt he could have engaged either of them in fascinating, if quite different, conversations, if the other had not been present. They all pulled their masks down around their necks, out of the way but instantly ready to hand.

They departed the garage's vehicle-lock without further delay, and the car rose in the air. Venier returned to his initial stiffly professional lecture mode, pointing out bits of project scenery. You *could* begin to see the terraforming from this modest altitude, in the faint smattering of Earth-green in the damp low places, and a fuzziness of lichen and algae on the rocks. Madame Vorsoisson, her face plastered to the canopy, asked enough intelligent questions of Venier that Miles did not have to strain his tired brain for any, for which he was very grateful.

"I'm surprised, Madame Vorsoisson, with your interest in botany, that you haven't leaned on your husband for a job in his department," said Miles after a while.

"Oh," she said, as if this was a new idea to her. "Oh, I couldn't do that."

"Why not?"

"Wouldn't it be nepotism? Or some kind of conflict of interest?"

"Not if you did your job well, which I'm sure you would. After all, the whole Barrayaran Vor system runs on nepotism. It's not a vice for us, it's a lifestyle."

Venier suppressed an unexpected noise, possibly a snort, and glanced at Miles with increased interest.

"Why should you be exempt?" Miles continued.

"It's only a hobby. I don't have nearly enough technical training. I'd need much more chemistry, to start."

"You could start in a technical assistant position—take evening classes to fill in your gaps. Bootstrap yourself up to something interesting in no time. They have to hire someone." Belatedly, it occurred to Miles that if she, not Vorsoisson, was the carrier of the Vorzohn's Dystrophy, there might be quelling reasons why she had not plunged into such a time- and energy-absorbing challenge. He sensed an elusive energy in her, as if it were tied in knots, locked down, circling back to exhaust itself destroying itself; had fear of her coming illness done that to her? Dammit, which of them *was* it? He was supposed to be such a hotshot investigator now, he ought to be able to figure this one out.

Well, he could do so easily; all he had to do was cheat, and call ImpSec Komarr, and request a complete background medical check on his hosts. Just wave his magical Auditor-wand and invade all the privacy he wanted to. *No.* All this had nothing to do with the accident to the soletta array. As this morning's embarrassment with her comconsole had demonstrated, he needed to start keeping his personal and professional curiosity just as strictly separated as his personal and Imperial funds. *Neither a peculator nor a voyeur be.* He ought to get a plaque engraved with that motto and hang it on his wall for a reminder. At least money didn't tempt him. He could smell her faint perfume, organic and floral against the plastic and metal and recycled air. . . .

To Miles's surprise, Venier said, "You really should consider it, Madame Vorsoisson."

Her expression, which during the flight had gradually become animated, grew reserved again. "I . . . we'll see. Maybe next year. After . . . if Tien decides to stay."

Vorsoisson's voice, over the intercom from the front compartment, interrupted to point out the upcoming peat bog, lining a long narrow valley below. It was a more impressive sight than Miles had expected. For one thing, it was a true and bright Earth-green; for another, it ran on for kilometers.

"This strain produces six times the oxygen of its Earth ancestor," Venier noted with pride.

"So . . . if you were trapped outside without a breath mask, could you crawl around in it and survive till you were rescued?" Miles asked practically.

"Mm . . . if you could hold your breath for about a hundred more years."

Miles began to suspect Venier of concealing a sense of humor beneath that twitchy exterior. In any case, the aircar spiraled down toward a rocky outcrop, and Miles's attention was taken up by their landing site. He'd had unpleasant and deep, so to speak, personal experience with the treachery of arctic bogs. But Vorsoisson managed to put the car down with a reassuring crunchy jar on solid rock, and they all adjusted their breath masks. The canopy rose to admit a blast of chill unbreatheable outside air, and they exited for a clamber over the rocks and down to personally examine the squishy green plants. They were squishy green plants, all right. There were lots of them. Stretching to the horizon. Lots. Squishy. Green. With an effort, Miles stopped his back-brain from composing a lengthy Report to the Emperor in this style, and tried instead to appreciate Venier's highly technical disquisition on potential deep-freeze damage to the something-chemical cycle.

After a little more time spent regarding the view—it didn't change, and Nikki, though he sprang around like a flea, with his mother laboring after him, didn't quite manage to fall into the bog—they all reboarded the aircar. After a flyover of a neighboring green valley, and a pass across another dull brown unaltered one for comparison and contrast, they turned for the Serifosa Dome.

A largish installation featuring its own fusion reactor, and a riot of assorted greens spilling away from it, caught Miles's attention on the leftward horizon. "What's that?" he asked Venier.

"It's Waste Heat's main experiment station," Venier replied.

Miles touched the intercom. "Any chance of dropping in for a visit down there?" he called the forward compartment.

Vorsoisson's voice hesitated. "I'm not sure we could get back to the dome before dark. I don't like to take the chance."

Miles hadn't thought night flight was that hazardous, but perhaps Vorsoisson knew his own limitations. And he did have his wife and child aboard, not to mention all that Imperial load in the somewhat unprepossessing persons of Miles and the Professor. Still, surprise inspections were always the most fun, if you wanted to turn up the good stuff. He toyed with the idea of insisting, Auditorially.

"It would certainly be interesting," murmured Venier. "I haven't been out there in person in years."

"Perhaps another day?" suggested Vorsoisson.

Miles let it go. He and Vorthys were playing visiting firemen here, not inspectors general; the real crisis was topside. "Perhaps. If there's time."

Another ten minutes of flight brought Serifosa Dome up over the horizon. It was vast and spectacular in the gathering dusk, with its glittering strings of lights, looping bubble-car tubes, warm glow of domes, sparkling towers. *We humans don't do too badly,* Miles thought, *if you catch us at the right angle.* The aircar slid back through the vehicle lock and settled again to the garage pavement.

Venier went off with the aircar, and Vorsoisson collected the spare breath masks. Madame Vorsoisson's face was bright and glowing, exhilarated by her field trip. "Don't forget to put your mask back on the recharger," she chirped to her husband as she handed him hers.

Vorsoisson's face darkened. "Don't. Nag. Me," he breathed through set teeth.

She recoiled slightly, her expression closing as abruptly as a shutter. Miles stared off through the pillars, politely pretending not to have heard or noticed this interplay. He was hardly an expert on marital miscommunication, but even he could see how that one had gone awry. Her perhaps unfortunately-chosen expression of love and interest had been received by the obviously tense and tired Vorsoisson as a slur on his competence. Madame Vorsoisson deserved a better hearing, but Miles had no advice to offer. *He* had never even come near to capturing a wife to miscommunicate with. Not for lack of trying. . . .

"Well, well," said Uncle Vorthys, also heartily pretending not to have noticed the byplay. "Everyone will feel better with a little supper aboard, eh, Ekaterin? Let me treat you all to dinner. Do you have another favorite place as splendid as the one where we ate lunch?"

The moment of tension was successfully extinguished in another Betan debate over the dinner destination; this time, Nikki was successfully overruled by the adults. Miles wasn't hungry, and the temptation to relieve Vorthys of the day's collection of data disks and escape back to some comconsole was strong, but perhaps with another drink or three he could endure one more family dinner with the Vorsoisson clan. The last, Miles promised himself.

A trifle drunker than he had intended to be, Miles undressed for another night in the rented grav-bed. He piled the new stack of data disks on the comconsole to wait for morning, coffee, and better mental coherence. The last thing he did was rummage in his case and fish out his controlled-seizure stimulator. He sat cross-legged on the bed and regarded it glumly.

The Barrayaran doctors had found no cure for the post-cryonic seizure disorder that had finally ended his military career. The best they had been able to offer was this: a triggering device to bleed off his convulsions in smaller increments, in controlled private times and places, instead of grandly, randomly, and spectacularly in moments of public stress. Checking his neurotransmitter levels was now a nightly hygienic routine, just like brushing his teeth, the doctors had suggested. He felt his right temple for the implant and positioned the read-contact. His only sensation was a faint spot of warmth.

The levels were not yet in the danger zone. A few more days before he had to put in the mouth-guard and do it again. Having left his Armsman, Pym, who usually played valet and general servant, back on Barrayar, he would have to find another spotter. The doctors had insisted he have a spotter, when he did this ugly little thing. He would much prefer to be helpless and out-of-consciousness—and twitching like a fish, he supposed, though of course *he* was the one person who never got to watch—in complete privacy. Maybe he would ask the Professor.

If you had a wife, she could be your spotter.

Gee, what a treat for her.

He grimaced, and put the device carefully away in its case, and crawled into bed. Perhaps in his dreams the space wreckage would reassemble itself, just like in a vid reconstruction, and reveal the secrets of its fate. Better to have visions of the wreckage than the bodies.

Chapter Five

Ekaterin studied Tien warily as they undressed for bed. The frowning tension in his face and body made her think she had better offer sex very soon. Strain in him frightened her, as always. It was past time to defuse him. The longer she waited, the harder it would be to approach him, and the tenser he would become, ending in some angry explosion of muffled, cutting words.

Sex, she imagined wistfully, should be romantic, abandoned, self-forgetful. Not the most tightly self-disciplined action in her world. Tien demanded response of her and worked hard to obtain it, she thought; not like men she'd heard about who took their own pleasure, then rolled over and went to sleep. She sometimes wished he would. He became upset—with himself, with her?—if she failed to participate fully. Unable to act a lie with her body, she'd learned to erase herself from herself, and so unblock whatever strange neural channel it was that permitted flesh to flood mind. The inward erotic fantasies required to absorb her self-consciousness had become stronger and uglier over time; was that a mere unavoidable side-effect of learning more about the ugliness of human possibility, or a permanent corruption of the spirit?

I hate this.

Tien hung up his shirt and twitched a smile at her. His eyes remained strained, though, as they had been all evening. "I'd like you to do me a favor tomorrow."

Anything, to delay the moment. "Certainly. What?"

"Take the brace of Auditors out and show 'em a good time. I'm about saturated with them. This downside holiday of theirs has been incredibly disruptive to my department. We've lost a week altogether, I bet, pulling together that show for them yesterday. Maybe they can go poke at something else, till they go back topside."

"Take them where, show them what?"

"Anything."

"I already took Uncle Vorthys around."

"Did you show him the Sector University district? Maybe he'd like that. Your uncle is interested in lots of things, and I don't think the Vor dwarf cares what he's offered. As long as it includes enough wine."

"I haven't the first clue what Lord Vorkosigan likes to do."

"Ask him. Suggest something. Take him, I don't know, take him shopping."

"Shopping?" she said doubtfully.

"Or whatever." He trod over to her, still smiling tightly. His hand slipped behind her back, to hold her, and he offered a tentative kiss. She returned it, trying not to let her dutifulness show. She could feel the heat of his body, of his hands, and how thinly stretched his affability was. Ah, yes, the work of the evening, defusing the unexploded Tien. Always a tricky business. She began to pay attention to the practiced rituals, key words, gestures, that led into the practiced intimacies.

Undressed and in bed, she closed her eyes as he caressed her, partly to concentrate on the touch, partly to block out his gaze, which was beginning to be excited and pleased. Wasn't there some bizarre mythical bird or other, back on Earth, who fancied that if it couldn't see you, you couldn't see it? And so buried its head in the sand, odd image. While still attached to its neck, she wondered?

She opened her eyes, as Tien reached across her and lowered the lamplight to a softer glow. His avid look made her feel not beautiful and loved, but ugly and ashamed. How could you be violated by mere eyes? How could you be lovers with someone, and yet feel every moment alone with them intruded upon your privacy, your dignity? *Don't look, Tien.* Absurd. There really was something wrong with her. He lowered himself beside her; she parted her lips, yielding quickly to his questing mouth. She hadn't always been this self-conscious and cautious. Back in the beginning, it had been different. Or had it been she alone who'd changed?

It became her turn to sit up and return caresses. That was easy enough; he buried his face in his pillow, and did not talk for a while, as her hands moved up and down his body, tracing muscle and tendon. Secretly seeking symptoms. The tremula seemed reduced tonight; perhaps last evening's shakes really had been a false alarm, merely the hunger and nerves he had claimed.

She knew when the shift had occurred in her, of course, back about four, five jobs ago now. When Tien had decided, for reasons she still didn't understand, that she was betraying him—with whom, she had never understood either, since the two names he'd finally mentioned as his suspects were so patently absurd. She'd had no idea such a sexual mistrust had taken over his mind, until she'd caught him following her, watching her, turning up at odd times and bizarre places when he was supposed to be at work—and had that perhaps had something to do with why *that* job had ended so badly? She'd finally had the accusation out of him. She'd been horrified, deeply wounded, and subtly frightened. Was it stalking, when it was your own husband? She had not had the courage to ask who to ask. Her one source of security was the knowledge that she'd never so much as been alone in any private place with another man. Her Vor-class training had done her that much good, at least. Then he had accused her of sleeping with her women friends.

That had broken something in her at last, some will to desire his good opinion. How could you argue sense into someone who believed something not because it was true, but because he was an idiot? No amount of panicky protestation or indignant denial or futile attempt to prove a negative was likely to help, because the problem was not in the accused, but in the accuser. She began then to believe he was living in a different universe, one with a different set of physical laws, perhaps, and an alternate history. And very different people from the ones she'd met of the same name. Smarmy dopplegangers all.

Still, the accusation alone had been enough to chill her friendships, stealing their innocent savor and replacing it with an unwelcome new level of awareness. With the next move, time and distance attenuated her contacts. And on the move after that, she'd stopped trying to make new friends.

To this day she didn't know if he'd taken her disgusted refusal to defend herself for a covert admission of guilt. Weirdly, after the blowup the subject had been dropped cold; he didn't bring it up again, and she didn't deign to. Did he think her innocent, or himself insufferably noble for forgiving her for nonexistent crimes?

Why is he so impossible?

She didn't want the insight, but it came nonetheless. *Because he fears losing you.* And so in panic blundered about destroying her love, creating a self-fulfilling prophecy? It seemed so. *It's not as though you can pretend his fears have no foundation.* Love was long gone, in her. She got by on a starvation diet of loyalty these days.

I am Vor. I swore to hold him in sickness. He is sick. I will not break my oath, just because things have gotten difficult. That's the whole point of an oath, after all. Some things, once broken, cannot ever be repaired. Oaths. Trust. . . .

She could not tell to what extent his illness was at the root of his erratic behavior. When they returned from the galactic treatment, he might be much better emotionally as well. Or at least she would at last be able to tell how much was Vorzohn's Dystrophy, and how much was just . . . Tien.

They switched positions; his skilled hands began working down her back, probing for her relaxation and response. An even more unhappy thought occurred to her then. Had Tien been, consciously or unconsciously, putting off his treatment because he realized on some obscure level that his illness, his vulnerability, was one of the few ties that still bound her to him? *Is this delay my fault?* Her head ached.

Tien, still valiantly rubbing her back, made a murmur of protest. She was failing to relax; this wouldn't do. Resolutely, she turned her thoughts to a practiced erotic fantasy, unbeautiful, but one which usually worked. Was it some weird inverted form of frigidity, this thing bordering on self-hypnosis she seemed to have to do in order to achieve sexual release despite Tien's too-near presence? How could you tell the difference between not liking sex, and not liking the only person you'd ever done sex with?

Yet she was almost desperate for touch, mere affection untainted by the indignities of the erotic. Tien *was* very good about that, massaging her for quite unconscionable lengths of time, though he sometimes sighed in a boredom for which she could hardly blame him. The touch, the make-it-better, the sheer catlike comfort, eased her body and then her heart, despite it all. She could absorb hours of this—she slitted one eye open to check the clock. Better not get greedy. So mind-wrenching, for Tien to demand a sexual show of her on the one hand, and accuse her of infidelity on the other. Did he want her to melt, or want her to freeze? *Anything you pick is wrong.* No, this wasn't helping. She was taking much too long to cultivate her arousal. Back to work. She tried again to start her fantasy. He might have rights upon her body, but her mind was hers alone, the one part of her into which he could not pry.

It went according to plan and practice, after that, mission accomplished all around. Tien kissed her when they'd finished. "There, all better," he murmured. "We're doing better these days, aren't we?"

She murmured back the usual assurances, a light, standard script. She would have preferred an honest silence. She pretended to doze, in postcoital lassitude, till his snores assured her he was asleep. Then she went to the bathroom to cry.

Stupid, irrational weeping. She muffled it in a towel, lest he, or Nikki, or her guests hear and investigate. *I hate him. I hate myself. I hate him, for making me hate myself. . . .*

Most of all, she despised in herself that crippling desire for physical affection, regenerating like a weed in her heart no matter how many times she tried to root it out. That neediness, that dependence, that love-of-touch must be broken first. It had betrayed her, worse than all the other things. If she could kill her need for love, then all the other coils which bound her, desire for honor, attachment to duty, above all every form of fear, could be brought into line. Austerely mystical, she supposed. *If I can kill all these things in me, I can be free of him.*

I'll be a walking dead woman, but I will be free.

She finished the weep, and washed her face, and took three painkillers. She could sleep now, she thought. But when she slipped back into the bedroom, she found Tien lying awake, his eyes a faint gleam in the shadows. He turned up the lamp at the whisper of her bare feet on the carpet. She tried to remember if insomnia was listed among the early symptoms of his disease. He raised the covers for her to slip beneath. "What were you doing in there all that time, going for seconds without me?"

She wasn't sure if he was waiting for a laugh, if that was supposed to be a joke, or her indignant denial. Evading the problem, instead she said, "Oh, Tien, I almost forgot. Your bank called this afternoon. Very strange. Something about requiring my countersignature and palm-print to release your pension account. I told them I didn't think that could be right, but that I would check with you and get back to them."

He froze in the act of reaching for her. "They had no business calling you about that!"

"If this was something you wanted me to do, you might have mentioned it earlier. They said they'd delay releasing it till I got back to them."

"Delayed, no! You idiot bitch!" His right hand clenched in a gesture of frustration.

The hateful and hated epithet made her sick to her stomach. All that effort to pacify him tonight, and here he was right back on the edge. . . . "Did I make a mistake?" she asked anxiously. "Tien, what's wrong? What's going on?" She prayed he wasn't about to put his fist through the wall again. The noise—would her uncle hear, or that Vorkosigan fellow, and how could she explain—

"No . . . no. Sorry." He rubbed his forehead instead, and she let out a covert sigh of relief. "I forgot about it being under Komarran rules. On Barrayar, I never had any trouble signing out my pension accumulation when I left any job, any job that offered a pension, anyway. Here on Komarr I think they want a joint signature from the designated survivor. It's all right. Call them back first thing in the morning, though, and clear it."

"You're not leaving your job, are you?" Her chest tightened in panic. Dear no, not another move so soon. . . .

"No, no. Hell, no. Relax." He smiled with one side of his mouth.

"Oh. Good." She hesitated. "Tien . . . do you have any accumulation from your old jobs back on Barrayar?"

"No, I always signed it out at the end. Why let them have the use of the money, when we could use it ourselves? It served to tide us over more than once, you know." He smiled bitterly. "Under the circumstances, you have to admit, the idea of saving for my old age is not very compelling. And you wanted that vacation to South Continent, didn't you?"

"I thought you said that was a termination bonus."

"So it was, in a sense."

So . . . if anything horrible happened to Tien, she and Nikolai would have nothing. *If he doesn't get treatment soon, something horrible is going to happen to him.* "Yes, but . . ." The realization struck her. Could it be . . . ? "Are you getting it out for—we're going for the galactic treatment, yes? You and me and Nikolai? Oh, Tien, good! Finally. Of course. I should have realized." So that's what he needed the money for, yes, at last! She rolled over and hugged him. But would it be enough? If it was less than a year's worth . . . "Will it be enough?"

"I . . . don't know. I'm checking."

"I saved a little out of my household allowance, I could put that in," she offered. "If it will get us underway sooner."

He licked his lips, and was silent for a moment. "I'm not sure. I don't like to let you . . ."

"This is exactly what I saved it for. I mean, I know I didn't earn it in the first place, but I managed it—it can be my contribution."

"How much do you have?"

"Almost four thousand Imperial marks!" She smiled, proud of her frugality.

"Oh!" He looked as though he were making an inner calculation. "Yes, that would help significantly."

He dropped a kiss on her forehead, and she relaxed further. She said, "I never thought about raiding your pension for the medical quest. I didn't realize we could. How soon can we get away?"

"That's . . . the next thing I'll have to find out. I would have checked it out this week, but I was interrupted by my department suffering a severe outbreak of Imperial Auditors."

She smiled in brief appreciation of his wit. He'd used to make her laugh more. If he had grown more sour with age, it was understandable, but the blackness of his humor had gradually come to weary her more than amuse her. Cynicism did not seem nearly so impressively daring to her now as it had when she was twenty. Perhaps this decision had lightened his heart, too.

Do you really think he'll do what he says, this time? Or will you be a fool? Again. No . . . if suspicion was the deadliest possible insult, then trust was always right, even if it was mistaken. Provisionally relieved by his new promise, she snuggled into the crook of his body, and for once his heavy arm flung across her seemed more comfort than trap. Maybe this time, they would finally be able to put their lives on a rational basis.

✧ ✧ ✧

"Shopping?" Lord Vorkosigan echoed over the breakfast table the next morning. He had been the last of the household to arise; Uncle Vorthys was already busy on the comconsole in Tien's study, Tien had left for work, and Nikki was off to school. Vorkosigan's mouth stayed straight, but the laugh lines at the corners of his eyes crinkled. "That's an offer seldom made to the son of my mother. . . . I'm afraid I don't need—no, wait, I do need something, at that. A wedding present."

"Who do you know who's getting married?" Ekaterin asked, relieved her suggestion had taken root, primarily because she didn't have a second one to offer. She prepared to be helpful.

"Gregor and Laisa."

It took her a moment to realize mean he meant the Emperor and his new Komarran fiancée. The surprising betrothal had been announced at Winterfair; the wedding was to be at Midsummer. "Oh! Uh . . . I'm not sure you can find anything in the Serifosa Dome that would be appropriate—maybe in Solstice they would have the kind of shops . . . oh, dear."

"I have to come up with something, I'm supposed to be Gregor's Second and Witness on their wedding circle. Maybe I could find something that would remind Laisa of home. Though possibly that's not a good idea—I'm not sure. I don't want to chance making her homesick on her honeymoon. What do you think?"

"We could look, I suppose . . ." There were exclusive shops she'd never dared enter in certain parts of the dome. This could be an excuse to venture inside.

"Duv and Delia, too, come to think of it. Yes, I've gotten way behind on my social duties."

"Who?"

"Delia Koudelka's a childhood friend of mine. She's marrying Commodore Duv Galeni, who is the new Chief of Komarran Affairs for Imperial Security. You may not have heard of him yet, but you will. He's Komarran-born."

"Of Barrayaran parents?"

"No, of Komarran resistance fighters. We seduced him to the service of the Imperium. We've agreed it was the shiny boots that turned the trick."

He was so utterly deadpan, he had to be joking. Hadn't he? She smiled uncertainly.

Uncle Vorthys lumbered into her kitchen then, murmuring, "More coffee?"

"Certainly." She poured for him. "How is it going?"

"Variously, variously." He sipped, and gave her a thank-you smile.

"I take it the morning courier has been here," said Vorkosigan. "How was last night's haul? Anything for me?"

"No, happily, if by that you mean more body parts. They brought back quite a bit of equipment of various sorts."

"Does it make any difference in your pet scenarios so far?"

"No, but I keep hoping it will. I dislike the way the vector analysis is shaping up."

Vorkosigan's eyes became notably more intent. "Oh? Why?"

"Mm. Take Point A as all things a moment before the accident—intact ship on course, soletta passively sitting in its orbital slot. Take Point B to be some time after the accident, parts of all masses scattering off in all directions at all speeds. By good old classical physics, B must equal A plus X, X being whatever forces—or masses—were added during the accident. We know A, pretty much, and the more of B we collect, the more we narrow down the possibilities for X. We're still missing some control systems, but the topside boys have by now retrieved most of the initial mass of the system of ship-plus-mirror. By the partial accounting done so far, X is . . . very large and has a very strange shape."

"Depending on when and how the engines blew, the explosion could have added a pretty damned big kick," said Vorkosigan.

"It's not the magnitudes of the missing forces that are so puzzling, it's their direction. Fragments of anything given a kick in free fall generally travel in a *straight* line, taking into account local gravities of course."

"And the ore ship pieces didn't?" Vorkosigan's brows rose. "So what do you have in mind for an outside force?"

Uncle Vorthys pursed his lips. "I'm going to have to contemplate this for a while. Play around with the numbers and the visual projections. My brain is getting too old, I think."

"What's the . . . the *shape* of the force, then, that makes it so strange?" asked Ekaterin, following all this with deep interest.

Uncle Vorthys set his cup down and placed his hands side by side, half open. "It's . . . a typical mass in space creates a gravitational well, a funnel if you will. This looks more like a *trough*."

"Running from the ore ship to the mirror?" asked Ekaterin, trying to picture this.

"No," said Uncle Vorthys. "Running from that nearby wormhole jump point to the mirror. Or vice versa."

"And the ore ship, ah, fell in?" said Vorkosigan. He looked momentarily as baffled as Ekaterin felt.

Uncle Vorthys did not look much better. "I should not like to say so in public, that's certain."

Vorkosigan asked, "A gravitational force? Or maybe . . . a gravitic imploder lance?"

"Eh," said Uncle Vorthys neutrally. "It's certainly not like the force map of any imploder lance I've ever seen. Ah, well." He picked up his coffee, and prepared to depart for his comconsole again.

"We were just planning an outing," said Ekaterin. "Would you like to see some more of Serifosa? Pick up a present for the Professora?'"

"I would, but I think it's my turn to stay in and read this morning," said her uncle. "You two go and have a good time. Though if you do see anything you think would please your aunt, I'd be extremely grateful if you'd purchase it, and I'll reimburse you."

"All right . . ." Go out with Vorkosigan alone? She'd assumed she would have her uncle along as chaperone. Still, if they stayed in public places, it should be enough to assuage any incipient suspicion on Tien's part. Not that Tien seemed to see Vorkosigan as any sort of threat, oddly. "You didn't need to see any more of Tien's department, did you?" Oh, dear, she hadn't phrased that well—what if he said yes?

"I haven't even reviewed their first stack of reports yet." Her uncle sighed. "Perhaps you'd care to take those on, Miles . . . ?"

"Yeah, I'll have a go at them." His eyes flicked up to Ekaterin's anxious face. "Later. When we get back."

Ekaterin led Lord Vorkosigan across the domed park that fronted her apartment building, heading for the nearest bubble-car station. His legs might be short, but his steps were quick, and she found she did not have to moderate her pace; if anything, she needed to lengthen her stride. That stiffness which she had seen impede his motion seemed to be something that came and went over the course of the day. His gaze, too, was quick, as he looked all around. At one point he even turned and walked backward a moment, studying something that had caught his eye.

"Is there anyplace in particular you would like to go?" she asked him.

"I don't know a great deal about Serifosa. I throw myself on your mercy, Madame, as my native guide. The last time I went shopping in any major way, it was for military ordnance."

She laughed. "That's very different."

"It's not as different as you might think. For the really high-ticket items they send sales engineers halfway across the galaxy to wait upon you. It's exactly the way my Aunt Vorpatril shops for clothes— in her case, come to think of it, also high-ticket items. The couturiers send their minions to her. I've become fond of minions, in my old age."

His old age was no more than thirty, she decided. A new-minted thirty much like her own, still worn uncomfortably. "And is that the way your mother the Countess shops, too?" How had *his* mother dealt with the fact of his mutations? Rather well, judging from the results.

"Mother just buys whatever Aunt Vorpatril tells her to. I've always had the impression she'd be happier in her old Betan Astronomical Survey fatigues."

The famous Countess Cordelia Vorkosigan was a galactic expatriate, of the most galactic possible sort, a Betan from Beta Colony. Progressive, high-tech, glittering Beta Colony, or corrupt, dangerous, sinister Beta Colony, take your pick of political views. No wonder Lord Vorkosigan seemed tinged with a faint galactic air; he literally was half galactic. "Have you ever been to Beta Colony? Is it as sophisticated as they say?"

"Yes. And no."

They arrived at the bubble-car platform, and she led them to the fourth car in line, partly because it was empty and partly to give herself an extra few seconds to select their destination. Quite automatically, Lord Vorkosigan hit the switch to close and seal the bubble canopy as soon as they'd settled into the front seat. He was either accustomed to his privacy, or just hadn't yet encountered the "Share the Ride" campaign now going on in Serifosa Dome. In any case, she was glad not to be bottled up with any Komarran strangers this trip.

Komarr had been a galactic trade crossroads for centuries, and the bazaar of the Barrayaran Empire for decades; even a relative backwater like Serifosa offered an abundance of wares at least equal to Vorbarr Sultana. She pursed her lips, then slotted in her credit chit and punched up the Shuttleport Locks District as their destination on the bubble-car's control panel. After a moment, they bumped into the tube and began to accelerate. The acceleration was slow, not a good sign.

"I believe I've seen your mother a few times on the holovid," she offered after a moment. "Sitting next to your father on reviewing platforms and the like. Mostly some years ago, when he was still Regent. Does it seem strange . . . does it give you a very different view of your parents, to see them on vid?"

"No," he said. "It gives me a very different view of holovids."

The bubble-car swung into a walled darkness lit by side-strips, flickering past the eye, then broke abruptly into sunlight, arching toward the next air-sealed complex. Halfway up the arc, they slowed still further; ahead of them, in the tube, Ekaterin could see other bubble-cars bunching to a crawl, like pearls on a string. "Oh, dear, I was afraid of that. Looks like we're caught in a blockage."

Vorkosigan craned his neck. "An accident?"

"No, the system's just overloaded. At certain times of day on certain routes, you can get held up from twenty to forty minutes. They're having a local political argument over the bubble-car system funding right now. One group wants to shorten the safety margins between cars and increase speeds. Another one wants to build more routes. Another one wants to ration access."

His eyes lit with amusement. "Ah, yes, I understand. And how many years has this argument been ongoing without issue?"

"At least five, I'm told."

"Isn't local democracy wonderful," he murmured. "And to think the Komarrans imagined we were doing them a *favor* to leave their downside affairs under their traditional sector control."

"I hope you don't mind heights," she said uncertainly, as the bubble-car moaned almost to a halt at the top of the arc. Through the faint distortions of the canopy and tube, half of Serifosa Dome's chaotic patchwork of structures seemed spread out to their view. Two cars ahead of them, a couple seized this opportunity to indulge in some heavy necking. Ekaterin studiously ignored them. "Or . . . small enclosed spaces."

He smiled a little grimly. "As long as the small enclosed space is above freezing, I can manage."

Was that a reference to his cryo-death? She hardly dared ask. She tried to think of a way to work the conversation back to his mother, and thence to how she'd dealt with his mutations. "Astronomical Survey? I thought your mother served in the Betan Expeditionary Force, in the Escobar War."

"Before the war, she had an eleven-year career in their Survey."

"Administration, or . . . She didn't go out on the blind wormhole jumps, did she? I mean, all spacers are a little strange, but wormhole wildcatters are supposed to be the craziest of the crazy."

"That's quite true." He glanced out, as with a slight jerk the bubble-car began to move once more, descending toward the next city section. "I've met some of 'em. I confess, I never thought of the government Survey as in the same league with the entrepreneurs. The independents make blind jumps into possible death hoping for a staggering fortune. The Survey . . . makes blind jumps into possible death for a salary, benefits, and a pension. Hm." He sat back, looking suddenly bemused. "She made ship captain, before the war. Maybe she had more practice for Barrayar than I'd realized. I wonder if she got tired of playing wall, too. I'll have to ask her."

"Playing wall?"

"Sorry, a personal metaphor. When you've taken chances a few too many times, you can get into an odd frame of mind. Adrenaline is a hard habit to kick. I'd always assumed that my, um, former taste for that kind of rush came from the *Barrayaran* side of my genetics. But near-death experiences tend to cause you to reevaluate your priorities. Running that much risk, that long . . . you'd end up either damn sure who you were and what you wanted, or you'd be, I don't know, anesthetized."

"And your mother?"

"Well, she's certainly not anesthetized."

She grew more daring still. "And you?"

"Hm." He smiled a small, elusive smile. "You know, *most* people, when they get a chance to corner me, try to pump me about my *father*."

"Oh." She flushed with embarrassment, and sat back. "I'm sorry. I was rude."

"Not at all." Indeed, he did not look or sound annoyed, his posture open and inviting as he leaned back and watched her. "Not at all."

Thus encouraged, she decided to be daring again. When would she ever repeat such a chance, after all? "Perhaps . . . what happened to you was a different kind of wall for her."

"Yes, it makes sense that you would see it from her point of view, I guess."

"What . . . exactly did happen . . . ?"

"To me?" he finished. He did not grow stiff as he had in that prickly moment over dinner the other night, but instead regarded her thoughtfully, with a kind of attentive seriousness that was almost more alarming. "What do you know?"

"Not a great deal. I'd heard that the Lord Regent's son had been born crippled, in the Pretender's War. The Lord Regent was noted for keeping his private life very private." Actually, she'd heard his heir was a mutie, and kept out of sight.

"That's *all*?" He looked almost offended—that he wasn't more famous? Or infamous?

"My life didn't much intersect that social set," she hastened to explain. "Or any other. My father was just a minor provincial bureaucrat. Many of Barrayar's rural Vor are a lot more rural than they are Vor, I'm afraid."

His smile grew. "Quite. You should have met my grandfather. Or . . . perhaps not. Well. Hm. There's not a great deal to tell, at this late date. An assassin aiming for my father managed to graze both my parents with an obsolete military poison gas called soltoxin."

"During the Pretendership?"

"Just prior, actually. My mother was five months pregnant with me. Hence this mess." A wave of his hand down his body, and that nervous jerk of his head, both summed himself and defied the viewer. "The damage was actually teratogenic, not genetic." He shot her an odd sidelong look. "It used to be very important to me for people to know that."

"Used to be? And not now?" Ingenuous of him—he'd managed to tell *her* quickly enough. She was almost disappointed. Was it true that only his body, and not his chromosomes, had been damaged?

"Now . . . I think maybe it's all right if they think I'm a mutie. If I can make it *really* not matter, maybe it will matter less for the next mutie who comes after me. A form of service that costs me no additional effort."

It cost him something, evidently. She thought of Nikolai, heading into his teens soon, and what a hard time of life that was even for normal children. "Were you made to feel it? Growing up?"

"I was of course somewhat protected by Father's rank and position."

She noted that *somewhat*. *Somewhat* was not the same as *completely*. Sometimes, *somewhat* was the same as *not at all*.

"I moved a few mountains, to force myself into the Imperial Military Service. After, um, a few false starts, I finally found a place for myself in Imperial Security, among the irregulars. The rest of the irregulars. ImpSec was more interested in results than appearances, and I found I could deliver results. Except—a slight miscalculation— all the achievements upon which I'd hoped to be rejudged disappeared into ImpSec's classified files. So I fell out at the end of a thirteen-year career, a medically discharged captain whom nobody knew, almost as anonymous as when I started." He actually sighed.

"Imperial Auditors aren't anonymous!"

"No, just discreet." He brightened. "So there's some hope yet."

Why did he make her want to laugh? She swallowed the impulse. "Do you wish to be famous?"

His eyes narrowed in a moment of introspection. "I would have said so, once. Now I think . . . I just wanted to be someone in my own right. Make no mistake, I like being my father's son. He is a great man. In every sense, and it's been a privilege to know him. But there is, nevertheless, a secret fantasy of mine, where just once, in some history somewhere, Aral Vorkosigan gets introduced as being principally important because he was Miles Naismith Vorkosigan's father."

She did laugh then, though she muffled it almost immediately with a hand over her mouth. But he did not seem to take offense, for his eyes merely crinkled at her. "It is pretty amusing," he said ruefully.

"No . . . no, not that," she hastily denied. "It just seems like some kind of hubris, I guess."

"Oh, it's all kinds of hubris." Except that he did not look in the least daunted by the prospect, merely calculating.

His thoughtful look fell on her then; he cleared his throat, and began, "When I was working on your comconsole yesterday morning—" The deceleration of the bubble-car interrupted him.

The little man craned his neck as they slid to a halt in the station. "Damn," he murmured.

"Is something wrong?" she asked, concerned.

"No, no." He hit the pad to raise the canopy. "So, let's see this Docks and Locks district . . ."

Lord Vorkosigan seemed to enjoy their stroll through the organized chaos of the Shuttleport Locks district, though the route he chose was decidedly nonstandard; he zig-zagged by preference down to what Ekaterin thought of as the underside of the area, where people and machines loaded and unloaded cargo, and where the less well-off sorts of spacers had their hostels and bars. There were plenty of odd-looking people in the district, in all colors and sizes, wearing strange clothes; snatches of conversations in utterly strange languages teased her ear in passing. The looks they gave the two Barrayarans were noted but ignored by Vorkosigan. Ekaterin decided that his lack of offense wasn't because the galactics stared less—or more—at him, it was that they stared equally at everybody.

She also discovered that he was attracted by the dreadful, among the galactic wares cramming the narrow shops into which they ducked. He actually appeared to seriously consider for several minutes what was claimed to be a genuine twentieth-century reproduction lamp, of Jacksonian manufacture, consisting of a sealed glass vessel containing two immiscible liquids which slowly rose and fell in the convection currents. "It looks just like red blood corpuscles floating in plasma," Vorkosigan opined, staring in fascination at the underlit blobs.

"But as a *wedding* present?" she choked, half amused, half appalled. "What kind of message would people take it for?"

"It would make Gregor laugh," he replied. "Not a gift he gets much. But you're right, the wedding present proper needs to be, er, proper. Public and political, not personal." With a regretful sigh, he returned the lamp to its shelf. After another moment, he changed his mind again, bought it, and had it shipped. "I'll get him *another* present for the wedding. This can be for his birthday."

After that, he let Ekaterin lead him into the more sophisticated end of the district, with shops displaying well-spread-out and well-lit jewelry and artwork and antiques, interspersed with discreet couturiers of the sort, she thought, who might send minions to his aunt. He seemed to find it much less interesting than the galactic rummage sale a few streets and levels away, the animation fading from his face, until his eye was caught by an unusual display in a jeweler's kiosk.

Tiny model planets, the size of the end of her thumb, turned in a grav-bubble against a black background. Several of the little spheres were displayed under various levels of magnification, where they proved to be perfectly-mapped replicas of the worlds they represented, right down to the one-meter scale. Not just rivers and mountains and seas, but cities and roads and dams, were represented in realistic colors. Furthermore, the terminator moved across their miniature landscapes in real-time for the planetary cycle in question; cities lit the night side like living jewels. They could be hung in pairs as earrings, or displayed in pendants or bracelets. Most of the planets in the wormhole nexus were available, including Beta Colony and an Earth that included as an option its famous moon circling a handspan away, though how this pairing was to be hung on someone's body was not entirely clear. The prices, at which Vorkosigan did not even glance, were alarming.

"That's rather fine," he murmured approvingly, staring in fascination at the little Barrayar. "I wonder how they do that? I know where I could have one reverse-engineered. . . ."

"They seem more like toys than jewels, but I have to admit, they're striking."

"Oh, yes, a typical tech toy—high-end this year, everywhere next year, nowhere after that, till the antiquarians' revival. Still . . . it would be fun to make up an Imperial set, Barrayar, Komarr, and Sergyar. I don't know any women with three ears . . . two earrings and a pendant, perhaps, though then you'd have the socio-political problem of how to rank the worlds."

"You could put all three on a necklace."

"True, or . . . I think my mother would definitely like a Sergyar. Or Beta Colony . . . no, might make her homesick. Sergyar, yes, very apropos. And there's Winterfair, and birthdays coming up—let's see, there's Mother, Laisa, Delia, Aunt Alys, Delia's sisters, Drou—maybe I ought to order a dozen sets, and a have a couple to spare."

"Uh," said Ekaterin, contemplating this burst of efficiency, "do all these women know each other?" Were any of them his lovers? Surely he wouldn't mention such in the same breath with his mother and aunt. Or might he be a suitor? But . . . to *all* of them?

"Oh, sure."

"Do you really think you ought to get them all the *same* present?"

"No?" he asked doubtfully. "But . . . they all know *me*. . . ."

In the end, he restrained himself, purchasing only two earring sets, one each of Barrayars and Komarrs, and swapping them out, for the brides of the two mixed marriages. He added a Sergyar on a fine chain for his mother. At the last moment, he bolted back for another Barrayar, for which woman on his lengthy list he did not say. The packets of tiny planets were made up and gift-wrapped.

Feeling a little overwhelmed by the Komarran bazaar, Ekaterin led him off for a look at one of her favorite parks. It bounded the end of the Locks district, and featured one of the largest and most naturally landscaped lakes in Serifosa. Ekaterin mentally planned a stop for coffee and pastry, after they circumnavigated the lake along its walking trails.

They paused at a railing above a modest bluff, where a view across the lake framed some of the higher towers of Serifosa. The crippled soletta array was in full view overhead now, through the park's transparent dome, creating dim sparkles on the lake's wavelets. Cheerful voices echoed distantly across the water, from families playing on an artificially-natural swimming beach.

"It's very pretty," said Ekaterin, "but the maintenance cost is terrific. Urban forestry is a full-time specialty here. Everything's consciously created, the woods, the rocks, the weeds, everything."

"World-in-a-box," murmured Vorkosigan, gazing out over the reflecting sheet. "Some assembly required."

"Some Serifosans think of their park system as a promise for the future, ecology in the bank," she went on, "but others, I suspect, don't know the difference between their little parks and real forests. I sometimes wonder if, by the time the atmosphere is breathable, the Komarrans' great-grandchildren will all be such agoraphobes, they won't even venture out in it."

"A lot of Betans tend to think like that. When I was last there—" His sentence was shattered by a sudden crackling boom; Ekaterin started, till she identified the noise as a load dropped from a mag-crane working on some construction, or reconstruction, back over their shoulders beyond the trees. But Vorkosigan jumped and spun like a cat; the package in his right hand went flying, his left made to push her behind him, and he drew a stunner she hadn't even known he was carrying half out of his trouser pocket before he, too, identified the source of the bang. He inhaled deeply, flushed, and cleared his throat. "Sorry," he said to her wide-eyed look. "I overreacted a trifle there." Though they both surreptitiously examined the dome overhead; it remained placidly intact. "Stunner's a pretty useless weapon anyway, against things that go bump like that." He shoved it back deep into his pocket.

"You dropped your planets," she said, looking around for the white packet. It was nowhere in sight.

He leaned out over the railing. "Damn."

She followed his gaze. The packet had bounced off the boardwalk, and fetched up a meter down the bluff, caught on a bit of hanging foliage, a thorny bittersweet plant dangling over the water.

"I think maybe I can reach it . . ." He swung over the railing past the sign admonishing CAUTION: STAY ON THE TRAIL and flung himself flat on the ground over the edge before she could squeak, *But your good suit—* Vorkosigan was not, she suspected, a man who routinely did his own laundry. But his blunt fingers swung short of the prize they sought. She had a hideous vision of an Imperial Auditor under her guest-hold landing head-down in the pond. Could she be accused of treason? The bluff was barely four meters high; how deep was the water here?

"My arms are longer," she offered, climbing after him.

Temporarily thwarted, he scrambled back to a sitting position. "We can fetch a stick. Or better yet, a minion with a stick." He glanced dubiously at his wrist comm.

"I *think*," she said demurely, "calling ImpSec for this might be overkill." She lay prone, and reached as he had. "It's all right, I think I can . . ." Her fingers too swung short of the packet, but only just. She inched forward, feeling the precarious pull of the undercut slope. She stretched . . .

The root-compacted soil of the edge sagged under her weight, and she began to slide precipitously forward. She yelped; pushing backward fragmented her support totally. One wildly back-grappling arm was caught suddenly in a viselike grip, but the rest of her body turned as the soil gave way beneath her, and she found herself dangling absurdly feet-down over the pond. Her other arm, swinging around, was caught, too, and she looked up into Vorkosigan's face above her. He was lying prone on the slope, one hand locked around each of her wrists. His teeth were clenched and grinning, his gray eyes alight.

"Let go, you idiot!" she cried.

The look on his face was weirdly, wildly exultant. "Never," he gasped, "again—"

His half-boots were locked around . . . nothing, she realized, as he began to slide inexorably over the edge after her. But his death-grip never slackened. The exalted look on his face melted to sudden horrified realization. The laws of physics took precedence over heroic intent for the next couple of seconds; dirt, pebbles, vegetation, and two Barrayaran bodies all hit the chilly water more or less simultaneously.

The water, it turned out, was a bit over a meter deep. The bottom was soft with muck. She wallowed upright onto her feet, one shoe gone who knew where, sputtering and dragging her hair from her eyes and looking around frantically for Vorkosigan. *Lord* Vorkosigan. The water came to her waist, it ought not to be over his head—no half-booted feet were sticking up like waving stumps anywhere—could he *swim*?

He popped up beside her, and blew muddy water out of his mouth, and dashed it from his eyes to clear his vision. His beautiful suit was sodden, and a water-plant dangled over one ear. He clawed it away, and located her, his hand going toward her and then stopping.

"Oh," said Ekaterin faintly. "Drat."

There was a meditative pause before Lord Vorkosigan spoke. "Madame Vorsoisson," he said mildly at last, "has it ever occurred to you that you may be just a touch oversocialized?"

She couldn't stop herself; she laughed out loud. She clapped her hand over her mouth, and waited fearfully for some masculine explosion of wrath.

None came; he merely grinned back at her. He looked around till he spotted his packet, now dangling mockingly overhead. "Ha. Now gravity's on our side, at least." He waded underneath the remains of the overhang, disappeared into the water again, and came up holding a couple of rocks. He shied them at the thorn plant till he dislodged his package, and caught it one-handed as it fell, before it could hit the water. He grinned again, and splashed back to her, and offered her his other arm for all the world as though they were about to enter some ambassadorial reception. "Madame, will you wade with me?"

His humor was irresistible; she found herself laying her hand upon his sleeve. "My pleasure, my lord."

She abandoned her surreptitious toe-prodding for her lost shoe. They sloshed off toward the nearest low place on shore, with the most serenely cockeyed dignity Ekaterin had ever experienced. Packet in his teeth, he scrambled ahead of her, grabbed a narrow out-leaning tree trunk for support, and handed her up through the mud with the air of an Armsman-driver helping his lady from the rear compartment of her groundcar. To Ekaterin's intense relief, no one across the lake appeared to have noticed their show. Could Vorkosigan's Imperial authority save them from arrest for swimming in a no-swimming zone?

"You aren't upset about the accident?" she inquired timorously as they regained the path, still hardly able to believe her good fortune in his admittedly odd reaction. A passing jogger stared at them, turning and bouncing backward a moment, but Vorkosigan waved him genially onward.

He tucked his packet under his arm. "Madame Vorsoisson, trust me on this one. Needle grenades are accidents. *That* was just an amusing inconvenience." But then his smile slipped, his face stiffened, and his breath drew in sharply. He added in a rush, "I should mention, I've lately become subject to occasional seizures. I pass out and have convulsions. They last about five minutes, and then go away, and I wake up, no harm done. If one should occur, don't panic."

"Are you about to have one now?" she asked, panicked.

"I feel a little strange all of a sudden," he admitted.

There was a bench nearby, along the trail. "Here, sit down—" She led him to it. He sat abruptly, and hunched over with his face in his hands. He was beginning to shiver with the wet cold, as was she, but his shudders were long and deep, traveling the length of his short body. Was a seizure starting now? She regarded him with terror.

After a couple of minutes, his ragged breathing steadied. He rubbed his face, hard, and looked up. He was extremely pale, almost gray-faced. His pasted-on smile, as he turned toward her, was so plainly false that she almost would rather he'd have frowned. "I'm sorry. I haven't done anything like that in quite a while, at least not in a waking state. Sorry."

"Was that a seizure?"

"No, no. False alarm entirely. Actually, it was a, um, combat flashback, actually. Unusually vivid. Sorry, I don't usually . . . I haven't done . . . I don't usually do things like this, really." His speech was scrambled and hesitant, entirely unlike himself, and failed signally to reassure her.

"Should I go for help?" She was sure she needed to get him somewhere warmer, as soon as possible. He looked like a man in shock.

"Ha. No. Worlds too late. No, really, I'll be all right in a couple of minutes. I just need to think about this for a minute." He looked sideways at her. "I was just stunned by an insight, for which I thank you."

She clenched her hands in her lap. "Either stop talking gibberish, or stop talking at all," she said sharply.

His chin jerked up, and his smile grew a shade more genuine. "Yes, you deserve an explanation. If you want it. I warn you, it's a bit ugly."

She was so rattled and exasperated by now, she'd have cheerfully choked explanations out of his cryptic little throat. She took refuge in the mockery of formality which had extracted them so nobly from the pond. "If you please, my lord!"

"Ah, yes, well. Dagoola IV. I don't know if you've heard much about it . . . ?"

"Some."

"It was an evacuation under fire. It was an unholy mess. Shuttles lifting with people crammed aboard. The details don't matter now, except for one. There was this woman, Sergeant Beatrice. Taller than you. We had trouble with our shuttle's hatch ramp, it wouldn't retract. We couldn't dog the hatch and lift above the atmosphere till we'd jettisoned it. We were airborne, I don't know how high, there was thick cloud cover. We got the damaged ramp loosened, but she fell after it. I grabbed for her. Touched her hand, even, but I missed."

"Did . . . was she killed?"

"Oh, yes." His smile now was utterly peculiar. "It was a long way down by then. But you see . . . something *I* didn't see until about five minutes ago. I've spent five, six years walking around with this picture in my head. Not all the time, you understand, just when I chanced to be reminded. If only I'd been a little quicker, grabbed a little harder, hadn't lost my grip, I might have pulled her in. Instant replay on an endless repeat. In all those years, I never once pictured what would *really* have happened if I'd made my grab good. She was almost twice my weight."

"She'd have pulled you out," said Ekaterin. For all the simplicity of his words, the images they evoked were intense and immediate. She rubbed at the deep red marks aching now on her wrists. *Because you would not have let go.*

He looked for the first time at the marks. "Oh. I'm sorry."

"It's all right." Self-conscious, she stopped massaging them.

This didn't help, because *he* took her hand, and rubbed gently at the blotches, as if he might erase them. "I think there must be something askew with my body image," he said.

"Do you think you're six feet tall, inside your head?"

"Apparently my dream-self thinks so."

"Does that—realizing the truth—make it any better?"

"No, I don't think so. Just . . . different. Stranger."

Both their hands were freezing cold. She sprang to her feet, eluding his arresting touch. "We have to go get dry and warm, or we'll both . . . be in a state." *Catch your death,* was her great-aunt's old phrase for it, and a singularly inept phrase it would be to use just now. She dropped her useless remaining shoe in the first trash bin they passed.

On their way to the bubble-car stop near the public beach, Ekaterin darted into a kiosk and bought a stack of colorful towels. In the bubble-car, she turned the heat up to its stingy maximum.

"Here," she said, shoving towels at Lord Vorkosigan as the car accelerated. "Get out of that sopping tunic, at least, and dry off a bit."

"Right." Tunic, silk shirt, and thermal undershirt hit the floor with a wet splat, and he rubbed his hair and torso vigorously. His skin had a blotched purple-blue tinge; pink and white scars sprang out in high contrast to their darkened background. There were scars on scars on scars, mostly very fine and surgically straight, in criss-crossing layers running back through time, growing fainter and paler: on his arms, on his hands and fingers, on his neck and running up under his hair, circling his ribcage and paralleling his spine, and, most pinkly and recently, an unusually ragged and tangled mess centered on his chest.

She stared in covert astonishment; his glance caught hers. By way of apology, she said, "You weren't joking about needle grenades, were you?"

His hand touched his chest. "No. But most of this is old surgery, from the brittle bones the soltoxin gifted me with. I've had practically every bone in my body replaced with synthetics, at one time or another. Very piecemeal, though I suppose it would not have been medically practical to just whip me off my skeleton, shake me out like a suit of clothes, and pop me back on over another one."

"Oh. My."

"Ironically enough, all this show represents the successful repairs. The injury that really took me out of the Service you can't even see." He touched his forehead and wrapped a couple of the towels around himself like a shawl. The towels had giant yellow daisies on them. His shivering was diminishing now, his skin growing less purple, though still blotchy. "I didn't mean to alarm you, back there."

She thought it through. "You should have told me sooner." Yes, what if one of his seizures had taken him by surprise, sometime along their route this morning? What in the world would she have done? She frowned at him.

He shifted uncomfortably. "You're quite right, of course. Um . . . quite right. Some secrets are unfair to keep from . . . people on your team." He looked away from her, looked back, smiled tensely, and said, "I started to tell you, earlier, but I rather lost my nerve. When I was working on your comconsole yesterday morning, I accidentally ran across your file on Vorzohn's Dystrophy."

Her breath seemed to freeze in her suddenly-paralyzed chest. "Didn't I—how could you accidentally . . ." Had she somehow left it open last time? Not possible!

"I could show you how," he offered. "ImpSec basic training is pretty basic. I think you could pick up that trick in about ten minutes."

The words blurted out before she could stop and think. "You opened it deliberately!"

"Well, yes." His smile now was false and embarrassed. "I was curious. I was taking a break from looking at vids of autopsies. Your, um, gardens are lovely, too, by the way."

She stared at him in disbelief. A mixture of emotions churned in her chest: violation, outrage, fear . . . and relief? *You had no right.*

"No, I had no right," he agreed, watching her obviously too-open expression; she tried to school her face to blankness. "I apologize. I can only plead that ImpSec training inculcates some pretty bad habits." He took a deep breath. "What can I do for you, Madame Vorsoisson? Anything you need to ask, or ask about . . . I am at your service." The little man half-bowed, an absurdly archaic gesture, sitting wrapped in his towels like some wizened old Count from the Time of Isolation in his robes of office.

"There's nothing you can do for me," Ekaterin said woodenly. She became aware that her legs and arms were tightly crossed, and she was starting to hunch over; she straightened with a conscious effort. Dear God, how would Tien react to her spilling, however inadvertently his deadly—well, *he* acted as though it were deadly— secret? Now of all times, when he seemed on the verge of overcoming his denial, or whatever it was, and taking effective action at last?

"I beg your pardon, Madame Vorsoisson, but I'm afraid I'm still uncertain exactly what your situation is. It's obviously very private, if even your uncle doesn't know, and I'd give odds he doesn't—"

"Don't tell him!"

"Not without your permission, I assure you, Madame. But . . . if you are ill, or expect to become ill, there is a great *deal* that can be done for you." He hesitated. "The contents of that file tell me you already know this. Is *anyone* helping you?"

Help. What a concept. She felt as though she might melt through the floor of the bubble car at the mere thought. She retreated from the terrible temptation. "I'm not ill. We don't require assistance." She raised her chin defiantly, and added with all the frost she could muster, "It was very wrong of you to read my private files, Lord Vorkosigan."

"Yes," he agreed simply. "A wrong I do not care to compound by either concealing my breach of trust, or failing to offer what help I can command."

Just *how much* help Imperial Auditor Vorkosigan might command . . . was not to be thought about. Too painful. Belatedly, she realized that declaring herself unaffected was tantamount to naming Tien afflicted. She was rescued from her confusion by the bubble-car sliding to a stop at her home station. "This is very much not your business."

"I beg you will think of your uncle as a resource, then. I'm certain he would wish it."

She shook her head, and hit the canopy release sharply.

They walked in stiff and chilled silence back to her apartment building, in awkward contrast, Ekaterin felt, to their earlier odd ease. Vorkosigan didn't look happy either.

Uncle Vorthys met them at the apartment door, still in shirtsleeves and with a data disk in his hand. "Ah! Vorkosigan! Back earlier than I expected, good. I almost rang your comm link." He paused, staring at their damp and bizarre bedragglement, but then shrugged and went on, "We had a visit from a second courier. Something for you."

"A second courier? Must be something hot. Is it a break in the case?" Vorkosigan shrugged an arm free of his towel-shawl and took the proffered disk.

"I'm not at all sure. They found another body."

"The missing were all accounted for. A body part, surely—a woman's arm, perhaps?"

Uncle Vorthys shook his head. "A body. Almost intact. Male. They're working on the identification now. They *were* all accounted for." He grimaced. "Now, it seems, we have a spare."

Chapter Six

Miles boiled himself in the shower for a long time, trying to regain control of his shocky body and scattered wits. He'd realized quickly, earlier, that all Madame Vorsoisson's anxious questions about his mother camouflaged oblique concerns about her son Nikolai, and he'd answered her as openly and carefully as he could. He'd been rewarded, through the extremely pleasant morning's expedition, by seeing her gradually relax and grow nearly open herself. When she'd laughed, her light blue eyes had sparkled. The animated intelligence had illuminated her face, and spilled over to loosen and soften her body from its original tight defensive density. Her sense of humor, creeping slowly out from hiding, had even survived his dropping them into that idiot pond.

Her brief appalled look when he'd half-stripped in the bubble-car had almost thrown him back into earlier modes of painful somatic self-consciousness, but not quite. It seemed he had grown comfortable at last in his own ill-used body, and the realization had given him a lunatic courage to try to clear things with her. So when all expression in her face shut down as he'd confessed his snooping . . . that had hurt.

He'd handled a bad situation as well as he could, hadn't he? Yes? No? He wished now he'd kept his mouth shut. *No.* His false stance with Madame Vorsoisson had been unbearable. *Unbearable? Isn't that a little strong? Uncomfortable*, he revised this hastily downward. Awkward, anyway.

But confession was supposed to be followed by absolution. If only the damned bubble-car had been delayed again, if only he'd had ten more minutes with her, he might have made it come out right. He shouldn't have tried to pass it off with that stupid joke, *I could show you how* . . .

Her icy, armored *We don't require assistance* felt like . . . missing a catch. He would be forced onward, she would spin down into the fog and never be seen again.

You're overdramatizing, boy. Madame Vorsoisson wasn't in a combat zone, was she?

Yes, she is. She was just falling toward death in exquisitely slow motion.

He wanted a drink desperately. Preferably several. Instead he dried himself off, dressed in another of his Auditor-suits, and went to see the Professor.

Miles leaned on the Professor's comconsole in the guest room which doubled as Tien Vorsoisson's home office, and studied the ravaged face of the dead man in the vid. He hoped for some revelation of expression, surprise or rage or fear, that would give a clue as to how the fellow had died. Besides suddenly. But the face was merely dead, its frozen distortions entirely physiological and familiar.

"First of all, are they sure he's really ours?" Miles asked, pulling up a chair for himself and settling in. On the vid, the anonymous medtech's examination recording played on at low volume, her voice-over comments delivered in that flat clinical tone universally used at moments like this. "He didn't drift in from somewhere else, I suppose."

"No, unfortunately," Vorthys said. "His speed and trajectory put him accurately at the site of our accident at the time of the smash-up, and his initial estimated time of death also matches."

Miles had wished for a break in the case, some new lead that would take him in a more speedily fruitful direction. He hadn't realized his desires were so magically powerful. *Be careful what you wish for* . . .

"Can they tell if he came from the ship, or the station?"

"Not from the trajectory alone."

"Mm, I suppose not. He shouldn't have been aboard either one. Well . . . we wait for the ID, then. News of this find has not yet been publicly released, I trust."

"No, nor leaked yet either, amazingly."

"Unless the explanation for his being there turns out to be rock-solid, I don't think secondhand reports are going to be enough on this one." He had read, God knew, enough reports in the last two weeks to saturate him for a year.

"Bodies are your department." The Professor ceded this one to him with a wave of his hand and a good will clearly laced with relief. Above the vid-plate, the preliminary examination wound to its conclusion; no one reached for the replay button.

Well, strictly speaking, political consequences were Miles's department. He really ought to visit Solstice soon, though in the planetary capital a visiting Auditor was more likely to get *handled*; he'd wanted this open provincial angle of view first, free of VIP choreographing.

"Engineering equipment," Vorthys added, "is mine. They've also just retrieved some of the ship's control systems I was waiting for. I'm think I'm going to have to go back topside soon."

"Tonight?" Miles could move out, and into a hotel, under the cover of that avuncular withdrawal. That would be a relief.

"If I went up now, I'd get there just in time for bed. I'll wait till morning. They've also found some odd things. Not accounted for in inventory."

"Odd things? New or old?" There had been tons of poorly inventoried junk equipment on the station, a century's accumulation of obsolete and worn-out technology that had been cheaper to store than haul away. If the probable-cause techs had the unenviable task of sorting it now, it must mean the highest-priority retrieval tasks were almost done.

"New. That's what's odd. And their trajectories were associated with this new body."

"I hardly ever saw a ship where somebody didn't have an unauthorized still or something operating in a closet somewhere."

"Nor a station either. But our Komarran boys are sharp enough to recognize a still."

"Maybe . . . I'll go up with you, tomorrow," Miles said thoughtfully.

"I would like that."

❖　　❖　　❖

Gathering up the remains of his nerve, Miles went to seek out Madame Vorsoisson. This would be, he guessed, his last chance to ever have a conversation alone with her. His footsteps echoed hollowly through the empty rooms, and his tentative speaking of her name went unanswered. She had left the apartment, perhaps to pick up Nikolai from school or something. *Missed again. Damn.*

Miles took the examination recording off to the comconsole in her workroom for a more careful second run-through, and stacked up the terraforming reports from yesterday next in line. With a self-conscious twinge, he keyed on the machine. His guilty conscience irrationally expected she might pop in at any moment to check up on him. But no, more likely she would avoid him altogether. He vented a depressed sigh and started the vid.

He found little to add to the Professor's synopsis. The mysterious eighth victim was middle-aged, of average height and build for a Komarran, if he was a Komarran. It was not possible at this point to tell if he had been handsome or ugly in life. Most of his clothing had been ripped or burned off in the disaster, including any handy pockets containing traceable credit chits, etcetera. The shreds that were left appeared to be anonymous ship-knits, common wear for spacers who might have to slide into a pressure suit at a moment's notice.

What was delaying the man's identification? Miles deliberately held in check the dozen theories his mind wanted to generate. He longed to gallop up immediately to the orbital station where the body had been taken, but his arrival in person topside, to breathe over the actual investigators' shoulders, would only distract them and slow things down. Once you had delegated the best people to do a job for you, you had to trust both them and your judgment.

What he could do without admitting impediment was go bother another useless high-level supervisor like himself. He punched up the private code for the Chief of Imperial Security—Komarr at his office in Solstice, which the man had properly sent him upon the Imperial Auditors' first arrival in Komarr local space.

General Rathjens appeared at once. He looked middle-aged, alert, and busy, all appropriate qualities for his rank and post. Interestingly, he took advantage of the latter and wore civilian Komarran-style street wear rather than Imperial undress greens, suggesting he was either subtly politically-minded, or preferred his comfort. Miles guessed the former. Rathjens was the ImpSec's top man on Komarr, reporting directly to Duv Galeni at ImpSec HQ in Vorbarr Sultana. "Yes, my Lord Auditor. What can I do for you?"

"I'm interested in the new corpse they found this morning topside in association, apparently, with our soletta disaster. You've heard of it?"

"Only just. I haven't had a chance to view the preliminary report yet."

"I just did. It's not very informative. Tell me, what's your standard operating procedure for identifying this poor fellow? How soon do you expect to have anything substantive?"

"The identification of a victim of an ordinary accident, topside or downside, would normally be left to the local civil security. Since this one came within our orbit as possible sabotage, we're running our own search in parallel with the Komarran authorities."

"Do you cooperate with each other?"

"Oh, yes. That is, they cooperate with us."

"I understand," said Miles blandly. "How long is ID likely to take?"

"If the man was Komarran, or if he was a galactic who came through Customs at one of the jump point stations, we should have something within hours. If he was Barrayaran, it may take a little longer. If he was somehow unregistered . . . well, that becomes another problem."

"I take it he hasn't been matched with any missing person report?"

"That would have sped things up. No."

"So he's been gone for almost three weeks, but nobody's missed him. Hm."

General Rathjens glanced aside at some readout on his own comconsole desk. "Do you know you are calling from an unsecured comconsole, Lord Vorkosigan?"

"Yes." That was why all his and the Professor's reports and digests from topside were being hand-carried to them from the local Serifosa ImpSec office. They hadn't expected to be here long enough to bother having ImpSec install their own secured machine. *Should have.* "I'm only seeking background information just now. When you do find out who this fellow is, how are the relatives notified?"

"Normally, local dome security sends an officer in person, if at all possible. In a case like this with potential ImpSec connections, we send an agent of our own with them, to make an initial evaluation and recommend further investigation."

"Hm. Notify me first, please. I may want to ride along and observe."

"It could come at an odd hour."

"That's fine." He wanted to feed his back-brain on something besides second-hand data; he wanted action for his restless body. He wanted out of this apartment. He'd thought it had been uncomfortable that first night because the Vorsoissons were strangers, but that was as nothing to how awkward it had become now he'd begun to know them.

"Very well, my lord."

"Thank you, General. That's all for now." Miles cut the com.

With a sigh, he turned again to the stack of terraforming reports, starting with Waste Heat Management's excessively complete report on dome energy flows. It was only in his imagination that the gaze from a pair of outraged light blue eyes burned into the back of his head.

He had left the workroom door open with the thought—hope?— that if Madame Vorsoisson just happened to be passing by, and just happened to want to renew their truncated conversation, she might realize she had his invitation to do so. The awareness that this left him sitting alone with his back to the door came to Miles simultaneously with the sense that he was no longer alone. At a surreptitious sniff from the vicinity of the doorway, he fixed his most inviting smile on his face and turned his chair around.

It was Nikki, hovering in the frame and staring at him in uncertain calculation. He returned Miles's misdirected smile shyly. "Hello," the boy ventured.

"Hello, Nikki. Home from school?"

"Yep."

"Do you like it?"

"Naw."

"Ah? How was today?"

"Boring."

"What are you studying, that's so dull?"

"Nothin'."

What a joy such monosyllabic exchanges must be to his parents, paying for that exclusive private school. Miles's smile twisted. Reassured, perhaps, by the glint of humor in his eye, the boy ventured within. He looked Miles up and down more openly than he had done heretofore; Miles bore being Looked At. *Yes, you can get used to me, kiddo.*

"Were you really a spy?" Nikki asked suddenly.

Miles leaned back, brows rising. "Now, wherever did you get that idea?"

"Uncle Vorthys *said* you were in ImpSec. Galactic operations," Nikki reminded him.

Ah, yes, that first night at the dinner table. "I was a courier officer. Do you know what that is?"

"Not . . . 'zactly. I thought a courier was a jumpship . . . ?"

"The ship is named after the job. A courier is a kind of glorified delivery man. I carried messages back and forth for the Imperium."

Nikki's brow wrinkled dubiously. "Was it dangerous?"

"It wasn't supposed to be. I generally got places only to have to turn around immediately and go back. I spent a lot of time en route reading. Composing reports. And, ah, studying. ImpSec would send these training programs along, that you were supposed to complete in your spare time, and turn back in to your superiors when you got home."

"Oh," said Nikki, sounding a little dismayed, possibly at the thought that even grownups weren't spared from homework. He regarded Miles more sympathetically. Then a spark rose in his eye. "But you got to go on *jumpships*, didn't you? Imperial fast couriers and things?"

"Oh, yes."

"*We* went on a jumpship, to come here. It was a Vorsmythe *Dolphin*-class 776 with quadruple-vortex outboard control nacelles and dual norm-space thrusters and a crew of twelve. It carried a hundred and twenty passengers. It was full up, too." Nikki's face grew reflective. "Kind of a barge, compared to Imperial fast couriers, but Mama got the jump pilot to let me come up and see his control room. He let me sit in his station chair and put on his headset." The spark had become a flame in the memory of this glorious moment.

Miles could recognize imprinting when he saw it. "You admire jumpships, I take it."

"I want to be a jump pilot when I grow up. Didn't you ever? Or . . . or wouldn't they let you?" A certain wariness returned to Nikki's face; had he been cautioned by the adults not to mention Miles's mutoid appearance? *Yes, let us all pretend to ignore the obvious. That ought to clarify the kid's worldview.*

"No, I wanted to be a strategist. Like my Da and my Gran'da. I couldn't have passed the physical for jump pilot anyway."

"My Da was a soldier. It sounded boring. He stayed on one base for practically the whole time. *I* want to be an Imperial pilot, in the fastest ships, and go places."

Very far away from here. Yes. Miles understood *that* one, all right. It occurred to him suddenly that even if nothing else was done between now and then, a military physical would reveal Nikki's Vorzohn's Dystrophy. And even if it was successfully treated, the defect would disqualify him for military pilot's training.

"Imperial pilot?" Miles let his brows rise in apparent surprise. "Well, I suppose . . . but if you really want to go places, the military's not your best route."

"Why not?"

"Except for a very few courier or diplomatic missions, the military jump pilots just go from Barrayar to Komarr to Sergyar and back. Same old routes, round and round. And you have to wait forever for your turn on the roster, my pilot acquaintances tell me. Now, if you really want experience, going out with the Komarran trade fleets would take you much farther afield—all the way to Earth, and beyond. And they go out for much longer, and there are many more berths to be had. There are more kinds of ships. Pilots get a lot more time in the hot-seat. *And* when you get to the interesting places, you're a lot freer to look around."

"Oh." Nikki digested this thoughtfully. "Wait here," he commanded abruptly, and darted out.

He was back in moments cradling a box jammed with model jumpships. "This is the *Dolphin*-776 we went on," he held one up for Miles's inspection. He rummaged for another. "Did you ride on fast couriers like this one?"

"The *Falcon*-9? Yes, a time or two." A model caught Miles's eye; automatically, he slid down onto the floor beside Nikki, who was arranging his collection for fleet inspection. "Good God, is that an RG freighter?"

"It's an antique." Nikki held it out.

Miles took it, his eye lighting. "I owned one of the very last of these, when I was seventeen. Now, *that* was a barge."

"A . . . a model like this?" asked Nikki uncertainly.

"No, a jumpship."

"You owned a real jumpship? Your*self*?" He inhaled alarmingly.

"Mm, me and a bunch of creditors." Miles smiled in reminiscence.

"Did you get to pilot it? In normal space, I mean, not in jump space."

"No, I wasn't even up to piloting shuttles then. I learned how to do that later, at the Academy."

"What happened to the RG? Do you still have it?"

"Oh, no. Or . . . well, I'm not just sure. It met with an accident in Tau Verde local space, ramming, um, colliding with another ship. Twisted hell out of its Necklin field generator rods. It was never going to jump again after that, so I leased it as a local-space freighter, and we left it there. If Arde—he's a jump pilot friend of mine—ever finds a set of replacement rods, I told him he can have the old RG."

"You had a *jumpship* and you *gave it away*?" Nikki's eyes widened in astonishment. "Do you have any *more*?"

"Not at present. Oh, look, a *General*-class cruiser." Miles reached for it. "My father commanded one of those, once, I believe. Do you have any Betan Survey ships . . . ?"

Heads bent together, they laid out the little fleet on the floor. Nikki, Miles was pleased to find, was well-up on all the tech-specs of every ship he owned; he expanded wonderfully, his voice, formerly shy around Miles-the-weird-adult-stranger, growing louder and faster in his unselfconscious enthusiasm as he detailed his machinery. Miles's stock rose as he was able to claim personal acquaintance with nearly a dozen of the originals for the models, and add a few interesting nonclassified jumpship anecdotes to Nikki's already impressive fund of knowledge.

"But," said Nikki after a slight pause for breath, "how do you get to be a pilot if you're not in the military?"

"You go through a training school and an apprenticeship. I know of at least four schools right here on Komarr, and a couple more at home on Barrayar. Sergyar doesn't have one yet."

"How do you get in?"

"Apply, and give them money."

Nikki looked daunted. "A lot of money?"

"Mm, no more than any other college or trade school. The biggest cost is getting your neurological interface surgically installed. It pays to get the best on that one." Miles added encouragingly, "You can do anything, but you have to make your chances happen. There are some scholarships and indenture-contracts that can grease your way in, if you hustle for them. You do have to be at least twenty years old, though, so you have lots of time to plan."

"Oh." Nikki seemed to contemplate this vast span of time, equal again to his whole life so far, stretching out before him. Miles could empathize; suppose someone told him he had to wait thirty more years for something he passionately desired? He tried to think of something he passionately desired. That he could have. The field was depressingly blank.

Nikki began to replace his models in their padded box. As he nestled the Falcon-9 into its space, his fingers caressed its Imperial military decals. He asked, "Do you still have your ImpSec silver eyes?"

"No, they made me give 'em back when I was fi—when I resigned."

"Why d'you quit?"

"I didn't want to. I had health problems."

"So they made you be an Auditor instead?"

"Something like that."

Nikki groped around for some way to continue this polite adult conversation. "Do you like it?"

"It's a little early to tell. It seems to involve a lot of homework." He glanced up guiltily at the stack of report disks waiting for him on the comconsole.

Nikki gave him a look of sympathy. "Oh. Too bad."

Tien Vorsoisson's voice made them both jump. "Nikki, what are you doing in here? Get up off the floor!"

Nikki scrambled to his feet, leaving Miles sitting cross-legged and abruptly conscious that his recently-chilled body had stiffened up again.

"Are you pestering the Lord Auditor? My apologies, Lord Vorkosigan! Children have no manners." Vorsoisson entered and loomed over them.

"Oh, his manners are fine. We were having an interesting discussion on the subject of jump ships." Miles contemplated the problem of standing gracefully in front of a fellow Barrayaran, without any unfortunate lurch or stumble to give a false impression of disability. He stretched, sitting, by way of preparation.

Vorsoisson grimaced wryly. "Ah, yes, the most recent obsession. Don't step barefoot on one of those damn things, it'll cripp—it'll hurt. Well, every boy goes through that phase, I suppose. We all outgrow it. Pick up all that mess, Nikki."

Nikki's eyes were downcast, but narrowed in brief resentment at this, Miles could see from his angle of view. The boy bent to scoop up the last of his miniature fleet.

"Some people grow into their dreams, instead of out of them," Miles murmured.

"That depends on whether your dreams are reasonable," said Vorsoisson, his lips twitching in rather bleak amusement. Ah, yes. Vorsoisson must be fully aware of the secret medical bar between Nikki and his ambition.

"No, it doesn't." Miles smiled slightly. "It depends on how hard you grow." It was difficult to tell just how Nikki took that in, but he heard it; his eyes flicked back to Miles as he carried his treasure box toward the door.

Vorsoisson frowned, suspicious of this contradiction, but said only, "Kat sent me to tell everyone supper is ready. Go wash your hands, Nikki, and tell your Uncle Vorthys."

Miles's last family dinner with the Vorsoisson clan was a strained affair. Madame Vorsoisson made herself very busy with serving admittedly excellent food, her faintly harried pose as effective as a placard saying *Leave me alone.* The conversation was left to the Professor, who was abstracted, and Tien, who, bereft of direction, spoke forcefully and without depth of local Komarran politics, authoritatively explaining the inner workings of the minds of people he had never, so far as Miles could discern, actually met. Nikolai, wary of his father, did not pursue the subject of jumpships in front of him.

Miles wondered now how he could have mistaken Madame Vorsoisson's silence for serenity, that first night, or Etienne Vorsoisson's tension for energy. Until seeing those brief glimpses of her animation earlier today, he had not guessed how much of her personality was missing from view, or how much went underground in the presence of her husband.

Now that he knew what clues to look for, he could see the faint grayness underlying Tien's dome-pallor, and spot his betraying tiny physical twitches masked as a big man's clumsiness with small objects. At first Miles had feared the illness was hers, and he'd been nearly ready to challenge Tien to a duel for his failure to take immediate and massive measures to solve the problem. If Madame Vorsoisson had been *his* wife . . . But apparently Tien was playing these little delaying head-games with his own condition. Miles knew, none better, the bone-deep Barrayaran fear of any genetic distortion. *Mortal embarrassment* was more than a turn of phrase. He didn't exactly go around advertising his own invisible seizure-disorder, either—though he'd been privately relieved to have that secret out with her. Not that it mattered, now that he was leaving. Denial was Tien's choice, stupid though it seemed; maybe the man was hoping to be hit by a meteor before his disease manifested itself. Miles's stifled impulse toward homicide was renewed with the thought, *But he's chosen the same for her Nikolai.*

Halfway through the main course—exquisitely aromatic vat-raised fish fillets baked on a bed of garlic potatoes—the door chimed. Madame Vorsoisson hastily rose to answer it. Feeling obscurely that it was bad security to send her off by herself, Miles followed. Nikolai, perhaps sensing adventure, tried to accompany them, but was roped back to face the remains of his dinner by his father. Madame Vorsoisson glanced at Miles over her shoulder, but said nothing.

She checked the welcome monitor beside the door. "It's another courier. Oh, it's a captain this time. Usually you get a sergeant." Madame Vorsoisson keyed open the hall door to reveal a young man in Barrayaran undress greens, with ImpSec's eye-of-Horus pins on his collar. "Do come in."

"Madame Vorsoisson." The man nodded to her, trod inside, and shifted his gaze to Miles. "Lord Auditor Vorkosigan. I'm Captain Tuomonen. I head up ImpSec's office here in Serifosa." Tuomonen appeared to be in his late twenties, dark haired and brown eyed like most Barrayarans, and a bit more trim and fit than the average desk soldier, though with dome-pale skin. He had a disk case in one hand and a larger case in the other, so nodded cordially rather than offering any salutelike gesture.

"Yes, General Rathjens mentioned you. We're honored to have such a courier."

Tuomonen shrugged. "ImpSec Serifosa is a very small office, my lord. General Rathjens directed you were to be informed as soon as possible after the new body was identified."

Miles's eye took in the secured disk case in the captain's hand. "Excellent. Come sit down." He led the captain to the conversation circle, a deeply-padded sunken bench which was the centerpiece of the Vorsoisson's living room. Like most of the rest of the furnishings, it was Komarran dome standard-issue. Did Madame Vorsoisson sometimes feel she was camping in a hotel, rather than making a home here? "Madame Vorsoisson, would you ask your uncle to join us? Let him finish eating first, though."

"I would like to speak with Administrator Vorsoisson, also, when he's finished," Tuomonen called after her. She nodded and withdrew, eyes dark with interest but posture still self-effacing, self-erasing, as if she wished she might become invisible to Miles's eyes.

"What do we have?" continued Miles, settling himself. "I told Rathjens I might like to accompany and observe the first ImpSec contact on this matter." He could pack his bag and take it along tonight, and not have to come back.

"Yes, my lord. That's why I'm here. Your mysterious body turns out to be a local fellow, from Serifosa. He is, or was, listed as an employee of the Terraforming Project here."

Miles blinked. "Not an engineer named Dr. Radovas, is it?"

Tuomonen stared at him, startled. "How did you know?"

"Wild-ass guess, because he went missing a few weeks ago. Oh, hell, I'll bet Vorsoisson could have identified him at a glance. Or . . . maybe not. He was pretty battered. Hm. Radovas's boss thought he'd eloped with his tech, a young lady named Marie Trogir. *Her* body hasn't turned up topside, has it?"

"No, my lord. But it sounds as though we ought to start looking for it."

"Yes. A full ImpSec search and background check, I think. Don't assume she's dead—if she's alive, we surely want to question her. Do you need a special order from me?"

"Not necessarily, but I'll bet it would expedite things." A faint enthusiastic gleam lit Tuomonen's eye.

"You have it, then."

"Thank you, my lord. I thought you'd want this." He handed Miles the secured case. "I pulled the complete dossier on Radovas before I left the office."

"Does ImpSec keep files on every Komarran citizen, or was he special?"

"No, we don't keep universal files. But we have a search program that can pull records of good depth from the information net very quickly. The first part of this is his public biography, school records, medical records, financial and travel documents, all the usual. I only had time to glance over it. But Radovas also does have a small ImpSec file, dating back to his student days during the Komarr Revolt. It was closed at the amnesty."

"Is it interesting?"

"I would not draw too many inferences from it alone. Half the population of Komarr of that age group was part of some student protest or would-be revolutionary group back then, including my mother-in-law." Tuomonen waited stiffly to see what response Miles would make to this tidbit.

"Ah, you married a local girl, did you?"

"Five years ago."

"How long have you been posted to Serifosa?"

"About six years."

"Good for you." *Yes! That leaves one more Barrayaran woman for the rest of us.* "You get along well with the locals, I take it."

Tuomonen's stiffness eased. "Mostly. Except for my mother-in-law. But I don't think that's entirely political." Tuomonen suppressed a small grin. "But our little daughter has her under complete control, now."

"I see." Miles smiled back at him. With a more thoughtful frown, he turned the case over, dug his Auditor's seal out of his pocket, and keyed it open. "Has your Analysis section red-flagged anything in this for me?"

"I *am* Serifosa's Analysis section," Tuomonen admitted ruefully. His glance at Miles sharpened. "I understand you're former ImpSec yourself, my lord. I think I'd rather let you read it over first, before I comment."

Miles's brows twitched up. Did Tuomonen not trust his own judgment, had the arrival of two Imperial Auditors in his sector unnerved him, or was he merely seizing the opportunity for some mutual brainstorming? "And what sort of dossier did you pull off the net on one Miles Vorkosigan, and speed-read before you left the office just now?"

"I did that day before yesterday, actually, my lord, when I was notified you would be arriving in Serifosa."

"And what was your analysis of it?"

"About two-thirds of your career is locked under a need-to-know seal that requires clearance from ImpSec HQ in Vorbarr Sultana to access. But your publicly recorded awards and decorations appear in a statistically significant pattern following supposedly routine courier missions assigned to you by the Galactic Affairs office. At approximately five times the density of the next most decorated courier in ImpSec history."

"And your conclusion, Captain Tuomonen?"

Tuomonen smiled faintly. "You were never a bloody courier, Captain Vorkosigan."

"Do you know, Tuomonen, I believe I am going to enjoy working with you."

"I hope so, sir." He glanced up as the Professor entered the living room, flanked by Tien Vorsoisson.

Vorthys finished wiping his mouth with his dinner napkin, stuffed it absently into his pocket, and greeted Tuomonen with a handshake, then introduced his nephew-in-law. As they all sat again, Miles said, "Tuomonen has brought us the identification of our extra body."

"Oh, good," said Vorthys. "Who was the poor fellow?"

Miles watched Tuomonen watch Tien and say, "Strangely enough, Administrator Vorsoisson, one of your employees. Dr. Barto Radovas."

Tien's grayness became a shade paler. "Radovas! What the hell was he doing up *there*?" The shock and horror on Tien's face was genuine, Miles would have sworn, the surprise in his voice unfeigned.

"I was hoping you might have some ideas, sir," said Tuomonen.

"My God. Well . . . was he aboard the station, or the ship?"

"We haven't determined that yet."

"I really can't tell you that much about the man. He was in Soudha's department. Soudha never made any complaints about his work to me. He got all his merit raises right to schedule." Tien shook his head. "But what the hell was he doing . . ." He glanced worriedly at Tuomonen. "He's not actually my employee, you know. He resigned several weeks ago."

"Five days before his death, according to our calculations," said Tuomonen.

Tien's brows wrinkled. "Well . . . he couldn't have been aboard that ore ship, then, could he? How could he have gotten all the way out to the second asteroid belt and boarded it before he even left Komarr?"

"He might have joined the ore ship en route," said Tuomonen.

"Oh. I suppose that's possible. My God. He's married. Was married. Is his wife still here in town?"

"Yes," said Tuomonen. "I'll be meeting shortly with the dome civil security officer who's taking the official notification of death to her."

"She's waited three weeks with no word from him," said Miles. "Another hour can't matter much at this point. I think I'd like to review your report before we leave, Captain."

"Please do, my lord."

"Professor, will you join me?"

They all ended up trooping into Vorsoisson's study. Miles privately felt he could do without Tien, but Tuomonen made no move to exclude him.

The report was not yet an in-depth analysis, but rather a wad of raw data bundled logically, with hasty preliminary notes and summations supplied by Tuomonen. A full analysis would doubtless arrive eventually from ImpSec-Komarr HQ. They all pulled up chairs and crowded around the vid display. After the initial overview, Miles let the Professor follow the thread of Radovas's career.

"He lost two years out of the middle of his undergraduate schooling to the Revolt," Vorthys noted. "Solstice University was shut down entirely, for a time then."

"But it looks like he made up some points with that two-year postgraduate stint on Escobar," Miles said.

"Anything could have happened to him there," opined Tien.

"But not much did, according to this," said Vorthys a bit dryly. "Commercial work in their orbital shipyards . . . he didn't even get a good research topic out of it. Solstice University did not renew his contract. Not a man with a gift for teaching, one feels."

"He was refused a job in the Imperial Science Institute because of his associations in the Revolt," Tuomonen pointed out, "despite the amnesty."

"All the amnesty promised was that he'd never be taken out and shot," said Miles a shade impatiently.

"But he was not refused it on the basis of inadequate technical competence," murmured Vorthys. "Here he goes on to a job rather below his educational level, in the Komarran orbital yards."

Miles checked. "He had three small children by then. He had to go for the money."

"Several bland years follow," the Professor droned on. "Changes companies only once, for a respectable increase in salary and position. Then he is hired by—Soudha was fairly new then, but hired by Soudha for the Terraforming Project, and moves downside permanently."

"No pay raise that time. Professor . . ." Miles said plaintively. He touched his finger to air on the vid display at this juncture in the late Dr. Radovas's career. "Doesn't this downside move strike you as a odd for a man trained and experienced in jump technologies? He was a five-space-math man."

Tuomonen smiled tightly, by which Miles deduced he had put his finger rather literally upon the same point that had bothered the captain.

Vorthys shrugged. "There could be many compelling reasons. He could have felt stale in his old work. He could have grown into new interests. Madame Radovas might have refused to live on a space station for one more day. I think you'll have to ask her."

"But it is unusual," said Tuomanen tentatively.

"Maybe," said Vorthys. "Maybe not."

"Well," sighed Miles after a long silence. "Let's go do the hard part."

The Radovas's apartment proved to be about a third of the way across the city from the Vorsoissons', but at this hour of the evening there were no delays in the bubble-car system. With Tuomonen leading, Miles, Vorthys, and Tien—whom Miles did not remember inviting, but who somehow had attached himself to the expedition—entered the lobby, where they found a youngish woman in a Serifosa Dome Security uniform waiting for them, none too patiently.

"Ah, the dome cop is female," Miles murmured to Tuomonen. He looked back over their cavalcade. "Good. We'll seem less like an invading army."

"So I hoped, my lord."

After brief introductions all around, they took a lift tube to a hallway nearly identical to every other dome residence building Miles had so far seen. The dome cop, who was styled Group-Patroller Rigby, rang the door chime.

After a pause long enough to start Miles wondering, *Is she home?* the door slid open. The woman framed there was slender and neatly dressed, appearing to Miles's Barrayaran eye to be in her mid-forties, which probably meant she was in her late fifties. She wore the usual Komarran trousers and blouse, and hunched into a heavy sweater. She looked pale and chilled, but there was certainly nothing else in her appearance to repel any husband.

Her eyes widened as she took in the uniformed people facing her, radiating the message *bad news.* "Oh," she sighed wearily. Miles, who had braced himself for hysterics, relaxed a little. She was going to be the underreacting type, it appeared. Her response would likely emerge oddly, and obliquely, and later.

"Madame Radovas?" the dome cop said. The woman nodded. "My name is Group-Patroller Rigby. I regret to inform you that your husband, Dr. Barto Radovas, has been found dead. May we please come in?"

Madame Radovas's hand went to her lips; she said nothing for a moment. "Well." She looked away. "I am not so pleased as I thought I'd be. What happened to him? That young woman—is she all right?"

"May we come in and sit down?" Rigby reiterated. "I'm afraid we are going to have to trouble you with some questions. We'll try to answer yours."

Madame Radovas's eye warily took in Tuomonen, in his ImpSec greens. "Yes. All right." She gave way, stepping backward, and gestured them all inside.

Her living room featured another standard conversation circle; Miles seated himself to one side, letting Tuomonen share line-of-sight across from Madame Radovas with the Group-Patroller, who introduced the rest of them. Tien joined them, folding himself onto the bench, a picture of awkward discomfort. Professor Vorthys shook his head slightly and remained standing, his gaze taking in the room.

"What happened to Barto? Was there an accident?" Madame Radovas's voice was husky, barely controlled, now that the news was sinking in.

"We're not certain," said Rigby. "His body was found in space, apparently associated with the disaster to the soletta three weeks ago. Did you know he had gone topside? Had he said anything before he left that would shed some light on this?"

"I . . ." She looked away. "He didn't speak to me before he left. I think he was not very brave about this. He left me a note on the comconsole. Until I found it, I thought this was an ordinary work trip."

"May we see it?" Tuomonen spoke for the first time.

"I erased it. Sorry." She frowned at him.

"The plan for this . . . leaving, do you think it was your husband's, or Marie Trogir's?" asked Rigby.

"You know all about them, I see. I have no idea. I was surprised. I don't know." Her voice grew sharper. "I wasn't consulted."

"Did he often make work trips?" asked Rigby.

"He went out on field tests fairly often. Sometimes he went to the terraforming conferences in Solstice. I usually went along on those." Her voice fluttered raggedly, then came back under her control.

"What did he take with him? Anything unusual?" asked Rigby patiently.

"Just what he normally took on a long field trip." She hesitated. "He took all his personal files. That's how I first knew for sure that he wasn't coming back."

"Did you talk to anyone at his work about this absence?"

Tien shook his head, but Madame Radovas replied, "I spoke to Administrator Soudha. After I found the note. Trying to figure out . . . what had gone wrong."

"Was Administrator Soudha helpful to you?" asked Tuomonen.

"Not very." She frowned again. "He didn't seem to feel it was any of his business what happened after Barto resigned."

"I'm sorry," said Vorsoisson. "Soudha didn't tell me about that part of it. I'll reprimand him. I didn't know."

And you didn't ask. But much as Miles would like to, even he found it hard to blame Tien for steering clear of what had looked to be an embarrassing domestic situation. Madame Radovas's frown at Vorsoisson became almost a glower.

"I understand you and your husband moved downside about four years ago," said Tuomonen. "It seemed an unusual change of careers, from five-space to what is effectively a form of civil engineering. Did he have a long-time interest in terraforming?"

She looked momentarily nonplused. "Barto cared about the future of Komarr. I . . . we were tired of station life. We wanted something more settled for the children. Dr. Soudha was looking for people for his team with different backgrounds, different kinds of problem-solving experience. He considered Barto's station experience valuable. Engineering is engineering, I suppose."

Professor Vorthys had been wandering gently around the room during this, one ear cocked toward the conversation, examining the travel mementos and portraits of children at various ages that were its principle decorations. He stopped before the library case on one wall, crammed with disks, and began randomly examining their titles. Madame Radovas gave him a brief curious glance.

"Due to the unusual situation in which Dr. Radovas's body was found, the law requires a complete medical examination," Rigby went on. "Given your personally awkward circumstances, when it's concluded, do you wish to have his body or his ashes returned to you, or to some other relative?"

"Oh. Yes. To me, please. There should be a proper ceremony. For the children's sake. For everyone's sake." She seemed very close to losing control now, tears standing in her eyes. "Can you . . . I don't know. Do you take care of this?"

"The Family Affairs counselor in our department will be glad to advise and assist you. I'll give you her number before we leave."

"Thank you."

Tuomonen cleared his throat. "Due to the mysterious circumstances of Dr. Radovas's death, ImpSec Komarr has also been asked to take an interest in the matter. I wonder if we might have your permission to examine your comconsole and personal records, to see if they suggest anything."

Madame Radovas touched her lips. "Barto took all his personal files. There's not much left but my own."

"Sometimes a technical examination can uncover more."

She shook her head, but said, "Well . . . I suppose so." She added more tartly, "Though I didn't think ImpSec had to bother with my permission."

Tuomonen did not deny this, but said, "I like to salvage what courtesies I can, Madame, from our crude necessities."

Professor Vorthys added in a distant tone from the far wall, his hands full of disks, "Get the library, too."

With a flash of bewildered anger, Madame Radovas said, "Why do you want to take away my poor husband's *library*?"

Vorthys looked up and gave her a kindly, disarming smile. "A man's library gives information about the shape of his mind the way his clothing gives information about the shape of his body. The cross-connections between apparently unrelated subjects may exist only in his thoughts. There is a sad disconnectedness that overcomes a library when its owner is gone. I think I should have liked to meet your husband when he was alive. In this ghostly way, perhaps I can, a little."

"I don't see why . . ." Her lips tightened in dismay.

"We can arrange for it to be returned to you in a day or two," Tuomonen said soothingly. "Is there anything you need out of it right away?"

"No, but . . . oh . . . I don't know. Take it. Take whatever you want, I don't care any more." Her eyes began to spill over at last. Group-Patroller Rigby handed her a tissue from one of her many uniform pockets and frowned at the Barrayarans.

Tien shifted uncomfortably; Tuomonen remained blandly professional. Taking her outburst for his cue, the ImpSec captain rose and carried his case over to the comconsole in the corner by the dining ell, opened it, and plugged an ImpSec standard black box into the side of the machine. At Vorthys' gesture, Rigby and Miles went to assist him in removing the library case intact from the wall, and sealing it for transport. Tuomonen, after sucking dry the comconsole, ran a scanner over the library, which Miles estimated contained close to a thousand disks, and generated a vid-receipt for Madame Radovas. She crumpled the plastic flimsy into the pocket of her gray trousers without looking at it, and stood with her arms crossed till the invaders assembled to depart.

At the last moment, she bit her lip and blurted, "Administrator Vorsoisson. There won't be . . . will I get . . . will there be any of the normal survivor's benefits coming from Barto's death?"

Was she in financial need? Her two youngest children were still in university, according to Tuomonen's files, and financially dependent on their parents; of course she was. But Vorsoisson shook his head sadly.

"I'm afraid not, Madame Radovas. The medical examiner seems to be quite clear that his death took place after his resignation."

If it had been the other way around, this would be a much more interesting problem for ImpSec. "She gets nothing, then?" asked Miles. "Through no fault of her own, she's stripped of all normal widow's benefits just because of her," he deleted a few pejorative adjectives, "late husband's fecklessness?"

Vorsoisson shrugged helplessly, and turned away.

"Wait," said Miles. He'd been of damned little use to anyone today so far. "Gregor does not approve of widows being left destitute. Trust me on this one. Vorsoisson, go ahead and run the benefits through for her anyway."

"I can't—how—do you want me to alter the date of his resignation?"

Thus creating the curious legal spectacle of a man resigning the day after his own death? By what method, spirit writing? "No, of course not. Simply make it by an Imperial order."

"There are no places on the forms for an Imperial order!" said Vorsoisson, taken aback.

Miles digested this. Tuomonen, looking faintly suffused, watched with wide-eyed fascination. Even Madame Radovas's eyebrows crimped with bemusement. She looked directly at Miles as if seeing him for the first time. At last, Miles said gently, "A design defect you shall have to correct, Administrator Vorsoisson."

Tien's mouth opened on some other protest, but then, intelligently, closed. Professor Vorthys looked relieved. Madame Radovas, her hand pressed to her check in something like wonder, said, "Thank you . . . Lord Vorkosigan."

After the usual If-you-think-of-anything-more-call-this-number farewells, the herd of investigators moved off down the hallway. Vorthys handed Tien the library case to lug. Back at the building's entrance lobby, the Group-Patroller prepared to go her own way.

"What, if anything, does ImpSec want us to do now?" she asked Tuomonen. "Dr. Radovas's death seems out of Serifosa's jurisdiction. Close relatives are automatically suspects in a mysterious death, but she's been here the whole time. I don't see any causal chain to that body in space."

"Neither do I, at present," Tuomonen admitted. "For now, continue with your normal procedures, and send my office copies of all your reports and evidence files."

"I don't suppose you'd care to return the favor?" Judging by the twist of her lips, Rigby thought she knew the answer.

"I'll see what I can do, if anything pertinent to Dome security turns up," Tuomonen promised guardedly. Rigby's brows rose at even this limited concession from ImpSec.

"I'm going to have to go back topside tomorrow morning," said Vorthys to Tuomonen. "I am not going to have time to do a thorough examination of this library myself. I shall have to trouble ImpSec for it, I'm afraid."

Tuomonen, his eye taking in the thousand-disk case, looked momentarily appalled. Miles added quickly, "On my authority, requisition a high-level analyst from HQ for that job. One of the basement boffins, with engineering and math certification, I think—right, Professor?"

"Yes, indeed, the best man you can get," said Vorthys.

Tuomonen looked very relieved. "What do you want him to look for, my Lord Auditor?"

"I don't quite know," said the Professor. "That's why I want an ImpSec analyst, eh? Essentially, I want him to generate an independent picture of Radovas from this data, which we may compare with impressions from other sources later."

"A candid view of the shape of the mind inside this library," mused Miles. "I see."

"I'm sure you do. Talk to the man, Miles, you know the kinds of things they do. And the kinds of things we want."

"Certainly, Professor."

They turned the library case over to Tuomonen, and Group-Patroller Rigby took her leave. It was approaching Komarran midnight.

"I'll take all this lot back to my office, then," said Tuomonen, looking at his assorted burdens, "and call HQ with the news. How much longer do you expect to be staying in Serifosa, Lord Vorkosigan?"

"I'm not sure. I'll stay on and have a talk with Soudha, and Radovas's other colleagues, at least, before I go up again. I, ah, think I'll move my things to a hotel tomorrow, after the Professor goes up."

"You are welcome to the hospitality of my home, Lord Vorkosigan," said Tien formally, and very unpressingly.

"Thank you anyway, Administrator Vorsoisson. Who knows, I may be ready to follow on topside as early as tomorrow night. We'll see what turns up."

"I'd appreciate it if you'd keep my office apprised of your movements," said Tuomonen. "It was of course your privilege to order no close security upon your person, Lord Vorkosigan, but now that your case seems to have acquired a local connection, I'd strongly request you reconsider that."

"ImpSec guards are generally charming fellows, but I really like not tripping over them every time I turn around," Miles replied. He tapped the ImpSec issue chrono-comm link, which looked oversized strapped around his left wrist. "Let's stick with our original compromise, for now. I'll yelp for help if I need you, I promise."

"As you wish, my lord," said Tuomonen disapprovingly. "Is there anything else you need?"

"Not tonight," said Vorthys, yawning.

I need all this to make sense. I need half a dozen eager informers. I want to be alone in a locked room with Marie Trogir and a hypo of fast-penta. I wish I might fast-penta that poor bitter widow, even. Rigby would require a court order for such an invasive and offensive step; Miles could do it on whim and his borrowed Imperial Voice, if he didn't mind being a very obnoxious Lord Auditor indeed. The justification was simply not yet sufficient. *But Soudha had better watch his step, tomorrow.* Miles shook his head. "No. Get some sleep."

"Eventually." Tuomonen smiled wryly. "Good night, my lords, Administrator."

They left the widow's building in opposite directions.

Chapter Seven

Ekaterin half-dozed, curled on the sunken living room couch, waiting for the men to return. She pushed back her sleeves and studied the deep bruises darkening on her wrists in the pattern of Lord Vorkosigan's grip.

She was not normally very body-conscious, she thought. She watched peoples' faces, giving a bare glance to anything below the neck beyond the social language of clothing. This . . . not aversion, screening . . . seemed a mere courtesy, and a part of her sexual fidelity as automatic as breathing. So it was doubly disturbing to find herself so very aware of the little man. And probably very rude, as well, given the oddness of his body. Vorkosigan's face, once she'd penetrated his first wary opacity, was . . . well, charming, full of dry wit only waiting to break into open humor. It was disorienting to find that face coupled with a body bearing a record of appalling pain. Was it some kind of perverse voyeurism, that her second reaction after shock had been a suppressed desire to persuade him to tell her all the stories about his war wounds? *Not from around here*, those hieroglyphs carved in his flesh had whispered, exotic with promise. And, *I have survived. Want to know how?*

Yes. I want to know how. She pressed her fingers to the bridge of her nose, as if she might press back the incipient headache gathering behind her eyes. Her body jolted at the faint *snick* and *shirr* of the hall door opening. But familiar voices, Tien's and her uncle's, reassured her it was only the expected return of the information-hunting party. She wondered what strange prey they had made a prize of. She sat up, and pushed down her sleeves. It was well after midnight.

Tuomonen was no longer with them, she found to her relief as she rounded the corner into the hallway. She could lock her household down for the night, like a proper chatelaine. Tien looked tense, Vorkosigan looked tired, and Uncle Vorthys looked the same as ever. Vorkosigan was murmuring, "I trust it goes without saying, Vorsoisson, that tomorrow will be a surprise inspection?"

"Certainly, my Lord Auditor."

"Did you find out anything interesting?" Ekaterin inquired generally, resetting the lock behind them.

"Mm, Madame Radovas had no suggestions as to how her wandering husband had wandered into our soletta wreck," said Uncle Vorthys. "I'd been hoping she might."

"It's so sad. They had seemed like such a nice couple, the few times I met them."

"Well, you know middle-aged men." Tien shrugged reprovingly, clearly excluding himself from the class.

Ah, Tien. Why couldn't you be the one to run off with a younger, richer woman? Maybe you'd be happier. You could scarcely be less happy. Why does your one virtue have to be fidelity? As far as she knew, anyway. Though she had wondered, during that thankfully-over weird period when he'd been accusing her, why an act she found unthinkable had so obsessed him. Maybe he didn't find it so unthinkable at all? She hardly had the energy to care.

She offered a late-night snack, an invitation only Uncle Vorthys accepted, and they all parted company for their respective sleeping quarters. By the time her uncle had finished eating and said good night, and she tidied up and made her way to her own bedroom, checking on Nikolai on the way, Tien was already in bed on his side with his eyes closed. Not sleeping yet; he had a very distinctive near-snore when he was truly asleep. When she slipped in beside him, he rolled over and flung his arm over her, and snugged her in tight.

He does love me, in some inept way. The thought almost made her want to weep. Yet what other human connections did Tien have, aside from her and Nikolai? His distant mother, remarried, and the ghost of his dead brother. Tien clutched her at night sometimes like a drowning man clutching his log.

If there was a hell, she hoped Tien's brother was in it. A Vor hell. He had done the proper thing, oh yes he had, cutting out his own mutation, and setting an example for Tien impossible to—so to speak—live up to. Tien had tried to emulate him, twice early on and once later, running up to suicide attempts so half-hearted as to barely qualify as gestures. The first two times she had been utterly terrified. For a period she had believed her loyalty and dependency were the only things holding him to life. By the third, she was numb. Much more of this, and she wouldn't be human at all. She felt barely human now.

Hoping to pretend her way to the real thing, she let her breathing slow, and feigned sleep. After a time, Tien, who was no more asleep than she, got up and went to the bathroom. But instead of returning to bed, he plodded quietly across the bedroom and out toward the kitchen. Maybe he'd changed his mind about that snack. Would he like it if she heated him some milk with brandy and spices in it? It was an old family recipe and remedy her great-aunt had brought to South Continent; comfort-drink for a visiting sick niece, though the larger of the generous portions had always somehow seemed to find its way into the old lady's own cup. Ekaterin smiled in memory, and padded after Tien.

Not the refrigerator but the kitchen comconsole terminal made the only faint light ahead of her. She paused in the doorway, puzzled. In her parent's household, the only allowable reason to call anyone at this hour of the night was to announce either a birth or a death, a rule she'd found she had internalized.

"What the hell was Radovas's body doing up there?" Tien, his back to her, spoke hoarsely and lowly to the torso over the vid-plate. Startled, Ekaterin recognized his subordinate Administrator Soudha. Soudha was not, as she would have expected, in pajamas, but still dressed for the day. Working this late at home? Well, engineers were like that. She drew back a little more into the shadows in the hallway. "You told me he'd quit."

"He did," said Soudha. "It's not our problem what happened to him afterward."

"The hell it's not. We're going to have frigging ImpSec all over the department tomorrow. The real thing, not just a VIP tour we can run around in circles and feed dinner and wave good-bye to. I could see Tuomonen getting this shitty-eyed look just thinking about it."

"We'll handle them. Go back to bed, Vorsoisson."

Lord Auditor Vorkosigan told you pointblank he wanted to make a surprise inspection, Tien. He speaks with the Emperor's Voice. What are you doing? She began to breathe through her mouth, soundlessly, starting to feel sick to her stomach.

"They're going to find out all about your sweet little scheme, and then we'll all be in it to our eyebrows," said Tien.

"No, they won't. We're tight in town. Just keep them away from the experiment station, and we'll grease them in and out without a squeak."

"The experiment station is a hollow shell. You haven't *got* a department, except in the files. What if they want to interview one of your ghost employees?"

"Such as yourself?" Soudha's mouth twisted in a thin smile. "Relax."

"I am not going down with you."

"You think you have a choice?" Soudha snorted. "Look. It'll be all right. They can audit all day long, and all they'll find is a lot of columns that add perfectly. Lena Foscol in Accounting is the most meticulous thief I've ever met. We're so far ahead of them they'll never catch up."

"Soudha, they're going to ask to interview people who *don't exist.* Then what?"

"Gone on vacation. Out on field work. We can stall."

"For how long? And then what?"

"Go to *bed*, Vorsoisson, and stop twitching."

"Goddammit, I've had two Imperial Auditors in my *house* for the last three days." He stopped and took a gulping breath; Soudha offered him a sympathetic shrug. Tien went on again in a lowered tone. "That's . . . another thing. I need an advance on my stipend. I need another twenty thousand marks. And I need it now."

"*Now?* Oh, sure, with ImpSec looking on, no doubt. Vorsoisson, you are gibbering."

"Dammit, I *have* to have the money. Or else."

"Or else what? Or else you're going to ImpSec and turn *yourself* in? Look, Tien." Soudha ran his hands through his hair in a harried swipe. "Lie low. Keep your mouth shut. Be sweet like sugar to the nice ImpSec lads, give them to me, and we'll handle them. Let's just take this one day at a time, all right?"

"Soudha, I know you can produce the twenty thousand. There has to be at least fifty thousand marks a month flowing out of your department's budget and into your pockets from the dummy employees alone, and God knows how much from the rest of it— though I'm sure your pet accountant does—what if they decide to fast-penta *her*?"

Ekaterin stepped backward, her bare feet seeking silence from the floor near the wall. *Dear God. What has Tien done now?* It was all too easy to fill in the blanks. Embezzlement and bribery at the very least, and on a grand scale. *How long has this been going on?*

The muffled voices from the kitchen exchanged a few more curt words, and the blue reflection from the holovid winked out, leaving the hallway obliquely lit only by the amber lights in the park outside. Heart pounding, Ekaterin slipped back down the hall into her bathroom and locked its door. She quickly flushed the commode and stood trembling at the sink, staring at her dim reflection in the glass. The faint nightlight made drowned sparks in her dilated eyes. After another minute, the bed creaked as Tien made his way back into it.

She waited a long time, but when she crept out, he was still awake.

"Hm?" he said muzzily as she slid under the covers again.

"Not feeling too well," she muttered. Truthfully.

"Poor Kat. Something you ate, you think?"

"Not sure." She curled up away from him, not having to pretend the sick ache in her belly.

"Take something, eh? If you're batting around all night, neither of us will get any sleep."

"I'll see." *I must know.* After a time she added, "Did you get anything arranged about our galactic trip today?"

"God, no. Much too busy."

Not too busy to complete the transfer of her funds to his own account, she'd noticed. "Would you . . . like me to take over making all the arrangements? There's no reason you should carry all that burden, I have plenty of time. I've already researched off-world medical facilities."

"Not *now*, Kat! We can deal with this later. Next week, after your uncle goes."

She let it drop, staring into the darkness. *Whatever it is he needs twenty thousand marks for, it's not to fulfill his word to me.*

Eventually, he slept, about two hours; Ekaterin watched the time ooze by, black and slow as tar. *I must know.*

And after you know, then what? Will you deal with it later, too? She lay waiting for the dawn's light.

The light is broken, remember?

The routine of dealing with Nikolai's needs steadied her in the morning. Uncle Vorthys left very early, to catch his orbital flight.

"Will you be coming back down?" she asked him a little wanly, helping him on with his jacket in the vestibule.

"I hope I might, but I can't promise. This investigation has already gone on longer than I expected, and has taken some peculiar turns. I really have no idea how long it will take to finish up." He hesitated. "If it drags on beyond the end of the term at the District University, perhaps the Professora might come out to join me for a time. Would you like that?"

Not trusting herself to speak, she nodded.

"Good. Good." He seemed about to say more, but then just shrugged and smiled, and hugged her good-bye.

She managed to evade almost all contact with Tien and Vorkosigan by accompanying Nikki to school in the bubble-car, an escort he scorned, and taking the long route home. As she had hoped, the apartment was empty on her return.

She washed down more painkillers with more coffee, then, with reluctant steps, entered Tien's office and sat before his comconsole. *I wish I'd taken Lord Vorkosigan up on his offer to teach me how to do this.* Her outrage at the mutie lord yesterday in the bubble-car now seemed to her all out of proportion. Misplaced. How much could her intimate knowledge of Tien make up for her lack of training in this sort of snooping? Not enough, she suspected, but she had to try.

Get started. You are deliberately delaying.

No. I am desperately delaying.

She keyed on the comconsole.

Tien's financial accounts, on this his personal machine, were not locked under a code seal. Income matched his salary; outgo . . . when all the routine outgo was accounted for, the amount left over should have been a modest respectable savings. Tien did not indulge himself with unshared luxuries. But the account was almost empty. Several thousand marks had disappeared without trace, including the transfer she had made to him yesterday morning. No, wait—that transfer was still on the list, hastily entered, not erased or hidden yet.

And it was a transfer, not an expenditure, to a file that had appeared nowhere else.

She followed its transfer marker to a hidden account. The comconsole produced a palm-lock form above the vid-plate.

When she and Tien had first set up their accounts on Komarr, less than a year ago, they had taken prudent thought for one or the other parent being temporarily disabled; each had emergency access to the other's accounts. Had Tien set this up entirely separately, or as a daughter-cell of his larger financial program, letting the machine do the work for him? *Maybe ImpSec covert ops doesn't have all the advantages*, she thought grimly, and placed her right hand in the light box. If only you were willing to betray a trust, why, the most amazing range of possible actions opened up to you.

So did the file.

She took a deep breath, and started reading.

By far the largest portion of what was under the seal turned out to be a huge research clip-file much like her own on the subject of Vorzohn's Dystrophy. But Tien's new obsession, it appeared, was Komarran trade fleets.

Komarr's economy was founded, of course, on its wormholes, and providing services to the trade ships of other worlds that passed through them. But once you had amassed all those profits, how to reinvest them? There were, after all, a physically limited number of wormholes in Komarr local space. So Komarr had gone on to develop its own trade fleets, going out into the wormhole nexus on long complicated circuits of months or even years, and returning, sometimes, with fabulous profits.

And sometimes not. Stories of all the best, most legendary returns were highlighted in Tien's files. The failures, admittedly fewer in number, were brushed aside. Tien was nothing if not an optimist, always. Every day was going to bring him his lucky break, the shot that would take him directly to the top with no intervening steps. As if he really believed that was how it was done.

Some of the fleets were closely held to the famous family corporations, Komarr's oligarchy, such as the Toscanes; others sold shares on the public market to any Komarran who cared to place his bet. Almost every Komarran did, at least in a small way; she'd heard one Barrayaran bureaucrat joke that it replaced the need for most other sorts of gambling in the Komarran state.

And when on Komarr, do as the Komarrans do? With dread in her heart, she switched to the financial portion of the file.

Where in God's name did Tien get a hundred thousand marks to buy fleet shares? His salary was barely five thousand marks a month. And then—having done so—why had he put all hundred thousand on the *same* fleet?

She turned her attention to the first question, which was at least potentially answerable with reference to facts of record, without requiring psychological theory. It took her some time to break the credit stream apart into its various sources. The partial answer was, he'd borrowed sixty thousand marks on short term at a disturbingly high interest rate, secured with his pension fund and forty thousand marks worth of fleet shares he'd bought with—what? With money that came from nowhere, apparently.

From Soudha? Was that what he had meant by a *ghost employee?*

Ekaterin read on. The fleet upon which Tien had placed this borrowed bet had departed with much hype and fanfare; shares had been trading on the secondary market at rising prices for weeks after it had departed Komarr. Tien had even made a multicolored graph to track his electronic gains. Then the fleet had encountered disaster: an entire ship, cargo, and crew lost hideously to a wormhole mishap. The fleet, now unable to complete many of its planned trade chains that had been based in the lost cargo, had rerouted and come home early, tail between its imaginary legs. Some fleets returned two for one to their investors, though the average was closer to ten percent; the Golden Voyage of Marat Galen in the previous century was famous for having returned a fabulous fortune of a hundred to one for every share its investors had purchased, founding at least two new oligarchic clans in the process.

Tien's fleet, however, had returned a loss of four for one.

With his twenty-five thousand marks of residue, Ekaterin's four thousand marks, his personal savings, and his meager pension fund, Tien had been placed to pay back only two-thirds of his loan, now due. Pressingly overdue, apparently, judging from the aggressively-worded dunning notices accumulating in the file. When he had cried to Soudha that he needed twenty thousand marks now, Tien had not been exaggerating. She could not help calculating how many years it would take to scrimp twenty thousand marks from her household budget.

What a nightmare. It was almost possible to feel sorry for the man.

Except for the little problem of the origin of that magical first forty thousand marks.

Ekaterin sat back and rubbed her numb face. She had a horrible feeling she could guess the hidden parts of this whole chain of reasoning. This apparently complex and deeply entrenched scam in the Terraforming Project had not, she thought, originated with Tien. All his previous dishonesties had been petty: wrong change not returned, a little padding here and there on expense reports, the usual minor erosion of character almost every adult suffered in weak moments. Not grand theft. Soudha had been here in his job for over five years. This was surely a home-grown Komarran crime. But Tien, newly made head of the Serifosa Sector, had perhaps stumbled upon it, and Soudha had bought his silence. So . . . had the previous Barrayaran Administrator whom Tien had replaced been on the take as well? A question for ImpSec, to be sure.

But Tien was in far over his head and must have realized it. Hence the gamble with the trade fleet shares. If the fleet had returned four for one, instead of the other way around, Tien would have been placed to return his bribe, make restitution, get out from under. Had some such panicked thought been in the back of his mind?

And if he had been lucky instead of unlucky, would the impulse have survived to become reality?

And if Tien had pulled a hundred thousand marks out of his hat, and told you he won them on trade fleet shares, would you have asked the first question about their origin? Or would you have been overjoyed and thought him a secret genius?

She sat now bent over, aching in every part of her body, up her back, her neck, inside and outside her head. In her heart. Her eyes were dry.

A Vor woman's first loyalty was supposed to be to her husband. Even unto treason, even unto death. The sixth Countess Vorvayne had followed her husband right up to the stocks in which he had been hung to die for his part in the Saltpetre Plot, and sat at his feet in a hunger strike, and died, in fact a day before him, of exposure. Great tragic story, that one—one of the best bloody melodramas from the history of the Time of Isolation. They'd made a holovid of it, though in the vid version the couple had died at the same moment, as if achieving mutual orgasm.

Has a Vor woman no honor of her own, then? Before Tien entered my life, did I not have integrity all the same?

Yes, and I laid it on my marriage oath. Rather like buying all your shares in one fleet.

If Tien had been afflicted with some great misguided political passion—thrown in his lot with the wrong side in Vordarian's Pretendership, whatever—if he had followed his convictions, she might well have followed him with all good will. But this was not allegiance to some greater truth, or even to some grandly tragic mistake.

It was just stupidity, piled on venality. It wasn't tragedy, it was farce. It was Tien all over. But if there was any honor to be regained by turning her own sick husband over to the authorities, she surely did not see it either.

If I grow much smaller, trying to keep my height under his, I believe I must soon disappear altogether.

But if she was not a Vor woman, what was she? To step away from her oath-sworn place at Tien's side was to step across a precipice into the dark, naked of any identity at all.

It was, what did they call it, a window of opportunity. If she left before the crisis broke, before this whole hideous mess came out in some public way, she would not be deserting Tien in his hour of greatest need, would she?

Ask your soldier's heart, woman. Is deserting the night before the battle any better than deserting in the heat?

Yet if she did not go, she tacitly acquiesced to this farce. Only ignorance was innocence, was bliss. Knowledge was . . . anything but power.

No one else would save her. No one else could. And even to open her lips and whisper "help" was to choose Tien's destruction.

She sat still as stone, in silence, for a very long time.

Chapter Eight

Captain Tuomonen arranged to rendezvous with Miles and Tien in the lobby of the Vorsoissons' residence building, rather than at the Terraforming Project offices, a blandly sociable gesture that did not fool Miles for a moment. The Imperial Auditor was to be saddled with an ImpSec guard whether he'd ordered one or not, it appeared. Miles almost looked forward to seeing the test of Tuomonen's polite ingenuity this security determination was doubtless going to demonstrate.

At the bubble-car platform across the park, Miles seized the opportunity to shunt Tien into another car and claim a private one for himself and Tuomonen, the better to decant the night's news from him. A few early morning commuters crowded in with the administrator, and his car slid away into the tubes. But as soon as the next pair of Komarrans, already hesitant at the sight of the green Imperial uniform, got close enough to make out the ImpSec eyes on the captain's collar, they sheered off hastily from any attempt to join Miles's little party.

"Do you always get a bubble-car to yourself?" Miles inquired of Tuomonen as the canopy closed and the car began to move.

"When I'm in uniform. Works like a charm." Tuomonen smiled slightly. "But if I want to eavesdrop on Serifosans, I make sure to wear civvies."

"Ha. So what's the status on Radovas's library this morning?"

"I dispatched one of the compound guards last night to hand-carry it to HQ in Solstice. Solstice is three time zones ahead of us; their analyst should have started on it by now."

"Good." Miles's brow wrinkled. *Compound guards?* "Um . . . just how big is ImpSec Serifosa, Captain Tuomonen?"

"Well . . . there's myself, my desk sergeant, and two corporals. We keep the data base, coordinate information flow to HQ, and provide support for any investigators HQ sends out on special projects. Then there is my lieutenant who commands the guards at the Sector Sub-Consulate compound. He has a unit of ten men to cover security there."

The Imperial Counselor was how the Barrayaran Viceroy of Komarr was styled, in deference to local custom. Miles's incognito arrival in Serifosa had excused him, or so he'd chosen to pretend, from a courtesy call on the Counselor's Serifosa Sector regional deputy. "Only ten men? For around the clock, all week?"

"I'm afraid so." Tuomonen smiled wryly. "Not much goes on in Serifosa, my lord. It was one of the least active Domes in the Komarr Revolt, a tradition of political apathy it has since maintained. It was the first Sector to have its occupying Imperial garrison withdrawn. One of my Komarran in-laws facetiously blames the lack of urban renewal in the Dome's central section on the previous generation's failure to arrange for it to have been leveled by Imperial forces." That aging and decrepit area was visible now in the distance, as the car reached the top of an arc and bumped into an intersecting tube. They rotated and began to descend toward Serifosa's newer rim.

"Still—apathetic or not—how do you stay on top of things?"

"I have a budget for paid informers. We used to pay them on a piecework-basis, till I discovered that when they had no real news to sell, they'd make some up. So I cut their numbers in half and put the best ones on a part-time regular salary, instead. We meet about once a week, and I give them a little security workshop and we have a gossip swap. I try to get them to think of themselves as low-level civilian analysts, rather than merely informers. It seems to have significantly helped the reliability of my information flow."

"I see. Do you have anyone planted in the Terraforming Project?"

"No, unfortunately. Terraforming is not considered security-critical. I do have people at the shuttleport, in the Locks district, in the Dome police, and a few in the local Dome government offices. We also cover the power plant, atmosphere cycling, and water treatment both independently and in cooperation with local authorities. They check their job applicants for criminal records and psychological instability, we check them for potentially dangerous political associations. Terraforming has always been just too damn far down the list for my budget to cover. I will say its employment background check standards are among the lowest in the civil service."

"Hm. Wouldn't that policy tend to concentrate the disaffected?"

Tuomonen shrugged. "Many intelligent Komarrans still do not love the Imperium. They have to do something for a living. To qualify for the Terraforming Project, it is perhaps enough that they love Komarr. They have simply no political motivation for sabotage there."

Barto cared about the future of Komarr, his widow had said. Might Radovas have been among the disaffected? And if he were, so what? Miles frowned in puzzlement as the car pulled into the stop in the station beneath the Terraforming Project offices.

As instructed, Tien Vorsoisson was waiting for them on the platform. He escorted them as before up through the atrium of his building to the floors of his domain; though a few doors were open on early morning activity in various departments as they passed, they were the first to arrive in Vorsoisson's office.

"Do you have any preference as to how to divide this up?" Miles asked Tuomonen, staring around meditatively as Vorsoisson brought up the lights.

"I managed to squeeze in a short interview with Andro Farr this morning," said Tuomonen. "He gave me some names of Marie Trogir's particular acquaintances at work. I believe I'd like to start with them."

"Good. If you want to start with Trogir, I'll start with Radovas, and we can meet in the middle. I want to begin by interviewing his boss, Soudha, I believe, Administrator Vorsoisson."

"Certainly, my Lord Auditor. Do you wish to use my office?"

"No, I think I want to see him in his own territory."

"I'll take you downstairs, then. I'll be at your disposal in just a moment, Captain Tuomonen."

Tuomonen seated himself at Vorsoisson's comconsole and eyed it thoughtfully. "Take your time, Administrator."

Vorsoisson, with a worried look over his shoulder, led Miles down one flight to the Department of Waste Heat Management. Soudha had not yet arrived; Miles dispatched Tien back to Tuomonen, then circled the engineer's office slowly, examining its decor and contents.

It was a rather bare place. Perhaps the department head had another, more occupied work area out at his experiment station. The book rack on the wall was sparsely filled, mostly with disks on management and technical references. There were works on space stations and their construction, to be sure close cousins of domes, but unlike Radovas's library, no more specialized texts on wormholes or five-space math than might be residue from Soudha's university days.

A heavy tread announced the room's owner; the curious look on Souda's face to find his office open and lit as he entered gave way to understanding as he saw Miles.

"Ah. Good morning, Lord Auditor Vorkosigan."

"Good morning, Dr. Soudha." Miles replaced the handful of disks in their former slots.

Soudha looked a bit tired; perhaps he was not a morning person. He gave Miles a weary smile of greeting. "To what do I owe the honor of this visit?" He muffled a yawn, pulled a chair up near his desk, and gave Miles a gesture of invitation to it. "Can I get you some coffee?"

"No, thank you." Miles sat, and let Soudha settle himself behind his comconsole desk. "I have some unpleasant news." Soudha's face composed itself attentively. "Barto Radovas is dead." He watched for Soudha's response.

Soudha blinked, his lips parting in dismay. "That's a shock. I thought he was in good health, for his age. Was it his heart? Oh, my, poor Trogir."

"No one's health stands up to exposure to vacuum without a pressure suit, regardless of their age." Miles decided not to include the details of the corpse's massive trauma, for now. "His body was found in space."

Soudha glanced up, his brows rising. "Do they think it has some connection to the soletta accident, then?".

Or why else would Miles be taking an interest, right. "Perhaps."

"Have they—what about Marie Trogir?" Soudha's lips thinned thoughtfully. "You didn't say she . . . ?"

"She's not been found. Or not yet. The probable-cause crews are continuing search sweeps topside, and ImpSec is now looking everywhere else. Their next task, of course, is to try to trace the couple from the time and place they were last seen, which was several weeks ago and here, apparently. We'll be requesting the cooperation of your department, of course."

"Certainly. This is . . . this is really a very horrifying turn of events. I mean, regardless of one's opinion of the way they chose to pursue their personal choices . . ."

"And what is your opinion, Dr. Soudha? I'd really like to get a sense of the man, and of Trogir. Do you have any ideas?"

Soudha shook his head. "I confess, this turn in their relationship took me by surprise. But I don't pry into my employees' private lives."

"So you've said. But you worked closely with the man for five years. What were his outside interests, his politics, his hobbies, his obsessions?"

"I . . ." Soudha shrugged in frustration. "I can give you his complete work record. Radovas was a quiet sort of fellow, never made trouble, did first-rate technical work—"

"Yes, why did you hire him? Waste Heat Management does not appear to have been his previous specialty."

"Oh, he had a great deal of station expertise—as you may know, getting rid of excess heat topside is a standard engineering challenge. I thought his technical experience might bring some new perspectives to our problems, and I was right. I was very pleased with his work—Section Two of the reports I gave you yesterday were mostly his, if you would like to examine them to get a real sense of the man. Power generation and distribution. Hydraulics, in Section Three, was mostly mine. The basis of heat exchange through liquid transfer is most promising—"

"I've looked over your report, thanks."

Soudha looked startled. "All of it? I had really understood Dr. Vorthys would be wanting it. I'm afraid it's a bit thick on the technical detail."

Oh, sure, I speed-read all two hundred thousand words before bed last night. Miles smiled blandly. "I accept your evaluation of Dr. Radovas's technical competence. But if he was so good, why did he leave? Was he bored, happy, frustrated? Why did this change in his personal circumstances lead to change in his work? I don't see a necessary connection."

"For that," said Soudha, "I'm afraid you will have to ask Marie Trogir. I strongly suspect the driving force in this peculiar decision came from her, though they both resigned and left together. She had far less to lose, leaving here, in pay and seniority and status."

"Tell me more about her."

"Well, I truly can't. Barto hired her himself and worked with her on a daily basis. She barely came to my attention. Her technical ability appears to have been adequate—although, come to think of it, those evaluations were all supplied by Barto. I don't know." Soudha rubbed his forehead. "This is all pretty upsetting. Barto, dead. *Why?*" The distress in his voice seemed genuine to Miles's experienced ear, but his shock appeared more surprise than the deep grief from loss of a close friend; Miles would, perhaps, have to look elsewhere for the insights into Radovas he now sought.

"I'd like to examine Dr. Radovas's office and work areas."

"Oh. I'm afraid his office was cleared and reassigned."

"Have you replaced him?"

"Not yet. I'm still collecting applications. I hope to start interviewing soon."

"Radovas must have been friends with somebody. I want to speak with his coworkers."

"Of course, my Lord Auditor. When would you like me to set up appointments?"

"I thought I'd just drop in."

Soudha pursed his lips. "Several of my people are on vacation, and several more are out at the experiment station, running a small test this morning. I don't expect them to be done before dark. But I can get you started with the people here, and have some more in by the time you're done with the first."

"All right. . . ."

With the air of a man throwing a sacrifice to the volcano god, Soudha called in two subordinates, whom Miles interviewed one at a time in the same conference chamber they'd used day before yesterday for the VIP briefing. Arozzi was a younger man, scarcely older than Miles, an engineer who was temporarily scrambling to take over Radovas's abandoned duties, and perhaps, he hinted, hoping for promotion into the dead man's shoes. Would my Lord Auditor like to see some of his work? No, he had not been close friends with his senior. No, the office romance had been a surprise to him, but then Radovas had been a private sort of fellow, very discreet. Trogir had been a bright woman, bright and beautiful;

Arozzi had no trouble appreciating what Radovas had seen in her. What had she seen in Radovas? He had no idea, but then, he wasn't a woman. Radovas dead? Dear God . . . No, he had no idea what the man had been doing topside. Maybe the couple had been trying to emigrate?

Cappell, the department's resident mathematician, was hardly more useful. He was a bit older than Arozzi, and a trifle more cynical. He took in the news of Radovas's death with less change of expression than either Arozzi or Soudha. He hadn't been close to Radovas or Trogir either, not on a social basis, though he worked often with the engineer, yes, checking calculations, devising projections. He'd be glad to show my Lord Auditor a few thousand more pages of his work. No? What was Trogir like? Well-enough looking, he supposed, but rather sly. Look what she'd done to poor Radovas, eh? Did he think Trogir might be dead as well? No, women were like cats, they landed on their feet. No, he'd never actually experimented with testing that old saying on live cats; he didn't have any pets himself. Nor a wife. No, he didn't want a kitten, thank you for the offer, my Lord Auditor. . . .

Miles met again with Tuomonen at lunchtime over mediocre cafeteria food in the executive dining room off the building's atrium; the displaced executives were forced to go elsewhere. They exchanged reports on their morning's conversations. Tuomonen hadn't found any breakthroughs either.

"No one expressed a dislike of Trogir, but she seems damned elusive," Tuomonen noted. "The Waste Heat department has a reputation for keeping itself to itself, apparently. The one woman in Waste Heat who was supposed to be her friend didn't have much to say. I wonder if I ought to get a female interrogator?"

"Mm, maybe. Though I thought Komarrans were supposed to be more egalitarian about such things. Maybe a Komarran female interrogator?" Miles sighed. "D'you know that according to the latest statistics, half of the Barrayaran women who take advanced schooling on Komarr don't go home again? There's a small group of alarmist bachelors who are trying to get the Emperor to deny them exit visas. Gregor has declined to hear their petition."

Tuomonen smiled slightly. "Well, there's more than one solution to that problem."

"Yes, how have your Komarran in-laws taken the announcement of the Emperor's betrothal to the Toscane heiress?"

"Some of them think it's romantic. Some of them think it's sharp business practice on Emperor Gregor's part. Coming from Komarrans, that's a warm compliment, by the way."

"Technically, Gregor owns the planet Sergyar. You might point that out to anyone who theorizes he's marrying Laisa for her money."

Tuomonen grinned. "Yes, but is Sergyar a *liquid* asset?"

"Only in the sense of Imperial funds gurgling down the drain, according to my father. But that's an entire other set of problems. And what do the Barrayaran expatriates around here think of the marriage?"

"In general, it's favored." Tuomonen smiled dryly into his coffee cup. "Five years ago, my colleagues thought I was cutting my career throat by my own marriage. I'd never get promoted out of Serifosa, they said. Now I am suspected of secret genius, and they've taken to regarding me with wary respect. I think . . . it's best if I be amused."

"Heh. You are a wise man, Captain." Miles finished off a starchy and gelid square of pasta-and-something, and chased it with the last of his cooling coffee. "So what did Trogir's friends think of Radovas?"

"Well, he's certainly managed to give a consistent impression of himself. Nice, conscientious guy, didn't make waves, kept to Waste Heat, his elopement a surprise to most. One woman thought it was your math fellow Cappell who was sweet on Trogir, not Radovas."

"He sounded more sour than sweet to me. Frustrated, perhaps?" Miles's back-brain sketched a nice, straightforward scenario of jealous murder, involving pushing Radovas out an airlock on a trajectory that only just by coincidence matched that of some soletta debris. *You can wish.* And anyway, it seemed more logical that any homicidal maniac wishing to clear a path to Trogir's side ought to have started with Andro Farr, and what the hell did any of this tragic romance have to do with an ore freighter swinging off course and smashing into the soletta array anyway? Unless the jealous maniac *was* Andro Farr . . . the Serifosa Dome police were supposed to be looking into that possibility.

Tuomonen grunted. "I will say, I got more of a sense of Trogir's personality from the few minutes I spent with Farr than I have from the rest of this crew all morning. I want to talk with him again, I think."

"*I* want to go topside, dammit. But whatever the end of the story is, up there, it certainly has to have begun here. Well . . . onward, I guess."

Soudha supplied Miles with more human sacrifices in the form of employees called back from the experiment station. They all seemed more interested in their work than in office gossip, but perhaps, Miles reflected, that was an observer-effect. By late afternoon, Miles was reduced to amusing himself wandering around the project offices and terrorizing employees by taking over their comconsoles at random and sampling data, and occasionally emitting ambiguous little "Hm . . ." noises as they watched him in fearful fascination. This lacked even the challenge of dissecting Madame Vorsoisson's comconsole, since the government-issue machines all opened everything immediately to the overrides in his Auditor's seal, regardless of their security classification. He mainly learned that terraforming was an enormous project with a centuries-long scientific and bureaucratic history, and that any individual who attempted to sort clues through sheer mass data assimilation had to be frigging insane.

Now, *delegating* that task, on the other hand . . . *Who do I hate enough in ImpSec?*

He was still pondering this question as he browsed through the files on Venier's comconsole in the Administrator's outer office. The nervous Venier had fled after about the fourth "Hm," apparently unable to stand the suspense. Tien Vorsoisson, who had intelligently left Miles pretty much to his own devices all day, poked his head around the corner and offered a tentative smile.

"My Lord Auditor? This is the hour at which I normally go home. Do you wish anything else from me?"

Departing employees had been trickling past the open doorway for the past several minutes, and office lights had been going out all down the corridor. Miles sat back and stretched. "I don't think so, Administrator. I want to look at a few more files, and talk to Captain Tuomonen. Why don't you go on. Don't wait your dinner." A mental picture of Madame Vorsoisson, moving gracefully about preparing delectable aromatic food for her husband's return, flashed unbidden in his brain. He suppressed it. "I'll be along later to collect my things." *Or better yet* . . . "Or I may send one of Tuomonen's corporals for them. Give your lady wife my best thanks for the hospitality of her household." There. That finished that. He wouldn't even have to say good-bye to her.

"Certainly, my Lord Auditor. Do you, ah, expect to be here again tomorrow?"

"That rather depends on what turns up overnight. Good evening, Administrator."

"Good evening, my lord." Tien withdrew quietly.

A few minutes later, Tuomonen wandered in, his hands full of data disks. "Finding anything, my lord?"

"I got all excited for a moment when I found a personal seal, but it turned out to be just Venier's file of Barrayaran jokes. Some of them are pretty good. Do you want a copy?"

"Is that the one that starts out: 'ImpSec Officer: What do you mean he got away? Didn't I tell you to cover all the exits?—ImpSec Guard: I did sir! He walked out through one of the entrances.'"

"Yep. And the next one goes, 'A Cetagandan, a Komarran, and a Barrayaran walked into a genetic counselor's clinic—'"

Tuomonen grimaced. "I've seen that collection. My mother-in-law sent it to me."

"Ratting on her disaffected Komarran comrades, was she?"

"I don't think that was her intent, no. I believe it was more of a personal message." Tuomonen looked around the empty office and sighed. "So, my Lord Auditor. When do we break out the fast-penta?"

"I've found nothing, here, really." Miles frowned thoughtfully. "I've found *too much* of nothing here. I may have to sleep on this overnight, let my back-brain play with it. The library analysis may provide some direction. And I certainly want to see Waste Heat's experiment station tomorrow morning, before I go back topside. Ah, Captain, it's tempting. Call out the guards, descend in force, freeze everything, full financial audit, fast-penta everyone in sight . . . turn this place upside down and shake it. But I need a *reason*."

"*I* would need a reason," said Tuomonen. "With full documentation, and my career on the line if I spent that much of ImpSec's budget and guessed wrong. But you, on the other hand, speak with the Emperor's Voice. *You* could call it a drill." There was no mistaking the envy in his voice.

"I could call it a quadrille." Miles smiled wryly. "It may come to that."

"I could call HQ, have them put a flying squad on alert," murmured Tuomonen suggestively.

"I'll let you know by tomorrow morning," Miles promised.

"I need to stop by my own office and tend to some routine matters," said Tuomonen. "Would you care to accompany me, my Lord Auditor?"

So you can guard me at your convenience? "I still want to potter around here a bit. There's something . . . something that's bothering me, and I haven't figured out what it is yet. Though I would like a chance to talk to the Professor on a secured channel before the evening is out."

"Perhaps, when you're ready to leave, you could call me and I can send one of my men to escort you."

Miles considered refusing this ingenuous offer, but on the other hand, they could swing by the Vorsoissons' apartment and collect Miles's clothes on the return trip; Tuomonen would have his security, and Miles would have a minion to carry his luggage, a win-win scenario. And having the guard in tow would give Miles an excuse not to linger. "All right."

Tuomonen, partially satisfied, nodded and took himself off. Miles turned his attention to the next layer of Venier's comconsole. Who knew, maybe there would be another joke list.

Chapter Nine

Ekaterin finished folding the last of Lord Vorkosigan's clothing into his travel bag, rather more carefully than their owner was wont to, judging from the stirred appearance of the layers beneath. She sealed his toiletries case and fitted it in, then the odd, gel-padded case containing that peculiar medical-looking device. She trusted it wasn't some sort of ImpSec secret weapon.

Vorkosigan's war story of his Sergeant Beatrice burned in Ekaterin's mind, as the marks on her wrists seemed to burn. O fortunate man, that his missed grasp had passed in a fraction of a second. What if he had had years to think about it first? Hours to calculate the masses and forces and the true arc of descent? Would it have been cowardice or courage to let go of a comrade he could not possibly have saved, to save himself at least? He'd had a command, he'd had responsibilities to others, too. *How much would it have cost you, Captain Vorkosigan, to have opened your hands and deliberately let go?*

She closed the bag and glanced at her chrono. Getting Nikolai settled at his friend's house "for overnight"—that first, before anything else—had taken longer than she'd planned, as had getting the rental company to come collect their grav-bed. Lord Vorkosigan had talked about removing to a hotel this evening, but done nothing toward it. When he returned with Tien, to find no dinner and his bed gone and his bags packed and waiting in the hall, surely he

131

would take the hint and decamp at once. Their good-bye would be formal and permanent, and above all, brief. She was almost out of time and had not even begun on her own things.

She dragged Vorkosigan's bag to the vestibule and returned to her workroom, staring around at the seedlings and cuttings, lights and equipment. It was impossible to pack all that in a bag she could carry. Another garden was going to be abandoned. At least they were getting smaller and smaller.

She'd once wanted to cultivate her marriage like a garden; one of the legendary great Vor parks that people came from Districts away to admire for color and beauty through the changing seasons, the sort that took decades to reach full fruition, growing richer and more complex each year. When all other desires had died, shreds of that ambition still lingered, to tempt her with, *If only I try one more time. . . .* Her lips twisted in bleak derision. Time to admit she had a black thumb for marriage. Plow it under, surface it with concrete, and be done.

She began as a minimum gesture to pull her library off the wall and fit it into a box. The urge to cram a few of her things hastily into some shopping bag and flee before Tien returned was strong. But sooner or later, she would have to face him. Because of Nikki, there would have to be negotiations, formal plans, eventually legal petitions, the uncertainty of which made her sick to her stomach. But she had been years coming to this moment. If she could not do this now, when her anger was high, how could she find the strength to face the rest in colder blood?

She walked through the apartment, staring at the objects of her life. They were few enough; the major furnishings had all come with the place and would stay with the place. Her spasmodic efforts at decoration, at creating some semblance of a Barrayaran home, the hours of work—it was like deciding what to grab in a fire, only slower. *Nothing. Let it all burn.*

The sole awkward exception was her great-aunt's bonsai'd skellytum. It was her one memento of her life before Tien, and it was in the nature of a sacred trust to the dead. Keeping something that foolish and ugly alive for seventy and more years . . . well, it was a typical Vor woman's job. She smiled bitterly, and brought it off the balcony into the kitchen, and began to look around for some way to transport it. At the sound of the hall door opening, she caught her breath, and schooled her features to as little expression as possible.

"Kat?" Tien ducked into the kitchen and stared around. "Where's dinner?"

My first question would have been, Where's Nikolai? I wonder how long it will take that thought to come to him. "Where is Lord Vorkosigan?"

"He stayed on at the office. He'll be along later, he said, to take his things away."

"Oh." She realized then that some tiny part of her had been hoping to conduct the impending conversation while Vorkosigan was still finishing up in her workroom or something; his presence providing some margin of safety, of social restraint upon Tien. Maybe it was better this way. "Sit down, Tien. I have to talk with you."

He raised dubious brows, but sat at the head of the table, around to her left. She would have preferred to have him opposite her.

"I am leaving you tonight."

"What?" His astonishment appeared genuine. "*Why?*"

She hesitated, reluctant to be drawn into argument. "I suppose . . . because I have come to the end of myself." Only now, looking back over the long draining years, did she become aware of how much of her there had been to use up. No wonder it had taken so long. *All gone now.*

"Why . . . why now?" At least he didn't say, *You must be joking.* "I don't understand, Kat." She could see him begin to grope, not toward understanding, but away from it, as far away as possible. "Is it the Vorzohn's Dystrophy? Damn, I knew—"

"Don't be stupid, Tien. If that was the issue, I'd have left years ago. I took oath to you in sickness and health."

He frowned and sat back, his brows lowering. "Is there someone else? There's someone else, isn't there!"

"I'm sure you wish there were. Because then it would be because of them, and not because of you." Her voice was level, utterly flat. Her stomach churned.

He was obviously shocked, and beginning to shake a little. "This is madness. I don't understand."

"I have nothing more to say." She began to rise, wishing nothing more than to be gone at once, away from him. *You could have done this over the comconsole, you know.*

No. I took my oath in the flesh. I will break it to pieces in the same way.

He rose with her, and his hand closed over hers, gripping it, stopping her. "There's more to it."

"You would know more about that than I would, Tien."

He hesitated now, beginning, she thought, to be really afraid. This might not be any safer for her. *He's never hit me yet, I'll give him that much credit.* Part of her almost wished he had. Then there would have been clarity, not this endless muddle. "What do you mean?"

"Let go of me."

"No."

She considered his hand on hers, tight but not grinding. But still much stronger than her own. He was half a head taller and outweighed her by thirty kilos. She did not feel as much physical fear as she had thought she would. She was too numb, perhaps. She raised her face to his. Her voice grew edged. "Let go of me."

A little to her surprise, he did so, his hand flexing awkwardly. "You have to tell me why. Or I'll believe it's to go to some lover."

"I no longer care what you believe."

"Is he Komarran? Some damned Komarran?"

Goading her in the usual spot, and why not? It had worked before to bring her into line. It half-worked still. She had sworn to herself that she wasn't even going to bring up the subject of Tien's actions and inactions. Complaint was a tacit plea for help, for reform, for . . . continuation. Complaint was to attempt to shuffle off the responsibility for action onto another. To act was to obliterate the need for complaint. She would act, or not act. She would not *whine.* Still in that dead-level voice, she said, "I found out about your trade shares, Tien."

His mouth opened, and shut again. After a moment he said, "I can make it up. I know what went wrong now. I can make the losses up again."

"I don't think so. Where did you get that forty thousand marks, Tien." Her lack of inflection made it not a question.

"I . . ." She could watch it in his face, as he ratcheted over his choice of lies. He settled on a fairly simple one. "Part I saved, part I borrowed. You're not the only one who can scrimp, you know."

"From Administrator Soudha?"

He flinched at the name, but said ingenuously, "How did you know?"

"It doesn't matter, Tien. I'm not going to turn you in." She stared at him in weariness. "I take no part in you anymore."

He paced, agitated, back and forth across the kitchen, his face working. "I did it for you," he said at last.

Yes. Now he will attempt to make me feel guilty. All my fault. It was as familiar as the steps of some well-practiced, poisonous dance. She watched silently.

"All for you. You wanted money. I worked my tail off, but it was never enough for you, was it?" His voice rose, as he tried to lash himself into a relieving, self-righteous anger. It fell a little flat to her experienced ear. "You pushed me into taking a chance, with your endless nagging and worrying. So it didn't work, and now you want to punish me, is that it? You'd have been quick enough to make up to me if it had paid off."

He was very good at this, she had to admit, his accusations echoing her own dark doubts. She listened to his patterned litany with a sort of detached appreciation, like a torture victim, gone beyond pain unbeknownst, admiring the color of her own blood. *Now he will attempt to make me feel sorry for him. But I'm done feeling sorry. I'm done feeling anything.*

"Money money money, is that what this is all about? What is it that you want to buy so damned much, Kat?"

Your health, as you may recall. And Nikki's future. And mine.

As he paced, sputtering, his eye fell on the bright red skellytum, sitting in its basin on the kitchen table. "You don't love me. You only love yourself. Selfish, Kat! You love your damned potted *plants* more than you love me. Here, I'll prove it to you."

He snatched up the pot and pressed the control for the door to the balcony. It opened a little too slowly for his dramatic timing, but he strode through nonetheless, and whirled to face her. "Which shall it be to go over the railing, Kat? Your precious plant, or me? Choose!"

She neither spoke nor moved. *Now he will attempt to terrify me with suicide gestures.* This made, what, the fourth time around for that ploy? His trump card, which had always before ended the game in his favor.

He brandished the skellytum high. "Me, or it?" He watched her face, waiting for her to break. An almost clinical curiosity prompted her to say *You*, just to see how he would wriggle out of his challenge, but she kept silent still. When she did not speak, he hesitated in confusion for a moment, then launched the ancient absurd thing over the side.

Five floors up. She counted the seconds in her head, waiting for the crash from below. It came as more of a distant, sodden thump, mixed with the crack of exploding pottery.

"You ass, Tien. You didn't even look to see if there was anyone below."

With a look of sudden alarm that almost made her want to laugh, he peeked fearfully over the side. Apparently he hadn't managed to kill anyone after all, for he inhaled deeply and turned back toward her, taking a few steps through the open airseal door into the kitchen, but not too near to her. "React, damn you! What do I have to do to get through to you?"

"Don't bother," she said levelly. "I cannot imagine anything you could do that would make me more angry than I am."

He had come to the end of his menu of tactics and stood at a loss. His voice grew smaller. "What do you want?"

"I want my honor back. But you cannot give it to me."

His voice grew smaller still; his hands opened in pleading. "I'm sorry about your aunt's skellytum. I don't know what . . ."

"Are you sorry about grand theft and petty treason, bribery and peculation?"

"I did it for *you*, Kat!"

"In eleven years," she said slowly, "you have apparently never figured out who I am. I don't understand that. How you can live with someone so intimately, so long, and yet never see them. Maybe you were living with some Kat holovid projection from your own mind, I don't know."

"What do you *want*, dammit? It's not like I can go back. I can't confess. That would be public dishonor! For me, you, Nikki, your uncle—you can't want that!"

"I want never to have to tell a lie again for as long as I live. What you do is your problem." She took a deep breath. "But know this. Whatever you do, or don't do, from now on had better be for yourself. Because it won't touch me." Done once, done for all time. She was never going through this again.

"I can—I can fix it."

Was he referring to her skellytum, their marriage, his crime? Wrong anyway, in all cases.

When she still did not respond, he blurted desperately, "Nikolai is mine, by Barrayaran law."

Interesting. Nikki was the one tactic he had never employed before, off limits. She knew then how deathly serious he knew her to be. Good. He glanced around, and added belatedly, "Where is Nikki?"

"Someplace safer."

"You can't keep him from me!"

I can if you're in prison. She didn't bother saying it aloud. Under the circumstances, Tien was perhaps unlikely to challenge her possession of Nikki before the law. But she wanted to keep Nikolai's concerns as far separated as possible from the ugliest part of this thing. She would not start that war, but if Tien dared to do so, she would finish it. She watched him more coldly than ever.

"I *will* fix it. I can. I have a plan. I've been thinking about it all day."

Tien with a plan was about as reassuring as a two-year-old with a charged plasma arc. *No. You are not to take responsibility for him anymore. That's what this is all about, remember? Let go.* "Do whatever you wish, Tien. I'm going to go finish packing now."

"Wait—" He swung around her. It disturbed her to have him between her and the door, but she did not let her fear show. "Wait. I'll make it up. You'll see. I'll fix it. Wait here!"

With an anxious wave of his hands, he made for the hall door, and was gone.

She listened to his retreating footsteps. Only when she heard the faint whisper from the lift tube did she step back onto the balcony and look over. Far below, the shattered remains of her skellytum made an irregular wet blotch on the pavement, the broken scarlet tendrils looking like spattered blood. A passer-by was staring curiously at it. After a minute, she saw Tien emerge from the building and stride across the park toward the bubble-car platform, almost breaking into a run from time to time. He twice looked back up toward their balcony, over his shoulder; she stepped back into the shadows. He disappeared into the station.

Every muscle of her body seemed to be spasming with tension. She felt close to vomiting. She returned to her—to the kitchen, and drank a glass of water, which helped settle her breathing and her stomach. She went to her work room to fetch a basket and some plastic sheeting and a trowel, to go scrape the mess off the walkway five floors down.

Chapter Ten

Miles sat at Administrator Vorsoisson's comconsole desk, methodically reading through the files of all the employees of the Waste Heat department. There seemed to be a lot of personnel, compared to some of the other departments; Waste Heat was definitely a favored child in the Project budget. Presumably most of them spent the bulk of their time out at the experiment station, since Waste Heat's offices here were modest. In hindsight, always acute, Miles wished he'd begun his survey of Radovas's life out there today, where there might have been some action to observe, instead of in this tower of bureaucratic boredom. More, he wished he'd dropped in on the experiment station during their first tour . . . well, no. He would not have known what to look for then.

And you know now? He shook his head in wry dismay and brought up another file. Tuomonen had taken a copy of the personnel list, and in due time would be interviewing most of these people, unless something happened to take the investigation off in another direction. Such as finding Marie Trogir—that was the first item now on Miles's wish list for ImpSec. Miles shifted to ease the twinge in his back; he could feel his body stiffening from sitting still in a cool room too long. Didn't these Serifosans know they needed to waste more heat?

Quick steps in the hallway paused and turned in at the outer office, and Miles glanced up. Tien Vorsoisson, a little out of breath, hung a moment in his office doorway, then plunged inside. He was carrying two heavy jackets, his own and the one of his wife's that Miles had used the other day, and a breath mask labeled *Visitor, Medium*. He smiled at Miles in suppressed agitation. "My Lord Auditor. So glad to still find you here."

Miles shut down the file and regarded Vorsoisson with interest. "Hello, Administrator. What brings you back tonight?"

"You, my lord. I need to talk with you right away. I have to . . . to show you something I've discovered."

Miles opened his hand, indicating the comconsole, but Vorsoisson shook his head. "Not here, my lord. Out at the Waste Heat experiment station."

Ah ha. "Right now?"

"Yes, tonight, while everyone is gone." Vorsoisson laid the spare breath mask on the comconsole, rummaged in a cabinet in the far wall, and came up with his own personal mask. He yanked the straps over his neck and hastily adjusted his chest harness to hold the supplementary oxygen bottle in place. "I've requisitioned a lightflyer, it's waiting downstairs."

"All right . . ." Now what was this going to be all about? Too much to hope Vorsoisson had found Marie Trogir locked in a closet out there. Miles checked his own mask—power and oxygen levels indicated it was fully recharged—and slipped it on. He took a couple of breaths in passing, to test its correct function, then slid it down out of the way under his chin and shrugged on the jacket.

"This way . . ." Vorsoisson led off with long strides, which annoyed Miles considerably; he declined to run to keep up with the man. The Administrator perforce waited for him at the lift tube, bouncing on his heels in impatience. This time, when they reached the garage sub-level, the vehicle was ready. It was a less-than-luxurious government issue two-passenger flyer, but appeared to be in perfectly good condition.

Miles was less certain of the driver. "What's this all about, Vorsoisson?"

Vorsoisson put his hand on the canopy and regarded Miles with an intensity of expression that was almost alarming. "What are the rules for declaring oneself an Imperial Witness?"

"Well . . . various, I suppose, depending on the situation." Miles was not, he realized belatedly, nearly as well up on the fine points of Barrayaran law as an Imperial Auditor ought to be. He needed to do more reading. "I mean . . . I don't think it's exactly something one does for oneself. It's usually negotiated between a potential witness and whatever prosecuting authority is in charge of the criminal case." *And rarely.* Since the end of the Time of Isolation, with the importation of fast-penta and other galactic interrogation drugs, the authorities no longer had to *bargain* for truthful testimony, normally.

"In this case, the authority is you," said Tien. "The rules are whatever you say they are, aren't they? Because you are an Imperial Auditor."

"Uh . . . maybe."

Vorsoisson nodded in satisfaction, raised the canopy, and slid into the pilot's seat. With reluctant fascination, Miles levered himself in beside him. He fastened his safety harness as the flyer lifted and glided toward the garage's vehicle lock.

"And why do you ask?" Miles probed delicately. Vorsoisson had all the air of a man anxious to spill something very interesting indeed. Not for three worlds did Miles wish to frighten him off at this point. At the same time, Miles would have to be extremely cautious about what he promised. *He's your fellow Auditor's nephew-in-law. You've just stepped onto an ethical tightrope.*

Vorsoisson did not answer right away, instead powering the lightflyer up into the night sky. The lights of Serifosa brightened the faint feathery clouds of valuable moisture above, which occluded the stars. But as they shot away from the dome city, the glowing haze thinned and the stars came out in force. The landscape away from the dome was very dark, devoid of the villages and homesteads that carpeted less climatically hostile worlds. Only a monorail streaked away to the southwest, a faint pale line against the barren ground.

"I believe," Vorsoisson said at last, and swallowed. "I believe I have finally accumulated enough evidence of an attempted crime against the Imperium for a successful prosecution. I hope I haven't waited too long, but I had to be sure."

"Sure of what?"

"Soudha has tried to bribe me. I'm not absolutely certain that he didn't bribe my predecessor, too."

"Oh? Why?"

"Waste Heat Management. The whole department is a scam, a hollow shell. I'm not really sure how long they've been able to keep this bubble going. They had *me* fooled for . . . for months. I mean . . .

a building full of equipment on a quiet day, how was I supposed to know what it did? Or didn't do? Or that there weren't anything *but* quiet days?"

"How long—" *have you known*, Miles bit off. That question was premature. "Just what are they doing?"

"They're bleeding off money from the project. For all I know, it may have started small, or by accident—some departed employee mistakenly kept on the roster, an accumulation of pay that Soudha figured out how to pocket. Ghost employees—his department is full of fictitious employees, all drawing pay. And equipment purchases for the ghost employees—Soudha suborned some woman in Accounting to go along with it. They have all the forms right, all the numbers match. They've slid it through I don't know how many fiscal inspections, because the accountants HQ sends out don't know how to check the science, only the forms."

"Who *does* check the science?"

"That's the thing, my Lord Auditor. The Terraforming Project isn't *expected* to produce quick results, not in any immediately measurable way. Soudha produces technical reports, all right, plenty of them, right to schedule, but I think he mostly does them by copying other sectors' previous-period results and fudging."

Indeed, the Komarran Terraforming Project was a bureaucratic backwater, far down the Barrayaran Imperium's urgent list. Not critical: a good place to park, say, incompetent Vor second sons out of the way of their families. Where they could do no harm to anyone, because the project was vast and slow, and they would cycle out and be gone again before the damage could even be measured. "Speaking of ghost employees—how does Radovas's death connect with this alleged scam?"

Vorsoisson hesitated. "I'm not sure it does. Except to draw ImpSec down on it and burst the bubble. After all, he quit days before he died."

"Soudha said he quit. Soudha, according to you, is a proven liar and data artist. Could Radovas have, say, threatened to expose Soudha and been murdered to assure his silence?"

"But Radovas was in on it. For years. I mean, all the technical people had to know. They couldn't *not* know they weren't doing the work the reports said."

"Mm, that may depend on how much of an artistic genius Soudha was, arranging his reports." Soudha's own personnel file certainly suggested he was neither stupid nor second-rate. Might he have cooked those records as well? *Oh, God. This means I'm not going to be able to trust any data off any comconsole in the whole damned department.* And he'd wasted *hours* today, decanting comconsoles. "Radovas might have had a change of heart."

"I don't *know*," said Vorsoisson plaintively. His glance flicked aside to Miles. "I want you to remember, I found this. I turned them in. Just as soon as I was sure."

His repeated insistence on that last point hinted broadly to Miles's ear that his knowledge of this fascinating piece of peculation predated his assurance by a noticeable margin. Had Soudha's bribe been not just offered, but accepted? Till the bubble burst. Was Miles witnessing an outbreak of patriotic duty on Vorsoisson's part, or an unseemly rush to get Soudha and Company before they got him?

"I'll remember," Miles said neutrally. Belatedly, it occurred to him that going off alone in the night with Vorsoisson to some deserted outpost, without even pausing to inform Tuomonen, might not be the brightest thing he'd ever done. Still, he doubted Vorsoisson would be nearly this forthcoming in the ImpSec captain's presence. It might be as well not to be too blunt with Vorsoisson about his chances of slithering out of this mess till they were safely back in Serifosa, preferably in the presence of Tuomonen and a couple of nice big ImpSec goons. Miles's stunner was a reassuring lump in his pocket. He would check in with Tuomonen via his wrist comm link as soon as he could arrange a quiet moment out of Vorsoisson's earshot.

"And tell Kat," Vorsoisson added.

Huh? What had Madame Vorsoisson to do with any of this? "Let's see this evidence of yours, then talk about it."

"What you'll mainly see is an absence of evidence, my lord," said Vorsoisson. "A great empty facility . . . there."

Vorsoisson banked the lightflyer, and they began to descend toward the Waste Heat experiment station. It was well lit with plenty of outdoor floodlamps, switched on automatically at dusk Miles presumed, and in high contrast to the surrounding dark. As they drew closer, Miles saw that its parking lot was not deserted; half a dozen lightflyers and aircars clustered in the landing circles. Windows glowed warmly here and there in the small office building, and more lights snaked through the airsealed tubes between sections. There were two big lift vans, one backing now into an opened loading bay in the large windowless engineering building.

"It looks pretty busy to me," said Miles. "For a hollow shell."

"I don't understand," said Vorsoisson.

Vegetation which actually stood higher than Miles's ankle struggled successfully against the cold here, but it was not quite abundant enough to conceal the lightflyer. Miles almost told Vorsoisson to douse the flyer's lights and bring them down out of sight over a small rise, despite the hike back it would entail. But Vorsoisson was already dropping toward an empty landing circle in the parking lot. He landed and killed the engine, and stared uncertainly toward the facility.

"Maybe . . . maybe you had better stay out of sight, at first," said Vorsoisson in worry. "They shouldn't mind me."

He was apparently unconscious of the world of self-revelation in this simple statement. They both adjusted their breath masks, and Vorsoisson popped the canopy. The chill night air licked Miles's exposed skin, above his breath mask, and prickled in his scalp. He dug his hands into his pockets as if to warm them, touched his stunner briefly, and followed the Administrator, a little behind him. Staying out of sight was one thing; letting Vorsoisson out of his sight was another.

"Try looking in the Engineering building first," Miles called, his voice muffled by his mask. "See if we can get a look at what's going on before you make contact with the en—er, try to speak to anyone."

Vorsoisson veered toward the loading bay's vehicle lock. Miles wondered if there was a chance anyone glancing out in the uncertain lighting might mistake him at first for Nikolai. The combination of Vorsoisson's dramatic mystery and his own natural paranoia was making him twitchy indeed, despite a better part of his mind that calculated high odds on a harmless scenario involving Vorsoisson being wildly mistaken.

They entered the pedestrian lock into the loading dock and cycled through. The pressure differential in his ears was slight. Miles kept his breath mask up temporarily as they rounded the parked lift van. He would call Tuomonen as soon as he ditched—

Miles skidded to a halt a moment too late to avoid being spotted in turn by the couple who stood quietly next to a float-pallet loaded with machinery. The woman, who had the pallet's control lead in her hand as she maneuvered the silently hovering load into the van, was

Madame Radovas. The man was Administrator Soudha. They both looked up in shock at their unexpected visitors.

Miles was torn for a moment between whacking his wrist-comm's screamer circuit or going for his stunner; but at Soudha's sudden movement toward his own vest Miles's combat reflexes took over, and his hand dove for his pocket. Vorsoisson half-turned, his mouth round with astonishment and the beginning of some warning cry. Miles would have thought *I've just been led into ambush by that idiot,* except that Vorsoisson was clearly much more surprised than he was.

Soudha managed to get his stunner out and pointed a half second before Miles did. *Oh, shit, I never asked Dr. Chenko what a stunner blast would do to my seizure stimulator—* the stunner beam took him full in the face. His head snapped back in an agony that was mercifully brief. He was unconscious before he hit the concrete floor.

Miles woke with a stunner migraine pinwheeling behind his eyes, metallic splinters of pure pain seemingly stuck quivering in his brain from his frontal lobes to his spinal column. He closed his eyes immediately against the too-bright glare of lights. He was nauseated to the point of vomiting. The realization immediately following, that he was still wearing his breath mask, caused his spacer's training to cut in; he swallowed and breathed deeply, carefully, and the dangerous moment passed. He was cold, and held upright in an awkward position by restraints pulling on his arms. He opened his eyes again and looked around.

He was outdoors in the chill Komarran dark, chained to a railing along the walkway on the blank side of what appeared to be the Waste Heat engineering building. Colored floodlights positioned in the vegetation two meters below, prettily illuminating the building and raised concrete walk, were the source of the eye-piercing light. Beyond them, the view was singularly uninformative, the ground falling away from the building and then rising, beyond it, into blank barrenness. The railing was a simple one, metal posts set into the concrete at meter intervals and a round metal handrail running between them. He was slumped to his knees, the concrete hard and cold beneath them, and his wrists were chained—chained? yes, chained, the links fastened with simple metal locks—to two successive posts, holding him half-spread-eagled.

His ImpSec comm-link was still strapped to his left wrist. He could not, of course, reach it with his right hand. Or—he tried—his head. He twisted his wrist around, to press it against the railing, but the screamer-button was recessed to prevent accidental bumps setting it off. Miles swore under his breath, and his breath mask. The mask appeared to be tightly fitted to his face, and he could feel the oxygen bottle still firmly strapped to his chest under his jacket—who had fastened his jacket up to his chin?—but he would have to be exquisitely careful not to jostle the mask till he had his hands free again to readjust it.

So . . . had the stunner beam induced a seizure while he was unconscious, or was he still working up to one? His next was almost due. He stopped swearing abruptly and took a couple of deep, calming breaths that fooled his body not at all.

A couple of meters to his right, he discovered Tien Vorsoisson similarly chained between two upright posts. His head lolled forward; he evidently wasn't awake yet. Miles tried to convince the knot of stressed terror in his solar plexus that this bit of cosmic justice was at least one bright point in the affair. He smiled grimly under his mask. All things considered, he'd rather Vorsoisson were free and able to try for help. Better still, leave Vorsoisson fastened there, free *himself* to try for help. But twisting his hands in their tight chains merely scraped his wrists raw.

If they wanted to kill you, you'd be dead now, he tried to convince his hyperventilating body. Unless, of course, they were sadists, out for a slow and studied revenge. . . . *What did I ever do to these people?* Besides the usual offense of being Barrayaran in general and Aral Vorkosigan's son in particular. . . .

Minutes crept by. Vorsoisson stirred and groaned, then fell back into flaccid unconsciousness, at least assuring Miles he wasn't dead. Yet. At length, the sound of footsteps on the concrete made Miles turn his head carefully.

Because of the approaching figure's breath mask and padded jacket Miles was not at first sure if it was a man or a woman, but as it neared he recognized the curly gray-blond hair and brown eyes of a woman who'd been at that first VIP orientation meeting—it was the accountant, the meticulous one who'd been sure to have a duplicate copy of her department's records for Miles, hah. *Foscol,* read the name on her breath mask.

She saw his open eyes. "Oh, good evening, Lord Auditor Vorkosigan." She raised her voice to a good loud clarity, to be sure her words penetrated the muffling of her mask.

"Good evening, Madame Foscol," he managed in return, matching her tone. If only he could get her talking, and listening –

She drew her hand from her pocket, and held up something glittering and metallic. "This is the key to your wrist locks. I'll set it over here, out of the way." She placed it carefully on the concrete walkway about halfway between Miles and the Administrator, next to the wall of the building. "Don't let anyone accidentally kick it over the side. You'd have a heck of a time finding it down there." She glanced thoughtfully over the rail at the dark vegetation below.

Implying that someone might be expected: a rescue party? Also implying that Foscol, Soudha, and Madame Radovas—*Madame Radovas, what is she doing here?*—did not expect to be around to supply the key in person when that happened.

She rummaged in her pocket again and came up with a data disk wrapped in protective plastic. "This, my Lord Auditor, is the complete record of Administrator Vorsoisson's acceptance of bribes, in the amount of some sixty thousand marks over the last eight months. Account numbers, data trail, where his money was embezzled in the first place—everything you should need for a successful prosecution. I'd been going to mail it to Captain Tuomonen, but this is better." Her eyes crinkled in a smile at him, above her breath mask. She bent and taped it securely to the back of Vorsoisson's jacket. "With my compliments, my lord." She stepped back and dusted her hands in the gesture of a dirty job well done.

"What are you doing?" Miles began. "What are you people doing out here, anyway? Why is Madame Radovas with—"

"Come, come, Lord Vorkosigan," Foscol interrupted him briskly. "You don't imagine that I'm going to stand around and *chat* with you, do you?"

Vorsoisson stirred, groaned, and belched. Despite the utter contempt in her eyes, lingering on his huddled figure, she waited a moment to be sure he wasn't going to vomit into his breath mask. Vorsoisson stared blearily at her, blinking in bewilderment and, Miles had no doubt, pain.

Miles clenched his fists and jerked against his chains. Foscol glanced at him and added kindly, "Don't hurt yourself, trying to get loose. Someone will be along eventually to collect you. I only regret I won't be able to watch." She turned on her heel and strode away, down the walk and around the corner of the building. After another minute, the faint sounds of a lift-van taking to the air drifted around the building. But they were on the opposite side of the building to the approach from Serifosa, and the departing van did not cross into Miles's limited line of sight.

Soudha's a competent engineer. I wonder if he's set the reactor here to destroy itself? was the next inspired thought to enter Miles' mind. That would erase all the evidence, Vorsoisson, and Miles, too. If he timed it just right, Soudha might be able to take out the ImpSec rescue squad as well . . . but it seemed Foscol meant the evidence pinned to Vorsoisson's back to survive, at least, which argued against a scenario that would turn the experiment station into a glowing glass hole in the landscape resembling the lost city of Vorkosigan Vashnoi. Soudha and Company did not seem to be thinking militarily. Thank God. This scene seemed engineered for maximum humiliation, and one could not embarrass the dead.

Their next-of-kin, however . . . Miles thought of his father and shuddered. And Ekaterin and Nikolai, and, of course, Lord Auditor Vorthys. Oh, yes.

Vorsoisson, coming to full consciousness at last, reared up and discovered the limits of his bonds. He swore muzzily, then with increasing clarity of expression, yanked his arms against their chains. After about a minute, he stopped. He stared around and found Miles.

"Vorkosigan. What the hell is going on here?"

"We appear to have been parked out of the way while Soudha and his friends finish decamping from the experiment station. They seem to have realized their time had run out." Miles wondered if he ought to mention to Vorsoisson what was taped to his back, then decided against it. The man was already breathing heavily from his struggles. Vorsoisson swore some more, monotonously, but after a bit seemed to become aware that he was repeating himself, and ran down.

"Tell me more about this embezzlement scheme of Soudha's," Miles said into the eerie silence. No insect or bird chirps enlivened the Komarran night, and no tree leaves rustled in the faint, chill breeze. No further sounds came from the buildings behind them. The only noise was the susurration of their breath masks' powered fans, filters, and regulators. "When did you find out about it?"

"Just . . . yesterday. A week ago yesterday. Soudha panicked, I think, and tried to bribe me. I didn't want to embarrass Kat's Uncle Vorthys by blowing it wide open while he was here. And I had to be sure, before I started accusing people right and left."

Foscol says you lie. Miles wasn't sure which of them he trusted least by now. Foscol could have invented her evidence against Vorsoisson using the same skills she had apparently called on to hide Soudha's thefts. He would have to let the ImpSec forensic specialists sort it out, and carefully.

Miles simultaneously sympathized with and was deeply suspicious of Vorsoisson's claimed hesitation, a dizzying state of mind to endure on top of a stunner migraine. He had never thought of fast-penta as a medicine for headache, but he wished he had a hypospray of it to jab in Vorsoisson's ass right now. *Later,* he promised himself. *Without fail.* "Is that all that's going on, d'you think?"

"What do you mean, all?"

"I don't quite . . . if I were Soudha and his group, fleeing the scene of our crime . . . they did have some lead time to prepare their retreat. Maybe as long as three or four weeks, if they knew Radovas's body was likely to be found topside." *And what the hell was Radovas's body doing up there anyway? I still don't have a clue.* "Longer, if they kept their emergency backup plans up to date, and Soudha is an engineer if ever I met one; he's got to have had fail-safes incorporated into his schemes. Wouldn't it make more sense to scatter, travel light, try to get out of the Empire in ones and twos . . . not leave in a bunch with two lift-vans full of . . . whatever the hell they needed two lift-vans to transport? Not their money, surely."

Vorsoisson shook his head, which shifted his breath mask slightly; he had to rub his face against the railing to reseat it. After a few minutes he said in a small voice, "Vorkosigan . . . ?"

Miles hoped from the humbler tone the man might be going to edge toward true confession after all. "Yes?" he said encouragingly.

"I'm almost out of oxygen."

"Didn't you check—" Miles tried to bring up the image in his pulsing brain of the moment Vorsoisson had snatched his breath mask out of the cabinet, back in his office, and donned it. No. He hadn't checked anything about it. A fully-charged mask would support twelve to fourteen hours of vigorous outdoor activity, under normal circumstances. Miles's visitor's mask had presumably been taken from a central store, where some tech had the job of processing and recharging used masks before setting them on the rack ready for reuse. *Don't forget to put your mask on the recharger,* Vorsoisson's wife had said to him, and been snapped at for nagging. Was Vorsoisson in the habit of stuffing his equipment away uncleaned? In his office, Madame Vorsoisson couldn't very well pick up after him the way she doubtless did at home

At one time, Miles could have crushed his own fragile hand bones and drawn his hand out through a restraint before his flesh began to swell enough to trap it again. He'd actually done that once, on a hideously memorable occasion. But the bones in his hands were all sturdy synthetics now, less breakable even than normal bone. All that his applied strength could do was make his chafed wrists bleed.

Vorsoisson's wrists began to bleed too, as he struggled more frantically against his chains.

"Vorsoisson, hold still!" Miles called urgently to him. "Conserve your oxygen. There's supposed to be someone coming. Go limp, breathe shallowly, make it last." Why hadn't the idiot mentioned this earlier, to Miles, to *Foscol* even . . . had Foscol intended this result? Maybe she'd meant both Miles and Vorsoisson to die, one after the other . . . *how long* till the promised someone came to collect them? A couple of days? Murdering an Imperial Auditor in the middle of a case was considered an act of treason worse than murdering a ruling District Count and only barely short of assassinating the Emperor himself. Nothing could be more surely calculated to send ImpSec's entire forces in frenzied pursuit of the fleeing embezzlers, with an implacable concentration reaching, potentially, across decades and distance and diplomatic barriers. It was a suicidal gesture, or unbelievably foolhardy. "How much do you have left?"

Vorsoisson wriggled his chin and tried to peer down over his nose into the dim recesses of his jacket to see the top of the canister strapped there. "Oh, God. I think it's reading zero."

"Those things always have some safety margin. Stay still, man! Try for some self-control!"

Instead Vorsoisson began to struggle ever more frantically. He threw himself forward and backward with all his considerable strength, trying to break the railing. Blood drops flew from the flayed skin of his wrists, and the railing reverberated and bent, but it did not break. He pulled up his knees and then flung himself down through the meter-wide opening between the posts, trying to propel his full body weight against the chains. They held, and then his backward-scrambling legs could not regain the walkway. His boot heels scraped and scrabbled on the wall. His dizzied choking, at the last, led to vomiting inside his breath mask. When it slipped down around his neck in his final paroxysms, it seemed almost a mercy, except for the way it revealed his distorted, purpling features. But the screams and pleas stopped, and then the gasps and gulpings. The kicking legs twitched, and hung limply.

Miles had been right; Vorsoisson might have had a full twenty or thirty minutes more oxygen if he had hunkered down quietly. Miles stood very still, and breathed very shallowly, and shivered in the cold. Shivering, he recalled dimly, used more oxygen, but he could not make himself stop. The silence was profound, broken only by the hiss of Miles's regulators and filters, and the beating of the blood in his own ears. He had seen many deaths, including his own, but this was surely one of the ugliest. The shocky shudders traveled up and down his body, and his thoughts spun uselessly: they kept circling back to the spuriously calm observation that a barrel of fast-penta would be no damned use to him now.

If he went into a convulsion and dislodged his breath mask in the process, he could be well on his way to asphyxiating before he even returned to consciousness. ImpSec would find him hanging there beside Vorsoisson, choked identically on his own spew. And nothing was more likely to set off one of his seizures than stress.

Miles watched the slime begin to freeze on the sagging corpse's face, scanned the dark skies in the wrong direction, and waited.

Chapter Eleven

Ekaterin set down her cases next to Lord Vorkosigan's in the vestibule, and turned for one last automatic check of the premises, one last patrol of her old life. All lights were out. All windows were sealed. All appliances were off . . . the comconsole chimed just as she was leaving the kitchen.

She hesitated. *Let it go. Let it all go.* But then she reflected it might be Tuomonen or someone, trying to reach Lord Vorkosigan. Or Uncle Vorthys, though she was not sure she even wanted to talk to him, tonight. She turned back to the machine, but her hand hesitated again with the thought that it might be Tien. *In that case, I will simply cut the com.* If it was Tien, about to attempt some other plea or threat or persuasion, at least it was a guarantee he was someplace else, and not here, and she could still walk away.

But the face that formed over the vid-plate at her reluctant touch was that of a Komarran woman from Tien's department, Lena Foscol. Ekaterin had only met her in person a couple of times, but Soudha's words over this same vid-plate last night leapt to her mind: *Lena Foscol in Accounting is the most meticulous thief I've ever met.* Oh, God. She was one of *them.* The background was out of focus, but the woman was wearing a parka, thrown open over dome-wear, suggesting she was either on her way to or on her way back from some outside expedition. Ekaterin regarded her with concealed revulsion.

"Madame Vorsoisson?" Foscol said brightly. Without waiting for Ekaterin's answer, she went on, "Please come pick up your husband at the Waste Heat experiment station. He'll be waiting for you outside on the northwest side of the Engineering building."

"But—" What was Tien doing out there at this time of night? "How did he get out there, doesn't he have a flyer? Can't he get a ride back with someone else?"

"Everyone else has left." Her smile widened, and she cut the com.

"But—" Ekaterin raised a hand in futile protest, too late. "Drat." And then, after a moment, "*Damn* it!"

Retrieving Tien from the experiment station would be a two-hour chore, at least. She would first have to take a bubble-car to a public flyer livery, and rent a flyer, since she had no authority to requisition one from Tien's department. She'd been seriously considering sleeping on a park bench tonight, just to save her pittance of funds for the uncertain days to come until she found some form of paying work, except that the dome patrollers didn't permit vagrants to loiter in any of the places where she might feel safe. Foscol hadn't said if Lord Vorkosigan was with Tien, which suggested he was not, which meant that she'd have to fly back to Serifosa alone with Tien, who would insist on taking the controls, and what if he finally got serious about his suicide threats when they were halfway back, and decided to take her down with him? No. It wasn't worth the risk. Let him rot out there till morning, or let him call someone else.

Her hand upon her case again, she reconsidered. Still hostage to fortune in this mess, or at least to everyone's good behavior, was Nikki. Tien's relationship to his son was mostly neglectful, interspersed with occasional bullying, but with enough spasms of actual attention that Nikki, at least, still seemed to show attachment to him. The two of them were always going to have a relationship separate from her own. She and Tien would be forced to cooperate for Nikki's sake: an iron-cladding of surface courtesy that must never crack. Tien's anger or potential brutality were no more of a threat to her future than some belated attempt on his part at affection or placation. She could face down either, now, she thought, with equal stoniness.

I am not here to vent my feelings. I am here to achieve my goals. Yes. She could foresee that was going to be her new mantra, in the weeks to come. With a grimace, she opened her case and retrieved her personal breath mask, checked its reservoirs, pulled on her parka, and headed out for the bubble-car station.

The delays were every bit as aggravating as Ekaterin had foreseen. Komarrans sharing her bubble-car forced two extra stops. She suffered a thirty-minute clog in the system within sight of her goal; by the time it spat her out at the westernmost dome lock, she was quite ready to chuck her plan of courtesy and go back to the apartment, except for the thought of facing another thirty-minute delay en route. The lightflyer they issued to her was elderly and not very clean. Alone at last, flying through the vast silence of the Komarran night, her heart eased a little, and she toyed with the fantasy of flying somewhere *else*, anywhere, just to extend the heavenly solitude. There might be more to pleasure than the absence of pain, but she couldn't prove it just now. The absence of pain, of other human beings and their needs pressing down upon her, seemed paradise enough. A paradise just out of reach.

Besides, she had no *elsewhere*. She could not even return to Barrayar with Nikki without first earning enough to pay for their passage, or borrowing the money from her father, or her distant brothers, or Uncle Vorthys. Distasteful thought. *What you feel doesn't count, girl*, she reminded herself. *Goals. You'll do whatever you have to do.*

The bright lights of the experiment station, isolated in this barren wilderness, made a glow on the horizon that drew the eye from kilometers off. She followed the black silky gleam of the river that wound past the facility. As she neared, she made out several vehicles grounded in the station's lot and frowned in anger. Foscol had lied about there being no one left at the station to give Tien a lift. On the other hand, this raised the possibility that Ekaterin might get a ride back to Serifosa with someone else . . . she checked her impulse to turn the flyer around in midair, and landed in the lot instead.

She adjusted her breath mask, released the canopy, and walked to the office building, hoping to arrange another ride before she saw Tien. The airlock opened to her touch on the control pad. There was not much reason to leave anything locked up way out here. She turned up the first well-lit hallway, calling, "Hello?"

No one answered. No one appeared to be here. About half the rooms were bare and empty; the rest were rather messy and disorganized, she thought. A comconsole was opened up, its insides torn out . . . melted, in fact. That must have been a spectacular malfunction. Her footsteps echoed hollowly as she crossed through the pedestrian tube to the engineering building. "Hello? Tien?" No answer here, either. The two big assembly rooms were shadowed and sinister, and deserted. "Anyone?" If Foscol hadn't lied after all, why were all those aircars and flyers in the lot? Where had their owners gone, and in what?

He'll be waiting for you outside on the northwest side. . . . She had only a vague idea which side of the building was the northwest; she'd half-expected Tien to be waiting in the parking lot. She sighed uneasily, and adjusted her breath mask again, and stepped out through the pedestrian lock. It would only take a few minutes to circle the building. *I want to fly back to Serifosa, right now. This is weird.* Slowly, she started around the building to her left, her footsteps sounding sharp on the concrete in the chill and toxic night air. A raised walkway, really the level edge of the building's concrete foundation, skirted the wall, with a railing along the outside as the ground fell away below. It made her feel as though she were being herded into some trap, or a corral. She rounded the second corner.

Halfway down the walk, a small human shape huddled on its knees, arms outflung, its forehead pressed against the railing. Another bigger shape hung by its wrists between two wide-spaced posts, its body dangling down over the edge of the raised concrete foundation, feet a half-meter from the ground. *What is this?* The dark seemed to pulsate. She swallowed her panic and hastened toward the odd pair.

The dangling figure was Tien. His breath mask was off, twisted around his neck. Even in the colored half-light from the spots in the vegetation below, she could see his face was mottled and purple, with a cold doughy stillness. His tongue protruded from his mouth; his bulging eyes were fixed and frozen. Very, very dead. Her stomach churned and knotted in shock, and her heart lumped in her chest.

The kneeling figure was Lord Vorkosigan, wearing her second-best jacket that she had been unable to find while packing a short eternity ago. His breath mask was still up—he turned his head, his eyes going wide and dark as he saw her, and Ekaterin melted with relief. The little Lord Auditor was still alive, at least. She was frantically grateful not to be alone with *two* corpses. His wrists, she saw at last, were chained to the railing's posts just as Tien's were. Blood oozed from them, soaking darkly into the jacket's cuffs.

Her first coherent thought was unutterable relief that she had not brought Nikki with her. *How am I going to tell him?* Tomorrow, that was a problem for tomorrow. Let him play away tonight in the bubble of another universe, one without this horror in it.

"Madame Vorsoisson." Lord Vorkosigan's voice was muffled and faint in his breath mask. "Oh, God."

Fearfully, she touched the cold chains around his wrists. The torn flesh was swollen up around the links, almost burying them. "I'll go inside and look for some cutters." She almost added, *Wait here,* but closed her lips on that inanity just in time.

"No, wait," he gasped. "Don't leave me alone—there's a key . . . supposedly . . . on the walk back there." He jerked his head.

She found it at once, a simple mechanical type. It was cold, a slip of metal in her shaking fingers. She had to try several times to get it inserted in the locks that fastened the chains. She then had to peel the chain out of Vorkosigan's blood-crusted flesh as if from a rubber mold, before his hand could fall. When she released the second one, he nearly pitched head-first over the edge of the concrete. She grabbed him and dragged him back toward the wall. He tried to stand, but his legs would not at first unbend, and he fell over again. "Give yourself a minute," she told him. Awkwardly, she tried to massage his legs, to restore circulation; even through the fabric of his gray trousers she could feel how cold and stiff they were.

She stood, holding the key in her hand, and stared in bewilderment at Tien's body. She doubted she and Vorkosigan together could lift that dead weight back up to the walk.

"It's much too late," said Vorkosigan, watching her. His brows were crooked with concern. "I'm s-sorry. Leave him for Tuomonen."

"What is this on his back?" She touched the peculiar arrangement, what appeared to be a plastic packet fixed in place with engineering tape.

"Leave that," said Lord Vorkosigan more sharply. "Please." And then, in more of a rush, stuttering in his shivering, "I'm sorry. I'm sorry. I c-couldn't b-break the chains. Hell, he couldn't either, and he's s-stronger than I am. . . . I thought I c-could break my hand and get it out, but I couldn't. I'm sorry. . . ."

"You need to come inside, where it's warm. Here." She helped pull him to his feet; with a last look over his shoulder at Tien, he suffered himself to be led, hunched over, leaning on her and lurching on his unsteady legs.

She led him through the airlock into the office building, and guided him to an upholstered chair in the lobby. He more fell than sat in it. He shivered violently. "B-b-button," he muttered to her, holding up his hands like paralyzed paws toward her.

"What?"

"Little button on the s-side of wrist com. Press it!"

She did so; he sighed and relaxed against the seat back. His stiff hands yanked at his breath mask; she helped him pull it off over his head, and pulled down her own mask.

"*God* I am glad to get out of that thing. Alive. I th-thought I was gonna have a seizure out there. . . ." He rubbed his pale face, scrubbing at the red pressure-lines engraved in the skin from the edges of the mask. "And it *itched*." Ekaterin spotted the control on a nearby wall and hastily tapped in an increase of the lobby's temperature. She was shivering too, though not from the cold, in suppressed shocky shudders.

"Lord Vorkosigan?" Captain Tuomonen's anxious voice issued thinly from the wrist com. "What's going on? Where the hell *are* you?!"

Vorkosigan lifted his wrist toward his mouth. "Waste Heat experiment station. Get out here. I need you."

"What are you— Should I bring a squad?"

"Don't need guns now, I don't think. You'll need forensics, though. And a medical team."

"Are you injured, my lord?" Tuomonen's voice grew sharp with panic.

"Not to speak of," he said, apparently oblivious to the blood still leaking from his wrists. "Administrator Vorsoisson is dead, though."

"What the hell—*you didn't check in with me before you left the dome, dammit!* What the hell is going on out there?!"

"We can discuss my failings at length, later. Carry on, Captain. Vorkosigan out." He let his arm fall, wearily. His shivering was lessening, now. He leaned his head back against the upholstery; the dark smudges of exhaustion under his eyes looked like bruises. He stared sadly at Ekaterin. "I am sorry, Madame Vorsoisson. There was nothing I could do."

"I would scarcely think so!"

He looked around, squinting, and added abruptly, "Power plant!"

"What about it?" asked Ekaterin.

"Gotta check before the troops arrive. I spent a lot of time wondering if it might have been sabotaged, when I was tied up out there."

His legs were still not working right. He almost fell over again as he tried to turn on his heel; she rose and just caught him, under his elbow.

"Good," he said vaguely to her, and pointed. "That way."

She was evidently drafted as support. He hobbled off in determination, clinging to her arm without apology. The forced action actually helped her to recover, if not calm, a sort of tenuous physical coherence; her shudders damped out, and her incipient nausea passed, leaving her belly feeling hot and odd. Another pedestrian tube led down to the power plant, next to the river. The river was the largest in the Sector, and the proximate reason for siting the experiment station here. By Barrayaran standards it would have been called a creek. Vorkosigan barged awkwardly around the power plant's control room, examining panels and readouts. "Nothing *looks* abnormal," he muttered. "I wonder why they didn't set it to self-destruct? *I* would have. . . ." He fell into a station chair.

She pulled up another one, and sat opposite him, watching him fearfully. "What *happened*?"

"I—we came out, Tien brought me out here—how the devil did *you* come here?"

"Lena Foscol called me at home, and told me Tien wanted a ride. She almost didn't catch me. I'd been about to leave. She didn't even tell me *you* were out here. You might still be . . ."

"No . . . no, I'm almost certain she'd have made some other arrangement, if she'd missed you altogether." He sat up straighter, or tried to. "What time is it now?"

"A little before 2100."

"I . . . would have guessed it was much later. They stunned us, you see. I don't know how long . . . What time did she call you?"

"It was just after 1900 hours."

His eyes squeezed shut, then opened again. "It was too late. It was already too late by then, do you understand?" he asked urgently. His hand jerked toward hers, on her knee as she leaned toward him to catch his hoarse words, but then fell back.

"No . . ."

"There was something questionable going on in the Waste Heat department. Your husband brought me out here to show me—well, I don't quite know what he thought he was going to show me, but we ran headlong into Soudha and his accomplices in the process of decamping. Soudha got the drop on me—stunned us both. I came to, chained to that railing out there. I don't think—I don't know. . . . I don't think they meant to kill your husband. He hadn't checked his breath mask, y'see. His reservoirs were almost empty. The Komarrans didn't check it either, before they left us. I didn't know, no one did."

"Komarrans wouldn't," Ekaterin said woodenly. "Their mask-check procedures are ingrained by the time they're three years old. They'd never imagine an adult would go outside the dome with deficient equipment." Her hands clenched, in her lap. She could picture Tien's death now.

"It was . . . quick," Vorkosigan offered. "At least that."

It was not. Neither quick nor clean. "Please do not lie to me. Please do not ever lie to me."

"All right . . ." he said slowly. "But I don't think . . . I don't *think* it was murder. To set up that scene, and then call *you* . . ." He shook his head. "Manslaughter at most. Death by misadventure."

"Death from stupidity," she said bitterly. "Consistent to the end."

He glanced up at her, his eyes not so much startled as aware, and questioning. "Ah?"

"Lord Auditor Vorkosigan." She swallowed; her throat was so tight it felt like a muscle spasm. The silence in the building, and outside, was eerie in its emptiness. She and Vorkosigan might as well have been the only two people left alive on the planet. "You should know, when I said Foscol called as I was leaving . . . I was *leaving*. Leaving Tien. I'd told him so, when he came home from the department tonight, and just before he went back, I suppose, to get you. What did he do?"

He took this in without much response at first, as if thinking it over. "All right," he echoed himself softly at last. He glanced across at her. "Basically, he came in babbling about some embezzlement scheme which had been going on in Waste Heat Management, apparently for quite some time. He sounded me out about declaring him an Imperial Witness, which he seemed to think would save him from prosecution. It's not quite that simple. I didn't commit myself."

"Tien would hear what he wanted to hear," she said softly.

"I . . . so I gathered." He hesitated, watching her face. "How long . . . what do you know about it?"

"And how long have I known it?" Ekaterin grimaced, and rubbed her face free of the lingering irritation of her own mask. "Not as long as I should have. Tien had been talking for months . . . You have to understand, he was irrationally afraid of anyone finding out about his Vorzohn's Dystrophy."

"I actually do understand that," he offered tentatively.

"Yes . . . and no. It's Tien's older brother's fault, in part. I've cursed the man for years. When *his* symptoms began, he took the Old Vor way out and crashed his lightflyer. It made an impression on Tien he never shook off. Set an impossible example. We'd had no idea his family carried the mutation, till Tien, who was his brother's executor, was going through the records and effects, and we realized both that the accident was deliberate, and why. It was just after Nikki was born . . ."

"But wouldn't it have . . . I'd wondered when I read your file—the defect should have turned up in the gene scan, before the embryo was started in the uterine replicator. Is Nikki affected, or . . . ?"

"Nikki was a body-birth. No gene scan. The Old Vor way. Old Vor have *good* blood, you know, no need to check anything."

He looked as if he'd bitten into a lemon. "Whose bright idea was *that*?"

"I don't . . . quite remember how it was decided. Tien and I decided together. I was young, we were just married, I had a lot of stupid romantic ideas . . . I suppose it seemed heroic to me at the time."

"How old were you?"

"Twenty."

"Ah." His mouth quirked in a expression she could not quite interpret, a sad mixture of irony and sympathy. "Yes."

Obscurely encouraged, she went on. "Tien's scheme for dealing with the dystrophy without anyone ever finding out he had it was to go get galactic treatment, somewhere far from the Imperium. It made it much more expensive than it needed to be. We'd been trying to save for years, but somehow, something always went wrong. We never made much progress. But for the past six or eight months, Tien's been telling me to stop worrying, he had it under control. Except . . . Tien always talks like that, so I scarcely paid attention. Then last night, after you went to sleep . . . I heard you tell him straight out you wanted to make a surprise inspection of his department today, I *heard* you—he got up in the night and called

Administrator Soudha, to warn him. I listened . . . I heard enough to gather they had some sort of payroll falsification scheme going, and I'm very much afraid . . . no. I'm certain Tien was taking bribes. Because—" she stopped and took a breath "—I broke into Tien's comconsole this morning and looked at his financial records." She glanced up, to see how Vorkosigan would take this. His mouth renewed the crooked quirk. "I'm sorry I ripped at you the other day, for looking through mine," she said humbly.

His mouth opened, and closed; he merely gave her a little encouraging wave of his fingers and slumped down a bit more in his chair, listening with an air of uttermost attention. *Listening*.

She went on hurriedly, not before her nerve broke, for she scarcely felt anything now, but before she dragged to a halt from sheer exhaustion. "He'd had at least forty thousand marks that I couldn't see where they'd come from. Not from his salary, certainly."

"Had?"

"If the information on the comconsole was right, he'd taken all forty thousand and borrowed sixty more, and lost it all on Komarran trade fleet shares."

"*All?*"

"Well, no, not quite all. About three-quarters of it." At his astonished look, she added, "Tien's luck has always been like that."

"I always used to say you made your own luck. Though I've been forced to eat those words often enough, I don't say it so much anymore."

"Well . . . I think it must be true, or how else could his luck have been so *consistently* bad? The only common factor in all the chaos *was* Tien." She leaned her head back wearily. "Though I suppose it might have been me, somehow." *Tien often said it was me.*

After a little silence, he said hesitantly, "Did you love your husband, Madame Vorsoisson?"

She didn't want to answer this. The truth made her ashamed. But she was done with dissimulation. "I suppose I did, once. In the beginning. I can hardly remember anymore. But I couldn't stop . . . caring for him. Cleaning up after him. Except my caring got slower and slower, and finally it . . . stopped. Too late. Or maybe too soon, I don't know." But if, of course, she had not broken from Tien just then, in just that way, he would not tonight have . . . and, and, and, along the whole chain of events that led to this moment. That *if-only* could, of course, be said equally for any link in the chain. Not more, not less. Not repairable. "I thought, if I let go, he would fall." She stared at her hands. "Eventually. I didn't expect it to happen so soon."

It began to be borne in upon her what a mess Tien's death was going to leave in her lap. She would be trading the painful legalities of separation for the equally painful and difficult legalities of sorting out his probably bankrupt estate. And what was she supposed to do about his body, or any kind of funeral, and how to notify his mother, and . . . yet solving the worst problem without Tien seemed already a thousand times easier than solving the simplest *with* Tien. No more deferential negotiations for permission or approval or consensus. She could just *do* it. She felt . . . like a patient coming out of some paralysis, stretching her arms wide for the first time, and surprised to discover they were strong.

She frowned in puzzlement. "Will there be charges? Against Tien?"

Vorkosigan shrugged. "It is not customary to try the dead, though I believe it was done occasionally in the Time of Isolation. Lord Vorventa the Twice-Hung springs to mind. No. There will be investigations, there will be reports, oh my head the reports, ImpSec's and my own and possibly the Serifosa Sector's security—I anticipate argument over jurisdiction—there may be testimony required of you in the prosecution of other persons . . ." He broke off, to hitch himself around with difficulty in his chair, and shove a now somewhat less stiff-from-cold hand into his pocket. "Persons who I suppose got away with my stunner . . ." His expression changed to one of dismay, and he spasmed to his feet and turned out both his trouser pockets, then checked his jacket, shucked it off, and patted his gray tunic. "*Damn.*"

"What?" asked Ekaterin in alarm.

"I think the bastards took my Auditor's seal. Unless it just fell out of my pocket, somewhere in all the horsing around tonight. Oh, God. It'll open any government or security comconsole in the Empire." He took a deep breath, then brightened. "On the other hand, it has a locator-circuit. ImpSec can trace it, if they're close enough—ImpSec can trace *them*. Ha!" With difficulty, he forced his red and swollen fingers to open a channel on his comm link. "Tuomonen?" he inquired.

"We're on our way, my lord," Tuomonen's voice came back instantly. "We're in the air, about halfway there I estimate. Will you *please* leave your channel open?"

"Listen. I think my assailants have taken off with my Auditor's seal. Delegate someone to start trying to track it at once. Find it and you'll find them, if it's not just been dropped around here somewhere. You can check that possibility when you get here."

Vorkosigan then insisted on a tour of the building, drafting Ekaterin once more as occasional support, though he stumbled very little now. He frowned at the melted comconsole, and at the empty rooms, and stared with narrowed eyes at the jumbles of equipment. Tuomonen and his men arrived just as they were reentering the lobby.

Lord Vorkosigan's lips twitched in bemusement as two half-armored guards, stunners at the ready, leaped through the airseal door. They gave Vorkosigan anxious nods, which he acknowledged with a wry salutelike gesture, then pelted after each other through the facility for a rather noisy security check. Vorkosigan hitched himself into a deliberately more relaxed posture, leaning against an upholstered chair. Captain Tuomonen, another Barrayaran soldier in half-armor, and three men in medical gear followed into the lobby.

"My lord!" said Tuomonen, pulling down his breath mask. His tone of voice sounded familiarly maternal to Ekaterin's ear, halfway between *Thank God you're safe* and *I'm going to strangle you with my bare hands*.

"Good evening, Captain," said Vorkosigan genially. "So glad to see you."

"You didn't notify me!"

"Yes, it was entirely my mistake, and I'll be certain to note your exoneration in my report," Vorkosigan said soothingly.

"It's not that, dammit!" Tuomonen strode over to him, motioning a medic in his wake. He took in Vorkosigan's macerated wrists and bloody hands. "Who did that to you?"

"I did it to myself, rather, I'm afraid." Vorkosigan's pose of studied ease slipped back into his original grimness. "It could have been worse, as I will show you directly. Around back. I want you to record everything, a complete scan. Anything you're in doubt of, leave for the experts from HQ. I want a top forensics team scrambled from Solstice immediately. Two teams, one for out here, one for those royally buggered comconsoles at the Terraforming offices. But first, I think," he glanced at the medtechs, and at Ekaterin, "we should get Administrator Vorsoisson's body down."

"Here's the key," said Ekaterin numbly, producing it from her pocket.

"Thank you," said Vorkosigan, taking it from her. "Wait here, please." He jerked up his chin, checked and pulled up his mask, and led the still-protesting Tuomonen back out the airseal doors, imperiously motioning the medics to follow. Ekaterin could still hear the clattering and strained sharp voices of the armed guards, echoing from distant corridors deeper in the office building.

She huddled into the chair Vorkosigan had vacated, feeling very odd not to be following the men to Tien. But someone else was going to be cleaning up the mess this time, it appeared. A few tears leaked from her eyes, residue of her body-shock she supposed, for she surely felt no more emotion than if she'd been a lump of lead.

After a long while, the men returned to the lobby, where Tuomonen finally persuaded Vorkosigan to sit down and let the senior medic attend to his injured wrists.

"This isn't the treatment I'm most concerned about just now," Vorkosigan complained, as a hypospray of synergine hissed into the side of his neck. "I have to get back to Serifosa. There's something I really need out of my luggage."

"Yes, my lord," said the medtech soothingly, and went on cleaning and bandaging.

Tuomonen went out to his aircar to relay some terse communication with his ImpSec superiors in Solstice, then returned to lean on the back of the chair and watch the medtech finish up.

Vorkosigan eyed Ekaterin, across the medtech. "Madame Vorsoisson. In retrospect, thinking back, did your husband ever say anything that indicated this scam had to do with something more than money?"

Ekaterin shook her head.

Tuomonen, in gruff tones, put in, "I'm afraid, Madame Vorsoisson, that ImpSec is going to have to take charge of your late husband's body. There must be a complete examination."

"Yes, of course," Ekaterin said faintly. She paused. "Then what?"

"We'll let you know, Madame." He turned to Vorkosigan, evidently continuing a conversation. "So what else did you think of, when you were tied up out there?"

"All I could really think about was when my next seizure was due," said Vorkosigan ruefully. "It became kind of an obsession, after a while. But I don't think Foscol knew about that hidden defect, either."

"I still want to call it murder and attempted murder, for the all-Sectors alert order," said Tuomonen, evidently continuing a debate. "And the attempted murder of an Imperial Auditor makes it treason, which disposes of any arguments about requisitions."

"Yes, very good," sighed Vorkosigan in acquiescence. "Make sure your reports have the facts clear, though, please."

"As I see them, my lord." Tuomonen grimaced, then burst out, "Damn, to think how long this thing must have been going on, right under my nose . . . !"

"Not your jurisdiction, Captain," observed Vorkosigan. "It was the Imperial Accounting Office's job to spot this kind of fraud in the civil service. Still . . . there's something very wrong here."

"I should say so!"

"No, I mean beyond the obvious." Vorkosigan hesitated. "They abandoned all their personal effects, yet took at least two air-vans of equipment."

"To . . . sell?" Ekaterin posited. "No, that makes no sense. . . ."

"Mm, and they left in a group, didn't split up. These people seemed to me to be Komarran patriots, of a sort. I can see where they might classify theft from the Barrayaran Imperium as something between a hobby and a patriotic duty, but . . . to steal from the Komarran Terraforming Project, the hope of their future generations? And if it wasn't just to line their pockets, what the *devil* were they using all the money *for*?" He scowled. "That will be for ImpSec's forensic accounting team to sort out, I suppose. And I want engineering experts in here, to see if they can make anything at all from the mess that's been left. And not left. It's clear Soudha's crew put *something* together in the Engineering building, and I don't think it had anything to do with waste heat." He rubbed his forehead, and muttered, "I'll bet Marie Trogir could tell us. *Damn* but I wish I'd fast-penta'd Madame Radovas when I had the chance."

Ekaterin swallowed a lump of dread and humiliation. "I'm going to have to tell my uncle."

Vorkosigan glanced up at her. "I'll take over that task, Madame Vorsoisson."

She frowned, torn between what seemed to her weak gratitude, and a dreary sense of duty, but could not muster the energy to argue with him. The medic finished winding the last medical tape around Vorkosigan's wrists.

"I must leave you in charge here, Captain, and return to Serifosa. I don't dare fly myself. Madame Vorsoisson, would you be so kind . . . ?"

"You *will* take a guard," said Tuomonen, a little dangerously.

"I have to get the flyer back," said Ekaterin. "It's rented." She squinted, realizing how stupid that sounded. But it was the only fragment of order in this mortal chaos it was presently in her power to restore. And then, belatedly, the realization came: *I can go home. It's safe to go home.* Her voice strengthened. "Certainly, Lord Vorkosigan."

The presence of the hulking young guard crowded into the flyer behind them, Vorkosigan's exhaustion, and Ekaterin's emotional disorientation combined to blunt conversation on the flight back to Serifosa. She drew stares, turning the flyer back in at the rental desk while trailed politely by a large, fully-armed, half-armored soldier and a dwarfish man with bloody clothes and bandages on his wrists, but on the other hand, they had a bubble-car all to themselves for the ride back to the apartment. There were no delays in the system on this return leg, Ekaterin noted with weary irony. She wondered if there would be any point, later when this all got sorted out, to check if Vorkosigan's insistence that it had already been too late for Tien when Foscol had called her was precisely true.

Her steps quickened in the hallway of her apartment; she felt like an injured animal, wanting nothing more than to go hide in her burrow. She came to an abrupt halt at her door, and her breath drew in. The palm-lock panel was hanging partway out of the wall, and the sliding door was not entirely closed. A thin line of light leaked along its edge. She backed up a step, and pointed.

Vorkosigan took it all in at once and motioned to the guard who, equally silently, stepped up to the door and drew his stunner. Vorkosigan put his finger to his lips, took her by the arm, and drew her back halfway to the lift-tubes. The automatic door wasn't working; the guard had to grasp it awkwardly and lean, to push it back into its slot. Stunner raised and visor lowered, he slipped inside. Ekaterin's heart hammered.

After a few minutes, the ImpSec guard, his visor up again, poked his head back out the door. "Someone's been through here right enough, m'lord. But they're gone now." Vorkosigan and Ekaterin followed him inside.

Both Vorkosigan's cases and her own, which she had left sitting by the door in the vestibule, had been broken open. Their clothing was scattered in mixed heaps all around on the floor. Little else in the apartment appeared to have been touched; some drawers were opened, their contents stirred, but aside from the disorder nothing had been vandalized. Was it a violation, when she herself had all but vacated this space, abandoned those possessions? She scarcely knew.

"This is not how I left my things," Vorkosigan observed mildly to her when they fetched up in the vestibule again after their first short survey.

"It's not how I left them either," she said a bit desperately. "I thought you would be coming back with Tien, and then leaving, so I'd packed them all for you, ready to take away."

"Touch nothing, especially the comconsoles, till the forensics folks get here," Vorkosigan told her. She nodded understanding. They both shucked their heavy jackets; automatically, Ekaterin hung them up.

Vorkosigan then proceeded to ignore his own dictate, and kneel in the vestibule to sort through the heaps. "Did you pack my code-locked data case?"

"Yes."

"It's gone now." He sighed, rose, and raised his wrist-comm to report these new developments to Captain Tuomonen, still at the experiment station. The overburdened Tuomonen, apprised, swore briefly and ordered his soldier to stick with the Lord Auditor like glue until relieved. For once, Vorkosigan didn't object.

Vorkosigan returned to the mess, turning over an untidy pile of Ekaterin's clothing. "Ha!" he cried, and pounced on the gel-pack case which contained that odd device. He opened it hurriedly, his hands shaking a little. "Thank God they didn't take *this*." He looked up at her, measuringly. "Madame Vorsoisson . . ." his normally forceful tone grew uncertain. "I wonder if I could trouble you to . . . assist me in this."

She almost said *Yes*, without thinking, but managed to alter the word to "What?" before it left her mouth.

He smiled tightly. "I mentioned my seizure disorder to you. It doesn't have a cure, unfortunately. But my Barrayaran doctors came up with a palliative, of sorts. I use this little machine to stimulate seizures, bleed them off in a controlled time and place, so they don't happen in an uncontrolled time and place. They tend to be exacerbated by stress." By his grimace, she could see him picturing the cold walkway on the backside of the Engineering building. "I suspect I'm now overdue. I would like to get it over with at once."

"I understand. But what do I do?"

"I'm supposed to have a spotter. To see I don't spit out my mouth guard, or, or injure myself or damage anything while I'm out. There shouldn't be much to it."

"All right . . ."

Under the dubious eye of the ImpSec guard, she followed him to the living room. He headed for the curved couch. "If you lie on the floor," Ekaterin suggested diffidently, still not sure how spectacular a show to expect, "you can't fall any further."

"Ah. Right." He settled himself on the carpet, the case open in his hand. She made sure the space around them was clear, and knelt beside him.

He unfolded the device, which resembled a set of headphones with a pad on one end and a mysterious knob on the other. He fitted it over his head and adjusted it to his temples. He smiled at Ekaterin in what she belatedly realized was extreme embarrassment, and muttered, "I'm afraid this looks a little stupid," fitted a plastic mouthguard onto his teeth, and lay back.

"Wait," said Ekaterin suddenly as his hand reached for his temple.

"Wha'?"

"Could . . . whoever came in here have tampered with that thing? Maybe it ought to be checked first."

His wide eyes met hers; as certainly as if she had been telepathic, she knew she shared with him at that moment a vision of his head being blown off at the touch of his hand on the stimulator's trigger. He ripped it back off his head, sat up, spat out his mouthguard, and cried, "Shit!" He added after a moment, in a tone level but about half an octave higher than his norm, "You're quite right. Thank you. I wasn't thinking. I made . . . many cosmic promises, that if I made it back here, I'd do this first thing, and *never never never* put it off just one extra day again." Hyperventilating, he stared in consternation at the device clutched in his hand.

Then his eyes rolled up, and he fell over backwards. Ekaterin caught his head just before it banged into the carpet. His lips were drawn back in a strange grin. His body shuddered, in waves passing down to his toes and fingertips, but he did not flail wildly about as she'd half-expected. The guard hovered, looking panicked. She rescued the mouth guard, and fitted it back over his teeth, not as difficult a task as it at first appeared; despite an impression to that effect, he was not rigid.

She sat back on her heels, and stared. *Triggered by stress. Yes. I see.* His face was . . . altered, his personality clearly not present but in a way that resembled neither sleep nor death. It seemed terribly rude to watch him so, in all his vulnerability; courtesy urged her to look away. But he had explicitly appointed her to this task.

She checked her chrono. About five minutes, he'd said these things lasted. It seemed a small eternity, but was in fact less than three minutes when his body stilled. He lay slumped in alarmingly flaccid unconsciousness for another minute beyond that, then drew in a shuddering breath. His eyes opened and stared about in palpable incomprehension. At least his dilated pupils were the same size.

"Sorry. Sorry . . ." he muttered inanely. "Didn't mean to do that." He lay staring upward, his eyebrows crooked. He added after a moment, "What *does* it look like, anyway?"

"Really strange," Ekaterin answered him honestly. "I like your face better when you're at home in your head." She had not realized how powerfully his personality enlivened his features, or how subtly, until she'd seen it removed.

"I like my *head* better when I'm at home in it, too," he breathed. He squeezed his eyes shut, and opened them again. "I'll get out of your way now." His hands twitched, and he tried to sit up.

Ekaterin didn't think he ought to be trying to do *anything* yet. She pressed him firmly back down with a hand on his chest. "Don't you dare take away that guard till my door gets fixed." Not that its expensive electronic lock had appeared to do the least good.

"Oh. No, of course not," he said faintly.

It was abundantly apparent that Vorkosigan's implicit claim that he bounced back out of his seizures with no ill effects was a, well, if not a lie, a gross exaggeration. He looked terrible.

She raised her gaze to catch that of the disturbed guard. "Corporal. Would you please help me to get Lord Vorkosigan to bed until he is more recovered. Or at least until your people arrive."

"Sure, ma'am." He seemed relieved to have this direction provided for him, and helped her pull Vorkosigan to his unsteady feet.

Ekaterin made a lightning calculation. Nikki's bed was the only one instantly available, and his room had no comconsole. If Vorkosigan went to sleep, which he obviously desperately needed to do after this night's ordeal, there was a chance he might be let to stay that way even when the ImpSec forensic invasion arrived. "This way," she nodded to the guard, and led them down the hall.

The incoherence of Vorkosigan's mumbled protests assured Ekaterin that she was doing precisely the right thing. He was shivering again. She helped him off with his tunic, made him lie down, dragged off his boots, covered him with extra blankets, turned the room's heat up to high, doused the lights, and withdrew.

There was no one to put *her* to bed, but she did not care to attempt conversation with the guard, who took up station in her living room to wait for his overextended reinforcements. Her whole body felt as though it had been beaten. She took some painkillers and lay down fully dressed in her own bedroom, a thousand uncertainties and conflicting scenarios for what she must do next jostling in her mind.

Tien's body, which had breathed beside her in this space last night, must be in the hands of the ImpSec medical examiner by now, laid out naked and still on a cold metal tray in some clinical laboratory here in Serifosa. She hoped they would treat his congealed husk with some measure of dignity, and not the nervous jocularity death sometimes evoked.

When this bed had been impossible to bear in the night, it had been her habit to sneak off to her workroom and fiddle with her virtual gardens. The Barrayaran garden had increasingly been her choice, of late. It lacked the texture, the smell, the slow dense satisfactions of the real, but it had soothed her mind nonetheless. But first Vorkosigan had occupied the room, and now he'd ordered her not to touch the comconsoles till ImpSec had drained them. She sighed and turned over, huddled in her accustomed corner of the bed even though the rest was unoccupied. *I want to leave this place as soon as I can. I want to be someplace where Tien has never been.*

She did not expect to sleep, but whether from the pain meds or exhaustion or the combination, she fell into a doze at last.

Chapter Twelve

Miles could tell right away that he wasn't going to enjoy waking up. A bad seizure usually left him with hangover-like symptoms the following day, and the lingering effects of heavy stun included muscle aches, muscle spasms, and pseudo-migraines. The combination, it appeared, was downright synergistic. He groaned, and tried to regain unconsciousness. A gentle touch on his shoulder thwarted his intent.

"Lord Vorkosigan?"

It was Ekaterin Vorsoisson's soft voice. His eyes sprang open on thankfully-dim lighting. He was in her son Nikki's room, and could not remember how he'd arrived here. He rolled over and blinked up at her. She had changed clothes since his last memory of her, kneeling beside him on her living room floor; she now wore a soft, high-necked beige shirt and darker-toned trousers in the Komarran style. Her long dark hair lay loose in damp new-washed strands on her shoulders. *He* still had on his blood-stained shirt and wrinkled trousers from yesterday's nightmare.

"I'm sorry to wake you," she continued, "but Captain Tuomonen is here."

"Ah," said Miles thickly. He struggled upright. Madame Vorsoisson was holding out a tray with a large mug of black coffee and a bottle of painkiller tablets. Two tablets had already been extracted from the bottle, and lay ready for ingestion beside the cup.

Only in his imagination did a heavenly choir supply background music. "Oh. My."

She didn't say anything more till he had fumbled the tablets to his lips and swallowed them. His swollen hands weren't working too well, but did manage to clutch the mug in something resembling a death-grip. A second swallow scalded away a world of nastiness lingering in his mouth, well worth the challenge to the queasiness in his stomach. "Thank you." After a third gulp, he achieved, "What time is it?"

"It's about an hour after dawn."

He'd been out of the loop for about four hours, then. All sorts of events could occur in four hours. Not parting with the mug, he kicked his legs out of the bed. His sock-clad feet groped for the floor. Walking was going to be a chancy business for the first few minutes.

"Is Tuomonen in a hurry?"

"I can't tell. He looks tired. He says they found your seal."

That decided it; Tuomonen before a shower. He swallowed more coffee, handed the mug back to Ekater—to Madame Vorsoisson—and levered himself to his feet. After an awkward smile at her, he did a few bends and stretches, to be certain he could walk down the hall without falling over in front of ImpSec.

He had not the first idea what to say to her. *I'm sorry I got your husband killed* was inaccurate on a couple of counts. Up to the point he had been stunned, Miles might have done half a dozen different things to have altered last night's outcome; if only Vorsoisson had checked his own damned breath mask before going out, the way he was supposed to, Miles was pretty certain he would still have been alive this morning. And the more he learned about the man, the less convinced he was that his death was any disservice to his wife. Widow. After a moment he essayed, "Are you all right?"

She smiled wanly, and shrugged. "All things considered."

Thin lines etched parallels between her eyes. "Did you, um . . ." he gestured at the bottle of tablets, "get any of those for yourself?"

"Several. Thank you."

"Ah. Good." *Harm has been done you, and I don't know how to fix it.* It was going to take a hell of a lot more than a couple of pills, though. He shook his head, regretted the gesture instantly, and staggered out to see Tuomonen.

The Imp Sec captain was waiting on the circular couch in the living room, also gratefully sucking down Madame Vorsoisson's coffee. He appeared to consider standing at some sort of quasiattention, when the Lord Auditor entered the room, but then thought better of it. Tuomonen gestured, and Miles seated himself across the table from the captain; they each mumbled their good-mornings. Madame Vorsoisson followed with Miles's half-empty coffee cup and set it before him, then, after a wary glance at Tuomonen, quietly seated herself. If Tuomonen wanted her to leave, he was going to have to ask her himself, Miles decided. And then justify the request.

In the event, Tuomonen merely nodded thanks to her, and shifted around and drew a plastic packet from his tunic. It contained Miles's gold-encased Auditor's electronic seal. He handed it across to Miles.

"Very good, Captain," said Miles. "I don't suppose you were so fortunate as to find it on the person of its thief?"

"No, more's the pity. You'll never guess where we *did* find it."

Miles squinted and held the plastic bag up to the light. A sheen of condensation fogged the inside. "In a sewer pipe halfway between here and the Serifosa Dome waste treatment plant, would be my first guess."

Tuomonen's jaw fell open. "How did you know?"

"Forensic plumbing was once a sort of hobby of mine. Not to sound ungrateful, but has anyone washed it?"

"Yes, in fact."

"Oh, thank you." Miles opened the packet and shook the heavy little device into his palm. It appeared undamaged.

Tuomonen said, "My lieutenant had its signal traced, or at any rate, triangulated, within half an hour of your call. He led an assault team down into the utility tunnels after it. I wish I could have seen it, when they finally figured out what was going on. You would have appreciated it, I'm almost certain."

Miles grinned despite his headache. "I was in no shape last night to appreciate anything, I'm afraid."

"Well, they made an impressive delegation when they went to wake up the Serifosa Dome municipal engineer. She's Komarran, of course. ImpSec coming for her in the middle of the night—her husband about had a heart spasm. My lieutenant finally got him calmed down, and got across to her what we needed . . . I'm afraid she found it an occasion for, er, considerable irony. We are all grateful that my lieutenant didn't yield to his first impulse, which was to have his team blast open the pipe section in question with their assault plasma rifles. . . ."

Miles almost choked on a swallow of coffee. "Ex*ceed*ingly grateful." He stole a glance at Ekaterin Vorsoisson, who was leaning back against the cushions listening to this, eyes alight, a hand pressed to her lips. His painkillers were cutting in; she didn't look so blurry now.

"There was no sign by then of our human quarry, of course," Tuomonen finished with a sigh. "Long gone."

Miles stared at his distorted reflection in the dark surface of his drink. "One sees the scenario. You should be able to work out the timetable quite precisely. Foscol and an unknown number of accomplices pick my pocket, tie me and the Administrator to the railing, fly back to Serifosa, call Madame Vorsoisson. Probably from someplace nearby. As soon as she vacates her apartment, they break in, knowing they have at least an hour to explore before the alarm goes up. They use my seal to open the data case and access my report files. Then they flush the seal down the toilet and leave. Not even breathing hard."

"Too bad they weren't tempted to keep it."

"Mm, they clearly realized it was traceable. Hence their little joke." He frowned. "But . . . why my data case?"

"They might have been looking for something about Radovas. What all *was* in your data case, my lord?"

"Copies of all the classified technical reports and autopsies from the soletta accident. Soudha's an engineer. He doubtless had a very good idea what was in there."

"We're going to have an interesting time later this morning at the Terraforming Project offices," said Tuomonen glumly, "trying to figure out which employees are absent because they fled, and which ones are absent because they are fictional. I need to get over there as soon as possible, to supervise the preliminary interrogations. We'll have to fast-penta them all, I suppose."

"I predict it will be a great waste of time and drugs," agreed Miles. "But there's always the chance of someone knowing more than they think they know."

"Mm, yes." Tuomonen glanced at the listening woman. "Speaking of which—Madame Vorsoisson—I'm afraid I'm going to have to ask you to cooperate with a fast-penta interrogation as well. It's standard operating procedure, in a mysterious death of this nature, to question the closest relatives. The Dome police may also be wanting in on it, or at least demand a copy, depending on what decisions are made about jurisdiction by my superiors."

"I understand," said Madame Vorsoisson, in a colorless voice.

"There was nothing mysterious about Administrator Vorsoisson's death," Miles pointed out uneasily. "I was standing right next to him." Well, kneeling, technically.

"She's not a *suspect*," Tuomonen said. "A witness."

And a fast-penta interrogation would help to keep it that way, Miles realized with reluctance.

"When do you wish to do this, Captain?" Madame Vorsoisson asked quietly.

"Well . . . not immediately. I'll have a better set of questions after this morning's investigations are complete. Just don't go anywhere."

Her glance at him silently inquired, *Am I under house arrest?* "At some point, I have to go get my son Nikolai. He was staying overnight at a friend's home. He hasn't been told anything about this yet. I don't want to tell him over the comconsole, and I don't want him to hear it first on the news."

"That won't happen," said Tuomonen grimly. "Not yet, anyway. Though I expect I'll have the information services badgering us soon enough. Someone is bound to notice that the most boring ImpSec post on Komarr is suddenly boiling with activity."

"I must either go get him, or call and arrange for him to stay longer."

"Which would you prefer?" Miles put in before Tuomonen could say anything.

"I . . . if you are going to do the interrogation here, today, I'd rather wait till its over with to get Nikki. I'll have to explain to his friend's mother something of the situation, at least that Tien was . . . killed in an accident last night."

"Have you bugged her comconsoles?" Miles asked Tuomonen bluntly.

Tuomonen's look queried this revelation, but he cleared his throat, and said, "Yes. You should be aware, Madame Vorsoisson, that ImpSec will be monitoring all calls in and out of here for a few days."

She looked blankly at him. "Why?"

"There is the possibility that someone, either from Soudha's group or some other connection we haven't yet discovered, not yet realizing the Administrator is dead, might try to communicate."

She accepted this with a slightly dubious nod. "Thank you for warning me."

"Speaking of calls," Miles added, "please have one of your people bring me a secured vid-link here. I have a few calls to make myself."

"Will you be staying here, my lord?" asked Tuomonen.

"For a while. Till after your interrogation, and until Lord Auditor Vorthys gets downside, as he will surely wish to do. That's the first call I want to make."

"Ah. Of course."

Miles looked around. His seizure stimulator, its case, and his mouthguard were still lying where they'd been dropped a few hours ago. Miles pointed. "And if you please, could you have your lab check my medical gear for any sign of tampering, then return it to me."

Tuomonen's brows rose. "Do you suspect it, my lord?"

"It was just a horrible thought. But I think it's going to be a very bad idea to underestimate either the intelligence or the subtlety of our adversaries in this thing, eh?"

"Do you need it urgently?"

"No." *Not anymore.*

"The data packet Foscol left on Administrator Vorsoisson's person—have you had a chance to look at it?" Miles went on. He managed to avoid glancing at Madame Vorsoisson.

"Just a quick scan," said Tuomonen. He did look at Madame Vorsoisson, and away, spoiling Miles's effort at delicacy. Her lips thinned only a little. "I turned it over to the ImpSec financial analyst—a colonel, no less—that HQ sent out to take charge of the financial part of the investigation."

"Oh, good. I was going to ask if HQ had sent you relief troops yet."

"Yes, everything you requested. The engineering team arrived on site at the experiment station about an hour ago. The packet Foscol left seems to be documentation of all the financial transactions relating to the, um, payments made by Soudha's group to the Administrator. If it's not all lies, it's going to be an amazing help in sorting out the whole embezzlement part of the mess. Which is really very odd, when you think about it."

"Foscol clearly had no love for Vorsoisson, but surely everything that incriminates him, incriminates the Komarrans equally. Quite odd, yes." If only his brain hadn't been turned to pulsing oatmeal, Miles felt, he could follow out some line of logic from this. Later.

An ImpSec tech wearing black fatigues emerged from the back of the apartment. He carried a black box identical to—in fact, possibly the same as—the one which Tuomonen had used at Madame Radovas's, and said to his superior, "I've finished all the comconsoles, sir."

"Thank you, Corporal. Go back to the office and transfer copies to our files, to HQ Solstice, and to Colonel Gibbs."

The tech nodded and trod out through the, Miles noticed, still-ruined door.

"And, oh yes, would you please detail a tech to repair Madame Vorsoisson's front door," Miles added to Tuomonen. "Possibly he could install a somewhat better-quality locking system while he's about it." She shot him a quietly grateful look.

"Yes, my lord. I will of course keep a guard on duty while you are here."

A duenna of sorts, Miles supposed. He must try to get Madame Vorsoisson something rather better. Suspecting he'd loaded poor sleepless Tuomonen with enough chores and orders for one session, Miles requested only that he be notified at once if ImpSec caught up with Soudha or any member of his group, and let the captain go off to his suddenly multiplied duties.

By the time he'd showered and dressed in his last good gray suit, the painkillers had achieved their full effect, and Miles felt almost human. When he emerged, Madame Vorsoisson invited him to her kitchen; Tuomonen's door guard stayed in the living room.

"Would you care for some breakfast, Lord Vorkosigan?"

"Have you eaten?"

"Well, no. I'm not really hungry."

Likely not, but she looked as pale and washed-out as he felt. Tactically inspired, he said, "I'll have something if you will. Something bland," he added prudently.

"Groats?" she suggested diffidently.

"Oh, yes please." He wanted to say, *I can get them*—mixing up a packet of instant groats was well within his ImpSec survival-trained capabilities, he could have assured her—but he didn't want to risk her going away, so he sat, an obedient guest, and watched her move about. She seemed uneasy, in what should have been this core place of her domain. Where *would* she fit? *Someplace much larger.*

She set up and served them both; they exchanged commonplace courtesies. When she'd eaten a few bites, she worked up an unconvincing smile, and asked, "Is it true fast-penta makes you . . . rather foolish?"

"Mm. Like any drug, people have varied reactions. I've conducted any number of fast-penta interrogations in the line of my former duties. And I've had it given to me twice."

Her interest was clearly piqued by this last statement. "Oh?"

"I, um . . ." He wanted to reassure her, but he had to be honest. *Don't ever lie to me,* she'd said, in a voice of suppressed passion. "My own reaction was idiosyncratic."

"Don't you have that allergy ImpSec is supposed to give to its— well, no, of course not, or you wouldn't be here."

ImpSec's defense against the truth drug was to induce a fatal allergic response in its key operatives. One had to agree to the treatment, but as it was a gateway to larger responsibilities and hence promotions, the security force had never lacked for volunteers. "No, in fact. Chief Illyan never asked me to undergo it. In retrospect, I can't help wondering if my father had a hand, there. But in any case, it doesn't make me truthful so much as it makes me hyper. I babble. Fast-foolish, I guess. The one, um, hostile interrogation I underwent, I was actually able to beat, by continually reciting poetry. It was a very bizarre experience. In normal people, the degree of, well, ugliness, depends a lot on whether you fight it or go along with it. If you feel that the questioner is on your side, it can be just a very relaxing way of giving the same testimony you would anyway."

"Oh." She did not look reassured enough.

"I can't claim it doesn't invade your reserve," and she possessed a reserve oceans-deep, "but a properly conducted interview ought not to," *shame you,* "be too bad." Though if last night's events had not shaken her out of her daunting self-control . . . He hesitated, then added, "How *did* you learn to underreact the way you do?"

Her face went blank. "Do I underreact?"

"Yes. You are very hard to read."

"Oh." She stirred her black coffee. "I don't know. I've been this way for as long as I can remember." A more introspective look stilled her features for a time. "No . . . no, there was a time . . . I suppose it goes back to . . . I had, I have, three older brothers."

A typical Vor family structure of their generation: too damned many boys, a token girl added as an afterthought. Hadn't any of those parents possessed a) foresight and b) the ability to do simple arithmetic? Hadn't any of them wanted to be *grandparents*?

"The eldest two were out of my range," she went on, "but the youngest was close enough in age to me to be obnoxious. He discovered he could entertain himself mightily by teasing me to screaming tantrums. Horses were a surefire subject; I was horse-mad at the time. I couldn't fight back—I hadn't the wits then to give as good as I got, and if I tried to hit him, he was enough bigger than me—I'm thinking of the time when I was about ten and he was about fourteen—he could just hold me upside down. He had me so well-trained after a while, he could set me off just by whinnying." She smiled grimly. "It was a great trial to my parents."

"Couldn't they stop him?"

"He usually managed to be witty enough, he got away with it. It even worked on me—I can remember laughing and trying to hit him at the same time. And I think my mother was starting to be ill by then, though neither of us knew it. What my mother told me—I can still see her, holding her head—was the way to get him to stop was for me to just not react. She said the same thing when I was teased at school, or upset about most anything. Be a stone statue, she said. Then it wouldn't be any fun for him, and he would stop.

"And he did stop. Or at least, he grew out of being a fourteen-year-old lout, and left for university. We're friends now. But I never unlearned to respond to attack by turning to stone. Looking back now, I wonder how many of the problems in my marriage were due to . . . well." She smiled, and blinked. "My mother was wrong, I think. She certainly ignored her own pain for far too long. But I'm stone all the way through, now, and it's too late."

Miles bit his knuckles, hard. Right. So at the dawn of puberty, she'd learned no one would defend her, she could not defend herself, and the only way to survive was to pretend to be dead. Great. And if there were a more fatally wrong move some awkward fellow could possibly make at this moment than to take her in his arms and try to comfort her, it escaped his wildest imaginings. If she needed to be stone right now because it was the only way she knew how to survive, let her be marble, let her be granite. *Whatever you need, you take it, Milady Ekaterin; whatever you want, you've got it.*

What he finally came up with was, "I like horses." He wondered if that sounded as idiotic as it . . . sounded.

Her dark brows crinkled in amused bafflement, so apparently it did. "Oh, I outgrew that years ago."

Outgrew, or gave up? "I was an only child, but I had a cousin—Ivan—who was as loutish as they come. And, of course, much bigger than me, though we're about the same age. But when I was a kid, I had a bodyguard, one of the Count-my-Father's Armsmen. Sergeant Bothari. He had no sense of humor at all. If Ivan had ever tried anything like your brother, no amount of wit would have saved him."

She smiled. "Your own bodyguard. Now, there's an idyllic childhood indeed."

"It was, in a lot of ways. Not the medical parts, though. The Sergeant couldn't help me there. Nor at school. Mind you, I didn't appreciate what I had at the time. I spent half of my time trying to figure out how to get away from his protection. But I succeeded often enough, I guess, to know I *could* succeed."

"Is Sergeant Bothari still with you? One of those crusty Old Vor family retainers?"

"He probably would be, if he were still alive, but no. We were, uh, caught in a war zone on a galactic trip when I was seventeen, and he was killed."

"Oh. I'm sorry."

"It was not exactly my fault, but my decisions were pretty prominent in the causal chain that led to his death." He watched for her reaction to this confession; as usual, her face changed very little. "But he taught me how to survive, and go on. The last of his very many lessons." *You have just experienced destruction; I know survival. Let me help.*

Her eyes flicked up. "Did you love him?"

"He was a . . . difficult man, but yes."

"Ah."

He offered after a time, "However you came by it, you are very level-headed in emergencies."

"I am?" She looked surprised.

"You were last night."

She smiled, clearly touched by the compliment. Dammit, she shouldn't take in this mild observation as if it were great praise. *She must be starving half to death, if such a scrap seems a feast.*

It was the most nearly unguarded conversation she'd ever granted him, and he longed to extend the moment, but they'd run out of groats to push around in the bottom of their dishes, their coffee was cold, and the tech from ImpSec arrived at this moment with the secured comconsole uplink Miles had requested. Madame Vorsoisson pointed out to the tech her late husband's office as a private space to set up the machine. The forensics people had been and gone while Miles slept; after briefly watching the new installation she retreated into housewifery like a red deer into underbrush, apparently intent on erasing all traces of their invasion of her space.

Miles turned to face the next most difficult conversation of the morning.

It took several minutes to establish the secure link with Lord Auditor Vorthys aboard the probable-cause team's mothership, now docked at the soletta array. Miles settled himself as comfortably as his aching muscles would allow, and prepared to cultivate patience in the face of the irritating several-second time lag between every exchange. Vorthys, when he at last appeared, was wearing standard-issue ship-knits, evidently in preparation for donning a pressure suit; the close-fitting cloth did not flatter his bulky figure. But he seemed to be well up for the day. The standard-meridian Solstice time kept topside was a few hours ahead of Serifosa's time zone.

"Good morning, Professor," Miles began. "I trust you've had a better night than we did. At the top of the bad news, your nephew-in-law Etienne Vorsoisson was killed last night in a breath-mask mishap at the Waste Heat experiment station. I'm here now at Ekaterin's apartment; she's holding up all right so far. I'll have a very long transmission in explanation. Over to you."

The trouble with the time lag was just how agonizingly long one had in which to anticipate the change of expression, and of people's lives, occasioned by the arrival of words one had sent but could no longer call back and edit. Vorthys looked every bit as shocked as Miles had expected when the message reached him. "My God. Go ahead, Miles."

Miles took a deep breath and began a blunt precis of yesterday's events, from the futile hours of being given the royal runaround at the Terraforming offices, to Vorsoisson's hasty return to drag him out to the experiment station, the revelation of his involvement with the embezzlement scheme, their encounter with Soudha and

Madame Radovas, the waking up chained to the railing. He did not describe Vorsoisson's death in detail. Ekaterin's arrival. ImpSec teams called out in force, too late. The business with his seal. Vorthys's expression changed from shocked to appalled as the details mounted.

"Miles, this is horrible. I'll come downside as soon as I can. Poor Ekaterin. Do please stay with her till I get there, won't you?" He hesitated. "Before this came up, I was actually thinking of requesting you to come topside. We've found some very odd pieces of equipment up here, which have undergone some quite incredible physical distortions. I'd wondered if you might have seen anything like it in your galactic military experiences. There are some traceable serial numbers left here and there in the debris, though, which I'd hoped may prove a lead. I'll just have to leave them to my Komarran boys for the moment."

"Odd equipment, eh? Soudha and his friends left with a lot of odd equipment, too. At least two lift-vans full. Have your Komarran boys send those serial numbers to Colonel Gibbs, care of ImpSec Serifosa. He's going to be tracing a lot of serial numbers in Terraforming Project purchases that—may not be as bogus as I'd first assumed. There's got to be more connections between here and there than just poor Radovas's body. Look, um . . . ImpSec here wants to fast-penta Ekaterin, on account of Tien's involvement. Do you want me to delay that till you arrive? I thought you might wish to supervise her interrogation, at least."

Lag. Vorthys's brow wrinkled in worried thought. "I . . . dear God. No. I want to, but I should not. My niece—a clear conflict of interest. Miles, my boy, do you suppose . . . would you be willing to sit in on it, and see that they don't get carried away?"

"ImpSec hardly ever uses those lead lined rubber hoses anymore, but yes, I planned to do just that. If you do not disapprove, sir."

Lag. "I should be excessively relieved. Thank you."

"Of course. I also should very much like to have your evaluation of whatever the ImpSec engineering team turns up out at the experiment station. At the moment I have very little evidence and lots of theories. I'm itching to reverse the proportions."

Professor Vorthys smiled dry appreciation of this last line, when it arrived. "Aren't we all."

"I have another suggestion, sir. Ekaterin seems very alone, here. She doesn't seem to have any close Komarran women friends that

I've seen so far, and of course, no female relatives . . . I wondered if it might not be a good idea for you to send for the Professora."

Vorthys's face lit when this one registered. "Not only good, but wise and kind. Yes, of course, at once. Given a family emergency of this nature, her assistant can surely supervise her final exams. The idea should have occurred to me directly. Thank you, Miles."

"Everything else can wait till you get downside, unless something breaks in the case on ImpSec's end. I'll get Ekaterin in here before I close the transmission. I know she longs to talk with you, but . . . Tien's involvement in this mess is pretty humiliating for her, I suspect."

The Professor's lips tightened. "Ah, Tien. Yes. I understand. It's all right, Miles."

Miles was silent for a time. "Professor," he began at last, "about Tien. Fast-penta interrogations tend to be a lot more controllable if the interrogator has some clue what he's getting into. I don't want . . . um . . . can you give me some sense of what Ekaterin's marriage looked like from her family's point of view?"

The time lag dragged, while Vorthys frowned. "I don't like to speak ill of the dead before their offering is even burned," he said at last.

"I don't think we're going to have a lot of choice, here."

"Huh," he said glumly when Miles's words reached him. "Well . . . I suppose it seemed like a good idea to everyone at the time. Ekaterin's father, Shasha Vorvayne, had known Tien's late father—he was recently deceased then. A decade ago already, my word the time has gone fast. Well. The two older men had been friends, both officers in the District government, the families knew each other . . . Tien had just quit the military, and had used his veteran's rights to obtain a job in the District civil service. Good-looking, healthy . . . seemed poised to follow in his father's footsteps, you know, though I suppose it ought to have been a clue that he had put in his ten years and never risen beyond the rank of lieutenant." Vorthys pursed his lips.

Miles reddened slightly. "There can be a lot of reasons—never mind. Go on."

"Vorvayne had begun to recover from my sister's untimely death. He had met a woman, nothing unseemly, an older woman, Violie Vorvayne is a charming lady—and begun to think of remarriage. He wanted, I suppose, to see Ekaterin properly settled—to honorably tie off the last of his obligations to the past, if you will. My nephews were all out on their own by then. Tien had called on him, in part as courtesy to his late father's friend, in part to get a reference for his District service application . . . they struck up as much of an acquaintance as might be between two men of such dissimilar ages. My brother-in-law doubtless spoke highly of Ekaterin. . . ."

"Settled in her father's mind equated with married, I take it. Not, say, graduated from University and employed at an enormous salary?"

"Only for the boys. My brother-in-law can be more Old Vor than you high Vor, in a lot of ways." Vorthys sighed. "But Tien sent a reputable Baba to arrange the contracts, the young people were permitted to meet . . . Ekaterin was excited. Flattered. The Professora was distressed that Vorvayne hadn't waited a few more years, but . . . young people have no sense of *time*. Twenty is old. The first offer is the last chance. All that nonsense. Ekaterin didn't know how attractive she was, but her father was afraid, I think, that she might settle on some inappropriate choice."

"Non-Vor?" Miles interpreted this.

"Or worse. Maybe even a mere tech, who knew?" Vorthys permitted himself one tiny ironic glint. Ah, yes. Until his Auditorial apotheosis three years ago, so startling to his relatives, Vorthys had had a most un-Vorish career himself. And marriage. And he'd started both back when the Old Vor were a lot more Old Vor than they were now—Miles thought of his grandfather, by way of exemplar, and suppressed a shudder.

"And the marriage seemed to start out well," the Professor went on. "She seemed busy and happy, there was little Nikki come along . . . Tien changed jobs rather often, I thought, but he was new in his career; sometimes it takes a few false starts to find your legs. Ekaterin grew out of touch with us, but when we did see her, she was . . . quieter. Tien never did settle down, always chasing some rainbow no one else could see. I think all the moves were hard on her." He frowned, as if thinking back for missed clues.

Miles did not dare explain about the Vorzohn's Dystrophy without Ekaterin's express permission, he decided. It was not his right. He confined himself to remarking, "I think Ekaterin may feel free to explain more of it now."

The Professor squinted worriedly at him. "Oh . . . ?"

I wonder what answers I'd get to those same questions if I could ask the Professora? Miles shook his head, and went to call Ekaterin to the comconsole.

Ekaterin. He tasted the syllables of her name in his mind. It had been so easy, speaking with her uncle, to slip into the familiar form. But she had not yet invited him to use her first name. Her late husband had called her *Kat.* A pet name. A little name. As if he hadn't had time to pronounce the whole thing, or wished to be bothered. It was true her full array, *Ekaterin Nile Vorvayne Vorsoisson,* made an impractical mouthful. But *Ekaterin* was light on the teeth and the tip of the tongue, yet elegant and dignified and entirely worth an extra second of, of anyone's time.

"Madame Vorsoisson?" he called quietly down the hall.

She emerged from her workroom; he gestured to the secured vid-link. Her face was grave, and her steps reluctant; he closed the office door softly on her, and left her and her uncle in private. Privacy was going to be a rare and precious element for her in the days to come, he could foresee.

The repair tech arrived at last, along with another duty guard. Miles took them aside for a word.

"I want you both to stay here till I get back, understand? Madame Vorsoisson is not to be left unguarded. Um . . . when you're done with the door, find out from her if there are any other repairs she needs done around here, and take care of them for her."

"Yes, my lord."

Trailed by his own guard, Miles took himself off to the Terraforming Project offices. He passed ImpSec guards on the bubble-car platform, in the building lobby, and at the corridor entrances to Terraforming's floors. Miles was put glumly in mind of an Old Vor aphorism about posting a guard on the picket line after the horses were stolen. Once within, the ImpSec personnel shifted from steely-eyed goons to intent techs and clerks, efficiently downloading comconsoles and examining files. Terraforming Project employees watched them in suppressed terror.

Miles found Colonel Gibbs set up in Vorsoisson's outer office, with his own imported comconsole planted firmly therein; rather to his surprise, the rabbity Venier was dancing worried attendance upon the ImpSec financial analyst. Venier shot Miles a look of dislike as he strode in.

"Good morning, Vennie; I didn't expect to see you, somehow," Miles greeted him cordially. He was oddly glad the fellow hadn't been one of Soudha's. "Hello, Colonel. I'm Vorkosigan. Sorry for dragging you out on such short notice."

"My Lord Auditor. I am at your disposal." Gibbs stood, formally, and took Miles's proffered hand for a dry handshake. Gibbs was a delight to Miles's eye; a spare, middle-aged man with graying hair and a meticulous manner who despite his Imperial undress greens looked every bit an accountant. Even having held his new rank for almost three whole months, it still felt odd to Miles to accept the older man's deference.

"I trust Captain Tuomonen has briefed you, and passed on the interesting data packet we acquired last night."

Gibbs, drawing up a chair for the Lord Auditor, nodded. Venier took the opportunity to excuse himself, and fled without further prompting at Gibbs' wave of permission. They seated themselves, and Miles went on, "How are you doing so far?" He glanced at the stacks of flimsies the comconsole desk had already acquired.

Gibbs gave him a faint smile. "For the first three hours work, I am reasonably pleased. We have managed to sort out most of Waste Heat Management's fictitious employees. I expect tracking their false accounts to go quickly. Your Madame Foscol's report on the late Administrator Vorsoisson's receipts is very clear. Verifying its truth should not present a serious problem."

"Be *very* cautious about any data which may have passed through her hands," Miles warned.

"Oh, yes. She's quite good. I suspect I am going to find it a pleasure and a privilege to work with her, if you take my meaning, my lord." Gibb's eyes glinted.

So nice to meet a man who loves his job. Well, he'd asked Solstice HQ to send him their best. "Don't speak too soon about Foscol. I have what promises to be a tedious request for you."

"Ah?"

"In addition to fictitious employees, I have reason to believe Waste Heat made a lot of fictitious equipment purchases. Phony invoices and the like."

"Yes. I've turned up three dummy companies they appear to have used for them."

"Already? That was quick. How?"

"I ran a data match of all invoices paid by the Terraforming Project with a list of all real companies in the tax registry of the Empire. Not, you understand, routine for in-house audits, though I believe I'll forward a suggestion that it should be added to the list of procedures in future. There were three companies left over. My field people are checking them out. I should have confirmation for you by the end of today. It is, I believe, not excessively optimistic to hope we may track every missing mark in a week."

"My most urgent concern is not actually the money." Gibb's brows rose at this; Miles forged on. "Soudha and his coconspirators also left with a large amount of equipment. It has crossed my mind that if we had a reliable list of Waste Heat's equipment and supply purchases, and subtracted from it the current physical inventory of what's out there at their experiment station, the remainder *ought* to include everything they took with them."

"So it should." Gibbs eyed him with approval.

"It's a brute-force approach," Miles said apologetically. "And not, alas, quite as simple as a data match."

"That," murmured Gibbs, "is why enlisted men were invented."

They smiled at each other in pleased understanding. Miles continued, "This will only work if the supply list is truly accurate. I want you to hunt particularly for phony invoices covering real, but nonstandard, nonaccounted equipment purchases. I want to know if Soudha smuggled in anything . . . odd."

Gibbs's head tilted in interest; his eyes narrowed thoughtfully. "Easy enough for them to have used their dummy companies also to launder those."

"If you find anything like that, red-flag it and notify myself or Lord Auditor Vorthys at once. And *especially* if you turn up any matches with the equipment Vorthys's probable-cause crew are presently finding at the site of the soletta accident."

"Ah! The connection begins to come clear. I must say, I had been wondering why this intense Imperial interest in a mere embezzlement scheme. Though it's a very *nice* embezzlement scheme," he hastened to assure Miles. "Professional."

"Quite. Consider that equipment list your top priority, please, Colonel."

"Very good, my lord."

Leaving Gibbs frowning—rather interestedly, Miles thought—at a fountain of data displays on his comconsole, Miles went to find Tuomonen.

The tired-looking ImpSec captain reported no surprises uncovered so far this morning. The field agents had not yet picked up Soudha's trail. HQ had sent in a major with an interrogation unit, who had taken over the systematic examination of the department's remaining employees; the inquisition was now going on in the conference chamber. "But it's going to take days to work through them all," Tuomonen added.

"Do you still want to do Madame Vorsoisson this afternoon?"

Tuomonen rubbed his face. "Yes, in all."

"I'll be sitting in."

Tuomonen hesitated. "That is your privilege, my lord."

Miles considered going to watch the employee interrogations, but decided that in his current physical state he would not contribute anything coherent. Everything seemed to be under control, for the moment, except for himself. The morning's painkillers were beginning to wear off, and the corridor was getting wavery around the edges. If he was going to be useful to anyone later in the day, he'd better give his battered body a rest. "I'll see you back at Madame Vorsoisson's, then," he told Tuomonen.

Chapter Thirteen

Ekaterin seated herself at the comconsole in her workroom and began to triage the shambles of her life. It was actually simpler than her first fears had supposed—there was so little of it, after all. *How did I grow so small?*

She made a list of her resources. At the top, and most vital: medical care for the dependents of a deceased project employee was guaranteed till the end of the quarter, a few weeks away yet. A time window, of sorts. She counted the days in her head. It would be time enough for Nikki, if she didn't waste any.

A few hundred marks remained in her household account, and a few hundred marks in Tien's. Her use of this apartment also ran till the end of the quarter, when she must vacate it to make way for the next administrator to be appointed to Tien's position. That was fine; she didn't want to stay here longer. No pension, of course. She grimaced. Guaranteed passage back to Barrayar, unavailable while Tien was alive, was due her and Nikki as another death benefit, and thank heavens Tien hadn't figured out how to cash *that* in.

The physical objects she owned were more burden than asset, given that she must transport them by jumpship. The free weight limit was not generous. She'd apportion Nikki the bulk of their weight allowance; his little treasures meant more to him than most of her larger ones did to her. It was stupid to let herself feel overwhelmed by a few rooms of things she'd been willing to abandon altogether bare hours ago. She could still abandon them, if she chose. She'd frequented a certain secondhand shop in a seedier part of the dome to clothe herself and Nikki. She could sell Tien's clothing and ordinary effects there, a chore which need only take a few hours. For herself, she longed to travel light.

On the other side of the ledger, her debts too were simple, if overwhelming. First were the twenty thousand marks Tien had borrowed and not paid back. Then—was she honor-bound, for the sake of Vor pride and Nikki's family name, to make restitution to the Imperium for the bribe money Tien had accepted? *Well, you can't do it today. Pass on to what you can do.*

She had researched the medical resources on Komarr for treating genetic disorders till the information had worn grooves in her brain, fantasized solutions that Tien's paranoias—and his legal control of his heir—had blocked her from carrying out. Technically, Nikki's legal guardian now was some male third cousin of Tien's back on Barrayar whom Ekaterin had never met. Nikki not being heir to a fortune or a Countship, the transfer of his guardianship back to her was probably hers for the asking. She would deal with that legal kink later, too. For now, it took her something under nine minutes to contact the top clinic on Komarr, in Solstice, and browbeat them into setting up Nikki's first appointment for the day after tomorrow, instead of the five weeks from today they first tried to offer her.

Yes.

So simple. She shook with a spasm of rage, at Tien, and at herself. This could have been done months ago, when they'd first come to Komarr, as easily as this, if only she'd mustered the courage to defy Tien.

Next she must notify Tien's mother, his closest living relative. Ekaterin could leave it to her to spread the news to Tien's more distant relatives back on Barrayar. Not feeling up to recording a vid message, she put it in writing, hoping it would not appear too cold. An accident with a breath mask, which Tien had failed to check. Nothing about the Komarrans, nothing about the embezzlement, nothing to which ImpSec could object. Tien's mother might never need to know of Tien's dishonor. Ekaterin humbly requested her preferences as to ceremonies and the disposition of the remains. Most likely she would want them returned to Barrayar to bury beside Tien's brother. Ekaterin could not help imagining her own feelings, in some future scene, if she entrusted Nikki to his bride with all bright promise only to have him returned to her later as a heap of ashes in a box. With a note. No, she would have to see this through in person. All that also must come later. She sent the message on its way.

The physical was easy; she could be finished and packed in a week. The financial was . . . no, not impossible, just not possible to solve at once. Presumably she must take out a loan on longer terms to pay off the first one—assuming anyone would loan money to a destitute and unemployed widow. Tien's antilegacy clouded the glimmerings of the new future she ached to claim for herself. She imagined a bird, released from ten years in a cage, told she could at last fly free—as soon as these lead weights were attached to her feet.

This bird's going to get there if she has to walk every step.

The comconsole chimed, startling her from this determined reverie. A man, soberly dressed in the Komarran style, appeared over the vid-plate at her touch. He wasn't anyone she knew from Tien's department.

"How do you do, ma'am," he said, looking at her uncertainly. "My name is Ser Anafi, and I represent the Rialto Sharemarket Agency. I'm trying to reach Etienne Vorsoisson."

She recognized the name of the company whose money Tien had lost on the trade fleet shares. "He's . . . not available. I'm Madame Vorsoisson. What is your question?"

Anafi's gaze at her grew more stern. "This is the fourth reminder notice of his outstanding loan balance, now overdue. He *must* either pay in full, or take immediate action to set up a new repayment schedule."

"How do you normally set up such a schedule?"

Anafi appeared surprised at this measured response. Had he dealt with Tien before this? He unbent slightly, leaning back in his chair. "Well . . . we normally calculate a percentage of the customer's salary, mitigated by any available collateral they may be able to offer."

I have no salary. I have no possessions. Anafi, she suspected, would not be pleased to learn this. "Tien . . . died in an accident last night. Things are in some disarray here today."

Anafi looked taken aback. "Oh. I'm sorry, Madame," he managed.

"I don't suppose . . . was the loan insured?"

"I'll check, Madame Vorsoisson. Let us hope . . ." Anafi turned to his comconsole; after a moment, he frowned. "I'm sorry to say, it was not."

Ah, Tien. "How should I pay it back?"

Anafi was silent a long moment, as if thinking. "If you would be willing to cosign for the loan, I could set up a payment schedule today for you."

"You can do that?"

At a tentative knock on the door frame of her workroom, she glanced around. Lord Vorkosigan had returned and stood leaning in the opening. How long had he been standing there? He gestured inside, and she nodded. He walked in and eyed Anafi over her shoulder. "Who is this guy?" he murmured.

"His name's Anafi. He's from the company Tien owes for the fleet shares loan."

"Ah. Allow me." He stepped up to the comconsole and tapped in a code. The view split, and a gray-haired man with colonel's tabs and Eye-of-Horus pins on his green uniform collar appeared.

"Colonel Gibbs," said Lord Vorkosigan genially. "I have some more data for you regarding Administrator Vorsoisson's financial affairs. Ser Anafi, meet Colonel Gibbs. ImpSec. He has a few questions for you. Good day."

"ImpSec!" said Anafi in startled horror. "ImpSec? What does—" He blipped out at Lord Vorkosigan's flourishing gesture.

"No more Anafi," he said, with some satisfaction. "Not for the next several days, anyway."

"Now, was that nice?" asked Ekaterin, amused in spite of herself. "They loaned that money to Tien in all good faith."

"Nevertheless, don't sign anything till you take legal advice. If you knew nothing of the loan, it's possible Tien's estate is liable for it, and not you. His creditors must squabble with each other for the pieces, and when it's gone, it's gone."

"But there's nothing in Tien's estate but debts." *And dishonor.*

"Then the squabble will be short."

"But is it fair?"

"Death is an ordinary business risk—in some businesses more than others, of course. . . ." He smiled briefly. "Ser Anafi was getting ready to have you sign on the spot. This suggests to me that he was perfectly aware of his risk, and thought he might hustle you into taking over a debt not rightfully yours while you were still in shock. *Not* fair. In fact, not ethical at all. Yes, I think we can leave him to ImpSec."

This was all rather high-handed, but . . . it was hard not to respond to the enthusiastic glint in Vorkosigan's eye as he'd annihilated her adversary.

"Thank you, Lord Vorkosigan. But I really need to learn how to do these things for myself."

"Oh, yes," he agreed without the least hesitation. "I wish Tsipis were here. He's been my family's man of business for thirty years. He *adores* tutoring the uninitiated. If I could turn him loose on you, you'd be up to speed in no time, and he'd be just ecstatic. I'm afraid he found me a frustrating pupil in my youth. I only wanted to learn about the military. He finally managed to smuggle in some economic education by presenting it as logistics and supply problems." He leaned against the comconsole desk, and crossed his arms, and tilted his head. "Do you think you will be returning to Barrayar anytime soon?"

"Just as soon as I possibly can. I can hardly bear being in this place."

"I think I understand. Where, ah, would you go, on Barrayar?"

She stared broodingly at the empty vid-plate. "I'm not sure yet. Not to my father's household." To be crammed back into the status of a child again. . . . She pictured herself arriving penniless and without resources, to batten upon her father or one of her brothers. They'd let her batten, all right, generously, but they would also act as if her dependence deprived her of rights and dignity and even intelligence. They would then arrange her life for her own good. . . . "I'm sure I'd be welcome, but I'm afraid his solution to my problems would be to try to marry me off again. The idea makes me gag, just now."

"Oh," said Lord Vorkosigan.

A brief silence fell.

"What would you do if you could do anything?" he asked suddenly. "No limited resources to juggle, no practical considerations. Anything at all."

"I don't . . . I usually start with the possible, and pare away from there."

"Try for more scope." A vague wave of his arm taking in the planet from zenith to horizon indicated his idea of scope.

She thought back, all the way back, to the point in her life where she had made that fatal wrong turn. So many years lost. "Well. I suppose . . . I would go back to university. But *this* time, I'd know what I was about. Formal training in horticulture and in art, for garden design; chemistry and biochemistry and botany and genetic manipulation. *Real* expertise, the kind that means you can't be intimidated or, or . . . persuaded to go along with something stupid because you think everyone in the universe knows more than you do." She frowned ruefully.

"So you could design gardens for pay?"

"More than that." Her eyes narrowed, as she struggled for her inner vision.

"Planets? Terraforming?"

"Oh, good heavens. *That* training takes ten years, and another ten years of internship beyond it, before you can even begin to grasp the complexities."

"So? They have to hire someone. Good God, they hired Tien."

"He was only an administrator." She shook her head, daunted.

"All right," he said cheerfully. "Bigger than a garden, smaller than a planet. That still leaves sufficient scope, I'd say. A Barrayaran District could be a good start. One with incomplete terraforming, say, and, and forestry projects, and, oh, damaged land reclamation, and a crying need for a touch of beauty. And," he went on, "you could work *up* to planets."

She had to laugh. "What is this obsession with planets? Will nothing smaller do, for you?"

"Elli Qu—a friend of mine used to say, 'Aim high. You may still miss the target but at least you won't shoot your foot off.'" His grin winked at her. He hesitated, then said more slowly, "You know . . . your father and brothers aren't your only relatives. The Professor and the Professora are boundless in their enthusiasm for education. You can't convince me they wouldn't be pleased to shelter you and Nikki in their home while you got your new start. And you'd be right there in Vorbarr Sultana, practically next door to the University and, um, everything. Good schools for Nikki."

She sighed. "It would be such a lovely change for him to stay in one place for a while. He could finally cultivate friends he wouldn't have to abandon. But . . . I've come to despise dependency."

He eyed her shrewdly. "Because it betrayed you?"

"Or lured me into betraying myself."

"Mm. But surely there is a qualitative difference between, um, a greenhouse and a cryochamber. Both provide shelter, but the first promotes growth, while the second merely, um . . ." He seemed to have become a little tangled in his metaphor.

"Retards decay?" Ekaterin politely tried to help unwind him.

"Just so." His brief grin again. "Anyway, I'm pretty sure the Professors are a human greenhouse. All those students—they're used to people growing up and moving on. They regard it as normal. I'd think you'd *like* it there." He wandered to her window and glanced out.

"I did like it there," she admitted wistfully.

"Then it all sounds perfectly possible to me. Good, that's settled. Have you had lunch?"

"What?" She laughed, and clutched her hair.

"Lunch," he repeated, deadpan. "Many people eat it at about this time of day."

"You're mad," she said with conviction, ignoring this willful piece of misdirection. "Do you always dispose of people's futures in that offhand fashion?"

"Only when I'm hungry."

She gave up. "I suppose I have something I can fix—"

"Certainly not!" he said indignantly. "I sent a minion. I just spotted him returning across the park, with a very promising large bag. The guards have to eat too, you see."

She contemplated, briefly, the spectacle of a man who casually sent ImpSec for carry-out. There probably were security concerns about meals on duty, at that. She let Vorkosigan shepherd her into her own kitchen, where they selected from a dozen containers. Ekaterin snitched a flaky apricot tart to set aside for Nikki, and they sent the remainder to the living room for the guards to picnic off. The only thing Vorkosigan permitted her to do was supply fresh tea.

"Did you find out anything new this morning?" she asked him, when they were settled at the table. She tried not to think about her last conversation here with Tien. *Oh, yes, I want to go home.* "Any word on Soudha and Foscol?"

"Not yet. Part of me expects ImpSec to catch up with them at any moment. Part of me . . . is not so optimistic. I keep wondering just how long they had to plan their departure."

"Well . . . I don't think they were expecting Imperial Auditors to arrive in Serifosa. That, at least, came as a surprise to them."

"Hm. Ah! *I* know why this whole thing feels so odd. It's as though my entire brain is suffering a time lag, and it's not just the bloody seizures. I'm on the wrong side. I'm on the damned defense, not the offense. One step behind all the time, reacting not acting—and I'm horribly afraid it may be an intrinsic condition of my new job." He downed a bite of sandwich. "Unless I can sell Gregor on the idea of an Auditor Provocateur . . . Well, anyway, I did have one idea, which I propose to spring on your uncle when he gets downside." He paused; silence fell. After a moment he added, "If you make an encouraging noise, I'll go on."

He'd caught her with her mouth full. "Hmm?"

"Lovely, yes. You see, suppose . . . suppose this thing of Soudha's is more than a mere embezzlement scheme. Maybe they were diverting all those Imperial funds to support a real research and development project, although nothing to do with Waste Heat Management. It may be a prejudice of my military background, but I keep thinking they might have been building a weapon. Some new variation on the gravitic imploder lance, I don't know." He gulped tea.

"I never had the impression that Soudha or any of the other Komarrans in the Terraforming Project were very military-minded. Quite the opposite."

"They needn't be, for an act of sabotage. Some grand stupid vile gesture—I keep worrying about Gregor's wedding coming up."

"Soudha isn't grandiose," said Ekaterin slowly. "Nor vile, particularly." She didn't doubt that Tien's death had been unintended.

"Nor stupid." Vorkosigan sighed regretfully. "I merely suggest that timetable to make myself nervous. Keeps me awake. But suppose it was a weapon. Did they perhaps *attack* that ore ship, as a test? Vile enough. Did their smoke test go very wrong? Was the subsequent damage to the mirror accidental, or deliberate? Or was it the other way around? The condition of Radovas's body suggests *something* backfired. A falling-out among thieves? Anyway, to anchor this spate of speculation to some sort of physical fact, I plan to get a list of every piece of equipment Soudha bought for his department, subtract from it everything they left there, and produce a parts list for their secret weapon. At this point my brilliance fails, and I plan to dump it on your uncle."

"Oh!" said Ekaterin. "He'll like that. He'll growl at you."

"Is that a good sign?"

"Yes."

"Hm. So, positing a secret-weapon sabotage-attack . . . how close are they to success? I keep coming back—sorry—to Foscol's odd behavior in providing that data packet of evidence against Tien. It seems to proclaim: it doesn't matter if the Komarrans are incriminated, because—fill in the blank. Because *why*? Because they will not be here to suffer the consequences? That suggests flight, which runs counter to the weapon hypothesis, which requires that they linger to use it."

"Or that they believed you would not be here to inflict the consequences," said Ekaterin. Had they meant Vorkosigan to die, too? Or . . . what?

"Oh, nice. *That's* reassuring." He bit rather aggressively into the last of his sandwich.

She rested her chin on her hand and regarded him with wry curiosity. "Does ImpSec know you babble like this?"

"Only when I'm very tired. Besides, I like to think out loud. It slows it down so I can get a good look at it. It gives you some idea of what living in my head is like. I admit, very few people can stand to listen at length." He shot her an odd sideways look. Indeed, whenever his animation slowed—which was not often—a gray weariness flashed underneath. "Anyway, you encouraged me. You sang *Hmm*."

She stared in amused indignation and refused to rise to the bait.

"Sorry," he said in a smaller voice. "I think I'm a little disoriented just now." He gave her an apologetic grimace. "I actually came back here to rest. Is that not sensible of me? I must be getting old."

Both their lives were out of phase with their chronological ages, Ekaterin realized bemusedly. She now possessed the education of a child and the status of a dowager. Vorkosigan . . . was young for his post, to be sure. But this whole posthumous second life of his was surely as old as you could be at any age. "Time is out of joint," she murmured; he looked up sharply, and seemed about to speak.

Voices from the vestibule interrupted whatever he'd been about to say. Ekaterin's head turned. "Tuomonen, so soon?"

"Do you want to put this off?" Vorkosigan asked her.

She shook her head. "No. I want to get it over with. I want to go get Nikki."

"Ah." He drained his tea mug and rose, and they both went out to her living room. It was indeed Captain Tuomonen. He nodded to Vorkosigan, and greeted her politely. He had brought a female medtech with him, in the uniform of the Barrayaran military medical auxiliary, whom he also introduced. She carried a medkit, which she placed on the round table and opened. Ampoules and hyposprays glittered in their gel slots. Other first-aid supplies hinted at more sinister possibilities.

Tuomonen indicated Ekaterin should sit on the circular couch. "Are you ready, Madame Vorsoisson?"

"I suppose so." Ekaterin watched with concealed fear and some loathing as the medtech loaded her hypospray and showed it to Tuomonen to cross-check.

The medtech laid a second hypospray out at the ready, and pulled a small, burr-like patch off a plastic strip. "Would you hold out your wrist, Madame?"

Ekaterin did so; the woman pressed the allergy test patch firmly against her skin, then peeled it up again. She continued to hold Ekaterin's wrist while she marked time on her chrono. Her fingers were dry and cold.

Tuomonen dispatched the two guards to the perimeter, namely the hallway and the balcony, and set up a vid recorder on a tripod. He then turned to Vorkosigan, and with a rather odd emphasis, said, "May I remind you, Lord Vorkosigan, that more than one questioner can create unnecessary confusion in a fast-penta interrogation."

Vorkosigan gave him an acknowledging hand wave. "Quite. I know the drill. Go ahead, Captain."

Tuomonen glanced at the medtech, who stared closely at Ekaterin's wrist, then released it. "She's clear," the woman reported.

"Proceed, please."

At the medtech's direction, Ekaterin rolled up her sleeve. The hypospray hissed against her skin with a cold bite.

"Count backwards slowly from ten," Tuomonen told her.

"Ten," Ekaterin said obediently. "Nine . . . eight . . . seven . . ."

Chapter Fourteen

Two . . . one . . ." Ekaterin's voice, almost inaudible at first, grew more firm as she counted down.

Miles thought he could almost mark Ekaterin's heartbeats, as the drug flooded her system. Her tightly clenched hands loosened in her lap. Tension in her face, neck, shoulders, and body melted away like snow in the sun. Her eyes widened and brightened, her pale cheeks flushed with soft color; her lips parted and curved, and she looked up at Miles, beyond Tuomonen, with an astonished sunny smile.

"Oh," she said, in a surprised voice. "It doesn't *hurt*."

"No, fast-penta doesn't hurt," said Tuomonen, in a level, reassuring tone.

That isn't what she means, Tuomonen. If a person lived in hurt like a mermaid in water, till hurt became as invisible as breath, its sudden removal—however artificial—must come as a stunning event. Miles breathed covert relief that Ekaterin apparently wasn't going to be a giggler or a drooler, nor was she one of the occasional unfortunates in whom the drug released a torrent of verbal obscenities, or an almost equally embarrassing torrent of tears.

No. The kicker here is going to be when we take it away again. The realization chilled him. *But my God, isn't she beautiful when she is not in pain?* Her open, smiling warmth looked strangely familiar to him, and he tried to remember just when he'd seen that sweet air about her before. Not today, not yesterday . . .

It was in your dream.

Oh.

He sat back and rested his chin in his hand, fingers across his mouth, as Tuomonen started down the list of standard neutral questions: name, birth date, parents' names, the usual. The purpose was not only to give the drug time to take full effect, but also to set up a rhythm of question-and-answer which would help carry the interrogation along when the questions, and answers, became more difficult. Ekaterin's birthday was just three weeks before his own, Miles noted in passing, but the War of Vordarian's Pretendership, which had so disrupted their mutual birth year in the regions around Vorbarr Sultana, had scarcely touched the South Continent.

The medtech had settled herself on a chair drawn up outside the conversation circle, out of the line of sight between interrogator and subject, but not, alas, entirely out of earshot. Miles trusted she had suitable top security clearances. He didn't know, and decided not to ask, if her gender represented delicacy on Tuomonen's part, tacit acknowledgment that a fast-penta interrogation could be a mind-rape. Physical brutality did not mix with fast-penta interrogation, which had helped to eliminate certain unsavory psychological types from successful careers as interrogators. But physical assault was not the only possible kind, nor even necessarily the worst. Or maybe she'd just been next up on the roster of available personnel.

Tuomonen moved on to more recent history. Exactly when had Tien acquired his Komarran post, and how? Had he known anyone in his department-to-be, or met with anyone in Soudha's group, before they'd left Barrayar? No? Had she seen any of his correspondence? Ekaterin, growing ever more cheerful in fast-penta elation, rattled on as confidingly as a child. She'd been so excited about the appointment, about the promised proximity to good medical facilities, certain she would get galactic-class help for Nikki at last. She had agonized over Tien's application and helped him to write it. Well, yes, written most of it for him. Serifosa Dome was fascinating, and their assigned apartment much larger and nicer than she'd been led to expect. Tien said the Komarrans were all techno-snobs, but she had not found them to be so . . .

Gently, Tuomonen led her back to the issue at hand. Just when had she discovered her husband's involvement in the embezzlement scheme, and how? She repeated the same story about Tien's midnight call to Soudha she had given Miles last night, larded with more extraneous details—among other things she insisted on giving Tuomonen a complete recipe for spiced brandied milk. Fast-penta did do odd things to one's memory, even though it did not, despite rumor, give one perfect recall. Her report of the overheard conversation sounded nearly verbatim, though. Despite his obvious fatigue, Tuomonen was skillful and patient, allowing her to ramble on at length, alert for the hidden gem of critical information in these flowing associations an interrogator always hoped would turn up, but usually didn't.

Her description of breaking into her husband's comconsole the following morning included the mulish side comment, "If Lord Vorkosigan could do it, *I* could do it," which at Tuomonen's alert query triggered an embarrassing detour into her views of Miles's earlier ImpSec-style raid on her own comconsole. Miles bit his lip and met Tuomonen's raised brows blandly.

"He did say he liked my gardens, though. Nobody else in my family wants to even look at them." She sighed, and smiled shyly at Miles. Dared he hope he was forgiven?

Tuomonen consulted his plastic flimsy. "If you didn't discover your husband's debts until yesterday morning, why did you transfer almost four thousand marks into his account on the previous morning?" His attention sharpened at Ekaterin's look of drunken dismay.

"He lied to me. Bastard. Said we were going for the galactic treatment. No! He *didn't* say it, damn it. Fool, me. I wanted it to be true so much. Better a fool than a liar. Is it? I didn't want to be *like* him."

Tuomonen sought enlightenment of Miles with a quick baffled glance. Miles blew out his breath. "Ask her if it was Nikki's money."

"Nikki's money," she confirmed with a quick nod. Despite the fast-penta wooze, she frowned fiercely.

"This make sense to you, my lord?" Tuomonen murmured.

"I'm afraid so. She had saved just that sum out of her household accounts toward her son's medical treatment. I saw the account in her files, when I was taking that, um, unfortunate tour. I take it that her husband, claiming to be using it for that purpose, instead relieved her of it to stave off his creditors." *Embezzlement indeed.* Miles exhaled, to bring his blood pressure back down. "Have you traced it?"

"Tien transferred it upon receipt to the Rialto Sharemarket Agency."

"There's no getting it back, I suppose?"

"Ask Gibbs, but I don't think so."

"Ah." Miles bit his knuckle, and nodded for Tuomonen to proceed. Now armed with the right questions, Tuomonen confirmed this interpretation explicitly, and went on to draw out all the intensely personal details about the Vorzohn's Dystrophy.

In exactly the same neutral tone, Tuomonen asked, "Did you arrange your husband's death?"

"No." Ekaterin sighed.

"Did you ask anyone, or pay anyone, to kill him?"

"No."

"Did you know he was to be killed?"

"No."

Fast-penta frequently made subjects bloody literal-minded; you always asked the important questions, the ones you were hot about, in a number of different ways, to be sure.

"Did you kill him yourself?"

"No."

"Did you love him?"

Ekaterin hesitated. Miles frowned. Facts were ImpSec's rightful prey; feelings, maybe less so. But Tuomonen wasn't quite out of line yet.

"I think I did, once. I must have. I remember the wonderful look on his face, the day Nikki was born. I must have. He wore it out. I can hardly remember that time."

"Did you hate him?"

"No . . . yes . . . I don't know. He wore that out too." She looked earnestly at Tuomonen. "He never hit me, you know."

What an obituary. *When I go down into the ground at last, as God is my judge, I pray my best-beloved may have better to say of me than, "He didn't hit me."* Miles set his jaw and said nothing.

"Are you sorry he died?"

Watch it, Tuomonen. . . .

"Oh, but it was such a relief. What a nightmare today would have been if Tien were still alive. Though I suppose ImpSec would have taken him away. Theft and treason. But I would have had to go see him. Lord Vorkosigan said I could not have saved him. There was not enough time after Foscol called me. I'm so glad. It's so ugly to be so glad. I suppose I should forgive Tien for everything, because he's dead now, but I'll never forgive him for turning me into something so ugly." Despite the drug, tears were leaking from her eyes now. "I didn't use to be this kind of person, but now I can't go back."

Some truths cut deeper than even fast-penta could soak. Expressionlessly, Miles reached past Tuomonen and handed Ekaterin a tissue. She blotted the moisture in owlish distress.

"Does she need more drug?" the medtech whispered.

"No." Miles made a hand-down gesture for silence.

Tuomonen asked some more neutral questions, till something like his subject's original sunny and confiding air returned. *Yeah. Nobody should have to do this much truth all at once.*

Tuomonen looked at his flimsy, glanced uneasily at Miles, licked his lips, and said, "Your cases and Lord Vorkosigan's were found together in your vestibule. Were you planning to leave together?"

Shock and fury flushed through Miles in a hot wave. *Tuomonen, you dare—!* But the memory of sorting through all that mixed underwear under the eye of the ImpSec guard stopped his words; so, yes, it *could* have looked odd, to someone who didn't know what was going on. He converted his boiling words to a slow breath, which he let out in a trickle. Tuomonen's eyes flicked sideways, wary of that sigh.

Ekaterin blinked at him in some confusion. "I'd hoped to."

What? Oh. "She means, at the same time," Miles gritted through his teeth to Tuomonen. "Not together. Try that."

"Was Lord Vorkosigan planning to take you away?"

"Away? Oh, what a lovely idea. Nobody was taking me away. Who would? I had to take myself away. Tien threw my aunt's skellytum over the balcony, but he didn't quite dare throw me. He wanted to, I think."

Miles was diverted to brood on these last words. How much physical courage had it taken her, to stand up to Tien at the last? Miles did not underestimate just what nerve it took face down large angry men who had the power to pick you up and pitch you across the room. Nerve and wit and never letting yourself get within arm's reach, nor blocked from the door. The calculations were automatic. And you had to stay in practice. For Ekaterin, it must have felt like landing a fully-loaded freight shuttle on her very first flying lesson.

Tuomonen, trying desperately for clarity and still with one eye on Miles, repeated, "Were you going to elope with Lord Vorkosigan?"

Her brows flew up. "No!" she said in astonishment.

No, of course not. Miles tried to recapture his first properly stunned reaction to the accusation, except that it now came out, *What a great idea. Why didn't I think of it?* which rather blunted the fine edge of his outrage. Anyway, she'd never have run off with him. It was all he could do to get a Barrayaran woman to walk down the street with a sawed-off mutie like him. . . .

Oh hell. Have you fallen in love with this woman, idiot boy?

Um. Yeah.

He'd been falling for days, he realized in retrospect. It was just that he'd finally hit the ground. He should have recognized the symptoms. *Oh, Tuomonen. The things we learn under fast-penta.*

He could finally see what Tuomonen was getting at, though, all complete. A nice neat little conspiracy: murder Tien, blame it on the Komarrans, run off with his wife over his dead body . . . "A most flattering scenario, Tuomonen," Miles breathed to the ImpSec captain. "Quick work on my part, considering I only met her five days ago. I thank you." *Was ever woman in this humor wooed? Was ever woman in this humor won? I think not.*

Tuomonen shot him a flat-lipped glower. "If my guard could think of it, and I could think of it, so could someone else. Best to knock the notion in the head as soon as possible. It's not as though I could fast-penta you. My lord."

No, not even if Miles volunteered. His known idiosyncratic reaction to the drug, so historically useful in evading hostile interrogation, also made it impossible for him to use it clear himself of any accusation. Tuomonen was just doing his job, and doing it well. Miles leaned back, and growled, "Yeah, yeah, all right. But you're optimistic, if you think even fast-penta is fast enough to compete with titillating rumor. As a courtesy to his Imperial Majesty's Auditors' reputations, do have a word with that guard of yours after this."

Tuomonen didn't argue, or pretend to misunderstand. "Yes, my lord."

Temporarily undirected, Ekaterin was burbling along on her free-association tangent. "I wonder if the scars below his belt are as interesting as the ones above. I could hardly have got him out of his trousers in that bubble-car, I suppose. I had a chance last night, and I didn't even think of it. Mutie Vor. How does he do it . . . ? I wonder what it would be like to sleep with someone you actually liked . . . ?"

"Stop," said Tuomonen belatedly. She fell silent and blinked at him.

Just when it was getting really interesting . . . Miles quelled a narcissistic, or perhaps masochistic, impulse to encourage her to go on in this strain. He'd invited himself along on this interrogation to keep *ImpSec* from abusing its opportunities.

"I'm finished, my lord," Tuomonen said aside to him in a low voice. He did not quite meet Miles's eyes. "Is there anything else you think I should ask, or that you wish to ask?"

Could you ever love me, Ekaterin? Alas, questions of future probability were unanswerable, even under fast-penta.

"No. I would ask you to note, nothing she's said under fast-penta substantially contradicts anything she's told us straight out. The two versions are in fact unusually congruent, compared to other interrogations in my experience."

"Mine as well," Tuomonen allowed. "Very good." He motioned to the silently waiting medtech. "Go ahead and administer the antagonist."

The woman stepped forward, adjusted the new hypospray, and pressed it against the inside of Ekaterin's arm. The lizard-hiss of the anti-drug going in licked Miles's ears. He counted Ekaterin's heartbeats again, one, two, three . . .

It was a horribly vampiric thing to watch, as if life itself were being sucked out of her. Her shoulders drew in, her whole body hunched in renewed tension, and she buried her face in her hands. When she raised it again, it was flushed and damp and strained, but she was not weeping, merely utterly exhausted, and closed again. He had thought she would weep. *Fast-penta doesn't hurt, eh?* Couldn't prove it now.

Oh, Milady. Can I ever make you look that happy without drugs? Of more immediate importance, would she forgive him for being a party to her ordeal?

"What a very odd experience," Madame Vorsoisson said neutrally. Her voice was hoarse.

"It was a well-conducted interview," Miles assured the room at random. "All things considered. I've . . . seen much worse."

Tuomonen gave him a dry look, and turned to Ekaterin. "Thank you, Madame Vorsoisson, for your cooperation. This has been extremely useful to the investigation."

"Tell the investigation it is welcome."

Miles was not just sure how to interpret that one. Instead he said to Tuomonen, "That *will* be all for her, won't it?"

Tuomonen hesitated, obviously trying to sort out whether that was a question or an order. "I hope so, my lord."

Ekaterin looked across at Miles. "I'm sorry about the suitcases, Lord Vorkosigan. I never thought how it might look."

"No, why should you have?" He hoped his voice didn't sound as hollow as it felt.

Tuomonen said to Ekaterin, "I both suggest and request you rest for a while, Madame Vorsoisson. My medtech will stay with you for about half an hour, to be sure you're fully recovered and don't have any further drug reactions."

"Yes, I . . . that would probably be wise, Captain." Rubbery-legged, she rose; the medtech went to her side and escorted her off toward her bedroom.

Tuomonen shut down his vid recorder. He said gruffly, "Sorry about that last round of questions, my Lord Auditor. It was not my intention to offer an insult to either you or Madame Vorsoisson."

"Yeah, well . . . don't worry about it. What's next, from ImpSec's point of view?"

Tuomonen's weary brow wrinkled. "I'm not sure. I wanted to make certain I conducted this interrogation myself. Colonel Gibbs has everything in hand at the Terraforming offices, and Major D'Emorie hasn't called to complain yet about anything at the experiment station. What we *need* next, preferably, is for the field agents to catch up with Soudha and his friends."

"I can't be in all three places," Miles said reluctantly. "Barring an arrest coming through . . . the Professor is en route, and has had the advantage of a full night's sleep. You, I believe, have had none. My field instincts say this is the time to knock off for a while. Do I need to make that an order?"

"No," Tuomonen assured him earnestly. "You have your wrist-comm, I have mine . . . Field has our numbers and orders to report the news. I'll be glad to get home for a meal, even if it is last night's dinner. And a shower." He rubbed his stubbled chin.

He finished packing the recorder, exchanged farewells with Miles, and went off to consult with his guards, hopefully to apprise them of Madame Vorsoisson's change of status from suspect/witness to free woman.

Miles considered the couch, rejected it, and wandered into Ekaterin's—Madame Vorsoisson's. . . . Ekaterin's, dammit, in his mind if not on his lips—Ekaterin's workroom. Automatic lighting still sustained the assortment of young plantings on the trellised shelves in the corners. The grav-bed was gone; oh yes, he'd forgotten she'd had it removed. The floor looked remarkably inviting, though.

A flash of scarlet in the trash bin caught his eye. Investigating, he found the remains of the bonsai'd skellytum bundled up in a square of plastic sheeting, mixed with pieces of its pot and damp loose dirt. Curiously, he dug it out and cleared a place on Ekaterin's work table, and unrolled the plastic . . . botanical body bag, he supposed.

The fragments put him in mind of the soletta array and the ore ship, and also of a couple of the more distressing autopsies he'd recently reviewed. Methodically, he began to sort them out. Broken tendrils in one pile, root threads in another, shards of the poor burst barrel of the thing in another. The five-floor plunge had had something of the same effect on the liquid-conserving central structure of the skellytum as a sledgehammer applied to a watermelon. Or a needle-grenade exploding inside someone's chest. He picked out sharp potsherds, and made tentative tries at piecing the bits of plant into place, like a jigsaw puzzle. Was there a botanical equivalent of surgical glue, which could hold it all together again and allow it to heal? Or was it too late? A brownish tinge to the pale interior lumps suggested rot already in progress.

He brushed the damp soil from his fingers, and realized suddenly that he was touching Barrayar. This bit of dirt had come from South Continent, dug up, perhaps, from a tart old Vor lady's backyard. He dragged over the station chair from the comconsole, climbed precariously up onto it, and retrieved what proved to be an empty pan from an upper shelf. Safely on his feet again, he carefully gathered up as much of the soil as he could, and dumped it in the pan.

He stood back, hands on his hips, and studied his work so far. It made a sad pile. "Compost, my Barrayaran friend, you're destined to be compost, for all of me. A decent burial may be all I can do for you. Though in your case, that might actually be the answer to your prayers. . . ."

A faint rustle and an indrawn breath made him suddenly aware that he was not alone. He turned his head to find Ekaterin, on her feet again and pausing in the doorway. Her color looked better now than it had immediately after the interrogation, her skin not so puffy and lined, though she still looked very tired. Her brows were drawn down in puzzlement. "What are you doing, Lord Vorkosigan?"

"Um . . . visiting a sick friend?" Reddening, he gestured to his efforts laid out on her work bench. "Has the medtech released you?"

"Yes, she's just left. She was very conscientious."

Miles cleared his throat. "I was wondering if there was any way to put your skellytum back together. Seemed a shame not to try, seventy years old and all that." He drew back respectfully as she came up to the bench and turned over a fragment. "I know you can't sew it up like a person, but I can't help thinking there ought to be something. I'm afraid I'm not much of a gardener. My parents let me try, once, when I was a little kid, back behind Vorkosigan House. I was going to grow flowers for my Betan mother. Sergeant Bothari ended up doing the spade work, as I recall. I dug the seeds up twice a day to see if they'd sprouted yet. My plants did not thrive, for some reason. After that we gave up and turned it into a fort."

She smiled, a real smile, not a fast-penta grin. *We did not break her after all.*

"No, you can't put it back together," she said. "The only way is to start over. What I could do is take the strongest root fragments— several of them, to make sure," her long hands sorted through his pile, "and set them to soak in a hormone solution. And then when it starts to put out new growth, repot it."

"I saved the dirt," Miles pointed out hopefully. *Idiot. Do you know what an idiot you sound like?*

But she merely said, "Thank you." Following up on her words, she rummaged in her shelves and found a shallow basin, and filled it with water from the work bench's little sink. Another cupboard yielded a box of white powder; she sprinkled a tiny amount into the water and stirred it with her fingers. Taking a knife from her tool drawer, she trimmed the most promising root fragments and pushed them into the solution. "There. Maybe something will come of that." She stretched to set the basin carefully out of the way on the shelf Miles had had to reach by standing on the chair, and shook the pan of dirt into a plastic bag, which she sealed and put next to the basin. She then rolled up the decaying remains in their tarp again, to take over and shake into another bin; the plastic went back into the trash. "By the time I'd thought of this poor skellytum again, it would have gone out with the organic recycle, and been too late. I'd abandoned hope for it last night, when I thought I had to leave with just what I could carry."

"I didn't mean to burden you. Will it be awkward, to carry home on the jumpship?"

"I'll put it in a sealed container. By the time I reach my destination, it should be just about ready to replant." She washed and dried her hands; Miles followed suit.

Damn Tuomonen anyway, for forcing to Miles's consciousness a desire his back-brain had known very well was too unripe and out of season for any fruitful result. *Time is out of joint*, she'd said. Now he was going to have to deal with it. Now he was going to have to *wait*. How long? *How about till after Tien is buried, for starters?* His intentions were honorable enough, at least some of them were, but his timing was *lousy*. He shoved his hands deep into his pockets and rocked on his heels.

Ekaterin folded her arms, leaned against the counter, and stared at the floor. "I wish to apologize, Lord Vorkosigan, for anything I might have said under fast-penta that was not appropriate."

Miles shrugged. "I invited myself along. But I thought you could use a spotter. You did as much for me, after all."

"A spotter." She looked up, her expression lightening. "I had not thought of it like that."

He opened his hand and smiled hopefully.

She smiled briefly in return, but then sighed. "I'd been so frantic, all day, for ImpSec to be done so I could go get Nikki. Now I think they were doing me a favor. I dread this part. I don't know what to tell him. I don't know how much I *should* tell him about Tien's mess. As little as possible? The whole truth? Neither feels right."

Miles said slowly, "We're still in the middle of a classified case, here. You can't burden a nine-year-old boy with government secrets, or that kind of judgment call. I don't even know yet how much of this will eventually become public knowledge."

"Things not done right away get harder." She sighed. "As I'm finding now."

Miles drew up the comconsole chair for her, and motioned her into it, and pulled out the stool from under the work bench. He perched on it, and asked, "Had you told him you were leaving Tien?"

"Not even that, yet."

"I think . . . that for today, you should only tell him that his father suffered an accident with his breath mask. Leave the Komarrans out of it. If he asks for more details than you know how to deal with, send him to me, and I'll take the job of telling him he can't know, or can't know yet."

Her level look asked, *Can I trust you?* "Take care you don't stir up more curiosity than you quell."

"I understand. The problem of the whole truth is as much a question of when as what. But after we both get back to Vorbarr Sultana, I would like, with your permission, to take you to talk with Gr—with a close friend of mine. He's Vor, too. He had the experience of being in something like Nikki's position. His father died under, ah, grievous circumstances, when he was much too young to be told the details. When he stumbled across some of the uglier facts, in his early twenties, it was pretty traumatic. I'll bet he'll have a better feel than either of us for what to tell Nikki and when. He has a fine judgment."

She gave him a provisional nod. "That sounds right. I would like that very much. Thank you."

He returned her a half-bow, from his perch. "Glad to be of service, Madame." He'd wanted to introduce her to Gregor the man, his foster-brother, not Emperor Gregor the Imperial Icon, anyway. This might serve more than one purpose.

"I also have to tell Nikki about his Vorzohn's Dystrophy, and I can't put that off. I made an appointment for him at a clinic in Solstice for the day after tomorrow."

"He does not know he carries it?"

She shook her head. "Tien would never let me tell him." She studied him gravely. "I think you were in something like Nikki's position, too, when you were a child. Did you have to undergo a great many medical procedures then?"

"God, yes, years of 'em. What can I say that's useful? Don't lie about whether it's going to hurt. Don't leave him alone for long periods." *Or you, either . . .* There was finally something he *could* do for her. "Events permitting, may I ride along with you to Solstice and render what assistance I can? I can't spare your uncle to you—he's going to be buried in technical problems by day after tomorrow, if my parts list takes shape."

"I can't take you away from your duties!"

"My experience suggests to me that if Soudha hasn't been arrested by then, what I will be doing by day after tomorrow is spinning my mental wheels. A day away from the problems may be just what I will need to give me a fresh approach. You would be doing me a service, I assure you."

She pursed her lips doubtfully. "I admit . . . I would be grateful for the company."

Did she mean any company, generally, or his company particularly? *Down, boy. Don't even think about it.* "Good."

Voices drifted in from the vestibule: one of the guards, and a familiar rumble. Ekaterin jumped up. "My uncle is here!"

"He made very good time." Miles followed her into the hallway.

Professor Vorthys, his broad face wrinkled with concern, gave his valise over to the guard and folded his niece in his arms, murmuring condolences. Miles watched in exquisite envy. Her uncle's warm sympathy almost broke her down, as all of ImpSec's cool professionalism had not; Miles made a mental note. Cool and practical, that was the ticket. She dashed tears from her eyes, dispatched the guard with his case to Tien's old office as before, and led her uncle to the living room.

After a very brief conference, it was decided the Professor would accompany her to go collect Nikolai. Miles seconded this despite what he ironically recognized as his present lovesick mania for volunteerism. Vorthys had a family right, and Miles himself was too close to Tien's death. He was also swaying on his feet as the set of painkillers and stimulants he'd taken before lunch wore off. Taking a third dose today would be a bad mistake. Instead he saw the Professor and Ekaterin out, then checked in with ImpSec HQ in Solstice on the secured comconsole.

No new news. He wandered back toward the living room. Ekaterin's uncle was here; Miles should go, now. Collect his things and decamp to that mythical hotel he'd been gassing about for the last week. There was no room for him in this little apartment, with Vorthys reinstalled in the guest room. Nikki would need his own bed back, and he was damned if he was going to trouble Ekaterin to rustle up another grav-bed, or worse, for his Vor lordly use. What *had* she been expecting, when she'd ordered in that thing? He should definitely go. He was obviously not being as civilly neutral toward his hostess as he'd imagined, if that blasted guard could make whatever comment it had been that had set off Tuomonen on that list of embarrassing questions about the suitcases.

"Do you need anything, my lord?" The door guard's voice at Miles's elbow startled him awake.

"Um . . . yeah. Next time one of your boys comes over from Solstice HQ, have him bring me a standard military-issue bedroll."

In the meanwhile, Miles staggered over and curled up on the couch after all. He was asleep in minutes.

Miles awoke when the little party returned with Nikki He sat up and managed to be reasonably composed by the time he had to face the boy. Nikki looked subdued and scared, but was not weeping or hysterical; he evidently turned his reactions inward rather than outward. Like his mother.

In the absence of female friends of Ekaterin's bearing casseroles and cakes in the Barrayaran manner, Miles caused ImpSec to supply dinner. The three adults kept the conversation neutral in front of Nikki, after which he went off to play by himself in his room, and Miles and the Professor retired to the study for a data-exchange. The new equipment found topside was indeed peculiar, including some power-transfer equipment heavy-duty enough for a small jumpship, parts of which had ripped apart, melted, and apparently exploded in a shower of plasma. The Professor called it, "Truly interesting," an engineering code-phrase that caught Miles's full attention.

In the middle of this, Colonel Gibbs reported in via comconsole. He smiled dryly at both Imperial Auditors, an expression which Miles was beginning to recognize as Gibbs's version of ecstasy.

"My Lord Vorkosigan. I have the first documented connection you were looking for. We've traced the serial numbers of a pair of hastings converters my Lord Vorthys's people found topside back through the chain to a Waste Heat purchase eight months ago. The converters were originally delivered to their experiment station."

"Right," breathed Miles. "Finally, more of a link than just Radovas's body. We have hold of the real string, all right. Thank you, Colonel. Carry on."

Chapter Fifteen

Ekaterin slept better than she'd expected to, but woke to the realization that she'd got through most of yesterday on adrenaline. Today, with its enforced wait for action, was going to be harder. *I've been waiting nine years. I can manage nineteen more hours.* Lying in bed allowed a kind of numb, foggy grief to descend, despite her release from the late chaos of Tien's life. So she rose, dressed carefully, ducked around the guard in her living room, made breakfast, and waited.

The Auditors stirred soon thereafter and came out gratefully for food, but carried off their coffee to the secured comconsole. She ran out of things to clean up, and went out to her balcony, but found the presence of another guard on post inhibited her from resting there. So she gave the guards coffee, and retreated to her kitchen, and waited some more.

Lord Vorkosigan emerged again. He fended off her offers of more coffee, and instead seated himself at her table. "ImpSec sent me the autopsy report on Tien this morning. How much do you want to know about it?"

The vision of Tien's congealed body, hanging in the frost, flashed in her memory. "Was there anything unexpected?"

"Not with respect to cause of death. They found his Vorzohn's Dystrophy, of course."

"Yes. Poor Tien. To spend all those years in a suppressed panic over his disease, only to die of another cause altogether." She shook her head. "So much effort, so *misplaced*. How far advanced was it, could they tell?"

"The nervous lesions were very distinct, according to the examiner. Though how they can tell one microscopic blob from another . . . The outward symptoms, if I interpret the medical jargon correctly, would have been impossible to conceal very soon."

"Yes. I think I knew that. It was the inward progress I wondered about. When did it start. How much of Tien's, oh, bad judgment and other behavior was his disease." Should she have somehow held on longer? *Could* she have? Until what other desperate denouement had played itself out?

"The damage builds slowly for a long time. Which parts of the brain are affected varies from person to person. For what it's worth, his seemed concentrated in the motor regions and peripheral nervous system. Though it may be possible to blame some of his actions on the disease, later, if a face-saving gesture is needed."

"How . . . politic. Face-saving for whom? I don't wish it."

He smiled a bit grimly. "I didn't think you did. But I have the unpleasant conviction that this case is going to shift from its nice clean engineering parameters into some very messy politics sooner or later. I never discard a possible reserve." He looked down at his hands, clasped loosely before him on the table. His gray sleeves imperfectly concealed the white bandages ringing his wrists. "How did Nikki take the news, last night?"

"That was hard. He started out—before I told him—trying to argue me into letting him stay and play another night. Getting passionate and sulking, you know how kids are. I so much wished I could simply let him go on, not having to know. I wasn't able to prepare him as much as I would have liked. I finally had to sit him down and tell him straight out, *Nikki, you have to come home now. Your Da was killed in a breath mask accident last night.* It just . . . wiped him blank. I almost wished for the whining back." Ekaterin looked away. She wondered what oblique forms Nikki's reactions might eventually take, and whether she would recognize them. Or handle them well. Or not . . . "I don't know how it's going to go in the long run. When I lost my mother . . . I was older, and we knew it was coming, but it was still a shock, *that* day, *that* hour. I always thought there would be more time."

"I've not yet lost a parent," said Vorkosigan. "Grandparents are different, I think. They are old, it's their destiny, somehow. I was shaken when my grandfather died, but my world was not. I think my father's was, though."

"Yes," she looked up gratefully, "that's the difference exactly. It's like an earthquake. Something that isn't supposed to move suddenly dumps you over. I think the world is going to be a scarier place for Nikki this morning."

"Have you hit him with his Vorzohn's Dystrophy news yet?"

"I'm letting him sleep. I'll tell him after breakfast. I know better than to stress a kid who has low blood sugar."

"Odd, I feel the same way about troops. Is there anything . . . can I help? Or would you prefer to be private?"

"I'm not sure. He doesn't have school today anyway. Weren't you taking my uncle out to the experiment station this morning?"

"Directly. It can wait an extra hour for this."

"I think . . . I would like it if you can stay. It's not good to make of the disease something all secret that's too awful to even talk about. That was Tien's mistake."

"Yes," he said encouragingly. "It's just a thing. You deal with it."

Her brows rose. "As in, one damn thing after another?"

"Yes, very like." He smiled at her, his gray eyes crinkling. Through whatever combination of luck and clever surgery, no scars marred his face, she realized. "It works, as tactics if not strategy."

True to his offer, Lord Vorkosigan drifted back into her kitchen as Nikki was finishing his breakfast. He lingered suggestively, stirring the coffee he took black and leaning against the far counter. Ekaterin took a deep breath and settled beside Nikki at the table, her own half-empty and cold cup a mere prop. Nikki eyed her warily.

"You won't be going to school tomorrow," she began, hoping to strike a positive note.

"Is that when Da's funeral is? Will I have to burn the offering?"

"Not yet. Your Grandmadame has asked that we bring his body back to Barrayar, to bury beside your uncle who died when you were little." Tien's mother's return message had come in by comconsole this morning, beamed and jumped through the wormhole-relays. In writing, as Ekaterin's had been, and perhaps for similar reasons; writing allowed one to leave so much out. "We'll do all the ceremonies and burn the offering then, when everyone can be there."

"Will we have to take him on the jumpship with us?" asked Nikki, looking disturbed.

From the side of the room Lord Vorkosigan said, "In fact, ImpS—the Imperial Civil Service will take care of all those arrangements, with your permission, Madame Vorsoisson. He will probably be back home before you are, Nikki."

"Oh," said Nikki.

"Oh," Ekaterin echoed. "I . . . I was wondering. I thank you."

He sketched a bow. "Allow me to pass on your mother-in-law's address and instructions. You have enough other things to do."

She nodded, and turned back to her son. "Anyway, Nikki . . . you and I are going to Solstice tomorrow, to visit a clinic there. We never mentioned this to you before, but you have a condition called Vorzohn's Dystrophy."

Nikki made an uncertain face. "What's *that*?"

"It's a disorder where, with age, your body stops making certain proteins in quite the right shape to do their job. Nowadays the doctors can give you some retrogenes that produce the proteins correctly, to make up for it. You're too young to have any symptoms, and with this fix, you never will." At Nikki's age, and on the first pass, it was probably not yet necessary to go into the complications it would entail for his future reproduction. She noticed dryly how she had managed to get through the long-anticipated spiel without once using the word *mutation*. "I've collected a lot of articles about Vorzohn's Dystrophy, which you can read when you want to. Some of them are too technical, but there are a couple I think you could get through with a little help." There. If she could avoid setting off his homework alarms, that ought to set up a reasonably neutral way to give him the information to which he had a right, and he could pursue it at his own pace thereafter.

Nikki looked worried. "Will it hurt?"

"Well, they will certainly have to draw blood, and take some tissue samples."

Vorkosigan put in, "I've had both done to me, what seems like a thousand times over the years, for various medical reasons. The blood draw hurts for a moment, but not later. The tissue sampling doesn't hurt because they use a medical micro-stun, but when the stun wears off, it aches for a while. They only need a tiny sample from you, so it won't be much."

Nikki appeared to digest this. "Do *you* have Vorzohn's thing, Lord Vorkosigan?"

"No. My mother was poisoned with a chemical called soltoxin, before I was born. It damaged my bones, mainly, which is why I'm so short." He wandered over to the table and sat down with them.

Ekaterin was expecting Nikki's next to be something along the lines of, *Will I be short?* but instead, his brown eyes widened in extreme worry. "Did she *die?*"

"No, she recovered completely. Fortunately. For us all. She's fine now."

He took this in. "Was she scared?"

Nikki, Ekaterin realized, had not yet sorted out just who Lord Vorkosigan's mother was, in relation to the people he'd heard about in his history lessons. Vorkosigan's brows rose in some bemusement. "I don't know. You can ask her yourself, someday, when—if you meet her. I'd be fascinated to hear the answer." He caught Ekaterin's unsettled gaze, but his eyebrows remained unrepentant.

Nikki regarded Lord Vorkosigan dubiously. "Did they fix your bones with retrogenes?"

"No, more's the pity. It would have been much easier on me, if it had been possible. They waited till they thought I was done growing, and then they replaced them with synthetics."

Nikki was diverted. "How d'you replace bones? How do you get them *out?*"

"Cut me open," Vorkosigan made a slicing motion with his right hand along his left arm from elbow to wrist, "chop the old bone out, pop the new one in, reconnect the joints, transplant the marrow to the new matrix, glue it up and wait for it to heal. Very messy and tedious."

"Did it hurt?"

"I was asleep—anesthetized. You're lucky you can have retrogenes. All *you* have to have are a few fiddling injections."

Nikki looked vastly impressed. "Can I see?"

After an infinitesimal hesitation, Vorkosigan unfastened his shirt cuff and pushed back his left sleeve. "That pale little line there, see?" Nikki stared with interest, both at Vorkosigan's arm and, speculatively, at his own. He wriggled his fingers, and watched his arm flex as the muscles and bones moved beneath his skin.

"I have a scab," he offered in return. "Want to see?" Awkwardly, he pushed up his pant leg to display the latest playground souvenir on his knee. Gravely, Vorkosigan inspected it, and agreed it was a good scab, and would doubtless fall off very soon now, and yes, perhaps there would be a scar, but his mother was very right to tell him not to pick it. To Ekaterin's relief, everyone then refastened their clothes and the contest went no further.

The conversation lagging after that high point, Nikki pushed a few last smears of groats and syrup artistically around the bottom of his dish, and asked, "Can I be excused?"

"Of course," said Ekaterin. "Wash the syrup off your hands," she called after his retreating form. She watched him—run, not walk—out, and said uncertainly, "That went better than I expected."

Vorkosigan smiled reassurance. "You were matter-of-fact, so you gave him no reason to be otherwise."

After a little silence Ekaterin said, "Was she scared? Your mother."

His smile twisted. "Spitless, I believe." His eyes warmed, and glinted. "But not, I understand, witless."

The two Auditors left for an on-site inspection of the Waste Heat experiment station shortly thereafter. Waiting carefully for a natural break in Nikki's quiet play in his room, Ekaterin called him in to her workroom to read the simplest and most straightforward article she had found on the subject of Vorzohn's Dystrophy. She sat him in her lap in her comconsole station chair, something she seldom did any more now he had become so leggy. It was a measure of his hidden unease this morning, she thought, that he did not resist the cuddle, nor her direction. He read through the article with fair understanding, stopping now and then to demand pronunciations and meanings of unfamiliar terms, or for her to rephrase or interpret some baffling sentence. If he had not been on her lap, she would not have detected the slight stiffening of his body as he read the line: . . . *later investigations concluded this natural mutation first appeared in Vorinnis's District near the end of the Time of Isolation. Only with the arrival of galactic molecular biology was it determined that it was unrelated to several old Earth genetic diseases which its symptoms sometimes mimic.*

"Any questions?" Ekaterin asked, when they'd finally wended to the end of the thing.

"Naw." Nikki elbowed off her lap and slid to his feet.

"You can read more whenever you want."

"Huh."

With difficulty, Ekaterin restrained herself from pursuing some more definite response from him, realizing she wanted it more for her sake than his own. *Are you all right, is it all right, do you forgive me?* He would not, could not, work through it all in an hour, or a day, or even a year; each day must have the challenge and response appropriate to it. *One damn thing after another,* Vorkosigan had said. But not, thank heavens, all things simultaneously.

The addition of Lord Vorkosigan to the expedition to Solstice made startling alterations in Ekaterin's carefully calculated travel plans. Instead of rising in the middle of the night to catch economy-class seats on the monorail, they awoke at a leisurely hour to take passage on an ImpSec suborbital courier shuttle which waited their pleasure, and would cover the intervening time zones with an hour to spare for lunch before Nikki's appointment.

"I love the monorail," Vorkosigan had confided apologetically at her first startled protest at the news of this change, sprung on her late in the evening when the two Auditors returned from their day's investigations. "In fact, I'm thinking of urging my brother Mark to invest in some of the companies trying to build more of them on Barrayar. But with this case heating up, ImpSec's made it pretty clear they would rather I did not travel by public transportation just now thank you very much my lord."

They also had two bodyguards. They wore discreet Komarran-style civilian clothes, which made them look exactly like a pair of Barrayaran military bodyguards in civvies. Vorkosigan seemed equally able to deal easily with them, or ignore them as though they were invisible, at will. He brought reports to read on the flight, but only glanced over them, seeming a little distracted. Ekaterin wondered if Nikki's restlessness broke his concentration, and if she ought to try and suppress the boy. But a quiet word from Vorkosigan at apogee won an excited Nikki an invitation to come forward and spend ten minutes in the pilot's compartment.

"How is the case going this morning?" Ekaterin asked him during this private interlude.

"Exactly as I predicted, unfortunately," he said. "ImpSec's failure to catch up with Soudha is growing more disturbing by the hour. I really thought they'd have nailed him by now. Between Colonel

Gibbs's group, and that team of earnest ImpSec boys we have counting widgets out at the experiment station, my parts list is starting to take shape, but it will be at least another day before it's complete."

"Did my uncle like the idea?"

"Heh. He said it was tedious, which I already knew. And then he appropriated it from me, which I take to indicate approval." He rubbed his lips, introspectively. "Thanks to your uncle, we did get one spot of encouragement last night. He'd thought to confiscate Radovas's personal library, when we visited Madame Radovas, and we sent it off to ImpSec HQ for analysis. Their analyst confirmed Radovas's primary interest in jumpship technology and wormhole physics, which does not surprise me much, but then we got a bonus.

"Soudha or his techs did a superb job of erasing everyone's comconsoles before ImpSec got to them, but evidently no one thought of the library. Some of the technical volumes had notes entered in the margin boxes. The Professor was quite excited about the mathematical fragments, but more obviously, there were reminders to confide this or that thought or calculation to some names jotted next to them. Mostly members of the Waste Heat group, but also a couple of others, including one who appears to be one of the late members of the station-keeping crew at the soletta array. We're now positing that Radovas and his equipment, with inside help, had been smuggled up to the soletta for whatever it was they were trying to do, rather than being aboard the ore freighter. So was the soletta essential to what they were doing, or were they only using it for a test platform? ImpSec has agents out all over the planet today, questioning and requestioning colleagues, relatives, and friends of everyone on the soletta or having anything to do with their resupply shuttle. Tomorrow, I will get to read all *those* reports."

Nikki's return dried up this amiable flow of information, and they soon landed at one of ImpSec's own private shuttleports on the edge of the vast sealed city of Solstice. Instead of taking a public bubble-car, they were provided with a floater and driver, who took them down into the restricted tunnels by some dizzying back route that brought them to their destination in about two-thirds the time of the bubble-car system.

The first stop was a restaurant atop one of Solstice's highest towers, providing diners a spectacular view of the capital glittering halfway to the horizon; though the place was crowded, no one was seated near them while they ate, Ekaterin observed. The bodyguards did not join in the meal.

The menu had no prices, triggering a moment of panic in Ekaterin's heart. She had no way to direct Nikki, or herself, for that matter, to the cheaper selections. *If you have to ask, you can't afford it.* Her initial determination to argue possession of her portion of the bill with Vorkosigan sagged.

Vorkosigan's height and appearance drew the usual covert double-takes. For the first time in his company, she became aware of being mistaken for a couple or even a family. Her chin rose defensively. What, did they think him too odd to attach a woman? It was none of their business anyway.

The next stop—and Ekaterin was very grateful she did not have to navigate to it herself—was the clinic, a comfortable quarter hour early. Vorkosigan did not appear to notice anything in the least remarkable about the whole magic carpet ride, though Nikki had been enthusiastically diverted throughout. Had Vorkosigan planned that? The boy grew suddenly very much quieter as they took the lift-tubes up to the clinic lobby.

When they were ushered to the booth of an admissions clerk, Vorkosigan pulled up a chair for himself just behind Ekaterin and Nikki, and the bodyguards faded discreetly out of range. Ekaterin presented identification and civil service payment documentation, and all seemed to go smoothly, until they came to the information that Nikki's father was lately deceased, and the clinic comconsole demanded formal permissions from Nikki's legal guardian.

That thing is much too well programmed, Ekaterin thought, and embarked on an explanation of the distance to Tien's third cousin back on Barrayar, and the time-constrained need for Nikki's treatment to be completed before their return. The Komarran clerk listened with understanding and sympathy, but the comconsole program did not agree, and after a couple of attempts to override it, the clerk went off to fetch her supervisor. Ekaterin bit her lip and rubbed her palms on her trouser knees. To come so far, to be so close, to get hung up on some legal technicality *now . . .*

The supervisor, a pleasant young Komarran man, returned with the clerk, and Ekaterin gave her explanation again. He listened, and rechecked all the documentation, and turned to her with an air of earnest regret.

"I'm sorry, Madame Vorsoisson. If you were a Komarran planetary shareholder, instead of a Barrayaran subject, the rules would be very different."

"All Komarran planetary shareholders are Barrayaran subjects," Vorkosigan pointed out from behind her, in a bland tone.

The supervisor managed a pained smile. "I'm afraid that's not quite what I meant. The thing is, a similar problem came up for us just a few months ago, regarding treatment under quasi-emergency conditions of a Vor child of Komarr-resident Barrayarans. We went with what seemed to us to be the common-sense approach. The child's legal guardian later disagreed, and the judicial, er, negotiations are still going on. It proved to be a very costly error of judgment for the clinic. Given that Vorzohn's Dystrophy is a chronic and not an immediately life-threatening condition, and that you should in theory be able to obtain your legal permissions in a week or two, I'm afraid I'm going to have to ask you to reschedule."

Ekaterin took a deep breath, whether to argue or scream she was not sure. But Lord Vorkosigan leaned past her shoulder and smiled at the supervisor.

"Hand me that read-pad, will you?"

The puzzled supervisor did so; Vorkosigan rummaged in his pocket and pulled out his gold Auditor's seal, which he uncapped and pressed to the pad, along with his right palm. He spoke into the vocorder. "By my order, and for the good of the Imperium, I request and require all assistance, to wit, suitable medical treatment for Nikolai Vorsoisson. Vorkosigan, Imperial Auditor." He handed it back. "See if that doesn't make your machine happier." He murmured aside to Ekaterin, "Just like swatting flies with a laser cannon. The aim's a bit tricky, but it sure takes care of the flies."

"Lord Vorkosigan, I can't . . ." Her tongue stumbled to a halt. *Can't what?* This wasn't like waffling over the lunch bill; Tien's benefits would be paying for Nikki's treatment, if only the Komarrans could be persuaded to disgorge it. Vorkosigan's offered contribution was entirely intangible.

"Nothing your esteemed uncle would not have done for you, if I could have spared him to you today." He gave her one of his ghost-bows, seated.

The supervisor's expression changed from suspicious to stunned as his comconsole digested this new data. "You are Lord Auditor Vorkosigan?"

"At your service."

"I . . . er . . . uh . . . in what capacity are you here, my lord?"

"Friend of the family." Vorkosigan's smile twisted just slightly. "Red tape cutter and general expediter."

To his credit, the supervisor managed not to gibber. He dismissed the clerk and sped them through processing, and himself escorted them upstairs and into the hands of the medtechs in the genetics department. He then vanished, but things ran amazingly quickly thereafter.

"It almost seems unfair," Ekaterin murmured, when Nikki was whisked away briefly by a tech to pee into a sampler. "I think Nikki just jumped the queue, there."

"Yes, well . . . I found last winter that an Auditor's seal had the same enlivening effect on ImpMil's veteran's treatment division, whose hallways are much draftier and drabber than these, and whose queue times are legendary. Quite miraculous. I was charmed." Vorkosigan's face grew more introspective, and sober. "I'm afraid I've not quite found my balance with this Imperial Auditor thing yet. What is the just use of power, what is its abuse? I could have ordered Madame Radovas to be fast-penta'd, or ordered Tien to land us at the experiment station that first evening, and events would now be . . . well, I don't quite know what they would now be, except different than this. But I did not wish to . . ." He trailed off, and for just a flash, Ekaterin caught an impression of a much younger man beneath his habitual mask of irony and authority. *He is no older than me, after all.*

"Did you anticipate that problem with the permissions? I should have thought of it, I suppose, but they took all the information when I made the appointment, and didn't say anything, so I thought, I assumed –"

"Not specifically. But I hoped I might have a chance to do some little service or another today. I'm pleased it was so easy."

Yes, she realized enviously, he could just wave all ordinary problems out of his path. Leaving only the extraordinary ones . . . her envy ebbed. It occurred belatedly to Ekaterin that he too might feel some guilt about Tien's death, and that was why he was going to such lengths to assist Tien's widow and orphan. So intense a concern seemed unnecessary, and she wondered how to reassure him that she did not blame him without creating more awkwardness than she erased.

A battery of tests was completed upon Nikki in about half the time Ekaterin had mentally allotted for them. The Komarran physician met with them in her comfortable office very shortly thereafter; Vorkosigan dismissed the bodyguards to lurk in the corridor.

"Nikki's gene scan shows the dystrophy complex to be very much in the classic mode," the doctor told them, when Ekaterin and Nikki were seated side by side in front of her comconsole desk. Vorkosigan, as usual, took a backseat and just watched. "He has a few idiosyncratic complications, but nothing *our* lab can't handle."

She illustrated her talk with a holovid of the actual offending chromosomes, and a computer-generated vid of exactly how the retrovirus would deliver the splice that would work to supplement their deficiencies. Nikki did not ask as many questions as Ekaterin had hoped he would—was he intimidated, weary, bored?

"I believe our gene techs can have the retrovirus personalized for Nikki in about a week," the doctor concluded. "I'm going to have you return for the injection then, Nikki. Plan to stay overnight in Solstice for a recheck the following day, Madame Vorsoisson, and if possible, visit us again just before you leave Komarr. Nikki will need to be reexamined monthly thereafter for three months, which you can have done at a clinic I will recommend to you in Vorbarr Sultana. We'll give you a disk with all the records, and they should be able to pick it up from there. After that, assuming all goes well, a yearly checkup should suffice."

"That's all?" said Ekaterin, weak with relief.

"That's all."

"There was no damage yet? We are in time?"

"No, he's fine. It's hard to project, with Vorzohn's Dystrophy, but I would guess in his case the onset of detectable gross cellular damage would have begun to appear in his late teens or early twenties. You are in good time."

Ekaterin held Nikki's hand hard as they exited, her steps firm, to keep her feet from dancing. With an, "Aw, Mama," Nikki extracted himself, and walked with independent dignity beside her. Vorkosigan, his hands shoved deep in his gray trouser pockets, followed smiling.

✦　✦　✦

Nikki fell asleep in the shuttle, with his head pillowed on Ekaterin's lap. She watched him fondly, and stroked his hair, lightly so as not to wake him.

Vorkosigan, sitting across from them with his reader on his knees again, watched her in turn, and murmured, "Is it well?"

"It's well," she said softly. "But it feels so strange . . . Nikki's illness has been the whole focus of my life for so long. I gradually pared away all the other impossibilities to concentrate wholly on this, the one main thing. It feels as though I had been steeling myself to batter down some unscaleable wall. And then, when I finally took a deep breath and put my head down and charged, it just . . . fell, all in a heap, like that. And now I'm stumbling around in the dust and the bricks, blinking. I feel very unbalanced. Where am I now? *Who* am I now?"

"Oh, you'll find your center. You can't have mislaid it totally, even if you have been revolving around other people. Give yourself time."

"I thought my center was to be Vor, like the women before me." She glanced across at him, feeling inarticulate and urgent. "When I chose Tien . . . you have to understand, it *was* my choice. My marriage was arranged, offered, but it wasn't forced. I wanted it, wanted to have children, form a family, carry on the pattern. Make my place in this, I don't know, generational pageant."

"I am the eleventh of my name. I know about the Vor pageant."

"Yes," she said gratefully. "It wasn't that I didn't choose what I wanted, or gave away my center, or any of those things. But somehow, I didn't end up with the beautiful Vor pattern-weave I was trying to make. I ended up with this . . . tangle of strings." Her fingers wriggled in air, miming chaos.

His lips quirked, introspective and ironic. "I know tangles, too."

"But do you know—well, of course you would, but . . . The business with the brick wall. Failure, failure was grown familiar to me. Comfortable, almost, when I stopped struggling against it. I did not know achievement was so devastating."

"Huh." He was leaning back, now, his reader forgotten on his lap, regarding her with his entire attention. "Yes . . . vertigo at apogee, eh? And the reward for a job well done is another job, and what have you done for us lately, and is that *all*, Lieutenant Vorkosigan, and . . . yes. Achievement is devastating, or at least disorienting, and they don't warn you in advance. It's the sudden change of momentum and direction, I think."

She blinked. "How very strange. I expected you to tell me I was being foolish."

"Deny your perfectly correct perception? Why should you expect that?"

"Habit . . . I suppose."

"Mm. You can learn to enjoy the sensation of winning, you know, once you get over the initial queasiness. It's an acquired taste."

"How long did it take you to acquire it?"

He smiled slowly. "Once."

"That's not a taste, that's an addiction."

"It's one that would look well on you."

His eyes were uncomfortably bright. Challenging? She smiled in confusion, and stared out the port at the darkening Komarran sky as the shuttle began its descent. He rubbed his lips, not quite erasing their odd quirk, and returned his attention to his reports.

Uncle Vorthys met them at the apartment door, data disks in his hand and a vague distracted smile on his face. He gave Ekaterin's hand a warm grasp, and fended off Nikki's immediate attempt to appropriate him and carry him off to hear about the wonders of the ImpSec shuttle.

"Just a moment, Nikki. We shall go to the kitchen for dessert, and you can tell me all about it. Ekaterin. I've heard from the Professora. She's taken ship on Barrayar, and will be here in three days' time. I didn't like to tell you till she was sure she could get away."

"Oh!" Ekaterin almost jumped with delight, mitigated immediately by concern. "Oh, no, sir, do you meant to say you are dragging that poor woman through five wormhole jumps from Barrayar to Komarr for *me*? She gets so jumpsick!"

"It was Lord Vorkosigan's idea, actually," said Uncle Vorthys.

Vorkosigan put on a bright, trapped smile at this, and shrugged warily.

"Although I had fully intended to drag her here for my own sake," Uncle Vorthys continued, "at the end of the term. This just advanced the timetable. She does like Komarr, once she gets here and has a day to recover from the jump-lag. I thought you would like it."

"You shouldn't have—but oh, I do like it, very much."

Vorkosigan straightened at these words, and his smile relaxed into a self-satisfaction that amused her vastly. Ekaterin wasn't sure if she was reading the subtleties of his expression better now, or if he was concealing them less.

"If I get you a ticket, would you go out to meet her at the jump-point station?" Uncle Vorthys added. "I'm afraid I won't have time, and she hates traveling alone. You could see her a day earlier, and have some time together on the last leg downside."

"Certainly, sir!" Ekaterin almost shivered with the realization of how much she longed to see her aunt. She'd been living in Tien's orbit so long, she'd become used to her isolation as the norm. Ekaterin counted the Professora as one of the few nondisheartening relatives she possessed. A friend—an ally! The Komarran women Ekaterin had met were nice enough, but there was so much they didn't understand. . . . Aunt Vorthys might make acerbic comments, but she understood deeply.

"Yes, yes, Nikki—" said Uncle Vorthys. "Miles. When you are ready, I'll meet you in my room, and we can go over today's progress on the comconsole."

"Have we some? Is it interesting?"

Uncle Vorthys made a balancing gesture with his free hand. "I'd be interested in what pattern you see emerging, if any."

"At your convenience. Knock on my door when you're ready." Vorkosigan smiled at Nikki, gave the Professor a vague salutelike gesture, and withdrew.

Nikki, impatiently waiting his turn, now dragged his great-uncle off to the kitchen as promised; Ekaterin could only be grateful that of his day's events the ImpSec shuttle seemed to loom so much larger than the medical examinations. She followed, satisfied.

Chapter Sixteen

Early the next morning Miles, in shirt and trousers but bare foot, stepped into the hallway with his toiletries case in hand. He must remind Tuomonen to return his medical kit. The ImpSec techs couldn't have found any interesting explosive devices in it, or he would have been informed by now. His bleary meditations suffered a check when he discovered Ekaterin, still dressed in a robe and with her hair in unusual but fetching disarray, leaning against the hall bathroom door.

"Nikki," she hissed. "Open this door at once! You can't hide all day in there."

A muffled young voice returned mulishly, "Yes, I can."

Lips tight, she tapped again, urgently but quietly, then jumped a little as she saw Miles, and clutched the neck of her robe.

"Oh. Lord Vorkosigan."

"Good morning, Madame Vorsoisson," he said civilly. "Ah . . . trouble?"

She nodded ruefully. "I thought yesterday went awfully easily. Nikki tried to insist he was too sick to go to school today, because of his Vorzohn's Dystrophy. I explained again it didn't work that way, but he got more and more stubborn. He begged to stay home. No, not just stubborn. Scared, I think. This isn't the usual malingering." She jerked her head toward the locked door. "I tried getting firm. It was not the right tactic. Now he's panicked."

Miles bent to glance at the lock, which was an ordinary mechanical one. Too bad it wasn't a palm lock; he knew some tricks with those. This one didn't even have screws, but some kind of rivets. It was going to take a pry bar. Or subterfuge . . .

"Nikki," called Ekaterin hopefully. "Lord Vorkosigan is out here. He needs to get washed and dressed, so he can go to work."

Silence.

"I'm torn," murmured Ekaterin in lower tones. "We're leaving in a few weeks. A few missed lessons wouldn't matter, but . . . that's not the point."

"I went to a private Vor school rather like his, when I was his age," Miles murmured back. "I know what he's afraid of. But I think your instincts are correct." He frowned thoughtfully, then set his case down and rummaged for his tube of depilatory cream, which he smeared liberally over his night's bristles. "Nikki?" he called more loudly. "Can I come in? I'm all over depilatory cream, and if I don't wash it off, it'll start eating through my skin."

"Won't he realize you can wash in the kitchen?" Ekaterin whispered.

"Maybe. But he's only nine, I'm gambling depilation is still a bit of a mystery."

After a moment Nikki's voice came, "You can come in. But I'm not coming out. And I'm locking it again."

"That's fair," Miles allowed.

Some rustling near the door. "Should I grab him when it opens?" Ekaterin asked, very dubiously.

"Nope. It would violate our tacit agreement. I'll go in, then we'll see what happens. At least you'll have a spy inside the gate, at that point."

"It seems wrong to use you so."

"Mm, but kids only dare defy those whom they really trust. The fact that I'm still mostly a stranger to him gives me an advantage, which I invite you to use."

"True enough. Well . . . all right."

The door opened a cautious crack. Miles waited. It opened a little wider. He sighed, turned sideways, and slipped through. Nikki shut it again immediately,and snapped the lock.

The boy was dressed for school, in his braided uniform of sober gray and maroon, but minus his shoes. The shoes presumably had been the sticking point, with their implicit commitment to going out. Nikki backed up and seated himself on the edge of the tub; Miles laid out his toiletries kit on the counter and rolled up his sleeves, trying to think fast before coffee. Or think at all. His eloquence had inspired his soldiers to face death, in the past, or so he dimly recalled. *Now let's try something really hard.* Playing for time and inspiration, he methodically brushed his teeth, by which time the depilatory had finished working. He washed off the resultant goo, rubbed his face dry with the towel, flung it over his shoulder, and leaned with his back against the door, slowly unrolling his sleeves and fastening his cuffs.

"So, Nikki," he said at last. "What's the trouble with going to school this morning?"

Moisture smeared around the boy's defiant eyes glistened when it caught the light. "I'm sick. I've got Vorzohn's thing."

"It's not catching. You can't give it to anybody." *Except for the way you got it.* From the blank look on Nikki's face, the idea of being dangerous to anyone else had never crossed his mind. Ah, the self-centeredness of childhood. Miles hesitated, wondering how to approach the real problem. For almost the first time, he wondered how certain aspects of his childhood had looked from his parents' point of view. The doubled vision was dizzying. *How the devil did I wind up on the enemy side?*

"You know," Miles essayed, "no one will even know you have it unless you tell them. It's not like they can smell it on you, eh?"

The mulish look redoubled. "That's what Mama said."

Scratch that trial balloon. There was an inherent problem in suggesting secrecy anyway, as Tien's life demonstrated. Suppressing a passing desire to strangle the boy for inflicting yet more distress on Ekaterin just now, Miles asked, "Have you had breakfast yet?"

"Yeah."

Starving him out or bribing him with food would be too slow, then. "Well . . . deal. I won't tell you you're blowing it all out of proportion if you won't tell me I don't understand."

Nikki glanced up from his seat, his attention arrested. *Yeah. See me, kid.* Miles considered, and immediately discarded, any argument that smacked of threat, that attempted to chivvy Nikki in the right direction by upping the pressure. For instance, the one that started out, *How do you ever expect to have the courage to jump through wormholes if you haven't the courage to face this?* Nikki was up against the wall now, driven into this untenable retreat. Upping the pressure would just squash him. The trick was to lower the wall. "I went to a private school a bit like yours. I can't remember a time I wasn't dealing with being a mutie Vor, in my classmates' eyes. By the time I was your age, I had a dozen strategies. Some of them were pretty counterproductive, I admit."

He'd gone through medical hell in his childhood with a stiff lip. But a few still-remembered playfellows, upon discovering that his brittle bones made physical harassment too dangerous—to themselves, when they found they couldn't conceal the evidence— had learned to reduce him to humiliated tears with words alone. Sergeant Bothari, delivering Miles daily to this academic purgatory, quickly made a routine of an expert shakedown, relieving him of weapons ranging from kitchen knives to a military stunner stolen from Captain Koudelka's holster. After that, Miles had gone to war in a subtler fashion. It had taken almost two years to teach certain of his classmates to leave him alone. Learning all round. Upon reflection, offering his own age nine-to-twelve solutions might not be the best idea . . . in fact, letting Nikki even find out what some of them had been could be a supremely bad idea. "But that was twenty years ago, on Barrayar. Times have changed. What exactly do you think your friends here will do to you?"

Nikki shrugged. "Dunno."

"Well, give me some guesses. You can't plan a strategy without good intelligence."

Nikki shrugged again. After a time he added, "It's not what they'll do. It's what they'll think."

Miles blew out his breath. "That's . . . a little tenuous for me to work with, y'know. What you fear someone will think, in the future. I usually have to use fast-penta to find out what people really think. And even fast-penta won't tell me what they're *going* to think."

Nikki hunched. Miles regretfully gave up the notion of telling him that if he kept making those turtle-backed gestures, his spine would freeze like that, just as Miles's had. There was a faint, awful possibility the boy might believe him.

"What we need," Miles sighed, "is an ImpSec agent. Someone to scout unknown territory, not knowing what the strangers they meet are going to do or think. Listen carefully, watch and remember, report back. And they have to do it over and over, in new places all the time. It's bloody daunting, the first time."

Nikki looked up. "How do you know? You said you were a courier."

Damn, the kid was sharp. "I'm, um, not supposed to talk about it. You're not cleared. But do you think your school is as dangerous as, say, Jackson's Whole, or Eta Ceta? Just to pick a couple of, ah, random examples."

Nikki stared in silent and, Miles feared, justified scorn of this adult floundering.

"Tell you something I did learn, though."

Nikki was drawn, or at least, looked up.

Go with it; he won't give you more. "It's not as daunting the second time. I wished later I could have started with the second time. But the only way to get to the second time is to do the first time. Seems paradoxical, that the fastest way to get to easy is through hard. In any case, I can't spare you an ImpSec agent to check out your school for antimutant activity."

Nikki snorted warily, alive to the least hint of patronization.

Miles's grin twisted in bleak appreciation. "Besides, it would be overkill, don't you think?"

"Prob'ly." Grouchy hunching.

"The ideal ImpSec scout would be someone who could blend in, anyway. Someone who knew the territory like that back of his hand, and wouldn't make dangerous mistakes out of ignorance. Someone who could keep his own counsel and not let his assumptions get in the way of his observations. And not get into fights, because it would blow his cover. Very practical people, the successful Imperial agents I've known." He eyed Nikki meditatively. This was not going well. Try another. "The youngest subagent I ever employed was about ten. It wasn't on Barrayar, needless to say, but I don't think you're any less bright or competent than she was."

"Ten?" said Nikki, temporarily startled out of his surly knot. "*She?*"

"It was for a spot of simple courier duty. She could pass unnoticed where a uniformed mercen—where a uniformed adult could not. Now, I'm willing to be your tactical consultant on this, ah, school-penetration mission, but I can't work without intelligence. And the best agent to collect it, in this case, is already in place. Do you dare?"

Nikki shrugged. But his lip-biting stony look had faded into one of speculation. "Ten . . . a *girl* . . ."

A hit, a very palpable hit. "I put her down on my ImpSec expenditures log as a local informant. She was paid, of course. Same rates as an adult. A small but measurable contribution to speeding that particular mission to a successful conclusion." Miles stared off into the middle distance for a moment, with an air of reminiscence of the sort which usually preceded long, boring adult stories. When he judged the hook was set, he feigned to come back to himself and smiled faintly at Nikki. "Well, that's enough of that. Duty drives. *I* haven't had breakfast. If you decide to come out, I'll be here for another ten minutes or so."

Miles unlatched the lock and let himself out. He didn't think Nikki had bought more than one word of his in three, though for a change and in contrast to several of his historic negotiations, it had all been true. But at least he'd managed to offer a line of retreat from an impossible position.

Ekaterin was waiting in the hall. He put his finger to his lips and waited a moment. The door stayed closed, but the lock did not click again. Miles motioned Ekaterin to follow, and tiptoed away to the living room.

"Whew," said Miles. "I think that's the toughest audience I've ever played to."

"What happened?" demanded Ekaterin anxiously. "Is he coming out?"

"Not sure yet. I gave him a couple of new things to think about. He didn't seem as panicked. And it's going to get really boring in there after a bit. Let's give him some time and see."

Miles was just finishing his groats and coffee when Nikki cautiously poked his head around the kitchen door. He lingered in the doorway, kicking his heel against the frame. Ekaterin, seated across from Miles, put her hand to her lips and waited.

"Where're my shoes?" asked Nikki after a moment.

"Under the table," said Ekaterin, maintaining, with obvious effort, a perfectly neutral tone. Nikki crawled under to retrieve them, and sat cross-legged on the floor by the door to put them on.

When he stood up again, Ekaterin said carefully, "Do you want anyone to go with you?"

"Naw." His gaze crossed Miles's just briefly, then he slouched into the living room to collect his school bag and let himself out the front door.

Ekaterin, turning back from her arrested half-rise from her chair, sank down limply. "My word. I wonder if I ought to call the school to make sure he arrives."

Miles thought it over. "Yes. But don't let Nikki know you checked."

"Right." She swirled the coffee around in the bottom of her cup, and added hesitantly, "How did you *do* that?"

"Do what?"

"Get him out of there. If it had been Tien . . . they were both stubborn. Tien would get so frustrated with Nikki sometimes, not without cause. He would have threatened to take the door down and drag Nikki to school; I would have run around in circles placating, frantically afraid things would get out of hand. Though they never quite seemed to. I don't know if that was because of me, or . . . Tien would always be a little ashamed later, not that he would ever apologize, but he would buy . . . well, it doesn't matter now."

Miles made a crosshatch pattern in the bottom of his dish with his spoon, hoping his desire for her approval was not too embarrassingly obvious. "Physical solutions have never come easily to me. I just . . . played with his mind, eased him out. I try never to take away somebody's face when I'm negotiating."

"Not even a child's?" Her lips quirked, and her brows flicked up in an expression he wasn't sure how to interpret. "A rare approach."

"So, maybe my tactics had the novelty of surprise. I admit, I did *think* of ordering my ImpSec minions into the breach, but it would have looked like a very silly order. Nikki's dignity wasn't the only one on the line."

"Well . . . thank you for being so patient. One doesn't normally expect busy and important men to take the time for kids."

Her voice was warm; she *was* pleased. Oh, good. He babbled in relief, "Well, *I* do. Expect it, that is. My Da always did, you see—take time for me. Later, when I learned not everyone's Da did the same, I just assumed it was only a trait of the *most* busy and *most* important men."

"Hm." She looked down at her hands, resting on either side of her cup, and smiled crookedly.

Professor Vorthys lumbered in, dressed for the day in his comfortable rumpled suit, scarcely more form-fitting than his pajamas. It was tailor-made garb, appropriate to his status as an Imperial Voice, but he must, Miles reflected, have driven his tailor to despair before coaxing *just* the fit he wanted, *With lots of room in the pockets*, as he'd once explained to Miles while the Professora rolled her eyes heavenward. Vorthys was stuffing data disks into these capacious compartments. "Are you ready, Miles? ImpSec just called to say they'll have an aircar and driver waiting for us at the West Locks."

"Yes, very good." With an apologetic smile to Ekaterin, Miles tossed off the last of his coffee and rose. "Will you be all right today, Madame Vorsoisson?"

"Yes, of course. I have a lot to do. I have an appointment with an estate law counselor, and any amount of sorting and packing . . . the guard won't have to go with me, will he?"

"Not unless you wish. We are leaving one man on duty here, by your leave. But if our Komarrans had wanted hostages, they could have taken me and Tien that first night." And bought themselves loads more trouble. If only they *had*, Miles reflected regretfully. His case could be ever so much further along by now. Soudha was too damned smart. "If I thought you and Nikki were in any possible danger—" *I'd figure some way to use you for bait*— no, no. "If you are in the least uncomfortable, I'd be happy to assign you a man."

"No, indeed."

That faint smile again. Miles felt he could happily spend the rest of the morning studying all the subtle expressions of her lips. *Equipment lists. You're going to go study equipment lists.* "Then I bid you good morning, Madame."

Lord Auditor Vorthys, after his first survey of the new situation, had chosen to set up his personal headquarters out at the Waste Heat experiment station. Miles had to admit, the security there was great; no one was likely to blunder in by accident, or wander across its bleak surroundings unobserved. Well, he and Tien had, but the occupants had been distracted at the time, and Tien had apparently possessed a dire luck which amounted to antigenius. Miles wondered which had come first, for Soudha; had the administrative acquisition of such a perfect site for secret work triggered the idea for his shadow project, or had he had the idea first, and then maneuvered himself into the right promotion to capture control of the station? Just one of a long list of questions Miles was itching to ask the man, under fast-penta.

After the ImpSec aircar delivered the two Auditors, Miles went off first to check the progress of his, or rather, ImpSec Engineering

Major D'Emorie's, inventory crews. The sergeant in charge promised completion of the tedious identification, counting, and cross-check of every portable object in the station before the end of today. Miles then returned to Vorthys, who had set up a sort of engineer's nest in one of the long upstairs workrooms in the office section, with roomy tables, lots of light, and a proliferating array of high-powered comconsoles. The Professor grunted greetings from behind a multicolored spaghetti-array of mathematical projections, glimmering above his vid-plate. Miles settled down in a comconsole station chair to study the growing list of real objects Colonel Gibbs claimed Waste Heat had paid for, but which were no longer to be found on Waste Heat's premises, hoping some subliminally familiar ordnance pattern might emerge.

After a while, the Professor shut off his holovid display and sighed. "Well, no doubt they built *something*. The topside crews picked up some more fragments yesterday, mostly melted."

"So does our inventory represent one something, destroyed along with Radovas, or two somethings?" Miles wondered aloud.

"Oh, I should think two, at least. Though the second may not have been assembled yet. If one thinks it through from Soudha's point of view, one realizes he's been having a very bad month."

"Yes, if that whole mess topside wasn't some really bizarre suicide mission, or internecine sabotage, or. . . . and where *is* Marie Trogir, blast it? I'm not at all sure the Komarrans knew, either. When he talked to me, Soudha seemed to be angling to find out if I knew anything of her. Unless that was just more of his misdirection."

"Are you seeing anything in your inventory yet?" asked Vorthys.

"Mm, not exactly what I'm looking for. The final autopsy report on Radovas revealed some cellular distortions, in addition to the gross, and I use that term advisedly, damage. They reminded me a little of what happens to human bodies which have suffered a near-miss from a gravitic imploder beam. A hit, of course, is very distinctive, in a messy and violently-distributed way, but a near-miss can kill without actually bursting the body. I've been wondering since I first saw the cell scans if Soudha has reinvented the gravitic imploder lance, or some other gravitic field weapon. Scaling them down to personnel size has been an ongoing ambition of the weapons boffins, I know. But . . . the parts list doesn't quite jibe. There's a load of heavy-duty power transmission equipment among this stuff, but I'm damned if I see what they're transmitting it *to*."

"The math fragments found in Radovas's library intrigue me very much," said Vorthys. "You spoke to Soudha's mathematician, Cappell—what was your impression of him?"

"It's hard to say, now that I know he was lying through his teeth at me through the whole interview," said Miles ruefully. "I deduce that Soudha trusted him to keep his head, at a time when the whole team must have been scrambling like hell to complete their withdrawal. Soudha was very selective, I now realize, in just who he gated through to me." Miles hesitated, not just sure he could lay out the logic of his next conclusion. "I think Cappell was a key man. Maybe next after Soudha himself. Although the accountant, Foscol . . . no. I give you a foursome. Soudha, Foscol, Cappell, and Radovas. They're the core. I'll bet you Betan dollars to sand the farrago about a love affair between Radovas and Trogir was a complete fabrication, a convincing smoke screen they developed after the accident, to buy time. But in that case, where *is* Trogir now?" After a moment he added, "And were they planning to use their thing, or sell it? If sell, they'd almost have to find a customer out of the Empire. Maybe Trogir double-crossed everyone and took off with the specs to some high bidder. ImpSec's got a tight watch for our missing Komarrans on all the jump-point exits from the Empire. They only had a couple hours start, they *can't* have got out before the lid clamped down. But Trogir had a two-week headstart. She could be long gone by now."

Vorthys shook his head, declining to reason in advance of his data; Miles sighed, and returned to his list.

By the end of an hour, Miles was cross-eyed from staring at meters and meters of really supremely boring inventory readouts. His mind wandered, revolving a plan to go attach himself like a hyperactive leech to *all* the field agents searching for the fugitive Komarrans. Sequentially, he supposed; he had learned not to wish to be twins, or any other multiple of himself. Miles thought of the old Barrayaran joke about the Vor lord who jumped on his horse and rode off in all directions. Forward momentum only worked as a strategy if one had correctly identified which way was *forward*. After all, Lord Auditor Vorthys didn't run around in circles; he sat composedly in the center and let it all come to him.

Miles's meditations on the proven disadvantages of cloning were interrupted when Colonel Gibbs called them. Gibbs was sporting a demure smile of amazing smugness. The Professor wandered over into range of the vid pickup and leaned on the back of Miles's chair as Gibbs spoke.

"My Lord Auditor. My Lord Auditor." Gibbs nodded to them both. "I've found something odd I expect you want. We finally succeeded in tracing the real purchase orders of Waste Heat's largest equipment expenditures. They have, over the last two years, bought five custom-designed Necklin field generators from a Komarran jumpship powerplant firm. I have the company's name and address, and copies of the invoices. Bollan Design—that's the builder— still has the tech specs on file."

"Soudha was building a jump ship?" Miles muttered, trying to picture it. "Wait a minute, Necklin rods come in pairs . . . maybe they broke one? Colonel, has ImpSec visited Bollan yet?"

"We did, to confirm the invoice forgery. Bollan Design appears to be a perfectly legitimate, though small, company; they've been in business about thirty years, which rather predates this embezzlement operation. They're unable to compete head to head with the major builders like Toscane Industries, so they've specialized in odd and experimental designs and custom repairs of out-system and obsolete jumpship rods. Bollan as a company does not appear to have violated any regulation, and seems to have dealt with Soudha as a customer in all good faith. The invoices at the time they left Bollen were not yet altered; that was done when they arrived on Foscol's comconsole, apparently. Nevertheless . . . the chief design engineer who worked on the order directly with Soudha has not been to work for three days, nor did my field agent find him at home."

Miles swore under his breath. "Ducking fast-penta interrogation, you bet. Unless his body turns up dead in a ditch. Could be either, at this point. You have a detainment order out on him, I trust?"

"Certainly, my lord. Shall I download everything we've acquired so far this morning on your secured channel?"

"Yes, please," said Miles.

"Especially the tech specs," put in Vorthys over his shoulder. "After I look at them, I may want to talk to the people at Bollen who *are* still there. May I trouble ImpSec to be sure none of the rest of them go on an extempore vacation before I get in touch with them, Colonel?"

"Already been done, my lord."

Still looking smug, Gibbs signed off, to be replaced by the promised financial and technical data. Vorthys tried to foist the financial records off on Miles, who promptly filed them and went to look at Vorthys's tech readouts.

"Well," said Vorthys, when, after a cursory initial scan, he was able to pull up a holovid schematic, which rotated slowly and colorfully in three dimensions above his vid-plate. "What the hell is that?"

"I was hoping you'd tell me," Miles breathed, now hanging in turn over the back of Vorthys's station chair. "Sure doesn't look like any Necklin rod I've ever seen." The lines turning in air sketched out a shape like a cross between a corkscrew and a funnel.

"All the designs are slightly different," noted Vorthys, bringing up four more shapes to hang in series beside the first. "Judging by the dates, they were scaling up with each subsequent model."

According to the attached measurements, the first three were relatively smaller, a couple of meters long and a meter or so wide. The fourth was double the dimensions of the third. The fifth, probably four meters wide at the larger end and six meters in length. Miles pictured the size of the assembly room doors in the building next to this one. Wherever that last one had been delivered to—four weeks ago?—it hadn't been here. And one did not leave a delicate precision device like a Necklin rod out in the wind and rain.

"Those things generate Necklin fields?" said Miles. "What shape? With a pair of jumpship rods, the fields counter-rotate and fold the ship through five-space." He held his hands out parallel with each other, palm up, then pressed them inward. In the metaphor he'd been given, the field wrapped around its ship to create a five-space needle of infinitesimal diameter and unlimited length, to punch through that area of five-space weakness called a wormhole, and unfold again into three-space on the other side. He'd also been dragged through a more convincing mathematical demonstration, in his last term at the Academy, all details of which, never called on subsequently thereafter, had evaporated out of his brain shortly after the final exam. That was long before his cryo-revival, so it was one bit of memory loss he could not blame on the sniper's needle-grenade. "I used to know this stuff . . ." he muttered plaintively.

Despite this broad hint, the Professor did not break into an enlightening lecture. He just sat in his station chair, his chin cupped in his palm. After a moment, he leaned forward and called up a dizzying succession of data files from the probable-cause investigation. "Ah. Here it is." A wriggly graph appeared, flanked by a list of elements and percentages running down one side. A fast pass through the data from Bollen produced another, similar list. The Professor leaned back. "I'll be damned."

"*What?*" said Miles.

"I did not expect to get this lucky. That," he pointed to the first graph, "is an analysis of the composition of a very melted and distorted mass fragment we picked up topside. It has nearly the same composition fingerprint as this fourth device, here. The figures which are a tiny bit off are just the sort of lighter and more volatile elements I'd expect to lose in such a melt. Huh. I didn't think we'd *ever* be able to reconstruct the source of those blobs. Now we don't have to."

"If that was the fourth," said Miles slowly, "where's the fifth?"

The Professor shrugged. "The same place as the first, second, and third?"

"Do you have enough information from the inventory to reconstruct its power supply? At that point, we'd have the whole machine mapped, wouldn't we?"

"Mm, maybe. It will certainly supply some parameters. How much power? Continuous, or phased? Bollen had to know, to supply the proper coupler . . . ah." He noodled again with the specs and fell into a study of the complicated diagram.

Miles rocked impatiently on his heels. When he felt could no longer maintain his respectful silence without the top of his head blowing off, he said, "Yes, but what does it *do*?"

"Just what it says, presumably. Generates a five-space distortion field."

"Which does what? *To* what?"

"Ah." The Professor sank back in his station chair and rubbed his chin ruefully. "Answering that may take a little longer."

"Can't we run comconsole simulations?"

"To be sure. But to get the right answer, one must first correctly frame the question. I want—humph!—a mathematical physicist specializing in five-space theory. Probably Dr. Riva, she's at the University of Solstice."

"If she's Komarran, ImpSec will object."

"Yes, but she's here on-planet. I've consulted her before, when I investigated a politically suspicious wormhole jump accident on the

Sergyar route two years ago. She thinks sideways better than any of the other five-space people I know."

Miles was under the impression that all five-space math experts thought sideways to the rest of humanity, but he nodded understanding of the importance of this character trait.

"I want her; I shall have her. But before I drag her out of her comfortable academic routine, I think I want to visit Bollen in person. Your Colonel Gibbs is very good, but he can't have asked all the questions."

Miles considered denying personal ownership of ImpSec and anyone in it, but recognized ruefully that he was now identified as the authority on ImpSec among the Auditors just as Vorthys was identified as the engineering expert. *It's an ImpSec problem,* he pictured some future conclave of his colleagues concluding. *Give it to Vorkosigan.* "Right."

The trip to Bollen Design's plant did not prove as enlightening as Miles had hoped. A hop in a suborbital shuttle to a dome one Sector west of Serifosa soon brought Miles and Vorthys face-to-face with Bollen's upset owners. Since they'd already thrown open all their records to ImpSec that morning, they had little more to offer the Imperial Auditors. The administrative people knew only of financial and contractual details with Soudha's mythical "private research institute" that had supposedly ordered the work; some techs who'd worked in the fabrication shop had very little to add to the specs already in Vorthys's possession. If the missing engineer had been as innocent of the true identity of the customer and purpose of the device as were the rest of the Bollen employees, he'd have had no reason to flee; Bollen Design had committed no crime that Miles could identify.

However, the techs were able to recall dates of several visits from men answering to descriptions of Soudha, Cappell, and Radovas, definitely one from Soudha as recently as the previous week. Their supervisor had never included them in these conferences. They had been told never to discuss the odd Necklin generators outside their work group, as the devices were experimental and not yet patented, trade secrets soon to transmute into profit (or loss). The progression so far had looked a lot more like loss than profit.

The customers had always picked up the finished devices from the plant themselves, not had them delivered anywhere. Miles made a note to find out if Waste Heat had owned their own large transport, and if not, to have ImpSec check out recent lift-van rentals of anything big enough to have hauled those last two generators.

Nosing around the plant while the Professor went off to speak High Engineering to the bilingual, Miles felt himself increasingly drawn to the hypothesis that the chief designer had gone missing voluntarily. Upon closer examination it had been found that many of the man's personal notes had apparently gone with him. Bollen's plant security was not military grade, but it would be a stretch to imagine Soudha's hurried Komarrans first murdering the man, then smoothly and surgically removing quite so many comconsole records from quite so many locations without inside help. Anyway, Miles didn't wish the man dead in a ditch. He wished him very much alive, at the business end of Tuomonen's hypospray. That was the trouble, people *anticipated* fast-penta now. Modern conspirators were a lot more tight-lipped than back in the bad old days of mere physical torture. Three days ago, if someone had told Miles that Gibbs was going to hand him what amounted to complete design specs of Soudha's secret weapon on a platter, he would have been delighted to imagine his case nearly solved. Ha.

Miles and Vorthys arrived back at Ekaterin's apartment that night too late for dinner, but in time for a hand-made dessert obviously tailored to the Professor's tastes, involving chocolate, cream, and quantities of hydroponic pecans. They all sat around Ekaterin's kitchen table to devour it. Whatever Nikki had encountered from his playmates today, it hadn't been unpleasant enough to affect his appetite, Miles noted with approval.

"How was school today?" Miles asked him, ashamed to let such a deadly boring triteness fall from his lips, but how else was he supposed to find out?

"All right," Nikki said around a mouthful of cream.

"Think you'll have any trouble tomorrow?"

"Naw." The tone of his monosyllables had returned to their normal preadolescent adult-wary indifference; no more the breathy panicked edge of this morning.

"Good," Miles said affably. Ekaterin's eyes were smiling, Miles noted out of the corner of his own. *Good.*

When Nikki finished bolting his dessert and galloped off, she added wryly, "And how was work today? I wasn't sure if the extra hours represented progress, or the reverse."

How was work today. Her tone seemed to apologize for the prosaic quality of the question. Miles wondered how to explain to her that he found it altogether delightful, and wished she'd do it again. And again and . . . Her perfume was making his reptile-brain want to roll over and do tricks, and he wasn't even sure she was wearing any. This mind-melting mixture of lust and domesticity was entirely novel to him. Well, half novel; he knew how to handle lust. It was the domesticity that had ambushed his guard. "We have advanced to new and surprising levels of bafflement," Miles told her.

The Professor opened his mouth, closed it, then said, "That about sums it up. Lord Vorkosigan's hypothesis has proved correct; the embezzlement scheme was got up to support the production of a, um, novel device."

"Secret weapon," Miles corrected. "I said secret weapon."

The Professor's eyes glinted in amusement. "Define your terms. If it's a weapon, then what's the target?"

"It's so secret," Miles explained to Ekaterin, "we can't even figure out what it does. So I'm at least half right." He glanced after Nikki. "I take it once Nikki got into his usual routine, things smoothed out?"

"Yes. I'd been almost certain they would," said Ekaterin. "Thank you so much for your help this morning, Lord Vorkosigan. I'm very grateful that—"

Miles was saved from certain embarrassment by the chime of the hall door. Ekaterin rose and went to answer it and the Professor followed, blocking Miles from his planned counterbid, *How did things go with the estate law counselor? I was sure you could get on top of it.* The ImpSec guard was now on post in the hallway, Miles reminded himself; he didn't need to make a parade out of this. Tucking the line away in his head for the next conversation-opener, he tapped open the airseal door and wandered out onto the balcony.

Both sun and soletta had set hours ago. Only the city itself gave a glow to the night. A few pedestrians still crossed the park below, moving in and out of the shadows, hurrying on their way to or from the bubble-car platform, or strolling more slowly in pairs. Miles leaned on the railing and studied one sauntering couple, his arm draped across her shoulders, her arm circling his waist. In zero gee, a height difference like that would cancel out, by God. And how did the space-dwelling four-armed quaddies manage these moments? He'd met a quaddie musician once. He was certain there must be a quaddie equivalent to a grip so humanly universal . . .

His idle envious speculations were derailed by the sound of voices within the apartment. Ekaterin was welcoming a guest. A man's voice, Komarran accented: Miles stiffened as he recognized the rabbity Venier's quick speech.

"—ImpSec didn't take as long to release his personal effects as I would have imagined. So Colonel Gibbs said I might bring them to you."

"Thank you, Venier," Ekaterin's voice replied, in the soft tone Miles had come to associate with wariness in her. "Just put the box down on the table, why don't you? Now, where did he go . . . ?"

A clunk. "Most of it is nothing, styluses and the like, but I figured you would want the vidclipper with all the holos of you and your son."

"Yes, indeed."

"Actually, there is more to my visit than just cleaning out Administrator Vorsoisson's office." Venier took a deep breath. "I wanted to speak to you privately."

Miles, who had been about to reenter the kitchen from the balcony, froze. Dammit, ImpSec had questioned and cleared Venier, hadn't they? What new secret could he be about to offer, and to Ekaterin of all people? If Miles entered, would he clam up?

"Well . . . well, all right. Um, why don't you sit down?"

"Thank you." The scrape of chairs.

Venier began again, "I've been thinking about how awkward your situation here has become since the Administrator's death. I'm so very sorry, but I couldn't help being aware, watching you over the months, that things were not what they should have been between you and your late husband."

"Tien . . . was difficult. I didn't realize it showed."

"Tien was an ass," Venier stated flatly. "*That* showed. Sorry, sorry. But it's true, and we both know it."

"It's moot now." Her tone was not encouraging.

Venier forged on. "I heard about how he played fast and loose with your pension. His death has plunged you into a monstrous situation. I understand you are being forced to return to Barrayar."

Ekaterin said slowly, "I plan to return to Barrayar, yes."

He ought to clear his throat, Miles thought. Trip over a balcony chair. Pop back through the door and cry, *Vennie, fancy meeting you here!* He began breathing through his mouth, for silence, instead.

"I realize this is a bad time to bring this up, much too soon," Venier went on. "But I've been watching you for months. The way you were treated. Practically a prisoner, in a traditional Barrayaran marriage. I could not tell how willing a prisoner you were, but now—have you considered staying on Komarr? *Not* going back into your cell? You have this chance, you see, to escape."

Miles could feel his heart begin to beat, in a free-form panic. Where was Venier going with this?

"I . . . the economics . . . our return passage is a death benefit, you see." That same wary softness.

"I have an alternative to offer you." Venier swallowed; Miles swore he could hear the slight gurgle in his narrow neck. "Marry me. It would give you the legal protection you need to stay here. No one could force you back, then. I could support you, while you train up to your full strength, botany or chemistry or anything you choose. You could be so much. I can't tell you how it's turned my stomach, to see so much human potential wasted on that clown of a Barrayaran. I realize that for you it would have to start as a marriage of convenience, but as a Vor, that's surely not an alien idea for you. And it could grow to be more, in time, I'm certain it could. I know it's too soon, but soon you'll be gone and then it will be too late!"

Venier paused for breath. Miles bent over, mouth still open, in a sort of silent scream. *My lines! My lines! Those were all my lines, dammit!* He'd expected Vorish rivals for Ekaterin's hand to come pouring out of the woodwork as soon as the widow touched down in Vorbarr Sultana, but my God, she hadn't even got off Komarr yet! He hadn't thought of Venier, or any other Komarran, as possible competition. He wasn't competition, the idea of Vennie as competition was laughable. Miles had more power, position, money, rank, all to lay at her feet when the time was finally ripe—Venier wasn't even taller than Ekaterin, he was a good four centimeters shorter—

The one thing Miles couldn't offer, though, was less Barrayar. In that, Venier had an advantage Miles could never match.

There followed a long, terrifying silence, during which Miles's brain screamed, *Say no, say no! say NO!*

"That's very kindly offered," Ekaterin said at last.

What the hell is that supposed to mean? And was Venier wondering the same thing?

"Kindness has nothing to do with it. I—" Venier cleared his throat again "—admire you very much."

"Oh, dear."

He added eagerly, "I've applied for the administrative position as head of terraforming here. I think I have a good chance. Because of the disruption in the department, HQ is surely going to be looking for some continuity. Or if the mud has splattered on the innocent as well as the guilty, I'll do whatever I have to do to get another shot, a chance to clear my professional reputation—I can make Serifosa Sector a showcase, I know I can. If you stay, I can get you voting shares. We could do it together; we could make this place a garden. Stay here and help build a world!"

Another long, terrifying silence. Then Ekaterin said, "I suppose you'd be assigned this apartment, if you succeeded to Tien's position."

"It goes with it," said Venier in an uncertain voice. Right, that wasn't a selling point, though Miles wasn't sure if Venier knew it. *I can hardly bear being in this place*, she'd said.

"You offer is kind and generous, Venier. But you have mistaken my situation, somewhat. No one is forcing me to return home. Komarr . . . I'm afraid these domes give me claustrophobia, anymore. Every time I pull on a breath mask, I'm going to think about the ugly way Tien died."

"Ah," said Venier. "I can understand that, but perhaps, in time . . . ?"

"Oh, yes. Time. Vor custom calls for a widow to mourn for one year." Miles could not guess what gesture, what facial expression, went with these words. A grimace? A smile?

"Do you hold to that archaic custom? Must you? Why? I never understood it. I thought in the Time of Isolation they tried to keep all women married all the time."

"Actually, I think it was practical. It gave time to be certain any pregnancy that might have been started could be completed while the woman was still under the control of her late husband's family, so they could be sure of claiming custody of any male issue. But still, whether I believe in formal mourning or not won't matter. As long as people think I do, I can use it to defend myself from—from unwanted suits. I so much need a quiet time and place to find my balance again."

There was a short silence. Then Venier said, more stiffly, "Defend? I did not mean my proposal as an attack, Kat."

"Of course I don't think that," she replied faintly.

Lie, lie. Of course she bloody well did. Ekaterin had experienced marriage as one long siege of her soul. After ten years of Tien, she probably felt about matrimony the way Miles felt about needle-grenade launchers. This was very bad for Venier. Good. But it was equally bad for Miles. Bad. Good. Bad. Good. Bad . . .

"Kat, I . . . I won't make a pest of myself. But think about it, think about all your alternatives, before you do anything irrevocable. I'll still be here."

Another awful silence. Then, "I don't wish to give you pain, who never gave me any, but it's wrong to make people live on false hopes." A long, indrawn breath, as if she was mustering all her strength. "No."

Yes!

And then, added more weakly, "But thank you so much for caring about me."

Longer silence. Then Venier said, "I meant to help. I can see I've made it worse. I really must be going, I still have to pick up dinner on the way home . . ."

Yes, and eat it alone, you miserable rabbit! Ha!

"Madame Vorsoisson, good night."

"Let me see you to the door. Thank you again for bringing Tien's things. I do hope you get Tien's job, Venier, I'm sure you could do it well. It's time they started promoting Komarrans into the higher administrative positions again . . ."

Miles slowly unfroze, wondering how he was going to slip past her now. If she went on to check Nikki, as she might, he could nip into her workroom without her seeing him, and pretend he'd been there all the time—

Instead, he heard her steps return to the kitchen. A scrape and rattle, a sigh, then a louder rattle as the contents of a box were, apparently, dumped wholesale into the trash chute. A chair being pulled or pushed. He inched forward, to peek around the door port. She had sat again for a moment, her hands pressed against her eyes. Crying? Laughing? She rubbed her face, threw back her head, and stood, turning toward the balcony.

Miles hastily backed up, looked around, and sat in the nearest chair. He extended his legs and threw back his head artistically, and closed his eyes. Dare he try to fake a snore, or would that be overdoing it?

Her steps paused. Oh, God, what if she sealed the door, locking him out like a strayed cat? Would he have to bang on the glass, or stay out here all night? Would anyone miss him? Could he climb down and come back in the front door? The thought made him shudder. He wasn't due for another seizure, but you never knew, that was part of what made his disorder *so* much fun. . . .

Her steps continued. He let his mouth hang slack, then he sat up, blinking and snorting. She was staring at him in surprise, her elegant features thrown into strong relief by the half-light from the kitchen. "Oh! Madame Vorsoisson. I must have been more tired than I thought."

"Were you asleep?"

His *Yes* mutated to a weak "Mm," as he recalled his promise not to lie to her. He rubbed his neck. "I'd have been half-paralyzed in that position."

Her brows drew down quizzically, and she crossed her arms. "Lord Vorkosigan. I didn't think Imperial Auditors were supposed to prevaricate like that."

"What . . . badly?" He sat all the way up and sighed. "I'm sorry. I'd stepped out to contemplate the view, and I didn't think anything when I first heard Vennie enter, and then I thought it might be something to do with the case, and then it was too late to say anything without embarrassing us all. As bad as the business with your comconsole all over again, sorry. Accidents, both. I'm not like this, really."

She cocked her head, a weird quirky smile tilting her mouth. "What, insatiably curious and entirely free of social inhibitions? Yes, you are. It's not the ImpSec training. You're a natural. No wonder you did so well for them."

Was this a compliment or an insult? He couldn't quite tell. Good, bad, good-bad-good . . . ? He rose, smiled, abandoned the idea of asking her about the estate law session, bid her a polite good night, and fled in ignominy.

Chapter Seventeen

Ekaterin made an early start the following morning to meet her aunt inbound from Barrayar. The ferry from Komarr to the wormhole jump station broke orbit before noon Solstice time. Ekaterin settled into her private sleeper-cell aboard the ferry with a contented, guilty sigh.

It was just like Uncle Vorthys to have provided this comfort for her; he did nothing by halves. *No artificial shortages*, she could almost hear him enthusiastically booming, though he usually recited that slogan in reference to desserts. So what if she could stand in the middle of the cabinette and touch both walls. She was glad not to be rubbing shoulders with the crowds in the economy seats as she had done on her first passage, even if it was only an eight-hour flight from Komarr orbit to jump station dock. She had sat then between Tien and Nikki at the climax of a seven-day passage from Barrayar, and been hard-pressed to name which of them had been more tired, tense, and cranky, including herself.

If only she'd accepted Venier's proposal, she wouldn't be facing a repeat of that wearing journey, a point in his favor Vennie could not have guessed at. Just as well. She thought of his unexpected offer last night in her kitchen, and her lips twisted in remembered embarrassment, amusement, and an odd little flash of anger. How had Venier ever got the idea that she was available? In wariness of Tien's irrational jealousy, she'd thought she had tamped out any possible come-on signal from her manner long ago. Or did she really look so pitiful that even a modest soul like Vennie could imagine himself her rescuer? If so, that surely wasn't his fault. Neither Venier's nor Vorkosigan's enthusiastic plans for her future education and employment were distasteful to her, indeed, they matched her own aspirations, and yet . . . both somehow implied, *You can become a real person, but only if you play our game.*

Why can't I be real where I am?

Drat it, she was not going to let this churning mess of emotions spoil her precious slice of solitude. She dug her reader out of her carry-on, arranged the generous allotment of cushions, and stretched out on the bunk. At a moment like this, she could really wonder why solitary confinement was considered such a severe punishment. Why, no one could get *at* you. She wriggled her toes, luxuriating.

The guilt was for Nikki, left ruthlessly behind with one of his school friends, putatively so that he would miss no classes. If, as Ekaterin sometimes felt, she really did do nothing of value all day long, why did she have to inconvenience so many people to take over her duties when she left? Something didn't add up. Not that Madame Vortorren, whose husband was an aide to the Imperial Counsellor's Serifosa Deputy, hadn't seemed cordially willing to help out the new widow. Nor was adding Nikki to her household any great strain on its resources—she had four children of her own, whom she somehow managed to feed, clothe, and direct amidst a general chaos which never seemed to ruffle her air of benign absent-mindedness. Madame Vortorren's children had learned early to be self-reliant, and was that so bad? Nikki had been fended off in his plea to accompany Ekaterin with the reminder that the ferry pilots had strict rules against allowing passengers on the flight deck, and anyway, it wasn't even a jumpship. In reality, Ekaterin looked forward to a private time to talk frankly with her aunt about her late life with Tien without Nikki overhearing every word. Her pent-up thoughts felt like an over-filled reservoir, churning in her head with no release.

She could barely sense the acceleration as the ferry sped onward. She popped the book-disk the law counselor had recommended to her on estate and financial management into her viewer, and settled back. The counselor had confirmed Vorkosigan's shrewd guess about Tien's debts ending with his estate. She would be walking away after ten years with exactly nothing, empty-handed as she had come. Except for the value of the experience . . . she snorted. Upon reflection, she actually preferred to be beholden to Tien for nothing. Let all debts be canceled.

The management disk was dry stuff, but a disk on Escobaran water gardens waited as her reward when she was done with her homework. It was true she had no money to manage as yet. That too must change. Knowledge might not be power, but ignorance was definitely weakness, and so was poverty. Time and past time to stop assuming she was the child, and everyone else the grownups. *I've been down once. I'm never going down again.*

She finished one book and half the other, got in an exquisite uninterrupted two-hour nap, and waked and tidied herself by the time the ferry arrived and began maneuvering to dock. She repacked her overnight bag, hitched up its shoulder strap, and went off to watch through the lounge viewports as they approached the transfer station and the jump point it served.

This station had been built nearly a century ago, when fresh explorations of the wormhole had yielded up the rediscovery of Barrayar. The lost colony had been found at the end of a complex multijump route entirely different from the one through which it had originally been settled. The station had undergone modification and enlargement during the period of the Cetagandan invasion; Komarr had granted the ghem lords right of passage in exchange for massive trade concessions throughout the Cetagandan Empire and a slice of the projected profits of the conquest, a bargain it later came to regret. A quieter period had followed, till the Barrayarans, graduates of the harsh school of the failed Cetagandan occupation, had poured through in turn.

Under the new Barrayaran Imperial management, the station had grown again, into a far-flung and chaotic structure housing some five thousand resident employees, their families, and a fluctuating number of transients, and serving some hundreds of ships a week on the only route to and from cul-de-sac Barrayar. A new long docking bar was under construction, sticking out from the bristling structure. The Barrayaran military station was a bright dot in the distance, bracketing the invisible five-space jump point. Ekaterin could see half a dozen ships in flight between civilian station and jump point, maneuvering to or from dock, and a couple of local-space freighters chugging off with cargoes to transfer at one of the other wormhole jump points. Then the ferry itself slid into its docking bay, and the looming station occluded the view.

The tedious business of customs checks having been got through back in Komarr orbit before boarding, the ferry's passengers disembarked freely. Ekaterin checked her holocube map, very necessary in this fantastic maze of a place, and went off to assure a hostel room for the night for herself and her aunt, and to drop off her luggage there. The hostel room was small but quiet, and should do nicely to give poor Aunt Vorthys time to recover from her jump sickness before completing the last leg of her journey. Ekaterin wished she'd had such a luxury available on her own inbound passage. Realizing that the last thing the Professora would want to face immediately was a meal, Ekaterin prudently paused for a snack in an adjoining concourse cafe, then went off to wait her ship's docking in the disembarkation lounge nearest its assigned bay.

She selected a seat with a good view of the airseal doors, and faintly regretted not bringing her reader, in case of delays. But the station and its denizens were a fascinating distraction. Where were all these people going, and why? Most arresting to her eye were the obvious galactics, not-from-around-here in strange planetary garb; were they passing through for business, diplomacy, refuge, recreation? Ekaterin had seen two worlds, in her life; would she ever see more? Two, she reminded herself, was one more than most people ever got. *Don't be greedy.*

How many had Vorkosigan seen . . . ?

Her idle thoughts circled back to her own personal disaster, like a flood victim sorting through her ruined possessions after the waters have receded. Was the Old Vor ideal of marriage and family an intrinsic contradiction of a woman's soul, or was it just Tien who'd been the source of her shrinkage? It was not clear how to sort out the answer without multiple trials, and marriage was not an experiment she cared to repeat. Yet the Professora seemed to be proof of the possible. She had public achievement—she was a historian, teacher, scholar in four languages—she had three grown children, and a marriage heading for the half-century mark. Had she made secret compromises? She had a solid place in her profession—might she have had a place at the top? She had three children—might she have had six?

We are going to have a race, Madame Vorsoisson. Do you wish to run with your right leg chopped off, or your left leg chopped off?

I want to run on both legs.

Aunt Vorthys had run on both legs, reasonably serenely—Ekaterin had lived in her household, and didn't think she overidealized her aunt—but then, she'd been married to Uncle Vorthys. One's career might depend solely on one's own efforts, but marriage was a lottery, and you drew your lot in late adolescence or early adulthood at a point of maximum idiocy and confusion. Perhaps it was just as well. If people were too sensible, the human race might well come to an end. Evolution favored the maximum production of children, not of happiness.

So how did you end up with neither?

She snorted self-derision, then sat up as the doors slid open and people began trickling through. Most of the tide had passed when Ekaterin spotted the short woman with the wobbly step, assisted by a shipping line porter who saw her through the doors and handed her the leash of the float pallet holding her luggage. Ekaterin rose, smiling, and started forward. Her aunt looked thoroughly frazzled, her long gray hair escaping its windings atop her head to drift about her face, which had lost its usual attractive pink glow in favor of a greenish-gray tinge. Her blue bolero and calf-length skirt looked rumpled, and the matching embroidered travel boots were perched precariously atop the pile of luggage, replaced on her feet with what were obviously bedroom slippers.

Aunt Vorthys fell into Ekaterin's hug. "Oh! So good to see you."

Ekaterin held her out, to search her face. "Was the trip very bad?"

"Five jumps," said Aunt Vorthys hollowly. "And it was such a fast ship, there wasn't as much time to recover between. Be glad you're one of the lucky ones."

"I get a touch of nausea," Ekaterin consoled her, on the theory that misery might appreciate company. "It passes off in about half an hour. Nikki is the lucky one—it doesn't seem to affect him at all." Tien had concealed his symptoms in grouchiness. Afraid of showing something he construed as weakness? Should she have tried to . . . *It doesn't matter now. Let it go.* "I have a nice quiet hostel room waiting for you to lie down in. We can get tea there."

"Oh, lovely, dear."

"Here, why is your luggage riding and you walking?" Ekaterin rearranged the two bags on the float pallet and flipped up the little seat. "Sit down, and I'll tow you."

"If it's not too dizzy a ride. The jumps made my feet swell, of all things."

Ekaterin helped her aboard, made sure she felt secure, and started off at a slow walk. "I apologize for Uncle Vorthys dragging you all the way out here for me. I'm only planning to stay a few more weeks, you see."

"I'd meant to come anyway, if his case went on much longer. It doesn't seem to be going as quickly as he expected."

"No, well . . . no. I'll tell you all the horrible details when we get in." A public concourse was not the venue for discussing it all.

"Quite, dear. You look well, if rather Komarran."

Ekaterin glanced down at her dun vest and beige trousers. "I've found Komarran dress to be comfortable, not the least because it lets me blend in."

"Someday, I'd love to see you dress to stand out."

"Not today, though."

"No, probably not. Do you plan on traditional mourning garb, when you get home?

"Yes, I think it would be a very good idea. It might save . . . save dealing with a lot of things I don't want to deal with just now."

"I understand." Despite her jump sickness, Aunt Vorthys stared around with interest at the passing station, and began updating Ekaterin on the lives of her Vorthys cousins.

Her aunt had grandchildren, Ekaterin thought, yet still seemed late-middle-aged rather than old. In the Time of Isolation, a Barrayaran woman would have been old at forty-five, waiting for death—if she made it even that far. In the last century, women's life expectancies had doubled, and might even be headed toward the triple-portion taken for granted by such galactics as the Betans. Had Ekaterin's own mother's early death given her a false sense of time, and of timing? *I have two lives for my foremothers' one.* Two lives in which to accomplish her dual goals. If one could stretch them out, instead of piling them atop one another . . . And the arrival of the uterine replicator had changed everything, too, profoundly. Why had she wasted a decade trying to play the game by the old rules? Yet a decade at twenty did not seem quite a straight trade for a decade at ninety. She needed to think this through. . . .

Away from the docks and locks area, the crowds thinned to an occasional passer-by. The station did not run so much on a day-and-night rhythm, as on a ships in dock, everybody switch, load and unload like mad because time was money, ships-out, quiet falls again pattern which did not necessarily match the Solstice-standard time kept throughout Komarr local-space.

Ekaterin turned up a narrow utility corridor she'd discovered earlier which provided a shortcut to the food concourse and her hostel beyond. One of the kiosks baked traditional Barrayaran breads and cannily vented their ovens into the concourse, for advertising; Ekaterin could smell yeast and cardamom and hot brillberry syrup. The combination was redolent of Barrayaran Winterfair, and a wave of homesickness shook her.

Coming down the otherwise-unpeopled corridor toward them along with the aromas was a man, wearing stationer-style dock-worker coveralls. The commercial logo on his left breast read SOUTHPORT TRANSPORT LTD., done in tilted, speedy-looking letters with little lines shooting off. He carried two large bags crammed with meal-boxes. He stopped short and stared in shock, as did she. It was one of the engineers from Waste Heat Management—Arozzi was his name.

He recognized her at once, too, unfortunately. "Madame Vorsoisson!" And, more weakly, "Imagine meeting you here." He stared around with a frantic, trapped look. "Is the Administrator with you . . . ?"

Ekaterin was just mustering a plan for, *I'm sorry, I don't believe I know you?* followed by dancing around him blankly, walking away without looking back, turning the corner, and dashing madly for the nearest emergency call box. But Arozzi dropped his bags, dug a stunner out of his pocket, and fumbled it right way round before she'd made it any further than, "I'm sorry—"

"So am I," he said with evident sincerity, and fired.

Ekaterin's eyes opened on a cockeyed view of the corridor ceiling. Her whole body felt like pins and needles, and refused to obey her urgent summons to move. Her tongue felt like a wadded-up sock, stuffed in her mouth.

"Don't make me stun you," Arozzi was pleading with someone. "I will."

"I believe you," came Aunt Vorthys's breathless voice, from just behind Ekaterin's ear. Ekaterin realized she was now aboard the float pallet, half-sitting up against her aunt's chest, her legs hung limply over the rearranged luggage in front of her. The Professora's hand gripped her shoulder. Arozzi, after a desperate look around, set his meal-boxes in her lap, picked up the float pallet's lead, and started off down the corridor as fast as the whining, overburdened pallet would follow.

Help, thought Ekaterin. *I'm being kidnapped by a Komarran terrorist.* Her cry, as they turned down another corridor and passed a woman in a food service uniform, came out a low moan. The woman barely glanced at them. Not an unusual sight, this, two very jumpsick transients being towed to their connecting ship, or to a hostel, or maybe to the infirmary. Or the morgue . . . Heavy stun, Ekaterin had been given to understand, knocked people out for hours. This must be light stun. Was this a favor? She could not feel her limbs, but she could feel her heart beating, thudding heavily in her chest as adrenaline struggled uselessly with her unresponsive peripheral nervous system.

More turns, more drops, more levels. Was her map cube still in her pocket? They passed out of passenger-country, into more utilitarian levels devoted to freight and ship repair. At last they turned in at a door labeled SOUTHPORT TRANSPORT, LTD. in the same logo style as on the coveralls, and AUTHORIZED PERSONNEL ONLY in larger red print. Arozzi led them around a turn, through some more airseal doors, and down a ramp into a large loading bay. It smelled cold, all oil and ozone and a sharp sick scent of plastics. They were at the outermost skin of the station, anyway, whatever direction they'd come. She'd seen the Southport logo before, Ekaterin realized; it was one of those minor, shoestring-budgeted local-space shipping companies that eked out a living in the few interstices left by the big Komarran family firms.

A tall, squarely-built man, also in worker's coveralls, trod across the bay toward them, his footsteps echoing. It was Dr. Soudha. "Dinner at last," he began, then he caught sight of the float pallet. "What the hell . . . ? Roz, what is this? Madame Vorsoisson!" He stared at her in astonishment. She stared back at him in muzzy loathing.

"I ran smack into her when I was coming away from the food concourse," explained Arozzi, grounding the float pallet. "I couldn't help it. She recognized me. I couldn't let her run and report, so I stunned her and brought her here."

"Roz, you fool! The last thing we need right now is hostages! She's sure to be missed, and how soon?"

"I didn't have a choice!"

"Who's this other lady?" He gave the Professora a weirdly polite, harried, how-d'you-do nod.

"My name is Helen Vorthys," said the Professora.

"Not Lord Auditor Vorthys's wife—?"

"Yes." Her voice was cold and steady, but as sensation returned Ekaterin could feel the slight tremble in her body.

Soudha swore under his breath.

Ekaterin swallowed, ran her tongue around her mouth, and struggled to sit up. Arozzi rescued his boxes, then belatedly drew his stunner again. A woman, attracted by the raised voices, approached around a stack of equipment. Middle-aged, with frizzy gray-blond hair, she also wore Southport Transport coveralls. Ekaterin recognized Lena Foscol, the accountant.

"Ekaterin," husked Aunt Vorthys, "who are these people? Do you know them?"

Ekaterin said loudly, if a little thickly, "They're the criminals who stole a huge sum of money from the Terraforming Project and murdered Tien."

Foscol, startled, said "What? We did no such thing! He was alive when I left him!"

"Left him chained to a railing with an empty oxygen canister, which you never checked. And then called *me* to come get him. An hour and a half too late." Ekaterin spat scorn. "An exquisite setup. Madame. Mad Emperor Yuri would have considered it a work of art."

"Oh," Foscol breathed. She looked sick. "Is this true? You're lying. No one would go out-dome with an empty canister!"

"You knew Tien," said Ekaterin. "What do you think?"

Foscol fell silent.

Soudha was pale. "I'm sorry, Madame Vorsoisson. If that was what happened, it was an accident. We intended him to live, I swear to you."

Ekaterin let her lips thin, and said nothing. Sitting up, with her legs swung out to the deck, she was able to get a less dizzying view of the loading bay. It was some thirty meters across and twenty deep, strongly lit, with catwalks and looping power lines running across the ceiling, and a glass-walled control booth on the opposite side from the broad entry ramp down which they'd come. Equipment lay scattered here and there around a huge object dominating the center of the chamber. Its main part seemed to consist of a wriggly trumpet-shaped cone made of some dark, polished substance— metal? glass?—resting in heavily padded clamps on a grounded float cradle. A lot of power connections slotted in at its narrow end. The mouth of the bell was more than twice as tall as Ekaterin. Was this the "secret weapon" Lord Vorkosigan had posited?

And *how* had they ever got it, and themselves, past the ImpSec manhunt? ImpSec was surely checking every shuttle that left the planetary surface—now, Ekaterin realized. This thing could have been transported weeks ago, before the hunt even started. And ImpSec was probably concentrating its attention on jumpships and their passengers, not on freight tugs trapped in local space. Soudha's conspirators had had years to develop their false ID. They acted as though they owned this place—maybe they did.

Foscol spoke to Ekaterin's fraught silence, almost as tight-lipped as Ekaterin herself. "We are not murderers. Not like you Barrayarans."

"I've never killed anyone in my life. For not-murderers, your body count is getting impressive," Ekaterin shot back. "I don't know what happened to Radovas and Trogir, but what about the six poor people on the soletta crew, and that ore freighter pilot—and Tien. That's eight at least, maybe ten." *Maybe twelve, if I don't watch my step.*

"I was a student at Solstice University during the Revolt," Foscol snarled, clearly very rattled by the news about Tien. "I saw friends and classmates shot in the streets, during the riots. I remember the out-gassing of the Green Park Dome. Don't you dare—a Barrayaran!—sit there and make mouth at me about murder."

"I was five years old at the time of the Komarr Revolt," said Ekaterin wearily. "What do you think I ought to have done about it, eh?"

"If you want to go back in history," the Professora put in dryly, "you Komarrans were the people who let the Cetagandans in on us. Five million Barrayarans died before the first Komarran ever did. Crying for your past dead is a piece of one-downsmanship a Komarran cannot win."

"That was longer ago," said Foscol a little desperately.

"Ah. I see. So the difference between a criminal and a hero is the *order* in which their vile crimes are committed," said the Professora, in a voice dripping false cordiality. "And justice comes with a sell-by date. In that case, you'd better hurry. You wouldn't want your heroism to spoil."

Foscol drew herself up. "We aren't planning to kill anyone. All of us here saw the futility of *that* kind of heroics twenty-five years ago."

"Things don't seem to be running exactly according to plan, then, do they?" murmured Ekaterin, rubbing her face. It was becoming less numb. She wished she could say the same for her wits. "I notice you don't deny being thieves."

"Just getting some of our own back," glinted Foscol.

"The money poured into Komarran terraforming doesn't do Barrayar any direct good. You were stealing from your own grandchildren."

"What we took, we took to make an investment for Komarr that will pay back incalculable benefit to our future generations," Foscol returned.

Had Ekaterin's words stung her? Maybe. Soudha looked as though he was thinking furiously, eyeing the two Barrayaran women. *Keep them arguing*, Ekaterin thought. People couldn't argue and think at the same time, or at least, a lot of people she'd met seemed to have that trouble. If she could keep them talking while her body recovered a little more from the stun, she could . . . what? Her eye fell on a fire and emergency alarm at the base of the entry ramp, maybe ten steps away. Alarm, false alarm, the attention of irate authorities drawn to Southport Transport . . . Could Arozzi stun her again in less than ten steps? She leaned back against her aunt's legs, trying to look very limp, and let one hand curl around the Professora's ankle, as if for comfort. The novel device loomed silently and mysteriously in the center of the chamber.

"So what are you planning to do," Ekaterin said sarcastically, "shut down the wormhole jump and cut us off? Or are you going to make—" Her voice died as the shocked silence her words had created penetrated. She stared around at the three Komarrans, staring at her in horror. In a suddenly smaller voice she said, "You can't do that. Can you?"

There was a military maneuver for rendering a wormhole temporarily impassable, which involved sacrificing a ship—and its pilot—at a mid-jump node. But the disruption damped out in a short time. Wormholes opened and closed, yes, but they were astrographic features like stars, involving time scales and energies beyond the present human capacity to control. "You can't do that," Ekaterin said more firmly. "Whatever disruption you create, sooner or later it will become passable again, and then you'll be in twice as much trouble as before." Unless Soudha's conspiracy was just the tip of an iceberg, with some huge coordinated plan behind it for all of Komarr to rise against Barrayaran rule in a new Komarr Revolt. More war, more blood under glass—the domes of Komarr might give her claustrophobia, but the thought of her Komarran neighbors going down to destruction in yet another round of this endless struggle made her sick to her stomach. The revolt had done vile things to Barrayarans, too. If new hostilities were ignited and went on long enough, Nikki would come of an age to be sucked into them. . . . "You can't hold it closed. You can't hold out here. You have no defenses."

"We can, and we will," said Soudha firmly.

Foscol's brown eyes shone. "We're going to close the wormhole *permanently.* We'll get rid of Barrayar forever, without firing a shot. A completely bloodless revolution, and there will be nothing they can do about it."

"An engineer's revolution," said Soudha, and a ghost of a smile curved his lips.

Ekaterin's heart hammered, and the echoing loading bay seemed to tilt. She swallowed, and spoke with effort: "You're planning to shut the wormhole to Barrayar with the Butcher of Komarr and three-fourths of Barrayar's space-based military forces on *this side,* and you actually think you're going to get a *bloodless* revolution? And what about all the people on Sergyar? You are idiots!"

"The original plan," said Soudha tightly, "was to strike at the time of the Emperor's wedding, when the Butcher of Komarr and three-fourths of the space forces would have been safely in Barrayar orbit."

"Along with a lot of innocent galactic diplomats. And not a few Komarrans!"

"I cannot think of a better fate for all the top collaborators," said Foscol, "than to be locked in with their lovely Barrayaran friends. The Old Vor lords are always saying how much better they had it back in their Time of Isolation. We're just giving them their wish."

Ekaterin squeezed the Professora's ankle and climbed slowly to her feet. Upright, she swayed, wishing her unbalance really were artistic fakery to put the Komarrans off-guard. She spoke with deadly venom. "In the Time of Isolation, I would have been dead at forty. In the Time of Isolation, it would have been my job to cut my mutant infants' throats, while my female relatives watched. I guarantee at least half the population of Barrayar does not agree with the Old Vor lords, including most of the Old Vor ladies. And you would condemn us all to go back to that, and you dare to call it bloodless!"

"Then count yourself lucky you're on the Komarran side," said Soudha dryly. "Come on, folks, we have work to do, and less time than ever to do it. Starting from now, all sleep shifts are canceled. Lena, go wake up Cappell. And we have to figure out how to lock these ladies down safely out of the way for a while."

The Komarrans were no longer waiting for the Emperor's wedding to provide their ideal tactical moment, it appeared. *How close* were they to putting their device into action? Close enough, it appeared, that even the arrival of two unwanted hostages wasn't enough to divert them.

Aunt Vorthys was trying to sit up straighter; Arozzi's eye had returned to the boxes of cooling food at his feet. Now.

Ekaterin launched herself forward, barreling into Arozzi and dashing onward. Arozzi swung around after her, but was temporarily distracted by a blue boot, thrown with surprising accuracy if limited strength by Aunt Vorthys, which bounced off the side of his head. Soudha and Foscol both began sprinting after her, but Ekaterin made it to the alarm and yanked down the lever hard, hanging on it as Arozzi's wavering stun beam found her. It hurt more, this time. Her hands spasmed open, and she fell. The first beat of the klaxon smote her ears before the shock and blackness took her away again.

Ekaterin opened her eyes to see her aunt's face, sideways. She realized she was lying with her head on the Professora's lap. She blinked and tried to lick her lips. Her body was all pins and needles and deep aches. A wave of nausea wrenched her stomach, and she struggled to lean sideways. A couple of spasms did not result in vomiting, however, and after a muffled belch, she rolled back. "Are we rescued?" she mumbled. They did not look rescued to her. They appeared to be sitting on the floor of a tiny lavatory, chilly and hard.

"No," said the Professora in a tone of disgust. Her face was tense and pale, with red bruises showing in the soft skin of her face and neck. Her hair was half down, straggling over her brow. "They gagged me, and dragged us both over behind that thing. The station squad burst in all right, but Soudha made all sorts of fast-talk apologies. He claimed it was an accident when Arozzi stumbled into the wall, and agreed to pay some enormous fine or another for turning in false alarms. I tried to make a noise, but it didn't do any good. Then they locked us in here."

"Oh," said Ekaterin. "Drat." Oversocialized, maybe, but stronger words seemed just as inadequate.

"Just so, dear. It was a good try, though. For a moment, I thought it would work, and so did your Komarrans. They were very upset."

"It will make the next try harder."

"Very likely," agreed her aunt. "We must think carefully what it ought to be. I don't think we can count on a third chance. Brutality does not seem to come naturally to them, but they do act very stressed. I don't believe those are safe people, just now, for all that they know you. When do you think we will be missed?"

"Not very soon," said Ekaterin regretfully. "I sent a message to Uncle Vorthys when I first got in to the station hostel. He may not expect another till we fail to get off the ferry tomorrow night."

"Something will happen then," said the Professora. Her tone of quiet confidence was undercut when she added more faintly, "Surely."

Yes, but what will happen between now and then? "Yes," Ekaterin echoed. She stared around the locked lavatory. "Surely."

Chapter Eighteen

Professor Vorthys's requested experts were due to arrive at the Serifosa shuttleport at nearly the same early hour as Ekaterin departed for her connection with the jump station ferry, so Miles managed to invite himself along on what would otherwise have been a family farewell. Ekaterin did not discuss last night's visit from Venier with her uncle; Miles had no opportunity to urge her, *Don't accept any marriage proposals from strangers while you're out there.* The Professor loaded her with verbal messages for his wife, and got a good-bye hug. Miles stood with his hands shoved in his pockets, and nodded a cordial safe-journey to her.

What Miles thought of as the *Boffin Express*, a commercial morning flight from Solstice, landed a short time later. The five-space expert, Dr. Riva, turned out to be a thin, intense, olive-skinned woman of about fifty, with bright black eyes and a quick smile. A stout, sandy young man she had in tow whom Miles first pegged as an undergraduate student was revealed as a mathematics professor colleague, Dr. Yuell.

A high-powered ImpSec aircar waited to whisk them directly out to the Waste Heat experiment station. When they arrived, the Professor led them all upstairs to his nest, which seemed to have acquired more comconsoles, stacks of flimsies, and tables littered with machine parts overnight. To everyone's discomfort, but not to Miles's surprise, ImpSec Major D'Emorie took formal recorded oaths

267

of loyalty and secrecy from the two Komarran consultants. Miles thought the loyalty oath was redundant, since neither academic could have held their current posts without having taken one previously. As for the secrecy oath . . . Miles wondered if either of the Komarrans had noticed yet that they had no way of leaving the experiment station except by ImpSec transport.

The five of them all then sat down to a lecture conducted by Lord Auditor Vorthys, which seemed halfway between a military briefing and an academic seminar, with a tendency to drift toward the latter. Miles wasn't sure if D'Emorie was there as participant or observer, but then, Miles didn't have much to say either, except to confirm one or two points about the autopsies when he was cued by Vorthys. Miles wondered again whether he might be more useful elsewhere, such as out with the field agents; he could hardly be less useful here, he realized glumly as the mathematical references began flying over his head. *When you folks convert all that to the pretty colored shapes on the comconsole, show me the picture. I like my storybooks to have pictures in them.* Perhaps he ought to go back to school for two or three years himself, and brush up. He consoled himself with the reflection that it was seldom he found himself in company who made him feel this stupid. It was probably good for his soul.

"The power that's fed into the—I suppose we can call it the horn—of the Necklin field generator is pulsed, definitely pulsed," Vorthys told the Komarrans. "Highly directional, rapid, and adjustable—I almost want to say, tunable."

"That's so very odd," said Dr. Riva. "Jumpship rods have a steady power—in fact, keeping unwanted fluctuations out of the power is a major design concern. Let's try some simulations with the various hypotheses . . ."

Miles woke up, and bent closer, as the assorted theories began to take visible form as three-dimensional vector maps above the vid-plate. Professor Vorthys provided some limiting parameters based on the projected nature of the power supply. The boffins did indeed produce some pretty pictures, but except for aesthetic considerations involving color contrasts, Miles didn't see what was to choose among them.

"What happens if somebody stands in front of the directional five-space pulses from that thing?" he asked at last. "At various distances, say. Or runs an ore freighter in front of it."

"Not much," said Riva, staring at the whirls and lines with an intensity at least equal to Miles's. "I'm not sure it would be good for you on the cellular level to be that close to any power generator of this magnitude, but it is, after all, a *five-space* field pulse. Any three-space effects would be due to some defocus on the fringe, and doubtless take the energy form of gravitational waves. Artificial gravity is a five-space/three-space interface phenomenon, as is your military gravitic imploder lance."

D'Emorie twitched slightly, but trying to keep a five-space physicist from knowing about the principles of the imploder lance was an exercise in futility right up there with trying to keep weather secret from a farmer. The best the military could hope for was to keep the engineering details under wraps for a time.

"Could it be, I don't know . . . that we're looking at *half* the weapon?"

Riva shrugged, but looked interested rather than scornful, so Miles hoped it wasn't a stupid question. "Have you determined if it is meant to be a weapon at all?" she said.

"We've got some very dead people to account for," Miles pointed out.

"That, alas, does not necessarily require a weapon." Professor Vorthys sighed. "Carelessness, stupidity, haste, and ignorance are quite as powerfully destructive of forces as homicidal intent. Though I must confess a special distaste for intent. It seems so unnecessarily redundant. It's . . . *anti*-engineering."

Dr. Riva smiled.

"Now," said Vorthys, "what I want to know is what happens if you aim this device *at* a wormhole, or, possibly, activate it while jumping *through* a wormhole. One would in that case also have to take into account effects due to the Necklin field it was traveling inside."

"Hmm . . ." said Riva. She and the sandy-haired youth went into close math-gibberish-mode, punctuated by some reprogramming of the simulation console. The first colorful display was rejected by them both with the muttered comment, "*That's* not right. . . ." A couple more went by. Riva sat back at last, and ran her hands through her short curls. "Any chance of taking this home to sleep on overnight?"

"Ah," said Lord Auditor Vorthys. "I'm afraid I was unclear to you over the comconsole last night. This is something in the nature of a crash program, here. We have reason to suspect time could be of the essence. We're all here for the duration, till we figure this out. No data leave this building."

"What, no dinner at the Top of the Dome in Serifosa?" said Yuell, sounding disappointed.

"Not tonight," Vorthys apologized. "Unless someone gets really inspired. Food and bedding will be supplied by the Emperor."

Riva glanced around the room, and by implication the facility. "Is this going to be the ImpSec Budget Hostel again? Bedrolls and ready-meals?"

The Professor smiled wryly. "I'm afraid so."

"I should have remembered that part from the last time. . . . Well, it's motivation of a sort, I suppose. Yuell, that's enough of this comconsole for now. Something's not right. I need to pace."

"The corridor is at your disposal," Professor Vorthys told her cordially. "Did you bring your walking shoes?"

"Certainly. I did remember *that* from our last date." She stuck out her legs, displaying comfortable thick-soled shoes, and rose to go off to the hallway. She began walking rapidly up and down, murmuring to herself from time to time.

"Riva claims to think better while walking," Vorthys explained to Miles. "Her theory is that it pumps the blood up to her brain. My theory is that since no one can keep up with her, it cuts down on the distracting interruptions."

A kindred spirit, by God. "Can I watch?"

"Yes, but please don't talk to her. Unless she talks to you, of course."

Both Vorthys and Yuell returned to fooling with their comconsoles. The Professor appeared to be trying to refine his hypothetical design for the missing power-supply system for the novel device. Miles wasn't sure but what Yuell was playing some sort of mathematical vid game. Miles leaned back in his station chair, stared out the window, and addressed his imagination to the question, *If I were a Komarran conspirator with ImpSec on my tail and a novel device the size of a couple of elephants, where would I hide it?* Not in his luggage, for damn sure. He scratched out ideas on a flimsy, and drew rejecting lines through most of them. D'Emorie studied the Professor's work and reran some of the earlier simulations.

After about three-quarters of an hour, Miles became aware that the echo of soft rapid footsteps from the corridor had ceased. He rose, and went and poked his head out the door. Dr. Riva was seated on a window ledge at the end of the corridor, gazing pensively out over the Komarran landscape. It fell away toward the stream, here, and was much less bleak than the usual scene, being liberally colonized by Earth green. Miles ventured to approach her.

She looked up at him with her quick smile as he neared, which he returned. He hitched his hip over the low ledge, and followed her gaze out the sealed window, then turned to study her profile. "So," he said at last. "What are you thinking?"

Her lips twisted wryly. "I'm thinking . . . that I don't believe in perpetual motion."

"Ah." Well, if it had been easy, or even just moderately difficult, the Professor would not have called for reinforcements, Miles reflected. "Hm."

She turned her gaze from the scenery to him, and said after a moment, "So, you're really the son of the Butcher?"

"I'm the son of Aral Vorkosigan," he replied steadily. "Yes." Her version of the perpetual question was neither the accidental social blunder of Tien, nor the deliberate provocation of Venier. It seemed something more . . . scientific. What was she testing for?

"The private life of men of power isn't what we expect, sometimes."

He jerked up his chin. "People have some very odd illusions about power. Mostly it consists of finding a parade and nipping over to place yourself at the head of the band. Just as eloquence consists of persuading people of things they desperately want to believe. Demagoguery, I suppose, is eloquence sliding to some least moral energy level." He smiled bleakly at his boot. "Pushing people uphill is one hell of a lot harder. You can break your heart, trying that." Literally, but he saw no point in discussing the Butcher's medical history with her.

"I was given to understand that power politics had chewed you up."

Surely she could not see scars through his gray suit. "Oh," Miles shrugged, "the prenatal damage was just the prologue. The rest I did to myself."

"If you could go back in time and change things, would you?"

"Prevent the soltoxin attack on my pregnant mother? If I could only pick one event to change . . . maybe not."

"What, because you wouldn't want to risk missing an Auditorship at thirty?" Her tone was only faintly mocking, softened by her wry smile. What the devil had Vorthys told her about him, anyway? She was highly aware, though, of the power of an Emperor's Voice.

"I almost arrived at thirty in a coffin, a couple of times. An Auditorship was never an ambition of mine. That appointment was a caprice of Gregor's. I wanted to be an admiral. It's not that." He paused, and drew in breath, and let it out slowly. "I've made a lot of grievous mistakes in my life, getting here, but . . . I wouldn't trade my journey now. I'd be afraid of making myself smaller."

She cocked her head, measuring his dwarfishness, not missing his meaning. "That's as fair a definition of satisfaction as any I've ever heard."

He shrugged. "Or loss of nerve." Dammit, he'd come out here to pick *her* brain. "So what do you think of the novel device?"

She grimaced, and rubbed her hands slowly, palm to palm. "Unless you want to posit that it was invented for the purpose of giving headaches to physicists, I think . . . it's time to break for lunch."

Miles grinned. "Lunch, we can supply."

Lunch, as threatened, was indeed military-issue ready-meals, though of the highest grade. They all sat around one of the tables in the long room, pushed aside chunks of equipment to make space, and tore off the wrappers from the self-heating trays. The Komarrans eyed their food dubiously; Miles explained how it could have been much worse, getting a giggle from Riva. The conversation became general, touching on husbands and wives and children and tenure and an exchange of scurrilous anecdotes about the fecklessness of former colleagues. D'Emorie had a couple of good ones about early ImpSec cases. Miles was tempted to top them with a few about his cousin Ivan, but nobly refrained, though he did explain how he'd once sunk himself and his personal vehicle in several meters of arctic mud. This led to the subject of the progress of Komarran terraforming, and so by degrees back to work. Riva, Miles noticed, grew quieter and quieter.

She maintained her silence as they all took to the comconsoles again after lunch. She did not resume her pacing. Miles watched her covertly, then less covertly. She reran several simulations, but did not play with further alterations. Miles knew damn well one couldn't hurry insight. This kind of problem-solving was a lot more like fishing than like hunting: waiting patiently and, to a degree, helplessly, for things to rise up out of the depths of the mind.

He thought about the last time he'd been fishing.

He considered Riva's age. She'd been in her teens at the time of the Barrayaran conquest of Komarr. In her twenties at the time of the Revolt. She'd survived, she'd endured, she'd cooperated; her years under Imperial rule had been good, including an obviously successful life of the mind, and a single marriage. She'd compared children with Vorthys, and spoken of an eldest daughter's upcoming wedding. No Komarran terrorist, she.

If you could go back in time and change things . . .

The only moment in time you could change things was the elusive *now*, which slipped through your fingers as fast as you could think about it. He wondered if she was thinking about that right now, too. Now.

Now, the Professora's ship from Barrayar would be getting ready for its final wormhole jump. Now, Ekaterin's ferry would be approaching the jump-point station. Now, Soudha and his crew of earnest techs would be doing . . . what? Where? Now, he was sitting in a room on Komarr watching a quietly brilliant woman who had stopped thinking.

He rose, and went to touch Major D'Emorie on his green-uniformed shoulder. "Major, can I have a word with you outside."

Surprised, D'Emorie shut down his comconsole, where he'd been checking out some question about available power transformers Vorthys had put to him. He followed Miles into the hall and down the corridor.

"Major, do you have a fast-penta interrogation kit available?"

D'Emorie's brows rose. "I can check, my lord."

"Do so. Get one and bring it to me, please."

"Yes, my lord."

D'Emorie went off. Miles lingered by the window. It was twenty minutes before D'Emorie returned, but he had the familiar case in his hand.

Miles took it. "Thank you. Now I would like you to take Dr. Youell for a walk. Discreetly. I'll let you know when you can come back in."

"My lord . . . if it's a matter for fast-penta, I'm sure ImpSec would want me to observe."

"I know what ImpSec wants. You may be assured, I will tell them what they need to know, afterward." Turnabout, hah, for all those briefings with vital pieces missing Lieutenant Vorkosigan had once endured . . . life was good, sometimes. Miles smiled a little sourly; D'Emorie, intelligently, veered off.

"Yes, my Lord Auditor."

Miles stood aside for D'Emorie to exit with Dr. Youell. When he entered the long room, he locked the door after himself. Both Professor Vorthys and Dr. Riva looked up at him in puzzlement.

"What's that for?" Dr. Riva asked, as he set the case on the table and opened it.

"Dr. Riva, I request and require a somewhat franker conversation with you than the one we had earlier." He held up the hypospray and calibrated the dosage for her estimated body mass. Allergy check? He didn't think he needed it, but it was standard operating procedure; if he didn't have to guess, he didn't have to guess wrong. He tore off a test-dot from the coiled strip of them and walked over to her station chair. She was too startled to resist at first when he took her hand, turned it over, and pressed the tester to the inside of her wrist, but she jerked back her arm at the prickle. He let it go.

"Miles," said Professor Vorthys in an agitated voice, "what is this? You can't fast-penta . . . Dr. Riva is my invited guest!"

That wording was one step away from the sort of Vor challenge that used to result in duels, in the bad old days. Miles took a deep breath. "My Lord Auditor. Dr. Riva. I have made two serious errors of judgment on this case so far. If I'd avoided either of them, your nephew-in-law would still be alive, we'd have nailed Soudha before he got away with all his equipment, and we would not now all be sitting at the bottom of a deep tactical hole playing with jigsaw puzzles. They were both at heart the same error. The first day we toured the Terraforming Project, I did not insist on Tien landing the aircar here, though I wanted to see the place. And on the second night, I did not insist on a fast-penta interrogation of Madame Radovas, though I wanted to. You're the failure analyst, Professor; am I wrong?"

"No . . . But you could not have known, Miles!"

"Oh, but I could have known. That's the whole point. But I didn't choose to do what was necessary, because I did not want to appear to use or abuse my Auditorial power in an offensive way. Especially not on here on Komarr, where everyone is watching me, the son of the Butcher, to see what I'll do. Besides, I spent a career fighting the powers-that-be. Now I am them. Naturally, I was a little confused."

Riva's hand was to her mouth; there was no hive or red streak on the inside of her arm. Well and good. Miles returned to the table and picked up the hypospray.

"Lord Vorkosigan, I do not consent to this!" said Riva stiffly as he approached her.

"Dr. Riva, I did not ask you to." His left hand guarded his right as in knife-play; the hypospray darted in to touch her neck even as she turned and began to rise from her chair. "It would be too cruel a dilemma." She sank back, glaring at him. Angry, but not desperate; she was divided in her own mind, then, which had doubtless saved them both the embarrassment of him chasing her around the room. Even at her age and dignity she could probably outrun him if she were truly determined to do so.

"Miles," said the Professor dangerously, "it may be your Auditorial privilege, but you had better be able to justify this."

"Hardly a privilege. Only my duty." He stared into Riva's eyes as her pupils dilated and she sank back limply in her chair. He didn't bother with the standard opening litany of neutral questions while waiting for the drug to cut in, but merely watched her lips. Their thin tension slowly softened to the stereotypical fast-penta smile. Her eyes remained more focused than those of the usual subject; he bet she could make this a lengthy and circuitous interrogation, if she chose. He'd do his best to cut that circuit as short as possible. The shortest way across a hostile District was around three sides.

"This was a really interesting five-space problem that Professor Vorthys set you," Miles observed to her. "Sort of a privilege to be brought in on it."

"Oh, yes," she agreed cordially. She smiled, frowned, her hands twitched, then her smile settled in more securely.

"Could be prizes and academic preferment, when it's all sorted out at last."

"Oh, better than that," she assured him. "New physics only come along once in a lifetime, and usually you're too young or too old."

"Strange, I've heard military careerists make the same complaint. But won't Soudha get the credit?"

"I doubt it was Soudha who thought of it. I'd bet it was the mathematician, Cappell, or maybe poor Dr. Radovas. It should be named after Radovas. He died for it, I suspect."

"I don't want anybody else to die for it."

"Oh, no," she agreed earnestly.

"What did you say it was, again, Professor Riva?" Miles did his best to pitch his voice like a bewildered undergraduate's. "I didn't understand."

"The wormhole collapsing technique. There ought to be a better name for it. I wonder if your Dr. Soudha calls it something shorter."

Lord Auditor Vorthys, who'd been watching with slit-eyed disapproval, sat slowly upright, his eyes widening, his lips moving.

The last time Miles had felt his stomach behave like this, he'd been on a combat drop from low orbit. *Wormhole collapsing technique? Does this mean what I think it does?*

"Wormhole collapsing technique," he repeated blandly, in his best fast-penta interrogator style. "Wormholes collapse, but I didn't think anything people could do could cause them to. Wouldn't it take an awful lot of power?"

"They seem to have found a way around that. Resonance, five-space resonance. Amplitude augmentation, you see. Shut it down forever. Don't think it would work in reverse, though. Can't be anti-entropic."

Miles glanced at Vorthys. The words obviously meant something to *him*. Good.

Dr. Riva waved her hands dreamily in front of her. "Higher and higher and higher and—boop!" She giggled. It was a very fast-penta'ish sort of giggle, the disturbing sort which suggested that on some other level, in her drug-scrambled brain, she was not giggling at all. Maybe she was screaming. As Miles was. . . . "Except," she added, "that there's something very wrong somewhere."

No lie. He walked over and picked up they hypospray of antagonist, and glanced up at Vorthys. "Anything you want to add while she'd still under? Or is it time to go back to normal mode?"

Vorthys still had an abstracted, inward look, his mind obviously ratcheting over everything he'd learned during the investigation in light of this new, revolutionary idea. He glanced up and over at the goofily grinning Riva. "I think we need all our wits about us." His brows drew down in something like pain. "One sees, of course, why she hesitated to confide her theory to us. In case it *is* right . . ."

Miles walked over to Riva with the second hypospray. "This is the fast-penta antagonist. It will neutralize the drug in your system in less than a minute."

To his astonishment, she threw up a restraining hand. "Wait. I had it. I could almost see it, in my mind . . . like a vid projection . . . energy transfers, flowing . . . field reservoir . . . wait."

She closed her eyes and leaned her head back; her feet tapped gently and rhythmically on the floor. Her smile came and went, came and went. Her eyes popped open at last, and she stared briefly and intently at Vorthys. "The keyword," she intoned, "is *elastic recoil.* Remember it." She glanced at Miles and held out a languid arm. "You may proceed, my lord." She giggled again.

He applied the hypospray over the blue vein inside her proffered elbow; it hissed briefly. He gave her an odd little half-bow, and stepped back, and waited. Her loose limbs tightened; she buried her face in her hands.

After about a minute, she looked up again, blinking. "What did I just say?" she asked Vorthys.

"Elastic recoil," he repeated, watching her intently. "What does it mean?"

She was silent a moment, staring at her feet. "It means . . . I compromised myself for nothing." Her lips thinned bitterly. "Soudha's device doesn't work. Or at any rate, it doesn't work to collapse a wormhole." She sat up, and shook herself out, stretching, the sense of her body doubtless coming back to her as the last of the antagonist chased through her system. "I thought that stuff would make me sick."

"Reactions vary wildly from subject to subject," said Miles. Indeed, he'd never seen one quite like *that* before. "A woman we interrogated the other day said she found it very restful."

"It had the *strangest* effect on my internal visualizations." She stared at the hypospray with speculative respect. "I may try it on purpose someday."

I want to be there if you do. Miles had a sudden exciting vision of using the drug to augment his own insights—instant brains!—then remembered to his extreme disappointment that fast-penta didn't work like that on him.

Riva glanced at Miles. "If I ever get out of a Barrayaran prison. Am I under arrest now?"

Miles chewed his lip. "What for?"

"Isn't violating loyalty and security oaths treason?"

"You haven't violated any security oath. Yet. As for the other . . . when two Imperial Auditors say they didn't see something, it can become remarkably invisible."

Vorthys smiled suddenly.

"I thought you were sworn to tell the truth, Lord Auditor."

"Only to Gregor. What we tell the rest of the universe is negotiable. We just don't advertise the fact."

"That, alas, is true." Vorthys sighed.

"How will you explain the missing drug doses to ImpSec?"

"One, I am an Imperial Auditor, I don't have to explain anything to anyone. Least of all ImpSec. Two, we used it experimentally to enhance scientific insight. Which I gather is the truth, so I return to Go *and* collect my tokens."

Her lips twisted up in a genuine, if wryly baffled, smile. "I see. I think."

"In short, this never happened, you are not under arrest, and we have work to do. For my curiosity, though, before I call our junior colleagues back in—can you give me a quick synopsis of your chain of reasoning? In nonmathematical terms, please."

"It's only *in* nonmathematical terms so far. If I can't run some real numbers in under this—well, I'll just have to dismiss it as an interesting hallucination."

"You were convinced enough to dry up on us."

"I was stunned. Not so much convinced as breathless."

"With hope?"

"With . . . I don't quite know." She shook her head. "I may yet be proved wrong, and it wouldn't be the first time. But you are familiar, I assume, with examples of positive feedback loops in resonant phenomena—sound, for example?"

"Feedback squeals, yes."

"Or a pure note that breaks a wineglass. And in structures—you know why soldiers must break step when marching across a bridge? So that the resonance of their steps doesn't collapse the structure?"

Miles grinned. "I actually saw that happen once. It involved a squad of Imperial Junior Scouts, a flag ceremony, a wooden footbridge, and my cousin Ivan. Dumped twenty really obnoxious teenage boys into a creek." He added aside to the Professor, "They wouldn't let me march with my squad that evening because, they said, my height would mess up their symmetry. So I was watching from the back benches. It was glorious. I think I was about thirteen, but I'll treasure the memory forever."

"Did you see it coming, or did it take you by surprise?" asked the Professor curiously.

"I saw it coming, though not, I admit, very far in advance."

"Hm."

Riva's brows twitched; she licked her lips and began. "Wormholes resonate in five-space. Very slightly, and at a very high rate. I *believe* that the function of Soudha's device is to emit a five-space energy pulse precisely tuned to the natural frequency of a wormhole. The pulse's power is low, compared to the latent energies involved in the wormhole's structure, but if properly tuned it might—no, *would,* gradually build up the amplitude of the wormhole's resonance until it exceeded its phase boundaries and collapsed. Or rather, I think Soudha's group thought it must collapse. What I think actually happened is more complex."

"Elastic recoil?" Vorthys prodded hopefully.

"In a sense. What *I* think happened is that the pulse amplified the resonance energies until the phase boundaries recoiled, and the energy was abruptly returned to three-space in the form of a directed gravitational wave."

"Good God," said Miles. "Do you mean to say Soudha's found a way to turn an entire wormhole into a giant imploder lance?"

"Mmmm . . ." said Riva. "Er . . . maybe. What I don't know is if that was what he *meant* to do. The first theory made more political sense to me . . . as a Komarran. It quite seduced me. I wonder if they were seduced as well? If he *did* mean the wormhole to act as a sort of imploder lance, I don't see that he's found a way to aim it. I think the gravitational pulse was returned back along the initial path. I don't know if Radovas committed suicide, but I'm very much afraid he may have shot himself."

"My word," breathed Vorthys. "And the ore ship—"

"If their test platform was indeed aboard the soletta array, the involvement of the ore ship was sheer bad luck. Bad timing. It blundered into the gravitational pulse and was ripped apart, then was funneled toward and struck the soletta array and thoroughly confused the issue. If the device was aboard the ore ship—well, same result."

"Including the confusion," said Vorthys ruefully.

"But . . . but there's still something very wrong. You have presumably calculated most of the energy vectors involved in the soletta accident?

"Over and over."

"You trust the numbers you gave me?"

"Yes."

"And you've put limits on what energies the device can have transferred, over various lengths of time."

"There are some fairly strict and obvious engineering limits to its potential peak power output," agreed Vorthys. "What we don't know is how long they could run it."

"Well," the five-space physicist took a deep breath, "unless they were running it for weeks, and Radovas and Trogir were seen downside much later than that, I think you've got more energy out of the wormhole than went into it."

"From where?"

"Presumably from the wormhole's deep structure. *Somehow.* Unless you want to posit that Soudha has invented perpetual motion as well, which is against my religion."

Vorthys was looking wildly excited. "This is wonderful! Miles, call Youell. Call D'Emorie. We *must* check those numbers."

When D'Emorie returned with Youell, all the tech folk were too entranced with the breakthrough regarding the novel device to broach any embarrassing questions about where the fast-penta had gone. D'Emorie would doubtless think to ask later; Miles would be bland and uninformative, he decided. Riva clearly didn't want to waste time and mental energy on anger when there was physics to be had, but if she decided to be pissed at him later, he would grovel as needed. For now, Miles sat back, watched, and listened, feeling that he understood perhaps one sentence in three.

So did Soudha now imagine that he possessed a wormhole collapser—or a giant imploder lance? He had stolen much of the technical data from the accident investigation; he had a lot of the same numbers Vorthys did, and the same amount of time to look them over. While simultaneously managing a complex evacuation of some dozen persons and several tons of equipment, Miles reminded himself. Soudha had been rather busy. Of course, *he* hadn't had to waste time reconstructing the plans of his device from scattered specs.

But the gravitational backlash from the test wormhole near the soletta array must have surprised Radovas—however briefly—and Soudha. The accident had stopped their research, brought Auditors down upon them, compelled their flight. It made no sense, none, to posit the destruction of the soletta as deliberate sabotage and suicide. If one wanted to blow up Barrayarans, there were much more inviting targets around. Such as the military stations guarding each wormhole exit from Komarr local space. As an imploder lance variant, the device wasn't going to make a very useful military weapon till they figured out how to aim it at someone besides themselves. Though if one could set it up in secret aboard a military station, turn it on, and flee before the blast occurred . . .

Had Soudha figured out what had happened yet? He had data, yes, but his five-space man was dead. Arozzi was only a junior engineer, and Cappell the math man did not show any special brilliance in his academic record. Vorthys had been able to tap the top five-space expert on the planet, not to mention Youell the Wonderboy, who, Miles noted, was just at this moment arguing math with Vorthys and winning. Given the data and enough time, Radovas might have made the same conceptual breakthrough as Riva, but Soudha in his flight was not equipped to. Unless he'd found a replacement for Radovas . . . Miles made a note to tell ImpSec to check for the disappearance of any other Komarran five-space experts in the last weeks.

Soudha's flight, Miles decided, had to be following one of three logic branches. Either they had abandoned all and fled, or they'd withdrawn to hide, painfully rebuild their safe base, and try again another day. *Or* they had moved up their timetable and elected to risk all on an early strike of some kind. Miles wondered if they'd put what should have been a technically-driven decision to a vote. They were Komarrans, after all, and apparently volunteers. Amateur conspirators, not that it was exactly a licensed trade. Option One didn't feel right, given what Miles had seen so far. Option Two seemed more likely, but gave ImpSec time enough to do their job. The Komarrans might have thought so too.

If you're going to worry, worry about Option Three. There was a lot to worry about, in Option Three. Panicked and desperate people were capable of very strange moves indeed; look at some of the incidents in his own career.

"Professor Vorthys. Dr. Riva." Miles had to repeat himself, more loudly, before they looked up. "So you aim this device at a wormhole, and switch it on, and it starts pumping in energy. At some point, it builds up to a break-point and bounces back at you. What happens if you turn it off before that point?"

"I am not certain," said Riva, "that that wasn't exactly what happened. The backlash may have been triggered by either exceeding the phase boundaries, or by Radovas turning off the pulse source. It is unclear if the phase-boundary deaugmentation is discontinous or not."

"So . . . once activated, the device may become in effect its own dead-man switch? Turning it off sets it off?"

"I'm not sure. It would be a good point to test."

From a suitable distance. "Well . . . if you figure it out, please let me know, eh? Carry on."

After a moment to either digest his question, or wait to see if he'd pop out with any other interruption, the conversation around the table returned to its original polyglot of English, mathematics, and engineering. Miles settled back, feeling anything but reassured.

If Soudha had perfected his device with an eye to using the wormholes as power sources to blow up the military stations that guarded them, as a surprise opening for a shooting war . . . the way to do it would be to blow up all six at once, coordinated with a Komarr-wide uprising on the scale of the ill-fated Komarr Revolt. Miles was not totally pleased with ImpSec's performance in this case so far, but Soudha's had been a small group, running close to the ground. The signs of a massive revolt brewing must be too widespread for even ImpSec to miss. Besides, the chief conspirators were all of an age to have been through that once. Anyone who'd experienced the debacle of the Komarr Revolt on the Komarr side had reason to mistrust their fellows almost as much as they mistrusted Barrayarans. The last people Soudha would want in on his plot were a bunch more Komarrans. And . . . they didn't have six devices. They'd had five, the fourth was destroyed, and the three earlier ones seemed to have been smaller-scale prototypes.

It was like having a gun with one bullet in it. You'd want to pick your target very carefully.

Suppose Soudha still imagined he possessed a wormhole-collapser, albeit one with a few bugs in the design. There were six active wormholes in Komarr local space, but Miles hadn't any doubt which one Soudha would go for.

The sole jump to Barrayar. *Cut us off at one stroke, yeah*. From a Komarran viewpoint *that* was a plot worth all of these five years of devotion, all the sweat and risk: closing Barrayar's only gate to the galactic wormhole nexus. A bloodless revolution, by God, sure to appeal to these tech types. They'd return Komarr to the good old days of its glory a century ago— and Barrayar to its bad old days, in a new Time of Isolation. Whether everyone, or indeed, anyone on either Komarr or Barrayar wanted to go there or not. Did the conspirators imagine they'd be permitted to *live*, once the truth was unraveled?

Probably not. But if Riva spoke straight, the process was not reversible; the wormhole, once collapsed, could not be reopened. The deed would be done, and no tears or prayers would undo it. Like an assassination. Soudha and his friends might imagine themselves as a new and more effective generation of Martyrs, content to be enshrined after death. They had seemed too practical, but who knew? One could be hypnotized by the hard choices in ways that had nothing to do with one's intelligence.

Yes. Miles now knew where the Komarrans were going, if they weren't there already. The civilian—or the military? No, the civilian transfer station which served the wormhole jump to Barrayar.

You just sent Ekaterin there. She's there now.

So was the Professora, and so were several thousand other innocent people, he reminded himself. He fought panic, to follow out his thread of thought to the end. Soudha might have a bolt-hole of some kind set up on the station, prepared perhaps months or years in advance. He would plan to set up his novel device, aim it at the wormhole, draw power from—where? If from the station, someone might notice. If they mounted it aboard a ship, (and it had to have been on some kind of ship to get out there), they could draw ship's power. But traffic control and the Barrayaran military were unlikely to tolerate any ship hanging around the wormhole without a filed flight plan, from which it had better not deviate.

Ship, or station? He had insufficient data to decide. But if Soudha had not seriously modified his device, the plot which began with a bloodless plan to collapse the wormhole could end in the bloody chaos of a major disaster to the transfer station. Miles had seen space disasters on various scales. He didn't want to ever see another.

Miles could imagine a dozen different scenarios from the data they had in hand, but only this one gave him no time or room to be wrong. *Go.* He reached for the secured comconsole and punched up ImpSec Komarr HQ at Solstice.

"This is Lord Auditor Vorkosigan. Give me General Rathjens, immediately. It's an emergency."

Vorthys looked up from the long table. "What?"

"I've just figured out that if there's any action coming up, it's got to be at the transfer station by the Barrayar jump."

"But Miles—surely Soudha would not be so foolish as to try again, after his initial disaster!"

"I don't trust Soudha in any way. Have you heard from Ekaterin or your wife?"

"Yes, Ekaterin messaged when you were out getting your, ah, supplies. She'd reached her hostel safely and was off to meet the Professora."

"Did she leave a number?'

"Yes, it's on the comconsole—"

General Rathjen's face appeared above the vid-plate. "My Lord Auditor?"

"General. I have new data suggesting our escaped Komarrans are at or are heading for the Barrayar Transfer Station. I want a max-penetration ImpSec search-sweep for them on the station and aboard any in-bound traffic, to commence as quickly as possible. I want ImpSec courier transport for myself out to there as fast as you can scramble it. I'll give you the details once I'm en route. When all that's in motion, I want to send a tight-beam personal message to, um—" he did a quick search "—this number."

Rathjens's brows rose, but he said only, "Yes, my Lord Auditor. I'll be most interested in those details."

"Indeed you will. Thanks."

Rathjens's face vanished; in a few moments, the tight-beam link blinked its go-ahead.

"Ekaterin," Miles spoke rapidly and with all his will into the vid pickup, as if he might so speed the message. "Take the Professora and get yourselves aboard the first out-bound transport you can find, any local space destination—Komarr orbit, one of the other stations, anywhere. We'll arrange to pick you both up later and get you home right and tight. Just get yourselves off the station, and go at once."

He hesitated over his closing; no, this was not the time or place to declare, *I love you*, no matter what dangers he imagined threatening her. By the time this message arrived, she might well be back in her hostel room, with the Professora listening over her shoulder. "Be careful. Vorkosigan out."

As Miles rose to go, Vorthys said doubtfully, "Do you think I should go with you?"

"No. I think you all should stay here and figure out what the hell happens when somebody tries to turn that infernal device off. And when you do, please tight-beam me the instructions."

Vorthys nodded. Miles gave the lot of them an ImpSec analyst's salute, which was a vague wave of the hand in the vicinity of one's forehead, turned, and strode for the door.

Chapter Nineteen

Ekaterin watched morosely as the sonic toilet ate her shoes with scarcely a burp.

"It was worth a try, dear," said Aunt Vorthys, glancing at her expression.

"There are too many fail-safe systems on this space station," Ekaterin said. "This worked for *Nikki*, on the jumpship coming out here. What an uproar there was. The ship's steward was so upset with us."

"My grandchildren could make short work of this, I'll bet," agreed the Professora. "It's too bad we don't have a few nine-year-olds with us."

"Yes," sighed Ekaterin. *And no.* That Nikki was safely back on Komarr right now was a source of liberating joy in some secret level of her mind. But there ought to be some way to sabotage a sonic toilet that would light up a station tech's board and bring an investigation. How to turn a sonic toilet into a weapon was just not in Ekaterin's job training. *Vorkosigan* probably knew how, she reflected bitterly. Just like a man, to be underfoot in her life for days and then a quarter of a solar system away when she really needed him.

For the tenth time, she felt the walls, tried the door, inventoried their clothes. Practically the only flammable item in the room was the women's hair. Setting a fire in a room in which one was locked did not much recommend itself to Ekaterin's mind, though it was a possible last resort. She stuck her hands in the wall slot and turned them, letting the sonic cleaner loosen the dirt, and the UV light bathe away the germs, and the air fan, presumably, whisk their little corpses away. She drew her hands out again. The engineers might swear the system was more effective, but it never made her feel as fresh as an old-fashioned water wash. And how were you supposed to put a baby's bottom in the thing? She glowered at the sanitizer. "If we had any kind of a tool at all, we ought to be able to do *something* with this."

"I had my Vorfemme knife," said the Professora sadly. "It was my best enameled one."

"Had?"

"It was in my boot-sheath. The boot I threw, I believe."

"Oh."

"You don't carry yours, these days?"

"Not on Komarr. I was trying to be, I don't know, modern." Her lips twisted. "I do wonder about the cultural message in the Vorfemme knife. I mean, yes, it made you better armed than the peasants, but never as well-armed as the two-sword men. Were the Vor lords afraid of their wives getting the drop on them?"

"Remembering my grandmother, it's possible," said the Professora.

"Mm. And my Great-Aunt Vorvayne." Ekaterin sighed, and glanced worriedly at her present aunt.

The Professora was leaning on the wall with one hand supporting her, looking still very pale and shaky. "If you are done with the attempted sabotage, I think I would like to sit down again."

"Yes, of course. It was a stupid idea anyway."

The Professora sank gratefully onto the only seat in the tiny lavatory, and Ekaterin took her turn leaning on the wall. "I am so sorry I dragged you into this. If you hadn't been with me . . . One of us *must* get away."

"If you see a chance, Ekaterin, take it. Don't wait for me."

"That would still leave Soudha with a hostage."

"I don't think that's the most important issue, just now. Not if the Komarrans were telling the truth about what that great ugly thing out there does."

Ekaterin rubbed her toe over the smooth gray deck of the lav. In a quieter voice, she asked, "Do you suppose our own side would sacrifice us, if it came to a standoff?"

"For this? Yes," said the Professora. "Or at any rate . . . they certainly ought to. Do the Professor and Lord Auditor Vorkosigan and ImpSec *know* what the Komarrans have built?"

"No, not as of yesterday. That is, they knew Soudha had built something—I gather they had almost managed to reconstruct the plans."

"Then they *will* know," said the Professora firmly. And a little less firmly, "Eventually . . ."

"I hope they won't think we ought to sacrifice ourselves, like in the Tragedy of the Maiden of the Lake."

"She was actually sacrificed by her brother, as the tradition would have it," said the Professora. "I do wonder if it was quite so voluntary as he later claimed."

Ekaterin reflected dryly on the old Barrayaran legend. As the tale went, the town of Vorkosigan Surleau, on the Long Lake, had been besieged by the forces of Hazelbright. Loyal vassals of the absent Count, a Vor officer and his sister, had held out till the last. On the verge of the final assault, the Maiden of the Lake had offered up her pale throat to her brother's sword rather than fall to the ravages of the enemy troops. The very next morning, the siege was unexpectedly lifted by the subterfuge of her betrothed—one of their Auditor Vorkosigan's distant ancestors, come to think of it, the latterly famous General Count Selig of that name—who sent the enemy hurriedly marching away to meet the false rumor of another attack. But it was, of course, too late for the Maiden of the Lake. Much Barrayaran historical sympathy, in the form of plays and poems and songs, had been expended upon the subsequent grief of the two men; Ekaterin had memorized one of the shorter poems for a school recitation, in her childhood. "I've always wondered," said Ekaterin, "if the attack really had taken place the next day, and all the pillage and rape had proceeded on schedule, would they have said, 'Oh, that's all right, then'?"

"Probably," said Aunt Vorthys, her lips twitching.

After a time, Ekaterin remarked, "I want to go home. But I don't want to go back to Old Barrayar."

"No more do I, dear. It's wonderful and dramatic to read about. So nice to be able to read, don't you know."

"I know girls who pine for it. They like to play dress-up and pretend being Vor ladies of old, rescued from menace by romantic Vor youths. For some reason they never play *dying in childbirth*, or *vomiting your guts out from the red dysentery,* or *weaving till you go blind and crippled from arthritis and dye poisoning,* or *infanticide.* Well, they do die romantically of disease sometimes, but somehow it's always an illness that makes you interestingly pale and everyone sorry and doesn't involve losing bowel control."

"I've taught history for thirty years. One can't reach them all, though we try. Send them to my class, next time."

Ekaterin smiled grimly. "I'd love to."

Silence fell for a time, while Ekaterin stared at the opposite wall and her aunt leaned back with her eyes closed. Ekaterin watched her in growing worry. She glanced at the door, and said at last, "Do you suppose you could pretend to be much sicker than you really are?"

"Oh," said Aunt Vorthys, not opening her eyes, "that would not be at all difficult."

By which Ekaterin deduced that she was already pretending to be much less sick than she really was. The jump-nausea seemed to have hit her awfully hard, this time. Was that gray-faced fatigue really all due to travel-sickness? Stunner fire could be unexpectedly lethal for a weak heart—was there a reason besides bewilderment that her aunt had not tried to struggle or cry out under Arozzi's threats?

"So . . . how is your heart, these days?" Ekaterin asked diffidently.

Aunt Vorthys's eyes popped open. After a moment, she shrugged. "So-so, dear. I'm on the waiting list for a new one."

"I thought new organs were easy to grow, now."

"Yes, but surgical transplant teams are rather less so. My case isn't that urgent. After the problems a friend of mine had, I decided I'd rather wait for one of the more proven groups to have a slot available."

"I understand." Ekaterin hesitated. "I've been thinking. We can't do anything locked in here. If I can get anyone to come to the door, I thought we might try to feign you were dangerously sick, and get them to let us out. After that—who knows? It can't be worse than this. All you'd have to do is go limp and moan convincingly."

"I'm willing," said Aunt Vorthys.

"All right."

Ekaterin fell to pounding on the door as loudly as she could, and calling the Komarrans urgently by name. After about ten minutes of this, the lock clicked, the door slid back, and Madame Radovas peeked in from a slight distance. Arozzi stood behind her with his stunner in his hand.

"What?" she demanded.

"My aunt is ill," said Ekaterin. "She can't stop shivering, and her skin is getting clammy. I think she may be going into shock from the jump-sickness and her bad heart and all this stress. She has to have a warm place to lie down, and a hot drink, at least. Maybe a doctor."

"We can't get you a doctor right now." Madame Radovas peered worriedly past Ekaterin at the limp Professora. "We could arrange the other, I guess."

"Some of us wouldn't mind having the lav back," Arozzi muttered. "It's not so good, all of us having to parade up and down the corridor to the nearest public one."

"There's no other safe place to lock them up," said Madame Radovas to him.

"So, put them out in the middle of the room and keep an eye on them. Stick them back in here later. One's sick, the other has to take care of her, what can they do? It's no good if the old lady dies on us."

"I'll see what I can do," said Madame Radovas to Ekaterin, and closed the door again.

In a little while she came back, to escort the two Barrayaran women to a cot and a folding chair set up at the edge of the loading bay, as far as possible from any emergency alarm. Ekaterin and Madame Radovas supported the stumbling Professora to the cot, and helped her lie down, and covered her up. Leaving Arozzi to guard them, Madame Radovas went off and returned with a steaming mug of tea and set it down; Arozzi then turned the stunner over to her and returned to his work. Madame Radovas drew up another folding chair and sat down a few prudent meters away from her captives. Ekaterin supported her aunt's shoulders while she drank the tea, blinked gratefully, and sank back with a moan. Ekaterin made play of feeling the Professora's forehead, and rubbing her chill hands, and looking very concerned. She stroked the tousled gray hair, and stared covertly around the loading bay she'd merely glimpsed before.

The device still sat in its float cradle, but more power lines snaked across the floor to it now; Soudha was overseeing the attachment of one such cable to the awkward array of converters at the base of the horn. A man she did not recognize busied himself in the glass-walled control booth. At his gestures, Cappell drew careful chalk lines on the deck near the device. When he finished, he consulted with Soudha, and Soudha himself took the float cradle's remote control, stepped back, and with exquisite care set the cradle to lift, move forward till it almost touched the outer wall, and gently land again in precise alignment with the chalk marks. The horn was now aimed not quite square-on with the inner door of the large freight lock. Were they getting ready to load it aboard a ship, and take it out to point at the wormhole? Or could they use it right from here?

Ekaterin drew her map cube from her pocket. Madame Radovas sat up in alarm, aiming the stunner, saw what it was, and settled back uneasily, but did not move to take the map from her. Ekaterin checked the location of the Southport Transport docks and locks; the company had leased three loading bays in a line, and Ekaterin was not sure just which she was now in. The three-dimensional vid projection did not supply any exterior orientation, but she rather thought they were on the same side of the station as the wormhole, which might well put this lock in line-of-sight to it. *I don't think there's very much time left at all.*

In addition to the ramp by which she'd entered and the door to the lavatory, there appeared to be two other airsealed exits from the bay. One was clearly a personnel lock to the exterior, next to the freight lock. Another went back into a section which might be offices, if this was indeed the center bay of the three. Ekaterin mentally traced a route through it to the nearest public corridor. Several Komarrans had come and gone through that door; perhaps they were all camping back there. In any case, it seemed more heavily populated than the door she'd come in. But closer. The control booth was a dead end.

Ekaterin eyed her fellow-widow. Strange to think that their different domestic paths had brought them both to the same place in the end. Madame Radovas looked tired and worn. *This has been a nightmare for everyone.*

"How do you imagine you're going to get away, after this?" Ekaterin asked her curiously. *Will you take us along?* Surely the Komarrans would have to.

Madame Radovas's lips thinned. "We hadn't planned to. Till you two came along. I'm almost sorry. It was simpler before. Collapse the wormhole and die. Now it's all possibilities and distractions and worries again."

"Worries? Worse than expecting to die?"

"*I* left three children back on Komarr. If I were dead, ImpSec would have no reason to . . . bother them."

Hostages all round, indeed.

"Besides," said Madame Radovas, "I voted for it. I could do no less than my husband did."

"You took a *vote*? On what? And how do you divide up Komarran-style voting shares in a revolt? You had to have taken everyone along—if anyone who knew anything had been left to be questioned under fast-penta, it would have been all up."

"Soudha, Foscol, Cappell, and my husband were considered the primary shareholders. They decided I had inherited my husband's voting stock. The choices were simple enough—surrender, flee, or fight to the last. The count was three to one for this."

"Oh? Who voted against it?"

She hesitated. "Soudha."

"How *odd*," said Ekaterin, startled. "He's your chief engineer now—doesn't that worry you?"

"Soudha," said Madame Radovas tartly, "has no children. He wanted to wait and try again later, as though there would be a later. If we do not strike now, ImpSec will shortly hold all our relatives hostage. But if we close the wormhole and die, there will be no one left for ImpSec to threaten with their harm. My children will be safer, even if I never see them again." Her eyes were bleak and sincere.

"What about all the Barrayarans on Komarr and Sergyar who will never see their families again? Cut off, not ever knowing their fate . . ." *Mine, for instance.* "They'll be the same as dead, to each other. It will be the Time of Isolation all over again." She shivered in horror at the cascading images of shock and grief.

"So be glad you're on the good side of the wormhole," Madame Radovas snapped. At Ekaterin's cold stare, she relented a little. "It won't be like your old Time of Isolation at all. You have a fully developed planetary industrial base, now, and a much larger population, which has experienced a hundred-year-long inflow of new genes. There are plenty of other worlds which scarcely maintain any galactic contact, and they get along just fine."

The Professora's eyes slitted open. "I think you are underestimating the psychological impact."

"What you Barrayarans do to each other, afterwards, is not my responsibility," said Madame Radovas. "As long as you can never do it to *us* again."

"How . . . do you expect to die?" asked Ekaterin. "Take poison together? Walk out an airlock?" *And will you kill us first?*

"I expect you Barrayarans will take care of those details, when you figure out what happened," said Madame Radovas. "Foscol and Cappell think we will escape, afterwards, or that we might be permitted to surrender. *I* think it will be the Solstice Massacre all over again. We even have our very own Vorkosigan for it. I'm not afraid." She hesitated, as if contemplating her own brave words. "Or at any rate, I'm too tired to care anymore."

Ekaterin could understand *that*. Unwilling to murmur agreement with the Komarran woman, she fell silent, staring unseeing across the loading bay.

Dispassionately, she considered her own fear. Her heart beat, yes, and her stomach knotted, and her breath came a bit too fast. Yet these people did not frighten her, deep down, nearly as much as she thought they ought to.

Once upon a time, shortly after one of Tien's unfathomable uncomfortable jealous jags had subsided back to whatever fantasy world it came from, he'd earnestly assured her that he had thrown his nerve disruptor (illegally owned because he did not carry it in issuance from their District liege lord) from a bridge one night, and got rid of it. She hadn't even known he'd possessed it. These Komarrans were desperate, and dangerous in their desperation. But she had slept beside things that scared her more than Soudha and all his friends. *How strange I feel.*

There was a tale in Barrayaran folklore about a mutant who could not be killed, because he hid his heart in a box on a secret island far from his fortress. Naturally, the young Vor hero talked the secret out of the mutant's captive maiden, stole the heart, and the poor mutant came to the usual bad end. Maybe her fear failed to paralyze her because Nikki was her heart, and safe away, far from here. Or maybe it was because for the first time in her life, she owned herself whole.

A few meters away across the loading bay, Soudha crossed again to the novel device, aimed the remote at the float cradle, and adjusted its position fractionally. Cappell called some question from the other side of the bay, and Soudha set the remote down on the edge of the cradle and paced along one of the power cables, examining it closely, till he reached the wall slot Cappell was fussing over. They bent their heads together over some loose connection or other. Cappell yelled a question to the man in the glass booth, who shook his head, and went out to join them.

If I think about this, the chance will be gone. If I think about this, even my mutant's heart will fail me.

Had she the right to take this much risk upon herself? *That* was the real fear, yes, and it shook her to her core. This wasn't a task for her. This was a task for ImpSec, the police, the army, a Vor hero, anyone but her. *Who are not here.* But oh, if she tried and failed, she failed for all Barrayar, for all time. And who would take care of Nikki, if he lost both parents in the space of barely a week? The safe thing to do was to wait for competent grownup male people to rescue her.

Like Tien, yeah?

"Are you getting any warmer now, Aunt Vorthys?" Ekaterin asked. "Have you stopped shivering?" She rose, and bent over her aunt with her back to Madame Radovas, and pretended to tuck the blanket tighter, while actually loosening it. Madame Radovas was shorter than Ekaterin, and slighter, and twenty-five years older. *Now*, Ekaterin mouthed to the Professora.

Moving smoothly but not suddenly, she turned, paced toward Madame Radovas, and flung the blanket over the woman's head as she jumped to her feet. The chair banged over backward. Another two paces and she was able to wrap her arms around the smaller woman, pinning her arms to her side. The stunner's beam splashed, buzzing, on the deck at their feet, and the nimbus made Ekaterin's legs tingle. She lifted Madame Radovas off her feet and shook her. The stunner clattered to the deck, and Ekaterin kicked it toward her aunt, who was fighting to get upright on her cot. Ekaterin flung the blanket-muffled Komarran woman away from her as hard as she could, turned, and sprinted for the float cradle.

She snatched up the remote control and spun away toward the glass control booth as fast as her legs could push her, her sweating bare feet firm against the smooth surface. The men at the wall outlet shouted and started toward her. She didn't look back.

She galloped around the corner and up the two stairs to the booth in one leap. She batted frantically at the door control pad. The door took forever to slide shut; Cappell was almost to the steps before she was able, after two tries with her shaking fingers, to activate the lock. Cappell hit the door with a resounding thud and began pounding on it.

She did not, dared not, look back to see what was happening to the Professora. Instead, she raised the remote and pointed it through the glass at the float cradle. The controls included six buttons and a four-pronged knob. She'd never been good at this sort of coordination. Fortunately, subtlety was not her object now.

The third stab of her fingers on a button found the *up* vector. All too slowly, the float cradle began to rise off the loading bay deck. Perhaps there were some sort of sensors in it which kept it level; the first four combinations she tried seemed to do nothing. Finally, she was able to make the thing begin to rotate. It bumped into the catwalks above, making nasty grinding noises. Good. Power cables snapped off and whipped around; the strange man barely dodged the spitting sparks. Soudha was screaming, trying to jump up at the glass wall in front of her. She could barely hear him. The glass, after all, was supposed to stand up to vacuum. He scrambled back and aimed a stunner at her. The beam splashed harmlessly off the window.

At last, she was able to make the sensor program appear on the remote's little readout. She canceled its running instructions, and then the cradle became more lively. She'd achieved an almost 180-degree rotation, bottom to top. Then she turned the cradle's power off.

It was only about a four-meter drop from the catwalks to the deck. She had no idea what material the huge horn was fabricated from. She anticipated having to try a couple of times, to achieve some dent or crack Soudha could not repair in the day it would take for her and her aunt to be missed at the ferry. Instead, the bell burst like—like a flower pot.

The boom shook the bay. Shards big and small skittered off across the deck like shrapnel. One jagged piece whanged past centimeters from Soudha's head and smacked into the booth's glass, and Ekaterin ducked involuntarily. But the glass held. Amazing material. She was glad the device's horn hadn't been cast of it. Laughter bubbled out of her throat, bravura berserker joy. She wanted to destroy a *hundred* devices. She turned on the float cradle's power again and bounced the smashed remains on the deck a few more times, just because she could. *The Maiden of the Lake fires back!*

The Professora was sitting on the deck by the far wall, bent over. Not running away, not even close to making an escape. Not good. Madame Radovas was on her feet and had recovered her stunner.

Cappell the mathematician was beating on the control booth's door with a meter-long high-torque wrench he'd found somewhere. Arozzi, his face running with blood from a flying piece of horn-shrapnel, dissuaded him before he rendered it unopenable; Soudha came running up with a handful of electronic tools, and he and Arozzi disappeared below the door's window. Scratchy sounds penetrated by the door lock, more sinister even than Cappell's frantic blows.

Ekaterin caught her breath and looked around the control booth. She couldn't empty the air from the loading bay, her aunt was out there, too. There, there was the comconsole. Should she have gone for it first? No, she was doing this in the right order. No matter how screwed up ImpSec's response was, no matter how misapplied or incompetent their tactics, they could not possibly lose Barrayar now.

"Hello, Emergency?" Ekaterin panted as the vid-plate activated. "My name is Ekaterin Vorsoisson—" She had to stop, as the automated system tried to route her to her choice of traveler's aids. She rejected Lost & Found, selected Security, and started over, not certain she'd reached a human yet, and praying it would all be recorded. "My name is Ekaterin Vorsoisson. Lord Auditor Vorthys is my uncle. I'm being held prisoner, along with my aunt, by Komarran terrorists at the Southport Transport docks and locks. I'm in a loading bay control booth right now, but they're getting the door open." She glanced over her shoulder. Soudha had defeated the lock; the airseal door, bent from Cappell's efforts with the wrench, whined and refused to retreat into its slot. Soudha and Arozzi put their shoulders to it, grunting, and it inched open. "Tell Lord Auditor Vorkosigan—tell ImpSec—"

Then the swearing Soudha slipped sideways through the door, followed by Cappell still clutching his wrench. Laughing hysterically, tears running down her cheeks, Ekaterin turned to face her fate.

Chapter Twenty

Miles barely restrained himself from pressing his face to his courier ship's airlock window, while waiting for the tube seals from the jump station to finish seating themselves. When the door hissed open at last he swung himself through in one motion, to land on his feet with a thump, and glare around the hatch corridor. His reception committee at the private lock, the ranking ImpSec man aboard and a fellow in blue-and-orange civilian security garb, both braced to attention after only the briefest beat of surprise at his height—he could tell by the way their eyes had to track downward to meet his face—and appearance.

"Lord Auditor Vorkosigan," the strained-looking ImpSec man, Vorgier, acknowledged Miles. "This is Group-Commander Husavi, who heads Station Security."

"Captain Vorgier. Commander Husavi. Are there any new developments in the situation in the last," he glanced at his chrono, "fifteen minutes?" Almost a full three hours had passed since the first message from Vorgier had turned his journey from Komarr orbit into this viscous nightmare of suppressed panic. Never had an ImpSec courier ship seemed to move so slowly, and since no amount of Auditorial screaming at the crew could change the laws of physics, Miles had perforce seethed in silence.

"My men, backed by those of Commander Husavi, are almost into position for our assault," Vorgier assured him. "We believe we can get an emergency tube seal into place over the outer door of the airlock containing the Vor women before, or almost before, the Komarrans can evacuate the air. The moment the hostages are retrieved, our armored men can enter the Southport bay at will. It will be over in minutes."

"Too bloody likely," snapped Miles. "Several engineers have had several hours to prepare for you. These Komarrans may be desperate, but I guarantee they are not stupid. If I can think of putting a pressure-sensitive explosive in the airlock, so can they."

What a set of mental images Vorgier's words conjured—a tube seal misapplied or applied too late to the outer skin of the station, Ekaterin's and the Professora's bodies blown outward into space— some space-armored ImpSec goon missing his catch—Miles could almost hear his embarrassed, bass *Oops* over the audio link now, in his mind's ear. Such a blessing that Vorgier hadn't confided these details earlier, when Miles would have had all those hours en route to reflect upon them, stuck aboard his courier ship. "The Vor ladies are not expendable. Madame Dr. Vorthys has a weak heart, her husband Lord Auditor Vorthys tells me. And Madame Vorsoisson is—just not expendable. And the Komarrans are the least expendable of all. We want them alive for questioning. Sorry, Captain, but I mislike your plan."

Vorgier stiffened. "My Lord Auditor. I appreciate your concern, but I believe this will be most quickly and effectively concluded as a military operation. Civilian authority can help best by staying out of the way and letting the professionals do their job."

The ImpSec deck had dealt him two men in a row of exceptional competence, Tuomonen and Gibbs; why, oh why, couldn't good things come in threes? They were supposed to, dammit. "This is *my* operation, Captain, and I will answer personally to the Emperor for every detail of it. I spent the last ten years as an ImpSec galactic agent and I've dealt with more damned *situations* than anyone else on Simon Illyan's roster and I know just *exactly* how fucked-up a *professional* operation can get." He tapped his chest. "So climb down off your Vor horse and brief me properly."

Vorgier looked considerably taken aback; Husavi tamped out a smile, which told Miles all too much about how things had been going here. To Vorgier's credit, he recovered almost instantly, and said, "Come this way, my Lord Auditor, to the operations center. I'll show you the details, and you can judge for yourself."

Better. They started off down the corridor, almost quickly enough for Miles's taste. "Has there been any change or increase in power-draw into the Southport Transport area?"

"Not yet," Husavi answered. "As you ordered, my engineers shut down their lines to just that necessary to run their life support. I don't know how much power the Komarrans are able to tap from the local system freighter they have docked there. Soudha has said if we try to capture or remove the ship, they'll open the airlock on the Vor ladies, so we've waited. Our remote sensors don't indicate any unusual readings from there yet."

"Good." Baffling, but good. Miles could not imagine why the Komarrans hadn't switched on their wormhole-collapsing device yet, in a last-ditch effort to accomplish their long-sought goal. Had Soudha figured out its inherent defect? Corrected it, or tried to? Was it not quite ready yet, and the Komarrans even now frantically preparing it? In any case, once it was powered up they were all in deep-deep, because the Professor and Riva had concluded, with some pretty unreassuring hand-waving, something like a fifty percent probability of an immediate gravitational back-blow from the wormhole the moment it was switched off, ripping the station apart. When Miles had inquired what the technical difference was between *a fifty-fifty chance* and *we don't know,* he hadn't got a straight answer from them. Further theoretical refinements had come to an abrupt halt, when the news had come through about the stand-off here; the Professor was on his way now to the jump point, just a few hours behind Miles.

They turned a corner and entered a lift-tube. Miles asked, "What's the current status of the station evacuation?"

Husavi replied, "We've waved off all incoming ships that could be diverted. A couple had to dock in order to refuel, or they couldn't have made it to an alternate station." He waited till they'd exited into another corridor before continuing. "We've managed to remove most of the transient passengers and about five hundred of our nonessential personnel so far."

"What story are you giving them?"

"We're telling them it's a bomb scare."

"Excellent." *And effectively true.*

"Most are cooperating. Some aren't."

"Hm."

"But there's a serious problem with transportation. There are simply not enough ships in range to remove everyone in less than ten hours."

"If the power-draw to the Southport bay spikes suddenly, you'll have to start shuttling people over to the military station." Though Miles was by no means sure the gravitational event, if it occurred, wouldn't suck in and damage or destroy the military station as well. "They'll have to help out."

"Captain Vorgier and I discussed this possibility with the military commander, my lord. He wasn't happy with the prospect of a sudden influx of, um, randomly selected, uncleared persons onto his station."

Miles bet not. "I'll speak with him." He sighed.

Vorgier's "operations center" turned out to be the local ImpSec offices; the central communications chamber did indeed bear a passing resemblance to a warship's tactics room, Miles had to allow. Vorgier called up a holovid display of the Southport docks and locks area, one with rather better technical detail than the one Miles had spent the last hour studying. He ran over the expected placement of his men and the projected timing and technique of his assault. It wasn't a bad plan, as assaults went. In his youth, out on covert ops, Miles had come up with things just as bravura and idiotic on equally short notice. All right . . . more idiotic, he admitted ruefully to himself. *Someday, Miles*, his boss ImpSec Chief Simon Illyan had once said to him, *I hope you live to have a dozen subordinates just like you*. Miles hadn't realized till now that had been a formal curse on Illyan's part.

Vorgier's sales pitch kept fading out in Miles's mind, displaced by an instant-replay of the recording of the last message from Ekaterin, which Vorgier had thoughtfully supplied Miles by tight-beam. He'd memorized every nuance of it in the last three hours. *I'm in a loading bay control booth—they're getting the door open--* She hadn't said anything about the novel device. Unless some report had been going to follow the *Tell Lord Vorkosigan—tell ImpSec*—part, which had been so rudely interrupted by the red-faced Soudha's paw abruptly descending on the comconsole control. Nothing could be seen in the fuzzy background, however computer-enhanced, but the dull control booth. And the mathematician, Cappell, gripping a wrench he looked ready to use for something other than tightening bolts, but evidently hadn't; ImpSec had received vids via the loading bay airlock's safety channel of both women being bundled alive into it, before Soudha had cut off the signal feed. Those brief images too burned in Miles's brain.

"All right, Captain Vorgier," Miles interrupted. "Hold your plan as a possible last resort."

"To be implemented under what circumstances, my Lord Auditor?"

Over my dead body, Miles did not reply. Vorgier might not understand it wasn't a joke. "Before we start blowing walls down, I want to try to negotiate with Soudha and his friends."

"These are Komarran terrorists. Madmen—you can't negotiate with them!"

The late Baron Ryoval had been a madman. The late Ser Galen had been a madman, without question. And the late General Metzov hadn't exactly been rowing with both oars in the water, either, come to think of it. Miles had to admit, there had been a definite negative trend to all those negotiations. "I'm not without experience in the problem, Vorgier. But I don't think Dr. Soudha is a madman. He's not even a mad scientist. He's merely a very upset engineer. These Komarrans may in fact be the most sensible revolutionaries I've ever met."

He stood a moment, staring unseeing at Vorgier's colorful, ominous tactical display, the logistics of the station evacuation warring in his head with guesses about the Komarrans' state of mind. Delusion, political passion, personality, judgment . . . visions of Ekaterin's terror and despair spun in his back-brain. If so spacious a containment as a Komarran dome gave her claustrophobia . . . *stop it*. He pictured a thick sheet of glass sliding down between him and that personal maelstrom of anxiety. If his authority here was absolute, so was his obligation to keep his thinking clear.

"Every hour buys lives. We'll play for time. Get me a channel to the military station's commander," Miles ordered. "After that, we'll see whether Soudha will answer his comconsole."

The deliberately blank chamber in which Miles sat might as easily have been on the nearby military station, or a ship lying several thousand kilometers off-station, as the few hundred meters from the Southport bay it actually was. Soudha's location, when his face formed at last over the vid-plate, was not so anonymous; he sat in the same glass-walled control booth from which Ekaterin had sent her alarm. Miles wondered what techs were monitoring the corridors for moves on ImpSec's part, and who was keeping a nervous finger on the personnel airlock's outer door control. Had they arranged it as a dead-man's switch?

Soudha's face was drawn and sincerely weary, no more the bland bluff liar. Lena Foscol sat tensely to the right of his station chair on a rolling stool, looking like some frumpy vizier. Madame Radovas too looked on, her face half-shadowed behind him, and Cappell stood off to the side, almost out of focus. Good. A Komarran stockholders' voting quorum, if he read the signs right. At least they honored his Imperial Auditor's authority to that extent.

"Good evening, Dr. Soudha," Miles began.

"You're out here?" Soudha's brows rose as he took in the lack of transmission lag.

"Yes, well, unlike Administrator Vorsoisson, I got out of my chains at the experiment station alive. I still don't know if you intended me to survive."

"He didn't really die, did he?" Foscol interrupted.

"Oh, yes." Miles made his voice deliberately soft. "I got to watch, just as you arranged. Every filthy minute of it. It was a remarkably ugly death."

She fell silent; Soudha said, "This is all beside the point now. The only message we want to receive from you people is that you have the jumpship ready to transport us to the nearest neutral space—Pol, or Escobar—whereupon you will get your Vor ladies back. If it's not that, I'm cutting this com."

"I have a few pieces of free information for you, first," said Miles. "I don't think they're ones you anticipate."

Soudha's hand hovered. "Go on."

"I'm afraid your wormhole-collapser no longer qualifies as a secret weapon. We caught up with your specs on file at Bollen Design. Professor Vorthys invited Dr. Riva, of Solstice University, in to consult. Are you aware of her reputation?"

Soudha nodded warily; Cappell's eyes widened. Madame Radovas stared wearily. Foscol looked deeply suspicious.

"Well, putting together your specs, the data from the soletta accident, and Riva's physics—there was a mathematician by the name of Dr. Youell in there too, if the name means anything to you—the Empire's top failure analyst and the Empire's top five-space expert have concluded that you did not, in fact, manage to invent a wormhole-collapser. What you managed to invent was a wormhole-boomerang. Riva says that when the five-space waves amplified the wormhole's resonance past its phase boundaries, instead of collapsing, the wormhole returned the energy to three-space in the form of a gravitational pulse. Tangling with this pulse was what destroyed the soletta array and the ore ship, and—I'm sorry, Madame Radovas—killed Dr. Radovas and Marie Trogir. The probable-cause crew finally found her body a few hours ago, I regret to report, wrapped up in some of the wreckage they'd retrieved almost a week back."

Only a puff of breath from Cappell marked his grief, but water glittered in his eyes. *Check*, thought Miles. *I thought he'd protested too much*. Nobody looked surprised, merely oppressed.

"So if you succeed in getting your thing working, what you will actually do is destroy this station, the five thousand or so people aboard, and yourselves. And tomorrow morning, Barrayar will still be there." Miles let his voice fall to a near whisper. "All for nothing, and less than nothing."

"He lies," said Foscol fiercely into the shocked silence. "He lies."

Soudha gave a weird snort, ran his hands through his hair, and shook his head. Then, to Miles's dismay, he laughed out loud.

Cappell stared at his colleague. "Do you really think that's why? That it malfunctioned like that?"

"It would explain," began Soudha. "It would explain . . . oh, God." He trailed off. "I thought it was the ore ship," he said at last. "Interfering somehow."

"I should also mention," Miles put in, still uneasily watching Soudha's odd reaction, "that ImpSec has arrested all the Waste Heat personnel and their families you left back at the Southport Transport facility at Solstice. And then there are all your other relatives and friends, the innocents who knew nothing. The hostage game is a bad game, a sad and ugly game that's a lot easier to start than end. The worst versions I've seen ended up with neither side in control, or getting anything they wanted. And the people who stand to lose the most in it frequently aren't even playing."

"Barrayaran threats." Foscol lifted her chin. "Do you think, after all this, we can't stand up to you?"

"I'm sure you can, but for what reason? There aren't too many prizes left in this mess. The biggest one is gone; you can't shut off Barrayar. You can't keep your secret or shield anyone you left behind on Komarr. About the only thing you can do now is kill more innocent people. Great goals can call for great sacrifices, yes, but your possible rewards are steadily shrinking." Yes, that was it; don't raise the pressure, lower the wall.

"We did not," husked Cappell, rubbing his eyes with the back of his hand, "go through all this just to deliver the weapon of the century straight into Barrayaran hands."

"It's already there. As a weapon, it appears to have some fundamental defects, so far. But Riva says there's evidence you got more power out of the wormhole than you put into it. This suggests possible future peaceful, economic uses, when the phenomena are better understood."

"Really?" said Soudha, sitting up. "How did she figure? What are her numbers?"

"Soudha!" said Foscol reprovingly. Madame Radovas winced, and Soudha subsided, albeit reluctantly, staring at Miles through narrowed eyes.

"On the other hand," Miles continued, "until further research assures us that collapsing a wormhole is indeed quite impossible, none of you are going anywhere, and especially not to any other planetary government. It's one of those ugly military decisions, y'know? And I'm afraid it's mine." *The Vor ladies are not expendable,* he'd told Vorgier. Was he lying then, or now? Well, if he couldn't figure it out, maybe the Komarrans wouldn't either.

"You are all headed, inexorably, for a Barrayaran prison," he went on. "The devil's bargain part about being Vor, which a lot of people including some Vor overlook, is that our lives are made for sacrifice. There is no threat, no torture, no slow murder you can apply to two Barrayaran women that will change your outcome."

Was this the right tack? Above the vid-plate their listening images were undersized, a little ghostly, hard to read. Miles wished he were having this conversation face-to-face. Half the subliminal clues, of body language, of the subtle nuances of expression and voice, were washed out in transmission and unavailable to his instincts. But handing himself over to them in person to augment their hostage collection could only have served to stiffen their wavering resolve. The memory of a woman's hand, slipping through his fingers into a screaming fog, flickered through his mind; his fists clenched helplessly in his lap. *Never again, you said. Not expendable, you said.* He watched the Komarrans' faces intently for all flickers of expression he could get, reflections of truth, lies, belief, suspicion, trust.

"There are advantages to prisons," he went on persuasively. "Some of them are comfortably furnished, and unlike graves, sometimes, eventually, you can get out of them again. Now, I am willing, in exchange for your peaceful surrender and cooperation, to personally guarantee your lives. Not, note, your freedom—that will have to wait. But time passes, old crises are succeeded by new ones, people change their minds. Live ones do, anyway. There are always those amnesties, in celebration of this or that public event—the birth of an Imperial heir, for instance. I doubt any of you will be forced to spend as much as a full decade in prison."

"Some offer," said Foscol bitterly.

Miles let his brows rise. "It's an honest one. You have a better hope of amnesty than Tien Vorsoisson does. That ore freighter pilot will enjoy no visits from her children. I reviewed her autopsy, did I mention? All the autopsies. If I have a moral qualm, it's that I'm bargaining away the rights of the dead soletta-keepers' families to any justice for their slain. There ought to be civil trials for manslaughter over this."

Even Foscol looked away at these words.

Good. Go on. The more time he burned, the better, and they were tracking his arguments; as long as he could keep Soudha from cutting the com, he was making some twisty sort of progress. "You bitch endlessly about Barrayaran tyranny, but somehow I don't think you folks took a vote of all Komarran planetary shareholders, before you attempted to seal—or steal—their future. And if you could have, I don't think you would have dared. Twenty years ago, even fifteen years ago, maybe you could have counted on majority support. By ten years ago, it was already too late. Would your fellows really want to close off their nearest market now, and lose all that trade? Lose all their relatives who've moved to Barrayar, and their half-Barrayaran grandchildren? Your trade fleets have found their Barrayaran military escorts bloody useful often enough. Who are the true tyrants here—the blundering Barrayarans who seek, however awkwardly, to include Komarr in their future, or the Komarran intellectual elitists who seek to exclude all but themselves from it?" He took a deep breath to control the unexpected anger which had boiled up with his words, aware he was teetering on the edge with these people. *Watch it, watch it.* "So all that remains for us is to try and salvage as many lives as possible from the wreckage."

After a little time, Madame Radovas asked, "How would you guarantee our lives?" They were the first words she had spoken, though she had listened intently throughout.

"By my order, as an Imperial Auditor. Only Emperor Gregor himself could gainsay it."

"So . . . why won't Emperor Gregor gainsay it?" asked Cappell skeptically.

"He's not going to be happy about any of this," Miles answered frankly. *And I'm going to have to give him the report, God help me.* "But . . . if I lay my word on the line, I don't think he'll deny me." He hesitated. "Or else I will have to resign."

Foscol snorted. "How nice for us, to know that after we are dead, you will resign. What a consolation."

Soudha rubbed his lips, watching Miles . . . watching his truncated image, Miles reminded himself. He was not the only one missing body cues. The engineer was silent, thinking . . . what?

"Your word?" Cappell grimaced. "Do you know what a Vorkosigan's word means to us?"

"Yes," said Miles levelly. "Do you know what it means to me?"

Madame Radovas tilted her head, and her quiet stare became, if possible, more focused.

Miles leaned forward into the vid pickup. "My *word* is all that stands between you and ImpSec's aspiring heroes coming through your walls. They don't need the corridors, you know. My *word* went down on my Auditor's oath, which holds me at this moment unblinking to a duty I find more horrific than you can know. I only have one name's oath. It cannot be true to Gregor if it is false to you. But if there's one thing my father's heartbreaking experience at Solstice taught, it's that I'd better not put my word down on events I do not control. If you surrender quietly, I can control what happens. If ImpSec has to detain you by force, it will be up to chance, chaos, and the reflexes of some overexcited young men with guns and gallant visions of thwarting mad Komarran terrorists."

"We are not terrorists," said Foscol hotly.

"No? You've succeeded in terrifying *me*," Miles said bleakly.

Her lips thinned, but Soudha looked less certain.

"If you unleash ImpSec, the consequences will be your doing," said Cappell.

"Almost correct," Miles agreed. "If I unleash ImpSec, the consequences will be my responsibility. It's that devil's distinction between being in charge and being in control. I'm in charge; you're in control. You can imagine how much this thrills me."

Soudha snorted. One corner of Miles's mouth tilted up in unwilling response. *Yeah, Soudha knows all about that one, too.*

Foscol leaned forward. "This is all a smoke screen. Captain Vorgier said they were sending for a jumpship. Where is it?"

"Vorgier was lying for time, which was his clear duty. There will not be a jumpship." Shit, that did it. There were only two ways this could go now. *There were only two ways it could go before.*

"We have a pair of hostages. Do we have to space one of them to prove we're serious?"

"I believe you are deathly serious. Which one gets to watch, the aunt or the niece?" Miles asked softly, settling back again. "You claim to not be mad terrorists, and I believe you. You're not. Yet. You are also not murderers; I actually accept that all the deaths you've left in your wake were accidents. So far. But I also know that line gets easier to slip over with practice. Please observe that you have now gone as far as you can without turning yourselves into a perfect replica of enemy you set out to oppose."

He let those last words hang in the air for a time, for emphasis.

"Vorkosigan's right, I think," said Soudha unexpectedly. "We've come to the end of our choices. Or to the beginning of another set. One that isn't the set I signed up for."

"We have to stick together, or it's no good," said Foscol urgently. "If we have to space one of them, I vote for that hell-cat Vorsoisson."

"Would you do it with your own hands?" said Soudha slowly. "Because I think I decline."

"Even after what she did to us?"

What in God's name did gentle Ekaterin do to you? Miles kept his expression as blank as he could, his body still.

Soudha hesitated. "Seems it made no difference after all."

Cappell and Madame Radovas both began to speak at once, but Soudha held up a restraining hand. He blew out his breath like a man in pain. "No. Let us continue as we began. The choice is plain. Stop now—unconditional surrender—or call Vorkosigan's bluff. Now, it's no secret to you I thought the time to go into hiding for a later try was before we ever left Komarr."

"I'm sorry I voted against you the last time," Cappell said to Soudha.

Soudha shrugged. "Yeah, well . . . If we're going to quit, the time's come."

No, it hasn't, Miles thought frantically. This was too abrupt. There was time for another ten hours of chit chat at the very least. He wanted to slide them to surrender, not stampede them to suicide. Or murder. If they believed him about the defects of their device, as they appeared to, it must soon occur to them that they could hold the whole station hostage, if they didn't mind the self-immolating aspect. Well, if they weren't going to think of that themselves, far be it from him to point it out. He leaned back in his station chair, and chewed on the side of his finger, and watched, and listened.

"There's no benefit in waiting, either way," Soudha went on. "The risk increases every minute. Lena?"

"No surrender," said Foscol sturdily. "We go on." And more bleakly, "Somehow."

"Cappell?"

The mathematician hesitated a long time. "I can't stand that Marie died for nothing. Hold out."

"Myself . . ." Soudha let his big square hand fall open. "Stop. Now that we've lost surprise, this goes nowhere. The only question is how long it takes to arrive." He turned to Madame Radovas.

"Oh. My turn already? I didn't want to go last."

"Yours would be the tie-breaking vote in any case," said Soudha.

Madame Radovas fell silent, staring out the control booth's glass—at the airlock door, across the bay? Miles's gaze could not help following hers; her turn back caught him at it, and he flinched.

You've done it now, boy. Ekaterin's life and your soul's oath ride on a frigging Komarran shareholders' debate. How did you let this happen? This wasn't in the plans. . . . His eye relocated, and ignored, the code on his comconsole that would launch Vorgier and his waiting troops.

Madame Radovas's gaze returned to the window. She said, to no one in particular, "Our safety before always depended on secrecy. Now even if we get to Pol or Escobar, or further, ImpSec will follow us. There would not ever be a safe time to give up our hostages. In exile or not, it will be prisoners, always prisoners. I'm tired of being a prisoner, of hope or fear."

"You were not a prisoner!" said Foscol. "You were one of us. I thought."

Madame Radovas looked across at her. "I supported my husband. If I hadn't—he would still be alive. Lena, I'm *tired*."

Foscol said tentatively, "Maybe you should rest, before deciding."

The look she got from Madame Radovas in return for that line made her drop her eyes, and look away.

Madame Radovas said to Soudha, "Do you believe him, about the device not working?"

Soudha frowned deeply. "Yes. I'm afraid so. Or I would have voted differently."

"Poor Barto." She stared at Miles for a long time in an almost detached wonder.

Encouraged by her apparent dispassion, he asked curiously, "Why is your vote the tie-breaker?"

"The scheme was my husband's idea, originally. This obsession has dominated my life for seven years. His voting share was always considered the greatest."

How very Komarran. Then Soudha had actually been the second-in-command, forced into the dead man's shoes . . . it was all amazingly irrelevant now. *Maybe they'll name it after him. The Radovas Effect.* Belike. "We are both heirs, of a sort, then."

"Indeed." The widow's lips twisted. "You know, I will never forget the look on your face when that fool Vorsoisson told you there was no place on his forms for an Imperial order. I almost laughed out loud, despite it all."

Miles smiled briefly, scarcely daring to breathe.

Madame Radovas shook her head in disbelief, but not, he thought, of his promises. "Well, Lord Vorkosigan . . . I'll take your word. And find out what it's worth." She searched the faces of each of her three colleagues, but when she spoke, she looked at him. "I vote to stop now."

Miles waited tensely for signs of dissension, protest, internal revolt. Cappell struck his fist on the booth's glass wall, which reverberated, and turned away, his features working. Foscol buried her face in her hands. After that, silence.

"That's it, then," said Soudha, bleakly exhausted. Miles wondered if the news of the device's inherent defect had sapped his will more than any argument. "We surrender, on your word for our lives. Lord

Auditor Vorkosigan." He squeezed his eyes shut and opened them again. "Now what?"

"A lot of sensible slow moves. First I gently detach ImpSec from its vision of a heroic assault. They were getting pretty worked up, out here. Then you inform the rest of your group. Then disarm whatever booby-traps you've set, and pile any weapons you may possess well away from yourselves. Unlock the doors. Then sit down quietly on the loading bay floor with your hands behind your heads. At that point, I'll let the boys in." He added prudently, "Please avoid sudden movements, that sort of thing."

"So be it." Soudha cut his comm; the Komarrans winked out. Miles shuddered in sudden disorientation, alone again in his little sealed room. The screaming man behind the glass wall in his mind was getting out a battering ram, it felt like.

Miles opened the channel on his comconsole and ordered a medical squad to accompany the arresting officers from ImpSec and Station Security, who were to be armed with stunners and stunners only. He repeated that last command a couple of times, to be sure. He felt as if he'd spent a century in his station chair. When he tried to stand up, he nearly fell over. Then he ran.

Miles's only compromise with Vorgier's anxiety for the Imperial Auditor's personal safety was to march down the ramp into the Southport loading bay behind instead of in front of the security team. The ten or so Komarrans, sitting cross-legged on the floor, twisted around to watch as the Barrayarans entered. After Miles came the tech squad, which spread out looking for booby-traps, and behind them the medical team with a float pallet.

The first thing which caught Miles's eye after the live target inventory was the upside-down float cradle in the middle of the bay, atop a pile of tangled wreckage. He was able, barely, to recognize it from the diagrams he'd seen back on Komarr as the fifth novel device. His heart lifted at this inexplicable, welcome sight.

He walked around it, staring, and came up to where Soudha was being frisked down and restrained. "My goodness. Your wormhole-collapser appears to have met with an accident. But it won't do you any good. We have the plans."

Cappell and a man Miles recognized as the engineer who'd fled from Bollen Design stood nearby, glowering at him; Foscol struggled into earshot, barely controlled by her female arresting officer.

"It wasn't us," sighed Soudha. "It was *her.*"

A jerk of his thumb drew Miles's attention to the inner door of the bay's personnel airlock. A metal bar was placed crookedly across the airseal door's jamb; the ends were melted onto door and wall respectively.

Miles's eyes widened, and his lips parted in breathless anticipation. "Her?"

"The bitch from hell. Or Barrayar, which is almost the same thing to hear her tell it. Madame Vorsoisson."

"Remarkable." The source of several oddly tilted responses on the Komarrans' part to his recent negotiations began at last to come clear to Miles. "Um . . . *how?*"

All three Komarrans tried to answer him at once, with a medley of blame-casting which included a lot of phrases like, *If Madame Radovas hadn't let her out, If you hadn't let Radovas let her out, How was I supposed to know? The old lady looked sick to me. Still does, If you hadn't put the remote down right in front of her, If you hadn't left the damned control booth, If you had just moved faster, If you had run for the float cradle and cut the power, So why didn't you think of that, huh?* by which Miles slowly pieced together the most glorious mental picture he'd had all day. All year. For quite a long time, actually.

I'm in love. I'm in love. I just thought I was in love, before. Now I really am. I must, I must, I must have this woman! Mine, mine, mine. Lady Ekaterin Nile Vorvayne Vorsoisson Vorkosigan, yes! She'd left nothing here for ImpSec and all the Emperor's Auditors to do but sweep up the bits. He wanted to roll on the floor and howl with joy, which would be most undiplomatic of him, under the circumstances. He kept his face neutral, and very straight. Somehow, he didn't think the Komarrans appreciated the exquisite delight of it all.

"When we stuffed her in the airlock I *welded* it shut," said Soudha morosely. "I wasn't going to let her do us a *third* time."

"Third time?" Miles said. "If that was the second, what was the first?"

"When that idiot Arozzi first brought her down here, she damn near blew the whole thing right then by hitting the emergency alarm."

Miles glanced aside at the alarm on the nearby wall. "And then what happened?"

"We had a sudden influx of station accident control. I thought I'd never get rid of them."

"Ah. I see." *How curious. Vorgier never mentioned that part. Later.* "You mean we've spent the last five hours scrambling to evacuate this station for nothing?"

Soudha smiled sourly. "You coming to me for sympathy, Barrayaran?"

"Heh. Never mind."

Most of the prisoners were formed up and marched out; with a gesture, Miles ordered Soudha to be held behind.

"Moment of truth, Soudha. Have you booby-trapped this thing?"

"There is a motion-sensitive charge attached to the outer door. Opening it from this side should not set it off."

With iron self-control, Miles watched as an ImpSec tech torched off the metal bar. It fell to the deck with a clang. He paused in one last moment of sick fear.

"What are you waiting for?" asked Soudha curiously.

"Just pondering the depth of your political ingenuity. Suppose this is set to go off and snatch our prize from us at the last."

"Now? Why? It's over," said Soudha.

"Revenge. Manipulation. Maybe you figure to drive me berserk and trigger a repeat of the Solstice Massacre all over again, writ somewhat smaller. That could be a propaganda coup. Whether it would be worth spending your lives for is all in your point of view, of course. Properly massaged, the incident could help start a new Komarr Revolt, I suppose."

"You have a really twisted mind, Lord Vorkosigan," said Soudha, shaking his head. "Was it your upbringing, or your genetics?"

"Yes." Miles sighed. After a brief moment of reflection, Miles waved the guards on, and Soudha was marched out after his colleagues.

After a go-ahead nod from the Imperial Auditor, the tech tapped the control pad. The inner door whined, sticking halfway. Miles pressed it gently sideways with his boot, and it shuddered open.

Ekaterin was on her feet, between the inner door and the Professora, who sat on the deck wearing her niece's vest over her own bolero. Ekaterin's face bore a red bruise, her hair was hanging every which way, her fists were clenched, and she looked perfectly demented and altogether gorgeous, in Miles's personal opinion. Smiling broadly, he held out both his hands and leaned inside.

She glared back at him. "About time." She stalked past, muttering in a voice of loathing, "Men!"

After the briefest lurch, Miles managed to convert his open arms into a smooth bow toward the Professora. "Madame Dr. Vorthys. Are you all right?"

"Why, hello, Miles." She blinked at him, gray faced and very chilled looking. "I've been better, but I believe I'll survive."

"I have a float pallet for you. These sturdy young men will help you to it."

"Oh, thank you, dear."

Miles stood back and waved the medtechs forward. The Professora looked perfectly content to be whisked aboard the medical pallet and covered with warm wraps. A cursory examination and a few words of debate resulted in a half-dose of synergine for her, but no IV; then the pallet rose into the air.

"The Professor will be here shortly," Miles assured her. "In fact, he'll likely be along before you both are done at the station infirmary. I'll see he gets sent straight on to you."

"I'm so pleased." The Professora motioned him nearer; when he bent over her, she grabbed him by the ear and planted a kiss on his cheek. "Ekaterin was wonderful," she whispered.

"I know," he breathed. His eyes crinkled, and she smiled back.

He stepped back from the pallet to Ekaterin's side, hoping her aunt's example might inspire her—he wouldn't mind salvaging *some* little show of appreciation—"You didn't seem surprised to see me," he murmured. The pallet started off, under the guidance of a medtech, and he and Ekaterin followed in procession; the ImpSec technicians politely waited till they'd cleared the chamber to plunge in to the airlock to disarm the charge.

Ekaterin shoved a strand of hair back over one ear with a hand that trembled only slightly. Red bruises glared on her arms, too, as her sleeve slid back. Miles frowned at them. "I knew it had to be our side," she said simply. "Or else it would have been the *other* door."

"Eh. Quite." Three hours, she'd had, to contemplate that possibility. "My fast courier was slow."

They turned up the next corridor in reflective silence. Gratifying as it might have been to have her fling herself into his arms and weep relief into—well, if not his shoulder, at least the top of his head—in front of that herd of ImpSec fellows, he had to admit he admired this style even more. *So what is this thing you have about tall women and unrequited love?* His cousin Ivan would doubtless have some cutting things to say—he growled in anticipation, in his mind. He would deal with Ivan and other hazards to his courtship later.

"Do you know you saved about five thousand lives?" he asked her.

Her dark brows drew down. "What?"

"The novel device was defective. If the Komarrans had managed to get it started, the gravitational back-blow from the wormhole would have taken out this station just like the soletta array, possibly with as few survivors. And I shudder at the thought of the property damage bill. To think how Illyan used to complain about my equipment losses back when I was just covert ops. . . ."

"You mean . . . it didn't work after all? I did all that for *nothing*?" She stopped short, her shoulders sagging.

"What do you mean, nothing? I've met Imperial generals who completed their entire careers with less to show for them. You should get a bloody medal, *I* think. Except that this whole thing is going to end up so classified, they're going to have to invent a whole new level of classification just to put it in. And then classify the classification."

Her lips puffed, not quite mirthfully. "What would I do with so useless an object as a medal?"

He thought bemusedly of the contents a certain drawer at home in Vorkosigan House. "Frame it? Use it as a paperweight? Dust it?"

"Just what I always wanted. More clutter."

He grinned at her; she smiled back at last, clearly beginning to come off her adrenaline jag, and without breaking down, either. She drew breath and started forward again, and he kept pace. She had met the enemy, mastered her moment, hung three hours on death's doorstep, all that, and she'd emerged still on her feet and snarling. Oversocialized, hah. *Oh, yeah, Da, I want this one.*

He stopped at the door to the infirmary; the Professora vanished within, borne off by her medical minions like a lady on a palanquin. Ekaterin paused with him.

"I have to leave you for a time and check on my prisoners. The stationers will take care of you."

Her brow wrinkled. "Prisoners? Oh. Yes. How *did* you get rid of the Komarrans?"

Miles smiled grimly. "Persuasion."

She stared down at him, one side of her lovely mouth curving up. Her lower lip was split; he wanted to kiss it and make it well. *Not yet. Timing, boy. And one other thing.*

"You must be very persuasive."

"I hope so." He took a deep breath. "I bluffed them into believing that I wouldn't let them go no matter what they did to you and the Professora. Except that I wasn't bluffing. We could not have let them go." There. Betrayal confessed. His empty hands clenched.

She stared at him in disbelief; his heart shrank. "Well, of *course* not!"

"Eh . . . what?"

"Don't you know what they wanted to do to Barrayar?" she demanded. "It was a horror show. Utterly vile, and they couldn't even see it. They actually tried to tell me that collapsing the wormhole wouldn't hurt anyone! Monstrous fools."

"That's what I thought, actually."

"So, wouldn't you put *your* life on the line to stop them?"

"Yes, but I wasn't putting my life—I was putting yours."

"But I'm Vor," she said simply.

His smile and his heart revived, dizzy with delight. "True Vor, milady," he breathed.

A female medtech was approaching, murmuring anxiously, "Madame Vorsoisson?" Miles yielded to her shepherding motions, gave Ekaterin an analyst's salute, and turned away. He was humming, off-key, by the time he rounded the first corner.

Chapter Twenty-One

The station infirmary personnel insisted on keeping both Vor women overnight, a precaution with which neither argued. Despite her exhaustion Ekaterin did get dispensation to go pick up her valise from her never-used hostel room, under the watchful eye of a very young ImpSec guard who called her "Ma'am" in every sentence and was determined to carry her luggage.

One message waited on her hostel room's comconsole: an urgent order from Lord Vorkosigan for her to take her aunt and flee the station at once, delivered in a tone of such intense conviction as to almost send her scurrying off despite its obviously outdated content. Instructions only, she noted; no explanations whatsoever. He really must have once held military command. The contrast between this strained, forceful lord and the almost goofy geniality of the young man who'd bowed her out of the airlock bemused her; which was the real Lord Vorkosigan? For all his apparently self-revealing babble, the man remained as elusive as a handful of water. *Water in the desert.* The thought popped unbidden into her mind, and she shook her head to clear it.

After she returned to the infirmary, Ekaterin sat up for a while with her aunt, waiting for the Professor. Uncle Vorthys arrived in the next hour. He was unusually breathless and subdued as he sat on the edge of his wife's bed and embraced her. She hugged him back, tears starting in her eyes for almost the first time in this whole night's ordeal.

"You shouldn't frighten me like that, woman," he told her in mock severity. "Running around getting kidnapped, thwarting Komarran terrorists, putting ImpSec out of a job . . . Your premature demise would entirely disarrange my selfish plan to drop dead first and leave you to pick up after me. Kindly don't do that!"

She laughed shakily. "I'll try not to, dear." The patient gown she wore was not a very flattering fashion, but her color did look rather better, Ekaterin thought. Synergine, hot liquids, warmth, quiet, and safety were working to banish her more alarming symptoms without further medical intervention, so that even her anxious husband was fairly quickly reassured. Ekaterin let her aunt tell him most of the story of their harrowing hours with the Komarrans, only putting in a few murmurs of correction when she waxed too flattering of her niece's part in it all.

Ekaterin reflected with bleak envy on the nature of a marriage that its principals could regard as prematurely threatened after a mere forty-plus years. *Not for me. I've lost that option.* The Professor and the Professora were surely among the fortunate few. Whatever personal qualities it took to achieve this happy state, it was abundantly plain to Ekaterin that she did not possess them. So be it.

The Professor's booming voice and precise academic diction returned to usual as he proceeded to harry the medtechs, unnecessarily, on his wife's behalf. Ekaterin intervened to suggest firmly that what Aunt Vorthys needed most now was *rest*; after one last disruptive pass through the private room, he took himself off to find Lord Vorkosigan and tour the late battlefield at the Southport locks. Ekaterin didn't think she could ever sleep again, but after she cleaned up and crawled into her own infirmary bed, a medtech brought her a potion and invited her to drink it. Ekaterin was still complaining muzzily that such things didn't work for her when the bed sheets seemed to suck her right down.

Whether due to the potion, exhaustion, sheer nervous collapse, or the absence of a nine-year-old demanding services, she slept late. The restful residue of the morning, spent chatting desultorily with her aunt, had drifted toward noon when Lord Vorkosigan trooped into the infirmary room. He was clean as a cat and his fine gray suit was crisp and fresh, though his face was traced with fatigue. He carried an enormous and awkward flower arrangement under each arm. Ekaterin hurried to help relieve him of them, sliding them onto a table before he dropped them both.

"Good day, Madame Dr. Vorthys, you're looking much better. Excellent. Madame Vorsoisson." He ducked his head at her, and his white grin winked.

"Wherever did you find such gorgeous flowers on a space station?" Ekaterin asked, astonished.

"In a shop. It's a Komarran space station. They'll sell you anything. Well, not *anything*—that would be Jackson's Whole. But it stands to reason, with all the people meeting and greeting and parting through here, that there would be a market niche for this sort of thing. They grow them right here on the station, you know, along with all their truck garden vegetables. Why do they call them truck gardens, I wonder? I don't think they ever grew trucks in them, even back on Old Earth." He dragged over a chair and sat down near her, at the foot of the Professora's bed. "I believe that dark red fuzzy thing is a Barrayaran plant, by the way. It made me break out in hives when I touched it."

"Yes, bloody puffwad," she agreed.

"Is that its name, or a value judgment?"

She smiled. "I believe it refers to the color. It comes from South Continent, on the western slopes of the Black Escarpment."

"I was at the Black Escarpment for winter training once. Happily, these things must have been buried under several meters of snow at the time."

"How shall we ever get them home, Miles?" said the Professora, half laughing.

"Don't burden yourself," he recommended. "You can always give them to the medtechs when you leave."

"But they must be very expensive," said Ekaterin in worry. Ridiculously so, for something they could only enjoy for a few hours.

"Expensive?" he said blankly. "Automated weapons-control systems are expensive. Combat drop missions which go wrong are very expensive. These are cheap. Really. Anyway, it supports a business, which is good for the Imperium. If you get a chance, you ought to ask for a tour of the station's hydroponics section before you leave. I'd think you'd find it pretty interesting."

"We'll see if there's time," said Ekaterin. "It's been such a bizarre experience. It's strange to realize I'm not even late getting back to pick up Nikki yet. Just a few more days to complete his treatment, and I'm done with Komarr."

"Do you have everything in hand for that? Everything you need? Your aunt," he nodded at the Professora, "is with you now."

"I expect I'll be able to handle anything that comes up this time," Ekaterin assured him.

"I expect you will." That scimitar smile flickered over his face again.

"We only missed the ship we were originally scheduled to take this morning because Uncle Vorthys insisted we wait and travel back to Komarr with him in his fast courier. Do you know when that will be? I should send a message to Madame Vortorren."

"He has a few chores here yet. ImpSec Komarr sent us out a special squad of boffins and techs to clean up and document that mess you made in the Southport loading bay—"

"Oh, dear. I'm sorry—" she began automatically.

"No, no, it was a beautiful mess. Couldn't have made a better one myself, and I've made a few. Anyway, he will be overseeing them, and then returning to Komarr to set up a secret scientific commission to study the device, explore its limits and all that. And HQ sent me some high-powered interrogators whom I wanted to personally brief before they took charge of my prisoners. Captain Vorgier wasn't too happy that I wouldn't let any of his local people question our conspirators, but I've already declared all details of this case need-to-know under my Auditor's seal, so he's out of luck." He cleared his throat. "Your uncle and I have decided I get the job of going straight back to Vorbarr Sultana from here and making the preliminary report to Emperor Gregor in person. He's only been getting ImpSec digests."

"Oh," she said, startled. "Leaving so soon . . . ? What about all your things—you shouldn't go off without your seizure stimulator, should you?"

Half self-consciously, he rubbed his temple; the white bandages were gone from his wrists, she noticed, leaving only pale red rings of new scars. To add to his collection, presumably. "I had Tuomonen pack up all my kit and send it out here with the crew from HQ. It arrived a couple of hours ago, so I'm all set. Good old ImpSec, they do piss me off sometimes. Tuomonen is going to get a major black mark, because the conspiracy in Serifosa Terraforming took place on his watch, and he never caught it, even though it was really the

Imperial Accounting Office which should have been the first line of defense. And that idiot Vorgier is getting a commendation. There is no justice."

"Poor Tuomonen. I liked him. Isn't there anything you can do about that?"

"Mm, I turned down a chance to be in charge of ImpSec's internal affairs, so no, I think I'd better not."

"Will he keep his post?"

"It's uncertain at this time. I told him if he finds his military career at a stand, to look me up. I think I'm going to be able to use a good trained assistant in this Auditor job. The work will be irregular, though. The trend of my life."

He sucked thoughtfully on his lower lip, and glanced across at her. "The reclassification of this case from a peculation scam to something far more serious also affects what you can tell Nikki, I'm afraid. It's all headed into a security black hole as fast as we can stuff it in there, and it's going to stay there for quite some time. There will, therefore, be no public prosecutions and no need for you to testify, though ImpSec may be around for another interview or two—*not* under fast-penta. In retrospect, I'm very relieved I played it as close to my chest as I did. But for Nikki, and all Tien's relatives, and anyone else, the story is going to have to remain that he died in a simple breath mask accident from being caught outside with a low reservoir, and you don't know any more details than that. Madame Dr. Vorthys, this is for you, too."

"I understand," said the Professora.

"I am both relieved, and disturbed," said Ekaterin slowly.

"In time, the security considerations will soften. You will have to rejudge the problem then, when, well, when many things may have changed."

"I did wonder if, for Nikki's name's honor, I ought to try to pay back the Imperium all the bribe money Tien received."

He looked startled. "Good God, no. If anyone owes anything, it's Foscol. *She* stole it in the first place. And we certainly won't be getting anything back from her."

"Something is owed," she said gravely.

"Tien settled his debt with his life. He's quits with the Imperium, I assure you. In the Emperor's Voice, if necessary."

She took this in. Death did wipe out debt. It just didn't erase the memory of pain; time was still required for that healing. *Your time is your own, now. That* felt strange. She could take all the time she wanted, or needed. Riches beyond dreams. She nodded. "All right."

"The past is paid. Please notify me about Tien's funeral, though. I wish to attend, if I can." He frowned. "I too owe something there."

She shook her head mutely.

"In any case, do call me when you and your aunt get back to Vorbarr Sultana." He glanced again at the Professora. "She and Nikki *will* be staying with you for a time, yes?" Ekaterin was not quite sure if that was phrased as a question or a demand.

"Yes, indeed." Aunt Vorthys smiled.

"So here are all my addresses." He spoke again to Ekaterin, and handed her a plastic flimsy. "The numbers for the Vorkosigan residences in Vorbarr Sultana, Hassadar, and Vorkosigan Surleau, for Master Tsipis in Hassadar—my man of business, I believe I mentioned him to you—he usually knows where to get hold of me in a pinch, when I'm out in the District—and a drop-number through the Imperial Residence, which will *always* know how to reach me. Any time, day or night."

Aunt Vorthys leaned back, with her finger on her lips, and regarded him with growing bemusement. "Do you think those will be enough, Miles? Perhaps you can think of three or four more, just to be sure?"

To Ekaterin's surprise, he flushed a little. "I trust these will suffice," he said. "And of course, I should be able to reach you through your aunt, right?"

"Of course," murmured Aunt Vorthys.

"I'd like to show you over my District sometime," he added to Ekaterin, avoiding the Professora's eye. "There's a great deal to see there you might find of interest. There's a major forestry project going on in the Dendarii Mountains, and some radiation reclamation experiments. My family owns several maple syrup and winery operations. There's botany all over the damn place, in fact; you can hardly move without tripping over a plant."

"Perhaps later on," said Ekaterin uncertainly. "What *will* happen to the Terraforming Project, as a result of all this mess with the Komarrans?"

"Mm, not too much, I now suspect. The security classification is going to limit the immediate public political repercussions."

"In the long run, too?"

"Though the amount of money that was stolen from Serifosa Sector's budget was huge from the viewpoint of a private individual, from the standpoint of the bureaucracy it wasn't that big a bite. There are nineteen other Sectors, after all. The damage to the soletta array is actually going to be the biggest bill."

"Will the Imperium repair it properly? I've so hoped they would."

He brightened. "I had this great idea about that. I'm going to pitch it to Gregor that we should declare the soletta repair—and enlargement—as a wedding present, from Gregor to Laisa and from Barrayar to Komarr. I'm going to recommend its size be nearly doubled, adding the six new panels the Komarrans have been begging for since forever. I think this mischance can be turned into an absolute propaganda coup, with the right timing. We'll shove the appropriation through the Council of Counts and Ministers quickly, before Midsummer, while everyone in Vorbarr Sultana is still sentimentally wound up for the Imperial Wedding."

She clapped her hands in enthusiasm, then paused in doubt. "Will that work? I didn't think the crusty old Council of Counts was susceptible to what Tien used to call *romantic drivel*."

"Oh," he said airily, "I'm sure they are. I'm a cadet member of the Counts myself—we're only human, after all. Besides, we can point out that every time a Komarran looks up—well, half the time— they'll see this Barrayaran gift hanging overhead, and know what it's doing to create their future. The power of suggestion and all that. It could save us the expense of putting down the *next* Komarran conspiracy."

"I hope so," she said. "I think it's a lovely idea."

He grinned, clearly gratified. He looked over at the Professora, and away, shifted around, and drew a small packet from his trouser pocket. "I don't know, Madame Vorsoisson, whether Gregor will give you a medal or not, for your quick thinking and cool response in the Southport bay—"

She shook her head. "I don't need—"

"But I thought you should have something to remember it all by. This." He stuck out his hand.

She took the packet and laughed. "Do I recognize this?"

"Probably."

She unfolded the familiar wrapping and opened the box to reveal the little model Barrayar from the jeweler's shop in Serifosa, now on a slender chain of braided gold. She held it up; it spun in the light.

"Look, Aunt Vorthys," she said shyly, and handed it across for inspection and approval.

The Professora examined it with interest, squinting a trifle. "Very fine, dear. Very fine indeed."

"Call it the Lord Auditor Vorkosigan Award for Making His Job Easier," said Vorkosigan. "You really did, you know. If the Komarrans hadn't already lost their infernal device, they would never have surrendered, even if I'd talked myself blue. In fact, Soudha said something to that effect during our preliminary interrogations last night, so you may consider it confirmed. If not for you, this station would be in a million hurtling pieces by now."

She hesitated. Should she accept—? She glanced at her aunt, who was smiling at her benignly and without apparent misgivings about the propriety of it. Not that Aunt Vorthys was particularly passionate about propriety—that indifference was, in fact, one of the qualities which made her Ekaterin's favorite female relative. *Think on that.* "Thank you," she said sincerely to Lord Vorkosigan. "I will remember. And I do remember," she added.

"Um, you're supposed to forget the unfortunate part about the pond."

"Never." Her lips curved up. "It was the highlight of the day. Was it some sort of psychic precognition that you laid this by?"

"I don't think so. Chance favors the prepared and all that. Fortunately for my credit, from the outside most people can't tell the rapid exploitation of a belatedly recognized opportunity from deep-laid planning." He positively smirked as she slid the chain over her head. "You know, you're the first girlfr—female friend I've had I've ever succeeded in giving Barrayar to. Not for lack of trying."

Her eyes crinkled. "Have you had a great many girlfriends?" If he hadn't, she'd have to dismiss her whole gender as congenital idiots. The man could charm snakes from their holes, nine-year-olds from locked bathrooms, and Komarran terrorists from their bunkers. Why weren't females following him around in herds? Could no Barrayaran woman see past his surface, or their own cocked-up noses?

"Mmm . . ." A rather long hesitation. "The usual progression, I suppose. Hopeless first love, this and that over the years, unrequited mad crushes."

"Who was the hopeless first love?" she asked, fascinated.

"Elena. The daughter of one of my father's Armsmen, who was my bodyguard when I was young."

"Is she still on Barrayar?"

"No, she emigrated years ago. Had a galactic military career and retired with the rank of captain. She's a commercial shipmaster now."

"Jumpships?"

"Yes."

"Nikki would be so envious. Um . . . what exactly is this and that? If I may ask." Would he answer?

"Er. Well. Yes, I think you should, all things considered. Better sooner than later, belike."

He was growing terribly Barrayaran, she thought; that use of *belike* was pure Dendarii mountain dialect. This outburst of confidences was at least as entertaining as putting him on fast-penta might be. Better, given what he'd said about his weird reaction to the drug.

"There was Elli. She was a free mercenary trainee when I first met her."

"What is she now?"

"Fleet Admiral. Actually."

"So she was this. Who was that?"

"There was Taura."

"What was she, when you first met her?"

"A Jacksonian body-slave. Of House Ryoval—very bad news, House Ryoval used to be."

"I must ask more about those covert ops missions of yours sometime . . . So what is she now?"

"Master Sergeant in a mercenary fleet."

"The same fleet as, um, the this?"

"Yes."

Her brows rose, helplessly. Her Aunt Vorthys was leaning back with her finger over her lips again, her eyes alight with laughter; no, the Professora clearly wasn't going to interfere with this. "And . . . ?" she led him on, beginning to be immensely curious as to how long he'd keep going. Why in the world did he think all this romantic history was something she ought to know? Not that she would stop him . . . nor would Aunt Vorthys, apparently, not for a bribe of five kilos of chocolates. But her secret opinion of her gender began to rise.

"Mm . . . there was Rowan. That was . . . that was brief."

"And she was . . . ?"

"A technical serf of House Fell. She's a cryo-revival surgeon in an independent clinic on Escobar, now, though, I'm happy to say. Very pleased with her new citizenship."

Tien had protected her proudly, she reflected, in the little Vor-lady fortress of her household. Tien had spent a decade protecting her so hard, especially from anything that resembled growth, she'd felt scarcely larger at thirty than she'd been at twenty. Whatever it was Vorkosigan had offered to this extraordinary list of lovers, it hadn't been protection.

"Do you begin to notice a trend in all this, Lord Vorkosigan?"

"Yes," he replied glumly. "None of them would marry me and come live on Barrayar."

"So . . . what about the unrequited mad crush?"

"Ah. That was Rian. I was young, just a new lieutenant on a diplomatic mission."

"And what does she do, now?"

He cleared his throat. "Now? She's an empress." He added, under the pressure of Ekaterin's wide stare, "Of Cetaganda. They have several, you see."

A silence fell, and stretched. He shifted uneasily in his chair, and his smile flicked on and off.

She rested her chin in her hand, and regarded him; her brows quirked in quizzical delight. "Lord Vorkosigan. Can I take a number and get in line?"

Whatever it was he'd been expecting her to say, it wasn't that; he was so taken aback he nearly fell off his chair. Wait, she hadn't meant it to come out sounding quite like— His smile stuck in the *on* position, but decidedly sideways.

"The next number up," he breathed, "is 'one.'"

It was her turn to be taken aback; her eyes fell, scorched by the blaze in his. He had lured her into levity. His fault, for being so . . . luring. She stared wildly around the room, groping for some suitably neutral remark with which to retrieve her reserve. It was a space station: there was no weather. *My, the vacuum is hard out today. . . .* Not that, either. She gazed beseechingly at Aunt Vorthys. Vorkosigan observed her involuntary recoil, and his smile acquired a sort of stuffed apologetic quality; he too looked cautiously to the Professora.

The Professora rubbed one finger thoughtfully over her chin. "And are you traveling back to Barrayar on a commercial liner, Lord

Vorkosigan?" she asked him affably. The mutually alarmed parties blinked at her in suffused gratitude.

"No," said Vorkosigan. "Fast courier. In fact, it's waiting for me right now." He cleared his throat, jumped to his feet, and made a show of checking his chrono. "Yes, right now. Professora, Madame Vorsoisson, I trust I shall see you both back in Vorbarr Sultana?"

"Yes, certainly," said Ekaterin, barely avoiding breathlessness.

"I will look forward to it with great fascination," said the Professora piously.

His smile went crooked in trenchant appreciation of her tone; he backed out with a flourishing, self-conscious bow, a courtly effect slightly spoiled by his caroming off the doorjamb. His quick steps faded down the corridor.

"A nice young man," observed Aunt Vorthys, into a room seeming suddenly much emptier. "A pity he's so short."

"He's not so short," said Ekaterin defensively. "He's just . . . concentrated."

Her aunt's smile grew maddeningly bland. "I could see that, dear."

Ekaterin lifted her chin in what remained of her dignity. "I see you are feeling very much better. Shall we go ask about that hydroponics tour?"

A Civil Campaign

Chapter One

The big groundcar jerked to a stop centimeters from the vehicle ahead of it, and Armsman Pym, driving, swore under his breath. Miles settled back again in his seat beside him, wincing at a vision of the acrimonious street scene from which Pym's reflexes had delivered them. Miles wondered if he could have persuaded the feckless prole in front of them that being rear-ended by an Imperial Auditor was a privilege to be treasured. Likely not. The Vorbarr Sultana University student darting across the boulevard on foot, who had been the cause of the quick stop, scampered off through the jam without a backward glance. The line of groundcars started up once more.

"Have you heard if the municipal traffic control system will be coming on line soon?" Pym asked, apropos of what Miles counted as their third near-miss this week.

"Nope. Delayed in development again, Lord Vorbohn the Younger reports. Due to the increase in fatal lightflyer incidents, they're concentrating on getting the automated air system up first."

Pym nodded, and returned his attention to the crowded road. The Armsman was a habitually fit man, his graying temples seeming merely an accent to his brown-and-silver uniform. He'd served the Vorkosigans as a liege-sworn guard since Miles had been an Academy cadet, and would doubtless go on doing so till either he died of old age, or they were all killed in traffic.

333

So much for short cuts. Next time they'd go around the campus. Miles watched through the canopy as the taller new buildings of the University fell behind, and they passed through its spiked iron gates into the pleasant old residential streets favored by the families of senior professors and staff. The distinctive architecture dated from the last un-electrified decade before the end of the Time of Isolation. This area had been reclaimed from decay in the past generation, and now featured shady green Earth trees, and bright flower boxes under the tall narrow windows of the tall narrow houses. Miles rebalanced the flower arrangement between his feet. Would it be seen as redundant by its intended recipient?

Pym glanced aside at his slight movement, following his eye to the foliage on the floor. "The lady you met on Komarr seems to have made a strong impression on you, m'lord . . ." He trailed off invitingly.

"Yes," said Miles, uninvitingly.

"Your lady mother had high hopes of that very attractive Miss Captain Quinn you brought home those times." Was that a wistful note in Pym's voice?

"Miss Admiral Quinn, now," Miles corrected with a sigh. "So had I. But she made the right choice for her." He grimaced out the canopy. "I've sworn off falling in love with galactic women and then trying to persuade them to immigrate to Barrayar. I've concluded my only hope is to find a woman who can already stand Barrayar, and persuade her to like me."

"And does Madame Vorsoisson like Barrayar?"

"About as well as I do." He smiled grimly.

"And, ah . . . the second part?"

"We'll see, Pym." *Or not, as the case may be.* At least the spectacle of a man of thirty-plus, going courting seriously for the first time in his life—the first time in the Barrayaran style, anyway—promised to provide hours of entertainment for his interested staff.

Miles let his breath and his nervous irritation trickle out through his nostrils as Pym found a place to park near Lord Auditor Vorthys's doorstep, and expertly wedged the polished old armored groundcar into the inadequate space. Pym popped the canopy; Miles climbed out, and stared up at the three-story patterned tile front of his colleague's home.

Georg Vorthys had been a professor of engineering failure analysis at the Imperial University for thirty years. He and his wife had lived in this house for most of their married life, raising three children and two academic careers, before Emperor Gregor had appointed Vorthys as one of his hand-picked Imperial Auditors. Neither of the Professors Vorthys had seen any reason to change their comfortable lifestyle merely because the awesome powers of an Emperor's Voice had been conferred upon the retired engineer; Madame Dr. Vorthys still walked every day to her classes. *Dear no, Miles!* the Professora had said to him, when he'd once wondered aloud at their passing up this opportunity for social display. *Can you imagine moving all those books?* Not to mention the laboratory and workshop jamming the entire basement.

Their cheery inertia proved a happy chance, when they invited their recently-widowed niece and her young son to live with them while she completed her own education. Plenty of room, the Professor had boomed jovially, the top floor is so empty since the children left. So close to classes, the Professora had pointed out practically. *Less than six kilometers from Vorkosigan House!* Miles had exulted in his mind, adding a polite murmur of encouragement aloud. And so Ekaterin Nile Vorvayne Vorsoisson had arrived. *She's here, she's here!* Might she be looking down at him from the shadows of some upstairs window even now?

Miles glanced anxiously down the all-too-short length of his body. If his dwarfish stature bothered her, she'd shown no signs of it so far. Well and good. Going on to the aspects of his appearance he could control: no food stains spattered his plain gray tunic, no unfortunate street detritus clung to the soles of his polished half-boots. He checked his distorted reflection in the groundcar's rear canopy. Its convex mirroring widened his lean, if slightly hunched, body to something resembling his obese clone-brother Mark, a comparison he primly ignored. Mark was, thank God, not here. He essayed a smile, for practice; in the canopy, it came out twisted and repellent. No dark hair sticking out in odd directions, anyway.

"You look just fine, my lord," Pym said in a bracing tone from the front compartment. Miles's face heated, and he flinched away from his reflection. He recovered himself enough to take the flower arrangement and rolled-up flimsy Pym handed out to him with, he hoped, a tolerably bland expression. He balanced the load in his arms, turned to face the front steps, and took a deep breath.

After about a minute, Pym inquired helpfully from behind him, "Would you like me to carry anything?"

"No. Thank you." Miles trod up the steps and wiggled a finger free to press the chime-pad. Pym pulled out a reader, and settled comfortably in the groundcar to await his lord's pleasure.

Footsteps sounded from within, and the door swung open on the smiling pink face of the Professora. Her gray hair was wound up on her head in her usual style. She wore a dark rose dress with a light rose bolero, embroidered with green vines in the manner of her home District. This somewhat formal Vor mode, which suggested she was just on her way either in or out, was belied by the soft buskins on her feet. "Hello, Miles. Goodness, you're prompt."

"Professora." Miles ducked a nod to her, and smiled in turn. "Is she here? Is she in? Is she well? You said this would be a good time. I'm not too early, am I? I thought I'd be late. The traffic was miserable. You're going to be around, aren't you? I brought these. Do you think she'll like them?" The sticking-up red flowers tickled his nose as he displayed his gift while still clutching the rolled-up flimsy, which had a tendency to try to unroll and escape whenever his grip loosened.

"Come in, yes, all's well. She's here, she's fine, and the flowers are very nice—" The Professora rescued the bouquet and ushered him into her tiled hallway, closing the door firmly behind them with her foot. The house was dim and cool after the spring sunshine outside, and had a fine aroma of wood wax, old books, and a touch of academic dust.

"She looked pretty pale and fatigued at Tien's funeral. Surrounded by all those relatives. We really didn't get a chance to say more than two words each." *I'm sorry* and *Thank you*, to be precise. Not that he'd wanted to talk much to the late Tien Vorsoisson's family.

"It was an immense strain for her, I think," said the Professora judiciously. "She'd been through so much horror, and except for Georg and myself—and you—there wasn't a soul there to whom she could talk truth about it. Of course, her first concern was getting Nikki through it all. But she held together without a crack from first to last. I was very proud of her."

"Indeed. And she is . . . ?" Miles craned his neck, glancing into the rooms off the entry hall: a cluttered study lined with bookshelves, and a cluttered parlor lined with bookshelves. No young widows.

"Right this way." The Professora conducted him down the hall and out through her kitchen to the little urban back garden. A couple of tall trees and a brick wall made a private nook of it. Beyond a tiny circle of green grass, at a table in the shade, a woman sat with flimsies and a reader spread before her. She was chewing gently on the end of a stylus, and her dark brows were drawn down in her absorption. She wore a calf-length dress in much the same style as the Professora's, but solid black, with the high collar buttoned up to her neck. Her bolero was gray, trimmed with simple black braid running around its edge. Her dark hair was drawn back to a thick braided knot at the nape of her neck. She looked up at the sound of the door opening; her brows flew up and her lips parted in a flashing smile that made Miles blink. *Ekaterin.*

"Mil—my Lord Auditor!" She rose in a flare of skirt; he bowed over her hand.

"Madame Vorsoisson. You look well." She looked wonderful, if still much too pale. Part of that might be the effect of all that severe black, which also made her eyes show a brilliant blue-gray. "Welcome to Vorbarr Sultana. I brought these . . ." He gestured, and the Professora set the flower arrangement down on the table. "Though they hardly seem needed, out here."

"They're lovely," Ekaterin assured him, sniffing them in approval. "I'll take them up to my room later, where they will be very welcome. Since the weather has brightened up, I find I spend as much time as possible out here, under the real sky."

She'd spent nearly a year sealed in a Komarran dome. "I can understand that," Miles said. The conversation hiccuped to a brief stop, while they smiled at each other.

Ekaterin recovered first. "Thank you for coming to Tien's funeral. It meant so much to me."

"It was the least I could do, under the circumstances. I'm only sorry I couldn't do more."

"But you've already done so much for me and Nikki—" She broke off at his gesture of embarrassed denial and instead said, "But won't you sit down? Aunt Vorthys—?" She drew back one of the spindly garden chairs.

The Professora shook her head. "I have a few things to attend to inside. Carry on." She added a little cryptically, "You'll do fine."

She went back into her house, and Miles sat across from Ekaterin, placing his flimsy on the table to await its strategic moment. It half-unrolled, eagerly.

"Is your case all wound up?" she asked.

"That case will have ramifications for years to come, but I'm done with it for now," Miles replied. "I just turned in my last reports yesterday, or I would have been here to welcome you earlier." Well, that and a vestigial sense that he'd ought to let the poor woman at least get her bags unpacked, before descending in force.

"Will you be sent out on another assignment now?"

"I don't think Gregor will let me risk getting tied up elsewhere till after his marriage. For the next couple of months, I'm afraid all my duties will be social ones."

"I'm sure you'll do them with your usual flair."

God, I hope not. "I don't think flair is exactly what my Aunt Vorpatril—she's in charge of all the Emperor's wedding arrangements—would wish from me. More like, shut up and do what you're told, Miles. But speaking of paperwork, how's your own? Is Tien's estate settled? Did you manage to recapture Nikki's guardianship from that cousin of his?"

"Vassily Vorsoisson? Yes, thank heavens, there was no problem with that part."

"So, ah, what's all this, then?" Miles nodded at the cluttered table.

"I'm planning my course work for the next session at university. I was too late to start this summer, so I'll begin in the fall. There's so much to choose from. I feel so ignorant."

"Educated is what you aim to be coming out, not going in."

"I suppose so."

"And what will you choose?"

"Oh, I'll start with basics—biology, chemistry . . ." She brightened. "One real horticulture course." She gestured at her flimsies. "For the rest of the season, I'm trying to find some sort of paying work. I'd like to feel I'm not totally dependent on the charity of my relatives, even if it's only my pocket money."

That seemed almost the opening he was looking for, but Miles's eye caught sight of a red ceramic basin, sitting on the wooden planks forming a seat bordering a raised garden bed. In the middle of the pot a red-brown blob, with a fuzzy fringe like a rooster's crest growing out of it, pushed up through the dirt. If it was what he thought . . . He pointed to the basin. "Is that by chance your old bonsai'd skellytum? Is it going to live?"

She smiled. "Well, at least it's the start of a new skellytum. Most of the fragments of the old one died on the way home from Komarr, but that one took."

"You have a—for native Barrayaran plants, I don't suppose you can call it a green thumb, can you?"

"Not unless they're suffering from some pretty serious plant diseases, no."

"Speaking of gardens." Now, how to do this without jamming his foot in his mouth too deeply. "I don't think, in all the other uproar, I ever had a chance to tell you how impressed I was with your garden designs that I saw on your comconsole."

"Oh." Her smile fled, and she shrugged. "They were no great thing. Just twiddling."

Right. Let them not bring up any more of the recent past than absolutely necessary, till time had a chance to blunt memory's razor edges. "It was your Barrayaran garden, the one with all the native species, which caught my eye. I'd never seen anything like it."

"There are a dozen of them around. Several of the District universities keep them, as living libraries for their biology students. It's not really an original idea."

"Well," he persevered, feeling like a fish swimming upstream against this current of self-deprecation, "I thought it was very fine, and deserved better than just being a ghost garden on the holovid. I have this spare lot, you see . . ."

He flattened out his flimsy, which was a ground plot of the block occupied by Vorkosigan House. He tapped his finger on the bare square at the end. "There used to be another great house, next to ours, which was torn down during the Regency. ImpSec wouldn't let us build anything else—they wanted it as a security zone. There's nothing there but some scraggly grass, and a couple of trees that somehow survived ImpSec's enthusiasm for clear lines of fire. And a criss-cross of walks, where people made mud paths by taking short cuts, and they finally gave up and put some gravel down. It's an extremely boring piece of ground." So boring he had completely ignored it, till now.

She tilted her head, to follow his hand as it blocked out the space on the ground plan. Her own long finger made to trace a delicate curve, but then shyly withdrew. He wondered what possibility her mind's eye had just seen, there.

"Now, I think," he went on valiantly, "that it would be a splendid thing to install a Barrayaran garden—all native species—open to the public, in this space. A sort of gift from the Vorkosigan family to the city of Vorbarr Sultana. With running water, like in your design, and walks and benches and all those civilized things. And those discreet little name tags on all the plants, so more people could learn about the old ecology and all that." There: art, public service, education— was there any bait he'd left off his hook? Oh yes, money. "It's a happy chance that you're looking for a summer job," *chance, hah, watch and see if I leave anything to chance,* "because I think you'd be the ideal person to take this on. Design and oversee the installation of the thing. I could give you an unlimited, um, generous budget, and a salary, of course. You could hire workmen, bring in whatever you needed."

And she would have to visit Vorkosigan House practically *every day*, and consult *frequently* with its resident lord. And by the time the shock of her husband's death had worn away, and she was ready to put off her forbidding formal mourning garb, and every unattached Vor bachelor in the capital showed up on her doorstep, Miles could have a lock on her affections that would permit him to fend off the most glittering competition. It was too soon, wildly too soon, to suggest courtship to her crippled heart; he had that clear in his head, even if his own heart howled in frustration. But a straightforward business friendship just might get past her guard. . . .

Her eyebrows had flown up; she touched an uncertain finger to those exquisite, pale unpainted lips. "This is exactly the sort of thing I wish to train to do. I don't know how to do it *yet.*"

"On-the-job training," Miles responded instantly. "Apprenticeship. Learning by doing. You have to start sometime. You can't start sooner than now."

"But what if I make some dreadful mistake?"

"I do intend this be an *ongoing* project. People who are enthusiasts about this sort of thing always seem to be changing their gardens around. They get bored with the same view all the time, I guess. If you come up with better ideas later, you can always revise the plan. It will provide variety."

"I don't want to waste your money."

If she ever became Lady Vorkosigan, she would have to get over that quirk, Miles decided firmly.

"You don't have to decide here on the spot," he purred, and cleared his throat. *Watch that tone, boy. Business.* "Why don't you come to Vorkosigan House tomorrow, and walk over the site in person, and see what ideas it stirs up in your mind. You really can't tell anything by looking at a flimsy. We can have lunch, afterward, and talk about what you see as the problems and possibilities then. Logical?"

She blinked. "Yes, very." Her hand crept back curiously toward the flimsy.

"What time may I pick you up?"

"Whatever is convenient for you, Lord Vorkosigan. Oh, I take that back. If it's after twelve hundred, my aunt will be back from her morning class, and Nikki can stay with her."

"Excellent!" Yes, much as he liked Ekaterin's son, Miles thought he could do without the assistance of an active nine-year-old in this delicate dance. "Twelve hundred it will be. Consider it a deal." Only a little belatedly, he added, "And how does Nikki like Vorbarr Sultana, so far?"

"He seems to like his room, and this house. I think he's going to get a little bored, if he has to wait until his school starts to locate boys his own age."

It would not do to leave Nikolai Vorsoisson out of his calculations. "I gather then that the retro-genes took, and he's in no more danger of developing the symptoms of Vorzohn's Dystrophy?"

A smile of deep maternal satisfaction softened her face. "That's right. I'm so pleased. The doctors in the clinic here in Vorbarr Sultana report he had a very clean and complete cellular uptake. Developmentally, it should be just as if he'd never inherited the mutation at all." She glanced across at him. "It's as if I'd had a five-hundred-kilo weight lifted from me. I could fly, I think."

So you should.

Nikki himself emerged from the house at this moment, carrying a plate of cookies with an air of consequence, followed by the Professora with a tea tray and cups. Miles and Ekaterin hastened to clear a place on the table.

"Hello, Nikki," said Miles.

"Hi, Lord Vorkosigan. Is that your groundcar out front?"

"Yes."

"It's a barge." This observation was delivered without scorn, as a point of interest.

"I know. It's a relic of my father's time as Regent. It's armored, in fact—has a massive momentum."

"Oh yeah?" Nikki's interest soared. "Did it ever get shot at?"

"I don't believe that particular car ever did, no."

"Huh."

When Miles had last seen Nikki, the boy had been wooden-faced and pale with concentration, carrying the taper to light his father's funeral offering, obviously anxious to get his part of the ceremony right. He looked much better now, his brown eyes quick and his face mobile again. The Professora settled and poured tea, and the conversation became general for a time.

It became clear shortly that Nikki's interest was more in the food than in his mother's visitor; he declined a flatteringly grownup offer of tea, and with his great-aunt's permission snagged several cookies and dodged back indoors to whatever he'd been occupying himself with before. Miles tried to remember what age he'd been when his own parents' friends had stopped seeming part of the furniture. Well, except for the military men in his father's train, of course, who'd always riveted his attention. But then, Miles had been military-mad from the time he could walk. Nikki was jump-ship mad, and would probably light up for a jump pilot. Perhaps Miles could provide one sometime, for Nikki's delectation. A happily married one, he corrected this thought.

He'd laid his bait on the table, Ekaterin had taken it; it was time to quit while he was winning. But he knew for a fact that she'd already turned down one premature offer of remarriage from a completely unexpected quarter. *Had* any of Vorbarr Sultana's excess Vor males found her yet? The capital was crawling with young officers, rising bureaucrats, aggressive entrepreneurs, men of ambition and wealth and rank drawn to the empire's heart. But not, by a ratio of almost five to three, with their sisters. The parents of the preceding generation had taken galactic sex-selection technologies much too far in their foolish passion for male heirs, and the very sons they'd so cherished—Miles's contemporaries—had inherited the resulting mating mess. Go to any formal party in Vorbarr Sultana these days, and you could practically taste the damned testosterone in the air, volatilized by the alcohol no doubt.

"So, ah . . . have you had any other callers yet, Ekaterin?"

"I only arrived a week ago."

That was neither yes nor no. "I'd think you'd have the bachelors out in force in no time." Wait, he hadn't meant to point that out . . .

"Surely," she gestured down her black dress, "this will keep them away. If they have any manners at all."

"Mm, I'm not so sure. The social scene is pretty intense just now."

She shook her head and smiled bleakly. "It makes no difference to me. I had a decade of . . . of marriage. I don't need to repeat the experience. The other women are welcome to the bachelors; they can have my share, in fact." The conviction in her face was backed by an uncharacteristic hint of steel in her voice. "That's one mistake I don't have to make twice. I'll never remarry."

Miles controlled his flinch, and managed a sympathetic, interested smile at this confidence. *We're just friends. I'm not hustling you, no, no. No need to fling up your defenses, milady, not for me.*

He couldn't make this go faster by pushing harder; all he could do was screw it up worse. Forced to be satisfied with his one day's progress, Miles finished his tea, exchanged a few more pleasantries with the two women, and took his leave.

Pym hurried to open the groundcar door as Miles skipped down the last three steps in one jump. He flung himself into the passenger seat, and as Pym slipped back into the driver's side and closed the canopy, waved grandly. "Home, Pym."

Pym eased the groundcar into the street, and inquired mildly, "Go well, did it, m'lord?"

"Just exactly as I had planned. She's coming to Vorkosigan House tomorrow for lunch. As soon as we get home, I want you to call that gardening service—get them to get a crew out tonight and give the grounds an extra going-over. And talk to—no, *I'll* talk to Ma Kosti. Lunch must be . . . exquisite, yes. Ivan always says women like food. But not too heavy. Wine—does she drink wine in the daytime, I wonder? I'll offer it, anyway. Something from the estate. And tea if she doesn't choose the wine, I know she drinks tea. Scratch the wine. And get the house cleaning crew in, get all those covers off the first floor furniture—off all the furniture. I want to give her a tour of the house while she still doesn't realize . . . No, wait. I wonder . . . if the place was a dreadful bachelor mess, perhaps it would stir up her pity. Maybe instead I ought to clutter it up some more, used glasses strategically piled up, the odd fruit peel under the sofa—a silent appeal, *Help us! Move in and straighten this poor fellow out*—or would that be more likely to frighten her off? What do you think, Pym?"

Pym pursed his lips judiciously, as if considering whether it was within his Armsman's duties to spike his lord's taste for street theater. He finally said in a cautious tone, "If I may presume to speak for the household, I *think* we should prefer to put our best foot forward. Under the circumstances."

"Oh. All right."

Miles fell silent for a few moments, staring out the canopy as they threaded through the crowded city streets, out of the University district and across a mazelike corner of the Old Town, angling back toward Vorkosigan House. When he spoke again, the manic humor had drained from his voice, leaving it cooler and bleaker.

"We'll be picking her up tomorrow at twelve hundred. You'll drive. You will always drive, when Madame Vorsoisson or her son are aboard. Figure it in to your duty schedule from now on."

"Yes, m'lord." Pym added a carefully laconic, "My pleasure."

The seizure disorder was the last souvenir that ImpSec Captain Miles Vorkosigan had brought home from his decade of military missions. He'd been lucky to get out of the cryo-chamber alive and with his mind intact; Miles was fully aware that many did not fare nearly so well. Lucky to be merely medically discharged from the Emperor's Service, not buried with honors, the last of his glorious line, or reduced to some animal or vegetative existence. The seizure-stimulator the military doctors had issued him to bleed off his convulsions was very far from being a cure, though it was supposed to keep them from happening at random times. Miles drove, and flew his lightflyer—but only alone. He never took passengers anymore. Pym's batman's duties had been expanded to include medical assistance; he had by now witnessed enough of Miles's disturbing seizures to be grateful for this unusual burst of level-headedness.

One corner of Miles's mouth crooked up. After a moment, he asked, "And how did you ever capture Ma Pym, back in the old days, Pym? Did you put your best foot forward?"

"It's been almost eighteen years ago. The details have gone a bit fuzzy." Pym smiled a little. "I was a senior sergeant at the time. I'd taken the ImpSec advanced course, and was assigned to security duty at Vorhartung Castle. She had a clerk's job in the archives there. I thought, I wasn't some boy anymore, it was time I got serious . . . though I'm not just sure that wasn't an idea she put into my head, because she claims she spotted me first."

"Ah, a handsome fellow in uniform, I see. Does it every time. So why'd you decide to quit the Imperial Service and apply to the Count-my-father?"

"Eh, it seemed the right progression. Our little daughter'd come along by then, I was just finishing my twenty-years hitch, and I was facing whether or not to continue my enlistment. My wife's family was here, and her roots, and she didn't particularly fancy following the flag with children in tow. Captain Illyan, who knew I was District-born, was kind enough to give me a tip, that your father had a place open in his Armsmen's score. And a recommendation, when I nerved up to apply. I figured a Count's Armsman would be a more settled job, for a family man."

The groundcar arrived at Vorkosigan House; the ImpSec corporal on duty opened the gates for them, and Pym pulled around to the porte cochère and popped the canopy.

"Thank you, Pym," Miles said, and hesitated. "A word in your ear. Two words."

Pym made to look attentive.

"When you chance to socialize with the Armsmen of other Houses . . . I'd appreciate it if you wouldn't mention Madame Vorsoisson. I wouldn't want her to be the subject of invasive gossip, and, um . . . she's no business of everyone and his younger brother anyway, eh?"

"A loyal Armsman does not gossip, m'lord," said Pym stiffly.

"No, of course not. Sorry, I didn't mean to imply . . . um, sorry. Anyway. The other thing. I'm maybe guilty of saying a little too much myself, you see. I'm not actually courting Madame Vorsoisson."

Pym tried to look properly blank, but a confused expression leaked into his face. Miles added hastily, "I mean, not *formally*. Not *yet*. She's . . . she's had a difficult time, recently, and she's a touch . . . skittish. Any premature declaration on my part is likely to be disastrous, I'm afraid. It's a timing problem. Discreet is the watchword, if you see what I mean?"

Pym attempted a discreet but supportive-looking smile.

"We're just good friends," Miles reiterated. "Anyway, we're going to be."

"Yes, m'lord. I understand."

"Ah. Good. Thank you." Miles climbed out of the groundcar, and added over his shoulder as he headed into the house, "Find me in the kitchen when you've put the car away."

✦ ✦ ✦

Ekaterin stood in the middle of the blank square of grass with gardens boiling up in her head.

"If you excavated there," she pointed, "and piled it up on that side, you'd gain enough slope for the water flow. A bit of a wall there, too, to block off the street noise and to heighten the effect. And the walkway curving down—" She wheeled, to encounter Lord Vorkosigan watching her, smiling, his hands stuffed in his gray trouser pockets. "Or would you prefer something more geometrical?"

"Beg pardon?" He blinked.

"It's an aesthetic question."

"I, uh . . . aesthetics are not exactly my area of expertise." He said this in a tone of sad confession, as though it might be something of which she was previously unaware.

Her hands sketched the bones of the projected piece, trying to call structure out of the air. "Do you want an illusion of a natural space, Barrayar before it was touched by man, with the water seeming like rocks and a creek, a slice of backcountry in the city—or something more in the nature of a metaphor, with the Barrayaran plants in the interstices of these strong human lines—probably in concrete. You can do really wonderful things with water and concrete."

"Which is better?"

"It's not a question of better. It's a question of what you are trying to say."

"I hadn't thought of it as a political statement. I'd thought of it as a gift."

"If it's your garden, it will be seen as a political statement whether you intended it or not."

The corner of his lip quirked as he took this in. "I'll have to think about that. But there's no doubt in your mind something could be done with the area?"

"Oh, none." The two Earth trees, seemingly stuck in the flat ground at random, would have to go. That silver maple was punky in the heartwood and would be no loss, but the young oak was sound—perhaps it could be moved. The terraformed topsoil must also be salvaged. Her hands twitched with the desire to start digging into the dirt then and there. "It's an extraordinary space to find preserved in the middle of Vorbarr Sultana." Across the street, a commercial office building rose a dozen stories high. Fortunately, it angled to the north and did not block out much light. The hiss and huff of groundcar fans made continuous counterpoint along the busy thoroughfare crossing the top end of the block, where she'd mentally placed her wall. Across the park on the opposite side, a high gray stone wall topped with iron spikes was already in place; treetops rising beyond it half-screened from view the great house holding down the center of the block.

"I'd invite you to sit while I think about it," said Lord Vorkosigan, "but ImpSec never put in benches—they didn't want to encourage loitering around the Regent's residence. Suppose you run up both contrasting designs on your comconsole, and bring them to me for review. Meanwhile, shall we walk round to the house? I think my cook will have lunch ready soon."

"Oh . . . all right . . ." With only one backward glance at the entrancing possibilities, Ekaterin let him lead her away.

They angled across the park. Around the corner of the gray wall at Vorkosigan House's front entrance, a concrete kiosk sheltered a guard in Imperial Security undress greens. He coded open the iron gate for the little Lord Auditor and his guest, and watched them pass through it, exchanging a short formal nod for Vorkosigan's thank-you half-salute, and smiling pleasantly at Ekaterin.

The somber stone of the mansion rose before them, four stories high in two major wings. What seemed dozens of windows frowned down. The short semicircle of drive curled around a brilliantly healthy patch of green grass and under a portico, which sheltered carved double doors flanked by tall narrow windows.

"Vorkosigan House is about two hundred years old, now. It was built by my great-great-great grandfather, the seventh Count, in a moment of historically unusual family prosperity ended by, among other things, the building of Vorkosigan House," Lord Vorkosigan told her cheerfully. "It replaced some decaying clan fortress down in the old Caravanserai area, and not before time, I gather."

He started to hold his hand to a palm-lock, but the doors eased soundlessly open before he could even touch it. His brows twitched up, and he bowed her inside.

Two guardsmen in Vorkosigan brown-and-silver livery stood at attention, flanking the entrance to the black-and-white stone-paved foyer. A third liveried man, Pym, the tall driver whom she'd met when Vorkosigan had picked her up earlier, was just turning away from the door security control panel; he too braced before his lord. Ekaterin was daunted. She had not received the impression when she'd seen him on Komarr that Vorkosigan maintained the old Vor formalities to quite this extent. Though not totally formal—instead of being sternly expressionless, the large guardsmen all smiled down at them, in a friendly and most welcoming manner.

"Thank you, Pym," said Vorkosigan automatically, and paused. After a moment regarding them back with a quizzical bent to his brows, he added, "I thought you were on night shift, Roic. Shouldn't you be asleep?"

The largest and youngest of the guards stood more stiffly to attention, and murmured, "M'lord."

"*M'lord* is not an answer. *M'lord* is an evasion," Vorkosigan said, in a tone more of observation than censure. The guard ventured a subdued smile. Vorkosigan sighed, and turned from him. "Madame Vorsoisson, permit me to introduce the rest of the Vorkosigan Armsmen presently seconded to me—Armsman Jankowski, Armsman Roic. Madame Vorsoisson."

She ducked her head, and they both nodded back, murmuring, "Madame Vorsoisson," and "My pleasure, Madame."

"Pym, you can let Ma Kosti know we're here. Thank you, gentlemen, that *will* be all," Vorkosigan added, with peculiar emphasis.

With more subdued smiles, they melted away down the back passage. Pym's voice drifted back, "See, what did I tell you—" His further explication to his comrades, whatever it was, was quickly muffled by distance into an unintelligible mutter.

Vorkosigan rubbed his lips, recovered his hostly cordiality, and turned back to her again. "Would you like to take a walk around the house before lunch? Many people find it of historical interest."

Personally, she thought it would be utterly fascinating, but she didn't want to come on like some goggling backcountry tourist. "I don't wish to trouble you, Lord Vorkosigan."

His mouth flickered to dismay and back again to earnest welcome. "No trouble. A pleasure, in fact." His gaze at her grew oddly intent.

Did he want her to say yes? Perhaps he was very proud of his possessions. "Then thank you. I should like that very much."

It was the right answer. His cheer returned in force, and he immediately motioned her to the left. A formal antechamber gave way to a wonderful library running the length of the end of the wing; she had to tuck her hands in her bolero pockets to keep them from diving at the old printed books with leather bindings which lined parts of the room from floor to ceiling. He bowed her out glass doors at the end of the library and across a back garden where several generations of servitors had clearly left very little room for any improvements. She thought she might plunge her arm to the elbow into the soil of the perennial beds. Apparently determined to be thorough, he led on into the cross-wing and down to an enormous wine cellar stocked with produce of various Vorkosigan District country farms. They passed through a subbasement garage. The gleaming armored groundcar was there, and a red enameled lightflyer tucked into a corner.

"Is that yours?" Ekaterin said brightly, nodding to the lightflyer.

His answer was unusually brief. "Yes. But I don't fly it much any more."

Oh. Yes. His seizures. She could have kicked herself. Fearing that some tangled attempt to apologize could only make it worse, she followed his shortcut up through a huge and redolent kitchen complex. There Vorkosigan formally introduced her to his famous cook, a plump middle-aged woman named Ma Kosti, who smiled broadly at Ekaterin and thwarted her lord's attempt to sample his lunch-in-preparation. Ma Kosti made it plain she felt her vast domain was underutilized—but how much could one short man eat, after all? He should be encouraged to bring in more company; hope you will come again soon, and often, Madame Vorsoisson.

Ma Kosti benignly shooed them on their way again, and Vorkosigan conducted Ekaterin through a bewildering succession of formal receiving rooms and back to the paved foyer. "Those are the public areas," he told her. "The second floor is all my own territory." With an infectious enthusiasm, he hustled her up the curving staircase to show off a suite of rooms he assured her had once been occupied by the famous General Count Piotr himself, and which were now his own. He made sure to point out the excellent view of the back gardens from the suite's sitting room.

"There are two more floors, plus the attics. The attics of Vorkosigan House are something to behold. Would you like to see them? Is there anything you'd particularly like to see?"

"I don't know," she said, feeling a little overwhelmed. "Did you grow up here?" She stared around the well-appointed sitting room, trying to picture the child-Miles therein, and decide whether she was grateful he'd stopped short of hauling her through his bedroom, just visible through the end door.

"In fact, for the first five or six years of my life, we lived at the Imperial Residence with Gregor," he replied. "My parents and my grandfather had some little, um, disagreement in the early years of the Regency, but then they were reconciled, and Gregor went off to the preparatory academy. My parents moved back here; they claimed the third floor the way I've marked off the second. Heir's privilege. Several generations in one house works best if it's a very *large* house. My grandfather had these rooms till he died, when I was about seventeen. I had a room on my parents' floor, though not in the same wing. They chose it for me because Illyan said it had the worst angle of fire from . . . um, it has a good view of the garden too. Would you care to . . . ?" He turned, gestured, smiled over his shoulder, and led her out and up another flight, around a corner, and part way down a long hall.

The room into which they turned did have a good window on the garden, but any traces of the boy Miles had been were erased. It was now done up as a bland guest room, with scant personality beyond what was lent it by the fabulous house itself. "How long were you here?" she asked, staring around.

"Till last winter, actually. I moved downstairs after I was medically discharged." He jerked up his chin in his habitual nervous tic. "During the decade I served in ImpSec, I was home so seldom, I never thought to need more."

"At least you had your own bath. These houses from the Time of Isolation are sometimes—" She broke off, as the door she casually opened proved instead to be a closet. The door next to it must lead into the bath. A soft glow of light came on automatically.

The closet was stuffed with uniforms—Lord Vorkosigan's old military uniforms, she realized from the size of them, and the superior tailoring. He wouldn't have been able to use standard-issue gear, after all. She recognized black fatigues, Imperial dress and undress greens, and the glittering brilliance of the formal parade red-and-blues. An array of boots stood guard along the floor from side to side. They'd all been put away clean, but the close concentrated aroma of him still permeated the warm dry air that puffed against her face like a caress. She inhaled, stunned by the military-masculine patchouli. It seemed to flow from her nose to her body directly, circumventing her brain. He stepped anxiously to her side, watching her face; the well-chosen scent he wore that she'd noticed in the cool air of his groundcar, a flattering spicy-citrus overlying clean male, was suddenly intensified by his proximity.

It was the first moment of spontaneous sensuality she'd felt since Tien's death. *Oh, since years before Tien's death.* It was embarrassing, yet oddly comforting too. *Am I alive below the neck after all?* She was abruptly aware that this was a bedroom.

"What's this one?" She kept her voice from squeaking upward much, and reached to pull out an unfamiliar gray uniform on its hanger, a heavy short jacket with epaulettes, many closed pockets, and white trim, with matching trousers. The stripes on the sleeves and assorted collar-pins encoding rank were a mystery to her, but there seemed to be a lot of them. The fabric had that odd fire-proof feel one found only in seriously expensive field gear.

His smile softened. "Well, now." He slipped the jacket off the hanger she clutched, and held it up briefly. "You've never met Admiral Naismith, have you. He was my favorite covert ops persona. He—I—ran the Dendarii Free Mercenary Fleet for ImpSec for years."

"You pretended to be a galactic admiral?"

"—Lieutenant Vorkosigan?" he finished wryly. "It started as a pretense. I made it real." One corner of his mouth zigged up, and with a murmur of *Why not?*, he hung the jacket over the doorknob and slipped out of his gray tunic, revealing a fine white shirt. A shoulder holster she'd not guessed he wore held a hand-weapon flat to his left side. *Even here, he goes armed?* It was only a heavy-duty stunner, but he seemed to wear it as unselfconsciously as he wore his shirt. *I suppose if you are a Vorkosigan, that's how you dress every day.*

He traded the tunic for the jacket and pulled it on; his suit trousers were so close a color match, he hardly needed to don the uniform pants to present his effect, or effect his presentation. He stretched, and on the return came to a posture totally unlike anything she'd seen in him before: relaxed, extended, somehow filling the space beyond his undersized body. One arm came out to prop him casually against the doorframe, and his tilted smile turned into something blazing. In a deadpan-perfect flat Betan accent that seemed never to have heard of the concept of the Vor caste, he said, "Aw, don't let that dull dirt-sucking Barrayaran bring you down. Stick with me, lady, and I'll show you the galaxy." Ekaterin, startled, stepped back a pace.

He jerked up his chin, still grinning dementedly, and began fastening the clasps. His hands reached the jacket waist, straightened the band, and paused. The ends were a couple of centimeters short of meeting at the middle, and the clasp notably failed to seat itself even when he gave it a covert tug. He stared down in such obvious dismay at this treasonous shrinkage, Ekaterin choked on a giggle.

He glanced up at her, and a rueful smile lit his eyes in response to the crinkle of her own. His voice returned to Barrayaran-normal. "I haven't had this on for over a year. Seems we outgrow our past in more ways than one." He hitched back out of the uniform jacket. "Hm. Well, you met my cook. Food's not a job for her, it's a sacred calling."

"Maybe it shrank in the wash," she offered in attempted consolation.

"Bless you. No." He sighed. "The Admiral's deep cover was fraying badly even before he was killed. Naismith's days were numbered anyway."

His voice made light of this loss, but she'd seen the scars on his chest left by the needle-grenade. Her mind circled back to the seizure she'd witnessed, on the living room floor of her and Tien's cramped apartment on Komarr. She remembered the look in his eyes after the epileptic storm had passed: mental confusion, shame, helpless rage. The man had driven his body far past its limits, in the belief, apparently, that unsupported will could conquer anything.

So it can. For a time. Then time ran out—no. Time ran on. There was no end to time. *But you come to the end of yourself, and time runs on, and leaves you.* Her years with Tien had taught her that, if nothing else.

"I suppose I ought to give these to Nikki to play with." He gestured casually at the row of uniforms. But his hands carefully straightened the gray jacket again on its hanger, brushed invisible lint, and hooked it back into its place in the bar. "While he still can, and is young enough to want to. He'll outgrow them in another year or so, I think."

Her breath drew in. *I think that would be obscene.* These relics had clearly been life and death to him. What possessed him, to make-believe they were no more than a child's playthings? She couldn't think how to discourage him from this horrifying notion without sounding as though she scorned his offer. Instead, after the moment's silence threatened to stretch unbearably, she blurted, "Would you go back? If you could?"

His gaze grew distant. "Well, now . . . now that's the strangest thing. I think I would feel like a snake trying to crawl back into its shed dead skin. I miss it every minute, and I have no wish at all to go back." He looked up, and twinkled at her. "Needle grenades are a learning experience, that way."

This was his idea of a joke, apparently. She wasn't sure if she wanted to kiss him and make it well, or run away screaming. She managed a faint smile.

He shrugged on his plain civilian tunic, and the sinister shoulder holster disappeared from view again. Closing the closet door firmly, he took her on a spin around the rest of the third floor; he pointed out his absent parents' suite, but to Ekaterin's secret relief did not offer to take her inside the succession of rooms. It would have felt very odd to wander through the famous Count and Countess Vorkosigan's intimate space, as though she were some voyeur.

They finally fetched up back on "his" floor, at the end of the main wing in a bright room he called the Yellow Parlor, which he apparently used as a dining room. A small table was elegantly set up for lunch for two. Good, they were not expected to dine downstairs in that elaborately-paneled cavern with the table that extended to seat forty-eight; ninety-six in a squeeze, if a second table, cleverly secreted behind the wainscoting, was brought out in parallel. At some unseen signal, Ma Kosti appeared with luncheon on a cart: soup, tea, an exquisite salad involving cultured shrimp and fruit and nuts. She left her lord and his guest discreetly alone after the initial flourishing serving, though a large silver tray with a domed cover which she left sitting atop the cart at Lord Vorkosigan's elbow promised more delights to come.

"It's a great house," Lord Vorkosigan told Ekaterin between bites, "but it gets really quiet at night. Lonely. It's not meant to be this empty. It needs to be filled up with life again, the way it used to be in my father's heyday." His tone was almost disconsolate.

"The Viceroy and Vicereine will be returning for the Emperor's wedding, won't they? It should be full again at Midsummer," she pointed out helpfully.

"Oh, yes, and their whole entourage. *Everyone* will be back on planet for the wedding." He hesitated. "Including my brother Mark, come to think of it. I suppose I should warn you about Mark."

"My uncle once mentioned you had a clone. Is that him, um . . . it?"

"*It* is the preferred Betan pronoun for a hermaphrodite; definitely him. Yes."

"Uncle Vorthys didn't say why you—or was it your parents?—had a clone made, except that it was complicated, and I should ask you." The explanation that leapt most readily to mind was that Count Vorkosigan had wanted an undeformed replacement for his soltoxin-damaged heir, but that obviously wasn't the case.

"That's the complicated part. *We* didn't. Some Komarran expatriates exiled to Earth did, as part of a much-too-baroque plot against my father. I guess when they couldn't get up a military revolution, they thought they'd try some biological warfare on a budget. They got an agent to filch a tissue sample from me—it couldn't have been that hard, I'd had hundreds of medical treatments and tests and biopsies as a child—and farmed it out to one of the less savory clone lords on Jackson's Whole."

"My word. But Uncle Vorthys said your clone didn't look like you—did he grow up without your, um, prenatal damage, then?" She gave him a short nod, but kept her eyes politely on his face. She'd already encountered his somewhat erratic sensitivity about his birth defects. *Teratogenic, not genetic*, he'd made sure she understood.

"If it had been that simple . . . He actually started to grow as he should, so they had to body-sculpt him down to my size. And shape. It was pretty gruesome. They'd intended him to pass close inspection as my replacement, so when I did things like have my busted leg bones replaced with synthetics, his got surgically replaced too. I know exactly how much that must have hurt. And they forced him to study to pass for me. All the years I thought I was an only child, he was developing the worst case of sibling rivalry you ever saw. I mean, think about it. Never allowed to be yourself, constantly—under threat of torture, in fact—compared with your older brother . . . By the time the plot fell through, he was on a fair way to being driven crazy."

"I should think so! But . . . how did you rescue him from the Komarrans?"

He was silent for a little, then said, "He kind of turned up on his own, at the last. As soon as he came within my Betan mother's orbit—well, you can imagine. Betans have very strict and clear convictions about parental responsibilities to clones. It surprised the hell out of him, I think. He knew he had a brother, God knows he'd had his face ground into that fact, but he wasn't expecting parents. He certainly wasn't expecting Cordelia Vorkosigan. The family has adopted him, I suppose is the simplest way of thinking about it. He was here on Barrayar for a while, then last year my mother sent him off to Beta Colony, to attend university and get therapy under the supervision of my Betan grandmother."

"That sounds good," she said, pleased with the bizarre tale's happy ending. The Vorkosigans stood by their own, it seemed.

"Mm, maybe. Reports leaking back from my grandmother suggest it's been pretty rocky for him. You see, he's got this obsession— perfectly understandable—about differentiating himself from me, so's no one could ever mistake one of us for the other ever again. Which is fine by me, don't get me wrong. I think it's a great idea. But . . . but he could have gotten a facial mod, or body sculpture, or growth hormones, or changed his eye color or bleached his hair, or anything but . . . instead what he decided to do was gain a great deal of weight. At my height, the effect is damned startling. I think he likes it that way. Does it on purpose." He stared rather broodingly at his plate. "I thought his Betan therapy might do something about that, but apparently not."

A scrabble at the edge of the tablecloth made Ekaterin start; a determined-looking half-grown black-and-white kitten hauled itself up over the side, tiny claws like pitons, and made for Vorkosigan's plate. He smiled absently, picked a couple of remaining shrimp from his salad, and deposited them before the little beast; it growled and purred through its enthusiastic chewing. "The gate guard's cat keeps having these kittens," he explained. "I admire their approach to life, but they do turn up . . ." He picked the large cover off the tray, and deposited it over the creature, trapping it. The undaunted purr resonated against the silver hemisphere like some small machine stripping its gears. "Dessert?"

The silver tray was loaded with eight different dessert pastries, so alarmingly beautiful Ekaterin thought it an aesthetic crime to eat them without making a vid recording for posterity first. "Oh, my." After a long pause, she pointed at one with thick cream and glazed fruit like jewels. Vorkosigan slipped it onto a waiting plate, and handed it across. He stared at the array longingly, but did not select one for himself, Ekaterin noticed. He was not in the least fat, she thought indignantly; when he'd played Admiral Naismith he must have been practically emaciated. The pastry tasted as wonderful as it looked, and Ekaterin's contribution to the conversation ceased for a short time. Vorkosigan watched her, smiling in, apparently, vicarious pleasure.

As she was scraping up the last molecules of cream from her plate with her fork, footsteps sounded in the hall, and men's voices. She recognized Pym's rumble, saying, " . . . no, m'lord's in conference with his new landscape designer. I really don't think he wishes to be disturbed."

A drawling baritone replied, "Yeah, yeah, Pym. Nor did I. It's official business from m'mother."

A look of extreme annoyance flashed over Vorkosigan's face, and he bit off an expletive too muffled to quite make out. As his visitor loomed in the doorway to the Yellow Parlor, his expression went very bland.

The man Pym was failing to impede was a young officer, a tall and startlingly handsome captain in undress greens. He had dark hair, laughing brown eyes, and a lazy smile. He paused to sweep Vorkosigan a mocking half-bow, saying, "Hail, O Lord Auditor coz. My God, is that a Ma Kosti lunch I spy? Tell me I'm not too late. Is there anything left? Can I lick your crumbs?" He stepped inside, and his eye swept over Ekaterin. "Oh ho! Introduce me to your *landscape designer*, Miles!"

Lord Vorkosigan said, somewhat through his teeth, "Madame Vorsoisson, may I make you known to my feckless cousin, Captain Ivan Vorpatril. Ivan, Madame Vorsoisson."

Undaunted by this disapproving editorial, Vorpatril grinned, bowed deeply over her hand, and kissed it. His lips lingered an appreciative second too long, but at least they were dry and warm; she didn't have to overcome an impolite impulse to wipe her hand on her skirt, when he at last released it. "And are you taking commissions, Madame Vorsoisson?"

Ekaterin was not quite sure whether to be amused or offended at his cheerful leer, but amused seemed safer. She permitted herself a small smile. "I'm only just starting."

Lord Vorkosigan put in, "Ivan lives in an apartment. I believe there is a flowerpot on his balcony, but the last time I looked, its contents were dead."

"It was *winter*, Miles." A faint mewing from the silver dome at his elbow distracted him. He stared at the cover, curiously tilted it up on one side, said, "Ah. One of you," and let it back down. He wandered around the table, spied the unused dessert plate, smiled beatifically, and helped himself to two of the pastries and the leftover fork at his cousin's plate. Returning to the empty place opposite, he settled his spoils, dragged up a chair, and seated himself between Lord Vorkosigan and Ekaterin. He regarded the mews of protest rising in volume from the dome, sighed, retrieved the feline prisoner, and settled it on his lap atop the fine cloth napkin, occupying it with a liberal smear of cream on its paws and face. "Don't let me interrupt you," he added around his first bite.

"We were just finishing," said Vorkosigan. "Why are you *here*, Ivan?" He added under his breath, "And why couldn't three bodyguards keep you out? Do I have to give orders to shoot to kill?"

"My strength is great because my cause is just," Vorpatril informed him. "My mother has sent me with a list of chores for you as long as my arm. With footnotes." He drew a roll of folded flimsies from his tunic, and waved them at his cousin; the kitten rolled on its back and batted at them, and he amused himself briefly, batting back. "Tik-tik-tik!"

"Your determination is relentless because you're more afraid of your mother than you are of my guardsmen."

"So are you. So are your guardsmen," observed Lord Vorpatril, downing another bite of dessert.

Vorkosigan swallowed an involuntary laugh, then recovered his severe look again. "Ah . . . Madame Vorsoisson, I can see I'm going to have to deal with this. Perhaps we'd best break off for today." He smiled apologetically at her, and pushed back his chair.

Lord Vorkosigan doubtless had important security matters to discuss with the young officer. "Of course. Um, it was good to meet you, Lord Vorpatril."

Impeded by the kitten, the captain didn't rise, but he nodded a most cordial farewell. "Madame Vorsoisson, a pleasure. I hope we'll see each other again soon."

Vorkosigan's smile went thin; she rose with him, and he shepherded her out into the hall, raising his wristcom to his lips and murmuring, "Pym, please bring the car around front." He gestured onward, and fell into step beside her down the corridor. "Sorry about Ivan."

She didn't quite see what he felt the need to apologize for, so concealed her bewilderment in a shrug.

"So do we have a deal?" he went on. "Will you take on my project?"

"Maybe you'd better see a few possible designs, first."

"Yes, of course. Tomorrow . . . or you can call me whenever you're ready. You have my number?"

"Yes, you gave me several of them back on Komarr. I still have them."

"Ah. Good." They turned down the great stairway, and his face went thoughtful. At the bottom, he looked up at her and added, "And do you still have that little memento?"

He meant the tiny model Barrayar, pendant on a chain, souvenir of the grim events they couldn't talk about in any public forum. "Oh, yes."

He paused hopefully, and she was stricken that she couldn't pull the jewelry out of her black blouse and demonstrate it on the spot, but she'd thought it too valuable to wear everyday; it was put away, carefully wrapped, in a drawer in her aunt's house. After a moment, the sound of the groundcar came from the porte cochère, and he ushered her back out the double doors.

"Good day, then, Madame Vorsoisson." He shook her hand, firmly and without holding it for too long, and saw her into the groundcar's rear compartment. "I guess I'd better go straighten out Ivan." As the canopy closed and the car pulled away, he turned to stalk back indoors. By the time the car bore her smoothly out the gates, he'd vanished from view.

Ivan set one of the used salad plates down on the floor, and plunked the kitten next to it. He had to admit, a young animal of almost any kind made an excellent prop; he'd noted the way Madame Vorsoisson's cool expression had softened as he'd noodled with the furry little verminoid. Where had Miles found that astonishing widow? He sat back, and watched the kitten's pink tongue flash over the sauce, and reflected glumly on his own last night's outing.

His date had seemed such a *possible* young woman: University student, away from home for the first time, bound to be impressed with an Imperial Vor officer. Bold of gaze and not a bit shy; she'd picked *him* up in *her* lightflyer. Ivan was expert in the uses of a lightflyer for breaking down psychological barriers and creating the proper mood. A few gentle swoops and you could almost always evoke some of those cute little shrieks where the young lady clung closer, her chest rising and falling as her breath came faster through parted and increasingly-kissable lips. *This* girl, however . . . he hadn't come so near to losing his last meal in a lightflyer since being trapped by Miles in one of his manic phases for an updraft demonstration over Hassadar. She'd laughed, fiendishly, while Ivan had smiled helplessly through clenched teeth, his knuckles whitening on the seat straps.

Then, in the restaurant she'd picked, they'd met up oh-so-casually with that surly pup of a graduate student, and the playlet began to fall into place. She'd been *using* him, dammit, to test the pup's devotion to her cause; and the cur had rolled over and snarled right on cue. *How do you do, sir. Oh, isn't this your uncle you said was in the Service? I beg your pardon. . . .* The smooth way he'd managed to turn the overly respectful offer of a chair into a subtle insult had been worthy of, of Ivan's shortest relative, practically. Ivan had escaped early, silently wishing them joy of each other. Let the punishment fit the crime. He didn't know what was happening with young Barrayaran girls these days. They were turning almost . . . almost *galactic*, as if they'd been taking lessons from Miles's formidable friend Quinn. His mother's acerbic recommendation that he stick to women of his own age and class seemed almost to begin to make sense.

Light footsteps echoed from the hall, and his cousin appeared in the doorway. Ivan considered, and dismissed, an impulse to favor Miles with a vivid account of last night's debacle. Whatever emotion was tightening Miles's lips and pulling his head down into that bulldog-with-a-hair-up-its-butt look, it was very far from promising sympathy.

"Rotten timing, Ivan," Miles bit out.

"What, did I spoil your tête-à-tête? *Landscape designer*, eh? *I* could develop a sudden interest in a landscape like that, too. What a profile."

"Exquisite," Miles breathed, temporarily distracted by some inner vision.

"And her face isn't bad, either," Ivan added, watching him.

Miles almost took the bait right then, but he muffled his initial response in a grimace. "Don't get greedy. Weren't you telling me you have that sweetheart deal with Madame Vor-what's-her-name?" He pulled back his chair and slumped into it, crossing his arms and his ankles and watching Ivan through narrowed eyes.

"Ah. Yes. Well. That seems to have fallen through."

"You amaze me. Was the compliant husband not so compliant after all?"

"It was all so unreasonable. I mean, they're cooking up their kid in a uterine replicator. It's not like someone even *can* graft a little bastard onto the family tree these days. In any case, he's nailed down a post in the colonial administration, and is whisking her off to Sergyar. He scarcely even let us make a civil good-bye." It had been an unpleasant scene with oblique death threats, actually. It might have been mitigated by the slightest sign of regret, or even concern for Ivan's health and safety, on her part, but instead she'd spent the moment hanging on her husband's arm and looking impressed by his territorial trumpeting. As for the pubescent prole terrorist with the lightflyer whom he'd next tried to persuade to mend his broken heart . . . he suppressed a shudder.

Ivan shrugged off his retrospective moment of depression, and went on, "But a widow, a real live young widow! Do you know how hard they are to find these days? I know fellows in HQ who'd give their right hands for a friendly widow, except they have to save them for those long, lonely nights. However did you luck onto this honey-pot?"

His cousin didn't deign to answer. After a moment, he gestured to the flimsy, rolled up beside Ivan's empty plate. "So what's all this?"

"Ah." Ivan flattened it out, and handed it across the table. "It's the agenda for your upcoming meeting with the Emperor, the Empress-to-be, and my mother. She's pinning Gregor to the wall on all the final details about the wedding. Since you are to be Gregor's Second, your presence is requested and required."

"Oh." Miles glanced down the contents. A puzzled line appeared between his brows, and he looked up again at Ivan. "Not that this isn't important, but shouldn't you be on duty at Ops right now?"

"Ha," said Ivan glumly. "Do you know what those bastards have done to me?"

Miles shook his head, brows rising inquisitively.

"I have been formally seconded to my mother—my *mother*—as aide-de-camp till the wedding's over. I joined the Service to get *away* from my mother, blast it. And now she's suddenly my chain of command!"

His cousin's brief grin was entirely without sympathy. "Until Laisa is safely hitched to Gregor, and can take over her duties as his political hostess, your mother may be the most important person in Vorbarr Sultana. Don't underestimate her. I've seen planetary invasion plans less complex than what's being booted about for this Imperial Wedding. It's going to take all Aunt Alys's generalship to bring it off."

Ivan shook his head. "I knew I should have put in for off-planet duty while I still could. Komarr, Sergyar, some dismal embassy, anywhere but Vorbarr Sultana."

Miles's face sobered. "I don't know, Ivan. Short of a surprise attack, this is the most politically important event of—I was about to say, of the year, but I really think, of our lifetimes. The more little heirs Gregor and Laisa can put between you and me and the Imperium, the safer we'll be. Us *and* our families."

"We don't have families yet," Ivan pointed out. *So, is that what's on his mind with the pretty widow? Oh ho!*

"Would we have dared? *I* sure thought about the issue, every time I got close enough to a woman to . . . never mind. But this wedding needs to run on rails, Ivan."

"I'm not arguing with that," said Ivan sincerely. He reached down to dissuade the kitten, who had licked the plate clean, from trying to sharpen its claws on his polished boots. A few moments spent petting it in his lap bought it off from that enthusiasm, and it settled down, purring, to the serious business of digesting and growing more hairs to shed on Imperial uniforms. "So what's your widow's first name, say again?" Miles hadn't actually imparted that bit of information, yet.

"Ekaterin," Miles sighed. His mouth seemed to caress all four syllables before reluctantly parting with them.

Oh, yeah. Ivan thought back over every bit of chaff his cousin had ever inflicted upon him for his numerous love affairs. *Did you think I was a stone, for you to sharpen your wits upon?* Opportunities to even the score seemed to hover on the horizon like rain clouds after a long drought. "Grief-stricken, is she, you say? Seems to me she could use someone with a sense of humor, to cheer her up. Not you, you're clearly in one of your funks. Maybe I ought to volunteer to show her the town."

Miles had poured himself more tea and been just about to put his feet up on a neighboring chair; at this, they came back down with a thump. "Don't even think about it. This one is *mine*."

"Really? You secretly betrothed already? Quick work, coz."

"No," he admitted grudgingly.

"You have some sort of an understanding?"

"Not yet."

"So she is not, in point of fact, anyone's but her own. At present."

Uncharacteristically, Miles took a slow sip of tea before responding. "I mean to change that. When the time is right, which it surely is not yet."

"Hey, all's fair in love and war. Why can't I try?"

Miles snapped back, "If you step in this, it *will* be war."

"Don't let your exalted new status go to your head, coz. Even an Imperial Auditor can't order a woman to sleep with him."

"Marry him," Miles corrected frostily.

Ivan tilted his head, his grin spreading. "My God, you *are* gone completely over the edge. Who'd have guessed it?"

Miles bared his teeth. "Unlike you, *I* have never pretended to not be interested in that fate. *I* have no brave bachelor speeches to eat. Nor a juvenile reputation as a local stud to maintain. Or live down, as the case may be."

"My, we are snarky today."

Miles took a deep breath; before he could speak, Ivan put in, "Y'know, that head-down hostile scrunch makes you look more hunch-backed. You ought to watch that."

After a long, chill silence, Miles said softly, "Are you challenging my ingenuity . . . Ivan?"

"Ah . . ." It didn't take long to grope for the right answer. "No."

"Good," Miles breathed, settling back. "Good . . ." Another long and increasingly disturbing silence followed this, during which his cousin studied Ivan through narrowed eyes. At last, he seemed to come to some internal decision. "Ivan, I'm asking for your word as Vorpatril—just between you and me—that you will leave Ekaterin alone."

Ivan's brows flew up. "That's a little pushy, isn't it? I mean, doesn't she get a vote?"

Miles's nostrils flared. "You have no real interest in her."

"How do you know? How do *I* know? I barely had a chance to say hello before you hustled her out."

"I know you. For you, she's interchangeable with the next ten women you chance to meet. Well, she's not interchangeable for me. I propose a treaty. You can have all the rest of the women in the universe. I just want this one. I think that's fair."

It was one of those Miles-arguments again, which always seemed to result oh-so-logically in Miles getting whatever Miles wanted. Ivan recognized the pattern; it hadn't changed since they were five years old. Only the content had evolved. "The problem is, the rest of the women in the universe are not yours to dispense, either," Ivan pointed out triumphantly. After a couple of decades practice, he *was* getting quicker at this. "You're trying to trade something you don't have for—something you don't have."

Thwarted, Miles settled back in his chair and glowered at him.

"Seriously," said Ivan, "isn't your passion a trifle sudden, for a man who just parted company with the estimable Quinn at Winterfair? Where have you been hiding this Kat, till now?"

"Ekaterin. I met her on Komarr," Miles replied shortly.

"During your case? This *is* recent, then. Hey, you haven't told me all about your first case, Lord Auditor coz. I must say, all that uproar about their solar mirror sure seems to have petered out into nothing." He waited expectantly, but Miles did not pick up on this invitation. He must not be in one of his voluble moods. *Either you can't turn him on, or you can't turn him off.* Well, if there was a choice, taciturn was probably safer for the innocent bystanders than spring-wound. Ivan added after a moment, "So does she have a sister?"

"No."

"They never do." Ivan heaved a sigh. "Who is she, really? Where does she live?"

"She is Lord Auditor Vorthys's niece, and her husband suffered a ghastly death barely two months ago. I doubt she's in the mood for your humor."

She wasn't the only one so disinclined, it appeared. Damn, but Miles seemed stuck in prick-mode today. "Eh, he got mixed up in one of *your* affairs, did he? That'll teach him." Ivan leaned back, and grinned sourly. "That's one way to solve the widow shortage, I suppose. Make your own."

All the latent amusement which had parried Ivan's sallies till now was abruptly wiped from his cousin's face. His back straightened as much as it could, and he leaned forward, his hands gripping his chair arms. His voice dropped to an arctic pitch. "I will thank you, Lord Vorpatril, to take care not to repeat that slander. Ever."

Ivan's stomach lurched in surprise. He had seen Miles come the Lord Auditor a couple of times now, but never before at *him*. The freezing gray eyes suddenly had all the expression of a pair of gun barrels. Ivan opened his mouth, then closed it, more carefully. What the *hell* was going on here? And how did someone so short manage to project that much menace? Years of practice, Ivan supposed. *And conditioning.* "It was a *joke*, Miles."

"I don't find it very damned amusing." Miles rubbed his wrists, and frowned into the middle distance. A muscle jumped in his jaw; he jerked up his chin. After a moment, he added more bleakly, "I won't be telling you about the Komarran case, Ivan. It's slit-your-throat-before-reading stuff, and no horseshit. I will tell you this, and I expect it to go no further. Etienne Vorsoisson's death was a mess and a murder, and I surely failed to prevent it. But I did not cause it."

"For God's sake Miles, I didn't really think you—"

"However," his cousin raised his voice to override this, "all the evidence which proves this is now as classified as it's possible to be. It follows, that should such an accusation be made against me, I can't publicly access the facts or testimony to *disprove* it. Think about the consequences of that for one minute, *if* you please. Especially if . . . if my suit prospers."

Ivan sucked on his tongue for a moment, quelled. Then he brightened. "But . . . Gregor has access. Who could argue with him? Gregor could pronounce you clear."

"My foster-brother the Emperor, who appointed me Auditor as a favor to my father? Or so everyone says?"

Ivan shifted uncomfortably. So, Miles had heard that one, had he? "The people who count know better. Where *do* you pick this stuff up, Miles?"

A dry shrug, and a little hand-gesture, was the only reply he got. Miles was growing unnervingly political, these days. Ivan had slightly less interest in becoming involved with Imperial politics than in holding a plasma arc to his head and pulling the trigger. It wasn't that he ran away screaming whenever the loaded topics arose; that would draw too much attention. Saunter off slowly, that was the ticket. Miles . . . Miles the maniacal maybe had the nerve for a political career. The dwarf always did have that little suicidal streak. *Better you than me, boy.*

Miles, who had fallen into a study of his half-boots, looked up again. "I know I have no right to demand a damned thing from you, Ivan. I still owe you for . . . for the events of last fall. And the dozen other times you saved my neck, or tried to. All I can do is ask. Please.

I don't get many chances, and this one matters the world to me." A crooked smile.

Damn that smile. Was it Ivan's fault, that he had been born undamaged while his cousin had been born crippled? No, blast it. It was bloody bungled politics that had wrecked him, and you'd think it would be a lesson to him, but no. Demonstrably, even sniper fire couldn't stop the hyperactive little git. In between inspiring you to strangle him with your bare hands, he could make you proud enough to cry. At least, Ivan had taken care no one could see his face, when he'd watched from the Council floor as Miles had taken his Auditor's oath with that terrifying intensity, before all the assembled panoply of Barrayar last Winterfair. So small, so wrecked, so obnoxious. So incandescent. *Give the people a light, and they'll follow it anywhere.* Did Miles know how dangerous he was?

And the little paranoid actually believed Ivan had the magic to entice any woman Miles really wanted away from him. His fears were more flattering to Ivan than he would ever let on. But Miles had so few humilities, it seemed almost a sin to take this one away from him. Bad for his soul, eh.

"All right." Ivan sighed. "But I'm only giving you first shot, mind. If she tells you to take a hike, I think I should have just as much right to be next in line as the other fellow."

Miles half relaxed. "That's all I'm asking." Then tensed again. "Your word as Vorpatril, mind."

"My word as Vorpatril," Ivan allowed grudgingly, after a very long moment.

Miles relaxed altogether, looking much more cheerful. A few minutes of desultory conversation about the agenda for Lady Alys's planning session segued into an enumeration of Madame Vorsoisson's manifold virtues. If there was one thing worse than enduring his cousin's preemptive jealousy, Ivan decided, it was listening to his romantically hopeful *burbling*. Clearly, Vorkosigan House was not going to be a good place to hide out from Lady Alys this afternoon, nor, he suspected, for many afternoons to come. Miles wasn't even interested in a spot of recreational drinking; when he started to explain to Ivan his several new plans for gardens, Ivan pleaded duty, and escaped.

As he found his way down the front stairs, it dawned on Ivan that Miles had done him *again*. He'd obtained exactly what he wanted, and Ivan wasn't even sure how it had happened. Ivan hadn't had any intention of giving up his name's word on this one. The very suggestion had been quite offensive, when you looked at it from a certain angle. He frowned in frustration.

It was all wrong. If this Ekaterin woman was indeed that fine, she deserved a man who'd hustle for her. And if the widow's love for Miles was to be tested, it would certainly be better done sooner than later. Miles had no sense of proportion, of restraint, of . . . of self-preservation. How devastating it would be, if she decided to throw him back. It would be the ice-water bath therapy all over again. *Next time, I should hold his head under longer. I let him up too soon, that was my mistake . . .*

It would be almost a public service, to dangle the alternatives in front of the widow before Miles got her mind all turned inside out like he did everyone else's. But . . . Miles had extracted his word from Ivan, with downright ruthless determination. Forced it, practically, and a forced oath was no oath at all.

The way around this dilemma occurred to Ivan between one step and the next; his lips pursed in a sudden whistle. The scheme was nearly . . . Milesian. Cosmic justice, to serve the dwarf a dish with his own sauce. By the time Pym let him out the front door, Ivan was smiling again.

Chapter Two

Kareen Koudelka slid eagerly into the window seat of the orbital shuttle, and pressed her nose to the port. All she could see so far was the transfer station and its starry background. After endless minutes, the usual clanks and yanks signaled undocking, and the shuttle spun away from the station. The thrilling colored arc of Barrayar's terminator slid past her view as the shuttle began its descent. The western three-quarters of North Continent still glowed in its afternoon. She could see the *seas*. Home again, after nearly a year. Kareen settled back in her seat, and considered her mixed feelings.

She wished Mark were with her, to compare notes. And how did people like Miles, who had been off-world maybe fifty times, handle the cognitive dissonance? He'd had a student year on Beta Colony too, when even younger than she. She realized she had a lot more questions to ask him about it now, if she could work up the nerve.

So Miles Vorkosigan really was an Imperial Auditor now. It was hard to imagine him as one of those stiff old sticks. Mark had expended considerable nervous wit at the news, before sending off a congratulatory message by tight-beam, but then, Mark had a Thing about Miles. *Thing* was not accepted psychoscientific terminology, she'd been informed by his twinkling therapist, but there was scarcely another term with the scope and flexibility to take in the whole complexity of the . . . Thing.

Her hand drifted down in an inventory, tugging her shirt and smoothing her trousers. The eclectic mix of garb—Komarran-style pants, Barrayaran bolero, a syntha-silk shirt from Escobar—wasn't going to shock her family. She pulled an ash-blond curl out straight and looked up at it cross-eyed. Her hair was almost grown out again to the length and style she'd had when she'd left. Yes, all the important changes were on the inside, privately; she might reveal them or not, in her own time, as seemed right or safe. *Safe?* she queried herself in bemusement. She was letting Mark's paranoias rub off on her. Still . . .

With a reluctant frown, she drew her Betan earrings from her ears, and tucked them into her bolero pocket. Mama had hung around with Countess Cordelia enough; she might well be able to decode their Betan meaning. This was the style that said: Yes, I'm a consenting and contraceptive-protected adult, but I am presently in an exclusive relationship, so please do not embarrass us both by asking. Which was rather a lot to encrypt in a few twists of metal, and the Betans had a dozen more styles for other nuances; she'd graduated through a couple of them. The contraceptive implant the earrings advertised could now just ride along in secret, no one's business but her own.

Kareen considered briefly the comparison of Betan earrings with related social signals in other cultures: the wedding ring, certain styles of clothing or hats or veils or facial hair or tattoos. All such signals could be subverted, as with unfaithful spouses whose behavior belied their outward statement of monogamy, but really the Betans seemed very good about keeping congruent to theirs. Of course, they had so many choices. Wearing a false signal was highly disapproved, socially. *It screws it up for the rest of us,* a Betan had once explained to her. *The whole idea is to eliminate the weird guessing-games.* You had to admire their honesty. No wonder they did so well at the sciences. In all, Kareen decided, there was a lot about the sometimes appallingly sensible Betan-born Countess Cordelia Vorkosigan that she thought she might understand much better now. But Tante Cordelia wouldn't be back home to talk with till nearly the Emperor's wedding at Midsummer, sigh.

She set the ambiguities of the flesh abruptly aside as Vorbarr Sultana drew into view below. It was evening, and a glorious sunset painted the clouds as the shuttle made its final descent. City lights in the dusk made the groundscape magical. She could pick out dear,

familiar landmarks, the winding river, a *real* river after a year of
those measly fountains the Betans put in their underground world,
the famous bridges—the folk song in four languages about them
rippled through her mind—the main monorail lines . . . then the
rush of landing, and the final whine to a true stop at the shuttleport.
Home, home, I'm home! It was all she could do to keep from
stampeding over the bodies of all the slow old people ahead of her.
But at last she was through the flex-tube ramp and the last maze of
tube and corridor. *Will they be waiting? Will they all be there?*

They did not disappoint her. They were all there, every one,
standing in their own little squad, staking out the best space by the
pillars closest to the exit doors: Mama clutching a huge bouquet of
flowers, and Olivia, holding up a big decorated sign with rainbow
ribbons streaming that said WELCOME HOME KAREEN!, and Martya,
jumping up and down as she saw her, and Delia looking very cool
and grownup, and Da himself, still wearing his Imperial undress
greens from the day's work at HQ, leaning on his stick and grinning.
The group-hug was all that Kareen's homesick heart had ever
imagined, bending the sign and squashing the flowers. Olivia
giggled and Martya shrieked and even Da rubbed water from his
eyes. Passers-by stared; male passers-by stared longingly, and tended
to blunder into walls. Commodore Koudelka's all-blond commando
team, the junior officers from HQ joked. Kareen wondered if Martya
and Olivia still tormented them on purpose. The poor boys kept
trying to surrender, but so far, none of the sisters had taken
prisoners except Delia, who'd apparently conquered that Komarran
friend of Miles's at Winterfair—an ImpSec commodore, no less.
Kareen could hardly wait to get home and hear all the details of the
engagement.

All talking at once, except for Da, who'd given up years ago and
now just listened benignly, they herded off to collect Kareen's
luggage and meet the groundcar. Da and Mama had evidently
borrowed the big one from Lord Vorkosigan for the occasion, along
with Armsman Pym to drive it, so that they all might fit in the rear
compartment. Pym greeted her with a hearty welcome-home from
his liege-lord and himself, piled her modest valises in beside him,
and they were off.

"I thought you would come home wearing one of those topless
Betan sarongs," Martya teased her, as the groundcar pulled away
from the shuttleport and headed toward town.

"I thought about it." Kareen buried her grin in her armload of flowers. "It's just not warm enough here."

"You didn't actually wear one *there*, did you?"

Fortunately, before Kareen was forced to either answer or evade this, Olivia piped up, "When I saw Lord Vorkosigan's car I thought Lord Mark might have come home with you after all, but Mama said not. Won't he be coming back to Barrayar for the wedding?"

"Oh, yes. He actually left Beta Colony before I did, but he stopped on the way at Escobar to . . ." she hesitated, "to attend to some business of his." Actually, Mark had gone to cadge weight-loss drugs, more powerful than those his Betan therapist would prescribe for him, from a clinic of refugee Jacksonian doctors in which he had a financial interest. He would doubtless check out the business health of the clinic at the same time, so it wasn't an outright lie.

Kareen and Mark had come close to having their first real argument over this dubious choice of his, but it was, Kareen recognized, indeed his choice. Body-control issues lay near the core of his deepest troubles; she was developing an instinct—if she didn't flatter herself, close to a real understanding—of when she could push for his good. And when she just had to wait, and let Mark wrestle with Mark. It had been a somewhat terrifying privilege to watch and listen, this past year, as his therapist coached him; and an exhilarating experience to participate, under the therapist's supervision, in the partial healing he was achieving. And to learn there were more important aspects to love than a mad rush for connection: confidentiality, for one. Patience for another. And, paradoxically and most urgently in Mark's case, a certain cool and distant autonomy. It had taken her months to figure that one out. She wasn't about to try to explain it to her noisy, teasing, loving family in the back of a groundcar.

"You've become good friends . . ." her mother trailed off invitingly.

"He needed one." *Desperately.*

"Yes, but is he your *boy*friend?" Martya had no patience with subtlety, preferring clarity.

"He seemed sweet on you when he was here last year," Delia observed. "And you've been running around with him all year on Beta Colony. Is he slow off the gun?"

Olivia added, "I suppose he's bright enough to be interesting—I mean, he's Miles's twin, he has to be—but *I* thought he was a bit creepy."

Kareen stiffened. *If you'd been cloned a slave, raised by terrorists to be a murderer, trained by methods tantamount to physical and psychological torture, and had to kill people to escape, you'd likely seem a little creepy too. If you weren't a twitching puddle.* Mark was no puddle, more power to him. Mark was creating himself anew with an all-out effort no less heroic for being largely invisible to the outside observer. She pictured herself trying to explain this to Olivia or Martya, and gave up instantly. Delia . . . no, not even Delia. She needed only to mention Mark's four semiautonomous subpersonalities, each with his own nickname, for the conversation to slide downhill permanently. Describing the fascinating way they all worked together to support the fragile economy of his personality would not thrill a family of Barrayarans obviously testing for an acceptable in-law.

"Down, girls," Da put in, smiling in the dimness of the groundcar compartment, and earning Kareen's gratitude. But then he added, "Still, if we are about to receive a go-between from the Vorkosigans, I'd like some warning to prepare my mind for the shock. I've known Miles all his life. Mark . . . is another matter."

Could they picture no other role for a man in her life than potential husband? Kareen was by no means sure Mark was a potential husband. He was still working his heart out on becoming a potential human being. On Beta Colony, it had all seemed so clear. She could almost feel the murky doubt rising around her. She was glad now she'd ditched her earrings. "I shouldn't think so," she said honestly.

"Ah." He settled back, clearly relieved.

"Did he really get hugely fat on Beta Colony?" asked Olivia brightly. "I shouldn't think his Betan therapist would have let him. I thought they were supposed to fix that. I mean, he was fat when he left *here*."

Kareen suppressed an urge to tear her hair, or better still, Olivia's. "Where did you hear that?"

"Mama said Lady Cordelia said her mother said," Olivia recited the links of the gossip-chain, "when she was back here at Winterfair for Gregor's betrothal."

Mark's grandmother had been a good Betan godmother to both bewildered Barrayaran students this past year. Kareen had known that she was a pipeline of information to her concerned daughter about the progress of her strange clone-son, with the sort of frankness only two Betans could have; Gran'tante Naismith often talked about the messages she'd sent or received, and passed on news and greetings. The possibility of Tante Cordelia talking to Mama was the one she hadn't considered, Kareen realized. After all, Tante Cordelia had been on Sergyar, Mama was here. . . . She found herself frantically calculating backward, comparing two planetary calendars. Had she and Mark become lovers yet, by Barrayaran Winterfair when the Vorkosigans had last been home? No, whew. Whatever Tante Cordelia knew now, she hadn't known it then.

"I thought the Betans could tweak your brain chemistry around any way they wanted," said Martya. "Couldn't they just normalize him, blip, like that? Why's it take so long?"

"That's just the point," Kareen said. "Mark spent most of his life having his body and mind forcibly jerked around by other people. He needs the time to figure out who he is when people *aren't* pumping him full of stuff from the outside. Time to establish a baseline, his therapist says. He has a Thing about drugs, you see." Though not, evidently, the ones he got himself from refugee Jacksonians. "When he's ready—well, never mind."

"Did his therapy make *any* progress, then?" Mama asked dubiously.

"Oh, yes, lots," said Kareen, glad to be able to say something unequivocally positive about Mark at last.

"What kind?" asked her puzzled mother.

Kareen pictured herself gibbering, *Well, he's gotten completely over his torture-induced impotence, and been trained how to be a gentle and attentive lover. His therapist says she's terribly proud of him, and Grunt is just ecstatic. Gorge would be a reasonable gourmand, if it weren't for his being co-opted by Howl to meet Howl's needs, and it was me who figured out that was what was really going on with the eating binges. Mark's therapist congratulated me for my observation and insight, and loaded me down with catalogs for five different Betan therapist training programs, and told me she'd help me find scholarships if I was interested. She doesn't quite know what to do about Killer yet, but Killer doesn't bother me. I can't deal with Howl. And that's one year's progress. And oh yes, through all this private stress and strain Mark maintained top standing in his high-powered finance school, does anybody care?* "It's pretty complicated to explain," she managed at last.

Time to change the subject. Surely someone else's love interest could be publicly dissected. "Delia! Does your Komarran commodore know Gregor's Komarran fiancée? Have you met her yet?"

Delia perked up. "Yes, Duv knew Laisa back on Komarr. They shared some, um, academic interests."

Martya chimed in, "She's cute, short, and plump. She has the most striking blue-green eyes, and she's going to set a fashion in padded bras. *You'll* be right in. Did you gain weight this year?"

"We've all met Laisa," Mama intervened before this theme could be developed into acrimony. "She seems very nice. Very intelligent."

"Yes," said Delia, shooting Martya a look of scorn. "Duv and I hope Gregor doesn't waste her in public relations, though she'll have to do some, of course. She has Komarran training in economics. She could run Ministerial committees, Duv says, if they'd let her. At least the Old Vor can't shuffle her off to be a brood mare. Gregor and Laisa have already let it be quietly known they plan to use uterine replicators for their babies."

"Are they getting any argument about that from the high traditionalists?" Kareen asked.

"If they do, Gregor's said he'll send 'em to argue with Lady Cordelia." Martya giggled. "If they dare."

"She'll hand them back their heads on a plate if they try," Da said cheerfully. "And they know she can. Besides, we can always help out by pointing to Kareen and Olivia as proof positive that replicators give fine results."

Kareen grinned. Olivia smiled more faintly. Their family's own demographics marked the arrival of that galactic technology on Barrayar; the Koudelkas had been among the first ordinary Barrayarans to chance the new gestation method, for their two younger daughters. Being presented to all and sundry like a prize agricultural exhibit at a District Fair got to be a weary pain after a while, but Kareen supposed it was a public service. There'd been much less of that lately, as the technology became widely accepted, at least in the cities and by those who could afford it. For the first time, she wondered how the Control Sisters, Delia and Martya, had felt about it.

"What do the Komarrans think of the marriage, does your Duv say?" Kareen asked Delia.

"It's a mixed reception, but what else do you expect from a conquered world? The Imperial Household means to put all the positive propaganda spin on it they can, of course. Right down to doing the wedding over again on Komarr in the Komarran style, poor Gregor and Laisa. All ImpSec leaves are canceled from now till after the second ceremony, so that means Duv's and my wedding plans are on hold till then." She heaved a large sigh. "Well, I'd rather have his undivided attention when I do finally get it. He's scrambling to get on top of his new job, and as the first Komarran to head Komarran Affairs he knows every eye in the Imperium is on him. Especially if anything goes wrong." She grimaced. "Speaking of people's heads on plates."

Delia had changed, this past year. Last time she'd spoken of Imperial events, the conversation had revolved around what to wear, not that color-coordinating the Koudelkas wasn't a challenge in its own right. Kareen began to think she might like this Duv Galeni fellow. A brother-in-law, hm. It was a concept to get used to.

And then the groundcar rounded the last corner, and home loomed up. The Koudelkas' residence was the end house in a block-row, a capacious three stories high and with a greedy share of windows overlooking a crescent-shaped park, smack in the middle of the capital and not half a dozen blocks from Vorkosigan House itself. The young couple had purchased it twenty-five years ago, when Da had been personal military aide to the Regent, and Mama had quit her ImpSec post as bodyguard to Gregor and his foster-mother Lady Cordelia in order to have Delia. Kareen couldn't begin to calculate how much its value must have appreciated since then, though she bet Mark could. An academic exercise—who could bear to sell the dear old place, creaky as it was? She bounded out of the car, wild with joy.

It was late in the evening before Kareen had a chance to talk privately with her parents. First there had to be the unpacking, and the distribution of presents, and the reclaiming of her room from the stowage her sisters had ruthlessly dumped there during her absence. Then there was the big family dinner, with all three of her best old girlfriends invited. Everybody talked and talked, except Da of course, who sipped wine and looked smug to be sitting down to dinner with eight women. In all the camouflaging chatter Kareen only gradually became aware that she was wrapping away in private silence the things that mattered most intensely to her. That felt very strange.

Now she perched on the bed in her parents' room as they readied for sleep. Mama was running through her set series of isometric exercises, as she'd done every night for as long as Kareen could remember. Even after two body-births and all those years, she still maintained an athlete's muscle tone. Da limped across the room and set his swordstick up by his side of the bed, sat awkwardly, and watched Mama with a little smile. His hair was all gray now, Kareen noticed; Mama's braided mane still maintained her tawny blond without cosmetic assistance, though it was getting a silvery sheen to it. Da's clumsy hands began the task of removing his half-boots. Kareen's eye was having trouble readjusting. Barrayarans in their mid-fifties looked like Betans in their mid-seventies, or even mid-eighties; and her parents had lived hard in their youth, through war and service. Kareen cleared her throat.

"About next year's," she began with a bright smile, "school."

"You *are* planning on the District University, aren't you?" said Mama, chinning herself gently on the bar hung from the ceiling joists, swinging her legs out horizontally, and holding them there for a silent count of twenty. "We didn't pinch marks to provide you with a galactic education to have you quit halfway. That would be heartbreaking."

"Oh, yes, I want to keep going. I want to go back to Beta Colony." There.

A brief silence. Then Da, plaintively: "But you just got *home*, lovie."

"And I wanted to come home," she assured him. "I wanted to see you all. I just thought . . . it wasn't too soon to begin planning. Knowing it's a big thing."

"Campaigning?" Da raised an eyebrow.

She controlled irritation. It wasn't as though she were a little girl begging for a pony. This was her whole life on the line, here. "Planning. Seriously."

Mama said slowly, perhaps because she was thinking or perhaps because she was folding herself upside-down, "Do you know what you would study this time? The work you selected last year seemed a trifle . . . eclectic."

"I did well in all my classes," Kareen defended herself.

"All fourteen completely unrelated courses," murmured Da. "This is true."

"There was so *much* to choose from."

"There is much to choose from at Vorbarr Sultana District," Mama pointed out. "More than you could learn in a couple of lifetimes, even Betan lifetimes. And the commute is much less costly."

But Mark won't be at Vorbarr Sultana. He'll be back on Beta. "Mark's therapist was telling me about some scholarships in her field."

"Is that your latest interest?" asked Da. "Psycho-engineering?"

"I'm not sure," she said honestly. "It *is* interesting, the way they do it on Beta." But was it psychology in general that entranced her, or just Mark's psychology? She couldn't really say. Well . . . maybe she could. She just didn't entirely like how the answer sounded.

"No doubt," said Mama, "any practical galactic medical or technical training would be welcome back here. If you could focus on one long enough to . . . The problem is money, love. Without Lady Cordelia's scholarship, we couldn't have dreamed of sending you off world. And as far as I know, her next year's grant has already been awarded to another girl."

"I didn't expect to ask her for anything more. She's done so much for me already. But there is the possibility of a Betan scholarship. And I could work this summer. That, plus what you would have spent anyway on the District University . . . you wouldn't expect a little thing like money to stop, say, Lord Miles?"

"I wouldn't expect plasma arc fire to stop Miles." Da grinned. "But he is, shall we say, a special case."

Kareen wondered momentarily what fueled Miles's famous drive. Was it frustrated anger, like the kind now heating her determination? How *much* anger? Did Mark, in his exaggerated wariness of his progenitor and twin, realize something about Miles that had eluded her? "Surely we can come up with some solution. If we all try."

Mama and Da exchanged a look. Da said, "I'm afraid things are a bit in the hole to start with. Between schooling for all of you, and your late grandmother Koudelka's illness . . . we mortgaged the house by the sea two years ago."

Mama chimed in, "We'll be renting it out this summer, all but a week. We figure with all the events at Midsummer we'll hardly have time to get out of the capital anyway."

"And your mama is now teaching self-defense and security classes for Ministerial employees," Da added. "So she's doing all she can. I'm afraid there aren't too many sources of cash left that haven't already been pressed into service."

"I enjoy the teaching," Mama said. Reassuring him? She added to Kareen, "And it's better than selling the summer place to clear the debt, which for a time we were afraid we'd have to do."

Lose the house by the sea, focus of her childhood? Kareen was horrified. Lady Alys Vorpatril herself had given the house on the eastern shore to the Koudelkas for a wedding present, all those years ago; something about saving her and baby Lord Ivan's lives in the War of Vordarian's Pretendership. Kareen hadn't known finances were so tight. Until she counted up the number of sisters ahead of her, and multiplied their needs . . . um.

"It could be worse," Da said cheerfully. "Think of what floating this harem would have been like back in the days of dowries!"

Kareen smiled dutifully—he'd been making that joke for at least fifteen years—and fled. She was going to have to come up with another solution. By herself.

The decor of the Green Room in the Imperial Residence was superior to that of any other conference chamber in which Miles had ever been trapped. Antique silk wall coverings, heavy drapes and thick carpeting gave it a hushed, serious, and somewhat submarine air, and the elegant tea laid out in elaborate service on the inlaid sideboard beat the extruded-food-in-plastic of the average military meeting all hollow. Spring sunshine streamed through the windows to make warm golden bars across the floor. Miles had been watching them hypnotically shift as the morning stretched.

An inescapable military tone was lent to the proceedings by the presence of three men in uniform: Colonel Lord Vortala the Younger, head of the ImpSec task force assigned to provide security for the Emperor's wedding; Captain Ivan Vorpatril, dutifully keeping notes for Lady Alys Vorpatril, just as he would have done as aide to his commander at any military HQ conference; and Commodore Duv Galeni, chief of Komarran Affairs for ImpSec, preparing for the day when the whole show would be replayed on Komarr. Miles wondered if Galeni, forty and saturnine, was picking up ideas for his own wedding with Delia Koudelka, or whether he had enough sense of self-preservation to hide out and leave it all to the highly competent, not to mention assertive, Koudelka women. All five of them. Miles would offer Vorkosigan House to Duv as a sanctuary, except the girls would certainly track him there.

Gregor and Laisa seemed to be holding up well so far. Emperor Gregor in his mid-thirties was tall and thin, dark and dry. Dr. Laisa Toscane was short, with ash-blond curls and blue-green eyes that narrowed often in amusement, and a figure that made Miles, for one, just want to sort of fall over on top of her and burrow in for the winter. No treason implied; he did not begrudge Gregor his good fortune. In fact, Miles regarded the months of public ceremony which were keeping Gregor from that consummation as a cruelty little short of sadistic. Assuming, of course, that they *were* keeping . . .

The voices droned on; Miles's thoughts drifted further. Dreamily, he wondered where he and Ekaterin might hold their future wedding. In the ballroom of Vorkosigan House, in the eye of the Empire? The place might not hold a big enough mob. He wanted witnesses, for this. Or did he, as heir to his father's Countship, have a political obligation to stage it at the Vorkosigan's District capital of Hassadar? The modern Count's Residence at Hassadar had always seemed more like a hotel than a home, attached as it was to all those District bureaucratic offices lining the city's main square. The most romantic site would be the house at Vorkosigan Surleau, in the gardens overlooking the Long Lake. An outdoor wedding, yes, he bet Ekaterin would like that. In a sense, it would give Sergeant Bothari a chance to attend, and General Piotr too. *Did you ever believe such a day would come for me, Grandfather?* The attraction of that venue would depend on the time of year, of course—high summer would be glorious, but it wouldn't seem so romantic in a mid-winter sleet storm. He wasn't at all sure he could bring Ekaterin up to the matrimonial fence before fall, and delaying the ceremony till next spring would be as agonizing as what was being done to Gregor. . . .

Laisa, across the conference table from Miles, flipped over the next page of her stack of flimsies, read down it for a few seconds, and said, "You people can't be *serious!*" Gregor, seated beside her, looked alarmed, and leaned to peer over her shoulder.

Oh, we must have got to page twelve already. Quickly, Miles found his place again on the agenda, and sat up and tried to look attentive.

Lady Alys gave him a dry glance, before turning her attention to Laisa. This half-year-long nuptial ordeal, from the betrothal ceremonies this past Winterfair to the wedding upcoming at Midsummer, was the cap and crown of Lady Alys's career as Gregor's official hostess. She'd made it clear that Things Would Be Done Properly.

The problem came in defining the term *Properly.* The most recent wedding of a ruling emperor had been the scrambling mid-war union of Gregor's grandfather Emperor Ezar to the sister of the soon-to-be-late Mad Emperor Yuri, which for a number of sound historical and aesthetic reasons Alys was loath to take as a model. Most other emperors had been safely married for years before they landed on the throne. Prior to Ezar one had to go back almost two hundred years, to the marriage of Vlad Vorbarra le Savante and Lady Vorlightly, in the most gaudily archaic period of the Time of Isolation.

"They didn't really make the poor bride strip to the buff in front of all their wedding guests, did they?" Laisa asked, pointing out the offending passage of historical quotation to Gregor.

"Oh, Vlad had to strip too," Gregor assured her earnestly. "The in-laws would have insisted. It was in the nature of a warranty inspection. Just in case any mutations turned up in future offspring, each side wanted to be able to assert it wasn't *their* kin's fault."

"The custom has largely died out in recent years," Lady Alys remarked, "except in some of the backcountry districts in certain language groups."

"She means the Greekie hicks," Ivan helpfully interpreted this for offworld-born Laisa. His mother frowned at this bluntness.

Miles cleared his throat. "The Emperor's wedding may be counted on to reinvigorate any old customs it takes up and displays. Personally, I'd prefer that this not be one of them."

"Spoilsport," said Ivan. "*I* think it would reintroduce a lot of excitement to wedding parties. It could be a better draw than the competitive toasting."

"Followed later in the evening by the competitive vomiting," Miles murmured. "Not to mention the thrilling, if erratic, Vor crawling races. I think you won one of those once, didn't you, Ivan?"

"I'm surprised you remember. Aren't you usually the first to pass out?"

"Gentlemen," said Lady Alys coldly. "We have a *great* deal of material yet to get through in this meeting. And *neither* of you is leaving till we are finished." She let that hang quellingly in the air for a moment, for emphasis, then went on. "I wouldn't expect to exactly reproduce that old custom, Laisa, but I put it on the list because it does represent something of cultural importance to the more conservative Barrayarans. I was hoping we might come up with an updated version which would serve the same psychological purpose."

Duv Galeni's dark brows lowered in a thoughtful frown. "Publish their gene scans?" he suggested.

Gregor grimaced, but then took his fiancée's hand and gripped it, and smiled at her. "I'm sure Laisa's would be just fine."

"Well, of course it is," she began. "My parents had it checked before I ever went into the uterine replicator—"

Gregor kissed her palm. "Yes, and I'll bet you were a darling blastocyst."

She grinned giddily at him. Alys smiled faintly, in brief indulgence. Ivan looked mildly nauseated. Colonel Vortala, ImpSec trained and with years of experience on the Vorbarr Sultana scene, managed to look pleasantly blank. Galeni, nearly as good, appeared only a little stiff.

Miles took this strategic moment to lean across and ask Galeni in an undertone, "Kareen's home, has Delia told you?"

Galeni brightened. "Yes. I expect I'll see her tonight."

"I want to do something for a welcome-home. I was thinking of inviting the whole Koudelka clan for dinner soon. Interested?"

"Sure—"

Gregor tore his besotted gaze from Laisa's, leaned back, and said mildly, "Thank you, Duv. And what other ideas does anyone have?"

Gregor was clearly not interested in making his gene-scan public knowledge. Miles thought through several regional variants of the old custom. "You could make it a sort of a levee. Each set of parental in-laws, or whoever you think ought to have the right and the voice, plus a physician of their choice gets to visit the opposite member of the couple on the morning of the wedding, for a brief physical. Each delegation publicly announces itself satisfied at some appropriate point of the ceremony. Private inspection, public assurance. Modesty, honor, and paranoia all get served."

"And you could be given your tranquilizers at the same time," Ivan pointed out, with gruesome cheer. "Bet you'll both need 'em by then."

"Thank you, Ivan," murmured Gregor. "So thoughtful." Laisa could only nod in amused agreement.

Lady Alys's eyes narrowed in calculation. "Gregor, Laisa? Is that idea mutually acceptable?"

"It works for me," said Gregor.

"I don't think my parents would mind going along with it," said Laisa. "Um . . . who would stand in for your parents, Gregor?"

"Count and Countess Vorkosigan will be taking their place on the wedding circle, of course," said Gregor. "I'd assume it would be them . . . ah, Miles?"

"Mother wouldn't blink," said Miles, "though I can't guarantee she wouldn't make rude comments about Barrayarans. Father . . ."

A more politically-guarded silence fell around the table. More than one eye drifted to Duv Galeni, whose jaw tightened slightly.

"Duv, Laisa." Lady Alys tapped one perfectly enameled fingernail on the polished tabletop. "Komarran socio-political response on this one. Frankly, please."

"I have no *personal* objection to Count Vorkosigan," said Laisa.

Galeni sighed. "Any . . . ambiguity that we can sidestep, I believe we should."

Nicely put, Duv. You'll be a politician yet. "In other words, sending the Butcher of Komarr to ogle their nekkid sacrificial maiden would be about as popular as plague with the Komarrans back home," Miles put in, since no one else could. Well, Ivan maybe. Lady Alys would have had to grope for several more moments to come up with a polite locution for the problem. Galeni shot him a medium-grateful glower. "Perfectly understandable," Miles went on. "If the lack of symmetry isn't too obvious, send Mother and Aunt Alys as the delegation from Gregor's side, with maybe one of the female cousins from his mother Princess Kareen's family. It'll fly for the Barrayaran conservatives because guarding the genome always was women's work."

The Barrayarans around the table grunted agreement. Lady Alys smiled shortly, and ticked off the item.

A complicated, and lengthy, debate ensued over whether the couple should repeat their vows in all four of Barrayar's languages. After that came thirty minutes of discussion on how to handle domestic and galactic newsfeeds, in which Miles adroitly, and with Galeni's strong support, managed to avoid collecting any more tasks requiring his personal handling. Lady Alys flipped to the next page, and frowned. "By the way, Gregor, have you decided what you're going to do about the Vorbretten case yet?"

Gregor shook his head. "I'm trying to avoid making any public utterance on that one for the moment. At least till the Council of Counts gets done trampling about in it. Whichever way they fall out, the loser's appeal will doubtless land in my lap within minutes of their decision."

Miles glanced at his agenda in confusion. The next item read *Meal Schedules.* "Vorbretten case?"

"Surely you've heard the scandal—" began Lady Alys. "Oh, that's right, you were on Komarr when it broke. Didn't Ivan fill you in? Poor René. The whole family's in an uproar."

"Has something happened to René Vorbretten?" Miles asked, alarmed. René had been a couple of years ahead of Miles at the Academy, and looked to be following in his brilliant father's footsteps. Commodore Lord Vorbretten had been a star protégé of Miles's father on the General Staff, until his untimely, if heroic, death by Cetagandan fire in the war of the Hegen Hub a decade past. Less than a year later, old Count Vorbretten had died, some said in grief for the loss of his beloved eldest son; René had been forced to give up his promising military career and take up his duties as Count of his family's District. Three years ago, in a whirlwind romance that had been the delight of Vorbarr Sultana, he'd married the gorgeous eighteen-year-old daughter of the wealthy Lord Vorkeres. *Them what has, gets,* as they said in the backcountry.

"Well . . ." said Gregor, "yes and no. Um . . ."

"Um *what?*"

Lady Alys sighed. "Count and Countess Vorbretten, having decided it was time to start carrying out their family duties, very sensibly decided to use the uterine replicator for their first-born son, and have any detected defects repaired in the zygote. For which, of course, they both had complete gene scans."

"René found he was a mutie?" Miles asked, astonished. Tall, handsome, athletic René? René, who spoke four languages in a modulated baritone that melted female hearts and male resistance, played three musical instruments entrancingly, and had perfect singing pitch to boot? René, who could make *Ivan* grind his teeth in sheer physical jealousy?

"Not exactly," said Lady Alys, "unless you count being one-eighth Cetagandan ghem as a defect."

Miles sat back. "Whoops." He took this in. "When did this happen?"

"Surely you can do the math," murmured Ivan.

"Depends on which line it came through."

"The male," said Lady Alys. "Unfortunately."

Right. René's grandfather, the seventh Count-Vorbretten-to-be, had indeed been born in the middle of the Cetagandan occupation. The Vorbrettens, like many Barrayarans, had done what they needed to survive. . . . "So René's great-grandma was a collaborator. Or . . . was it something nastier?"

"For what it's worth," said Gregor, "what little surviving documentation ImpSec has unearthed suggests it was probably a voluntary and rather extended liaison, with one—or more—of the high-ranking ghem-officers occupying their District. At this range, one can't tell if it was love, self-interest, or an attempt to buy protection for her family in the only coin she had."

"It could have been all three," said Lady Alys. "Life in a war zone isn't simple."

"In any case," said Gregor, "it seems not to have been a matter of rape."

"Good God. So, ah, do they know which ghem-lord was René's ancestor?"

"They could in theory send his gene scan to Cetaganda and find out, but as far as I know they haven't elected to do so yet. It's rather academic. What is . . . something other than academic is the apparent fact that the seventh Count Vorbretten was not the son of the sixth Count."

"They were calling him René Ghembretten last week at HQ," Ivan volunteered. Gregor grimaced.

"I'm astounded the Vorbrettens let this leak out," said Miles. "Or was it the doctor or the medtechs who betrayed them?"

"Mm, therein hangs yet more of the tale," said Gregor. "They had no intention of doing so. But René told his sisters and his brother, thinking they had a right to know, and the young Countess told her parents. And from there, well, who knows. But the rumor eventually came to the ears of Sigur Vorbretten, who is the direct descendant of the sixth Count's younger brother, and incidentally the son-in-law of Count Boriz Vormoncrief. Sigur has somehow—and there's a counter-suit pending about his methods—obtained a copy of René's gene scan. And Count Vormoncrief has brought suit before the Council of Counts, on his son-in-law's behalf, to claim the Vorbretten descent and District for Sigur. And there it sits."

"Ow. Ow! So . . . is René still Count, or not? He was presented and confirmed in his person by the Council, with all the due forms— hell, I was there, come to think of it. A Count doesn't *have* to be the previous Count's son—there've been nephews, cousins, skips to other lines, complete breaks due to treason or war—has anyone mentioned Lord Midnight, the fifth Count Vortala's horse, yet? If a horse can inherit a Countship, I don't see what's the theoretical objection to a Cetagandan. Part-Cetagandan."

"I doubt Lord Midnight's father was married to his mother, either," Ivan observed brightly.

"Both sides were claiming that case as a precedent, last I heard," Lord Vortala, himself a descendant of the infamous fifth Count, put in. "One because the horse was confirmed as heir, t' other because the confirmation was later revoked."

Galeni, listening in fascination, shook his head in wonder, or something like that. Laisa sat back and gnawed gently on her knuckle, and kept her mouth straight. Her eyes only crinkled slightly.

"How's René taking it all?" asked Miles.

"He seems to have become rather reclusive lately," said Alys, in a worried tone.

"I . . . maybe I'll call on him."

"That would be a good thing," said Gregor gravely. "Sigur is attempting in his suit to attach everything René inherited, but he's let it be known he'd be willing to settle for just the Countship and its entailments. Too, I suppose there are some trifles of property inherited through the female lines which aren't under question."

"In the meanwhile," Alys said, "Sigur has sent a note to my office requesting his rightful place in the wedding procession and the oath-takings as Count Vorbretten. And René has sent a note requesting Sigur be barred from the ceremonies if the case has not yet been settled in his favor. So, Gregor? Which one lays his hands between

Laisa's when she's confirmed as Empress, if the Council of Counts hasn't made up what passes for its collective mind by then?"

Gregor rubbed the bridge of his nose, and squeezed his eyes shut briefly. "I don't know. We may have to have both of them. Provisionally."

"Together?" said Lady Alys, her lip curling in dismay. "Tempers are running high, I heard." She glowered at Ivan. "Exacerbated by the humor certain low-minded persons seem to find in what is actually an exquisitely painful situation."

Ivan began to smile, then apparently thought better of it.

"One trusts they will not choose to mar the dignity of the occasion," said Gregor. "Especially if their appeal to me is still hanging fire. I suppose I should find some way to let them know that, gently. I am presently constrained to avoid them . . ." His eye fell on Miles. "Ah, Lord Auditor Vorkosigan. This sounds like a task very much within your purview. Would you be so kind as to remind them both of the delicacy of their positions, if things look to be getting out of hand at any point?"

Since the official job description of an Imperial Auditor was, in effect, Whatever You Say, Gregor, Miles could hardly argue with this. Well, it could have been worse. He shuddered to think of how many chores he might have been assigned by now if he'd been so stupid as to *not* show up for this meeting. "Yes, Sire," he sighed. "I'll do my best."

"The formal invitations begin to go out soon," Lady Alys said. "Let me know if there are any changes." She turned over the last page. "Oh, and have your parents said yet exactly when they'll be arriving, Miles?"

"I've assumed you would know before I did. Gregor?"

"Two Imperial ships are assigned to the Viceroy's pleasure," said Gregor. "If there are no crises on Sergyar to impede him, Count Vorkosigan implied he'd like to be here in better time than last Winterfair."

"Are they coming together? I thought Mother might come early again, to support Aunt Alys," said Miles.

"I love your mother dearly, Miles," Lady Alys sighed, "but after the betrothal, when I suggested she come home to help me with these preparations, she suggested Gregor and Laisa ought to elope."

Gregor and Laisa both looked quite wistful at the thought, and held hands under the table. Lady Alys frowned uneasily at this dangerous breath of mutiny.

Miles grinned. "Well, of course. That's what *she* did. After all, it worked for her."

"I don't think she was serious, but with Cordelia, one can never quite tell. It's just appalling how this whole subject brings out the Betan in her. I can only be grateful she's on Sergyar just now." Lady Alys glowered at her flimsy, and added, "Fireworks."

Miles blinked, then realized this wasn't a prediction of the probable result of the clash in social views between his Betan mother and his Barrayaran aunt, but rather, the last—thank God—item on today's agenda.

"Yes!" said Gregor, smiling eagerly. All the Barrayarans round the table, including Lady Alys, perked up at this. An inherent cultural passion for things that went boom, perhaps.

"On what schedule?" Lady Alys asked. "There will of course be the traditional display on Midsummer Day, the evening after the Imperial Military Review. Do you want displays every night on the three days intervening till the wedding, as well as on the wedding night?"

"Let me see that budget," Gregor said to Ivan. Ivan called it up for him. "Hm. We wouldn't want the people to become jaded. Let other organizations, such as the city of Vorbarr Sultana or the Council of Counts, foot the displays on the intervening nights. And up the budget for the post-wedding display by fifty percent, from my personal purse as Count Vorbarra."

"Ooh," said Ivan appreciatively, and entered the changes. "Nice."

Miles stretched. Done at last.

"Oh, yes, I almost forgot," added Lady Alys. "Here is your meal schedule, Miles."

"My what?" Without thinking, he accepted the flimsy from her hand.

"Gregor and Laisa have dozens of invitations during the week between the Review and the Wedding from assorted organizations which wish to honor them—and themselves—ranging from the Imperial Veterans' Corps to the Honorable Order of City Bakers. And Bankers. And Brewers. And Barristers. Not to mention the rest of the alphabet. Far more than they can possibly accept, of course.

They will do as many of the most critical ones as they can fit in, but after that, you will have to take the next tier, as Gregor's Second."

"Did any of these people actually invite me, in my own person?" Miles asked, scanning down the list. There were at least thirteen meals or ceremonies in three days on it. "Or are they getting a horrible surprise? I can't eat all this!"

"Throw yourself on that unexploded dessert, boy!" Ivan grinned. "It's your duty to save the Emperor from indigestion."

"Of course they'll know. You may expect to be called upon to make a number of thank-you speeches appropriate to the various venues. And here," his mother added, "is your schedule, Ivan."

Ivan's grin faded into a look of dismay, as he stared at his own list. "I didn't know there were that many guilds in this damned town . . ."

A wonderful thought occurred to Miles—he might be able to take Ekaterin along to a sedate selection of these. Yes, let her see Lord Auditor Vorkosigan in action. And her serene and sober elegance would add no little validation to *his* consequence. He sat up straighter, suddenly consoled, and folded the flimsy and slipped it into his tunic.

"Can't we send Mark to some of these?" asked Ivan plaintively. "He'll be back in town for this bash. And he's a Vorkosigan too. Outranks a Vorpatril, surely. And if there's one thing the lad can do, it's eat."

Galeni's brows rose in reluctant agreement with this last assessment, though the look on his face was a study in grim bemusement. Miles wondered if Galeni too was reflecting that Mark's other notable talent was assassination. *At least he doesn't eat what he kills.*

Miles began to glower at Ivan, but Aunt Alys beat him to it. "Control your wit, if you please, Ivan. Lord Mark is neither the Emperor's Second, nor an Imperial Auditor, nor of any great experience in delicate social situations. And despite all Aral and Cordelia could do for him last year, most people still regard his position within the family as rather ambiguous. Nor is he, I'm given to understand, stable enough yet to be safely subjected to stress in very public arenas. Despite his therapy."

"It was a *joke*," Ivan muttered defensively. "How do you expect us to all get through this alive if we're not allowed to have a sense of humor?"

"Exert yourself," his mother advised him brutally.

On these daunting words, the meeting broke up.

Chapter Three

A cool spring drizzle misted onto Miles's hair as he stepped into the shelter of the Vorthys's doorway. In the gray air, the gaudy tile front of the house was subdued, becoming a patterned subtlety. Ekaterin had inadvertently delayed this meeting by sending him her proposed garden designs over the comconsole. Fortunately, he hadn't had to *feign* indecision over the choice; both layouts were very fine. He trusted they would still be able to spend hours this afternoon, heads bent together over the vid display, comparing and discussing the fine points.

A fleeting memory of the erotic dream from which he'd awoken this morning warmed his face. It had been a replay of his and Ekaterin's first meeting in the garden here, but in this version her welcome had taken a much more, um, exciting and unexpected turn. Except why had his stupid unconscious spent so much worry about tell-tale grass-stains on the knees of his trousers, when it could have been manufacturing even more fabulous moments of abundance for his dream-self? And then he'd woken up too damned soon. . . .

The Professora opened the door to him, and smiled a welcome. "Come in, Miles." She added, as he entered her hallway, "Have I ever mentioned before how much I appreciate the fact that you call before you visit?"

Her house did not have its usual hushed, librarylike quiet. There seemed to be a party going on. Startled, Miles swiveled his head toward the archway on his left. A clink of plates and glassware and the scent of tea and apricot pastries wafted from the parlor.

Ekaterin, smiling politely but with two little parallel lines of tension between her brows, sat enthroned in her uncle's overstuffed chair in the corner, holding a teacup. Ranged around the room, perched on more decorative chairs, were three men, two in Imperial undress greens and one in a civilian tunic and trousers.

Miles didn't recognize the heavy-set fellow who wore major's tabs, along with Ops pins, on his high collar. The other officer was Lieutenant Alexi Vormoncrief, whom Miles knew slightly. His pins, too, indicated he now worked in Ops. The third man, in the finely-cut civilian togs, was highly adept at avoiding work of any kind, as far as Miles knew. Byerly Vorrutyer had never joined the Service; he'd been a town clown for as long as Miles had been acquainted with him. Byerly had impeccable taste in everything but his vices. Miles would have been loath to introduce Ekaterin to him even *after* she was safely betrothed.

"Where did *they* come from?" Miles asked the Professora in an undertone.

"Major Zamori I had as an undergraduate student, fifteen years ago," the Professora murmured back. "He brought me a book he said he thought I would like. Which is true; I already had a copy. Young Vormoncrief came to compare pedigrees with Ekaterin. He thought they might be related, he said, as his grandmother was a Vorvane. Aunt to the Minister for Heavy Industries, you know."

"I know that branch, yes."

"They have spent the past hour establishing that, while the Vorvanes and the Vorvaynes are indeed of the same root stock, the families split off at least five generations back. I don't know why By Vorrutyer is here. He neglected to supply me with an excuse."

"There is no excuse for By." But Miles thought he could see exactly why the three of them were there, lame stories and all, and she was clutching her teacup in the corner and looking trapped. Couldn't they do better than those palpably transparent tales? "Is my cousin Ivan here?" he added dangerously. Ivan worked in Ops, come to think of it. Once was happenstance, twice was coincidence . . .

"Ivan Vorpatril? No. Oh, dear, is he likely to turn up? I'm out of pastries. I had bought them for the Professor's dessert tonight. . . ."

"I trust not," muttered Miles. He fixed a polite smile on his face, and swung into the Professora's parlor. She followed after him.

Ekaterin's chin came up, and she smiled and put down her cup-shield. "Oh, Lord Vorkosigan! I'm so glad you're here. Um . . . do you know these gentlemen?"

"Two out of three, Madame. Good morning, Vormoncrief. Hello, Byerly."

The three acquaintances exchanged guarded nods. Vormoncrief said politely, "Good morning, my Lord Auditor."

"Major Zamori, this is Lord Auditor Miles Vorkosigan," the Professora supplied.

"Good day, sir," said Zamori. "I've heard of you." His gaze was direct and fearless, despite his being so heavily outnumbered by Vor lords. But then, Vormoncrief was a mere stripling of a lieutenant, and Byerly Vorrutyer didn't rank at all. "Did you come to see Lord Auditor Vorthys? He just stepped out."

Ekaterin nodded. "He went for a walk."

"In the rain?"

The Professora rolled her eyes slightly, by which Miles guessed her husband had skipped off and left her to play duenna to her niece by herself.

"No matter," Miles went on. "In fact, I have some little business with Madame Vorsoisson." And if they took that to mean a Lord Auditor's Imperial business, and not merely Lord Vorkosigan's private business, who was he to correct them?

"Yes," Ekaterin nodded in confirmation of this.

"My apologies for interrupting you all," Miles added, by way of a broad hint. He did not sit down, but leaned against the frame of the archway, and crossed his arms. No one moved.

"We were just discussing family trees," Vormoncrief explained.

"At some length," murmured Ekaterin.

"Speaking of strange pedigrees, Alexi, Lord Vorkosigan and I were almost related much more closely," Byerly remarked. "I feel quite a familial attachment to him."

"Really?" said Vormoncrief, looking puzzled.

"Oh, yes. One of my aunts on the Vorrutyer side was once married to his father. So Aral Vorkosigan is actually some sort of virtual, if not virtuous, uncle to me. But she died young, alas—ruthlessly pruned from the tree—without bearing me a cousin to cut the future Miles out of his inheritance." Byerly cocked a brow at Miles. "Was she fondly remembered, in your family dinner conversations?"

"We never much discussed the Vorrutyers," said Miles.

"How odd. We never much discussed the Vorkosigans, either. Hardly at all, in fact. Such a resounding silence, one feels."

Miles smiled, and let just such a silence stretch between them, curious to see who would flinch first. By's eye began to glint appreciation, but the first whose nerve broke was one of the innocent bystanders.

Major Zamori cleared his throat. "So, Lord Auditor Vorkosigan. What's the final word on the Komarr accident, really? Was it sabotage?"

Miles shrugged, and let By and his habitual needling drop from his attention. "After six weeks of sifting through the data, Lord Auditor Vorthys and I returned a probable cause of pilot error. We debated the possibility of pilot suicide, but finally discarded the idea."

"And which was your opinion?" asked Zamori, sounding interested. "Accident or suicide?"

"Mm. I felt suicide would explain a lot about certain physical aspects of the collision," Miles replied, sending up a silent prayer of apology to the soul of the slandered pilot. "But since the dead pilot neglected to supply us with any supporting evidence, such as notes or messages or therapy records, we couldn't make it an official verdict. Don't quote me," he added, for verisimilitude.

Ekaterin, sheltered in her uncle's chair, nodded understanding to him of this official lie, perhaps adding it to her own repertoire of deflections.

"So what do you think of this Komarran marriage of the Emperor's?" Vormoncrief added. "I suppose you must approve of it—you're in it."

Miles took note of his dubious tone. Ah yes, Vormoncrief's uncle Count Boriz Vormoncrief, being just outside the spatter-zone, had inherited the leadership of the shrinking Conservative Party after the fall of Count Vortrifrani. The Conservative party's response to future-Empress Laisa had been lukewarm at best, though, prudently, no overt hostility had been permitted to leak into their public stances where someone—i.e., ImpSec—would have been compelled to take notice of it. Still, just because Boriz and Alexi were related didn't by any means guarantee they shared the same political views. "I think it's great," said Miles. "Dr. Toscane is brilliant and beautiful, and Gregor, well, it's high time he produced an heir. And you have to figure, if nothing else it leaves one more Barrayaran woman for the rest of us."

"Well, it leaves one more Barrayaran woman for *one* of us," Byerly Vorrutyer corrected this sweetly. "Unless you are proposing something delightfully outré."

Miles's smile thinned as he contemplated By. Ivan's wit, wearing as it could sometimes grow, was saved from being offensive by a certain ingenuousness. Unlike Ivan, Byerly never insulted anyone unintentionally.

"You gentlemen should all pay a visit to Komarr," Miles recommended genially. "Their domes are just chock full of lovely women, all with clean gene scans and galactic educations. And the Toscanes aren't the only clan fielding an heiress. Many of the Komarran ladies are rich—Byerly." He restrained himself from helpfully explaining to all present that Madame Vorsoisson's feckless late husband had left her destitute, first because Ekaterin was sitting right there, with her eyebrows tilted at him, and secondly because he couldn't imagine that By, for one, didn't already know it.

Byerly smiled faintly. "Money isn't everything, they say."

Check. "Still, I'm sure you could make yourself pleasant, if you ever chose to try."

By's lip quirked. "Your faith in me is touching, Vorkosigan."

Alexi Vormoncrief said sturdily, "A daughter of the Vor is good enough for me, thanks. I've no need or taste for off-world exotica."

While Miles was still trying to work out if this was an intended slur on his Betan mother—with By, he would have been sure, but Vormoncrief had never struck him as over-supplied with subtlety—Ekaterin said brightly, "I'll just step up to my room and get those data disks, shall I?"

"If you please, Madame." Miles trusted By had not made her the object of any of his guerrilla conversational techniques. If so, Miles might have a little private word with his ersatz cousin. Or maybe even send his Armsmen to do so, just like the good old days. . . .

She rose, and made her way to the hall and up the stairs. She did not return. Vormoncrief and Zamori eventually exchanged disappointed looks, and noises about *time to be going,* and made to rise. The military raincoat Vormoncrief shrugged on had had time to dry since his arrival, Miles noted with disapproval. The gentlemen courteously took their leave of their putative hostess, the Professora.

"Tell Madame Vorsoisson I'll bring that disk of jumpship designs around for Nikki as soon as I may," Major Zamori assured the Professora, glancing up the stairway.

Zamori's been here often enough to know Nikki already? Miles regarded his regular profile uneasily. He seemed tall, too, though not as tall as Vormoncrief; it was his bulk that helped make his presence loom like that. Byerly was slim enough that his height was not so apparent.

They lingered a moment in an awkward crowded gaggle in the tiled hall, but Ekaterin did not descend again, and at last they gave up and let themselves be shepherded out the front door. It was raining harder now, Miles saw with some satisfaction. Zamori plunged off into the shower, head-down. The Professora closed the door on them with a grimace of relief.

"You and Ekaterin can use the comconsole in my study," she directed Miles, and turned to start collecting the plates and cups left derelict in her parlor.

Miles trod across the hall into her office-cum-library, and looked around. Yes, this would be a fine and cozy spot for his conference. The front window was propped open to catch a fresh draft. Voices from the porch carried through the damp air with unfortunate clarity.

"By, you don't think *Vorkosigan* is dangling after Madame Vorsoisson, is he?" That was Vormoncrief.

Byerly Vorrutyer replied indifferently, "Why not?"

"You'd think she'd be revolted. No, it must be just some leftover business from his case."

"I wouldn't wager on that. I know women enough who would hold their noses and take the plunge for a Count's heir even if he came covered in green fur."

Miles's fist clenched, then carefully unclenched. *Oh, yeah? So why didn't you ever supply me with that list, By?* Not that Miles cared now . . .

"I don't claim to understand women, but Ivan's the catch I could see them going for," Vormoncrief said. "If the assassins had been a little more competent, way back when, *he* might have inherited the Vorkosigans' Countship. Too bad. My uncle says he'd be an ornament to our party, if he didn't have that family alliance with Aral Vorkosigan's damned Progressives."

"Ivan Vorpatril?" Byerly snorted. "Wrong type of party for him, Alexi. He only goes to the kind where the wine flows freely."

Ekaterin appeared in the archway and smiled crookedly at Miles. He considered slamming the window shut, hard. There were technical difficulties with that idea; it had a crank-latch. Ekaterin too had caught the voices—how soon? She drifted in, and cocked her head, and lifted an inquiring and unrepentant brow at him, as if to say, *At it again, are you?* Miles managed a brief embarrassed smile.

"Ah, here's your driver at last," Byerly added. "Lend me your coat, Alexi; I don't wish to damp my lovely new suit. What do you think of it? The color flatters my skin tone, no?"

"Hang your skin tone, By."

"Oh, but my tailor assured me it does. Thank you. Good, he's opening the canopy. Now for the dash through the wet; well, you can dash. I shall saunter with dignity, in this ugly but inarguably waterproof Imperial garment. Off we go now . . ." Two sets of footsteps faded into the drizzle.

"He *is* a character, isn't he?" said Ekaterin, half-laughing.

"Who? Byerly?"

"Yes. He's *very* snarky. I could scarcely believe the things he dared to say. Or keep my face straight."

"I scarcely believe the things By says either," said Miles shortly. He pulled a second chair around in front of the comconsole as close to the first as he dared, and settled her. "Where did they all come from?" Besides the Ops department of Imperial Headquarters, apparently. *Ivan, you rat, you and I are going to have a talk about what sort of gossip you sprinkle around at work. . . .*

"Major Zamori called on the Professora last week," said Ekaterin. "He seems a pleasant enough fellow. He had a long chat with Nikki—I was impressed with his patience."

Miles was impressed with his *brains.* Damn the man, for spotting Nikki as one of the few chinks in Ekaterin's armor.

"Vormoncrief first turned up a few days ago. I'm afraid he's a bit of a bore, poor man. Vorrutyer just came in with him this morning; I'm not sure he was exactly invited."

"He's found a new victim to sponge off, I suppose," said Miles. Vorrutyers seemed to come in two flavors, flamboyant and reclusive; By's father, the youngest son of his generation, was a misanthropic pinchmark of the second category, and never came near the capital if he could help it. "By's notoriously without visible means of support."

"He puts up a good front, if so," said Ekaterin judiciously.

Upper-class poverty was a dilemma with which Ekaterin could identify, Miles realized. He hadn't intended his remark as a ploy to gain sympathy for Byerly Vorrutyer. Blast.

"I think Major Zamori was a bit put out when they arrived on top of his visit," Ekaterin went on. She added fretfully, "I don't know why they're *here*."

Check your mirror, Miles refrained from advising her. He let his brows rise. "Truly?"

She shrugged, and smiled a little bitterly. "They mean well, I guess. Maybe I was naïve to think this," she gestured down her black dress, "would be enough to relieve me of having to deal with the nonsense. Thanks for trying to ship them to Komarr for me, though I'm not sure it took. My hints don't seem to be working. I don't wish to be rude."

"Why not?" said Miles, hoping to encourage this trend of thought. Though rudeness might not work on By; it would be just as likely to excite him into making it a contest. Miles suppressed a morbid urge to inquire if there'd been any *more* unattached gentlemen turn up on her front step this week, or if he'd just viewed the whole inventory. He really didn't want to hear the answer. "But enough of this, as you say, nonsense. Let's talk about my garden."

"Yes, let's," she said gratefully, and set up the two vid models, which they'd dubbed *the backcountry garden* and *the urban garden* respectively, on her aunt's comconsole. Their heads bent together side by side, just as Miles had pictured. He could smell the dusky perfume of her hair.

The backcountry garden was a naturalistic display, with bark pathways curling through thickly planted native species on contoured banks, a winding stream, and scattered wooden benches. The urban garden had strong rectangular terraces of poured plascrete, which were walks and benches and channels for the water all together. In a series of skillful, penetrating questions, Ekaterin managed to elicit from him that his heart really favored the backcountry garden, however much his eye was seduced by the plascrete fountains. As he watched in fascination, she modified the backcountry design to give the ground more slope and the stream more prominence, winding in an S-curve that originated in a rock fall and ended in a small grotto. The central circle where the paths intersected was transformed to traditional patterned brick, with the

Vorkosigan crest, the stylized maple leaf backed by the three overlapping triangles representing the mountains, picked out in contrasting paler brick. The whole was dropped further below street level, to give the banks more room to climb, and to muffle the city noise.

"Yes," he said at last, in considerable satisfaction. "That's the plan. Go with it. You can start lining up your contractors and bids."

"Are you sure you really want to go on?" said Ekaterin. "I'm now out of my experience, I'm afraid. All my designs have been virtual ones, till this."

"Ah," said Miles smugly, having anticipated this last-minute waffle. "Now is the moment to put you in direct touch with my man of business, Tsipis. He's had to arrange every sort of maintenance and building work on the Vorkosigan properties in the last thirty years. He knows who all the reputable and reliable people are, and where we can draw labor or materials from the Vorkosigan estates. He'll be delighted to walk you through the whole thing." *In fact, I've let him know I'll have his head if he's not delighted every minute.* Not that Miles had had to lean very hard; Tsipis found all aspects of business management utterly fascinating, and would drone on for hours about them. It made Miles laugh, if painfully, to realize how often in his space mercenary command he'd saved a day by drawing not on his ImpSec training, but on one of old Tsipis's scorned lessons. "If you're willing to be his pupil, he'll be your slave."

Tsipis, carefully primed, answered the comconsole in his office in Hassadar himself, and Miles made the necessary introductions. The new acquaintance went well; Tsipis was elderly, long married, and genuinely interested in the project at hand. He drew Ekaterin almost instantly out of her wary shyness. By the time he'd finished his first lengthy conversation with her, she'd shifted from *I can't possibly* mode to possession of a flow-chart checklist and a coherent plan which would, with luck, result in groundbreaking as early as the following week. Oh yes. This was going to do well. If there was one thing Tsipis appreciated, it was a quick study. Ekaterin was one of those *show once* people whom Miles, in his mercenary days, had found more precious than unexpected oxygen in the emergency reserve. And she didn't even know she was unusual.

"Good heavens," she remarked, organizing her notes after Tsipis had cut the com. "What an education that man is. I think I should be paying you."

"Payment," said Miles, reminded. "Yes." He drew a credit chit from his pocket. "Tsipis has set up the account for you to pay all expenses incurred. This is your own fee for the accepted design."

She checked it in the comconsole. "Lord Vorkosigan, this is too much!"

"No, it's not. I had Tsipis scout the prices for similar design work from three different professional companies." They happened to be the top three in the business, but would he have hired anything less for Vorkosigan House? "This is an average of their bids. He can show them to you."

"But I'm an amateur."

"Not for damn long."

Wonder of wonders, this actually won a smile of increasing self-confidence. "All I did was assemble some pretty standard design elements."

"So, ten percent of that is for the design elements. The other ninety percent is for knowing how to arrange them."

Hah, she didn't argue with *that*. You couldn't be that good and not know it, somewhere in your secret heart, however much you'd been abused into affecting public humility.

This was, he recognized, a good bright note on which to end. He didn't want to linger to the point of boring her, as Vormoncrief had evidently done. Was it too early to . . . no, he'd try. "By the way, I'm putting together a dinner party for some old friends of mine—the Koudelka family. Kareen Koudelka, who is a sort of protégé of my mother's, is just back from a school year on Beta Colony. She's hit the ground running, but as soon as I can determine a date when everyone's free, I'd like to have you come too, and meet them."

"I wouldn't want to intrude—"

"Four daughters," he overrode this smoothly, "Kareen's the youngest. And their mother, Drou. And Commodore Koudelka, of course. I've known them all my life. And Delia's fiancé, Duv Galeni."

"A family with five women in it? All at once?" An envious note sounded plainly in her voice.

"I'd think you'd enjoy them a lot. And vice versa."

"I haven't met many women in Vorbarr Sultana . . . they're all so busy . . ." She glanced down at her black skirt. "I really ought not to go to parties just yet."

"A *family* party," he emphasized, tacking handily into this wind. "Of course I mean to invite the Professor and the Professora." Why not? He had, after all, ninety-six chairs.

"Perhaps . . . that would be unexceptionable."

"Excellent! I'll get back to you on the dates. Oh, and be sure to call Pym to notify the House guards when your workmen are due, so he can add them to his security schedule."

"Certainly."

And on that carefully-balanced note, warm yet not too personal, he made his excuses and decamped.

So, the enemy was now thronging her gates. *Don't panic, boy.* By the time of the dinner party, he might have her up to the pitch of accepting some of his wedding-week engagements. And by the time they'd been seen publicly paired at half a dozen of those, well, who knew.

Not me, unfortunately.

He sighed, and sprinted off through the rain to his waiting car.

Ekaterin wandered back to the kitchen, to see if her aunt needed any more help with the clean up. She was guiltily afraid she was too late, and indeed she found the Professora sitting at the kitchen table with a cup of tea and stack of, judging by the bemused look on her face, undergraduate essays.

Her aunt frowned fiercely, and scribbled with her stylus, then looked up and smiled. "All done, dear?"

"More like, just started. Lord Vorkosigan chose the backcountry garden. He really wants me to go ahead."

"I never doubted it. He's a decisive man."

"I'm sorry for all the interruptions this morning." Ekaterin made a gesture in the direction of the parlor.

"I don't see why *you're* apologizing. You didn't invite them."

"Indeed, I didn't." Ekaterin held up her new credit chit, and smiled. "But Lord Vorkosigan has already paid me for the design! I can give you rent for Nikki and me now."

"Good heavens, you don't owe us rent. It doesn't cost us anything to let you have the use of those empty rooms."

Ekaterin hesitated. "You can't say the food we eat comes free."

"If you wish to buy some groceries, go ahead. But I'd much prefer you saved it toward your schooling in the fall."

"I'll do both." Ekaterin nodded firmly. Carefully managed, the credit chit would spare her having to beg her father for spending money for the next several months. Da was not ungenerous, but she didn't want to hand him the right to give her reams of unwanted advice and suggestions as to how to run her life. He'd made it plain at Tien's funeral that he was unhappy she hadn't chosen to come home, as befit a Vor widow, or gone to live with her late husband's mother, though the senior Madame Vorsoisson hadn't invited them.

And how had he imagined Ekaterin and Nikki could fit in his modest flat, or find any educational opportunities in the small South Continent town to which he'd retired? Sasha Vorvayne seemed a man oddly defeated by his life, at times. He'd always made the conservative choices. Mama had been the daring one, but only in the little ways she could fit into the interstices of her role as a bureaucrat's wife. Had the defeat become contagious, toward the end? Ekaterin sometimes wondered if her parents' marriage had been, in some subtler way, almost as much of a secret mismatch as her own.

A white-haired head passed the window; a rattle, and the back door opened to reveal her Uncle Vorthys, Nikki in tow. The Professor stuck his head inside, and whispered dramatically, "Are they gone? Is it safe to come back?"

"All clear," reported his wife, and he lumbered into the kitchen.

He was burdened with a large bag, which he dumped on the table. It proved to contain replacements, several times over, for the pastries that had been consumed earlier.

"Do you think we have enough now?" the Professora inquired dryly.

"No artificial shortages," declaimed her husband. "I remember when the girls were going through that phase. Up to our elbows in young men at all hours, and not a crumb left in the house at the end of the day. I never understood your generous strategy." He explained aside to Ekaterin, "I wanted to cut their numbers by offering them spotty vegetables, and chores. The ones who came back after *that*, we would know were serious. Eh, Nikki? But for some reason, the women wouldn't let me."

"Feel free to offer them all the rotten vegetables and chores you can think of," Ekaterin told him. *Alternately, we could lock the doors and pretend no one is home. . . .* She sat down glumly beside her aunt, and helped herself to a pastry. "Did you and Nikki get your share, finally?"

"We had coffee and cookies and milk at the bakery," her uncle assured her.

Nikki licked his lips happily, and nodded confirmation. "Uncle Vorthys says all those fellows want to marry you," he added in apparent disbelief. "Is that really true?"

Thank you, dear Uncle, Ekaterin thought wryly. She'd been wondering how to explain it all to a nine-year-old boy. Though Nikki didn't seem to find the idea nearly as horrifying as she did. "That would be illegal," she murmured. "Outré, even." She smiled faintly at By Vorrutyer's jibe.

Nikki scorned the joke. "You know what I mean! Are you going to pick one of 'em?"

"No, dear," she assured him.

"Good." He added after a moment of silence, "Though if you *did*, a major would be better than a lieutenant."

"Ah . . . why?"

Ekaterin watched with interest as Nikki struggled to evolve *Vormoncrief is a patronizing Vor bore*, but to her relief, the vocabulary escaped him. He finally fell back on, "Majors make more money."

"A very practical point," Uncle Vorthys observed, and, perhaps still mistrusting his wife's generosity, packed up about half of his new stock of pastries to carry off and hide in his basement laboratory. Nikki tagged along.

Ekaterin leaned her elbows on the kitchen table, rested her chin on her hands, and sighed. "Uncle Vorthys's strategy might not be such a bad idea, at that. The threat of chores might get rid of Vormoncrief, and would certainly repel Vorrutyer. I'm not so sure it would work on Major Zamori, though. The spotty vegetables might be good all round."

Aunt Vorthys sat back, and regarded her with a quizzical smile. "So what do you want me to do, Ekaterin? Start telling your potential suitors you're not at home to visitors?"

"Could you? With my work on the garden starting, it would be the truth," said Ekaterin, considering this.

"Poor boys. I almost feel sorry for them."

Ekaterin smiled briefly. She could feel the pull of that sympathy, like a clutching hand, drawing her back into the dark. It made her skin crawl.

Every night now, lying down alone without Tien, was like a taste of some solitary heaven. She could stretch her arms and legs out all the way to the sides of the bed, reveling in the smooth space, free of compromise, confusion, oppression, negotiation, deference, placation. Free of Tien. Through the long years of their marriage she had become almost numb to the ties that had bound her to him, the promises and the fear, his desperate needs, his secrets and lies. When the straps of her vows had been released at last by his death, it was as if her whole soul had come awake, tingling painfully, like a limb when circulation was restored. *I did not know what a prison I was in, till I was freed.* The thought of voluntarily walking back into such a marital cell again, and locking the door with another oath, made her want to run screaming.

She shook her head. "I don't need another dependent."

Her aunt's brows quirked. "You don't need another Tien, that's certain. But not all men are like Tien."

Ekaterin's fist tightened, thoughtfully. "But I'm still like me. I don't know if I can *be* intimate, and not fall back into the bad old ways. Not give myself away down to the very bottom, and then complain I'm empty. The most horrible thought I have, looking back on it all, is that it wasn't all Tien's fault. I *let* him get worse and worse. If he'd chanced to marry a woman who would have stood up to him, who would have *insisted* . . ."

"Your line of logic makes my head ache," her aunt observed mildly.

Ekaterin shrugged. "It's all moot now."

After a long moment of silence, the Professora asked curiously, "So what do you think of Miles Vorkosigan?"

"He's all right. *He* doesn't make me cringe."

"I thought—back on Komarr—he seemed a bit interested in you himself."

"Oh, that was just a joke," Ekaterin said sturdily. Their joke had gone a little beyond the line, perhaps, but they had both been tired, and punchy at their release from those days and hours of fearsome strain . . . his flashing smile, and the brilliant eyes in his weary face, blazed in her memory. It had to have been a joke. Because if it weren't a joke . . . she would have to run screaming. And she was much too tired to get up. "But it's been nice to find someone genuinely interested in gardens."

"Mmm," said her aunt, and turned over another essay.

The afternoon sun of the Vorbarr Sultana spring warmed the gray stone of Vorkosigan House into something almost mellow, as Mark's hired groundcar turned in to the drive. The ImpSec gate guard at the kiosk was not one of the men Mark had met last year. The guard was respectful but meticulous, going as far as checking Mark's palm print and retina scan before waving them through with a mumbled grunt that might have been an apologetic "M'lord." Mark stared up through the car's canopy as they wound up the drive to the front portico.

Vorkosigan House again. Home? His cozy student apartment back on Beta Colony seemed more like home now than did this vast stone pile. But although he was hungry, horny, tired, tense, and jump-lagged, at least he wasn't throwing up in a paroxysm of anticipated terror this time. It was just Vorkosigan House. He could handle it. And as soon as he got inside, he could call Kareen, yes! He released the canopy the instant the car sighed to the pavement, and turned to help Enrique unload.

Mark's feet had barely hit the concrete when Armsman Pym popped out of the front doors, and gave him a snappy, yet somehow reproachful, salute. "My Lord Mark! You should have called us from the shuttleport, m'lord. We'd have picked you up properly."

"That's all right, Pym. I don't think all our gear would have fit in the armored car anyway. Don't worry, there's still plenty for you to do." The hired freight van which had followed them from the shuttleport cleared the gate guard and chuffed up the drive to wheeze to a halt behind them.

"Holy saints," murmured Enrique out of the corner of his mouth, as Mark hurried to help him hoist the DELICATE crate, which had ridden between them in the ground car, out to the pavement. "You really *are* Lord Vorkosigan. I'm not sure I totally believed you, till now."

"I really am Lord *Mark*," Mark corrected this. "Get it straight. It matters, here. I am not now, nor do I ever aspire to be, the heir to the Countship." Mark nodded toward the new short figure exiting the mansion through the carved double doors, now swung welcoming-wide. "*He's* Lord Vorkosigan."

Miles didn't look half-bad, despite the peculiar rumors about his health which had leaked back to Beta Colony. Someone had taken a hand in improving his civilian wardrobe, judging by the sharp gray suit he wore, and he filled it properly, not so sickly-thin as he'd still been when Mark had last seen him here almost a year ago. He advanced on Mark with a grin, his hand held out. They managed to exchange a firm, brotherly handshake. Mark was desperate for a hug, but not from Miles.

"Mark, dammit, you took us by surprise. You're supposed to call from orbit when you get in. Pym would have been there to pick you up."

"So I've been advised."

Miles stood back and looked him over, and Mark flushed in self-consciousness. The meds Lilly Durona had given him had permitted him to piss away more fat in less time than was humanly natural, and he'd stuck religiously to the strict regimen of diet and liquids to combat the corrosive side effects. She'd said the drug-complex wasn't addictive, and Mark believed her; he couldn't wait to get off the loathsome stuff. He now weighed very little more than when he'd last set foot on Barrayar, just as planned. Killer was released from his fleshly cage, able to defend them again if he absolutely had to. . . . But Mark hadn't anticipated how flabby and gray he was going to look, as though he were melting and slumping like a candle in the sun.

And indeed, the next words out of his brother's mouth were, "Are you feeling all right? You don't look so good."

"Jump lag. It will pass." He grinned tightly. He wasn't sure if it was the drugs, Barrayar, or missing Kareen that put him more on edge, but he was sure of the cure. "Have you heard from Kareen? Did she get in all right?"

"Yes, she got here fine, last week. What's that peculiar crate with all the layers?"

Mark wanted to see Kareen more than anything in the universe, but first things first. He turned to Enrique, who was goggling in open fascination at him and his progenitor-twin.

"I brought a guest. Miles, I'd like you to meet Dr. Enrique Borgos. Enrique, my brother Miles, Lord Vorkosigan."

"Welcome to Vorkosigan House, Dr. Borgos," Miles said, and shook hands in automatic politeness. "Your name sounds Escobaran, yes?"

"Er, yes, er, Lord Vorkosigan."

Wonders, Enrique managed to get it right this time. Mark had only been coaching him on Barrayaran etiquette for ten straight days. . . .

"And what are you a doctor of?" Miles glanced again, worriedly, at Mark; Mark guessed he was evolving alarmed theories about his clone-brother's health.

"Not medicine," Mark assured Miles. "Dr. Borgos is a biochemist and genetic entomologist."

"Words . . . ? No, that's etymologist. Bugs, that's right." Miles's eye was drawn again to the big steel-wound shock-cushioned crate at their feet. "Mark, why does that crate have air holes?"

"Lord Mark and I are going to be working together," the gangling scientist told Miles earnestly.

"I assume we have some room to spare for him," Mark added.

"God, yes, help yourselves. The House is yours. I moved last winter to the big suite on the second floor of the east wing, so the whole of the north wing is unoccupied now above the ground floor. Except for the room on the fourth floor that Armsman Roic has. He sleeps days, so you might want to give him some margin. Father and Mother will bring their usual army with them when they get here towards Midsummer, but we can rearrange things then if necessary."

"Enrique hopes to set up a little temporary laboratory, if you don't mind," Mark said.

"Nothing explosive, I trust? Or toxic?"

"Oh, no, no, Lord Vorkosigan," Enrique assured him. "It's not like that at all."

"Then I don't see why not." He glanced down, and added in a fainter tone, "Mark . . . why do the air holes have *screens* in them?"

"I'll explain everything," Mark assured him airily, "as soon as we get unloaded and I pay off these hired drivers." Armsman Jankowski had appeared at Pym's elbow while the introductions had been going forth. "The big blue valise is mine, Pym. Everything else goes with Dr. Borgos."

By press-ganging the drivers, the van was unloaded quickly to the staging area of the black-and-white tiled entry hall. A moment of alarm occurred when Armsman Jankowski, tottering along under a load of what Mark knew to be hastily-packed laboratory glassware, stepped on a black-and-white kitten, well-camouflaged by the tiles. The outraged creature emitted an ear-splitting yowl, spat, and shot off between Enrique's feet, nearly tripping the Escobaran, who was just then balancing the very expensive molecular analyzer. It was saved by a grab from Pym.

They'd almost been caught, during their midnight raid on the padlocked lab that had liberated the all-important notes and irreplaceable specimens, when Enrique had insisted on going back for the damned analyzer. Mark would have taken it as some sort of cosmic I-told-you-so if Enrique had dropped it *now*. *I'll buy you a whole new lab when we get to Barrayar*, he'd kept trying to convince the Escobaran. Enrique had seemed to think Barrayar was still stuck in the Time of Isolation, and he wasn't going to be able to obtain anything here more scientifically complex than an alembic, a still, and maybe a trepanning chisel.

Settling in their digs took still more time, as the ideal spot Enrique immediately tried to select for his new lab was the mammoth, modernized, brilliantly-lit, and abundantly-powered kitchen. Upon Pym's inquiry, Miles hastily arrived to defend this turf for his cook, a formidable woman whom he seemed to regard as essential to the smooth running not only of his household but also of his new political career. After a low-voiced explanation from Mark that the phrase *The House is yours* was a mere polite locution, and not meant to be taken literally, Enrique was persuaded to settle for a secondary laundry room in the half-basement of the north wing, not nearly so spacious, but with running water and waste disposal facilities. Mark promised a shopping trip for whatever toys and tools and benches and hoods and lighting Enrique's heart desired just as soon as possible, and left him to start arranging his treasures. The scientist showed no interest whatsoever in the selection of a bedroom. Mark figured he'd probably end up dragging a cot into his new lab, and settling there like a brooding hen defending her nest.

Mark threw his valise into the same room he'd occupied last year, and returned to the laundry to make ready to pitch his proposal to his big brother. It had all seemed to make such splendid sense, back on Escobar, but Mark hadn't known Enrique so well then. The man was a genius, but God Almighty he needed a keeper. Mark thought he understood the whole mess with the bankruptcy proceedings and the fraud suits perfectly, now. "Let me do the talking, understand?" Mark told Enrique firmly. "Miles is an important man here, an Imperial Auditor, *and* he has the ear of the Emperor himself. His support could give us a big boost." More importantly, his active opposition could be fatal to the scheme; he could kill it with a word. "I know how to work him. Just agree with everything I say, and don't try to add any embellishments of your own."

Enrique nodded eagerly, and followed him like an over-sized puppy through the maze of the house till they tracked Miles down in the great library. Pym was just setting out a spread of tea, coffee, Vorkosigan wines, two varieties of District-brewed beer, and a tray of assorted hors d'oeuvres that looked like a stained-glass window done in food. The Armsman gave Mark a cordial welcome-home nod, and withdrew to leave the two brothers to their reunion.

"How handy," Mark said, pulling up a chair next to the low table. "Snacks. It just so happens I have a new product for you to taste-test, Miles. I think it could prove very profitable."

Miles flicked up an interested eyebrow, and leaned forward as Mark unwrapped a square of attractive red foil to reveal a soft white cube. "Some sort of cheese, is it?"

"Not exactly, though it is an animal product, in a sense. This is the unflavored base version. Flavors and colors can be added as desired, and I'll show you some of those later when we've had time to mix them up. It's nutritious as hell, though—a perfectly balanced blend of carbohydrates, proteins, and fats, with all the essential vitamins in their proper proportions. You could live on a diet of this stuff alone, and water, if you had to."

"I lived on it for three months straight!" Enrique put in proudly. Mark shot him a slight frown, and he subsided.

Mark seized one of the silver knives on the tray, cut the cube into four parts, and popped a portion into his mouth. "Try it!" he said around his chewing. He stopped short of a dramatic mumble of *yum, yum!* or other convincing sound effects. Enrique too reached for a piece. More cautiously, so did Miles. He hesitated, with the fragment at his lips, to find both his watchers hanging on his gesture. His brows twitched up; he chewed. A breathless silence fell. He swallowed.

Enrique, scarcely able to contain himself, said, "How d'you like it?"

Miles shrugged. "It's . . . all right. Bland, but you said it was unflavored. Tastes better than a lot of military rations I've eaten."

"Oh, military rations," said Enrique. "Now, there's an application I hadn't thought of—"

"We'll get to that phase later," said Mark.

"So what makes it so potentially profitable?" asked Miles curiously.

"Because, through the miracle of modern bioengineering, it can be made practically for free. Once the customer has purchased, or perhaps licensed, his initial supply of butter bugs, that is."

A slight but noticeable silence. "His what?"

Mark pulled out the little box from his jacket pocket, and carefully lifted the lid. Enrique sat up expectantly. "This," said Mark, and held the box out toward his brother, "is a butter bug."

Miles glanced down into the box, and recoiled. "*Yuk!* That is the most disgusting thing I've seen in my life!"

Inside the box, the thumb-sized worker butter bug scrabbled about on its six stubby legs, waved its antennae frantically, and tried to escape. Mark gently pushed its tiny claws back from the edges. It chittered its dull brown vestigial wing carapaces, and crouched to drag its white, soft, squishy-looking abdomen to the safety of one corner.

Miles leaned forward again, to peer in revolted fascination. "It looks like a cross between a cockroach, a termite, and a . . . and a . . . and a pustule."

"We have to admit, its physical appearance is not its main selling point."

Enrique looked indignant, but refrained from denying this last statement out loud.

"Its great value lies in its efficiency," Mark went on. It was a good thing they hadn't started out by showing Miles a whole colony of butter bugs. Or worse, a queen butter bug. They could work up to the queen butter bugs much later, once they'd dragged their prospective patron over the first few psychological humps. "These things eat almost any kind of low-grade organic feedstocks. Corn stalks, grass clippings, seaweed, you name it. Then, inside their gut, the organic matter is processed by a carefully-orchestrated array of symbiotic bacteria into . . . bug butter curds. Which the butter bugs regur—return through their mouths and pack into special cells, in their hive, all ready for humans to harvest. The raw butter curds—"

Enrique, unnecessarily, pointed to the last fragment still sitting on the foil.

"Are perfectly edible at this point," Mark went on more loudly, "though they can be flavored or processed further. We're considering more sophisticated product development by adding bacteria to provide desirable flavors to the curds right in the bug's guts, so even that processing step won't be necessary."

"Bug vomit," said Miles, working through the implications. "You fed me bug vomit." He touched his hand to his lips, and hastily poured himself some wine. He looked at the butter bug, looked at the remaining fragment of curd, and drank deeply. "You're insane," he said with conviction. He drank once more, carefully swishing the wine around in his mouth for a long time before swallowing.

"It's just like honey," Mark said valiantly, "only different."

Miles's brow wrinkled, as he considered this argument. "Very different. Wait. Is that what was in that crate you brought in, these vomit bugs?"

"*Butter* bugs," Enrique corrected frostily. "They pack most efficiently—"

"*How many* . . . butter bugs?"

"We rescued twenty queen-lines in various stages of development before we left Escobar, each supported by about two hundred worker bugs," Enrique explained. "They did very well on the trip—I was so proud of the girls—they more than doubled their numbers en route. Busy, busy! Ha, ha!"

Miles's lips moved in calculation. "You've carted upwards of *eight thousand* of those revolting things into *my house*?"

"I can see what you're worried about," Mark cut in quickly, "and I assure you, it won't be a problem."

"I don't think you can, but what won't be a problem?"

"Butter bugs are highly controllable, ecologically speaking. The worker bugs are sterile; only the queens can reproduce, and they're parthenogenetic—they don't become fertile till treated with special hormones. Mature queens can't even move, unless their human keeper moves them. Any worker bug that might chance to get out would just wander about till it died, end of story."

Enrique made a face of distress at this sad vision. "Poor thing," he muttered.

"The sooner, the better," said Miles coldly. "Yuk!"

Enrique looked reproachfully at Mark, and began in a low voice, "You promised he'd help us. But he's just like all the others. Short-sighted, emotional, unreasoning—"

Mark held up a restraining hand. "Calm down. We haven't even gotten to the main part yet." He turned to Miles. "Here's the real pitch. We think Enrique can develop a strain of butter bugs to eat *native Barrayaran* vegetation, and convert it into humanly-digestible food."

Miles's mouth opened, then shut again. His gaze sharpened. "Go on . . ."

"Picture it. Every farmer or settler out in the backcountry could keep a hive of these butter bugs, which would crawl around eating all that free alien food that you folks go to so much trouble to eradicate with all the burning and terraforming treatments. And not only would the farmers get free food, they would get free fertilizer as well. Butter bug guano is terrific for plants—they just sop it up, and grow like crazy."

"Oh." Miles sat back, an arrested look in his eyes. "I know someone who is very interested in fertilizers . . ."

Mark went on, "I want to put together a development company, here on Barrayar, to both market the existing butter bugs, and create the new strains. I figure with a science genius like Enrique and a business genius like me," *and let us not get the two mixed up,* "well, there's no limit to what we can get."

Miles frowned thoughtfully. "And what did you get on Escobar, if I may ask? Why bring this genius and his product all the way here?"

Enrique would have got about ten years in jail, if I hadn't come along, but let's not go into that. "He didn't have me to handle the business, then. And the Barrayaran application is just absolutely compelling, don't you think?"

"If it can be made to work."

"The bugs can work to process Earth-descended organic matter right now. We'll market that as soon as we can, and use the proceeds to finance the basic research on the other. I can't set a timetable for that till Enrique has had more time to study Barrayaran biochemistry. Maybe a year or two, to, ah, get all the bugs out." Mark grinned briefly.

"Mark . . ." Miles frowned at the butter bug box, now sitting closed on the table. Tiny scratching noises arose from it. "It sounds logical, but I don't know if logic is going to sell to the proles. Nobody will want to eat food that comes out of something that looks like *that.* Hell, they won't want to eat anything it *touches.*"

"People eat honey," argued Mark. "And that comes out of bugs."

"Honeybees are . . . sort of cute. They're furry, and they have those classy striped uniforms. And they're armed with their stings, just like little swords, which makes people respect them."

"Ah, I see—the insect version of the Vor class," Mark murmured sweetly. He and Miles exchanged edged smiles.

Enrique said, in a bewildered tone, "So do you think if I put stings on my butter bugs, Barrayarans would like them better?"

"No!" said Miles and Mark together.

Enrique sat back, looking rather hurt.

"So." Mark cleared his throat. "That's the plan. I'll be setting up Enrique in a proper facility as soon as I have time to find something suitable. I'm not sure whether here in Vorbarr Sultana or out in Hassadar would be better—if this takes off, it could bring in a lot of business, which you might like for the District."

"True . . ." allowed Miles. "Talk to Tsipis."

"I plan to. Do you begin to see why I think of them as money bugs? And do you think you might want to invest? Nothing like getting in on the ground floor, and all that."

"Not . . . at this time. Thanks all the same," said Miles neutrally.

"We, ah, do appreciate the temporary space, you know."

"No problem. Or at least . . ." his eye chilled, "it had better not be."

In the conversational lull that followed, Miles was apparently recalled to his place as a host, and he offered up the food and drinks. Enrique chose beer, and treated them to a dissertation on the history of yeast in human food production, going back to Louis Pasteur, with side comments on parallels between yeast organisms and the butter bugs' symbiotes. Miles drank more wine and didn't say much. Mark nibbled from the grand platter of delectable hors d'oeuvres and calculated the day when he would come to the end of his weight-loss drugs. Or maybe he would just flush the rest tonight.

Eventually Pym, who was apparently playing butler in Miles's reduced bachelor household, came in to collect the plates and glasses. Enrique eyed his brown uniform with interest, and asked about the meaning and history of the silver decorations on the collar and cuffs. This actually drew Miles out briefly, as he supplied Enrique with a few highlights of family history (politely omitting their prominent place in the aborted Barrayaran invasion of Escobar a generation ago), the past of Vorkosigan House, and the story of the Vorkosigan crest. The Escobaran seemed fascinated by the fact that the mountains-and-leaf design had originated as a Count's mark to seal the bags of District tax revenues. Mark was encouraged to believe Enrique was developing a social grace after all. Perhaps he would develop another one soon. One could hope.

When enough time had passed that, Mark calculated, he and Miles could feel they'd accomplished their unaccustomed and still awkward fraternal bonding ritual, he made noises about *finishing unpacking*, and the welcome-home party broke up. Mark guided Enrique back to his new lab, just to be sure he got there all right.

"Well," he said heartily to the scientist. "That went better than I expected."

"Oh, yes," said Enrique vaguely. He had that foggy look in his eyes that betokened visions of long-chain molecules dancing in his head: a good sign. The Escobaran was apparently going to survive his traumatic transplant. "And I've had this wonderful idea how to get your brother to like my butter bugs."

"Great," said Mark, somewhat at random, and left him to it. He headed up the back stairs two at a time to his bedroom and its waiting comconsole, to call Kareen, Kareen, *Kareen*.

Chapter Four

Ivan had finished his mission of delivering one hundred hand-calligraphed Imperial wedding invitations to Ops HQ for subsequent off-world distribution to select serving officers, when he encountered Alexi Vormoncrief, also passing out through the security scanners in the building's lobby.

"Ivan!" Alexi hailed him. "Just the man! Wait up."

Ivan paused by the automated doors, mentally composing a likely mission order from She Who Must Be Obeyed Till After The Wedding in case he needed to effect an escape. Alexi was not the most stultifying bore in Vorbarr Sultana—several gentlemen of the older generation currently vied for that title—but he certainly qualified as an understudy. On the other hand, Ivan was extremely curious to know if the seeds he'd dropped in Alexi's ear a few weeks back had borne any amusing fruit.

Alexi finished negotiating security and bustled over, a little breathless. "I'm just off duty, are you? Can I treat you to a round, Ivan? I have a bit of news, and you deserve to be the first to know." He rocked on his heels.

If Alexi was buying, why not? "Sure."

Ivan accompanied Alexi across the street to the convenient tavern that the Ops officers regarded as their collective property. The place was something of an institution, having gone into business some ten or fifteen minutes after Ops had opened its then-new building soon after the Pretender's War. The decor was calculatedly dingy, tacitly preserving it as a male bastion.

They slid into a table toward the back; a man in well-cut civvies lounging at the bar turned his head as they passed. Ivan recognized By Vorrutyer. Most town clowns didn't frequent the officers' bars, but By could turn up anywhere. He had the damnedest connections. By raised a hand in mock-salute to Vormoncrief, who, expansively, beckoned him over to join them. Ivan raised a brow. Byerly was on record as despising the company of his fellows who, as he put it, came unarmed to the battle of wits. Ivan couldn't imagine why he was cultivating Vormoncrief. Opposites attracting?

"Sit, sit," Vormoncrief told By. "I'm buying."

"In that case, certainly," said By, and settled in smoothly. He gave Ivan a cordial nod; Ivan returned it a trifle warily. He didn't have Miles present as a verbal shield-wall. By never baited Ivan while Miles was around. Ivan wasn't quite sure if it was because his cousin ran subtle interference, or because By preferred the more challenging target. Maybe Miles ran interference by *being* the more challenging target. On the other hand, maybe his cousin regarded Ivan as his own personal archery butt, and just didn't want to share. Family solidarity, or mere Milesian possessiveness?

They punched their orders into the server, and Alexi tapped in his credit chit. "Oh, my sincere condolences, by the way, on the death of your cousin Pierre," he said to Byerly. "I kept forgetting to mention that, because you don't wear your House blacks. You really should, you know. You have the right, your blood ties are close enough. Did they finally determine the cause of death?"

"Oh, yes. Heart failure, dropped him like a stone."

"Instant?"

"As far as anyone could tell. Being a ruling Count, his autopsy was thorough. Well, if the man hadn't been such an antisocial recluse, someone might have come across the body before his brain spoiled."

"So young, hardly fifty. It's a shame he died without issue."

"It's a greater shame that rather more of my Vorrutyer uncles didn't die without issue." By sighed. "I'd have a new job."

"I didn't know you hankered after the Vorrutyers' District, By," said Ivan. "Count Byerly? A political career?"

"God forfend. I have no desire whatsoever to join that hall full of fossils arguing in Vorhartung Castle, and the District bores me to tears. Dreary place. If only my fecund cousin Richars were not such a very complete son-of-a-bitch—no insult intended to my late aunt—I would wish him joy of his prospects. If he can obtain them. Unfortunately, he *does* take joy in them, which quite takes the joy out of it all for me."

"What's wrong with Richars?" asked Alexi blankly. "Seemed a solid enough fellow to me, the few times I've met him. Politically sound."

"Never mind, Alexi."

Alexi shook his head in wonderment. "By, don't you have any proper family feeling?"

By dismissed this with an airy what-would-you? gesture. "I haven't any proper family. My principal feeling is revulsion. With perhaps one or two exceptions."

Ivan's brow wrinkled, as he unraveled By's patter. "*If* he can obtain them? What impediment would Richars have?" Richars was eldest son of the eldest uncle, adult, and as far as Ivan knew, in his right mind. Historically, being a son-of-a-bitch had never been considered a valid excuse for exclusion from the Council of Counts, else it would have been a much thinner body. It was only being a bastard that eliminated one. "No one's discovered he's a secret Cetagandan, like poor René Vorbretten, have they?"

"Unfortunately, no." By glanced across at Ivan, an oddly calculating look starting in his eyes. "But Lady Donna—I believe you know her, Ivan—lodged a formal declaration of impediment with the Council the day after Pierre died, which has temporarily blocked Richars's confirmation."

"I'd heard something. Wasn't paying attention." Ivan hadn't seen Pierre's younger sister Lady Donna in the flesh—and what delicious flesh it had once been—since she'd divested her third spouse and semiretired to the Vorrutyer's District to become her brother's official hostess and unofficial District deputy. It was said she had more clout in the day-to-day running of the District than Pierre. Ivan could believe it. She must be almost forty now; he wondered if she'd started to run to fat yet. On her, it might look good. Ivory skin, wicked black hair to her hips, and smoldering brown eyes like embers. . . .

"Oh, I'd wondered why Richars's confirmation was taking so long," said Alexi.

By shrugged. "We'll see if Lady Donna can make her case stick when she gets back from Beta Colony."

"My mother thought it odd she left before the funeral," said Ivan. "She hadn't heard of any bad blood between Donna and Pierre."

"Actually, they got along rather well, for my family. But the need was urgent."

Ivan's own fling with Donna had been memorable. He'd been a callow new officer, she'd been ten years older and temporarily between spouses. They hadn't talked much about their relatives. He'd never told her, he realized, how her mind-melting lessons had saved his ass a few years later, during that near-disastrous diplomatic mission to Cetaganda. He really ought to call on her, when she got back from Beta Colony. Yes, she might be depressed about those accumulating birthdays, and need cheering up . . .

"So what's the substance of her declaration of impediment?" asked Vormoncrief. "And what's Beta Colony got to do with it?"

"Ah, we shall have to see how that plays out when Donna gets back. It will be a surprise. I wish her every success." A peculiar smile quirked By's lips.

Their drinks arrived. "Oh, very good." Vormoncrief raised his glass high. "Gentlemen, to matrimony. I have sent the Baba!"

Ivan paused with his glass halfway to his lips. "Beg pardon?"

"I've met a woman," said Alexi smugly. "In fact, I might say I have met *the* woman. For which I thank you, Ivan. I would never have known of her existence but for your little hint. By's seen her once—she's suitable in every way to be Madame Vormoncrief, don't you think, By? Great connections—she's Lord Auditor Vorthys's niece—how did you find out about her, Ivan?"

"I . . . met her at my cousin Miles's. She's designing a garden for him." *How did Alexi get so far, so fast?*

"I didn't know Lord Vorkosigan had any interest in gardens. No accounting for taste. In any case, I managed to get her father's name and address through this casual conversation about family trees. South Continent. I had to buy a round-trip ticket for the Baba, but she's one of the most exclusive go-betweens—not that there are many left—in Vorbarr Sultana. Hire the best, I say."

"Madame Vorsoisson has accepted you?" said Ivan, stunned. *I never intended it to go to this. . . .*

"Well, I assume she will. When the offer arrives. Almost no one uses the old formal system anymore. She'll take it as a romantic surprise, I hope. Bowl her right over." His smugness was tinged with anxiety, which he soothed with a large gulp of his beer. By Vorrutyer swallowed a sip of wine and whatever words he'd been about to utter.

"Think she'll accept?" Ivan said cautiously.

"A woman in her situation, why should she refuse? It will give her a household of her own again, which she must be used to, and how else can she get one? She's true Vor, she will surely appreciate the nicety. *And* it steals a march on Major Zamori."

She hadn't accepted yet. There was still hope. This wasn't celebration, this was nervous babbling seeking the sedation of drink. Sound idea—Ivan took a long gulp. Wait . . . "Zamori? I didn't tell Zamori about the widow."

Ivan had selected Vormoncrief with care, as a plausible enough threat to put the wind up Miles without actually posing a real danger to his suit. For status, a mere no-lord Vor surely couldn't compete with a Count's heir and Imperial Auditor. Physically . . . hm. Maybe he hadn't thought enough about that one. Vormoncrief was a well-enough looking man. Once Madame Vorsoisson was outside of Miles's charismatic jamming-field, the comparison might be . . . rather painful. But Vormoncrief was a blockhead—surely she couldn't pick him over . . . *and how many married blockheads do you know? Somebody picked 'em. It can't be that much of an impediment.* But Zamori—Zamori was a serious man, and no fool.

"Something I let slip, I fear." Vormoncrief shrugged. "No matter. He's not Vor. It gives me an edge with her family Zamori can't touch. She married Vor before, after all. And she must know a woman alone has no business raising a son. It'll be a financial stretch, but I think if I take a firm hand I can convince her to fire him off to a real Vor school soon after the knot is tied. Make a man of him, knock that little obnoxious streak right out of him before it becomes a habit."

They finished their beer; Ivan ordered the next round. Vormoncrief went off to find the head.

Ivan chewed on his knuckle, and stared at By.

"Problems, Ivan?" By inquired easily.

"My cousin Miles is courting Madame Vorsoisson. He told me to back off her under pain of his ingenuity."

By's brows twitched up. "Then watching him annihilate Vormoncrief should amuse you. Or would it be the other way around that would charm?"

"He's going to eviscerate me out my ass when he finds out I tipped Vormoncrief onto the widow. And Zamori, oh God."

By smiled briefly with one side of his mouth. "Now, now. I was there. Vormoncrief bored her to tears."

"Yes, but . . . maybe her situation isn't comfortable. Maybe she would take the first ticket out that was offered . . . wait, you? How did you come there?"

"Alexi . . . leaks. It's a habit of his."

"Didn't know you were wife-hunting."

"I'm not. Don't panic. Nor am I about to inflict a Baba—good lord, what an anachronism—on the poor woman. Though I may note that *I* did not bore her. She was even a little intrigued, I fancy. Not bad for a first reconnaissance. I may take Vormoncrief along on my future amorous starts, for flattering contrast." By glanced up, to be sure the object of their analysis was not on the way back, and leaned forward and lowered his voice to a more confidential tone. But he did not go on to carve the block further or more wittily. Instead he murmured, "You know, I think my cousin Lady Donna would be very glad of your support in her upcoming case. You could be of real use to her. You have the ear of a Lord Auditor—short, but surprisingly convincing in his new role, I was impressed—Lady Alys, Gregor himself. Important people."

"They're important. I'm not." Why the hell was By flattering *him*? He must want something—badly.

"Would you be willing to meet with Lady Donna, when she returns?"

"Oh." Ivan blinked. "That, gladly. But . . ." He thought it through. "I'm not quite sure what she expects to accomplish. Even if she blocks Richars, the Countship can only go to one of his sons or younger brothers. Unless you're planning mass murder at the next family reunion, which is more exertion than I'd expect of you, I don't see how it delivers any benefit to you."

By smiled briefly. "I said I don't want the Countship. Meet with Donna. She will explain it all to you."

"Well . . . all right. Good luck to her, anyway."

By sat back. "Good."

Vormoncrief returned, to dither about his Vor mating ploys into his second beer. Ivan tried without success to change the subject. Byerly drifted off just before it was his turn to buy the next round.

Ivan made excuses involving obscure Imperial duties, and escaped at last.

How to avoid Miles? He couldn't put in for transfer to some distant embassy till this damned wedding was over. That would be too late. Desertion was a possibility, he thought morosely—maybe he could go off and join the Kshatryan Foreign Legion. No, with all Miles's galactic connections, there wasn't a cranny of the wormhole nexus, no matter how obscure, sure to be safe from his wrath. And ingenuity. Ivan would have to trust to luck, Vormoncrief's stultifying personality, and for Zamori—kidnapping? Assassination? Maybe introduce him to more women? Ah, yes! Not to Lady Donna, though. That one, Ivan proposed to keep for himself.

Lady Donna. *She* was no pubescent prole. Any husband who dared to trumpet in her presence risked being sliced off at the knees. Elegant, sophisticated, assured . . . a woman who knew what she wanted, and how to ask for it. A woman of his own class, who understood the game. A little older, yes, but with lifespans extending so much these days, what of that? Look at the Betans; Miles's Betan grandmother, who must be ninety if she was a day, was reported to have a gentleman-friend of eighty. Why hadn't he thought of Donna earlier?

Donna. Donna, Donna, Donna. Mmm. This was one meeting he wouldn't miss for worlds.

"I set her to wait in the antechamber to the library, m'lord," Pym's familiar rumble came to Kareen's ears. "Would you like me to bring you anything, or ah, anything?"

"No. Thank you," came Lord Mark's lighter voice in reply from the front hall. "Nothing, that will be all, thank you."

Mark's footsteps echoed off the stone paving: three rapid strides, two skips, a slight hesitation, and a more measured footfall to the archway into the antechamber. *Skips? Mark?* Kareen bounced to her feet as he rounded the corner. Oh, my, *surely* it could not have been good for him to lose that much weight that quickly—instead of the familiar excessively round solidity, he looked all *saggy*, except for his grin, and his blazing eyes—

"Ah! Stand right there!" he ordered her, seized a footstool, placed it before her knees, climbed up, and flung his arms around her. She wrapped her arms around him in turn, and the conversation was buried for a moment in frantic kisses given and received and returned redoubled.

He came up for air long enough to inquire, "How did you get here?" then didn't let her answer for another minute.

"Walked," she said breathlessly.

"Walked! It must be a kilometer and a half!"

She put her hands on his shoulders, and backed off far enough to focus her eyes on his face. He was too pale, she thought disapprovingly, almost pasty. Worse, his buried resemblance to Miles was edging toward the surface with his bones, an observation she knew would horrify him. She kept it to herself. "So? My father used to walk to work here every day in good weather, stick and all, when he was the Lord Regent's aide."

"If you'd called, I would have sent Pym with the car—hell, better, I'd have come myself. Miles says I can use his lightflyer whenever I want."

"A lightflyer, for six blocks?" she cried indignantly, between a couple more kisses. "On a beautiful spring morning like this?"

"Well, they don't have slidewalks here . . . mmm. . . . Oh, that's good . . ." He nuzzled her ear, inhaled her tickling curls, and planted a spiral line of kisses from her earlobe to her collarbone. She hugged him tight. The kisses seemed to burn across her skin like little fiery footprints. "Missed you, missed you, missed you . . ."

"Missed you missed you missed you too." Though they *could* have traveled home together, if he hadn't insisted on his Escobaran detour.

"At least the walk made you all warm . . . you could come up to my room, and take off all those hot clothes . . . can Grunt come out to play, hmm . . . ?"

"*Here*? In *Vorkosigan House*? With all the Armsmen around?"

"It's where I live, presently." This time, he broke off and leaned back to eye-focusing distance. "And there's only three Armsmen, and one sleeps in the daytime." A worried frown started between his eyes. "Your house . . . ?" he ventured.

"Worse. It's full of parents. And sisters. *Gossipy* sisters."

"Rent a room?" he offered after a puzzled moment.

She shook her head, groping for an explanation of muddled feelings she hardly understood herself.

"We could borrow Miles's lightflyer . . ."

This brought an involuntary giggle to her lips. "There's *really* not enough room. Even if we both took your nasty meds."

"Yes, he can't have been thinking, when he purchased that thing. Better a huge aircar, with vast comfortable upholstered seats. That you can fold down. Like that armored groundcar he has, left over from the Regency—hey! We could crawl in the back, mirror the canopy . . ."

Kareen shook her head, helplessly.

"*Anywhere* on Barrayar?"

"That's the trouble," she said. "Barrayar."

"In orbit . . . ?" He pointed skyward in hope.

She laughed, painfully. "I don't *know*, I don't know . . ."

"Kareen, what's wrong?" He was looking very alarmed, now. "Is it something I've done? Something I said? What have I—are you still mad about the drugs? I'm sorry. I'm sorry. I'll stop them. I'll, I'll gain the weight back. Whatever you want."

"It's not *that*." She stepped back half a pace further, though neither let go of the other's hands. She cocked her head. "Though I *don't* understand why being a body narrower should make you suddenly look half a head shorter. What a bizarre optical illusion. Why should mass translate to height, psychologically? But no. It's not you. It's me."

He clutched her hands and stared in earnest dismay. "I don't understand."

"I've been thinking about it the whole ten days, waiting for you to get home here. About you, about us, about me. All week, I've been feeling stranger and stranger. On Beta Colony, it seemed so right, so logical. Open, official, approved. Here . . . I haven't been able to tell my parents about us. I tried to work up to it. I haven't even been able to tell my sisters. Maybe, if we'd come home together, I wouldn't have lost my nerve, but . . . but I did."

"Were . . . are you thinking about that Barrayaran folktale where the girl's lover ended up with his head in a pot of basil, when her relatives caught up with him?"

"Pot of basil? No!"

"*I* thought about it . . . I think your sisters could, y'know, if they teamed up. Hand me my head, I mean. And I know your mother could; she trained you all."

"How I wish Tante Cordelia were here!" Wait, that was perhaps an unfortunate remark, in the context. Pots of basil, good God. Mark was so paranoid . . . *quite*. Never mind. "I wasn't thinking of you, at all."

"Oh." His voice went rather flat.

"That's not what I mean! I was thinking of you day and night. Of us. But I've been so uncomfortable, since I got back. It's like I can just feel myself, folding back up into my old place in this Barrayaran culture-box. I can feel it, but I can't stop it. It's horrible."

"Protective coloration?" His tone suggested he could understand a desire for camouflage. His fingers noodled back along her collarbone, crept around her neck. One of his wonderful neck rubs would feel so good, just now . . . He'd worked so hard, to learn to touch and be touched, to overcome the panic and the flinching and the hyperventilation. He was breathing faster now.

"Something like that. But I hate secrets and lies."

"Can't you just . . . tell your family?"

"I tried. I just couldn't. Could you?"

He looked nonplused. "You want me to? It would be the basil for sure."

"No, no, I mean hypothetically."

"I could tell *my* mother."

"*I* could tell *your* mother. She's Betan. She's another world, the other world, the one where we were so right. It's *my* mother I can't talk to. And I always could, before." She found she was trembling, a little. Mark could feel it through her hands; she could tell by the stricken look in his eyes as he raised his face to hers.

"I don't understand how it can feel so right there, and so wrong here," Kareen said. "It should be not wrong here. Or not right there. Or something."

"That makes no sense. Here or there, what's the difference?"

"If there's no difference, why did you go to so much trouble to lose all that weight before you would set foot on Barrayar again?"

His mouth opened, and closed. He finally got out, "Well, so. It's only for a couple of months. I can take a couple of months."

"It gets worse. Oh, Mark! I can't go back to Beta Colony."

"What? Why not? We'd planned—you'd planned—is it that your parents suspect, about us? Have they forbidden you—"

"It's not that. At least, I don't think it is. It's just money. Or just no money. I couldn't have gone, last year, without the Countess's scholarship. Mama and Da say they're strapped, and I don't know how I can earn so much in just the few months." She bit her lip in renewed determination. "But I mean to think of something."

"But if you can't—but I'm not done yet, on Beta Colony," he said plaintively. "I have another year of school, and another year of therapy."

Or more. "But you do mean to come back to Barrayar, after, don't you?"

"Yes, I think. But a whole year apart—" He gripped her tighter, as though looming parents were bearing down upon them to rip her from his grasp on the spot. "It would be . . . excessively stressful, without you," he mumbled in muffled understatement into her flesh.

After a moment, he took a deep breath, and peeled himself away from her. He kissed her hands. "There's no need to panic," he addressed her knuckles earnestly. "There's months to figure something out. Anything could happen." He looked up, and feigned a normal smile. "I'm glad you're here anyway. You have to come see my butter bugs." He hopped down from the footstool.

"Your what?"

"Why does everyone seem to have so much trouble with that name? I thought it was simple enough. Butter bugs. And if I hadn't gone by Escobar, I would never have run across 'em, so that much good has come of it all. Lilly Durona tipped me on to them, or rather, onto Enrique, who was in a spot of trouble. Great biochemist, no financial sense. I bailed him out of jail, and helped him rescue his experimental stocks from the idiot creditors who'd confiscated 'em. You'd have laughed, to watch us blundering around in that raid on his lab. Come on, come see."

As he towed her by the hand through the great house, Kareen asked dubiously, "Raid? On Escobar?"

"Maybe raid is the wrong word. It was entirely peaceful, miraculously enough. *Burglary*, perhaps. I actually got to dust off some of my old training, believe it or not."

"It doesn't sound very . . . legal."

"No, but it was moral. They were Enrique's bugs—he'd made 'em, after all. And he loves them like pets. He cried when one of his favorite queens died. It was very affecting, in a bizarre sort of way. If I hadn't been wanting to strangle him at just that moment, I'd have been very moved."

Kareen was just starting to wonder if those cursed weight-loss meds had any psychological side-effects Mark hadn't seen fit to confide to her, when they arrived at what she recognized as one of Vorkosigan House's basement laundry rooms. She hadn't been back in this part of the house since she'd played hide-and-seek here with her sisters as children. The windows high in the stone walls let in a few strips of sunlight. A lanky fellow with crisp dark hair, who looked no older than his early twenties at the outside, was puttering distractedly about among piles of half-unpacked boxes.

"Mark," he greeted them. "I must have more shelving. And benches. And lighting. And more heat. The girls are sluggish. You promised."

"Check the attics first, before you go running out to buy stuff new," Kareen suggested practically.

"Oh, good idea. Kareen, this is Dr. Enrique Borgos, from Escobar. Enrique, this is my . . . my *friend*, Kareen Koudelka. My best friend." Mark held tightly and possessively to her hand as he announced this. But Enrique merely nodded vaguely at her.

Mark turned to a broad covered metal tray, balanced precariously on a crate. "Don't look yet," he said over his shoulder to her.

A memory of life with her older sisters whispered through Kareen's mind—*Open your mouth and close your eyes, and you will get a big surprise* . . . Prudently, she ignored his directive and advanced to see what he was doing.

He lifted the tray's cover to reveal a writhing mass of brown-and-white shapes, chittering faintly and crawling over one another. Her startled eye sorted out the details—insectoid, big, lots of legs and waving feelers—

Mark plunged his hand in amongst the heaving masses, and she blurted, "Eck!"

"It's all right. They don't bite or sting," he assured her with a grin. "Here, see? Kareen, meet butter bug. Bug, Kareen."

He held out a single bug, the size of her thumb, in his palm.

Does he really want me to touch that thing? Well, she'd got through Betan sex education, after all. What the hell. Torn between curiosity and revulsion, she held out her hand, and Mark tipped the bug into it.

Its little clawed feet tickled her skin, and she laughed nervously. It was quite the most incredibly ugly live thing she'd ever seen in her life. Though she had perhaps dissected nastier items in her Betan xenozoology course last year; nothing looked its best after pickling.

The bugs didn't smell too bad, just sort of green, like mown hay. It was the scientist who needed to wash his shirt.

Mark embarked on an explanation of how the bugs reprocessed organic matter in their really disgusting-looking abdomens, complicated by pedantic technical corrections about the biochemical details from his new friend Enrique. It all made sense biologically, as far as Kareen could tell.

Enrique pulled a single petal from a pink rose which lay piled with half a dozen others in a box. The box, also balanced on a stack of crates, bore the mark of one of Vorbarr Sultana's premier florists. He set the petal in her palm next to the bug; the bug clutched it in its front claws, and began nibbling off the tender edge. He smiled fondly at the creature. "Oh, and Mark," he added, "the girls need more food as soon as possible. I got these this morning, but they won't last the day." He waved at the florist's box.

Mark, who had been anxiously watching Kareen contemplate the bug in her hand, seemed to notice the roses for the first time. "Where did you get the flowers? Wait, you bought *roses* for *bug fodder?*"

"I asked your brother how to get some Earth-descended botanical matter that the girls would like. He said, call there and order it. Who is Ivan? But it was terribly expensive. We're going to have to rethink the budget, I'm afraid."

Mark smiled thinly, and seemed to count to five before answering. "I see. A *slight* miscommunication, I fear. Ivan is our cousin. You will doubtless not be able to avoid meeting him sooner or later. There is Earth-descended botanical matter available much more cheaply. I believe you can collect some outside—no, maybe I'd better not send you out alone. . . ." He stared at Enrique with an expression of deeply mixed emotion, rather the way Kareen stared at the butter bug in her palm. It was about halfway through munching down the rose petal now.

"Oh, and I *must* have a lab assistant as soon as possible," Enrique added, "if I am to plunge unimpeded into my new studies. And access to whatever the natives here may know about their local biochemistry. Mustn't waste precious time reinventing the wheel, you know."

"I believe my brother has some contacts at Vorbarr Sultana University. And at the Imperial Science Institute. I'm sure he could get you access to anything that isn't security-related." Mark chewed gently on his lip, his brows drawn down in a momentarily downright Milesian expression of furious thought. "Kareen . . . didn't you say you were looking for a job?"

"Yes . . ."

"Would *you* like a job as an assistant? You had those couple of Betan biology courses last year—"

"Betan training?" Enrique perked up. "Someone with Betan training, in this benighted place?"

"Only a couple of undergraduate courses," Kareen explained hastily. "And there are *lots* of folks on Barrayar with galactic training of all sorts." *What does he think this is, the Time of Isolation?*

"It's a start," said Enrique, in a tone of judicious approval. "But I was going to ask, Mark, do we have enough money to hire anyone yet?"

"Mm," said Mark.

"You, out of money?" said Kareen to Mark, startled. "What did you *do* on Escobar?"

"I'm not *out*. It's just tied up in a lot of nonliquid ways right now, and I spent quite a bit more than I'd budgeted—it's only a temporary cash-flow problem. I'll get it sorted out at the end of the next period. But I have to confess, I was really glad I could put Enrique and his project up here free for a little while."

"We could sell shares again," Enrique suggested. "That's what I did before," he added in an aside to Kareen.

Mark winced. "I think not. I know I explained to you about *closely-held*."

"People do raise venture capital that way," Kareen observed.

Mark informed her under his breath, "But they don't normally sell shares to five hundred and eighty percent of their company."

"Oh."

"I was going to pay them all back," Enrique protested indignantly. "I was so close to breakthrough, I couldn't stop then!"

"Um . . . excuse us a moment, Enrique." Mark took Kareen by her free hand, led her into the corridor outside the laundry room, and shut the door firmly. He turned to her. "He doesn't need an assistant. He needs a *mother*. Oh, God, Kareen, you have no idea what a boon it would be if you could help me ride herd on the man. I could give *you* the credit chits with a quiet mind, and you could keep the records and dole out his pocket-money, and keep him out of dark alleys and not let him pick the Emperor's flowers or talk back to

ImpSec guards or whatever suicidal thing he comes up with next. The thing is, um . . ." He hesitated. "*Would* you be willing to take shares as collateral against your salary, at least till the end of the period? Doesn't give you much spending money, I know, but you said you meant to save . . ."

She stared dubiously at the butter bug, still tickling her palm as it finished off the last of its rose petal. "Can you really give me shares? Shares of what? But . . . if this doesn't work out as you hope, I wouldn't have anything else to fall back on."

"It will work," he promised urgently. "I'll make it work. I own fifty-one percent of the enterprise. I'm having Tsipis help me officially register us as a research and development company, out of Hassadar."

She would be betting their future together on Mark's odd foray into bioentrepreneurship, and she wasn't even sure he was in his right mind. "What, ah, does your Black Gang think of all this?"

"It's not their department in any way."

Well, that was reassuring. This was apparently the work of his dominant personality, Lord Mark, serving the whole man, and not a ploy of one of his sub-personas for its own narrow ends. "Do you really think Enrique is that much of a genius? Mark, I thought that smell back in the lab was the bugs at first, but it was him. When was his last bath?"

"He probably forgot to take one. Feel free to remind him. He won't be offended. In fact, think of it as part of your job. Make him wash and eat, take charge of his credit chit, organize the lab, make him look both ways before crossing the street. *And* it would give you an excuse to hang out here at Vorkosigan House."

Put like that . . . besides, Mark was giving her that pleading-puppy-eyes look. In his own strange way Mark was almost as good as Miles at drawing one into doing things one suspected one would later regret deeply. Infectious obsession, a Vorkosigan family trait.

"Well . . ." A little chittering *burp* made her look down. "Oh, no, Mark! Your bug is sick." Several milliliters of thick white liquid dripped from the bug's mandibles onto her palm.

"What?" Mark surged forward in alarm. "How can you tell?"

"It's throwing up. Ick! Could it be jump-lag? That makes some people nauseous for days." She looked around frantically for a place to deposit the creature before it exploded or something. Would bug diarrhea be next?

"Oh. No, that's all right. They're supposed to do that. It's just producing its bug butter. *Good* girl," he crooned to the bug. At least, Kareen trusted he was addressing the bug.

Firmly, Kareen took his hand, turned it palm-up, and dumped the now-slimy bug into it. She wiped her hand on his shirt. "Your bug. You hold it."

"*Our* bugs . . . ?" he suggested, though he accepted it without demur. "Please . . . ?"

The goop didn't smell bad, actually. In fact, it had a scent rather like roses, roses and ice cream. She nevertheless found the impulse to lick the stickiness off her hand to be quite resistible. Mark . . . was less so. "Oh, very well." *I don't know how he talks me into things like this.* "It's a deal."

Chapter Five

Armsman Pym admitted Ekaterin to the grand front hall of Vorkosigan House. Belatedly, she wondered if she ought to be using the utility entrance, but in his tour of a couple of weeks ago Vorkosigan hadn't shown her where it was. Pym was smiling at her in his usual very friendly way, so perhaps it was all right for the moment.

"Madame Vorsoisson. Welcome, welcome. How may I serve you?"

"I had a question for Lord Vorkosigan. It's rather trivial, but I thought, if he was right here, and not busy . . ." She trailed off.

"I believe he's still upstairs, madame. If you would be pleased to wait in the library, I'll fetch him at once."

"I can find my way, thank you," she fended off his proffered escort. "Oh, wait—if he's still asleep, please don't—" But Pym was already ascending the stairs.

She shook her head, and wandered through the antechamber to the left toward the library. Vorkosigan's Armsmen seemed impressively enthusiastic, energetic, and attached to their lord, she had to concede. And astonishingly cordial to visitors.

She wondered if the library harbored any of those wonderful old hand-painted herbals from the Time of Isolation, and whether she might borrow—she came to a halt. The chamber had an occupant: a short, fat, dark-haired young man who crouched at a comconsole that sat so incongruously among the fabulous antiques. It was displaying a collection of colored graphs of some kind. He glanced up at the sound of her step on the parquet.

Ekaterin's eyes widened. *At my height,* Lord Vorkosigan had complained, *the effect is damned startling.* But it wasn't the soft obesity that startled nearly so much as the resemblance to, what did they call it for a clone, to his progenitor, which was half-buried beneath the . . . why did she instantly think of it as a barrier of flesh? His eyes were the same intense gray as Miles's—as Lord Vorkosigan's, but their expression was closed and wary. He wore black trousers and a black shirt; his belly burgeoned from an open backcountry-style vest which conceded the spring weather outside only by being a green so dark as to be almost black.

"Oh. You must be Lord Mark. I'm sorry," she spoke to that wariness.

He sat back, his finger touching his lips in a gesture very like one of Lord Vorkosigan's, but then going on to trace his doubled chin, pinching it between thumb and finger in an emphatic variation clearly all his own. "I, on the other hand, am tolerably pleased."

Ekaterin flushed in confusion. "I didn't mean—I didn't mean to intrude."

His eyebrows flicked up. "You have the advantage of me, milady." The timbre of his voice was very like his brother's, perhaps a trifle deeper; his accent was an odd amalgam, neither wholly Barrayaran nor wholly galactic.

"Not milady, merely Madame. Ekaterin Vorsoisson. Excuse me. I'm, um, your brother's landscape consultant. I just came in to check what he wants done with the maple tree we're taking down. Compost, firewood—" She gestured at the cold carved white marble fireplace. "Or if he just wants me to sell the chippings to the arbor service."

"Maple tree, ah. That would be Earth-descended botanical matter, wouldn't it?"

"Why, yes."

"I'll take any chopped-up bits he doesn't want."

"Where . . . would you want it put?"

"In the garage, I suppose. That would be handy."

She pictured the heap dumped in the middle of Pym's immaculate garage. "It's a rather large tree."

"Good."

"Do you garden . . . Lord Mark?"

"Not at all."

The decidedly disjointed conversation was interrupted by a booted tread, and Armsman Pym leaning around the doorframe to announce, "M'lord will be down in a few minutes, Madame Vorsoisson. He says, please don't go away." He added in a more confiding tone, "He had one of his seizures last night, so he's a little slow this morning."

"Oh, dear. And they give him such a headache. I shouldn't trouble him till he's had his painkillers and black coffee." She turned for the door.

"No, no! Sit down, madame, sit, please. M'lord would be right upset with me if I botched his orders." Pym, smiling anxiously, motioned her urgently toward a chair; reluctantly, she sat. "There now. Good. Don't move." He watched her a moment as if to make sure she wasn't going to bolt, then hurried off again. Lord Mark stared after him.

She hadn't thought Lord Vorkosigan was the sort of Old Vor who threw his boots at his servants' heads when he was displeased, but Pym did seem edgy, so who knew? She looked around again to find Lord Mark leaning back in his chair, steepling his fingers and watching her curiously.

"Seizures . . . ?" he said invitingly.

She stared back at him, not at all sure what he was asking. "They leave him with the most dreadful hangover the next day, you see."

"I'd understood they were practically cured. Is this not, in fact, the case?"

"Cured? Not if the one I witnessed was a sample. Controlled, he says."

His eyes narrowed. "So, ah . . . where did you see this show?"

"The seizure? It was on my living room floor, actually. In my old apartment on Komarr," she felt compelled to explain at his look. "I met him during his recent Auditorial case there."

"Oh." His gaze flicked up and down, taking in her widow's garb. Construing . . . what?

"He has this little headset device his doctors made for him, which is supposed to trigger them when he chooses, instead of randomly." She wondered if the one he'd had last night was medically induced, or if he'd left it for too long again and suffered the more severe, spontaneous version. He'd claimed to have learned his lesson, but—

"He neglected to supply me with all those complicating details, for some reason," Lord Mark murmured. An oddly unhumorous grin flashed over his face and was gone. "Did he explain to you how he came by them in the first place?"

His attention upon her had grown intent. She groped for the right balance between truth and discretion. "Cryo-revival damage, he told me. I once saw the scars on his chest from the needle grenade. He's lucky he's alive."

"Huh. Did he also mention that at the time he encountered the grenade, he was trying to save my sorry ass?"

"No . . ." She hesitated, taking in his defiantly lifted chin. "I don't think he's supposed to talk much about his, his former career."

He smiled thinly, and drummed his fingers on the comconsole. "My brother has this bad little habit of editing his version of reality to fit his audience, y'see."

She could understand why Lord Vorkosigan was loath to display any weakness. But was Lord Mark angry about something? Why? She sought to find some more neutral topic. "Do you call him your brother, then, and not your progenitor?"

"Depends on my mood."

The subject of their discussion arrived then, curtailing the conversation. Lord Vorkosigan wore one of his fine gray suits and polished half-boots, his hair was neatly combed but still damp, and the faint scent of his cologne carried from his shower-warmed skin. This dapper impression of greet-the-morning energy was unfortunately belied by his gray-toned face and puffy eyes; the general effect was of a corpse reanimated and dressed for a party. He managed a macabre smile in Ekaterin's direction, and a suspicious squint at his clone-brother, and lowered himself stiffly into an armchair between them. "Uh," he observed.

He looked appallingly just like that morning-after on Komarr, minus the bloodstains and scabs. "Lord Vorkosigan, you should not have gotten up!"

He gave her a little wave of his fingers which might have been either agreement or denial, then Pym arrived in his wake bearing a tray with coffeepot, cups, and a basket covered with a bright cloth from which wafted an enticing aroma of warm spiced bread. Ekaterin watched with fascination as Pym poured out the first cup and folded his lord's hand around it; Lord Vorkosigan sipped, inhaled—it looked like his first breath of the day—sipped again, and looked up and blinked. "Good morning, Madame Vorsoisson." His voice only sounded a little underwater.

"Good morning—oh—" Pym poured her a cup too before she could forestall him. Lord Mark shut off his comconsole graphs and added sugar and cream to his, and studied his progenitor-brother with obvious interest. "Thank you," Ekaterin said to Pym. She hoped Vorkosigan had ingested his painkillers upstairs, first thing; by his rapidly-improving color and easing movement, she was fairly sure he had.

"You're up early," Vorkosigan said to her.

She almost pointed out the time, in denial of this, then decided that might be impolitic. "I was excited to be starting my first professional garden. The sod crew are out rolling up the grass in the park this morning, and collecting the terraformed topsoil. The tree crew will be along shortly to transplant the oak. It occurred to me to ask if you wanted the maple for firewood, or compost."

"Firewood. Sure. We burn wood now and then, when we're being deliberately archaic for show—it impresses the hell out of my mother's Betan visitors—and there're always the Winterfair bonfires. There's a pile out back behind some bushes. Pym can show you."

Pym nodded genial confirmation.

"I've laid claim to the leaves and chippings," Lord Mark put in, "for Enrique."

Lord Vorkosigan shrugged, and held a hand palm-out in a warding gesture. "That's between you and your eight thousand little friends."

Lord Mark appeared to find no mystery in this obscure remark; he nodded thanks. Having, apparently, accidentally routed her employer out of bed, Ekaterin wondered if it would be too rude to dash out again immediately. She ought probably to stay long enough to drink at least one cup of Pym's coffee. "If all goes well, the excavation can start tomorrow," she added.

"Ah, good. Did Tsipis put you in the way of collecting all your water and power connection permits?"

"Yes, that's all under control. And I've learned more than I expected about Vorbarr Sultana's infrastructure."

"It's a lot older and stranger than you'd think. You should hear Drou Koudelka's war stories some time, about how they escaped through the sewers after collecting the Pretender's head. I'll see if I can get her going at the dinner party."

Lord Mark leaned his elbow on the comconsole, nibbled gently on his knuckle, and idly rubbed his throat.

"A week from tomorrow night seems to be the date I can round up everyone," Lord Vorkosigan added. "Will that work for you?"

"Yes, I think so."

"Good." He shifted around, and Pym hastened to pour him more coffee. "I'm sorry I missed the garden groundbreaking. I really meant to come out and watch that with you. Gregor sent me out-country a couple of days ago on what turned out to be a fairly bizarre errand, and I didn't get back till late last night."

"Yes, what was that all about?" Lord Mark put in. "Or is it an Imperial secret?"

"No, unfortunately. In fact, it's already gossip all over town. Maybe it will divert attention from the Vorbretten case. Though I'm not sure if you can call it a *sex* scandal, exactly." A tilted grimace. "Gregor told me, 'You're half-Betan, Miles, you're *just* the Auditor to handle this one.' I said, 'Thanks, Sire.'"

He paused for his first bite of sweet spiced bread, washed down with another swallow of coffee, and warmed to his theme. "Count Vormuir came up with this wonderful idea how to solve his District's underpopulation problem. Or so he imagined. Are you up on the latest hot demographic squabbles among the Districts, Mark?"

Lord Mark waved a negating hand, and reached for the bread basket. "I haven't been following Barrayaran politics for the past year."

"This one goes back further than that. Among our father's early reforms, when he was Regent, was that he managed to impose uniform simplified rules for ordinary subjects who wanted to change Districts, and switch their oaths to their new District Count. Since every one of the sixty Counts was trying to attract population to his District at the expense of his brother Counts, Da somehow greased this through the Council, even though everyone was also trying to prevent their own liege people from leaving them. Now, each Count has a lot of discretion about how he runs his District, how he structures his District government, how he imposes his taxes, supports his economy, what services he provides his people, whether Progressive or Conservative or a party of his own invention like that loon Vorfolse down on the south coast, and on and on. Mother describes the Districts as sixty sociopolitical culture dishes. I'd add, economic, too."

"That part, I've been studying," Lord Mark allowed. "It matters to where I place my investments."

Vorkosigan nodded. "Effectively, the new law gave every Imperial subject the right to vote local government with their feet. Our parents drank champagne with dinner the night the vote slipped through, and Mother grinned for days. I must have been about six, because we were living here by then, I remember. The long-term effect, as you can imagine, has been a downright biological competition. Count Vorenlightened makes it good for his people, his District grows, his revenues increase. His neighbor Count Vorstodgy makes it too tough, and he leaks people like a sieve, and his revenues drop. *And* he gets no sympathy from his brother Counts, because his loss is their gain."

"Ah, ha," said Mark. "And is the Vorkosigan's District winning or losing?"

"We're just treading water, I think. We've been losing people to the Vorbarr Sultana economy since forever. And a hell of a lot of loyalists followed the Viceroy to Sergyar last year. On the other hand, the District University and new colleges and medical complexes in Hassadar have been a big draw. Anyway, Count Vormuir has been a long-time loser in this demographic game. So, he implemented what he fondly imagined to be a wildly Progressive personal—I might say, very personal—solution."

Ekaterin's cup was empty, but she'd lost all desire to leave. She could listen to Lord Vorkosigan by the hour, she thought, when he was on like this. He was entirely awake and alive now, engrossed in his story.

"Vormuir," Vorkosigan went on, "bought himself thirty uterine replicators and imported some techs to run them, and started, ah, manufacturing his own liege people. His own personal crèche, as it were, but with only one sperm donor. Guess who."

"Vormuir?" Mark hazarded.

"None other. It's the same principle as a harem, I guess. Only different. Oh, and he's only making little girls, at present. The first batch of them are almost two years old. I saw them. Appallingly cute, en masse."

Ekaterin's eyes widened at this vision of a whole thundering cadre of little girls. The impact must be something like a child-garden—or, depending on the decibel level, a girl-grenade. *I always wanted daughters.* Not just one, lots—sisters, the like of which she had never had. *Too late now.* None for her, dozens for Vormuir—the pig, it wasn't fair! She was bemusedly aware that she ought to be feeling outrage, but what she really felt was outraged envy. What had Vormuir's wife—wait. Her brows lowered. "Where is he getting the eggs? His Countess?"

"That's the next little legal wrinkle in this mess," Vorkosigan went on enthusiastically. "His Countess, who has four half-grown children of her—and his—own, wants nothing to do with this. In fact, she isn't talking to him, and has moved out. One of his Armsmen told Pym, very privately, that the last time he attempted to impose a, um, conjugal visit upon her, and threatened to batter down her door, she dumped a bucket of water out the window on him—this was mid-winter—and then threatened to personally warm him with her plasma arc. And then threw down the bucket and screamed at him that if he was that much in love with plastic tubes, he could use that one. Do I have that right, Pym?"

"Not the precise quote I was given, but close enough, m'lord."

"Did she hit him?" Mark asked, sounding quite interested.

"Yes," said Pym, "both times. I understand her aim is superior."

"I suppose that made the plasma arc threat convincing."

"Speaking professionally, when one is standing next to the target, an assailant with *bad* aim is actually more alarming. Nevertheless, the Count's Armsmen persuaded him to come away."

"But we digress." Vorkosigan grinned. "Ah, thank you, Pym." The attentive Armsman, blandly, poured his lord more coffee, and refilled Mark and Ekaterin's cups.

Vorkosigan went on, "There is a commercial replicator crèche in Vormuir's District capital, which has been growing babies for the well-to-do for several years now. When a couple present themselves for this service, the techs routinely harvest more than one egg from the wife, that being the more complex and expensive part of the proceedings. The backup eggs are kept frozen for a certain length of time, and if not claimed by then, are discarded. Or they are supposed to be. Count Vormuir hit upon a clever economy. He had his techs collect all the viable discards. He was very proud of this angle, when he was explaining it all to me."

Now *that* was appalling. Nikki had been, to her cost, a body-birth, but it might well have been different. If Tien had had sense, or if she'd stood up for simple prudence instead of letting herself be seduced by the romantic drama of it all, they might have chosen a replicator-gestation. Imagine learning that her longed-for daughter was now the property of an eccentric like Vormuir . . . "Do any of the women know?" asked Ekaterin. "The ones whose egg cells were . . . can you call it stolen?"

"Ah, not at first. Rumors, however, had begun to leak out, hence the Emperor was moved to dispatch his newest Imperial Auditor to investigate." He bowed at her, sitting. "As for whether it can be called theft— Vormuir claims to have violated no Barrayaran law whatsoever. He claims it quite smugly. I shall be consulting with several of Gregor's Imperial lawyers over the next few days, and trying to figure out if that is in fact true. On Beta Colony, they could hang him out to dry for this, and his techs with him, but of course on Beta Colony, he'd never have got this far."

Lord Mark shifted in his station chair. "So how many little girls does Vormuir have by now?"

"Eighty-eight live births, plus thirty more coming along in the replicators. Plus his first four. A hundred and twenty-two children for that idiot, not one for—anyway, I gave him an order in the Emperor's Voice to start no more until Gregor had ruled on his ingenious scheme. He was inclined to protest, but I pointed out that since all his replicators were full anyway, and would be for the next seven or so months, he wasn't really much discommoded by this. He shut up, and went off to consult with *his* lawyers. And I flew back to Vorbarr Sultana and gave Gregor my verbal report, and went home to bed."

He'd left out confession of his seizure in this description, Ekaterin noted. What was Pym about, to have so pointedly mentioned it?

"There ought to be a law," Lord Mark said.

"There ought to be," his brother replied, "but there isn't. This is Barrayar. Lifting the Betan legal model wholesale strikes me as a recipe for revolution, and besides, a lot of their particular conditions don't apply here. There are a dozen galactic codes which address these issues in addition to the Betan. I left Gregor last night muttering about appointing a select committee to study them all and recommend a Joint Council ruling. And me on it, for my sins. I hate committees. I much prefer a nice clean chain of command."

"Only if you're at the top of it," Lord Mark observed dryly.

Lord Vorkosigan conceded this with a sardonic wave. "Well, yes."

Ekaterin asked, "But will you be able to corner Vormuir with a new law? Surely his situation would have to be, um . . . grandfathered."

Lord Vorkosigan grinned briefly. "Exactly the problem. We've got to nail Vormuir under some existing rule, bent to fit, to discourage imitators, while shoving the new law, in whatever form it finally takes, through the Counts and Ministers. We can't use a rape charge; I looked up all the technical definitions, and they just don't stretch that way."

Lord Mark asked, in a worried voice, "Did the little girls seem abused or neglected?"

Lord Vorkosigan glanced up at him rather sharply. "I'm not the expert on crèche care you are, but they seemed all right to me. Healthy . . . noisy . . . they screeched and giggled a lot. Vormuir told me he had two full-time nurturers for every six children, in shifts. He also went on about his frugal plans for having the older ones care for the younger ones, later on, which gave an unsettling hint of just how far he's thinking of expanding this genetic enterprise. Oh, and we can't get him for slavery, either, because they all really are actually his daughters. And the theft-of-the-eggs angle is extremely ambiguous under current rules." In a peculiarly exasperated tone he added, "Barrayarans!" His clone-brother gave him an odd look.

Ekaterin said slowly, "In Barrayaran customary law, when Vor-caste families split because of death or other reasons, the girls are supposed to go to their mothers or mother's kin, and the boys to their fathers. Don't these girls belong to their mothers?"

"I looked at that one, too. Leaving aside the fact that Vormuir isn't married to any of them, I suspect very few of the mothers would actually want the girls, and all of them would be pretty upset."

Ekaterin wasn't altogether sure about the first part of this, but he certainly had the second dead-to-rights.

"And if we forced them into their mothers' families, what punishment would there be in it to Vormuir? His District would still be richer by a hundred and eighteen girls, and he wouldn't even have to feed them." He set aside his half-eaten piece of spice bread, and frowned. Lord Mark selected a second, no, third slice, and nibbled on it. A glum silence fell.

Ekaterin's brows drew down in thought. "By your account, Vormuir is much taken with economies, of scale and otherwise." Only long after Nikki's birth had she wondered if Tien had pushed for the old-fashioned way because it had seemed much cheaper. *We won't have to wait until we can afford it* had been a potent argument, in her eager ears. Vormuir's motivation seemed as much economic as genetic: ultimately, wealth for his District and therefore for him. This techno-harem was intended to become future taxpayers, along with the husbands he no doubt assumed they would draw in, to support him in his old age. "In effect, the girls are the Count's acknowledged bastards. I'm sure I read somewhere . . . in the Time of Isolation, weren't Imperial and count-palatine female bastards entitled to a dowry, from their high-born father? And it required some sort of Imperial permission . . . the dowry almost was the sign of legal acknowledgment. I'll bet the Professora would know all the historical details, including the cases where the dowries had to be dragged out by force. Isn't an Imperial permission effectively an Imperial order? Couldn't Emperor Gregor set Count Vormuir's dowries for the girls . . . high?"

"Oh." Lord Vorkosigan sat back, his eyes widening with delight. "Ah." An evil grin leaked between his lips. "Arbitrarily high, in fact. Oh . . . *my*." He looked across at her. "Madame Vorsoisson, I believe you have hit on a possible solution. I will certainly pass the idea along as soon as I may."

Her heart lifted in response to his obvious pleasure—well, all right, actually it was a sort of razor-edged glee; anyway, he smiled at her smile at his smile. She could only hope she'd done some little bit to ease his morning-after headache. A chiming clock began sounding in the antechamber. Ekaterin glanced at her chrono. Wait, how could it possibly be this late? "Oh, my word, the time. My tree crew will be here any moment. Lord Vorkosigan, I must excuse myself."

She jumped to her feet, and made polite farewells to Lord Mark. Both Pym and Lord Vorkosigan escorted her personally to the front door. Vorkosigan was still very stiff; she wondered how much pain his forced motion denied, or defied. He encouraged her to stop in again, any time she had the least question, or needed anything at all, and dispatched Pym to show her where to have the crew stack the maple wood, and stood in the doorway and watched them both till they turned the corner of the great house.

Ekaterin glanced back over her shoulder. "He didn't look very well this morning, Pym. You really shouldn't have let him get out of bed."

"Oh, I know it, ma'am," Pym agreed morosely. "But what's a mere Armsman to do? I haven't the authority to countermand his orders. What he really needs, is looking after by someone who won't stand his nonsense. A proper Lady Vorkosigan would do the trick. Not one of those shy, simpering ingenues all the young lords seem to be looking to these days, he'd just ride right over her. He needs a woman of experience, to stand up to him." He smiled apologetically down at her.

"I suppose so," sighed Ekaterin. She hadn't really thought about the Vor mating scene from the Armsmen's point of view. Was Pym hinting that his lord had such an ingenue in his eye, and his staff was worried it was some sort of mismatch?

Pym showed her the wood cache, and made a sensible suggestion for placing Lord Mark's compost heap near it rather than in the underground garage, assuring her it would be just fine there. Ekaterin thanked him and headed back toward the front gates.

Ingenues. Well, if a Vor wanted to marry within his caste, he almost had to look to the younger cohort, these days. Vorkosigan did not strike her as a man who would be happy with a woman who was not up to his intellectual weight, but how much choice did he have? Presumably any woman with brains enough to be interesting to him in the first place would not be so foolish as to reject him for his physical . . . it was no business of hers, she told herself firmly. And it was absurd to allow the vision of this imaginary ingenue, offering him an imaginary devastating insult about his disabilities, to raise one's real blood pressure. Completely absurd. She marched off to oversee the dismantling of the bad tree.

Mark was just reaching to reactivate the comconsole when Miles wandered back into the library, smiling absently. Mark turned to watch his progenitor-brother start to fling himself back into his armchair, only to hesitate, and lower himself more carefully. Miles stretched his shoulders as if to loosen knotted muscles, leaned back, and stuck his feet out. He picked up his half-eaten piece of bread, remarked cheerfully, "That went well, don't you think?" and bit into it.

Mark eyed him doubtfully. "What went well?"

"The co'versation." Miles chased his bite with the last of his cold coffee. "So, you've met Ekaterin. Good. What did you two find to talk about, before I got downstairs?"

"You. Actually."

"Ah?" Miles's face lit, and he sat up a little straighter. "What did she say about me?"

"We mainly discussed your seizures," Mark said grimly. "She seemed to know a great deal more about them than you had seen fit to confide to me."

Miles subsided, frowning. "Hm. That's not the aspect of me I'm really anxious to have her dwell on. Still, it's good she knows. I wouldn't want to be tempted to conceal a problem of that magnitude again. I've learned my lesson."

"Oh, really." Mark glowered at him.

"I sent you the basic facts," his brother protested in response to this look. "You didn't need to dwell on all the gory medical details. You were on Beta Colony; there was nothing you could do about it anyway."

"They're my fault."

"Rubbish." Miles really did do a very good offended snort; Mark decided it was a touch of his—their—Aunt Vorpatril in it that gave it that nice upper-class edge. Miles waved a dismissive hand. "It was the sniper's doing, followed by more medical random factors than I can calculate. Done's done; I'm alive again, and I mean to stay that way this time."

Mark sighed, realizing reluctantly that if he wanted to wallow in guilt, he'd get no cooperation from his big brother. Who, it appeared, had other things on his mind.

"So what did you think of her?" Miles asked anxiously.

"Who?"

"*Ekaterin*, who else?"

"As a landscape designer? I'd have to see her work."

"No, no, no! Not as a landscape designer, though she's good at that *too*. As the next Lady Vorkosigan."

Mark blinked. "What?"

"What do you mean, *what*? She's beautiful, she's smart—dowries, ye gods, how perfect, Vormuir will split—she's incredibly level-headed in emergencies. Calm, y'know? A lovely calm. I adore her calm. I could swim in it. Guts *and* wit, in one package."

"I wasn't questioning her fitness. That was a merely a random noise of surprise."

"She's Lord Auditor Vorthys's niece. She has a son, Nikki, almost ten. Cute kid. Wants to be a jump-pilot, and I think he has the determination to make it. Ekaterin wants to be a garden designer, but I think she could go on to be a terraformer. She's a little too quiet, sometimes—she needs to build up her self-confidence."

"Perhaps she was just waiting to get a word in edgewise," Mark suggested.

Miles paused, stricken—briefly—by doubt. "Do you think I talked too much, just now?"

Mark waved his fingers in a little perish-the-thought gesture, and poked through the bread basket for any lurking spice bread crumbs. Miles stared at the ceiling, stretched his legs, and counter-rotated his feet.

Mark thought back over the woman he had just seen here. Pretty enough, in that elegant brainy-brunette style Miles liked. Calm? Perhaps. Guarded, certainly. Not very expressive. Round blondes were much sexier. Kareen was wonderfully expressive; she'd even managed to rub some of those human skills off on him, he thought in his more optimistic moments. Miles was plenty expressive too, in his own unreliable way. Half of it was horseshit, but you were never sure which half.

Kareen, Kareen, Kareen. He must *not* take her attack of nerves as a rejection of him. *She's met someone she likes better, and is dumping us,* whispered someone from the Black Gang in the back of his head, and it wasn't the lustful Grunt. *I know a few ways to get rid of excess fellows like that. They'd never even find the body.* Mark ignored the vile suggestion. *You have no place in this, Killer.*

Even if she had met someone else, say, on the way home, all lonely by herself because he'd insisted on taking that other route, she had the compulsive honesty to tell him so if it were so. Her honesty was at the root of their present contretemps. She was constitutionally incapable of walking around pretending to be a chaste Barrayaran maiden unless she was. It was her unconscious solution to the cognitive dissonance of having one foot planted on Barrayar, the other on Beta Colony.

All Mark knew was that if it came down to a choice between Kareen and oxygen, he'd prefer to give up oxygen, thanks. Mark considered, briefly, laying his sexual frustrations open to his brother for advice. Now would be the perfect opportunity, trading on Miles's newly-revealed infatuation. Trouble was, Mark was by no means sure which side Miles would be *on.* Commodore Koudelka had been Miles's mentor and friend, back when Miles had been a fragile youth hopelessly wild for a military career. Would Miles be sympathetic, or would he lead, Barrayaran-style, the posse seeking Mark's head? Miles was being terrifically Vorish these days.

Yes, and so after all his exotic galactic romances, Miles had finally settled on the Vor next door. If settled was the term—the man mouthed certainties that the twitching of his body belied. Mark's brow wrinkled in puzzlement. "Does Madame Vorsoisson know this?" he asked at last.

"Know what?"

"That you're, um . . . hustling her for the next Lady Vorkosigan." And what an *odd* way to say, *I love her, and I want to marry her.* It was very Miles, though.

"Ah." Miles touched his lips. "That's the tricky part. She's very recently widowed. Tien Vorsoisson was killed rather horribly less than two months ago, on Komarr."

"And you had what, to do with this?"

Miles grimaced. "Can't give you the details, they're classified. The public explanation is a breath-mask accident. But in effect, I was standing next to him. You know how that one feels."

Mark flipped up a hand, in sign of surrender; Miles nodded, and went on. "But she's still pretty shaken up. By no means ready to be courted. Unfortunately, that doesn't stop the competition around here. No money, but she's beautiful, and her bloodlines are impeccable."

"Are you choosing a wife, or buying a horse?"

"I am describing how my Vor rivals think, thank you. Some of them, anyway." His frown deepened. "Major Zamori, I don't trust. He may be smarter."

"You have rivals already?" *Down, Killer. He didn't ask for your help.*

"God, yes. And I have a theory about where they came from . . . never mind. The important thing is for me to make friends with her, get close to her, without setting off her alarms, without offending her. Then, when the time is right—well, then."

"And, ah, when are you planning to spring this stunning surprise on her?" Mark asked, fascinated.

Miles stared at his boots. "I don't know. I'll recognize the tactical moment when I see it, I suppose. If my sense of timing hasn't totally deserted me. Penetrate the perimeter, set the trip lines, plant the suggestion—strike. Total victory! Maybe." He counter-rotated his feet the other way.

"You have your campaign all plotted out, I see," said Mark neutrally, rising. Enrique would be glad to hear the good news about the free bug fodder. And Kareen would be here for work soon—her organizational skills had already had notable effect on the zone of chaos surrounding the Escobaran.

"Yes, exactly. So take care not to foul it up by tipping my hand, if you please. Just play along."

"Mm, I wouldn't dream of interfering." Mark made for the door. "Though I'm not at all sure *I'd* choose to structure *my* most intimate relationship as a war. Is she the enemy, then?"

His timing was perfect; Miles's feet had come down and he was still sputtering just as Mark passed the door. Mark stuck his head back through the frame to add, "I hope her aim is as good as Countess Vormuir's."

Last word: I win. Grinning, he exited.

Chapter Six

"Hello?" came a soft alto voice from the door of the laundry room-cum-laboratory. "Is Lord Mark here?"

Kareen looked up from assembling a new stainless steel rack on wheels to see a dark-haired woman leaning diffidently through the doorway. She wore very conservative widow's garb, a long-sleeved black shirt and skirt set off only by a somber gray bolero, but her pale face was unexpectedly young.

Kareen put down her tools and scrambled to her feet. "He'll be back soon. I'm Kareen Koudelka. Can I help you?"

A smile illuminated the woman's eyes, all too briefly. "Oh, you must be the student friend who is just back from Beta Colony. I'm glad to meet you. I'm Ekaterin Vorsoisson, the garden designer. My crew took out that row of amelanchier bushes on the north side this morning, and I wondered if Lord Mark wanted any more compost."

So that's what those scrubby things had been called. "I'll ask. Enrique, can we use any um, amel-whatsit bush chippings?"

Enrique leaned around his comconsole display and peered at the newcomer. "Is it Earth-descended organic matter?"

"Yes," replied the woman.

"Free?"

"I suppose. They were Lord Vorkosigan's bushes."

"We'll try some." He disappeared once more behind the churning colored displays of what Kareen had been assured were enzymatic reactions.

445

The woman stared curiously around the new lab. Kareen followed her gaze proudly. It was all beginning to look quite orderly and scientific and attractive to future customers. They'd painted the walls cream white; Enrique had picked the color because it was the exact shade of bug butter. Enrique and his comconsole occupied a niche in one end of the room. The wet-bench was fully plumbed, set up with drainage into what had once been the washtub. The dry-bench, with its neat array of instruments and brilliant lighting, ran along the wall all the way to the other end. The far end was occupied by racks each holding a quartet of meter-square custom-designed new bughouses. As soon as Kareen had the last set assembled, they could release the remaining queen-lines from their cramped travel box into their spacious and sanitary new homes. Tall shelves on both sides of the door held their proliferating array of supplies. A big plastic waste bin brimmed with a handy supply of bug fodder; a second provided temporary storage for bug guano. The bugshit had not proved nearly as smelly or abundant as Kareen had expected, which was nice, as the task of cleaning the bughouses daily had fallen to her. Not half bad for a first week's work.

"I must ask," said the woman, her eye falling on the heaped-up maple bits in the first bin. "What does he want all those chippings *for?*"

"Oh, come in, and I'll show you," said Kareen enthusiastically. The dark-haired woman responded to Kareen's friendly smile, drawn in despite her apparent reserve.

"I'm the Head Bug Wrangler of this outfit," Kareen went on. "They were going to call me the lab assistant, but I figured as a shareholder I ought to at least be able to pick my own job title. I admit, I don't have any other wranglers to be the head of, yet, but it never hurts to be optimistic."

"Indeed." The woman's faint smile was not in the least Vor-supercilious; drat it, she hadn't said if it was Lady or Madame Vorsoisson. Some Vor could get quite huffy about their correct title, especially if it was their chief accomplishment in life so far. No, if this Ekaterin were that sort, she would have made a point of the *Lady* at the first possible instant.

Kareen unlatched the steel-screen top of one of the bug hutches, reached in, and retrieved a single worker-bug. She was getting quite good at handling the little beasties without wanting to puke by now, as long as she didn't look too closely at their pale pulsing abdomens.

Kareen held out the bug to the gardener, and began a tolerably close copy of Mark's Better Butter Bugs for a Brighter Barrayar sales talk.

Though Madame Vorsoisson's eyebrows went up, she didn't shriek, faint, or run away at her first sight of a butter bug. She followed Kareen's explanation with interest, and was even willing to hold the bug and feed it a maple leaf. There was something very *bonding* about feeding live things, Kareen had to admit; she would have to keep that ploy in mind for future presentations. Enrique, his interest piqued by the voices drifting past his comconsole discussing his favorite subject, wandered over and did his best to queer her pitch by adding long, tedious technical footnotes to Kareen's streamlined explanations. The garden designer's interest soared visibly when Kareen got to the part about future R&D to create a Barrayaran-vegetation-consuming bug.

"If you could teach them to eat strangle-vines, South Continent farmers would buy and keep colonies for that alone," Madame Vorsoisson told Enrique, "whether they produced edible food as well or not."

"Really?" said Enrique. "I didn't know that. Are you familiar with the local planetary botany?"

"I'm not a fully-trained botanist—yet—but I have some practical experience, yes."

"Practical," echoed Kareen. A week of Enrique had given her a new appreciation for the quality.

"So let's see this bug manure," the gardener said.

Kareen led her to the bin and unsealed the lid. The woman peered in at the heap of dark, crumbly matter, leaned over, sniffed, ran her hand through it, and let some sift out through her fingers. "Good heavens."

"What?" asked Enrique anxiously.

"This looks, feels, and smells like the finest compost I've ever seen. What kind of chemical analysis are you getting off it?"

"Well, it depends on what the girls have been eating, but—" Enrique burst into a kind of riff on the periodic table of the elements. Kareen followed the significance of about half of it.

Madame Vorsoisson, however, looked impressed. "Could I have some to try on my plants at home?" she asked.

"Oh, yes," said Kareen gratefully. "Carry away all you want. There's getting to be rather a lot of it, and I'm really beginning to wonder where would be a safe place to dispose of it."

"Dispose of it? If this is half as good as it looks, put it up in ten-liter bags and sell it! Everyone who's trying to grow Earth plants here will be willing to try it."

"Do you think so?" said Enrique, anxious and pleased. "I couldn't get anyone interested, back on Escobar."

"This is Barrayar. For a long time, burning and composting was the only way to terraform the soil, and it's still the cheapest. There was never enough Earth-life based compost to both keep old ground fertile and break in new lands. Back in the Time of Isolation they even had a war over horse manure."

"Oh, yeah, I remember that one from my history class." Kareen grinned. "A *little* war, but still, very . . . symbolic."

"Who fought who?" asked Enrique. "And why?"

"I suppose the war was really over money and traditional Vor privilege," Madame Vorsoisson explained to him. "It had been the custom, in the Districts where the Imperial cavalry troops were quartered, to distribute the products of the stables free to any prole who showed up to cart it away, first-come first-served. One of the more financially pressed Emperors decided to keep it all for Imperial lands or sell it. This issue somehow got attached to a District inheritance squabble, and the fight was on."

"What finally happened?"

"In *that* generation, the rights fell to the District Counts. In the following generation, the Emperor took them back. And in the generation after that—well, we didn't have much horse cavalry anymore." She went to the sink to wash, adding over her shoulder, "There is still a customary distribution every week from the Imperial Stables here in Vorbarr Sultana, where the ceremonial cavalry squad is kept. People come in their groundcars, and carry off a bag or two for their flower beds, just for old time's sake."

"Madame Vorsoisson, I've lived for four years in butter bug guts," Enrique told her earnestly as she dried her hands.

"Mm," she said, and won Kareen's heart on the spot by receiving this declaration with no more risibility than a slight helpless widening of her eyes.

"We really need someone on the macro-level as a native guide to the native vegetation," Enrique went on. "Do you think *you* could help us out?"

"I suppose I could give you some sort of quick overview, and some ideas about where to go to next. But you'd really need a

District agronomy officer—Lord Mark can surely access the one in the Vorkosigan's District for you."

"There, you see already," cried Enrique. "I didn't even know there was such a thing as a District agronomy officer."

"I'm not sure Mark does, either," Kareen added doubtfully.

"I'll bet the Vorkosigans' manager, Tsipis, could guide you," Madame Vorsoisson said.

"Oh, do you know Tsipis? Isn't he a lovely man?" said Kareen.

Madame Vorsoisson nodded instant agreement. "I've not met him in person yet, but he's given me ever so much help over the comconsole with Lord Vorkosigan's garden project. I mean to ask him if I could come down to the District to collect stones and boulders from the Dendarii Mountains to line the stream bed—the water in the garden is going to take the form of a mountain stream, you see, and I fancied Lord Vorkosigan would appreciate the home touch."

"Miles? Yes, he loves those mountains. He used to ride up into them all the time when he was younger."

"Really? He hasn't talked much to me about that part of his life—"

Mark appeared at the door at that moment, tottering along under a large box of laboratory supplies. Enrique relieved him of it with a glad cry, and carried it off to the dry bench, and began unpacking the awaited reagents.

"Ah, Madame Vorsoisson," Mark greeted her, catching his breath. "Thank you for the maple chippings. They seem to be a hit. Have you met everyone?"

"Just now," Kareen assured him.

"She likes our bugs," said Enrique happily.

"Have you tried the bug butter yet?" Mark asked.

"Not yet," Madame Vorsoisson said.

"Would you be willing to? I mean, you did see the bugs, yes?" Mark smiled uncertainly at this new potential customer/test subject.

"Oh . . . all right." The gardener's return smile was a trifle crooked. "A small bite. Why not."

"Give her a taste test, Kareen."

Kareen pulled one of the liter tubs of bug butter from the stack on the shelf, and pried it open. Sterilized and sealed, the stuff would keep indefinitely at room temperature. She'd harvested this batch just this morning; the bugs had responded most enthusiastically to their new fodder. "Mark, we're going to need more of these containers. Bigger ones. A liter of bug butter per bughouse per day is going to add up to a lot of bug butter after a while." Pretty soon, actually. Especially when they hadn't been able to persuade anyone in the household to eat more than a mouthful apiece. The Armsmen had taken to avoiding this corridor.

"Oh, the girls will make more than that, now they're fully fed," Enrique informed them cheerfully over his shoulder from the bench.

Kareen stared thoughtfully at the twenty tubs she'd put up this morning, atop the small mountain from the last week. Fortunately, there was a lot of storage space in Vorkosigan House. She scrounged up one of the disposable spoons kept ready for sampling, and offered it to Madame Vorsoisson. Madame Vorsoisson accepted it, blinked uncertainly, scooped a sample from the tub, and took a brave bite. Kareen and Mark anxiously watched her swallow.

"Interesting," she said politely after a moment.

Mark slumped.

Her brows knotted in sympathy; she glanced at the stack of tubs. After a moment she offered, "How does it respond to freezing? Have you tried running it through an ice cream freezer, with some sugar and flavoring?"

"Actually, not yet," said Mark. His head tilted in consideration. "Hm. D'you think that would work, Enrique?"

"Don't see why not," responded the scientist. "The colloidal viscosity doesn't break down when exposed to subzero temperatures. It's thermal acceleration which alters the protein microstructure and hence texture."

"Gets kind of rubbery when you cook it," Mark translated this. "We're working on it, though."

"Try freezing," Madame Vorsoisson suggested. "With, um, perhaps a more dessert-sounding name?"

"Ah, marketing," Mark sighed. "That's the next step now, isn't it?"

"Madame Vorsoisson said she would test out the bug shit on her plants for us," Kareen consoled him.

"Oh, great!" Mark smiled again at the gardener. "Hey, Kareen, you want to fly down to the District with me day after tomorrow, and help me scout sites for the future facility?"

Enrique paused in his unpacking to unfocus his gaze into the air, and sigh, "*Borgos Research Park.*"

"Actually, I was thinking of calling it *Mark Vorkosigan Enterprises,*" Mark said. "D'you suppose I ought to spell it out in full?

MVK Enterprises might have some potential for confusion with Miles."

"*Kareen's Butter Bug Ranch*," Kareen put in sturdily.

"We'll obviously have to have a shareholder's vote." Mark smirked.

"But you'd win automatically," Enrique said blankly.

"Not necessarily," Kareen told him, and shot Mark a mock-glower. "Anyway, Mark, we were just talking about the District. Madame Vorsoisson has to go down there and collect rocks. And she told Enrique she could help him with figuring out Barrayaran native botany. What if we all go together? Madame Vorsoisson says she's never met Tsipis except over the comconsole. We could introduce her and make a sort of picnic out of it all."

And she wouldn't end up alone with Mark, and exposed to all sorts of . . . temptation, and confusion, and resolve-melting neck rubs, and back rubs, and ear-nibbling, and . . . she didn't want to think about it. They'd got on very *professionally* all week here at Vorkosigan House, very comfortably. Very busily. Busy was good. Company was good. Alone together was . . . um.

Mark muttered under his breath to her, "But then we'd have to take Enrique, and . . ." By the look on his face, *alone together* had been just what he'd had in mind.

"Oh, c'mon, it'll be fun." Kareen took the project firmly in hand. A very few minutes of persuasion and schedule-checking and she had the quartet committed, with an early start set and everything. She made a mental note to arrive at Vorkosigan House in plenty of time to make sure Enrique was bathed, dressed, and ready for public display.

Quick, light footsteps sounded from the corridor, and Miles rounded the doorjamb like a trooper swinging himself through a shuttle hatch. "Ah! Madame Vorsoisson," he panted. "Armsman Jankowski only just told me you were here." His gaze swept the room, taking in the demonstration in progress. "You didn't let them feed you that bug vom—bug stuff, did you? Mark—!"

"It's not half bad, actually," Madame Vorsoisson assured him, earning a relieved look from Mark, followed by a see-what-did-I-tell you jerk of his chin at his brother. "It may possibly need a little product development before it's ready to market."

Miles rolled his eyes. "Just a tad, yes."

Madame Vorsoisson glanced at her chrono. "My excavation crew will be back from lunch any minute. It was nice to meet you, Miss

Koudelka, Dr. Borgos. Until day after tomorrow, then?" She picked up the bag of tubs packed with bug manure Kareen had put up for her, smiled, and excused herself. Miles followed her out.

He was back in a couple of minutes, having evidently seen her to the door at the end of the corridor. "Good God, Mark! I can't believe you fed her that bug vomit. How could you!"

"Madame Vorsoisson," said Mark with dignity, "is a very sensible woman. When presented with compelling facts, *she* doesn't let a thoughtless emotional response overcome her clear reason."

Miles ran his hands through his hair. "Yeah, I know."

Enrique said, "Impressive, actually. She seemed to understand what I wanted to say even before I spoke."

"And after you spoke, too," said Kareen mischievously. "That's even more impressive."

Enrique grinned sheepishly. "Was I too technical, do you think?"

"Evidently not in this case."

Miles's brows drew down. "What's going on the day after tomorrow?"

Kareen answered sunnily, "We're all going down to the District together to visit Tsipis and look around for various things we need. Madame Vorsoisson's promised to introduce Enrique to Barrayaran native botany on site, so he can start to design what modifications he'll need to make to the new bugs later."

"*I* was going to take her on her first tour of the District. I have it all planned out. Hassadar, Vorkosigan Surleau, the Dendarii Gorge— I have to make exactly the right first impression."

"Too bad," said Mark unsympathetically. "Relax. We're only going to have lunch in Hassadar and scout around a bit. It's a big District, Miles, there'll be plenty left for you to show off later."

"Wait, I know! I'll go with you. Expedite things, yeah."

"There are only four seats in the lightflyer," Mark pointed out. "I'm flying, Enrique needs Madame Vorsoisson, and I'm damned if I'm going to leave Kareen behind in order to pack *you*." He somehow smiled fondly at her and glowered at his brother simultaneously.

"Yeah, Miles, you're not even a stockholder," Kareen supported this.

With a driven glare, Miles decamped, going off up the corridor muttering, " . . . can't *believe* he fed her *bug* vomit. If only I'd gotten here before—Jankowski, dammit, you and I are going to have a little—"

Mark and Kareen followed him out the door. They stood in the corridor watching this retreat. "What in the world's bit him?" Kareen asked in wonder.

Mark grinned evilly. "He's in love."

"With his gardener?" Kareen's brows rose.

"Causality's the other way around, I gather. He met her on Komarr during his recent case. He hired her as his gardener to create a little propinquity. He's courting her in secret."

"In secret? Why? She seems perfectly eligible to me—she's Vor, even—or is her rank only by marriage? But I shouldn't think that would matter to Miles. Or—are *her* relatives against it, because of his—?" A vague gesture down her body implied Miles's putative mutations. She frowned in outrage at the scent of this romantically doleful scenario. How dare they look down on Miles for—

"Ah, secret *from* her, as I understand it."

Kareen wrinkled her nose. "Wait, what?"

"You'll have to get him to explain it. It made no sense to me. Not even by Miles's standards of sense." Mark frowned thoughtfully. "Unless he's having a major outbreak of sexual shyness."

"Sexually shy, Miles?" Kareen scoffed. "You met that Captain Quinn he had in tow, didn't you?"

"Oh, yes. I've met several of his girlfriends, in fact. The most appalling bunch of bloodthirsty amazons you ever saw. God, they were frightening." Mark shuddered in memory. "Of course, they were all pissed as hell at me at the time for getting him killed, which I suppose accounts for some of it. But I was just thinking . . . you know, I really wonder if he picked them—or if they picked him? Maybe, instead of being such a great seducer, he's just a man who can't say no. It would certainly explain why they were *all* tall aggressive women who were used to getting what they wanted. But now—maybe for the first time—he's up against trying to pick for himself. And he doesn't know *how*. He hasn't had any practice." A slow grin spread across Mark's broad face at this vision. "Ooh. I wanna watch."

Kareen punched his shoulder. "Mark, that's not nice. Miles *deserves* to meet the right woman. I mean, he's not getting any younger, is he?"

"Some of us get what they deserve. Others of us get luckier than that." He captured her hand, and nuzzled the inside of her wrist, making the hairs stand up on her arm.

"Miles always says you make your own luck. Stop that." She repossessed her hand. "If sweat-equity is going to pay my way back to Beta Colony, I need to get back to work." She retreated into the lab; Mark followed.

"Was Lord Vorkosigan very upset?" Enrique asked anxiously as they reappeared. "But Madame Vorsoisson *said* she didn't mind trying our bug butter—"

"Don't worry about it, Enrique," Mark told him jovially. "My brother is just being a prick because he has something on his mind. If we're lucky, he'll go take it out on his Armsmen."

"Oh," said Enrique. "That's all right, then. I have a plan to bring him around."

"Yeah?" said Mark skeptically. "What plan?"

"It's a surprise," said the scientist, with a sly grin, or at any rate, as sly as he could bring off, which really wasn't very. "If it works, that is. I'll know in a few more days."

Mark shrugged, and glanced at Kareen. "You know what he's got up his sleeve?"

She shook her head, and settled herself on the floor once more with her rack-assembly project. "You might try pulling an ice cream freezer out of yours, though. Ask Ma Kosti first. Miles seems to have showered her with every piece of food service equipment imaginable. I think he was trying to bribe her into resisting the employment offers from all his friends." Kareen blinked, seized by inspiration.

Product development, too right. Never mind the appliances, the resource they had right here in Vorkosigan House was human genius. *Frustrated* human genius; Ma Kosti pressed the hard-working entrepreneurs to come to a special lunch in her kitchen every day, and sent trays of snacks to the lab betimes. And the cook was already soft on Mark, even after just a week; he so obviously appreciated her art. They were well on their way to bonding.

She jumped up and handed Mark the screwdriver. "Here. Finish this."

Grabbing six tubs of bug butter, she headed for the kitchen.

Miles climbed from the old armored groundcar, and paused a moment on the flower-bordered curving walkway to stare enviously at René Vorbretten's entirely modern townhouse. Vorbretten House perched on the bluff overlooking the river, nearly opposite to

Vorhartung Castle. Civil war as urban renewal: the creaky old fortified mansion which had formerly occupied the space had been so damaged in the Pretender's War that the previous Count and his son, when they'd returned to the city with Aral Vorkosigan's victorious forces, had decided to knock it flat and start over. In place of dank, forbidding, and defensively useless old stone walls, truly effective protection was now supplied by optional force-fields. The new mansion was light and open and airy, and took full advantage of the excellent views of the Vorbarr Sultana cityscape up and down stream. It doubtless had enough bathrooms for all the Vorbretten Armsmen. And Miles bet René didn't have troubles with *his* drains.

And if Sigur Vorbretten wins his case, René will lose it all. Miles shook his head, and advanced to the arched doorway, where an alert Vorbretten Armsman stood ready to lead Miles to his liege-lord's presence, and Pym, no doubt, to a good gossip downstairs.

The Armsman brought Miles to the splendid sitting room with the window-wall looking across the Star Bridge toward the castle. This morning, however, the wall was polarized to near-darkness, and the Armsman had to wave on lights as they entered. René was sitting in a big chair with his back to the view. He sprang to his feet as the Armsman announced, "Lord Auditor Vorkosigan, m'lord."

René swallowed, and nodded dismissal to his Armsman, who withdrew silently. At least René appeared sober, well-dressed, and depilated, but his handsome face was dead pale as he nodded formally to his visitor. "My Lord Auditor. How may I serve you?"

"Relax, René, this isn't an official visit. I just dropped by to say hello."

"Oh." René exhaled visible relief, the sudden stiffness in his face reverting to mere tiredness. "I thought you were . . . I thought Gregor might have dispatched you with the bad news."

"No, no, no. After all, the Council can't very well vote without telling you." Miles nodded vaguely toward the river, and the Council's seat beyond it; René, recalled to his hostly duties, depolarized the window and pulled chairs around for himself and Miles to take in the view while they talked. Miles settled himself across from the young Count. René had thought quickly enough to drag up a rather low chair for his august visitor, so Miles's feet didn't dangle in air.

"But you might have been—well, I don't know what you might have been," said René ruefully, sitting down and rubbing his neck. "I wasn't expecting you. Or anyone. Our social life has evaporated with amazing speed. Count and Countess Ghembretten are apparently not good people to know."

"Ouch. You've heard that one, have you?"

"My Armsmen heard it first. The joke's all over town, isn't it?"

"Eh, yeah, sort of." Miles cleared his throat. "Sorry I wasn't by earlier. I was on Komarr when your case broke, and I only heard about it when I got back, and then Gregor sent me up-country, and, well, screw the excuses. I'm sorry as hell this thing has happened to you. I can flat guarantee the Progressives don't want to lose you."

"Can you? I thought I had become a deep embarrassment to them."

"A vote's a vote. With turnover among the Counts literally a once-in-a-lifetime event—"

"Usually," René put in dryly.

Miles shrugged this off. "Embarrassment is a passing emotion. If the Progressives lose you to Sigur, they lose that vote for the next generation. They'll back you." Miles hesitated. "They are backing you, aren't they?"

"More or less. Mostly. Some." René waved an ironic hand. "Some are thinking that if they vote against Sigur and lose, they'll have made a permanent enemy in the Council. And a vote, as you say, is a vote."

"What do the numbers look like, can you tell yet?"

René shrugged. "A dozen certain for me, a dozen certain for Sigur. My fate will be decided by the men in the middle. Most of whom aren't speaking with the Ghembrettens this month. I don't think it looks good, Miles." He glanced across at his visitor, his expression an odd mix of sharpness and hesitancy. In a neutral tone he added, "And do you know how Vorkosigan's District is going to vote yet?"

Miles had realized he would have to answer that question if he saw René. So, no doubt, did every other Count or Count's Deputy, which also explained the sudden dip in René's social life lately; those who weren't avoiding him were avoiding the issue. With a couple of weeks to think it through behind him, Miles had his answer ready. "We're for you. Could you doubt it?"

René managed a rueful smile. "I had been almost certain, but then there is that large radioactive hole the Cetagandans once put in the middle of your District."

"History, man. Do I help your vote-count?"

"No," sighed René. "I'd already factored you in."

"Sometimes, one vote makes all the difference."

"It makes me crazy to think it might be that close," René confessed. "I hate this. I wish it were over."

"Patience, René," Miles counseled. "Don't throw away any advantage just because of an attack of nerves." He frowned thoughtfully. "Seems to me what we have here are two coequal legal precedents, jostling each other for primacy. A Count chooses his own successor, with the consent of the Council by their vote of approval, which is how Lord Midnight got in."

René's smile twisted. "If a horse's ass can be a Count, why not the whole horse?"

"I think that *was* one of the fifth Count Vortala's arguments, actually. I wonder if any transcripts of those sessions still exist in the archives? I must read them someday, if they do. Anyway, Midnight clearly established that direct blood relationship, though customary, was not required, and even if Midnight's case is rejected, there are dozens of other less memorable precedents on that score anyway. Count's choice before Count's blood, unless the Count has neglected to make a choice. Only then does male primogeniture come into play. Your grandfather was confirmed as heir in his . . . his mother's husband's lifetime, wasn't he?" Miles had been confirmed as his own father's heir during the Regency, while his father had been at the height of his power to ram it through the Council.

"Yes, but fraudulently, according to Sigur's suit. And a fraudulent result is no result."

"I don't suppose the old man might have known? And is there any way to prove it, if he did? Because if he knew your grandfather was not his son, his confirmation was legal, and Sigur's case evaporates."

"If the sixth Count knew, we haven't been able to find a scrap of evidence. And we've been turning the family archives inside out for weeks. I shouldn't think he could have known, or he would surely have killed the boy. And the boy's mother."

"I'm not so sure. The Occupation was a strange time. I'm thinking about how the bastard war played out in the Dendarii region." Miles blew out his breath. "Ordinary known Cetagandan by-blows were usually aborted or killed as soon as possible. Occasionally, the guerrillas used to make a sort of gruesome game of planting the little corpses for the occupying soldiers to find. Used to unnerve the hell out of the Cetagandan rank and file. First was their normal human reaction, and second, even the ones who were so brutalized by then as not to care realized anywhere we slipped in a dead baby, we could just as well have slipped in a bomb."

René grimaced distaste, and Miles realized belatedly that the lurid historical example might have acquired a new personal edge for him. He hurried on, "The Cetagandans weren't the only people to object to that game. Some Barrayarans hated it too, and took it as a blot on our honor—Prince Xav, for example. I know he argued vehemently with my grandfather against it. Your great—the sixth Count could well have been in agreement with Xav, and what he did for your grandfather a sort of silent answer."

René tilted his head, looking struck. "I never thought of that. He *was* a friend of old Xav's, I believe. But there's still no proof. Who knows what a dead man knew, but never spoke of?"

"If you have no proof, neither does Sigur."

René brightened slightly. "That's true."

Miles gazed again at the magnificent view along the urbanized river valley. A few small boats chugged up and down the narrowing stream. In former eras, Vorbarr Sultana had been as far inland as navigation from the sea could get, as the rapids and falls here blocked further commercial transport. Since the end of the Time of Isolation, the dam and locks just upstream from the Star Bridge had been destroyed and rebuilt three times.

Across from where they sat in Vorbretten House, Vorhartung Castle's crenellations loomed up through the spring-green treetops, gray and archaic. The traditional meeting-place of the Council of Counts had overlooked—in both senses of the word, Miles thought dryly—all these transformations. When there wasn't a war on, waiting for old Counts to die in order to effect change could be a slow process. One or two popped off a year, on average these days, but the pace of generational turnover was slowing still further as life spans extended. Having two seats open at once, and both up for grabs by either a Progressive or a Conservative heir, was fairly unusual. Or rather, René's seat was up for grabs between the two main parties. The other was more mysterious.

Miles asked René, "Do you have any idea what was the substance of Lady Donna Vorrutyer's motion of impediment against her cousin Richars taking the Vorrutyer Countship? Have you heard any talk?"

René waved a hand. "Not much, but then, who's talking to me, these days? Present company excepted." He shot Miles a covertly grateful look. "Adversity does teach who your real friends are."

Miles was embarrassed, thinking of how long it had taken him to get over here. "Don't take me for more virtuous than I am, René. I would have to be the last person on Barrayar to argue that carrying a bit of off-planet blood in one's veins should disqualify one for a Countship."

"Oh. Yes. You're half-Betan, that's right. But in your case, at least it's the correct half."

"Five-eighths Betan, technically. Less than half a Barrayaran." Miles realized he'd just left himself open for a pot shot about his height, but René didn't take aim. Byerly Vorrutyer would never have let a straight-line like that pass unexploited, and Ivan would have at least dared to grin. "I usually try to avoid bringing people's attention to the math."

"Actually, I did have a few thoughts on Lady Donna," René said. "Her case just might end up impinging on you Vorkosigans after all."

"Oh?"

René, drawn out of his bleak contemplation of his own dilemma, grew more animated. "She placed her motion of impediment and took off immediately for Beta Colony. What does that suggest to you?"

"I've been to Beta Colony. There are so many possibilities I can scarcely begin to sort them out. The first and simplest thought is that she's gone to collect some sort of obscure evidence about her cousin Richars's ancestry, genes, or crimes."

"Have you ever met Lady Donna? *Simple* isn't how I'd describe her."

"Mm, there's that. I should ask Ivan for a guess, I suppose. I believe he slept with her for a time."

"I don't think I was around town then. I was out on active duty during that period." A faint regret for his abandoned military career crept into René's voice, or maybe Miles was projecting. "But I'm not surprised. She had a reputation for collecting men."

Miles cocked an interested eyebrow at his host. "Did she ever collect you?"

René grinned. "I somehow missed that honor." He returned the ironic glance. "And did she ever collect you?"

"What, with *Ivan* available? I doubt she ever looked down far enough to notice me."

René opened his hand, as if to deflect Miles's little flash of self-deprecation, and Miles bit his tongue. He was an Imperial Auditor now; public whining about his physical lot in life sat oddly on the ear. He *had* survived. No man could challenge him now. But would even an Auditorship be enough to induce the average Barrayaran woman to overlook the rest of the package? *So it's a good thing you're not in love with an average woman, eh, boy?*

René went on, "I was thinking about your clone Lord Mark, and your family's push to get him recognized as your brother."

"He *is* my brother, René. My legal heir and everything."

"Yes, yes, so your family has argued. But what if Lady Donna has been following that controversy, and how you made it come out? I'll bet she's gone off to Beta Colony to have a clone made of poor old Pierre, and is going to bring it back to offer as his heir in place of Richars. Somebody had to try that, sooner or later."

"It's . . . certainly possible. I'm not sure how it would fly with the fossils. They damn near choked on Mark, year before last." Miles frowned in thought. Could this damage Mark's position? "I heard she was practically running the District for Pierre these last five years. If she could get herself appointed the clone's legal guardian, she could continue to run it for the next twenty. It's unusual to have a female relative be a Count's guardian, but there are some historical precedents."

"Including that Countess who was legally declared a male in order to inherit," René put in. "And then had that bizarre suit later about her marriage."

"Oh, yeah, I remember reading about that one. But there was a civil war on, at the time, which broke down the barriers for her. Nothing like being on the side of the right battalions. No civil war here except for whatever lies between Donna and Richars, and I've never heard an inside story on that feud. I wonder . . . if you're right—would she use a uterine replicator for the clone, or would she have the embryo implanted as a body-birth?"

"Body-birth seems weirdly incestuous," René said, with a grimace of distaste. "You do wonder about the Vorrutyers, sometimes. I hope she uses a replicator."

"Mm, but she never had a child of her own. She's what, forty or so . . . and if the clone were growing inside her own body, she'd at least be sure to have it—excuse me, him—as thoroughly personally guarded as possible. Much harder to take away from her, that way, or to argue that someone else should be his guardian. Richars, for example. Now that would be a sharp turn of events."

"With Richars as guardian, how long do you think the child would live?"

"Not past his majority, I suspect." Miles frowned at this scenario. "Not that his death wouldn't be impeccable."

"Well, we'll find out Lady Donna's plan soon," said René. "Or else her case will collapse by default. Her three months to bring her evidence are almost up. It seems a generous allotment of time, but I suppose in the old days they had to allow everyone a chance to get around on horseback."

"Yes, it's not good for a District to leave its Countship empty for so long." One corner of Miles's mouth turned up. "After all, you wouldn't want the proles to figure out they could live without us."

René's brows twitched acknowledgment of the jibe. "Your Betan blood is showing, Miles."

"No, only my Betan upbringing."

"Biology isn't destiny?"

"Not anymore, it's not."

The light music of women's voices echoed up the curving staircase into the sitting room. A low alto burble Miles thought he recognized was answered by a silvery peal of laughter.

René sat up, and turned around; his lips parted in a half smile. "They're back. And she's laughing. I haven't heard Tatya laugh in weeks. Bless Martya."

Had that been Martya Koudelka's voice? The thump of a surprising number of feminine feet rippled up the stairs, and three women burst into Miles's appreciative view. *Yes.* The two blond Koudelka sisters, Martya and Olivia, set off the dark good looks of the shorter third woman. The young Countess Tatya Vorbretten had bright hazel eyes, wide-set in a heart-shaped face with a foxy chin. And dimples. The whole delightful composition was framed by ringlets of ebony hair that bounced as she now did.

"Hooray, René!" said Martya, the owner of the alto voice. "You're *not* still sitting alone here in the dark and gloom. Hi, Miles! Did you finally come to cheer René up? Good for you!"

"More or less," said Miles. "I didn't realize you all knew each other so well."

Martya tossed her head. "Olivia and Tatya were in school together. I just came along for the ride, and to boot them into motion. Can you believe, on this beautiful morning, they wanted to stay *in*?"

Olivia smiled shyly, and she and Countess Tatya clung together for a brief supportive moment. Ah, yes. Tatya Vorkeres had not been a countess back in those private-school days, though she had certainly already been a beauty, and an heiress.

"Where all did you go?" asked René, smiling at his wife.

"Just shopping in the Caravanserai. We stopped for tea and pastries at a café in the Great Square, and caught the changing of the guard at the Ministry." The Countess turned to Miles. "My cousin Stannis is a directing officer in the fife and drum corps of the City Guard now. We waved at him, but of course he couldn't wave back. He was on duty."

"I was sorry we hadn't made you come out with us," said Olivia to René, "but now I'm glad. You would have missed Miles."

"It's all right, ladies," said Martya stoutly. "Instead I vote we make René escort us all to the Vorbarr Sultana Hall tomorrow night. I *happen* to know where I can get four tickets."

This was seconded and voted in without reference to the Count, but Miles couldn't see him offering much resistance to a proposal that he escort three beautiful women to hear music that he adored. And indeed, with a somewhat sheepish glance at Miles, he allowed himself to be persuaded. Miles wondered how Martya had cornered the tickets, which were generally sold out a year or two in advance, on such short notice. Was she drawing on her sister Delia's ImpSec connections, perhaps? This whole thing smelled of Team Koudelka in action.

The Countess smiled and held up a hand-calligraphed envelope. "Look, René! Armsman Kelso handed this to me as we came in. It's from Countess Vorgarin."

"Looks like an invitation to me," said Martya in a tone of vast satisfaction. "See, things aren't so bad as you feared."

"Open it," urged Olivia.

Tatya did so; her eyes raced down the handwriting. Her face fell. "Oh," she said in a flattened tone. The delicate paper half-crumpled in her tight fist.

"What?" said Olivia anxiously.

Martya retrieved the paper, and read down it in turn. "The cat! It's an *un*-invitation! To her baby daughter's naming party. ' . . . afraid you would not be comfortable,' my eye! The coward. The cat!"

Countess Tatya blinked rapidly. "That's all right," she said in a muffled voice. "I hadn't been planning to go anyway."

"But you said you were going to wear—" René began, then closed his mouth abruptly. A muscle jumped in his jaw.

"All the women—and their mothers—who missed catching René these last ten years are being just . . . just . . ." Martya sputtered to Miles, "*feline.*"

"That's an insult to cats," said Olivia. "*Zap* has better character."

René glanced across at Miles. "I couldn't help noticing . . ." he said in an extremely neutral voice, "we haven't received a wedding invitation from Gregor and Dr. Toscane as yet."

Miles held up a reassuring hand. "Local invitations haven't been sent out yet. I know that for a fact." This was not the moment to mention that inconclusive little political discussion on the subject he'd sat in on a few weeks ago at the Imperial Residence, Miles decided.

He stared around the tableau, Martya fuming, Olivia stricken, the Countess chilled, René flushed and stiff. Inspiration struck. *Ninety-six chairs.* "I'm giving a little private dinner party in two nights time. It's in honor of Kareen Koudelka and my brother Mark getting home from Beta Colony. Olivia will be there, and all the Koudelkas, and Lady Alys Vorpatril and Simon Illyan, and my cousin Ivan and several other valued friends. I'd be honored if you both would join us."

René managed a pained smile at this palpable charity. "Thank you, Miles. But I don't think—"

"Oh, Tatya, yes, you've got to come," Olivia broke in, squeezing her old friend's arm. "Miles is finally unveiling his lady-love for us all to meet. Only Kareen's seen her so far. We're all just dying of curiosity."

René's brows went up. "You, Miles? I thought you were as confirmed a bachelor as your cousin Ivan. Married to your career."

Miles grimaced furiously at Olivia, and twitched at René's last words. "I had this little medical divorce from my career. Olivia, where did you ever get the idea that Madame Vorsoisson—she's my landscape designer, you see, René, but she's Lord Auditor Vorthys's niece, I met her on Komarr, she's just recently widowed and *certainly* not—not ready to be anybody's lady-love. Lord Auditor Vorthys and the Professora will be there too, you see, a family party, nothing inappropriate for her."

"For who?" asked Martya.

"Ekaterin," escaped his mouth before he could stop it. All four lovely syllables.

Martya grinned unrepentantly at him. René and his wife looked at each other—Tatya's dimple flashed, and René pursed his lips thoughtfully.

"Kareen said Lord Mark said you said," Olivia said innocently. "Who was lying, then?"

"Nobody, dammit, but—but—" He swallowed, and prepared to run down the drill one more time. "Madame Vorsoisson is . . . is . . ." Why was this getting harder to explain with practice, instead of easier? "Is in formal mourning for her late husband. I have every intention of declaring myself to her when the time is right. The time is not right. So I have to wait." He gritted his teeth. René was now leaning his chin on his hand, his finger across his lips, and his eyes alight. "And I *hate waiting*," Miles burst out.

"Oh," said René. "I see."

"Is she in love with you too?" asked Tatya, with a furtive fond glance at her husband.

God, the Vorbrettens were as gooey as Gregor and Laisa, and after three years, too. This marital enthusiasm was a damned contagious disease. "I don't know," Miles confessed in a smaller voice.

"He told Mark he's courting her in secret," Martya put in to the Vorbrettens. "It's a secret *from* her. We're all still trying to figure that one out."

"Is the entire city party to my private conversations?" Miles snarled. "I'm going to strangle Mark."

Martya blinked at him with manufactured innocence. "Kareen had it from Mark. *I* had it from Ivan. Mama had it from Gregor. And Da had it from Pym. If you're trying to keep a secret, Miles, why are you going around telling everyone?"

Miles took a deep breath.

Countess Vorbretten said demurely, "Thank you, Lord Vorkosigan. My husband and I would be pleased to come to your dinner party." She dimpled at him.

His breath blew out in a, "You're welcome."

"Will the Viceroy and Vicereine be back from Sergyar?" René asked Miles. His voice was tinged with political curiosity.

"No. In fact. Though they're due quite soon. This is *my* party. My last chance to have Vorkosigan House to myself before it fills up with the traveling circus." Not that he didn't look forward to his parents' return, but his head-of-the-House role had been rather . . . pleasant, these past few months. Besides, introducing Ekaterin to Count and Countess Vorkosigan, her prospective future parents-in-law, was something he wished to choreograph with the utmost care.

He'd surely done his social duty by now. Miles rose with some dignity, and bid everyone farewell, and politely offered Martya and Olivia a ride, if they wished it. Olivia was staying on with her friend the Countess, but Martya took him up on it.

Miles gave Pym a fishy look as the Armsman opened the groundcar canopy for them to enter the rear compartment. Miles had always put down Pym's extraordinary ability to collect gossip, a most valuable skill to Miles in his new post, to Pym's old ImpSec training. He hadn't quite realized Pym might be *trading*. Pym, catching the look but not its cause, went a bit blander than usual, but seemed otherwise unaffected by his liege-lord's displeasure.

In the rear compartment with Martya as they pulled away from Vorbretten House and swung down toward the Star Bridge, Miles seriously considered dressing her down for roasting him about Ekaterin in front of the Vorbrettens. He was an Imperial Auditor now, by God—or at least by Gregor. But then he'd get no further information out of her. He controlled his temper.

"How do the Vorbrettens seem to be holding up, from your view?" he asked her.

She shrugged. "They're putting up a good front, but I think they're pretty shaken. René thinks he's going to lose the case, and his District, and everything."

"So I gathered. And he might, if he doesn't make more push to keep it." Miles frowned.

"He's hated the Cetagandans ever since they killed his da in the war for the Hegen Hub. Tatya says it just spooks him, to think the Cetagandans are *in* him." She added after a moment, "I think it spooks her a little, too. I mean . . . now we know why that branch of the Vorbrettens suddenly acquired that extraordinary musical talent, after the Occupation."

"I'd made that connection too. But she seems to be standing by him." Unpleasant, to think this mischance might cost René his marriage as well as his career.

"It's been hard on her too. She likes being a Countess. Olivia says, back in their school days, envy sometimes made the other girls mean to Tatya. Being picked out by René was kind of a boost for her, not that the rest of them couldn't see it coming, with her glorious soprano. She does adore him."

"So you think their marriage will weather this?" he asked hopefully.

"Mm . . ."

"Mm . . . ?"

"This whole thing began when they were going to start their baby. And they haven't gone ahead. Tatya . . . doesn't talk about that part of things. She'll talk about everything else, but not that."

"Oh." Miles tried to figure out what that might mean. It didn't sound very encouraging.

"Olivia is almost the only one of Tatya's old friends who've shown up, after all this blew up. Even René's sisters have kind of gone to ground, though for the opposite reason I suppose. It's like nobody wants to look her in the eye."

"If you go back far enough, we're all descended from off-worlders, dammit," Miles growled in frustration. "What's one-eighth? A tinge. Why should it disqualify one of the best people we have? Competence should count for something."

Martya's grin twisted. "If you want sympathy, you've come to the wrong store, Miles. If my da were a Count, it wouldn't matter how competent I was, I still wouldn't inherit. All the brilliance in the world wouldn't matter a bit. If you're just now finding out that this world is unjust, well, you're behind the times."

Miles grimaced. "It's not news to me, Martya." The car pulled up outside Commodore Koudelka's townhouse. "But justice wasn't my job, before." *And power isn't nearly as all-powerful as it looks from the outside.* He added, "But that's probably the one issue I can't help you on. I have the strongest personal reasons for not wanting to reintroduce inheritance through the female line into Barrayaran law. Like, my survival. I like my job very well. I don't want Gregor's."

He popped the canopy, and she climbed out, and gave him a sort of acknowledging salaam for both this last point and the ride. "See you at your dinner party."

"Give my best to the Commodore and Drou," he called after her.

She shot him a bright Team Koudelka smile over her shoulder, and bounced away.

Chapter Seven

Mark gently banked the lightflyer, to give the rear-seat passengers, Kareen and Madame Vorsoisson, a better view of the Vorkosigan's District capital of Hassadar glittering on the horizon. The weather was cooperating, a beautiful sunny day that breathed promise of imminent summer. Miles's lightflyer was a delight: sleek, fast, and maneuverable, knifing through the soft warm air, and best of all with the controls precisely aligned to be ergonomically perfect for a man just Mark's height. So what if the seat was a little on the narrow side. You couldn't have everything. *For example, Miles can't have this anymore.* Mark grimaced at the thought, and shunted it aside.

"It's lovely land," Madame Vorsoisson remarked, pressing her face to the canopy to take it all in.

"Miles would be flattered to hear you say so," Mark carefully encouraged this trend of thought. "He's pretty stuck on this place."

They were certainly viewing it in the best possible light, literally, this morning. A patchwork of spring verdure in the farms and woods—the woods no less a product of back-breaking human cultivation than the fields—rippled across the landscape. The green was broken up and set off by irregular slashes of Barrayaran native red-brown, in the ravines and creek bottoms and along uncultivable slopes.

Enrique, his nose also pressed to the canopy, said, "It's not at all what I was expecting, from Barrayar."

"What were you expecting?" asked Madame Vorsoisson curiously.

"Kilometers of flat gray concrete, I suppose. Military barracks and people in uniform marching around in lockstep."

"Economically unlikely for an entire planetary surface. Though uniforms, we do have," Mark admitted.

"But once it gets up to several hundred different kinds, the effect isn't so uniform anymore. And some of the colors are a little . . . unexpected."

"Yes, I feel sorry for those Counts who ended up having to pick their House colors last," Mark agreed. "I think the Vorkosigans must have fallen somewhere in the middle. I mean, brown and silver isn't *bad*, but I can't help feeling that the fellows with the blue and gold— or the black and silver—do have a sartorial edge." He could fancy himself in black and silver, with Kareen all blond and tall on his arm.

"It could be worse," Kareen put in cheerfully. "How do you think you'd look in a House cadet's uniform of chartreuse and scarlet, like poor Vorharopulos, Mark?"

"Like a traffic signal in boots." Mark made a wry face. "The lockstep is lacking too, I've gradually come to realize. More like, milling around in a confused herd. It was . . . almost disappointing, at first. I mean, even disregarding enemy propaganda, it's not the image Barrayar itself tries to project, now is it? Though I've learned to kind of like it this way."

They banked again. "Where is the infamous radioactive area?" Madame Vorsoisson asked, scanning the changing scene.

The Cetagandan destruction of the old capital of Vorkosigan Vashnoi had torn the heart out of the Vorkosigan's District, three generations ago. "Southeast of Hassadar. Downwind and downstream," Mark replied. "We won't pass it today. You'll have to get Miles to show it to you sometime." He suppressed a slightly snarky grin. Betan dollars to sand the blighted lands hadn't been on Miles's projected itinerary.

"Barrayar doesn't all look like this," Madame Vorsoisson told Enrique. "The part of South Continent where I grew up was flat as a griddlecake, even though the highest mountain range on the planet—the Black Escarpment—was just over the horizon."

"Was it dull, being so flat?" asked Enrique.

"No, because the horizon was boundless. Stepping outdoors was like stepping into the sky. The clouds, the light, the storms—we had the best sunrises and sunsets ever."

They passed the invisible barrier of Hassadar's air traffic control system, and Mark gave over navigation to the city computers. After a few more minutes and some brief coded transmissions, they were brought gently down on a very private and highly restricted landing pad atop the Count's Residence. The Residence was a large modern building faced with polished Dendarii mountain stone. With its connections to the municipal and District offices, it occupied most of one side of the city's central square.

Tsipis stood waiting by the landing ring, neat and gray and spare as ever, to receive them. He shook hands with Madame Vorsoisson as though they were old friends, and greeted off-worlder Enrique with the grace and ease of a natural diplomat. Kareen gave, and got, a familial hug.

They switched vehicles to a waiting aircar, and Tsipis shepherded them off for a quick tour of three possible sites for their future facility, whatever it was to be named, including an underutilized city warehouse, and two nearby farms. Both farm sites were untenanted because their former inhabitants had followed the Count to his new post on Sergyar, and no one else had wanted to take on the challenge of wrestling profit from their decidedly marginal land, one being swampy and the other rocky and dry. Mark checked the radioactivity plats carefully. They were all Vorkosigan properties already, so there was nothing to negotiate with respect to their use.

"You might even persuade your brother to forgo the rent, if you ask," Tsipis pointed out with enthusiastic frugality about the two rural sites. "He can; your father assigned him full legal powers in the District when he left for Sergyar. After all, the family's not getting any income from the properties now. It would conserve more of your capital for your other startup costs."

Tsipis knew precisely what budget Mark had to work with; they'd gone over his plans via comconsole earlier in the week. The thought of asking Miles for a favor made Mark twitch a little, but . . . was he not a Vorkosigan too? He stared around the dilapidated farm, trying to feel entitled.

He put his head together with Kareen, and they ran over the choices. Enrique was permitted to wander about with Madame Vorsoisson, being introduced to various native Barrayaran weeds. The condition of the buildings, plumbing, and power-grid connections won over condition of the land, and they settled at last on the site with the newer—relatively—and more spacious outbuildings. After one more thoughtful tour around the premises, Tsipis whisked them back to Hassadar.

For lunch, Tsipis led them to Hassadar's most exclusive locale—the official dining room of the Count's Residence, overlooking the Square. The remarkable spread which the staff laid on hinted that Miles had sent down a few urgent behind-the-scenes instructions for the care and feeding of his . . . gardener. Mark confirmed this after dessert when Kareen led Enrique and the widow off to see the garden and fountain in the Residence's inner courtyard, and he and Tsipis lingered over the exquisite vintage of Vorkosigan estate-bottled wine usually reserved for visits from Emperor Gregor.

"So, Lord Mark," said Tsipis, after a reverent sip. "What do you think of this Madame Vorsoisson of your brother's?"

"I think . . . she is not my brother's yet."

"Mm, yes, I'd understood *that* part. Or should I say, it has been explained to me."

"What all has he been telling you about her?"

"It is not so much what he says, as how he says it. And how often he repeats himself."

"Well, that too. If it were anyone but Miles, it would be hilarious. Actually, it's still hilarious. But it's also . . . hm."

Tsipis blinked and smiled in perfect understanding. "Heart-stopping . . . I think . . . is the word I should choose." And Tsipis's vocabulary was always as precise as his haircut. He stared out over the square through the room's tall windows. "I used to see him as a youngster rather often, when I was in company with your parents. He was constantly overmatching his physical powers. But he never cried much when he broke a bone. He was almost frighteningly self-controlled, for a child that age. But once, at the Hassadar District Fair it was, I chanced to see him rather brutally rejected by a group of other children whom he'd attempted to join." Tsipis took another sip of wine.

"Did he cry then?" asked Mark.

"No. Though his face looked very odd when he turned away. Bothari was watching with me—there was nothing the Sergeant could do either, there wasn't any physical threat about it all. But the next day Miles had a riding accident, one of his worst ever. Jumping, which he had been forbidden to do, on a green horse he'd been told not to ride . . . Count Piotr was so infuriated—and frightened—I thought he was going to have a stroke on the spot. I came later to wonder how much of an accident that accident was." Tsipis hesitated. "I always imagined Miles would choose a galactic wife, like his father before him. Not a Barrayaran woman. I'm not at all sure what Miles thinks he's doing with this young lady. Is he setting himself up to go smash again?"

"He claims he has a Strategy."

Tsipis's thin lips curved, and he murmured, "And doesn't he always . . ."

Mark shrugged helplessly. "To tell the truth, I've barely met the woman myself. You've been working with her—what do you think?"

Tsipis tilted his head shrewdly. "She's a quick study, and meticulously honest."

That sounded like faint praise, unless one happened to know those were Tsipis's two highest encomiums.

"Quite well-looking, in person," he added as an afterthought. "Not, ah, nearly as over-tall as I was expecting."

Mark grinned.

"I think she could do the *job* of a future Countess."

"Miles thinks so too," Mark noted. "And picking personnel was supposed to have been one of his major military talents." And the better he got to know Tsipis, the more Mark thought that might be a talent Miles had inherited from his—*their*—father.

"It's not before time, that's certain," Tsipis sighed. "One does wish for Count Aral to have grandchildren while he's still alive to see them."

Was that remark addressed to me?

"You will keep an eye on things, won't you?" Tsipis added.

"I don't know what you think I could do. It's not like I could *make* her fall in love with him. If I had that kind of power over women, I'd use it for myself!"

Tsipis smiled vaguely at the place Kareen had vacated, and back, speculatively, to Mark. "What, and here I was under the impression you had."

Mark twitched. His new-won Betan rationality had been losing ground on the subject of Kareen, this past week, his subpersonas growing restive with his rising tension. But Tsipis was his financial advisor, not his therapist. Nor even—this was Barrayar, after all—his Baba.

"So have you seen any sign at all that Madame Vorsoisson returns your brother's regard?" Tsipis went on rather plaintively.

474 Lois McMaster Bujold

"No," Mark confessed. "But she's very reserved." And was this lack of feeling, or just frightening self-control? Who could tell from this angle? "Wait, ha, I know! I'll set Kareen onto it. Women gossip to each other about that sort of thing. That's why they go off so long to the ladies' room together, to dissect their dates. Or so Kareen once told me, when I'd complained about being left bereft too long . . ."

"I do like that girl's sense of humor. I've always liked all the Koudelkas." Tsipis's eye grew glinty for a moment. "You *will* treat her properly, I trust?"

Basil alert, basil alert! "Oh, yes," Mark said fervently. Grunt, in fact, was aching to treat her properly to the limit of his Betan-trained skills and powers right now, if only she'd let him. Gorge, who made a hobby of feeding her gourmet meals, had had a good day today. Killer lurked ready to assassinate any enemy she cared to name, except that Kareen didn't make enemies, she just made friends. Even Howl was strangely satisfied, this week, everyone else's pain being his gain. On this subject, the Black Gang voted as one man.

That lovely, warm, open woman . . . In her presence he felt like some sluggish cold-blooded creature crawling from under a rock where it had crept to die, meeting the unexpected miracle of the sun. He might trail around after her all day, meeping piteously, hoping she would light him again for just one more glorious moment. His therapist had had a few stern words to him on the subject of this addiction—*It's not fair to Kareen to lay such a burden on her, now is it? You must learn to give, from sufficiency, not only take, from neediness.* Quite right, quite right. But dammit, even his *therapist* liked Kareen, and was trying to recruit her for the profession. Everyone liked Kareen, because Kareen liked everyone. They wanted to be around her; she made them feel good inside. They would do anything for her. She had in abundance everything Mark most lacked, and most longed for: good cheer, infectious enthusiasm, empathy, sanity. The woman had the most tremendous future in sales—what a team the two of them might make, Mark for analysis, Kareen for the interface with the rest of humanity . . . The mere thought of losing her, for any reason, made Mark frantic.

His incipient panic attack vanished and his breathing steadied as she reappeared safely, with Enrique and Madame Vorsoisson still in tow. Despite the loss of ambition on everyone's part due to lunch, Kareen got them all up and moving again for the second of the day's tasks, collecting the rocks for Miles's garden. Tsipis had rustled them up a holo-map, directions, and two large, amiable young men with hand tractors and a lift van; the lift van followed the lightflyer as Mark headed them south toward the looming gray spine of the Dendarii Mountains.

Mark brought them down in a mountain vale bordered by a rocky ravine. The area was still more Vorkosigan family property, entirely undeveloped. Mark could see why. The virgin patch of native Barrayaran—well, you couldn't call it forest, quite, though *scrub* summed it up fairly well—extended for kilometers along the forbidding slopes.

Madame Vorsoisson exited the lightflyer, and turned to take in the view to the north, out over the peopled lowlands of the Vorkosigan's District. The warm air softened the farthest horizon into a magical blue haze, but the eye could still see for a hundred kilometers. Cumulous clouds puffed white and, in three widely separated arcs, towered up over silver-gray bases like rival castles.

"Oh," she said, her mouth melting in a smile. "Now *that's* a proper sky. That's the way it should be. I can see why you said Lord Vorkosigan likes it up here, Kareen." Her arms stretched out, half-unconsciously, to their fullest extent, her fingers reaching into free space. "Usually hills feel like walls around me, but this—this is very fine."

The oxlike beings with the lift van landed beside the lightflyer. Madame Vorsoisson led them and their equipment scrambling down into the ravine, there to pick out her supply of aesthetically-pleasing genuine Dendarii rocks and stones for the minions to haul away to Vorbarr Sultana. Enrique followed after like a lanky and particularly clumsy puppy. Since what went down would have to puff and wheeze back up, Mark limited himself to a peek over the edge, and then a stroll around the less daunting grade of the vale, holding hands with Kareen.

When he slipped his arm around her waist and cuddled in close, she melted around him, but when he tried to slip in a subliminal sexual suggestion by nuzzling her breast, she stiffened unhappily and pulled away. Damn.

"Kareen . . ." he protested plaintively.

She shook her head. "I'm sorry. I'm sorry."

"Don't . . . apologize to me. It makes me feel very weird. I want you to want me too, or it's no damn good. I thought you did."

"I did. I do. I'm—" She bit off her words, and tried again. "I thought I was a real adult, a real person, back on Beta Colony. Then I came back here . . . I realize I'm dependent for every bite of food I put in my mouth, for every stitch of clothing, for everything, on my family, and this place. And I always was, even when I was on Beta. Maybe it was all . . . fake."

He clutched her hand; that at least he might not let go of. "You want to be good. All right, I can understand that. But you have to be careful who you let define your *good*. My terrorist creators taught me that one, for damn sure."

She clutched him back, at that feared memory, and managed a sympathetic grimace. She hesitated, and went on, "It's the mutually exclusive definitions that are driving me crazy. I can't be good for both places at the same time. I learned how to be a good girl on Beta Colony, and in its own way, it was just as hard as being a good girl here. And a lot scarier, sometimes. But . . . I felt like I was getting *bigger* inside, if you can see what I mean."

"I think so." He hoped he hadn't provided any of that scary, but suspected he had. All right, he knew he had. There had been some dark times, last year. Yet she had stuck with him. "But you have to choose Kareen's good, not Barrayar's . . ." he took a deep breath, for honesty, "Not even Beta's." *Not even mine?*

"Since I got back, it's like I can't even find myself to ask."

For her, this was a metaphor, he reminded himself. Though maybe he was a metaphor too, inside his head with the Black Gang. A metaphor gone metastatic. Metaphors could do that, under enough pressure.

"I want to go back to Beta Colony," she said in a low, passionate voice, staring out unseeing into the breath-taking space below. "I want to stay there till I'm a *real* grownup, and can be myself wherever I am. Like Countess Vorkosigan."

Mark's brows rose at this idea of a role model for gentle Kareen. But you had to say this for his mother, she didn't take any shit from any one for any reason. It would be preferable, though, if one could catch a bit of that quality without having to walk through war and fire barefoot to get it.

Kareen in distress was like the sun going dark. Apprehensively, he hugged her around the waist again. Fortunately, she read it as support, as intended, and not importunity again, and leaned into him in return.

The Black Gang had their place as emergency shock troops, but they made piss-poor commanders. Grunt would just have to wait some more. He could damn well set up a date with Mark's right hand or something. This one was too important to screw up, oh yeah.

But what if she finally became herself in a way that left no room for him . . . ?

There was nothing to eat, here. Change the subject, quick. "Tsipis seems to like Madame Vorsoisson."

Her face lightened with instant gratitude at this release. *Therefore, I must have been pressuring her.* Howl whimpered, from deep inside; Mark stifled him.

"Ekaterin? I do too."

So she was *Ekaterin* now: first names, good. He would have to send them off to the ladies' room some more. "Can you tell if she likes Miles?"

Kareen shrugged. "She seems to. She's working really hard on his garden and all."

"I mean, is she in love at all? I've never even heard her call him by his first name. How can you be in love with someone you're not on a first-name basis with?"

"Oh, that's a Vor thing."

"Huh." Mark took in this reassurance dubiously. "It's true Miles is being very Vor. I think this Imperial Auditor thing has gone to his head. But do you suppose you could kind of hang around her, and try to pick up some clues?"

"Spy on her?" Kareen frowned disapproval. "Did Miles set you on me for this?"

"Actually, no. It was Tsipis. He's a bit worried for Miles. And—I am too."

"I would like to be friends with her . . ."

Naturally.

"She doesn't seem to have very many. She's had to move a lot. And I think whatever happened to her husband on Komarr was more ghastly than she lets on. The woman is so full of silences, they spill over."

"But will she do for Miles? Will she be good for him?"

Kareen cocked an eyebrow down at him. "Is anyone bothering to ask if Miles will be good for her?"

"Um . . . um . . . why not? Count's heir. Well-to-do. An Imperial Auditor, for God's sake. What more could a Vor desire?"

"I don't know, Mark. It likely depends on the Vor. I do know I'd take you and every one of the Black Gang at their most obstreperous for a hundred years before I'd let myself get locked up for a week with Miles. He . . . *takes you over*."

"Only if you let him." But he warmed inside with the thought that she could really, truly prefer him to the glorious Miles, and suddenly felt less hungry.

"Do you have any idea what it takes to stop him? I still remember being kids, me and my sisters, visiting Lady Cordelia with Mama, and Miles told off to keep us occupied. Which was a really cruel thing to do to a fourteen-year-old boy, but what did I know? He decided the four of us should be an all-girl precision drill team, and made us march around in the back garden of Vorkosigan House, or in the ballroom when it was raining. I think I was four." She frowned into the past. "What Miles needs is a woman who will tell him to go soak his head, or it'll be a disaster. For her, not him." After a moment, she added sapiently, "Though if for her, for him too, sooner or later."

"Ow."

The amiable young men came panting back up out of the ravine then, and took the lift van back down into it. With clanks and thumps, they finished loading, and their van lumbered into the air and headed north. Some time later, Enrique and Madame Vorsoisson appeared, breathless. Enrique, who clutched a huge bundle of native Barrayaran plants, looked quite cheerful. In fact, he actually looked as if he had blood circulation. The scientist probably hadn't been outdoors for years; it was doubtless good for him, despite the fact that he was dripping wet from having fallen in the creek.

They managed to get the plants stuffed in the back, and Enrique half-dried, and everyone loaded up again as the sun slanted west. Mark took pleasure in trying the lightflyer's speed, as they circled the vale one last time and banked northward, back toward the capital. The machine hummed like an arrow, sweet beneath his feet and fingertips, and they reached the outskirts of Vorbarr Sultana again before dusk.

They dropped off Madame Vorsoisson first, at her aunt and uncle's home near the University, with many promises that she would stop in at Vorkosigan House on the morrow and help Enrique look up the scientific names of all his new botanical samples. Kareen hopped out at the corner in front of her family's townhouse, and gave Mark a little farewell kiss on the cheek. *Down, Grunt. That wasn't to your address.*

Mark slipped the lightflyer back into its corner in the subbasement garage of Vorkosigan House, and followed Enrique into the lab to help him give the butter bugs their evening feed and checkup. Enrique did stop short of singing lullabies to the little creepy-crawlies, though he was in the habit of talking, half to them and half to himself, under his breath as he puttered around the lab. The man had worked all alone for too damned long, in Mark's view. Tonight, though, Enrique hummed as he separated his new supply of plants according to a hierarchy known only to himself and Madame Vorsoisson, some into beakers of water and some spread to dry on paper on the lab bench.

Mark turned from weighing, recording, and scattering a few generous scoops of tree bits into the butter bug hutches to find Enrique settling at his comconsole and firing it up. Ah, good. Perhaps the Escobaran was about to commit some more futurely-profitable science. Mark wandered over, preparing to kibitz approvingly. Enrique was busying himself not with a vertigo-inducing molecular display, but with an array of closely-written text.

"What's that?" Mark asked.

"I promised to send Ekaterin a copy of my doctoral thesis. She *asked*," Enrique explained proudly, and in a tone of some wonder. "*Toward Bacterial and Fungal Suite-Synthesis of Extra-cellular Energy Storage Compounds*. It was the basis of all my later work with the butter bugs, when I finally hit upon them as the perfect vehicle for the microbial suite."

"Ah." Mark hesitated. *It's Ekaterin for you too, now?* Well, if Kareen had got on a first-name basis with the widow, Enrique, also present, couldn't very well have been excluded, could he? "Will she be able to read it?" Enrique wrote just the same way he talked, as far as Mark had seen.

"Oh, I don't expect her to follow the molecular energy-flow mathematics—my faculty advisors had a struggle with those—but she'll get the gist of it, I'm sure, from the animations. Still . . . perhaps I could do something about this abstract, to make it more attractive at first glance. I have to admit, it's a trifle dry." He bit his lip, and bent over his comconsole. After a minute he asked, "Can you think of a word to rhyme with *glyoxylate*?"

"Not . . . off-hand. Try *orange*. Or *silver*."

"Those don't rhyme with anything. If you can't be helpful, Mark, go away."

"What are you *doing*?"

"*Isocitrate*, of course, but that doesn't quite scan . . . I'm trying to see if I can produce a more striking effect by casting the abstract in sonnet form."

"That sounds downright . . . stunning."

"Do you think?" Enrique brightened, and started humming again. "Threonine, serine, polar, molar . . ."

"Dolor," Mark supplied at random. "Bowler." Enrique waved him off irritably. Dammit, Enrique wasn't supposed to be wasting his valuable brain-time writing poetry; he was supposed to be designing long-chain molecule interactions with favorable energy-flows or something. Mark stared at the Escobaran, bent like a pretzel in his comconsole station chair in his concentration, and his brows drew down in sudden worry.

Even Enrique couldn't imagine he might attract a woman with his dissertation, could he? Or was that, *only* Enrique could imagine . . . ? It was, after all, his sole signal success in his short life. Mark had to grant, any woman he *could* attract that way was the right sort for him, but . . . but not this one. Not the one Miles had fallen in love with. Madame Vorsoisson was excessively polite, though. She would doubtless say something kind no matter how appalled she was by the offering. And Enrique, who was as starved for kindness as . . . as someone else Mark knew all too well, would build upon it . . .

Expediting the removal of the Bugworks to its new permanent site in the District seemed suddenly a much more urgent task. Lips pursed, Mark tiptoed quietly out of the lab.

Padding up the hall, he could still hear Enrique's happy murmur, "Mucopolysaccharide, hm, there's a good one, like the rhythm, *mu-co-pol-ee-sacc-a-ride* . . ."

The Vorbarr Sultana shuttleport was enjoying a mid-evening lull in traffic. Ivan stared impatiently around the concourse, and shifted his welcome-home bouquet of musky-scented orchids from his right hand to his left. He trusted Lady Donna would not arrive too jump-lagged and exhausted for a little socialization later. The flowers should strike just the right opening note in this renewal of their acquaintance; not so grand and gaudy as to suggest desperation on his part, but sufficiently elegant and expensive to indicate serious interest to anyone as cognizant of the nuances as Donna was.

Beside Ivan, Byerly Vorrutyer leaned comfortably against a pillar and crossed his arms. He glanced at the bouquet and smiled a little By smile, which Ivan noted but ignored. Byerly might be a source of witty, or half-witty, editorial comment, but he certainly wasn't competition for his cousin's amorous attentions.

A few elusive wisps of the erotic dream he'd had about Donna last night tantalized Ivan's memory. He would offer to carry her luggage, he decided, or rather, some of it, whatever she had in her hand for which he might trade the flowers. Lady Donna did not travel light, as he recalled.

Unless she came back lugging a uterine replicator with Pierre's clone in it. That, By could handle all by himself; Ivan wasn't touching it with a stick. By had remained maddeningly closed-mouthed about what Lady Donna had gone to obtain on Beta Colony that she thought would thwart her cousin Richars's inheritance, but really, somebody had to try the clone-ploy sooner or later. The political complications might land in his Vorkosigan cousins' laps, but as a Vorpatril of a mere junior line, he could steer clear. *He* didn't have a vote in the Council of Counts, thank God.

"Ah." By pushed off from the pillar and gazed up the concourse, and raised a hand in brief greeting. "Here we go."

Ivan followed his glance. Three men were approaching them. The white-haired, grim-looking fellow on the right, returning By's wave, he recognized even out of uniform as the late Count Pierre's tough senior Armsman—what was his name?—Szabo. Good, Lady Donna had taken help and protection on her long journey. The tall fellow on the left, also in civvies, was one of Pierre's other guardsmen. His junior status was discernible both by his age and by the fact that he was the one towing the float pallet with the three valises aboard. He had an expression on his face with which Ivan could identify, a sort of covert crogglement common to Barrayarans just back from their first visit to Beta Colony, as if he wasn't sure whether to fall to the ground and kiss the concrete or turn around and run back to the shuttle.

The man in the center Ivan had never seen before. He was an athletic-looking fellow of middle height, more lithe than muscular, though his shoulders filled his civilian tunic quite well. He was soberly dressed in black, with the barest pale gray piping making salute to the Barrayaran style of pseudo-military ornamentation in men's wear. The subtle clothes set off his lean good looks: pale skin, thick dark brows, close-cropped black hair, and trim, glossy black beard and mustache. His step was energetic. His eyes were an electric brown, and seemed to dart all around as if seeing the place for the first time, and liking what they saw.

Oh, hell, had Donna picked up a Betan paramour? This could be annoying. The fellow wasn't a mere boy, either, Ivan saw as they came up to him and By; he was at least in his mid-thirties. There was something oddly familiar about him. Damned if he didn't look a true Vorrutyer—that hair, those eyes, that smirking swagger. An unknown son of Pierre's? The secret reason, revealed at last, why the Count had never married? Pierre would've had to have been about fifteen when he'd sired the fellow, but it was possible.

By exchanged a cordial nod with the smiling stranger, and turned to Ivan. "You two, I think, need no introduction."

"I think we do," Ivan protested.

The fellow's white grin broadened, and he stuck out a hand, which Ivan automatically took. His grip was firm and dry. "Lord Dono Vorrutyer, at your service, Lord Vorpatril." His voice was a pleasant tenor, his accent not Betan at all, but educated Barrayaran Vor-class.

It was the smiling eyes that did it at last, bright like embers.

"Aw, *shit*," hissed Ivan, recoiling, and snatching back his hand. "Donna, you *didn't*." Betan medicine, oh, yeah. And Betan surgery. They could, and would, do anything on Beta Colony, if you had the money and could convince them you were a freely consenting adult.

"If I have my way with the Council of Counts, soon to be Count Dono Vorrutyer," Donna—Dono—whoever—went on smoothly.

"Or killed on sight." Ivan stared at . . . him, in draining disbelief. "You don't seriously think you can make this fly, do you?"

He—she—twitched a brow at Armsman Szabo, who raised his chin a centimeter. Donna/Dono said, "Oh, believe me, we went over the risks in detail before starting out." She/he, whatever, spotted the orchids clutched forgotten in Ivan's left hand. "Why, Ivan, are those for *me*? How sweet of you!" she cooed, wrested them from him, and raised them to her nose. Beard occluded, she blinked demure black eyelashes at him over the bouquet, suddenly and horribly Lady Donna again.

"Don't *do* that in public," said Armsman Szabo through his teeth.

"Sorry Szabo." The voice's pitch plunged again to its initial masculine depth. "Couldn't resist. I mean, it's *Ivan*."

Szabo's shrug conceded the point, but not the issue.

"I'll control myself from now on, I promise." Lord Dono reversed the flowers in his grip and swept them down to his side as though holding a spear, and came to a shoulders-back, feet-apart posture of quasimilitary attention.

"Better," said Szabo judiciously.

Ivan stared in horrified fascination. "Did the Betan doctors make you taller, too?" He glanced down; Lord Dono's half-boot heels were not especially thick.

"I'm the same height I always was, Ivan. Other things have changed, but not my height."

"No, you *are* taller, dammit. At least ten centimeters."

"Only in your mind. One of the many fascinating psychological side effects of testosterone I am discovering, along with the amazing mood-swings. When we get home we can measure me, and I'll prove it to you."

"Yes," said By, glancing around, "I do suggest we continue this conversation in a more private place. Your groundcar is waiting as you instructed, Lord Dono, with your driver." He offered his cousin a little ironic bow.

"You . . . don't need me, to intrude on this family reunion," Ivan excused himself. He began to sidle away.

"Oh, yes we do," said By. With matching evil grins, the two Vorrutyers each took Ivan by an arm, and began to march him toward the exit. Dono's grip was convincingly muscular. The Armsmen followed.

They found the late Count Pierre's official groundcar where By had left it. The alert Armsman-driver in the Vorrutyers' famous blue-and-gray livery hurried to raise the rear canopy for Lord Dono and his party. The driver looked sidelong at the new lord, but appeared entirely unsurprised by the transformation. The younger Armsman finished stowing the limited luggage and slid into the front compartment with the driver, saying, "Damn, I'm glad to be home. Joris, you would not *believe* what I saw on Beta—"

The canopy lowered on Dono, By, Szabo, and Ivan in the rear compartment, cutting off his words. The car pulled smoothly away from the shuttleport. Ivan twisted his neck, and asked plaintively,

"Was that all your luggage?" Lady Donna used to require a second car to carry it all. "Where is the rest of it?"

Lord Dono leaned back in his seat, raised his chin, and stretched his legs out before him. "I dumped it all back on Beta Colony. One case is all my Armsmen are expected to travel with, Ivan. Live and learn."

Ivan noted the possessive, *my* Armsmen. "Are they—" he nodded at Szabo, listening, "are you all in on this?"

"Of course," said Dono easily. "Had to be. We all met together the night after Pierre died, Szabo and I presented the plan, and they swore themselves to me then."

"Very, um . . . loyal of them."

Szabo said, "We've all had a number of years to watch Lady Donna help run the District. Even my men who were less than, mm, personally taken with the plan are District men bred and true. No one wanted to see it fall to Richars."

"I suppose you all have had opportunities to watch him, too, over time," allowed Ivan. He added after a moment, "How'd he manage to piss you *all* off?"

"He didn't do it overnight," said By. "Richars isn't that heroic. It's taken him years of persistent effort."

"I doubt," said Dono in a suddenly clinical tone, "that anyone would care, at this late date, that he tried to rape me when I was twelve, and when I fought him off, drowned my new puppy in retaliation. After all, no one cared at the time."

"Er," said Ivan.

"Give your family credit," By put in, "Richars convinced them all the puppy's death had been your fault. He's always been very good at that sort of thing."

"*You* believed my version," said Dono to By. "Almost the only person to do so."

"Ah, but I'd had my own experiences with Richars by then," said By. He did not volunteer further details.

"I was not yet in your father's service," Szabo pointed out, possibly in self-exculpation.

"Count yourself lucky," sighed Dono. "To describe that household as *lax* would be overly kind. And no one else could impose order till the old man finally stroked out."

"Richars Vorrutyer," Armsman Szabo continued to Ivan, "observing Count Pierre's, er, nervous problems, has counted the

Vorrutyer Countship and District as his property anytime these last twenty years. It was never in his interest to see poor Pierre get better, or form a family of his own. I know for a fact that he bribed the relatives of the first young lady to whom Pierre was engaged to break it off, and sell her elsewhere. Pierre's second effort at courtship, Richars thwarted by smuggling the girl's family certain of Pierre's private medical records. The third fiancée's death in that flyer wreck was never proved to be anything but an accident. But Pierre didn't believe it was an accident."

"Pierre . . . believed a lot of strange things," Ivan noted nervously.

"I didn't think it was an accident either," said Szabo dryly. "One of my best men was driving. He was killed too."

"Oh. Um. But Pierre's own death is not suspected . . . ?"

Szabo shrugged. "I believe the family tendency to those circulatory diseases would not have killed Pierre if he hadn't been too depressed to take proper care of himself."

"I *tried*, Szabo," said Dono—Donna—bleakly. "After that episode with the medical records, he was so incredibly paranoid about his doctors."

"Yes, I know." Szabo began to pat her hand, caught himself, and gave him a soft consoling punch in the shoulder instead. Dono's smile twisted in appreciation.

"In any case," Szabo went on, "it was abundantly plain that no Armsman who was loyal to Pierre—and we all were, God help the poor man—would last five minutes in Richars's service. His first step—and we'd all heard him say so—would be to make a clean sweep of everything and everyone loyal to Pierre, and install his own creatures. Pierre's sister being the first to go, of course."

"If Richars had a gram of self-preservation," murmured Dono fiercely.

"Could he do that?" asked Ivan doubtfully. "Evict you from your home? Have you no rights under Pierre's will?"

"Home, District, and all." Dono smiled grimly. "Pierre made no will, Ivan. He didn't want to name Richars as his successor, wasn't all that fond of Richars's brothers or sons either, and was still, I think, even to the last, hoping to cut him out with an heir of his own body. Hell, Pierre might have expected to live forty more years, with modern medicine. All I would have had as Lady Donna was the pittance from my own dowries. The estate's in the most incredible mess."

"I'm not surprised," said Ivan. "But do you really think you can make this work? I mean, Richars *is* heir-presumptive. And whatever you are now, you weren't Pierre's younger brother at the moment Pierre died."

"That's the most important legal point in the plan. A Count's heir only inherits at the moment of his predecessor's death if he's already been sworn in before the Council. Otherwise, the District isn't inherited till the moment the Counts confirm it. And at that moment—some time in the next couple of weeks—I will be, demonstrably, Pierre's brother."

Ivan's mouth screwed up, as he tried to work this through. Judging by the smooth fit of the black tunic, the lovely great breasts in which he'd once . . . never mind—anyway, they were clearly all gone now. "You've really had surgery for . . . what did you do with . . . you didn't do that hermaphrodite thing, did you? Or where is . . . everything?"

"If you mean my former female organs, I jettisoned 'em with the rest of my luggage back on Beta. You can scarcely find the scars, the surgeon was so clever. They'd put in their time, God knows—can't say as I miss 'em."

Ivan missed them already. Desperately. "I wondered if you might have had them frozen. In case things don't work out, or you change your mind." Ivan tried to keep the hopeful tone out of his voice. "I know there are Betans who switch sexes back and forth three or four times in their lives."

"Yes, I met some of them at the clinic. They were most helpful and friendly, I must say."

Szabo rolled his eyes only slightly. Was Szabo acting as Lord Dono's personal valet now? It was customary for a Count's senior Armsman to do so. Szabo must have witnessed it all, in detail. *Two witnesses. She took two witnesses, I see.*

"No," Dono went on, "if I ever change back—which I have no plans to do, forty years were enough—I'd start all over with fresh cloned organs, just as I've done for this. I could be a virgin again. What a dreadful thought."

Ivan hesitated. He finally asked, "Didn't you need to add a Y chromosome from somewhere? Where'd you get it? Did the Betans supply it?" He glanced helplessly at Dono's crotch, and quickly away. "Can Richars argue that the—the inheriting bit is part-Betan?"

"I thought of that. So I got it from Pierre."

"You didn't have, um, your new male organs cloned from him?" Ivan boggled at this grotesque idea. It made his mind hurt. Was it some kind of techno-incest, or what?

"No, no! I admit, I did borrow a tiny tissue sample from my brother—he didn't need it, by then—and the Betan doctors did use part of a chromosome from it, just for my new cloned parts. My new testicles are a little less than two percent Pierre, I suppose, depending on how you calculate it. If I ever decide to give my prick a nickname, the way some fellows do, I suppose I ought to call it after him. I don't feel much inclined to do so, though. It feels very all-me."

"But are the chromosomes of your body still double-X?"

"Well, yes." Dono frowned uneasily, and scratched his beard. "I expect Richars to try to make a point with that, if he thinks of it. I did look into the retrogenetic treatment for complete somatic transformation. I didn't have time for it, the complications can be strange, and for a gene splice this large the result is usually no better than a partial cellular mosaic, a chimera, hit-or-miss. Sufficient for treating some genetic diseases, but not the legal disease of being some-little-cell-female. But the portion of my tissues responsible for fathering the next little Vorrutyer heir is certifiably XY, and incidentally, made free of genetic disease, damage, and mutation while we were about it. The next Count Vorrutyer won't have a bad heart. Among other things. The prick's always been the most important qualification for a Countship anyway. History says so."

By chuckled. "Maybe they'll just let the prick vote." He made an X gesture down by his crotch, and intoned sonorously, "*Dono, his mark.*"

Lord Dono grinned. "While it wouldn't be the first time a real prick has held a seat in the Council of Counts, I'm hoping for a more complete victory. That's where you come in, Ivan."

"Me? I don't have anything to do with this! I don't *want* anything to do with this." Ivan's startled protests were cut short by the car slowing in front of the Vorrutyers' townhouse and turning in.

Vorrutyer House was a generation older than Vorkosigan House and correspondingly notably more fortresslike. Its severe stone walls threw projections out to the sidewalk in a blunted star pattern, giving crossfire onto what had been a mud street decorated with horse dung in the great house's heyday. It had no windows on the ground floor at all, just a few gun-slits. Thick iron-bound planks, scorning carving or any other decorative effect, formed the double doors into its inner courtyard; they now swung aside at an automated signal, and the groundcar squeezed through the passage. The walls were marked with smears of vehicle enamel from less careful drivers. Ivan wondered if the murder-holes in the dark arched roof, above, were still functional. Probably.

The place had been restored with an eye to defense by the great general Count Pierre "Le Sanguinaire" Vorrutyer himself, who was principally famous as Emperor Dorca's trusted right arm/head thug in the civil war that had broken the power of the independent Counts just before the end of the Time of Isolation. Pierre had made serious enemies, all of whom he had survived into a foul-tongued old age. It had taken the invading Cetagandans and all their techno-weaponry to finally put an end to him, with great difficulty, after an infamous and costly siege—not of this place, of course. Old Pierre's eldest daughter had married an earlier Count Vorkosigan, which was where the Pierre of Mark's middle name had come down from. Ivan wondered what old Pierre would think of his offshoots now. Maybe he would like Richars best. Maybe his ghost still walked here. Ivan shuddered, stepping out onto the dark cobblestones.

The driver took the car off to its garage, and Lord Dono led the way, two steps at a time, up the green-black granite staircase out of the courtyard and into the house. He paused to sweep a glance back over the stony expanse. "First thing is, I'm going to get some more light out here," he remarked to Szabo.

"First thing is, get the title deed in your name," Szabo returned blandly.

"My new name." Dono gave him a short nod, and pushed onward.

The interior of the house was so ill-lit, one couldn't make out the mess, but apparently all had been left exactly as it had been dropped when Count Pierre had last gone down to his District some months ago. The echoing chambers had a derelict, musty odor. They fetched up finally, after laboring up two more gloomy staircases, in the late Count's abandoned bedroom.

"Guess I'll sleep here tonight," said Lord Dono, staring around dubiously. "I want clean sheets on the bed first, though."

"Yes, m'lord," said Szabo.

Byerly cleared a pile of plastic flimsies, dirty clothes, dried fruit rinds, and other detritus from an armchair, and settled himself comfortably, legs crossed. Dono prowled the room, staring rather sadly at his dead brother's few and forlorn personal effects, picking up and putting down a set of hairbrushes—Pierre had been balding—dried-up cologne bottles, small coins. "Starting tomorrow, I want this place cleaned up. I'm not waiting for the title deed for that, if I have to live here."

"I know a good commercial service," Ivan couldn't help volunteering. "They clean Vorkosigan House for Miles when the Count and Countess aren't in residence, I know."

"Ah? Good." Lord Dono made a gesture at Szabo. The Armsman nodded, and promptly collected the particulars from Ivan, noting them down on his pocket audiofiler.

"Richars made two attempts to take possession of the old pile while you were gone," Byerly reported. "The first time, your Armsmen stood firm and wouldn't let him in."

"Good men," muttered Szabo.

"Second time, he came round with a squad of municipal guardsmen and an order he'd conned out of Lord Vorbohn. Your officer of the watch called me, and I was able to get a counter-order from the Lord Guardian of the Speaker's Circle with which to conjure them away. It was quite exciting, for a little while. Pushing and shoving in the doorways . . . no one drew weapons, or was seriously injured, though, more's the pity. We might have been able to sue Richars."

"We've lawsuits enough." Dono sighed, sat on the edge of the bed, and crossed his legs. "But thanks for what you did, By."

By waved this away.

"Below the knees, if you must," said Szabo. "Knees apart is better."

Dono immediately rearranged his pose, crossing his ankles instead, but noted, "By sits that way."

"By is not a good male model to copy."

By made a moue at Szabo, and flipped one wrist out limply. "Really, Szabo, how can you be so cruel? And after I saved your old homestead, too."

Everyone ignored him. "How about Ivan?" Dono asked Szabo, eyeing Ivan speculatively. Ivan was suddenly unsure of where to put his feet, or his hands.

"Mm, fair. The very best model, if you can remember exactly how he moved, would be Aral Vorkosigan. Now, *that* was power in motion. His son doesn't do too badly, either, projecting beyond his real space. Young Lord Vorkosigan is just a bit studied, though. Count Vorkosigan just is."

Lord Dono's thick black brows snapped up, and he rose to stalk across the room, flip a desk chair around, and straddle it, arms crossed along its back. He rested his chin on his arms and glowered.

"Huh! I recognize that one," said Szabo. "Not bad, keep working on it. Try to take up more space with your elbows."

Dono grinned, and leaned one hand on his thigh, elbow cocked out. After a moment, he jumped up again, and went to Pierre's closet, flung the doors wide, and began rooting within. A Vorrutyer House uniform tunic sailed out to land on the bed, followed by trousers and a shirt; then one tall boot after another thumped to the bed's end. Dono reemerged, dusty and bright-eyed.

"Pierre wasn't that much taller than me, and I always could wear his shoes, if I had thick socks. Get a seamstress in here tomorrow—"

"Tailor," Szabo corrected.

"Tailor, and we'll see how much of this I can use in a hurry."

"Very good, m'lord."

Dono began unfastening his black tunic.

"I think it's time for me to go now," said Ivan.

"Please sit down, Lord Vorpatril," said Armsman Szabo.

"Yes, come sit by me, Ivan." Byerly patted his upholstered chair arm invitingly.

"Sit down, Ivan," Lord Dono growled. His burning eyes suddenly crinkled, and he murmured, "For old time's sake, if nothing else. You used to run *into* my bedroom to watch me undress, not out of it. Must I lock the door and make you play hunt the key again?"

Ivan opened his mouth, raised a furious admonishing finger in protest, thought better of it, and sank to a seat on the edge of the bed. *You wouldn't dare* seemed suddenly a really unwise thing to say to the former Lady Donna Vorrutyer. He crossed his ankles, then hastily uncrossed them again and set his feet apart, then crossed them again, and twined his hands together in vast discomfort. "I don't see what you need me for," he said plaintively.

"So you can witness," said Szabo.

"So you can testify," said Dono. The tunic hit the bed beside Ivan, making him jump, followed by a black T-shirt.

Well, Dono had spoken truly about the Betan surgeon; there weren't any visible scars. His chest sprouted a faint nest of black hairs; his musculature tended to the wiry. The shoulders of the tunic hadn't been padded.

"So you can *gossip*, of course," said By, lips parted in either some bizarre prurient interest, or keen enjoyment of Ivan's embarrassment, or more likely both at once.

"If you think I'm going to say one word about being here tonight to *anyone*—"

With a smooth motion, Dono kicked his black trousers onto the bed atop the tunic. His briefs followed.

"Well?" Dono stood before Ivan with an utterly cheerful leer on his face. "What do you think? Do they do good work on Beta, or what?"

Ivan glanced sidelong at him, and away. "You look . . . normal," he admitted reluctantly.

"Well, show *me* while you're at it," By said.

Dono turned before him.

"Not bad," said By judiciously, "but aren't you a trifle, ah, juvenile?"

Dono sighed. "It was a rush job. Quality, but rush. I went from the hospital straight to the jumpship for home. The organs are going to have to finish growing *in situ*, the doctors tell me. A few months yet to fully adult morphology. The incisions don't hurt anymore, though."

"Ooh," said By, "puberty. What fun for you."

"On fast-forward, at that. But the Betans have smoothed that out a lot for me. You have to give them credit, they're a people in control of their hormones."

Ivan conceded reluctantly, "My cousin Miles, when he had his heart and lungs and guts replaced, said it took almost a full year for his breathing and energy to be completely back to normal. They had to finish growing back to adult size after they were installed too. I'm sure . . . it will be all right." He added after a helpless moment, "So does it work?"

"I can piss standing up, yeah." Dono reached over and retrieved his briefs, and slid them back on. "As for the other, well, real soon now, I understand. I can hardly wait for my first wet dream."

"But will any woman want to . . . it's not like you're going to be keeping it a secret, who and what you were before . . . how will you, um . . . That's one place Armsman Pygmalion over there," Ivan waved at Szabo, "won't be able to coach you."

Szabo smiled faintly, the most expression Ivan had seen on his face tonight.

"Ivan, Ivan, Ivan." Dono shook his head, and scooped up the House uniform trousers. "I taught *you* how, didn't I? Of all the problems I expect to have . . . puzzling how to lose my male virginity isn't one of them. Really."

"It . . . doesn't seem fair," said Ivan in a smaller voice. "I mean, *we* had to figure all this stuff out when we were thirteen."

"As opposed to, say, twelve?" Dono inquired tightly.

"Um."

Dono buckled the trousers—they were not too snug across the hips after all—hitched into the tunic, and frowned at his reflection in the mirror. He bunched handfuls of extra fabric at the sides. "Yeah, that'll do. The tailor should have it ready by tomorrow night. I want to wear this when I go present my evidence of impediment at Vorhartung Castle."

The blue-and-gray Vorrutyer House uniform was going to look exceptionally good on Lord Dono, Ivan had to concede. Maybe that would be a good day to call in his Vor rights and get a ticket, and take a discreet back seat in the visitor's gallery at the Council of Counts. Just to see what happened, to use one of Gregor's favorite phrases.

Gregor . . .

"Does Gregor know about this?" Ivan asked suddenly. "Did you tell him your plan, before you left for Beta?"

"No, of course not," said Dono. He sat on the bed's edge, and began pulling on the boots.

Ivan could feel his teeth clench. "Are you out of your minds?"

"As somebody or another is fond of quoting—I think it was your cousin Miles—it is always easier to get forgiveness than permission." Dono rose, and went to the mirror to check the effect of the boots.

Ivan clutched his hair. "All right. You two—you three—dragged me up here because you claimed you wanted my help. I'm going to hand you a hint. Free." He took a deep breath. "You can blindside me, and laugh your heads off if you want to. It won't be the first time I've been the butt. You can blindside Richars with my good will. You can blindside the whole Council of Counts. Blindside my cousin Miles—please. I want to watch. But do not, if you value your chances, if you mean this to be anything other than a big, short joke, do *not* blindside Gregor."

Byerly grimaced uncertainly; Dono, turning before the mirror, shot Ivan a penetrating look. "Go to him, you mean?"

"Yes. I can't make you," Ivan went on sternly, "but if you don't, I categorically refuse to have anything more to do with you."

"Gregor can kill it all with a word," said Dono warily. "Before it even launches."

"He can," said Ivan, "but he won't, without strong motivation. Don't give him that motivation. Gregor does not like political surprises."

"I thought Gregor was fairly easy-going," said By, "for an emperor."

"No," said Ivan firmly. "He is not. He is merely rather quiet. It's not the same thing at all. You don't want to see what he's like pissed."

"What does he look like, pissed?" asked By curiously.

"Identical to what he looks like the rest of the time. That's the scary part."

Dono held up a hand, as By opened his mouth again. "By, aside from the chance to amuse yourself, you pulled Ivan in on this tonight because of his connections, or so you claimed. In my experience, it's a bad idea to ignore your expert consultants."

By shrugged. "It's not like we're paying him anything."

"*I* am calling in some old favors. This costs me. And it's not from a fund I can replace." Dono's glance swept to Ivan. "So what exactly do you suggest we do?"

"Ask Gregor for a brief interview. *Before* you talk to or see anyone else at all, even over the comconsole. Chin up, look him in the eye—" An ungodly thought occurred to Ivan then. "Wait, you didn't ever sleep with *him*, did you?"

Dono's lips, and mustache, twitched up with amusement. "No, unfortunately. A missed opportunity I now regret deeply, I assure you."

"Ah." Ivan breathed relief. "All right. Then just tell him what you plan to do. Claim your rights. He'll either decide to let you run, or he'll impound you. If he cuts you off, well, the worst will be over, and quickly. If he decides to let you run . . . you'll have a silent backer even Richars at his most vicious can't top."

Dono leaned against Pierre's bureau, and drummed his fingers in the dust atop it. The orchids now lay there in a forlorn heap. Wilted, like Ivan's dreams. Dono's lips pursed. "Can you get us in?" he asked at last.

"I, uh . . . I, uh . . ."

His gaze became more urgent, piercing. "Tomorrow?"

"Ah . . ."

"Morning?"

"Not *morning*," By protested faintly.

"Early," insisted Dono.

"I'll . . . seewhatIcando," Ivan managed at last.

Dono's face lit. "*Thank* you!"

The extraction of this reluctant promise had one beneficial side-effect: the Vorrutyers proved willing to let their captive audience go, the better for Ivan to hurry home and call Emperor Gregor. Lord Dono insisted on detailing his car and a driver to take Ivan the short distance to his apartment, thwarting Ivan's faint hope of being mugged and murdered in a Vorbarr Sultana alleyway on the way home and thus avoiding the consequences of this evening's revelations.

Blessedly alone in the back of the groundcar, Ivan entertained a brief prayer that Gregor's schedule would be too packed to admit the proposed interview. But it was more likely he'd be so shocked at Ivan breaking his rule of a low profile, he'd make room at once. In Ivan's experience, the only thing more dangerous to such innocent bystanders as himself than arousing Gregor's wrath was arousing his curiosity.

Once back safely in his little apartment, Ivan locked the door against all Vorrutyers past and present. He'd beguiled his time yesterday imagining entertaining the voluptuous Lady Donna here . . . what a waste. Not that Lord Dono didn't make a passable man, but Barrayar didn't *need* more men. Though Ivan supposed they might reverse Donna's ploy, and send the excess male population to Beta Colony to be altered into the more pleasing form . . . he shuddered at the vision.

With a reluctant sigh, he dug out the security card he'd managed to avoid using for the past several years, and ran it through his comconsole's read-slot.

Gregor's gatekeeper, a man in bland civilian dress who did not identify himself—if you had this access, you were supposed to know—answered at once. "Yes? Ah. Ivan."

"I would like to speak to Gregor, please."

"Excuse me, Lord Vorpatril, but did you mean to use this channel?"

"Yes."

The gatekeeper's brows rose in surprise, but his hand moved to one side, and his image blinked out. The comconsole chimed. Several times.

Gregor's image came up at last. He was still dressed for the day, relieving Ivan's alarmed visions of dragging him out of bed or the shower. The background showed one of the Imperial Residence's cozier sitting rooms. Ivan could just make out a fuzzy view of Dr. Toscane, in the background. She seemed to be adjusting her blouse. *Ulp. Keep it brief. Gregor clearly has better things to do tonight.*

I wish I did.

Gregor's blank expression changed to one of annoyance as he recognized Ivan. "Oh. It's you." The irritated look faded slightly. "You never call me on this channel, Ivan. Thought it had to be Miles. What's up?"

Ivan took a deep breath. "I just came from meeting . . . Donna Vorrutyer at the shuttleport. Back from Beta. You two need to see each other."

Gregor's brows rose. "Why?"

"I'm sure she'd much rather explain it all herself. I have nothing to do with this."

"You do now. Lady Donna's calling in old favors, is she?" Gregor frowned, and added a bit dangerously, "I am not a coin to be bartered in your love affairs, Ivan."

"No, Sire," Ivan agreed fervently. "But you want to see her. Really and truly. As soon as possible. Sooner. Tomorrow. Morning. Early."

Gregor cocked his head. Curiously. "Just how important is this?"

"That's entirely for you to judge. Sire."

"If *you* want nothing to do with it . . ." Gregor trailed off, and stared unnervingly at Ivan. His hand at last tapped on his comconsole control, and he glanced aside at some display Ivan could not see. "I could move . . . hm. How about eleven sharp, in my office."

"Thank you, Sire." *You won't regret this* seemed a much too optimistic statement to add. In fact, adding anything at all had all the appeal of stepping over a cliff without a grav-suit. Ivan smiled instead, and ducked his head in a little half-bow.

Gregor's frown grew more thoughtful still, but after a moment of further contemplation, he returned Ivan's nod, and cut the com.

Chapter Eight

Ekaterin sat before the comconsole in her aunt's study, and ran again through the seasonal succession of Barrayaran plants bordering the branching pathways of Lord Vorkosigan's garden. The one sensory effect the design program could not help her model was odor. For that most subtle and emotionally profound effect, she had to rely on her own experience and memory.

On a soft summer evening, a border of scrubwire would emit a spicy redolence that would fill the air for meters around, but its color was muted and its shape low and round. Intermittent stands of chuffgrass would break up the lines, and reach full growth at the right time, but its sickly citrus scent would clash with the scrubwire, and besides, it was on the proscribed list of plants to which Lord Vorkosigan was allergic. Ah—zipweed! Its blond and maroon stripes would provide excellent vertical visual interest, and its faint sweet fragrance would combine well, appetizingly even, with the scrubwire. Put a clump there by the little bridge, and there and there. She altered the program, and ran the succession again. *Much better.* She took a sip of her cooling tea, and glanced at the time.

She could hear her Aunt Vorthys moving about in the kitchen. Late-sleeper Uncle Vorthys would be down soon, and shortly afterwards Nikki, and aesthetic concentration would be a lost cause. She had only a few days for any last design refinements before she began working with real plants in quantity. And less than two hours

497

before she needed to be showered and dressed and onsite to watch the crew hook up and test the creek's water circulation.

If all went well, she could start laying her supply of Dendarii rocks today, and tuning the gentle burble of the water flow around and over and among them. The sound of the creek was another subtlety the design program could not help her with, though it had addressed environmental noise abatement. The walls and curving terraces were up onsite, and satisfactory; the city-noise-baffling effects were all she'd hoped for. Even in winter the garden would be hushed and restful. Blanketed with snow broken only by the bare up-reaching lines of the woodier scrub, the shape of the space would still please the eye and soothe the mind and heart.

By tonight, the bones of the thing would be complete. Tomorrow, the flesh, in the form of trucked-in, unterraformed native soils from remote corners of the Vorkosigan's District, would arrive. And tomorrow evening before Lord Vorkosigan's dinner party, just for promise, she would put the first plant into the soil: a certain spare rootling from an ancient South Continent skellytum tree. It would be fifteen years or more before it would grow to fill the space allotted for it, but what of that? Vorkosigans had held this ground for two hundred years. Chances were good Vorkosigans would still be there to see it in its maturity. Continuity. With continuity like that, you could grow a *real* garden. Or a real family . . .

The front door chimed, and Ekaterin jumped, abruptly aware she was still dressed in an old set of her uncle's ship knits for pajamas, with her hair escaping the tie at the nape of her neck. Her aunt's step sounded from the kitchen into the tiled hall, and Ekaterin tensed to duck out of the line of sight should it prove some formal visitor. Oh, dear, what if it was Lord Vorkosigan? She'd waked at dawn with garden revisions rioting through her head, sneaked quietly downstairs to work, and hadn't even brushed her teeth yet—but the voice greeting her aunt was a woman's, and a familiar one at that. *Rosalie, here? Why?*

A dark-haired, fortyish woman leaned around the edge of the archway and smiled. Ekaterin waved back in surprise, and rose to go to the hallway and greet her. It was indeed Rosalie Vorvayne, the wife of Ekaterin's eldest brother. Ekaterin hadn't seen her since Tien's funeral. She wore conservative day-wear, skirt and jacket in a bronze green that flattered her olive skin, though the cut was a little dowdy and provincial. She had her daughter Edie in tow, to whom she said,

"Run along upstairs and find your cousin Nikki. I have to talk to your Aunt Kat for a while." Edie had not quite reached the adolescent slouch stage, and thumped off willingly enough.

"What brings you to the capital at this hour?" Aunt Vorthys asked Rosalie.

"Is Hugo and everyone all right?" Ekaterin added.

"Oh, yes, we're all fine," Rosalie assured them. "Hugo couldn't get away from work, so I was dispatched. I plan to take Edie shopping later, but getting her up to catch the morning monorail was a real chore, believe me."

Hugo Vorvayne held a post in the Imperial Bureau of Mines northern regional headquarters in Vordarian's District, two hours away from Vorbarr Sultana by the express. Rosalie must have risen before light for this outing. Her two older sons, grown almost past the surly stage, presumably had been left to their own devices for the day.

"Have you had breakfast, Rosalie?" Aunt Vorthys asked. "Do you want any tea or coffee?"

"We ate on the monorail, but tea would be lovely, thank you, Aunt Vorthys."

Rosalie and Ekaterin both followed their aunt into her kitchen to offer assistance, and as a result all ended up seated around the kitchen table with their steaming cups. Rosalie brought them up to date upon the health of her husband, the events of her household, and the accomplishments of her sons since Tien's funeral. Her eyes narrowed with good humor, and she leaned forward confidingly. "But to answer your question, what brings me here is you, Kat."

"Me?" said Ekaterin blankly.

"Can't you imagine why?"

Ekaterin wondered if it would be rude to say, *No, how should I?* She compromised with an inquiring gesture, and raised eyebrows.

"Your father had a visitor a couple of days ago."

Rosalie's arch tone invited a guessing-game, but Ekaterin could only think of how soon she might finish the social niceties and get away to her work-site. She continued to smile dimly.

Rosalie shook her head in amused exasperation, leaned forward, and tapped her finger on the table beside her cup. "You, my dear, have a very eligible offer."

"Offer of what?" Rosalie wasn't likely to be bringing her a new garden design contract. But surely she couldn't mean—

"Marriage, what else? And from a proper Vor gentleman, too, I'm pleased to report. So old-fashioned of the man, he sent a Baba all the way from Vorbarr Sultana to your da in South Continent—it quite bowled the old man over. Your da called Hugo to pass on the particulars. We decided that after all that baba-ing rather than do it over the comconsole someone ought to tell you the good news in person. We're all so pleased, to think you might be settled again so soon."

Aunt Vorthys sat up, looking considerably startled. She put a finger to her lips.

A Vor gentleman from the capital, old-fashioned and highly conscious of etiquette, Da bowled over, who else could it be but—Ekaterin's heart seemed to stop, then explode. *Lord Vorkosigan? Miles, you rat, how could you do this without asking me first!* Her lips parted in a dizzying mixture of fury and elation.

The arrogant little—! But . . . he to pick *her*, to be his Lady Vorkosigan, chatelaine of that magnificent house and of his ancestral District—there was so much to be done in that beautiful District, so daunting and exciting—and Miles himself, oh, my. That fascinating scarred short body, that burning intensity, to come to *her* bed? His hands had touched her perhaps twice; they might as well have left scorch marks on her skin, so clearly did her body remember those brief pressures. She had not, had not dared, let herself think about him in that way, but now her carnal consciousness of him wrenched loose from its careful suppression and soared. Those humorous gray eyes, that alert, mobile, kissable mouth with its extraordinary range of expression . . . could be hers, all hers. But how *dare* he ambush her like this, in front of all her relatives?

"You're pleased?" Rosalie, watching her face closely, sat back and smiled. "Or should I say, thrilled? Good! And not completely surprised, I daresay."

"Not . . . completely." *I just didn't believe it. I chose not to believe it, because . . . because it would have ruined everything . . .*

"We were afraid you might find it early days, after Tien and all. But the Baba said he meant to steal a march on all his rivals, your da told Hugo."

"He doesn't have any rivals." Ekaterin swallowed, feeling decidedly faint, thinking of the remembered scent of him. But how could he imagine that she—

"He has good hopes for his postmilitary career," Rosalie went on.

"Indeed, he's said so." *It's all kinds of hubris*, Miles had told her once, describing his ambitions for fame to exceed his father's. She'd gathered he didn't expect that fact to slow him down in the least.

"Good family connections."

Ekaterin couldn't help smiling. "A *slight* understatement, Rosalie."

"Not as rich as others of his rank, but well-enough to do, and I never thought you were one to hold out for the money. Though I always did think you needed to look a bit more to your own needs, Kat."

Well, yes, Ekaterin had been dimly aware that the Vorkosigans were not as wealthy as many other families of Count's rank, but Miles had riches enough to drown in by her old straitened standards. She would never have to pinch and scrape again. All her energy, all her thought, could be freed for higher goals—Nikki would have every opportunity—"Plenty enough for me, good heavens!"

But how bizarre of him, to send a Baba all the way to South Continent to talk to her da . . . was he that shy? Ekaterin's heart was almost touched, but for the reflection that it might simply be that Miles gave no thought to how much his wants inconvenienced others. Shy, or arrogant? Or both at once? He could be a most ambiguous man sometimes—charming as . . . as no one she'd ever met before, but elusive as water.

Not just elusive; slippery. Borderline trickster, even. A chill stole over her. Had his garden proposal been nothing more than a trick, a ploy to keep her close under his eye? The full implications began to sink in at last. Maybe he didn't admire her work. Maybe he didn't care about his garden at all. Maybe he was merely manipulating her. She knew herself to be hideously vulnerable to the faintest flattery. Her starvation for the slightest scrap of interest or affection was part of what had kept her self-prisoned in her marriage for so long. A kind of Tien-shaped box seemed to loom darkly before her, like a pitfall trap baited with poisoned love.

Had she betrayed herself again? She'd so much wanted it to be true, wanted to take her first steps into independence, to have the chance to display her prowess. She'd imagined not just Miles, but all the people of the city, amazed and delighted by her garden, and new orders pouring in, the launch of a career. . . .

You can't cheat an honest man, the saying went. Or woman. If Lord Vorkosigan had manipulated her, he'd done so with her full cooperation. Her hot rage was douched with cold shame.

Rosalie was burbling on, " . . . want to tell Lieutenant Vormoncrief the good news yourself, or should we go round through his Baba again?"

Ekaterin blinked her back into focus. "What? Wait, *who* did you say?"

Rosalie stared back. "Lieutenant Vormoncrief. Alexi."

"*That* block?" cried Ekaterin in dawning horror. "Rosalie, never tell me you've been talking about Alexi Vormoncrief this whole time!"

"Why, yes," said Rosalie in dismay. "Who did you think, Kat?"

The Professora blew out her breath and sat back.

Ekaterin was so upset the words escaped her mouth without thought. "I thought you were talking about Miles Vorkosigan!"

The Professora's brows shot up; it was Rosalie's turn to stare. "Who? Oh, good heavens, you don't mean the Imperial Auditor fellow, do you? That grotesque little man who came to Tien's funeral and hardly said a word to anyone? No wonder you looked so odd. No, no, no." She paused to peer more closely at her sister-in-law. "You don't mean to tell me he's been courting you too? How embarrassing!"

Ekaterin took a breath, for balance. "Apparently not."

"Well, that's a relief."

"Um . . . yes."

"I mean, he's a mutie, isn't he? High Vor or no, the family would never urge you to match with a mutie just for money, Kat. Put that right out of your mind." She paused thoughtfully. "Still . . . they're not handing out too many chances to be a Countess. I suppose, with the uterine replicators these days, you wouldn't actually have to have any physical contact. To have children, I mean. And they could be gene-cleaned. These galactic technologies give the idea of a marriage of convenience a whole new twist. But it's not as though you were that desperate."

"No," Ekaterin agreed hollowly. *Just desperately distracted.* She was furious with the man; why should the notion of never ever having to have any physical contact with him make her suddenly want to burst into tears? Wait, no—if Vorkosigan *wasn't* the man who'd sent the Baba, her whole case against him, which had bloomed so violently in her mind just now, collapsed like a house of cards. He was innocent. She was crazy, or headed that way fast.

"I mean," Rosalie went on in a tone of renewed encouragement, "here's Vormoncrief, for instance."

"Here is *not* Vormoncrief," Ekaterin said firmly, grasping for the one certain anchor in this whirlwind of confusion. "Absolutely not. You've never met the man, Rosalie, but take it from me, he's a twittering idiot. Aunt Vorthys, am I right or not?"

The Professora smiled fondly at her. "I would not put it so bluntly, dear, but really, Rosalie, shall we say, I think Ekaterin can do better. There's plenty of time yet."

"Do you think so?" Rosalie took in this assurance doubtfully, but accepted her elder aunt's authority. "It's true Vormoncrief's only a lieutenant, and the descendant of a younger son at that. Oh, dear. What are we to tell the poor man?"

"Diplomacy's the Baba's job," Ekaterin pointed out. "All we have to supply is a straight *no*. She'll have to take it from there."

"That's true," Rosalie allowed, looking relieved. "One of the advantages of the old system, I suppose. Well . . . if Vormoncrief is not the one, he's not the one. You're old enough to know your own mind. Still, Kat, I don't think you ought to be too choosy, or wait too long past your mourning time. Nikki needs a da. And you're not getting any younger. You don't want to end up as one of those odd old women who eke out their lives in their relatives' attics."

Your attic is safe from me under any circumstances, Rosalie. Ekaterin smiled a bit grimly, but did not speak this thought aloud. "No, only the third floor."

The Professora's eyes flicked at her, reprovingly, and Ekaterin flushed. She was not ungrateful, she wasn't. It was just . . . oh, hell. She pushed back her chair.

"Excuse me. I have to go get my shower and get dressed. I'm due at work soon."

"Work?" said Rosalie. "Must you go? I'd hoped to take you out to lunch, and shopping. To celebrate, and look for bride clothes, in the original plan, but I suppose we could convert it to a consolation day instead. What do you say, Kat? I think you could use a little fun. You haven't had much, lately."

"No shopping," said Ekaterin. She remembered the last time she'd been shopping, on Komarr with Lord Vorkosigan in one of his more lunatic moods, before Tien's death had turned her life inside-out. She didn't think a day with Rosalie could match it. At Rosalie's look of distressed disappointment, she relented. The woman had got up before dawn for this fool's errand, after all. "But I suppose you and Edie could pick me up for lunch, and then bring me back."

"All right . . . where? Whatever are you doing these days, anyway? Weren't you talking about going back to school? You haven't exactly communicated with the rest of the family much lately, you know."

"I've been busy. I have a commission to design and implement a display garden for a Count's townhouse." She hesitated. "Lord Auditor Vorkosigan's, actually. I'll give you directions how to get there before you and Edie go out."

"Vorkosigan is employing you, too?" Rosalie looked surprised, then suddenly militantly suspicious. "He hasn't been . . . you know . . . pushing himself on you at all, has he? I don't care whose son he is, he has no right to impose on you. Remember, you have a brother to stand up for you if you need it." She paused, perhaps to reflect upon a vision of Hugo's probable appalled recoil at being volunteered for this duty. "Or I'd be willing to give him a piece of my mind myself, if you need help." She nodded, now on firmer ground.

"Thank you," choked Ekaterin, beginning to evolve plans for keeping Rosalie and Lord Vorkosigan as far apart as possible. "I'll keep you in mind, if it ever becomes necessary." She escaped upstairs.

In the shower, she tried to recover from the seething chaos Rosalie's misunderstood mission had generated in her brain. Her physical attraction for Miles—Lord Vorkosigan—*Miles*, was no news, really. She'd felt and ignored the pull of it before. It was by no means in despite of his odd body; his size, his scars, his energy, his *differences* fascinated her in their own right. She wondered if people would think her perverse, if they knew the strange way her tastes seemed to be drifting these days. Firmly, she turned the water temperature down to pure cold.

But flatline suppression of all erotic speculation was a legacy of her years with Tien. She owned herself now, owned her own sexuality at last. Free and clear. She could dare to dream. To look. To feel, even. Action was another matter altogether, but drat it, she could *want*, in the solitude of her own skull, and possess that wanting whole.

And he liked her, he did. It was no crime to like her, even if it was inexplicable. And she liked him back, yes. A little too much, even, but that was no one's business but her own. They could go on like this. The garden project wouldn't last forever. By midsummer, fall at the latest, she could turn it and a schedule of instructions over to Vorkosigan House's usual groundskeepers. She might drop by to check on it from time to time. They might even meet. From time to time.

She was starting to shiver. She turned the water temperature back up to as hot as she could stand, so the steam billowed in clouds.

Would it do any harm, to make of him a dream-lover? It seemed invasive. How would she like it, after all, if she discovered she was starring in someone else's pornographic daydreams? Horrified, yes? Disgusted, to be pawed over in some untrusted stranger's thoughts. She imagined herself so portrayed in Miles's thoughts, and checked her horror quotient. It was a little . . . weak.

The obvious solution was to bring dreams and reality into honest congruence. If deleting the dreams wasn't possible, what about making them real? She tried to imagine having a lover. How did people go *about* such things, anyway? She could barely nerve herself to ask for directions on a street corner. How in the world did you ask someone to . . . But reality—reality was too great a risk, ever again. To lose herself and all her free dreams in another long nightmare like her life with Tien, a slow, sucking, suffocating bog closing over her head forever . . .

She jerked the temperature down again, and adjusted the spray so the droplets struck her skin like spicules of ice. Miles was not Tien. He wasn't trying to own her, for heaven's sake, or destroy her; he'd only hired her to make him a garden. Entirely benign. She must be going insane. She trusted it was a temporary insanity. Maybe her hormones had spiked this month. She would just ride it out, and all these . . . unusual thoughts, would just go away on their own. She would look back on herself and laugh.

She laughed, experimentally. The hollow echoes were due to being in the shower, no doubt. She shut off the freezing water, and stepped out.

There was no reason she would have to see him today. He sometimes came out and sat on the wall a while and watched the crew's progress, but he never interrupted. She wouldn't have to talk with him, not till his dinner tomorrow night, and there would be lots of *other* people to talk with then. She had plenty of time to settle her mind again. In the meanwhile, she had a creek to tune.

✧   ✧   ✧

Lady Alys Vorpatril's office at the Imperial Residence, which handled all matters of social protocol for the Emperor, had expanded of late from three rooms to half of a third-floor wing. There Ivan found himself at the disposal of the fleet of secretaries and assistants Lady Alys had laid on to help handle the wedding. It had sounded a treat, to be working in an office with dozens of women, till he'd discovered they were mostly steely-eyed middle-aged Vor ladies who brooked even less nonsense from him than his mother did. Fortunately, he'd only dated two of their daughters, and both those ventures had ended without acrimony. It could have been much worse.

To Ivan's concealed dismay, Lord Dono and By Vorrutyer were in such good time for their Imperial appointment they stopped up to see him on the way in. Lady Alys's secretary summoned him curtly into the department's outer office, where he found the pair refraining from sitting down and making themselves comfortable. By was dressed in his usual taste, in a maroon suit conservative only by town clown standards. Lord Dono wore his neat Vor-style black tunic and trousers with gray piping and decoration, clearly mourning garb, which not coincidentally set off his newly masculinized good looks. The middle-aged secretary was giving him approving glances from under her eyelashes. Armsman Szabo, in full Vorrutyer House uniform, had taken up that I-am-furniture guard stance by the door, as if covertly declaring there were some kinds of lines of fire it wasn't his job to be in.

No one not on staff wandered the halls of the Imperial Residence by themselves; Dono and By had an escort, in the person of Gregor's senior major-domo. This gentleman turned from some conversation with the secretary as Ivan entered, and eyed him with new appraisal.

"Good morning, Ivan," said Lord Dono cordially.

"Morning, Dono, By." Ivan managed a brief, reasonably impersonal nod. "You, ah, made it, I see."

"Yes, thank you." Dono glanced around. "Is Lady Alys here this morning?"

"Gone off to inspect florists with Colonel Vortala," said Ivan, happy to be able to both tell the truth and avoid being drawn further into whatever schemes Lord Dono might have.

"I must chat with her sometime soon," mused Dono.

"Mm," said Ivan. Lady Donna had not been one of Alys Vorpatril's intimates, being half a generation younger and involved with a different social set than the politically active crowd over which Lady Alys presided. Lady Donna had discarded, along with her first husband, a chance to be a future Countess; though having met that lordling, Ivan thought he could understand the sacrifice. In any case, Ivan had not had any trouble controlling his urge to gossip about this new twist of events with either his mother or any of the sedate Vor matrons she employed. And fascinating as it would be to witness the first meeting of Lady Alys with Lord Dono and all the protocol puzzles he trailed, on the whole Ivan thought he would rather be safely out of range.

"Ready, gentlemen?" said the major-domo.

"Good luck, Dono," said Ivan, and prepared to retreat.

"Yes," said By, "good luck. I'll just stay here and chat with Ivan till you're done, shall I?"

"My list," said the major-domo, "has all of you on it. Vorrutyer, Lord Vorrutyer, Lord Vorpatril, Armsman Szabo."

"Oh, that's an error," said Ivan helpfully. "Only Lord Dono actually needs to see Gregor." By nodded confirmation.

"The list," said the major-domo, "is in the Emperor's own hand. This way, please."

The normally saturnine By swallowed a little, but they all dutifully followed the major-domo down two floors and around the corner to the north wing and Gregor's private office. The major-domo had not demanded Ivan vouch for Dono's identity, Ivan noted, by which he deduced the Residence had caught up with events overnight. Ivan was almost disappointed. He'd so wanted to see somebody else be as boggled as he'd been.

The major-domo touched the palm pad by the door, announced his party, and was bid to enter. Gregor shut down his comconsole desk and looked up as they all trod within. He rose and walked around to lean against it, cross his arms, and eye the group. "Good morning, gentlemen. Lord Dono. Armsman."

They returned a mumble averaging out to *Good morning, Sire,* except for Dono, who stepped forward with his chin up and said in a clear voice, "Thank you for seeing me on such short notice, Sire."

"Ah," said Gregor. "Short notice. Yes." He cast an odd look at By, who blinked demurely. "Please be seated," Gregor went on. He gestured to the leather sofas at the end of the room, and the major-domo hurried to pull around a couple of extra armchairs. Gregor took his usual seat on one of the sofas, turned a little sideways, that he might have full view of his guests' faces in the bright diffuse light from the north-facing windows overlooking his garden.

"I should be pleased to stand, Sire," Armsman Szabo murmured suggestively, but he was not to be permitted to hug the doorway and potential escape; Gregor merely smiled briefly, and pointed at a chair, and Szabo perforce sat, though on the edge. By took a second chair and managed a good simulation of his usual cross-legged ease. Dono sat straight, alert, knees and elbows apart, claiming a space no one disputed; he had the second couch entirely to himself, until Gregor opened an ironic palm, and Ivan was forced to take the place next to him. As far toward the end as possible.

Gregor's face wasn't giving much away, except the obvious fact that the chance of Donna/Dono taking him by surprise had passed sometime in the intervening hours since Ivan's call. Gregor broke the ensuing silence just before Ivan could panic and blurt something.

"So, whose idea was this?"

"Mine, Sire," Lord Dono answered steadily. "My late brother expressed himself forcibly many times—as Szabo and others of the household can witness—that he abhorred the idea of Richars stepping into his place as Count Vorrutyer. If Pierre had not died so suddenly and unexpectedly, he would surely have found a substitute heir. I feel I am carrying out his verbal will."

"So you, ah, claim his posthumous approval."

"Yes. If he had thought of it. Granted, he had no reason to entertain such an extreme solution while he lived."

"I see. Go on." This was Gregor in his classic give-them-enough-rope-to-hang-themselves mode, Ivan recognized. "What support did you assure yourself of, before you left?" He glanced rather pointedly at Armsman Szabo.

"I secured the approval of my Arms—of my late brother's Armsmen, of course," said Dono. "Since it was their duty to guard the disputed property until my return."

"You took their oaths?" Gregor's voice was suddenly very mild.

Ivan cringed. To receive an Armsman's oath before one was confirmed as a Count or Count's heir was a serious crime, a violation of one of the subclauses of Vorlopulous's Law which, among other things, had restricted a Count's Armsmen to a mere squad of twenty. Lord Dono gave Szabo the barest nod.

"We gave our personal words," Szabo put in smoothly. "Any man may freely give his personal word for his personal acts, Sire."

"Hm," said Gregor.

"Beyond the Vorrutyer Armsmen, the only two people I informed were my attorney, and my cousin By," Lord Dono continued. "I needed my attorney to put certain legal arrangements into motion, check all the details, and prepare the necessary documents. She and all her records are entirely at your disposal, of course, Sire. I'm sure you understand the tactical necessity for surprise. I told no one else before I left, lest Richars take warning and also prepare."

"Except for Byerly," Gregor prompted.

"Except for By," Dono agreed. "I needed someone I could trust in the capital to keep an eye on Richars's moves while I was out of range and incapacitated."

"Your loyalty to your cousin is most . . . notable, Byerly," murmured Gregor.

By eyed him warily. "Thank you, Sire."

"And your remarkable discretion. I do take note of it."

"It seemed a personal matter, Sire."

"I see. Do go on, Lord Dono."

Dono hesitated fractionally. "Has ImpSec passed you my Betan medical files yet?"

"Just this morning. They were apparently a little delayed."

"You mustn't blame that nice ImpSec boy who was following me. I'm afraid he found Beta Colony a trifle overwhelming. And I'm sure the Betans didn't offer them up voluntarily, especially since I told them not to." Dono smiled blandly. "I'm glad to see he rose to the challenge. One would hate to think ImpSec was losing its old edge, after Illyan's retirement."

Gregor, listening with his chin in his hand, gave a little wave of his fingers in acknowledgement of this, on all its levels.

"If you've had a chance to glance over the records," Dono went on, "you will know I am now fully functional as a male, capable of carrying out my social and biological duty of siring the next Vorrutyer heir. Now that the requirement of male primogeniture has been met, I claim the nearest right by blood to the Countship of the Vorrutyer's District, and in light of my late brother's expressed views, I claim Count's choice as well. Peripherally, I also assert that I will make a better Count than my cousin Richars, and that I will serve my District, the Imperium, and you more competently than he ever could. For evidence, I submit my work in the District on Pierre's behalf over the last five years."

"Are you proposing other charges against Richars?" asked Gregor.

"Not at present. The one charge of sufficient seriousness lacked sufficient proof to bring to trial at the time—" Dono and Szabo exchanged a glance.

"Pierre requested an ImpSec investigation of his fiancée's flyer accident. I remember reading the synopsis of the report. You are correct. There was no proof."

Dono managed to shrug acknowledgement without agreement. "As for Richars's lesser offenses, well, no one cared before, and I doubt they'll start caring now. I will not be charging that he is unfit—though I think he is unfit—but rather, maintaining that I am more fit and have the better right. And so I will lay it before the Counts."

"And do you expect to obtain any votes?"

"I would expect a certain small number of votes against Richars from his personal enemies even if I were a horse. For the rest, I propose to offer myself to the Progressive party as a future voting member."

"Ah?" Gregor glanced up at this. "The Vorrutyers were traditionally mainstays of the Conservatives. Richars was expected to maintain that tradition."

"Yes. My heart goes out to the old guard; they were my father's party, and his father's before him. But I doubt many of their hearts will go out to me. Besides, they are a present minority. One must be practical."

Right. And while Gregor was careful to maintain a façade of Imperial even-handedness, no one had any doubt the Progressives were the party he privately favored. Ivan chewed on his lip.

"Your case is going to create an uproar in the Council at an awkward time, Lord Dono," said Gregor. "My credit with the Counts is fully extended right now in pushing through the appropriations for the Komarran solar mirror repairs."

Dono answered earnestly, "I ask nothing of you, Sire, but your neutrality. Don't quash my motion of impediment. And don't permit the Counts to dismiss me unheard, or hear me only in secret. I want a public debate and a public vote."

Gregor's lips twisted, contemplating this vision. "Your case could set a most peculiar precedent, Lord Dono. With which I would then have to live."

"Perhaps. I would point out that I am playing exactly by the old rules."

"Well . . . perhaps not *exactly*," murmured Gregor.

By put in, "May I suggest, Sire, that if in fact dozens of Counts' sisters were itching to stampede out to galactic medical facilities and return to Barrayar to attempt to step into their brothers' boots, it would have likely happened before now? As a precedent, I doubt it would be all that popular, once the novelty wore off."

Dono shrugged. "Prior to our conquest of Komarr, access to that sort of medicine was scarcely available. Someone had to be the first. It wouldn't even have been me if things had gone differently for poor Pierre." He glanced across at Gregor, eye to eye. "Though I will certainly not be the last. Quashing my case, or brushing it aside, won't settle anything. If nothing else, taking it through the full legal process will force the Counts to explicitly examine their assumptions, and rationalize a set of laws which have managed to ignore the changing times for far too long. You cannot expect to run a galactic empire with rules that haven't been revised or even reviewed since the Time of Isolation." That awful cheerful leer ignited Lord Dono's face suddenly. "In other words, it will be good for them."

A very slight smile escaped Gregor in return, not entirely voluntarily, Ivan thought. Lord Dono was playing Gregor just right—frank, fearless, and up front. But then, Lady Donna had always been observant.

Gregor looked Lord Dono over, and pressed his hand to the bridge of his nose, briefly. After a moment he said ironically, "And will you be wanting a wedding invitation too?"

Dono's brows flicked up. "If I am Count Vorrutyer by then, my attendance will be both my right and my duty. If I'm not—well, then." After a slight silence, he added wistfully, "Though I always did like a good wedding. I had three. Two were disasters. It's so much nicer to watch, saying over and over to yourself, *It's not me! It's not me!* One can be happy all day afterward on that alone."

Gregor said dryly, "Perhaps your next one will be different."

Dono's chin lifted. "Almost certainly, Sire."

Gregor sat back, and stared thoughtfully at the crew arrayed before him. He tapped his fingers on the sofa arm. Dono waited gallantly, By nervously, Szabo stolidly. Ivan spent the time wishing he were invisible, or that he'd never run across By in that damned bar, or that he'd never met Donna, or that he'd never been born. He waited for the ax, whatever it was going to be, to fall, and wondered which way he ought to dodge.

Instead what Gregor said at last was, "So . . . what's it like?"

Dono's white grin flashed in his beard. "From the inside? My energy's up. My libido's up. I would say it makes me feel ten years younger, except I didn't feel like this when I was thirty, either. My temper's shorter. Otherwise, only the world has changed."

"Ah?"

"On Beta Colony, I scarcely noticed a thing. By the time I got to Komarr, well, the personal space people gave me had approximately doubled, and their response time to me had been cut in half. By the time I hit the Vorbarr Sultana Shuttleport, the change was phenomenal. Somehow, I don't think I got all that result just from my exercise program."

"Huh. So . . . if your motion of impediment fails, will you change back?"

"Not any time soon. I must say, the view from the top of the food chain promises to be downright panoramic. I propose to have my blood and money's worth of it."

Another silence fell. Ivan wasn't sure if everyone was digesting this declaration, or if their minds had all simply shorted out.

"All right . . ." said Gregor slowly at last.

The look of growing curiosity in his eyes made Ivan's skin crawl. *He's going to say it, I just know he is . . .*

"Let's see what happens." Gregor sat back, and gave another little wave of his fingers, as if to speed them on their way. "Carry on, Lord Dono."

"Thank you, Sire," said Dono sincerely.

No one waited around for Gregor to reiterate this dismissal. They all beat a prudent retreat to the corridor before the Emperor could change his mind. Ivan thought he could feel Gregor's eyes boring wonderingly into his back all the way out the door.

"Well," By exhaled brightly, as the major-domo led them down the corridor once more. "That went better than I'd expected."

Dono gave him a sidelong look. "What, was your faith failing, By? I think things went quite as well as I'd hoped for."

By shrugged. "Let's say, I was feeling a bit out of my usual depth."

"That's why we asked Ivan for help. For which I thank you once more, Ivan."

"It was nothing," Ivan denied. "I didn't do anything." *It's not my fault.* He didn't know why Gregor had put him on his short list for this meeting; the Emperor hadn't even asked him anything. Though Gregor was as bad as Miles for plucking clues out of, as far as Ivan could tell, thin air. He couldn't imagine what Gregor had construed from all this. He didn't *want* to imagine what Gregor had construed from all this.

The syncopated clomp of all their boots echoed as they rounded the corner into the East Wing. A calculating look entered Lord Dono's eyes, which put Ivan briefly in mind of Lady Donna, in the least reassuring way. "So what's your mama doing in the next few days, Ivan?"

"She's busy. Very busy. All this wedding stuff, you know. Long hours. I scarcely see her except at work, anymore. Where we are all very busy."

"I have no wish to interrupt her work. I need something more . . . casual. When were you going to see her again not at work?"

"Tomorrow night, at my cousin Miles's dinner party for Kareen and Mark. He told me to bring a date. I said I'd be bringing you as my guest. He was delighted." Ivan brooded on this lost scenario.

"Why, thank you, Ivan!" said Dono promptly. "How thoughtful of you. I accept."

"Wait, no, but that was before—before you—before I knew you—" Ivan sputtered, and gestured at Lord Dono in his new morphology. "I don't think he'll be so delighted now. It will mess up his seating arrangements."

"What, with *all* the Koudelka girls coming? I don't see how. Though I suppose some of them have taken young men in tow by now."

"I don't know about that, except for Delia and Duv Galeni. And if Kareen and Mark aren't—never mind. But I think Miles is trying to slant the sex ratio, to be on the safe side. It's really a party to introduce everyone to his gardener."

"I beg your pardon?" said Dono. They fetched up in the vestibule by the Residence's east doors. The major-domo waited patiently to see the visitors out, in that invisible and unpressing way he could project so well. Ivan was sure he was taking in every word to report to Gregor later.

"His gardener. Madame Vorsoisson. She's this Vor widow he's gone and lost his mind over. He hired her to put a garden in that lot next to Vorkosigan House. She's Lord Auditor Vorthys's niece, if you must know."

"Ah. Quite eligible, then. But how unexpected. Miles Vorkosigan, in love at last? I'd always thought Miles would fancy a galactic. He always gave one the feeling most of the women around here bored him to death. One was never quite certain it wasn't sour grapes, though. Unless it was self-fulfilling prophecy." Lord Dono's smile was briefly feline.

"It was getting a galactic to fancy Barrayar that was the hang-up, I gather," said Ivan stiffly. "Anyway, Lord Auditor Vorthys and his wife will be there, and Illyan with my mother, and the Vorbrettens, as well as all the Koudelkas and Galeni and Mark."

"René Vorbretten?" Dono's eyes narrowed with interest, and he exchanged a glance with Szabo, who gave a tiny nod in return. "I'd like to talk to *him*. He's a pipeline into the Progressives."

"Not this week, he's not." By smirked. "Didn't you hear what Vorbretten found dangling in his family tree?"

"Yes." Lord Dono waved this away. "We all have our little genetic handicaps. I think it would be fascinating to compare notes with him just now. Oh, yes, Ivan, you must bring me. It will be perfect."

For whom? With all that Betan education, Miles was about as personally liberal as it was possible for a Barrayaran Vor male to be, but Ivan still couldn't imagine that he would be thrilled to find Lord Dono Vorrutyer at his dining table.

On the other hand . . . so what? If Miles had something *else* to be irritated about, perhaps it would distract him from that little problem with Vormoncrief and Major Zamori. What better way to confuse the enemy than to multiply the targets? It wasn't as though Ivan would have any obligation to protect Lord Dono from Miles.

Or Miles from Lord Dono, for that matter. If Dono and By considered Ivan, a mere HQ captain, a valuable consultant on the social and political terrain of the capital, how much better a one was a real Imperial Auditor? If Ivan could, as it were, transfer Dono's affections to this new target, he might be able to crawl away entirely unobserved. *Yes.*

"Yes, yes, all right. But this is the last favor I'm going to do for you, Dono, is it understood?" Ivan tried to look stern.

"*Thank* you," said Lord Dono.

Chapter Nine

Miles stared at his reflection in the long antique mirror on his grandfather's former bedroom wall, now his own room, and frowned. His best Vorkosigan House uniform of brown and silver was much too formal for this dinner party. He would surely have an opportunity to squire Ekaterin to some venue for which it was actually appropriate, such as the Imperial Residence or the Council of Counts, and she could see and, he hoped, admire him in it then. Regretfully, he shucked the polished brown boots back off and prepared to return to the clothing he'd started with forty-five minutes before, one of his plain gray Auditor's suits, very clean and pressed. Well, slightly less pressed, now, with another House uniform and two Imperial uniforms from his late service tossed atop it on the bed.

He necessarily cycled back through naked, and frowned uneasily at himself again. Someday, if things went well, he must stand before her in his skin, in this very room and place, with no disguise at all.

A moment of panicked longing for Admiral Naismith's gray-and-whites, put away in the closet one floor above, passed over him. No. Ivan would be certain to hoot at him. Worse, Illyan might say something . . . dry. And it wasn't as though he wanted to explain the little Admiral to his other guests. He sighed, and redonned the gray suit.

Pym stuck his head back through the bedroom door, and smiled in approval, or perhaps relief. "Ah, are you ready now, m'lord? I'll just get these out of your way again, shall I?" The speed with which Pym whipped away the other garments assured Miles he'd made the right choice, or at least, the best choice available to him.

Miles adjusted the thin strip of white shirt collar above the jacket's neck with military precision. He leaned forward to peer suspiciously for gray in his scalp, relocated the couple of strands he'd noted recently, suppressed an impulse to pluck them out, and then combed his hair again. *Enough of this madness.*

He hurried downstairs to recheck the table arrangements in the grand dining room. The table glittered with Vorkosigan cutlery, china, and a forest of wineglasses. The linen was graced with no less than three strategically low, elegant flower arrangements, over which he could see, and which he hoped Ekaterin would enjoy. He'd spent an hour debating with Ma Kosti and Pym over how to properly seat ten women and nine men. Ekaterin would be seated at Miles's right hand, off the head of the table, and Kareen at Mark's, off the foot; that hadn't been negotiable. Ivan would be seated next to his lady guest, in the middle as far from Ekaterin and Kareen as possible, the better to block any possible move of his on anyone else's partner— though Miles trusted Ivan would be fully occupied.

Miles had been an envious bystander to Ivan's brief, meteoric affair with Lady Donna Vorrutyer. In retrospect, he thought perhaps Lady Donna had been more charitable and Ivan less suave than it had seemed to his then-twenty-year-old perspective, but Ivan had certainly made the most of his good luck. Lady Alys, still full of plans for her son's marriage to some more eligible Vor bud, had been a bit rigid about it all; but with all those years of frustrated matchmaking behind her Lady Alys might find Lady Donna looking much better now. After all, with the advent of the uterine replicator and associated galactic biotech, being forty-something was no bar to a woman's reproductive plans at all. Nor being sixty-something, or eighty-something . . . Miles wondered if Ivan had mustered the nerve to ask Lady Alys and Illyan if they had any plans for providing him with a half-sib, or if the possibility hadn't crossed his mind yet. Miles decided he would have to point it out to his cousin at some appropriate moment, preferably when Ivan's mouth was full.

But not tonight. Tonight, everything had to be perfect.

Mark wandered in to the dining room, also frowning. He too was showered and slicked, and dressed in a suit tailored and layered, black on black with black. It lent his short bulk a surprisingly authoritative air. He strolled up the table's side, reading place cards, and reached for a pair.

"Don't even touch them," Miles told him firmly.

"But if I just switch Duv and Delia with Count and Countess Vorbretten, Duv will be as far away from me as we can get him," Mark pleaded. "I can't believe he wouldn't prefer that himself. I mean, as long as he's still next to Delia . . ."

"No. I have to put René next to Lady Alys. It's a favor. He's politicking. Or he damn well should be." Miles cocked his head. "If you're serious about Kareen, you and Duv are going to have to deal, you know. He's going to be one of the family."

"I can't help thinking his feelings about me must be . . . mixed."

"Come now, you saved his life." *Among other things.* "Have you seen him, since you got back from Beta?"

"Once, for about thirty seconds, when I was dropping off Kareen at her home, and he was coming out with Delia."

"So what did he say?"

"He said, *Hello, Mark.*"

"That sounds pretty unexceptionable."

"It was his tone of voice. That dead-level thing he does, y'know?"

"Well, yes, but you can't deduce anything from that."

"Exactly my point."

Miles grinned briefly. And just how serious was Mark about Kareen? He was attentive to her to the point of obsession, and the sense of sexual frustration rising from them both was like heat off a pavement in high summer. Who knew what had passed between them on Beta Colony? *My mother does, probably.* Countess Vorkosigan had better spies than ImpSec did. But if they were sleeping together, it wasn't in Vorkosigan House, according to Pym's informal security reports.

Pym himself entered at this point, to announce, "Lady Alys and Captain Illyan have arrived, m'lord."

This formality was scarcely necessary, as Aunt Alys was right at Pym's elbow, though she nodded brief approval at the Armsman as she passed into the dining room. Illyan strolled in after her, and favored the room with a benign smile. The retired ImpSec chief looked downright dapper, in a dark tunic and trousers that set off the gray at his temples; since their late-life romance had bloomed, Lady Alys had taken a firm hand in improving his somewhat dire civilian wardrobe. The sharp clothes did a lot to camouflage the disturbing vague look that clouded his eyes now and then, damn the enemy who'd so disabled him.

Aunt Alys swept down the table, inspecting the arrangements with a cool air that would have daunted a drill sergeant. "Very good, Miles," she said at last. The *Better than I would have expected of you* was unspoken, but understood. "Though your numbers are uneven."

"Yes, I know."

"Hm. Well, it can't be helped now. I want a word with Ma Kosti. Thank you, Pym, I'll find my way." She bustled out the server's door. Miles let her go, trusting that she would find all in order below, and that she would refrain from prosecuting her ongoing campaign to hire away his cook in the middle of the most important dinner party of his life.

"Good evening, Simon," Miles greeted his former boss. Illyan shook his hand cordially, and Mark's without hesitation. "I'm glad you could make it tonight. Did Aunt Alys explain to you about Eka—about Madame Vorsoisson?"

"Yes, and Ivan had a few comments as well. Something on the theme of fellows who fall into the muck-hole and return with the gold ring."

"I haven't got to the gold ring part yet," said Miles ruefully. "But that's certainly my plan. I'm looking forward to you all meeting her."

"She's the one, is she?"

"I hope so."

Illyan's smile sharpened at Miles's fervent tone. "Good luck, son."

"Thanks. Oh, one word of warning. She's still in her mourning year, you see. Did Alys or Ivan explain—"

He was interrupted by the return of Pym, who announced that the Koudelka party had arrived, and he had conveyed them to the library, as planned. It was time to go play host in earnest.

Mark, who trod on Miles's heels all the way across the house, paused in the antechamber to the great library to give himself a desperate look in the mirror there, and smooth his jacket down over his paunch. In the library, Kou and Drou waited, all smiles; the Koudelka girls were raiding the shelves. Duv and Delia were seated together bent over an old book already.

Greetings were exchanged all around, and Armsman Roic, on cue, began bringing out the hors d'oeuvres and drinks. Over the years Miles had watched Count and Countess Vorkosigan host what seemed a thousand parties and receptions here in Vorkosigan House, scarcely one without some hidden or overt political agenda. Surely he could manage this little one in style. Mark, across the room, made himself properly attentive to Kareen's parents. Lady Alys arrived from her inspection tour, gave her nephew a short nod, and went to hang on Illyan's arm. Miles listened for the door.

His heart beat faster at the sound of Pym's voice and steps, but the next guests the Armsman ushered in were only René and Tatya Vorbretten. The Koudelka girls instantly made Tatya welcome. Things were certainly starting well. At the sound of action at the distant front door again, Miles abandoned René to make what he could of his opportunity with Lady Alys, and slipped out to check for the new arrivals. *This* time it was Lord Auditor Vorthys and his wife, and Ekaterin at last, yes!

The Professor and the Professora were gray blurs in his eyes, but Ekaterin glowed like a flame. She wore a sedate evening dress in some silky charcoal-gray fabric, but she was happily handing off a pair of dirty garden gloves to Pym. Her eyes were bright, and her cheeks bore a faint, exquisite flush. Miles concealed in a welcoming smile his thrill to see the pendant model Barrayar he'd given her lying skin-warmed against her creamy breast.

"Good evening, Lord Vorkosigan," she greeted him. "I'm pleased to report the first native Barrayaran plant is now growing in your garden."

"Clearly, I'll have to inspect it." He grinned at her. What a great excuse to nip out for a quiet moment together. Perhaps it might finally give him occasion to declare . . . no. No. Still much too premature. "Just as soon as I get everyone introduced, here." He offered her his arm, and she took it. Her warm scent made him a little dizzy.

Ekaterin hesitated at the party noise already pouring from the library as they approached, her hand tightening on his arm, but she took a breath, and plunged in with him. Since she already knew Mark and the Koudelka girls, whom Miles trusted would soon make her comfortable again, he made her known first to Tatya, who eyed her with interest and exchanged shy pleasantries. He then took her over to the long doors, took a slight breath himself, and introduced her to René, Illyan, and Lady Alys.

Miles was watching so anxiously for the signs of approval in Illyan's expression that he almost missed the blink of terror in Ekaterin's, as she found herself shaking the hand of the legend who'd run the dreaded Imperial Security for thirty iron years. But she rose to the occasion with scarcely a tremor. Illyan, who seemed blithely unconscious of his sinister effect, smiled upon her with all the admiration Miles could have hoped for.

There. Now people could mill about and drink and talk till it was time to herd them all in to be seated for dinner. Were they all in? No, he was still missing Ivan. And one other—should he send Mark to check—?

Ah, not necessary. Here came Dr. Borgos, all on his own. He poked his head around the door and entered diffidently. To Miles's surprise, he was all washed and combed and dressed in a perfectly respectable suit, if in the Escobaran style, that was entirely free of lab stains. Enrique smiled, and came up to Miles and Ekaterin. He reeked not of chemicals, but of cologne.

"Ekaterin, good evening!" he said happily. "Did you get my dissertation?"

"Yes, thank you."

His smile grew shyer still, and he stared down at his shoe. "Did you like it?"

"It was very impressive. Though it was a bit over my head, I'm afraid."

"I don't believe that. I'm sure you got the gist of it . . ."

"You flatter me, Enrique." She shook her head, but her smile said, *And you may flatter me some more.*

Miles went slightly stiff. *Enrique? Ekaterin? She doesn't even call me by my first name yet!* And she would never have accepted a comment on her physical beauty without flinching; had Enrique stumbled on an unguarded route to her heart that Miles had missed?

She added, "I think I followed the introductory sonnet, almost. Is that the usual style, for Escobaran academic papers? It seems very challenging."

"No, I made it up especially." He glanced up at her again, then down at his other shoe.

"It, um, scanned quite perfectly. Some of the rhymes seemed quite unusual."

Enrique brightened visibly.

Good God, Enrique was writing *poetry* to her? Yes, and why hadn't *he* thought of poetry? Besides the obvious reason of his absence of talent in that direction. He wondered if she'd like to read a really clever combat-drop mission plan, instead. Sonnets, damn. All he'd ever come up with in that line were limericks.

He stared at Enrique, who was now responding to her smile by twisting himself into something resembling a tall knotted bread-stick, with dawning horror. *Another* rival? And insinuated into his own household . . . ! *He's a guest. Your brother's guest, anyway. You can't have him assassinated.* Besides, the Escobaran was only twenty-four standard years old; she must see him as a mere puppy. *But maybe she likes puppies . . .*

"Lord Ivan Vorpatril," Pym's voice announced from the doorway. "Lord Dono Vorrutyer." The odd timbre in Pym's voice jerked Miles's head around even before his brain caught up with the unauthorized name accompanying Ivan. *Who?*

Ivan stood well clear of his new companion, but it was obvious by some remark the other was making that they'd come in together. Lord Dono was an intense-looking fellow of middle height with a close-trimmed black spade-beard, wearing Vor-style mourning garb, a black suit edged with gray which set off his athletic body. Had Ivan made a substitution in Miles's guest list without telling him? He should know better than to violate House Vorkosigan's security procedures like that . . . !

Miles strolled up to his cousin, Ekaterin still beside him—well, he hadn't exactly let go of her hand on his arm, but she hadn't tried to draw it from under his hand, either. Miles thought he knew on sight all his Vorrutyer relatives who could claim a lord's rank. Was this a more distant descendant of Pierre Le Sanguinaire, or some by-blow? The man was not young. Damn, where had he seen those electric brown eyes before . . . ?

"Lord Dono. How do you do." Miles proffered his hand, and the lithe man took it in a cheerful grip. Between one breath and the next the clue dropped, bricklike, and Miles added suavely, "You *have* been to Beta Colony, I perceive."

"Indeed, Lord Vorkosigan." Lord Dono's—Lady Donna who was, yes—white grin broadened in his black beard.

Ivan looked on with betrayed disappointment at this lack of a double-take.

"Or should I say, Lord Auditor Vorkosigan," Lord Dono went on. "I don't believe I've had the chance to congratulate you upon your new appointment."

"Thank you," said Miles. "Permit me to introduce my friend, Madame Ekaterin Vorsoisson . . ."

Lord Dono kissed Ekaterin's hand with slightly too enthusiastic panache, bordering on a mockery of the gesture; Ekaterin returned an uncertain smile. They gavotted through the social niceties, while Miles's wits went on overdrive. Right. Clearly, the former Lady Donna did not have a clone of brother Pierre tucked away in a uterine replicator after all. It was breathtakingly plain what his legal tactic against Pierre's putative heir Richars was going to be instead. *Well, somebody had to try it, sooner or later.* And it would be a privilege to watch. "May I wish you the best of luck in your upcoming suit, Lord Dono?"

"Thank you." Lord Dono met his gaze directly. "Luck, of course, has nothing to do with it. May I discuss it in more detail with you, later on?"

Caution tempered his delight; Miles sidestepped. "I am, of course, but my father's proxy in the Council. As an Auditor, I am obliged to avoid party politics on my own behalf."

"I quite understand."

"But, ah . . . perhaps Ivan could reintroduce you to Count Vorbretten over there. He's dealing with a suit in the Council as well; you could compare valuable notes. And Lady Alys and Captain Illyan, of course. Professora Vorthys would also be extremely interested, I think; don't overlook any comments she might have. She's a noted expert on Barrayaran political history. Carry on, Ivan." Miles nodded demurely disinterested dismissal.

"*Thank* you, Lord Vorkosigan." Lord Dono's eyes were alight with appreciation of all the nuances, as he passed cordially on.

Miles wondered if he could sneak out to the next room and have a laughing fit. Or if he'd better make a vid call . . . He grabbed Ivan in passing, and stood on tiptoe to whisper, "Does Gregor know about this yet?"

"Yes," Ivan returned out of the corner of his mouth. "I made sure of that, first thing."

"Good man. What did he say?"

"Guess."

"*Let's see what happens?*"

"Got it in one."

"Heh." Relieved, Miles let Lord Dono tow Ivan off.

"Why are you laughing?" Ekaterin asked him.

"I am not laughing."

"Your eyes are laughing. I can tell."

He glanced around. Lord Dono had buttonholed René, and Lady Alys and Illyan were circling in curiously. The Professor and Commodore Koudelka were off in a corner discussing, from the snatches of words Miles could overhear, quality control problems in military procurement. He motioned Roic to bring wine, led Ekaterin into the remaining free corner, and brought her up to speed on Lady Donna/Lord Dono and the impending motion of impediment in as few words as he could manage.

"Goodness." Ekaterin's eyes widened, and her left hand stole to touch the back of her right, as if the pressure of Lord Dono's kiss still lingered there. But she managed to keep her other reactions to no more than a quick glance down the room, where Lord Dono was now attracting a crowd including all the Koudelka girls and their mother. "Did you know about this?"

"Not at all. That is, everyone knew she'd spiked Richars and gone to Beta Colony, but not why. It makes perfect sense now, in an absurd kind of way."

"Absurd?" said Ekaterin doubtfully. "I should think it would have taken a great deal of courage." She took a sip of her drink, then added in a thoughtful tone, "And anger."

Miles back-pedaled quickly. "Lady Donna never suffered fools gladly."

"Really?" Ekaterin, an odd look in her eyes, drifted away down the room toward this new show.

Before he could follow her, Ivan appeared at his elbow, a glass of wine already half-empty in his hand. Miles didn't want to talk with Ivan. He wanted to talk with *Ekaterin*. He murmured nonetheless, "That's quite a date you brought. I would never have suspected you of such Betan breadth of taste, Ivan."

Ivan glowered at him. "I might have known I'd get no sympathy from you."

"Bit of a shock, was it?"

"I damn near passed out right there in the shuttleport. Byerly Vorrutyer set me up for it, the little sneak."

"By knew?"

"Sure did. In on it from the beginning, I gather."

Duv Galeni too drifted up, in time to hear this; seeing Duv detached from Delia at last, his future father-in-law Commodore Koudelka and the Professor joined them. Miles let Ivan explain the new arrival, in his own words. Miles's guess was confirmed that Ivan hadn't had any hint of this at the time he'd asked his host's permission to bring Donna to the dinner, smugly plotting his welcome-home campaign upon her, well, not virtue; oh, oh, oh, to have been the invisible eye at the moment Ivan discovered the change . . . !

"Did this catch ImpSec by surprise too?" Commodore Koudelka inquired blandly of Commodore Galeni.

"Wouldn't know. Not my department." Galeni took a firm sip of his wine. "Domestic Affairs' problem."

Both officers glanced around at a peal of laughter from the group at the far end of the room; it was Madame Koudelka's laugh. An echoing cascade of giggles hushed conspiratorially, and Olivia Koudelka glanced over her shoulder at the men.

"What *are* they laughing at?" said Galeni doubtfully.

"Us, probably," growled Ivan, and slouched off to find more wine for his empty glass.

Koudelka stared down the room, and shook his head. "Donna Vorrutyer, good God."

Every woman in the party including Lady Alys was now clustered in evident fascination around Lord Dono, who was gesturing and holding forth to them in lowered tones. Enrique was grazing the hors d'oeuvres, and staring at Ekaterin in bovine rapture. Illyan, abandoned by Alys, was leafing absently through a book, one of the illustrated herbals Miles had laid out earlier.

It was time to serve dinner, Miles decided firmly. Where Ivan *and* Lord Dono would be barricaded behind a wall of older, married ladies and their spouses. He broke away for a quiet word with Pym, who departed to pass the word belowstairs, and returned shortly to formally announce the meal.

The couples resorted themselves and shuffled out of the great library, across the anteroom and the paved hall, and through the intervening series of chambers. Miles, in the lead with Ekaterin recaptured on his arm, encountered Mark and Ivan conspiratorially exiting the formal dining room. They turned around and rejoined the throng. Miles's sudden suspicion was horribly confirmed, out of the corner of his eye, as he passed up the table; his hour of strategic planning with the place cards had just been disarranged.

All his carefully rehearsed conversational gambits were for people now on the other end of the table. Seating was utterly randomized—no, not randomized, he realized. Reprioritized. Ivan's goal had clearly been to get Lord Dono as far away from himself as possible; Ivan now was taking his chair at the far end of the table by Mark, while Lord Dono seated himself in the place Miles had intended for René Vorbretten. Duv, Drou, and Kou had somehow all migrated Miles-ward, farther from Mark. Mark still kept Kareen at *his* right hand, but Ekaterin had been bumped down the other side of the table, beyond Illyan, who was still on Miles's immediate left. It seemed no one had quite dared touch Illyan's card. Miles would now have to speak across Illyan to converse with her, no *sotto voce* remarks possible.

Aunt Alys, looking a little confused, seated herself at Miles's honored right, directly across from Illyan. She'd clearly noticed the switches, but failed Miles's last hope of help by saying nothing, merely letting her eyebrows flick up. Duv Galeni found his future mother-in-law Drou between himself and Delia. Illyan glanced at the cards and seated Ekaterin between himself and Duv, and the *accompli* was *fait*.

Miles kept smiling; Mark, ten places distant, was too far away to catch the *I-will-get-you-for-this-later* edge to it. Maybe it was just as well.

Conversations, though not the ones Miles had anticipated, began anew around the table as Pym, Roic, and Jankowski, playing butler and footmen, bustled about and began to serve. Miles watched Ekaterin with some concern for signs of stress, trapped as she was between her formidable ImpSec seatmates, but her expression remained calm and pleasant as the Armsmen plied her with excellent food and wine.

It wasn't until the second course appeared that Miles realized what was bothering him about the food. He had confidently left the details to Ma Kosti, but this wasn't quite the menu they'd discussed. Certain items were . . . different. The hot consommé was now an exquisite cold creamy fruit soup, decorated with edible flowers. In honor of Ekaterin, maybe? The vinegar-and-herb salad dressing had been replaced by something with a pale, creamy base.

The aromatic herb spread, passed around with the bread, bore no relation to butter . . .

Bug vomit. They've slipped in that damned bug vomit.

Ekaterin twigged to it, too, about the time Pym brought round the bread; Miles spotted it by her slight hesitation, glance through her lashes at Enrique and Mark, and completely dead-pan continuation in spreading her piece and taking a firm bite. By not the smallest other sign did she reveal that she knew what she was swallowing.

Miles tried to indicate to her that she didn't have to eat it by pointing surreptitiously at the little herbed bug-butter crock and desperately raising his eyebrows; she merely smiled and shrugged.

"Hm?" Illyan, between them, murmured with his mouth full.

"Nothing, sir," Miles said hastily. "Nothing at all." Leaping up and screaming, *Stop, stop, you're all eating hideous bug stuff!* to his high-powered guests, would be . . . startling. Bug vomit wasn't, after all, poisonous. If nobody told them, they'd never know. He bit into dry bread, and chased it with a large gulp of wine.

The salad plates were removed. Three-quarters of the way down the table, Enrique dinged on his wineglass with his knife, cleared his throat, and stood up.

"Thank you for your attention . . ." He cleared his throat again. "I've enjoyed the hospitality of Vorkosigan House, as I'm sure we all have tonight—" agreeing murmurs rose around the table; Enrique brightened and burbled on. "I have a gift of thanks I would like to present to Lord—to Miles, Lord Vorkosigan," he smiled at his successful precision, "and I thought that now would be a good time."

Miles was seized with certainty that whatever it was, now would be a *terrible* time. He stared down-table at Mark with an inquiring glower, *Do you know what the hell this is all about?* Mark returned an unreassuring *No clue, sorry,* shrug, and eyed Enrique with growing concern.

Enrique removed a box from his jacket and trod up the room to lay it between Miles and Lady Alys. Illyan and Galeni, across the table, tensed in ImpSec-trained paranoia; Galeni's chair slid back slightly. Miles wanted to reassure them that it wasn't likely to be explosive, but with Enrique, how could one be sure? It was bigger than the last box the butter-bug crew had presented to him. Miles prayed for maybe one of those tacky sets of gold-plated dress spurs that had been a brief rage a year ago, mostly among young men who'd never crossed a horse in their lives, anything but . . .

Enrique proudly lifted the lid. It wasn't a bigger butter bug; it was three butter bugs. Three butter bugs whose carapaces flashed brown and silver as they scrabbled over one another, feelers waving . . . Lady Alys recoiled and strangled a squeak; Illyan jerked upright in alarm for her. Lord Dono leaned forward around her in curiosity, and his black brows shot up.

Miles, mouth slightly open, bent to stare in paralyzed fascination. Yes, it was indeed the Vorkosigan crest stenciled in bright silver on each tiny, repulsive brown back; a lace-edge of silver outlined the vestigial wings in exact imitation of the decorations on the sleeves of his Armsmen's uniforms. The replication of his House colors was precise. You could identify the famous crest at a glance. You could probably identify it at a glance from two meters away. Dinner service ground to a halt as Pym, Jankowski, and Roic gathered to look over his shoulder into the box.

Lord Dono glanced from the butter bugs to Miles's face, and back. "Are they . . . are they perhaps a weapon?" he ventured cautiously.

Enrique laughed, and launched into an enthusiastic explanation of his new model butter bugs, complete with the totally unnecessary information that they were the source of the very fine improved bug butter base underlying the soup, salad dressing, and bread spread recipes. Miles's mental picture of Enrique bent over a magnifying glass with a teeny, tiny paintbrush shredded into vapor as Enrique explained that the patterns weren't, oh no, of course not, *applied*, but rather, genetically created, and would breed true with each succeeding generation.

Pym looked at the bugs, glanced at the sleeve of his proud uniform, stared again at the deadly parody of his insignia the creatures now bore, and shot Miles a look of heartbreaking despair, a silent cry which Miles had no trouble interpreting as, *Please, m'lord, please, can we take him out and kill him* now?

From the far end of the table he heard Kareen's worried voice whisper, "What's going on? Why isn't he saying anything? Mark, go look . . ."

Miles leaned back, and grated through his teeth to Pym at the lowest possible volume, "He didn't intend it as an insult." *It just came out that way. My father's, my grandfather's, my House's sigil on those pullulating cockroaches . . . !*

Pym returned him a fixed smile over eyes blazing with fury. Aunt Alys remained rather frozen in place. Duv Galeni had his head cocked to one side, his eyes crinkling and his lips parted in who-knew-what inner reflections, and Miles wasn't about to ask, either. Lord Dono was even worse; he now had his napkin half stuffed into his mouth, and his face was flushed as he snorted through his nose. Illyan watched with his finger to his lips, and almost no expression at all, except for a faint delight in his eyes that made Miles writhe inside. Mark arrived, and bent to look. His face paled, and he glanced sideways at Miles in alarm. Ekaterin had her hand over her mouth; her eyes upon him were dark and wide.

Of all his riveted audience, only one's opinion mattered.

This was the woman whose late unlamented husband had been given over to . . . what displays of temper? What public or private rages? Miles swallowed his gibbering opinion of Enrique, Escobarans, bioengineering, his brother Mark's insane notions of entrepreneurship, and Liveried Vorkosigan Vomit Bugs, blinked, took a deep breath, and smiled.

"Thank you, Enrique. Your talent leaves me speechless. But perhaps you ought to put the girls away now. You wouldn't want them to get . . . tired." Gently, he replaced the lid of the box, and handed it back to the Escobaran. Across from him, Ekaterin softly exhaled. Lady Alys's brows rose in impressed surprise. Enrique marched back happily to his place. Where he proceeded to explain and demonstrate his Vorkosigan butter bugs to everyone who had been seated too far away to see the show, including Count and Countess Vorbretten opposite him. It was a real conversation-stopper, except for an unfortunate crack of laughter from Ivan, quickly choked down at a sharp reproof from Martya.

Miles realized that food had ceased to appear in the previous smooth stream. He motioned the still-transfixed Pym over, and murmured, "Will you bring the next course now, please?" He added in a grim undertone, "*Check* it first."

Pym, jerked back to attention to his duties, muttered, "Yes, m'lord. I understand."

The next course proved to be poached chilled Vorkosigan District lake salmon, without bug butter sauce, just some hastily-cut lemon slices. Good. Miles breathed temporary relief.

Ekaterin at last worked up the nerve to attempt a conversational gambit upon one of her seatmates. One couldn't very well ask an ImpSec officer, *So, how was work today?* so she fell back on what she clearly thought was a more generalized opener. "It's unusual to meet a Komarran in the Imperial Service," she said to Galeni. "Does your family support your career choice?"

Galeni's eyes widened just slightly, and narrowed again at Miles, who realized belatedly that his predinner briefing to Ekaterin, designed to accentuate the positive, hadn't included the fact that most of Galeni's family had died in various Komarran revolts and their aftermaths. And the peculiar relation between Duv and Mark was something he hadn't even begun to figure out how to broach to her. He was frantically trying to guess how to telepathically convey this to Duv, when Galeni replied merely, "My new one does." Delia, who had stiffened in alarm, melted in a smile.

"Oh." It was instantly apparent from Ekaterin's face that she knew she'd misstepped, but not how. She glanced at Lady Alys, who, perhaps still stunned by the butter bugs, was bemusedly studying her plate and missed the silent plea.

Never one to let a damsel flounder in distress, Commodore Koudelka cut in heartily, "So, Miles, speaking of Komarr, do you think their solar mirror repair appropriations are going to fly in Council?"

Oh, perfect segue. Miles flashed his old mentor a brief smile of gratitude. "Yes, I think so. Gregor's thrown his weight behind it, as I'd hoped he would."

"Good," said Galeni judiciously. "That will help on all sides." He gave Ekaterin a short, forgiving nod.

The difficult moment passed; in the relieved pause while people marshaled their contributory bits of political gossip to follow up this welcome lead, Enrique Borgos's cheerful voice floated up the table, disastrously clear:

"—will make so much profit, Kareen, you and Mark can buy yourselves another one of those amazing trips to the Orb when you get back to Beta. As many as you want, in fact." He sighed enviously. "I wish *I* had somebody to go there with."

The Orb of Unearthly Delights was one of Beta Colony's most famous, or notorious, pleasure domes; it had a galactic reputation. If your tastes weren't quite vile enough to direct you on to Jackson's Whole, the range of licensed, medically supervised pleasures which could be purchased at the Orb was enough to boggle most minds. Miles entertained a brief, soaring hope that Kareen's parents had never heard of it. Mark could pretend it was a Betan science museum, anything but—

Commodore Koudelka had just taken a mouthful of wine to chase his last bite of salmon. The atomized spray arced nearly to Delia, seated across from her father. A lungful of wine in a man that age was an alarming event in any case; Olivia patted his back in hesitant worry, as he buried his reddening face in his napkin and gasped. Drou half-pushed her chair back, as she hesitated between going up around the table to assist her husband or, possibly, down the table to strangle Mark. Mark was no help at all; guilty terror drained his fat cheeks of blood, producing a suety, unflattering effect.

Kou got just enough breath back to gasp at Mark, "*You* took *my* daughter to the *Orb*?"

Kareen, utterly panicked, blurted, "It was part of his therapy!"

Mark, panicked worse, added in desperate exculpation, "We got a Clinic discount . . ."

Miles had often thought that he wanted to be there to see the look on Duv Galeni's face when he learned that Mark was his potential brother-in-law. Miles now took the wish back, but it was too late. He'd seen Galeni look frozen before, but never so . . . *stuffed*. Kou was breathing again, which would be reassuring if it weren't for the slight tinge of hyperventilation. Olivia stifled a nervous giggle. Lord Dono's eyes were bright with appreciation; he surely knew all about the Orb, possibly in both his current and former sexual incarnations. The Professora, next to Enrique, leaned forward to take a curious look up and down the table.

Ekaterin looked terribly worried, but not, Miles noted, surprised. Had Mark confided history to her that he hadn't seen fit to trust to his own brother? Or had she and Kareen already become close enough friends to share such secrets, one of those women-things? And if so, what had Ekaterin seen fit to confide to Kareen in return about *him*, and was there any way he could find out . . . ?

Drou, after a notable hesitation, sank back down. An ominous, blighted we-will-discuss-this-later silence fell.

Lady Alys was alive to every nuance; her social self-control was such that only Miles and Illyan were close enough to her to detect her wince. Well able to set a tone no one dared ignore, she weighed in at last with, "The presentation of the mirror repair as a wedding gift has proven most popular with—Miles, *what* has that animal got in its mouth?"

Miles's confused query of *What animal?* was answered before he even voiced it by the thump of multiple little feet across the dining room's polished floor. The half-grown black-and-white kitten was being chased by its all-black litter mate; for a catlet with its mouth stuffed full, it managed to emit an astonishingly loud *mrowr* of possession. It scrabbled across the wide oak boards, then gained traction on the priceless antique hand-woven carpet, till it caught a claw and flipped itself over. Its rival promptly pounced upon it, but failed to force it to give up its prize. A couple of insectoid legs waved feebly among the quivering white whiskers, and a brown-and-silver wing carapace gave a dying shudder.

"My butter bug!" cried Enrique in horror, shoved back his chair, and pounced, rather more effectively, on the feline culprit. "Give it up, you murderess!" He retrieved the mangled bug, much the worse for wear, from the jaws of death. The black kitten stretched itself up his leg, and waved a frantic paw, *Me, me, give me one too!*

Excellent! thought Miles, smiling fondly at the kittens. *The vomit bugs have a natural predator after all!* He was just evolving a rapid-deployment plan for Vorkosigan House's guardcats when his brain caught up with itself. The kitten had already had the butter bug in its mouth when it had scampered into the dining room. Therefore—

"Dr. Borgos, where did that cat find that bug?" Miles asked. "I thought you had them all locked down. In fact," he glanced down the table at Mark, "you promised me they would be."

"Ah . . ." Enrique said. Miles didn't know what chain of thought the Escobaran was thumbing down, but he could see the jerk when he got to the end. "Oh. Excuse me. There's something I have to check in the lab." Enrique smiled unreassuringly, dropped the kitten on his vacated chair, spun on his heel, and hurried out of the dining room toward the back stairs.

Mark said hastily, "I think I'd better go with him," and followed.

Filled with foreboding, Miles set his napkin down, and murmured quietly, "Aunt Alys, Simon, take over for me, would you?" He joined the parade, pausing only long enough to direct Pym to serve more wine. Lots more. Immediately.

Miles caught up with Enrique and Mark at the door of the laundry-cum-laboratory one floor below just in time to hear the Escobaran's cry of *Oh, no!* Grimly, he shouldered past Mark to find Enrique kneeling by a large tray, one of the butter bug houses, which now lay at an angle between the box upon which it had been perched, and the floor. Its screen top was knocked askew. Inside, a single Vorkosigan-liveried butter bug, which was missing two legs on one side, scrambled about in forlorn circles but failed to escape over the side-wall.

"What happened?" Miles hissed to Enrique.

"They're *gone*," Enrique replied, and began to crawl around the floor, looking under things. "Those cursed cats must have knocked the tray over. I'd pulled it out to select your presentation bugs. I wanted the biggest and best. It was all right when I left it . . ."

"*How many* bugs were in this tray?"

"All of them, the entire genetic grouping. About two hundred individuals."

Miles stared around the lab. No Vorkosigan-liveried bugs were visible anywhere. He thought about what a large, old, creaky structure Vorkosigan House really was. Cracks in the floors, cracks in the walls, tiny fissures of access everywhere; spaces under the floorboards, behind the wainscoting, up in the attics, inside the old plastered walls . . .

The worker bugs, Mark had said, *would just wander about till they died, end of story* . . . "You still have the queen, presumably? You can, ah, recover your genetic resource, eh?" Miles began to walk slowly along the walls, staring down intently. No brown-and-silver flashes caught his straining eye.

"Um," said Enrique.

Miles chose his words carefully. "You assured me the queens couldn't move."

"*Mature* queens can't move, that's true," Enrique explained, climbing to his feet again, and shaking his head. "*Immature* queens, however, can scuttle like lightning."

Miles thought it through; it took only a split-second. Vorkosigan-liveried vomit bugs. Vorkosigan-liveried vomit bugs *all over Vorbarr Sultana.*

There was an ImpSec trick, which involved grabbing a man by the collar and giving it a little half-twist, and doing a thing with the knuckles; applied correctly, it cut off both blood circulation and breath. Miles was absently pleased to see that he hadn't lost his touch, despite his new civilian vocation. He drew Enrique's darkening face down toward his own. Kareen, breathless, arrived at the lab door.

"Borgos. You will have every one of those god-damned vomit bugs, and *especially* their queen, retrieved and accounted for at least six hours before Count and Countess Vorkosigan are due to walk in the door tomorrow afternoon. Because five hours and fifty-nine minutes before my parents arrive here, I am calling in a professional exterminator to take care of the infestation, that means any and all vomit bugs left outstanding, do you understand? No exceptions, no mercy."

"*No, no!*" Enrique managed to wail, despite his lack of oxygen. "You *mustn't . . .*"

"Lord Vorkosigan!" Ekaterin's shocked voice came from the door. It had some of the surprise effect of being hit from ambush by a stunner beam. Miles's hand sprang guiltily open, and Enrique staggered upright again, drawing breath in a huge strangled wheeze.

"Don't stop on my account, Miles," said Kareen coldly. She stalked into the lab, Ekaterin behind her. "Enrique, you idiot, how *could* you mention the Orb in front of my parents! Have you no sense?"

"You've known him for this long, and you have to ask?" said Mark direfully.

"And how did you—" her angry gaze swung to Mark, "how did he find out about it anyway—Mark?"

Mark shrank slightly.

"Mark never said it was a secret—I thought it sounded romantic. Lord Vorkosigan, please! Don't call an exterminator! I'll get the girls all back, I promise! Somehow—" Tears welled in Enrique's eyes.

"Calm down, Enrique!" Ekaterin said soothingly. "I'm sure," she cast Miles a doubtful look, "Lord Vorkosigan won't order your poor bugs killed. You'll find them again."

"I have a *time* limit here . . ." Miles muttered through his teeth. He could just picture the scene, tomorrow afternoon or evening, of himself explaining to the returning Viceroy and Vicereine just what those tiny retching noises coming from their walls were. Maybe he could shove the task of apprising them onto Mark—

"If you like, Enrique, I'll stay and help you hunt," Ekaterin volunteered sturdily. She frowned at Miles.

The sensation was like an arrow through his heart, *Urk.* Now *there* was a scenario: Ekaterin and Enrique with their heads heroically, and closely, bent together to save the Poor Bugs from the evil threats of the villainous Lord Vorkosigan . . . Grudgingly, he back-pedaled. "After dinner," he suggested. "We'll all come back after dinner and help." Yes, if anyone was going to crawl around on the floor hunting bugs alongside Ekaterin, it would be him, dammit. "The Armsmen too." He pictured Pym's joy at the news of this task, and cringed inside. "For now, perhaps we had better return and make polite conversation and all that," Miles went on. "Except Dr. Borgos, who will be busy."

"I'll stay and help him," Mark offered brightly.

"What?" cried Kareen. "And send me back up there with my parents all alone? *And* my sisters—I'll never hear the end of this from them . . ."

Miles shook his head in exasperation. "Why in God's name did you take Kareen to the Orb in the first place, Mark?"

Mark stared at him in disbelief. "Why d'you *think*?"

"Well . . . yes . . . but surely you knew it wasn't, um, wasn't, um . . . proper for a young Barrayaran la—"

"Miles, you howling hypocrite!" said Kareen indignantly. "When Gran' Tante Naismith told us you'd been there yourself—*several* times . . . !"

"That was duty," Miles said primly. "It's astounding how much interstellar military and industrial espionage gets filtered through the Orb. You'd better believe Betan security tracks it, too."

"Oh, yeah?" said Mark. "And are we also supposed to believe you never once sampled the services while you were waiting for your contacts—?"

Miles could recognize the moment for a strategic retreat when he saw it. "I think we should all go eat dinner now. Or it will burn up or dry out or something, and Ma Kosti will be very angry with us for spoiling her presentation. And she'll go work for Aunt Alys instead, and we'll all have to go back to eating Reddi-Meals."

This hideous threat reached both Mark and Kareen. Yes, and who *had* inspired his cook to come up with all those tasty bug butter recipes? Ma Kosti surely hadn't volunteered on her own. It reeked of conspiracy.

He exhaled, and offered his arm to Ekaterin. After a moment of hesitation, and a worried glance back at Enrique, she took it, and Miles managed to get them all marshaled out of the lab and back upstairs to the dining room again without anyone bolting off.

"Was all well, belowstairs, m'lord?" Pym inquired in a concerned undervoice.

"We'll talk about it later," Miles returned, equally *sotto voce*. "Start the next course. And offer more wine."

"Should we wait for Dr. Borgos?"

"No. He'll be occupied."

Pym gave a disquieted twitch, but moved off about his duties. Aunt Alys, bless her etiquette, didn't ask for enlargement, but led the conversation immediately onto neutral topics; her mention of the Emperor's wedding diverted most people's thoughts at once. Possibly excepted were the thoughts of Mark and Commodore Koudelka, who eyed each other in wary silence. Miles wondered if he ought to privately warn Kou what a bad idea it would be to pull his swordstick on Mark, or whether that might do more harm than good. Pym topped up Miles's own wineglass before Miles could explain that his whispered instructions hadn't been meant to apply to himself. What the hell. A certain . . . numbness, was beginning to seem like an attractive state.

He was not at all sure if Ekaterin was having a good time; she'd gone all quiet again, and glanced occasionally toward Dr. Borgos's empty place. Though Lord Dono's remarks made her laugh, twice. The former Lady Donna made a startlingly good-looking man, Miles realized on closer study. Witty, exotic, and just possibly heir to a Countship . . . and, come to think of it, with the most appalling unfair advantage in love-making expertise.

The Armsmen cleared away the plates for the main course, which had been grilled vat beef fillet with a very quick pepper garnish, accompanied by a powerful deep red wine. Dessert appeared: sculpted mounds of frozen creamy ivory substance bejeweled with a gorgeous arrangement of glazed fresh fruit. Miles caught Pym, who had been avoiding his eye, by the sleeve in passing, and leaned over for a word behind his hand.

"Pym, is that what I think it is?"

"Couldn't be helped, m'lord," Pym muttered back in wary self-exculpation. "Ma Kosti said it was that or nothing. She's still right furious about the sauces, and says she wants a word with you after this."

"Oh. I see. Well. Carry on."

He picked up his spoon, and took a valiant bite. His guests followed suit doubtfully, except for Ekaterin, who regarded her portion with every evidence of surprised delight, and leaned forward to exchange a smile with Kareen, downtable; Kareen returned her a mysterious but triumphant high-sign. To make it even worse, the stuff was meltingly delicious, seeming to lock into every primitive pleasure-receptor in Miles's mouth at once. The sweet and potent golden dessert wine followed it with an aromatic shellburst on his palate that complemented the frozen bug stuff perfectly. He could have cried. He smiled tightly, and drank, instead. His dinner party limped on somehow.

Talk of Gregor and Laisa's wedding allowed Miles to supply a nice, light, amusing anecdote about his duties in obtaining, and transporting, a wedding gift from the people of his District, a life-sized sculpture of a guerilla soldier on horseback done in maple sugar. This won a brief smile from Ekaterin at last, this time toward the right fellow. He mentally marshaled a leading question about gardens to draw her out; she could sparkle, he was sure, if only she had the right straight line. He briefly regretted not priming Aunt Alys for this ploy, which would have been more subtle, but in his original plan, she hadn't been going to be seated right there—

Miles's pause had lasted just a little too long. Genially taking his turn to fill it, Illyan turned to Ekaterin.

"Speaking of weddings, Madame Vorsoisson, how long has Miles been courting you? Have you awarded him a date yet? Personally, I think you ought to string him along and make him work for it."

A chill flush plunged to the pit of Miles's stomach. Alys bit her lip. Even *Galeni* winced.

Olivia looked up in confusion. "I thought we weren't supposed to mention that yet."

Kou, next to her, muttered, "Hush, lovie."

Lord Dono, with malicious Vorrutyer innocence, turned to her and inquired, "What weren't we supposed to mention?"

"Oh, but if Captain Illyan said it, it must be all right," Olivia concluded.

Captain Illyan had his brains blown out last year, thought Miles. *He is not all right. All right is precisely what he is not . . .*

Her gaze crossed Miles's. "Or maybe . . ."

Not, Miles finished silently for her.

Ekaterin's face, animate and amused moments ago, was turning to sculpted marble. It was not an instantaneous process, but it was relentless, implacable, geologic. The weight of it, pressing on Miles's heart, was crushing. *Pygmalion in reverse; I turn breathing women to white stone. . . .* He knew that bleak and desert look; he'd seen it one bad day on Komarr, and had hoped never to see it in her lovely face again.

Miles's sinking heart collided with his drunken panic. *I can't afford to lose this one, I can't, I can't.* Forward momentum, forward momentum and bluff, those had won battles for him before.

"Yes, ah, heh, quite, well, so, that reminds me, Madame Vorsoisson, I'd been meaning to ask you—will you marry me?"

Dead silence reigned all along the table.

Ekaterin made no response at all, at first. For a moment, it seemed as though she had not even heard his words, and Miles almost yielded to a suicidal impulse to repeat himself more loudly. Aunt Alys buried her face in her hands. Miles could feel his breathless grin grow sickly, and slide down his face. *No, no. What I should have said—what I meant to say was . . . please pass the bug butter? Too late . . .*

She visibly unlocked her throat, and spoke. Her words fell from her lips like ice chips, singly and shattering. "How strange. And here I thought you were interested in gardens. Or so you told me."

You lied to me hung in the air between them, unspoken, thunderously loud.

So yell. Scream. Throw something. Stomp on me all up and down, it'll be all right, it'll hurt good—I can deal with that—

Ekaterin took a breath, and Miles's soul rocketed in hope, but it was only to push back her chair, set her napkin down by her half-eaten dessert, turn, and walk away up the table. She paused by the Professora only long enough to bend down and murmur, "Aunt Vorthys, I'll see you at home."

"But dear, will you be all right . . . ?" The Professora found herself addressing empty air, as Ekaterin strode on. Her steps quickened as she neared the door, till she was almost running. The Professora glanced back and made a helpless, how-could-you-do-this, or maybe that was, how-could-you-do-this-you-idiot, gesture at Miles.

The rest of your life is walking out the door. Do something. Miles's chair fell backwards with a bang as he scrambled out of it. "Ekaterin, wait, we have to talk—"

He didn't run till he passed the doorway, pausing only long enough to slam it, and a couple of intervening ones, shut between the dinner party and themselves. He caught up with her in the entry hall, as she tried the door and fell back; it was, of course, security-locked.

"Ekaterin, wait, listen to me, I can explain," he panted.

She turned to give him a disbelieving stare, as though he were a Vorkosigan-liveried butter bug she'd just found floating in her soup.

"I have to talk to you. You have to talk to me," he demanded desperately.

"Indeed," she said after a moment, white about the lips. "There is something I need to say. Lord Vorkosigan, I resign my commission as your landscape designer. As of this moment, you no longer employ me. I will send the designs and planting schedules on to you tomorrow, to pass on to my successor."

"What good will those do me?!"

"If a garden was what you really wanted from me, then they are all you'll need. Right?"

He tested the possible answers on his tongue. *Yes* was right out. So was *no*. Wait a minute—

"Couldn't I have wanted both?" he suggested hopefully. He continued more strongly, "I wasn't lying to you. I just wasn't saying everything that was on my mind, because, dammit, you weren't ready to hear it, because you aren't half-healed yet from being worked over for ten years by that ass Tien, and I could see it, and you could see it, and even your Aunt Vorthys could see it, and *that's* the truth."

By the jerk of her head, that one had hit home, but she only said, in a dead-level voice, "Please open your door now, Lord Vorkosigan."

"Wait, listen—"

"You have manipulated me enough," she said. "You've played on my . . . my *vanity*—"

"Not vanity," he protested. "Skill, pride, drive—anyone could see you just needed scope, opportunity—"

"You *are* used to getting your own way, aren't you, Lord Vorkosigan. Any way you can." Now her voice was horribly dispassionate. "Trapping me in front of everyone like that."

"That was an accident. Illyan didn't get the word, see, and—"

"Unlike everyone else? You're *worse* than Vormoncrief! I might just as well have accepted *his* offer!"

"Huh? What did Alexi—I mean, no, but, but—whatever you want, I want to give it to you, Ekaterin. Whatever you need. Whatever it is."

"You can't give me my own soul." She stared, not at him, but inward, on what vista he could not imagine. "The garden could have been *my* gift. You took that away too."

Her last words arrested his gibbering. What? Wait, now they were getting down to something, elusive, but utterly vital—

A large groundcar was pulling up outside, under the porte cochère. No more visitors were due; how had they got past the ImpSec gate guard without notification of Pym? Dammit, no interruptions, not *now*, when she was just beginning to open up, or at least open fire—

On the heels of this thought, Pym hurtled through the side doors into the foyer. "Sorry, m'lord—sorry to intrude, but—"

"*Pym.*" Ekaterin's voice was nearly a shout, cracking, defying the tears lacing it. "*Open the damned door and let me out.*"

"*Yes* milady!" Pym snapped to attention, and his hand spasmed to the security pad.

The doors swung wide. Ekaterin stormed blindly through, head-down, into the chest of a startled, stocky, white-haired man wearing a colorful shirt and a pair of disreputable, worn black trousers. Ekaterin bounced off him, and had her hands caught up by the, to her, inexplicable stranger. A tall, tired-looking woman in rumpled travel-skirts, with long roan-red hair tied back at the nape of her neck, stepped up beside them, saying, "What in the world . . . ?"

"Excuse me, miss, are you all right?" the white-haired man rumbled in a raspy baritone. He stared piercingly at Miles, lurching out of the light of the foyer in Ekaterin's wake.

"No," she choked. "I need—I want an auto-cab, please."

"Ekaterin, no, wait," Miles gasped.

"I want an auto-cab *right now.*"

"The gate guard will be happy to call one for you," the red-haired woman said soothingly. Countess Cordelia Vorkosigan, Vicereine of Sergyar—*Mother*—stared even more ominously at her wheezing son. "And see you safely into it. Miles, why are you harrying this young lady?" And more doubtfully, "Are we interrupting business, or pleasure?"

From thirty years of familiarity, Miles had no trouble unraveling this cryptic shorthand to be a serious query of, *Have we walked in on, perhaps, an official Auditorial interrogation gone wrong, or is this one of your personal screw-ups again?* God knew what Ekaterin made of it. One bright note: if Ekaterin never spoke to him again, he'd never be put to explain the Countess's peculiar Betan sense of humor to her.

"My dinner party," Miles grated. "It's just breaking up." *And sinking. All souls feared lost.* It was redundant to ask, *What are you doing here?* His parents' jumpship had obviously made orbit early, and they had left the bulk of their entourage to follow on tomorrow, while they came straight downside to sleep in their own bed. How had he rehearsed this vitally-important, utterly-critical meeting, again? "Mother, Father, let me introduce—*she's getting away!*"

As a new distraction rose from the hallway at Miles's back, Ekaterin slipped through the shadows all the way to the gate. The Koudelkas, having perhaps intelligently concluded that this party was over, were decamping en masse, but the wait-till-we-get-home conversation had undergone a jump-start. Kareen's voice was protesting; the Commodore's overrode it, saying, "You *will* come home now. You're not staying another minute in this house."

"I *have* to come back. I *work* here."

"Not any more, you don't—"

Mark's harried voice dogged along, "Please, sir, Commodore, Madame Koudelka, you mustn't blame Kareen—"

"You can't stop me!" Kareen declaimed.

Commodore Koudelka's eye fell on the returnees as the rolling altercation piled up in the hallway. "Ha—Aral!" he snarled. "Do you realize what your son has been up to?"

The Count blinked. "Which one?" he asked mildly.

The chance of the light caught Mark's face, as he heard this off-hand affirmation of his identity. Even in the chaos of his hopes pinwheeling to destruction, Miles was glad to have seen the brief awed look that passed over those fat-distorted features. *Oh, Brother. Yeah. This is why men follow this man—*

Olivia tugged her mother's sleeve. "Mama," she whispered urgently, "can I go home with Tatya?"

"Yes, dear, I think that might be a good idea," said Drou distractedly, clearly looking ahead; Miles wasn't sure if she was cutting down Kareen's potential allies in the brewing battle, or just the anticipated noise level.

René and Tatya looked as though they would have been glad to sneak out quietly under the covering fire, but Lord Dono, who had somehow attached himself to their party, paused just long enough to say cheerily, "*Thank* you, Lord Vorkosigan, for a most memorable evening." He nodded cordially to Count and Countess Vorkosigan, as he followed the Vorbrettens to their groundcar. Well, the operation hadn't changed Donna/Dono's vile grip on irony, unfortunately . . .

"Who was that?" asked Count Vorkosigan. "Looks familiar, somehow . . ."

A distracted-looking Enrique, his wiry hair half on-end, prowled into the great hall from the back entry. He had a jar in one hand, and what Miles could only dub Stink-on-a-Stick in the other: a wand with a wad of sickly-sweet scent-soaked fiber attached to its end, which he waved along the baseboards. "Here, buggy, buggy," he cooed plaintively. "Come to Papa, that's the good girls . . ." He paused, and peered worriedly under a side-table. "Buggy-buggy . . . ?"

"Now . . . *that* cries out for an explanation," murmured the Count, watching him in arrested fascination.

Out by the front gate, an auto-cab's door slammed; its fans whirred as it pulled away into the night forever. Miles stood still, listening amid the uproar, till the last whisper of it was gone.

"Pym!" The Countess spotted a new victim, and her voice went a little dangerous. "I seconded you to look after Miles. Would you care to explain this scene?"

There was a thoughtful pause. In a voice of simple honesty, Pym replied, "No, Milady."

"Ask Mark," Miles said callously. "He'll explain everything." Head down, he started for the stairs.

"You rat-coward—!" Mark hissed at him in passing.

The rest of his guests were shuffling uncertainly into the hallway.

The Count asked cautiously, "Miles, are you drunk?"

Miles paused on the third step. "Not yet, sir," he replied. He didn't look back. "Not nearly enough yet. Pym, see me."

He took the steps two at a time to his chambers, and oblivion.

Chapter Ten

"Good afternoon, Mark." Countess Vorkosigan's bracing voice spiked Mark's last futile attempts to maintain unconsciousness. He groaned, pulled his pillow from his face, and opened one bleary eye.

He tested responses on his furry tongue. *Countess. Vicereine. Mother.* Strangely enough, *Mother* seemed to work best. "G'fertn'n, M'thur."

She studied him for a moment further, then nodded, and waved at the maid who'd followed in her wake. The girl set down a tea tray on the bedside table and stared curiously at Mark, who had an urge to pull his covers up over himself even though he was still wearing most of last night's clothing. The maid trundled obediently out of Mark's room again at the Countess's firm, "Thank you, that will be all."

Countess Vorkosigan opened the curtains, letting in blinding light, and pulled up a chair. "Tea?" she inquired, pouring without waiting for an answer.

"Yeah, I guess." Mark struggled upright, and rearranged his pillows enough to accept the mug without spilling it. The tea was strong and dark, with cream, the way he liked it, and it scalded the glue out of his mouth.

The Countess poked doubtfully at the empty butter bug tubs piled on the table. Counting them up, perhaps, because she winced. "I didn't think you'd want breakfast yet."

"No. Thank you." Though his excruciating stomach-ache was calming down. The tea actually soothed it.

"Neither does your brother. Miles, possibly driven by his new-found need to uphold Vor tradition, sought *his* anesthetic in wine. Achieved it, too, according to Pym. At present, we're letting him enjoy his spectacular hangover without commentary."

"Ah." *Fortunate son.*

"Well, he'll have to come out of his rooms eventually. Though Aral advises not to look for him before tonight." Countess Vorkosigan poured herself a mug of tea too, and stirred in cream. "Lady Alys was very peeved at Miles for abandoning the field before his guests had all departed. She considered it a shameful lapse of manners on his part."

"It was a shambles." One that, it appeared, they were all going to live through. Unfortunately. Mark took another sluicing swallow. "What happened after . . . after the Koudelkas left?" Miles had bailed out early; Mark's own courage had broken when the Commodore had lost his grip to the point of referring to the Countess's mother as a *damned Betan pimp*, and Kareen had flung out the door proclaiming that she would sooner walk home, or possibly to the other side of the continent, before riding one meter in a car with a pair of such hopelessly uncultured, ignorant, benighted Barrayaran *savages*. Mark had fled to his bedroom with a stack of bug butter tubs and a spoon, and locked the door; Gorge and Howl had done their best to salve his shaken nerves.

Reversion under stress, his therapist would no doubt have dubbed it. He'd half hated, half exulted in the sense of not being in charge in his own body, but letting Gorge run to his limit had blocked the far more dangerous *Other*. It was a bad sign when Killer became nameless. He had managed to pass out before he ruptured, but only just. He felt spent now, his head foggy and quiet like a landscape after a storm.

The Countess continued, "Aral and I had an extremely enlightening talk with Professor and Professora Vorthys—now, *there's* a woman who has her head screwed on straight. I wish I'd made her acquaintance before this. They then left to see after their niece, and we had a longer talk with Alys and Simon." She took a slow sip. "Do I understand correctly that the dark-haired young lady who bolted past us last night was my potential daughter-in-law?"

"Not anymore, I don't think," said Mark morosely.

"Damn." The Countess frowned into her cup. "Miles told us practically nothing about her in his, I think I'm justified in calling them *briefs*, to us on Sergyar. If I'd known then half the things the Professora told me later, I'd have intercepted her myself."

"It wasn't my fault she ran off," Mark hastened to point out. "Miles opened his mouth and jammed his boot in there all by himself." He conceded reluctantly after a moment, "Well, I suppose Illyan helped."

"Yes. Simon was pretty distraught, once Alys explained it all to him. He was afraid he'd been told Miles's big secret and then forgot. *I'm* quite peeved at Miles for setting him up like that." A dangerous spark glinted in her eye.

Mark was considerably less interested in Miles's problems than in his own. He said cautiously, "Has, ah . . . Enrique found his missing queen, yet?"

"Not so far." The Countess hitched around in her chair and looked bemusedly at him. "I had a nice long talk with Dr. Borgos, too, once Alys and Illyan left. He showed me your lab. Kareen's work, I understand. I promised him a stay of Miles's execution order upon his girls, after which he calmed down considerably. I will say, his science seems sound."

"Oh, he's brilliant about the things that get his attention. His interests are a little, um, narrow, is all."

The Countess shrugged. "I've been living with obsessed men for the better part of my life. I think your Enrique will fit right in here."

"So . . . you've met our butter bugs?"

"Yes."

She seemed unfazed; *Betan, you know.* He could wish Miles had inherited more of her traits. "And, um . . . has the Count seen them yet?"

"Yes, in fact. We found one wandering about on our bedside table when we woke up this morning."

Mark flinched. "What did you do?"

"We turned a glass over her and left her to be collected by her papa. Sadly, Aral did not spot the bug exploring his shoe before he put it on. That one we disposed of quietly. What was left of her."

After a daunted silence, Mark asked hopefully, "It wasn't the queen, was it?"

"We couldn't tell, I'm afraid. It appeared to have been about the same size as the first one."

"Mm, then not. The queen would have been noticeably bigger."

Silence fell again, for a time.

"I will grant Kou one point," said the Countess finally. "I do have some responsibility toward Kareen. And toward you. I was perfectly aware of the array of choices that would be available to you both on Beta Colony. Including, happily, each other." She hesitated. "Having Kareen Koudelka as a daughter-in-law would give Aral and me great pleasure, in case you had any doubt."

"I never imagined otherwise. Are you asking me if my intentions are honorable?"

"I trust your honor, whether it fits in the narrowest Barrayaran definition or encompasses something broader," the Countess said equably.

Mark sighed. "Somehow, I don't think the Commodore and Madame Koudelka are ready to greet me with reciprocal joy."

"You *are* a Vorkosigan."

"A clone. An imitation. A cheap Jacksonian knock-off." *And crazy to boot.*

"A bloody expensive Jacksonian knock-off."

"Ha," Mark agreed darkly.

She shook her head, her smile growing more rueful. "Mark, I'm more than willing to help you and Kareen reach for your goals, whatever the obstacles. But you have to give me some clue of what your goals *are.*"

Be careful how you aim this woman. The Countess was to obstacles as a laser cannon was to flies. Mark studied his stubby, plump hands in covert dismay. Hope, and its attendant, fear, began to stir again in his heart. "I want . . . whatever Kareen wants. On Beta, I thought I knew. Since we got back here, it's been all confused."

"Culture clash?"

"It's not just the culture clash, though that's part of it." Mark groped for words, trying to articulate his sense of the wholeness of Kareen. "I think . . . I think she wants *time.* Time to be herself, to be where she is, who she is. Without being hurried or stampeded to take up one role or another, to the exclusion of all the rest of her possibilities. *Wife* is a pretty damned exclusive role, the way they do it here. She says Barrayar wants to put her in a box."

The Countess tilted her head, taking this in. "She may be wiser than she knows."

He brooded. "On the other hand, maybe I was her secret vice, back on Beta. And here I'm a horrible embarrassment to her. Maybe she'd like me to just shove off and leave her alone."

The Countess raised a brow. "Didn't sound like it last night. Kou and Drou practically had to pry her nails out of our door jamb."

Mark brightened slightly. "There is that."

"And how have your goals changed, in your year on Beta? In addition to adding Kareen's heart's desire to your own, that is."

"Not changed, exactly," he responded slowly. "Honed, maybe. Focused. Modified . . . I achieved some things in my therapy I'd despaired of, of ever making come right in my life. It made me think maybe the rest isn't so impossible after all."

She nodded encouragement.

"School . . . economics school was good. I'm getting quite a tool-kit of skills and knowledge, you know. I'm really starting to know what I'm doing, not just faking it all the time." He glanced sideways at her. "I haven't forgotten Jackson's Whole. I've been thinking about indirect ways to shut down the damned butcher cloning lords there. Lilly Durona has some ideas for life-extension therapies that might be able to compete with their clone-brain transplants. Safer, nearly as effective, *and* cheaper. Draw off their customers, disrupt them economically even if I can't touch them physically. Every scrap of spare cash I've been able to amass, I've been dumping into the Durona Group, to support their R and D. I'm going to own a controlling share of them, if this goes on." He smiled wryly. "And I still want enough money left that no one has power over me. I'm beginning to see how I can get it, not overnight, but steadily, bit by bit. I, um . . . wouldn't mind starting a new agribusiness here on Barrayar."

"And Sergyar, too. Aral was very interested in possible applications for your bugs among our colonists and homesteaders."

"*Was* he?" Mark's lips parted in astonishment. "Even with the Vorkosigan crest on them?"

"Mm, it would perhaps be wise to lose the House livery before pitching them seriously to Aral," the Countess said, suppressing a smile.

"I didn't know Enrique was going to do that," Mark offered by way of apology. "Though you should have seen the look on Miles's face, when Enrique presented them to him. It almost made it worth it. . . ." He sighed at the memory, but then shook his head in renewed despair. "But what good is it all, if Kareen and I can't get back to Beta Colony? *She's* stuck for money, if her parents won't support her. I could offer to pay her way, but . . . but I don't know if that's a good idea."

"Ah," said the Countess. "Interesting. Are you afraid Kareen would feel you had purchased her loyalty?"

"I'm . . . not sure. She's very conscientious about obligations. I want a lover. Not a debtor. I think it would be a bad mistake to accidentally . . . put her in another kind of box. I want to give her *everything*. But I don't know how!"

An odd smile turned the Countess's lip. "When you give each other everything, it becomes an even trade. Each wins all."

Mark shook his head, baffled. "An odd sort of Deal."

"The best." The Countess finished her tea and put down her cup, "Well. I don't wish to invade your privacy. But do remember, you're *allowed* to ask for help. It's part of what families are all about."

"I owe you too much already, milady."

Her smile tilted. "Mark, you don't pay back your parents. You can't. The debt you owe them gets collected by your children, who hand it down in turn. It's a sort of entailment. Or if you don't have children of the body, it's left as a debt to your common humanity. Or to your God, if you possess or are possessed by one."

"I'm not sure that seems fair."

"The family economy evades calculation in the gross planetary product. It's the only deal I know where, when you give more than you get, you aren't bankrupted—but rather, vastly enriched."

Mark took this in. And what kind of parent to him was his progenitor-brother? More than a sibling, but most certainly not his mother. . . . "Can you help Miles?"

"That's more of a puzzle." The Countess smoothed her skirts, and rose. "I haven't known this Madame Vorsoisson all her life the way I've known Kareen. It's not at all clear what I *can* do for Miles—I would say *poor boy*, but from everything I've heard he dug his very own pit and jumped in. I'm afraid he's going to have to dig himself back out. Likely it will be good for him." She gave a firm nod, as though a supplicant Miles were already being sent on his way to achieve salvation alone: *Write when you find good works.* The Countess's idea of maternal concern was damned unnerving, sometimes, Mark reflected as she made her way out.

He was conscious that he was sticky, and itchy, and needed to pee and wash. And he had a pressing obligation to go help Enrique hunt for his missing queen, before she and her offspring built a nest in the walls and started making *more* Vorkosigan butter bugs. Instead, he lurched to his comconsole, sat gingerly, and tried the code for the Koudelkas' residence.

He desperately aligned an array of fast talk in four flavors, depending on whether the Commodore, Madame Koudelka, Kareen, or one of her sisters answered the vid. Kareen hadn't called him this morning: was she sleeping, sulking, locked in? Had her parents bricked her up in the walls? Or worse, thrown her out on the street? Wait, no, that would be all right—she could come live *here*—

His subvocalized rehearsals were wasted. *Call Not Accepted* blinked at him in malignant red letters, like a scrawl of blood hovering over the vid plate. The voice-recognition program had been set to screen him out.

Ekaterin had a splitting headache.

It was all that wine last night, she decided. An appalling amount had been served, including the sparkling wine in the library and the different wines with each of the four courses of dinner. She had no idea how much she'd actually drunk. Pym had assiduously topped up her glass whenever the level had dropped below two-thirds. More than five glasses, anyway. Seven? Ten? Her usual limit was two.

It was a wonder she'd been able to stalk out of that overheated grand dining room without falling over; but then, if she'd been stone sober, could she ever have found the nerve—or was that, the ill-manners—to do so? *Pot-valiant, were you?*

She ran her hands through her hair, rubbed her neck, opened her eyes, and lifted her forehead again from the cool surface of her aunt's comconsole. All the plans and notes for Lord Vorkosigan's Barrayaran garden were now neatly and logically organized, and indexed. Anyone—well, any gardener who knew what they were doing in the first place—could follow them and complete the job in good order. The final tally of all expenses was appended. The working credit account had been balanced, closed, and signed off. She had only to hit the Send pad on the comconsole for it all to be gone from her life forever.

She groped for the exquisite little model Barrayar on its gold chain heaped by the vid plate, held it up, and let it spin before her eyes. Leaning back in the comconsole chair, she contemplated it, and all the memories attached to it like invisible chains. Gold and lead, hope and fear, triumph and pain . . . She squinted it to a blur.

She remembered the day he'd bought it, on their absurd and ultimately very wet shopping trip in the Komarran dome, his face alive with the humor of it all. She remembered the day he'd given it to her, in her hospital room on the transfer station, after the defeat of the conspirators. *The Lord Auditor Vorkosigan Award for Making His Job Easier*, he'd dubbed it, his gray eyes glinting. He'd apologized that it was not the real medal any soldier might have earned for doing rather less than what she'd done that awful night-cycle. It wasn't a gift. Or if it was, she'd been very wrong to accept it from his hand, because it was much too expensive a bauble to be proper. Though *he* had grinned like a fool, Aunt Vorthys, watching, hadn't batted an eye. It was, therefore, a prize. She'd won it herself, paid for it with bruises and terror and panicked action.

This is mine. I will not give it up. With a frown, she drew the chain back over her head and tucked the pendant planet inside her black blouse, trying not to feel like a guilty child hiding a stolen cookie.

Her flaming desire to return to Vorkosigan House and rip her skellytum rootling, so carefully and proudly planted mere hours ago, back out of the ground, had burned out sometime after midnight. For one thing, she would certainly have run afoul of Vorkosigan House's security, if she'd gone blundering about in its garden in the dark. Pym, or Roic, might have stunned her, and been very upset, poor fellows. And then carried her back inside, where . . . Her fury, her wine, and her over-wrought imagination had all worn off near dawn, running out at last in secret, muffled tears in her pillow, when the household was long quiet and she could hope for a scrap of privacy.

Why should she even bother? Miles didn't care about the skellytum—he hadn't even gone out to *look* at it last evening. She'd been lugging the awkward thing around in her life for fifteen years, in one form or another, since inheriting the seventy-year-old bonsai from her great-aunt. It had survived death, marriage, a dozen moves, interstellar travel, being flung off a balcony and shattered, more death, another five wormhole jumps, and two subsequent transplantations. It had to be as exhausted as she was. Let it sit there and rot, or dry up and blow away, or whatever its neglected fate was to be. At least she had dragged it back to Barrayar to finish dying. Enough. She was done with it. Forever.

She called her garden instructions back up on the comconsole, and added an appendix about the skellytum's rather tricky post-transplant watering and feeding requirements.

"Mama!" Nikki's sharp, excited voice made her flinch.

"Don't . . . don't *thump* so, dear." She turned in her station chair and smiled bleakly at her son. She was inwardly grateful she hadn't dragged him along to last night's debacle, though she could've pictured him enthusiastically joining poor Enrique on the butter bug hunt. But if Nikki had been present, she could not have left, and abandoned him. Nor yanked him along with her, halfway through his dessert and doubtless protesting in bewilderment. She'd have been mother-bound to her chair, there to endure whatever ghastly, awkward social torment might have subsequently played out.

He stood by her elbow, and bounced. "Last night, did you work out with Lord Vorkosigan when he's gonna take me down to Vorkosigan Surleau and learn to ride his horse? You said you would."

She'd brought Nikki along to the garden work-site several times, when neither her aunt nor uncle could be home with him. Lord Vorkosigan had generously offered to let him have the run of Vorkosigan House on such days, and they'd even hustled up Pym's youngest boy Arthur from his nearby home for a playmate. Ma Kosti had captured Nikki's stomach, heart, and slavish loyalty in very short order, Armsman Roic had played games with him, and Kareen Koudelka had let him help in the lab. Ekaterin had almost forgotten this off-hand invitation, issued by Lord Vorkosigan when he'd turned Nikki back over to her at the end of one workday. She'd made polite-doubtful noises at the time. Miles had assured her the horse in question was very old and gentle, which hadn't exactly been the doubt that had concerned her.

"I . . ." Ekaterin rubbed her temple, which seemed to anchor a lacework of shooting pain inside her head. *Generously . . . ?* Or just more of Miles's campaign of subtle manipulation, now revealed? "I really don't think we ought to impose on him like that. It's such a long way down to his District. If you're really interested in horses, I'm sure we can get you riding lessons somewhere much nearer Vorbarr Sultana."

Nikki frowned in obvious disappointment. "I dunno about horses. But he said he might let me try his lightflyer, on the way down."

"Nikki, you're much too young to fly a lightflyer."

"Lord Vorkosigan said *his* father let *him* fly when he was younger than me. He said his da said he needed to know how to take over the controls in an emergency just as soon as he was physically able. He said he sat him on his lap, and let him take off and land all by himself and everything."

"You're much too big to sit on Lord Vorkosigan's lap!" So was she, she supposed. But if he and she were to—*stop that.*

"Well," Nikki considered this, and allowed, "anyway, he's too little. It'd look goofy. But his lightflyer seat's just right! Pym let me sit in it, when I was helping him polish the cars." Nikki bounced some more. "Can you ask Lord Vorkosigan when you go to work?"

"No. I don't think so."

"Why not?" He looked at her, his brow wrinkling slightly. "Why didn't you go today?"

"I'm . . . not feeling very well."

"Oh. Tomorrow, then? Come on, Mama, *please*?" He hung on her arm, and twisted himself up, and made big eyes at her, grinning.

She rested her throbbing forehead in her hand. "No, Nikki. I don't think so."

"Aw, why *not*? You *said*. Come on, it'll be so great. You don't have to come if you don't want, I s'pose. Why not, why not, why not? Tomorrow, tomorrow, tomorrow?"

"I'm not going to work tomorrow, either."

"Are you that sick? You don't look that sick." He stared at her in startled worry.

"No." She hastened to address that worry, before he started making up dire medical theories in his head. He'd lost one parent this year. "It's just . . . I'm not going to be going back to Lord Vorkosigan's house. I quit."

"Huh?" Now his stare grew entirely bewildered. "*Why*? I thought you *liked* making that garden thing."

"I did."

"Then why'd you quit?"

"Lord Vorkosigan and I . . . had a falling-out. Over, over an ethical issue."

"What? What issue?" His voice was laced with confusion and disbelief. He twisted himself around the other way.

"I found he'd . . . lied to me about something." *He promised he'd never lie to me.* He'd feigned that he was very interested in gardens.

He'd arranged her life by subterfuge—and then told everyone else in Vorbarr Sultana. He'd pretended he didn't love her. He'd as much as promised he'd never ask her to marry him. He'd *lied*. Try explaining *that* to a nine-year-old boy. Or to any other rational human being of any age or gender, her honesty added bitterly. *Am I insane yet?* Anyway, Miles hadn't actually *said* he wasn't in love with her, he'd just . . . implied it. Avoided saying much on the subject at all, in fact. Prevarication by misdirection.

"Oh," said Nikki, eyes wide, daunted at last.

The Professora's blessed voice interrupted from the archway. "Now, Nikki, don't be pestering your mother. She has a very bad hangover."

"A *hangover*?" Nikki clearly had trouble fitting the words *mother* and *hangover* into the same conceptual space. "She said she was sick."

"Wait till you're older, dear. You'll doubtless discover the distinction, or lack of it, for yourself. Run along now." His smiling great-aunt guided him firmly away. "Out, out. Go see what your Uncle Vorthys is up to downstairs. I heard some very odd noises a bit ago."

Nikki let himself be chivvied out, with a disturbed backward glance over his shoulder.

Ekaterin put her head back down on the comconsole, and shut her eyes.

A clink by her head made her open them again; her aunt was setting down a large glass of cool water and holding out two painkiller tablets.

"I had some of those this morning," said Ekaterin dully.

"They appear to have worn off. Drink all the water, now. You clearly need to rehydrate."

Dutifully, Ekaterin did so. She set the glass down, and squeezed her eyes open and shut a few times. "That really was *the* Count and Countess Vorkosigan last night, wasn't it." It wasn't really a question, more a plea for denial. After nearly stampeding over them in her desperate flight out the door, she'd been halfway home in the auto-cab before her belated realization of their identity had dawned so horribly. The great and famous Viceroy and Vicereine of Sergyar. What business had they, to look so like ordinary people at a moment like that? *Ow, ow, ow.*

"Yes. I'd never met them to speak to at any length before."

"Did you . . . speak to them at length last night?" Her aunt and uncle had been almost an hour behind her, arriving home.

"Yes, we had quite a nice chat. I was impressed. Miles's mother is a very sensible woman."

"Then why is her son such a . . . never mind." *Ow.* "They must think I'm some sort of hysteric. How did I get the nerve to just stand up and walk out of a formal dinner in front of all those . . . and Lady *Alys Vorpatril* . . . and at *Vorkosigan House.* I can't believe I did that." After a brooding moment, she added, "I can't believe *he* did that."

Aunt Vorthys did not ask, *What?*, or *Which he?* She did purse her lips, and look quizzically at her niece. "Well, I don't suppose you had much choice."

"No."

"After all, if you hadn't left, you'd have had to answer Lord Vorkosigan's question."

"I . . . didn't . . . ?" Ekaterin blinked. Hadn't her actions been answer enough? "Under *those* circumstances? Are you mad?"

"He knew it was a mistake the moment the words were out of his mouth, I daresay, at least judging from that ghastly expression on his face. You could see everything just drain right out of it. Extraordinary. But I can't help wondering, dear—if you'd wanted to say *no,* why didn't you? It was the perfect opportunity to do so."

"I . . . I . . ." Ekaterin tried to collect her wits, which seemed to be scattering like sheep. "It wouldn't have been . . . *polite.*"

After a thoughtful pause, her aunt murmured, "You might have said, 'No, thank you.' "

Ekaterin rubbed her numb face. "Aunt Vorthys," she sighed, "I love you dearly. But please go away now."

Her aunt smiled, and kissed her on the top of her head, and drifted out.

Ekaterin returned to her twice-interrupted brooding. Her aunt was right, she realized. Ekaterin *hadn't* answered Miles's question. And she hadn't even noticed she hadn't answered.

She recognized this headache, and the knotted stomach that went with it, and it had nothing to do with too much wine. Her arguments with her late husband Tien had never involved physical violence directed against her, though the walls had suffered from his clenched fists a few times. The rows had always petered out into days of frozen, silent rage, filled with unbearable tension and a sort of grief, of two people trapped together in the same always-too-small space walking wide around each other. She had almost always broken first, backed down, apologized, placated, anything to make the pain stop. *Heartsick*, perhaps, was the name of the emotion.

I don't want to go back there again. Please don't ever make me go back there again.

Where am I, when I am at home in myself? Not here, for all the increasing burden of her aunt and uncle's charity. Not, certainly, with Tien. Not with her own father. With . . . Miles? She had felt flashes of profound ease in his company, it was true, brief perhaps, but calm like deep water. There had also been moments when she'd wanted to whack him with a brick. Which was the real Miles? Which was the real Ekaterin, for that matter?

The answer hovered, and it scared her breathless. But she'd picked wrong before. She had no judgment in these man-and-woman matters, she'd proved that.

She turned back to the comconsole. A note. She should write some sort of cover note to go with the returned garden plans.

I think they will be self-explanatory, don't you?

She pressed the Send pad on the comconsole, and stumbled back upstairs to pull the curtains and lie down fully dressed on her bed until dinner.

Miles slouched into the library of Vorkosigan House, a mug of weak tea clutched in his faintly trembling hand. The light in here was still too bright this evening. Perhaps he ought to seek refuge in a corner of the garage instead. Or the cellar. Not the wine cellar—he shuddered at the thought. But he'd grown entirely bored with his bed, covers pulled over his head or not. A day of that was enough.

He stopped abruptly, and lukewarm tea sloshed onto his hand. His father was at the secured comconsole, and his mother was at the broad inlaid table with three or four books and a mess of flimsies spread out before her. They both looked up at him, and smiled in tentative greeting. It would probably seem surly of him to back out and flee.

"G'evening," he managed, and shambled past them to find his favorite chair, and lower himself carefully into it.

"Good evening, Miles," his mother returned. His father put his console on hold, and regarded him with bland interest.

"How was your trip home from Sergyar?" Miles went on, after about a minute of silence.

"Entirely without incident, happily enough," his mother said. "Till the very end."

"Ah," said Miles. "That." He brooded into his tea mug.

His parents humanely ignored him for several minutes, but whatever they'd been separately working on seemed to not hold their attention anymore. Still, nobody left.

"We missed you at breakfast," the Countess said finally. "And lunch. And dinner."

"I was still throwing up at breakfast," said Miles. "I wouldn't have been much fun."

"So Pym reported," said the Count.

The Countess added astringently, "Are you done with that now?"

"Yeh. It didn't help." Miles slumped a little further, and stretched his legs out before him. "A life in ruins with vomiting is still a life in ruins."

"Mm," said the Count in a judicious tone, "though it does make it easy to be a recluse. If you're repulsive enough, people spontaneously avoid you."

His wife twinkled at him. "Speaking from experience, love?"

"Naturally." His eyes grinned back at her.

More silence fell. His parents did not decamp. Obviously, Miles concluded, he wasn't repulsive enough. Perhaps he should emit a menacing belch.

He finally started, "Mother—you're a woman—"

She sat up, and gave him a bright, encouraging Betan smile. "Yes . . . ?"

"Never mind," he sighed. He slumped again.

The Count rubbed his lips and regarded him thoughtfully. "Do you have anything to *do*? Any miscreants to go Imperially Audit, or anything?"

"Not at present," Miles replied. After a contemplative moment he added, "Fortunately for them."

"Hm." The Count tamped down a smile. "Perhaps you are wise." He hesitated. "Your Aunt Alys gave us a blow-by-blow account of your dinner party. With editorials. She was particularly insistent that I tell you she *trusts*," Miles could hear his aunt's cadences mimicked in his father's voice, "you would not have fled the scene of any other losing battle the way you deserted last night."

Ah. Yes. His parents had been left with the mopping up, hadn't they. "But there was no hope of being shot dead in the dining room if I stayed with the rear guard."

His father flicked up an eyebrow. "And so avoid the subsequent court martial?"

"Thus conscience doth make cowards of us all," Miles intoned.

"I am sufficiently your partisan," said the Countess, "that the sight of a pretty woman running screaming, or at least swearing, into the night from your marriage proposal rather disturbs me. Though your Aunt Alys says you scarcely left the young lady any other choice. It's hard to say what else she could have done *but* walk out. Except squash you like a bug, I suppose."

Miles cringed at the word *bug*.

"Just how bad—" the Countess began.

"Did I offend her? Badly enough, it seems."

"Actually, I was about to ask, just how bad *was* Madame Vorsoisson's prior marriage?"

Miles shrugged. "I only saw a little of it. I gather from the pattern of her flinches that the late unlamented Tien Vorsoisson was one of those subtle feral parasites who leave their mates scratching their heads and asking, *Am I crazy? Am I crazy?*" She wouldn't have those doubts if she married *him*, ha.

"Aah," said his mother, in a tone of much enlightenment. "One of *those*. Yes. I know the type of old. They come in all gender-flavors, by the way. It can take years to fight your way out of the mental mess they leave in their wake."

"I don't *have* years," Miles protested. "I've *never* had years." And then pressed his lips shut at the little flicker of pain in his father's eyes. Well, who knew what Miles's second life expectancy was, anyway. Maybe he'd started his clock all over, after the cryorevival. Miles slumped lower. "The hell of it is, I knew better. I'd had way too much to drink, I panicked when Simon . . . I never meant to ambush Ekaterin like that. It was *friendly* fire . . ."

He went on after a little, "I had this great plan, see. I thought it could solve everything in one brilliant swoop. She has this real passion for gardens, and her husband had left her effectively destitute. So I figured, I could help her jump-start the career of her dreams, slip her some financial support, and get an excuse to see her nearly every day, *and* get in ahead of the competition. I had to practically wade through the fellows panting after her in the Vorthys's parlor, the times I went over there—"

"For the purpose of panting after her in her parlor, I take it?" his mother inquired sweetly.

"No!" said Miles, stung. "To consult about the garden I'd hired her to make in the lot next door."

"Is *that* what that crater is," said his father. "In the dark, from the groundcar, it looked as though someone tried to shell Vorkosigan House and missed, and I'd wondered why no one had reported it to us."

"It is not a *crater*. It's a sunken garden. There's just . . . just no plants in it yet."

"It has a very nice shape, Miles," his mother said soothingly. "I went out and walked through it this afternoon. The little stream is very pretty indeed. It reminds me of the mountains."

"That was the idea," said Miles, primly ignoring his father's mutter of . . . *after a Cetagandan bombing raid on a guerilla position . . .*

Then Miles sat bolt upright in sudden horror. *Not quite no plants.* "Oh, God! I never went out to look at her skellytum! Lord Dono came in with Ivan—did Aunt Alys explain to you about Lord Dono?—and I was distracted, and then it was time for dinner, and I never had the chance afterwards. Has anyone watered—? Oh, shit, no wonder she was angry. I'm dead meat twice over—!" He melted back into his puddle of despair.

"So, let me get this straight," said the Countess slowly, studying him dispassionately. "You took this destitute widow, struggling to get on her own feet for the first time in her life, and dangled a golden career opportunity before her as bait, just to tie her to you and cut her off from other romantic possibilities."

That seemed an uncharitably bald way of putting it. "Not . . . not *just*," Miles choked. "I was trying to do her a good turn. I never imagined she'd quit—the garden was everything to her."

The Countess sat back, and regarded him with a horribly thoughtful expression, the one she acquired when you'd made the mistake of getting her full, undivided attention. "Miles . . . do you remember that unfortunate incident with Armsman Esterhazy and the game of cross-ball, when you were about twelve years old?"

He hadn't thought of it in years, but at her words, the memory came flooding back, still tinged with shame and fury. The Armsmen used to play cross-ball with him, and sometimes Elena and Ivan, in the back garden of Vorkosigan House: a low-impact game, of minimum threat to his then-fragile bones, but requiring quick reflexes and good timing. He'd been elated the first time he'd won a match against an actual adult, in this case Armsman Esterhazy. He'd been shaken with rage, when a not-meant-to-be-overheard remark had revealed to him that the game had been a setup. Forgotten. But not forgiven.

"Poor Esterhazy had thought it would cheer you up, because you were depressed at the time about some, I forget which, slight you'd suffered at school," the Countess said. "I still remember how furious you were when you figured out he'd *let* you win. Did you ever carry on about that one. We thought you'd do yourself a harm."

"He stole my victory from me," grated Miles, "as surely as if he'd cheated to win. *And* he poisoned every subsequent real victory with doubt. I had a *right* to be mad."

His mother sat quietly, expectantly.

The light dawned. Even with his eyes squeezed shut, the intensity of the glare hurt his head.

"Oh. Noooo," groaned Miles, muffled into the cushion he jammed over his face. "*I* did *that* to *her*?"

His remorseless parent let him stew in it, a silence sharper-edged than words.

"*I* did *that* to *her* . . ." he moaned, pitifully.

Pity did not seem to be forthcoming. He clutched the cushion to his chest. "Oh. God. That's exactly what I did. She said it herself. She said the garden could have been *her* gift. And I'd taken it away from her. Too. Which made no sense, since it was she who'd just quit . . . I thought she was starting to argue with me. I was so pleased, because I thought, if only she would argue with me . . ."

"You could win?" the Count supplied dryly.

"Uh . . . yeah."

"Oh, son." The Count shook his head. "Oh, poor son." Miles did not mistake this for an expression of sympathy. "The only way you win *that* war is to start with unconditional surrender."

"That *you* is plural, note," the Countess put in.

"I *tried* to surrender!" Miles protested frantically. "The woman was taking no prisoners! I tried to get her to stomp me, but she wouldn't. She's too dignified, too, oversocialized, too, too . . ."

"Too smart to lower herself to your level?" the Countess suggested. "Dear me. I think I'm beginning to like this Ekaterin. And I haven't even finished being properly introduced to her yet. *I'd like you to meet—she's getting away!* seemed a little . . . truncated."

Miles glared at her. But he couldn't keep it up. In a smaller voice, he said, "She sent all the garden plans back to me this afternoon, on the comconsole. Just like she'd said she would. I'd set it to code-buzz me if any call originating from her came in. I damn near killed myself, getting over to the machine. But it was just a data packet. Not even a personal note. *Die, you rat* would have been better than this . . . this *nothing*." After a fraught pause, he burst out, "What do I do *now*?"

"Is that a rhetorical question, for dramatic effect, or are you actually asking my advice?" his mother inquired tartly. "Because I'm not going to waste my breath on you unless you're finally paying attention."

He opened his mouth for an angry reply, then closed it. He glanced for support to his father. His father opened his hand blandly in the direction of his mother. Miles wondered what it would be like, to be in such practiced teamwork with someone that it was as though you coordinated your one-two punches telepathically. *I'll never get the chance to find out. Unless.*

"I'm paying attention," he said humbly.

"The . . . the kindest word I can come up with for it is *blunder*—was yours. You owe the apology. Make it."

"*How?* She's made it abundantly clear she doesn't want to speak to me!"

"*Not* in person, good God, Miles. For one thing, I can't imagine you could resist the urge to babble, and blow yourself up. Again."

What is it about all my relatives, that they have so little faith in—

"Even a live comconsole call is too invasive," she continued. "Going over to the Vorthys's in person would be much too invasive."

"The way *he's* been going about it, certainly," murmured the Count. "General Romeo Vorkosigan, the one-man strike force."

The Countess gave him a faintly quelling flick of her eyelash. "Something rather more controlled, I think," she continued to Miles. "About all you can do is write her a note, I suppose. A short, succinct note. I realize you don't do *abject* very well, but I suggest you exert yourself."

"D'you think it would work?" Faint hope glimmered at the bottom of a deep, deep well.

"*Working* is not what this is about. You can't still be plotting to make love and war on the poor woman. You'll send an apology because you owe it, to her and to your own honor. Period. Or else don't bother."

"Oh," said Miles, in a very small voice.

"Cross-ball," said his father. Reminiscently. "Huh."

"The knife is in the target," sighed Miles. "To the hilt. You don't have to twist." He glanced across at his mother. "Should the note be handwritten? Or should I just send it on the comconsole?"

"I think your *just* just answered your own question. If your execrable handwriting has improved, it would perhaps be a nice touch."

"Proves it wasn't dictated to your secretary, for one thing," put in the Count. "Or worse, composed by him at your order."

"Haven't got a secretary yet." Miles sighed. "Gregor hasn't given me enough work to justify one."

"Since work for an Auditor hinges on awkward crises arising in the Empire, I can't very well wish more for you," the Count said. "But no doubt things will pick up after the wedding. Which will have one less crisis because of the good work you just did on Komarr, I might say."

He glanced up, and his father gave him an understanding nod; yes, the Viceroy and Vicereine of Sergyar were most definitely in the need-to-know pool about the late events on Komarr. Gregor had undoubtedly sent on a copy of Miles's eyes-only Auditor's report for the Viceroy's perusal. "Well . . . yes. At the very least, if the conspirators had maintained their original schedule, there'd have been several thousand innocent people killed that day. It would have marred the festivities, I think."

"Then you've earned some time off."

The Countess looked momentarily introspective. "And what did Madame Vorsoisson earn? We had her aunt give us her eyewitness description of their involvement. It sounded like a frightening experience."

"The public gratitude of the Empire is what she *should* have earned," said Miles, in reminded aggravation. "Instead, it's all been buried deep-deep under the ImpSec security cap. No one will ever know. All her courage, all her cool and clever moves, all her bloody *heroism*, dammit, was just . . . made to disappear. It's not fair."

"One does what one has to, in a crisis," said the Countess.

"No." Miles glanced up at her. "Some people do. Others just fold. I've seen them. I know the difference. Ekaterin—she'll never fold. She can go the distance, she can find the speed. She'll . . . she'll *do*."

"Leaving aside whether we are discussing a woman or a horse," said the Countess—dammit, Mark had said practically the same thing, what was *with* all Miles's nearest and dearest?—"everyone has their folding-point, Miles. Their mortal vulnerability. Some just keep it in a nonstandard location."

The Count and Countess gave each other one of those Telepathic Looks again. It was extremely annoying. Miles squirmed with envy.

He drew the tattered shreds of his dignity around him, and rose. "Excuse me. I have to go . . . water a plant."

It took him thirty minutes of wandering around the bare, crusted garden in the dark, with his hand-light wavering and the water from his mug dribbling over his fingers, to even *find* the blasted thing. In its pot, the skellytum rootling had looked sturdy enough, but out here, it looked lost and lonely: a scrap of life the size of his thumb in an acre of sterility. It also looked disturbingly limp. Was it wilting? He emptied the cup over it; the water made a dark spot in the reddish soil that began to evaporate and fade all too quickly.

He tried to imagine the plant full grown, five meters high, its central barrel the size, and shape, of a sumo wrestler, its tendril-like branches gracing the space with distinctive corkscrew curves. Then he tried to imagine himself forty-five or fifty years old, which was the age to which he'd have to survive to see that sight. Would he be a reclusive, gnarled bachelor, eccentric, shrunken, invalidish, tended only by his bored Armsmen? Or a proud, if stressed, paterfamilias with a serene, elegant, dark-haired woman on his arm and half a dozen hyperactive progeny in tow? Maybe . . . maybe the hyperactivity could be toned down in the gene-cleaning, though he was sure his parents would accuse him of cheating. . . .

Abject.

He went back inside Vorkosigan House to his study, where he sat himself down to attempt, through a dozen drafts, the best damned *abject* anybody'd ever seen.

Chapter Eleven

Kareen leaned over the porch rail of Lord Auditor Vorthys's house and stared worriedly at the close-curtained windows in the bright tile front. "Maybe there's no one home."

"I said we should have called before we came here," said Martya, unhelpfully. But then came a rapid thump of steps from within—surely not the Professora's—and the door burst open.

"Oh, hi, Kareen," said Nikki. "Hi, Martya."

"Hello, Nikki," said Martya. "Is your mama home?"

"Yeah, she's out back. You want to see her?"

"Yes, please. If she's not too busy."

"Naw, she's only messing with the garden. Go on through." He gestured them hospitably in the general direction of the back of the house, and thumped back up the stairs.

Trying not to feel like a trespasser, Kareen led her sister through the hall and kitchen and out the back door. Ekaterin was on her knees on a pad by a raised flower bed, grubbing out weeds. The discarded plants were laid out beside her on the walk, roots and all, in rows like executed prisoners. They shriveled in the westering sun. Her bare hand slapped another green corpse down at the end of the row. It looked therapeutic. Kareen wished *she* had something to kill right now. Besides Martya.

Ekaterin glanced up at the sound of their footsteps, and a ghost of a smile lightened her pale face. She jammed her trowel into the dirt, and rose to her feet. "Oh, hello."

"Hi, Ekaterin." Not wishing to plunge too baldly into the purpose of her visit, Kareen added, with a wave of her arm, "This is pretty." Trees, and walls draped with vines, made the little garden into a private bower in the midst of the city.

Ekaterin followed her glance. "It was a hobby-project of mine, when I lived here as a student, years ago. Aunt Vorthys has kept it up, more or less. There are a few things I'd do differently now . . . Anyway," she gestured at the graceful wrought-iron table and chairs, "won't you sit down?"

Martya took prompt advantage of the invitation, seating herself and resting her chin on her hands with a put-upon sigh.

"Would you like anything to drink? Tea?"

"Thanks," said Kareen, also sitting. "Nothing to drink, thanks." This household lacked servants to dispatch on such errands; Ekaterin would have to go off and rummage in the kitchen with her own hands to supply her guests. And the sisters would be put to it to guess whether to follow prole rules, and all troop out to help, or impoverished-high-Vor rules, and sit and wait and pretend they didn't notice there weren't any servants. Besides, they'd just eaten, and her dinner still sat like a lump in Kareen's stomach even though she'd barely picked at it.

Kareen waited until Ekaterin was seated to venture cautiously, "I just stopped by to find out—that is, I'd wondered if, if you'd heard anything from . . . from Vorkosigan House?"

Ekaterin stiffened. "No. Should I have?"

"Oh." What, Miles the monomaniacal hadn't made it all up to her by now? Kareen had pictured him at Ekaterin's door the following morning, spinning damage-control propaganda like mad. It wasn't that Miles was so irresistible—she, for one, had always found him quite resistible, at least in the romantic sense, not that he'd ever exactly turned his attention on her—but he was certainly the most *relentless* human being she'd ever met. What was the man doing all this time? Her anxiety grew. "I'd thought—I was hoping—I'm awfully worried about Mark, you see. It's been almost two days. I was hoping you might have . . . heard something."

Ekaterin's face softened. "Oh, Mark. Of course. No. I'm sorry."

Nobody cared enough about Mark. The fragilities and fault lines of his hard-won personality were invisible to them all. They'd load him down with impossible pressures and demands as though he were, well, Miles, and assume he'd never break. . . . "My parents have forbidden me to call anyone at Vorkosigan House, or go over there or anything," Kareen explained, tight-voiced. "They insisted I give them my word before they'd even let me out of the house. And *then* they stuck me with a snitch." She tossed her head in the direction of Martya, now slumping with almost equal surliness.

"It wasn't *my* idea to be your bodyguard," protested Martya. "Did I get a vote? No."

"Da and Mama—especially Da—have gone all Time-of-Isolation over this. It's just crazy. They're all the time telling you to grow up, and then when you do, they try to make you stop. And shrink. It's like they want to cryofreeze me at twelve forever. Or stick me back in the replicator and lock down the lid." Kareen bit her lip. "And I don't fit in there anymore, *thank* you."

"Well," said Ekaterin, a shade of sympathetic amusement in her voice, "at least you'd be safe there. I can understand the parental temptation of that."

"You're making it worse for yourself, you know," said Martya to Kareen, with an air of sisterly critique. "If you hadn't carried on like a madwoman being locked in an attic, I bet they wouldn't have gone nearly so rigid."

Kareen bared her teeth at Martya.

"There's something to that in both directions," said Ekaterin mildly. "Nothing is more guaranteed to make one start acting like a child than to be treated like one. It's so infuriating. It took me the longest time to figure out how to stop falling into that trap."

"Yes, exactly," said Kareen eagerly. "You understand! So—how did *you* make them stop?"

"You can't make them—whoever your particular *them* is—do anything, really," said Ekaterin slowly. "Adulthood isn't an award they'll give you for being a good child. You can waste . . . years, trying to get someone to give that respect to you, as though it were a sort of promotion or raise in pay. If only you do enough, if only you are *good enough*. No. You have to just . . . take it. Give it to yourself, I suppose. Say, *I'm sorry you feel like that*, and walk away. But that's hard." Ekaterin looked up from her lap where her hands had been absently rubbing at the yard dirt smeared on them, and remembered to smile. Kareen felt an odd chill. It wasn't just her reserve that made Ekaterin daunting, sometimes. The woman went down and down, like a well to the middle of the world. Kareen bet even Miles couldn't shift her around at his will and whim.

How hard is it to walk away? "It's like they're *that* close," she held up her thumb and finger a few millimeters apart, "to telling me I have to choose between my family and my lover. And it makes me scared, and it makes me furious. Why shouldn't I have both? Would it be considered too much of a good thing, or what? Leaving aside that it'd be a horrid guilt to lay on poor Mark—he knows how much my family means to me. A family is something he didn't have, growing up, and he romanticizes it, but still."

Her flattened hands beat a frustrated tattoo on the garden tabletop. "It all comes back to the damned money. If I were a *real* adult, I'd have my own income. And I could walk away, and they'd know I could, and they'd have to back off. They think they have me trapped."

"Ah," said Ekaterin faintly. "That one. Yes. That one is very real."

"Mama accused *me* of only doing short-term thinking, but I'm not! The butter bug project—it's like school all over again, short-term deprivation for a really major pay-off down the line. I've studied the analyses Mark did with Tsipis. It's not a get-rich-quick scheme. It's a get-rich-*big* scheme. Da and Mama don't have a clue how big. They imagine I've spent my time with Mark playing around, but I've been working my tail off, and I know *exactly* why. Meanwhile I have over a month's salary tied up in shares in the basement of Vorkosigan House, and *I don't know what's happening over there!*" Her fingers were white where they gripped the table edge, and she had to stop for breath.

"I take it you haven't heard from Dr. Borgos, either?" said Martya cautiously to Ekaterin.

"Why . . . no."

"I felt almost sorry for him. He was trying so hard to please. I hope Miles hasn't really had all his bugs killed."

"Miles never threatened *all* his bugs," Kareen pointed out. "Just the escapees. As for me, I wish Miles *had* strangled him. I'm sorry you made him stop, Ekaterin."

"Me!" Ekaterin's lips twisted with bemusement.

"What, Kareen," scoffed Martya, "just because the man revealed to everybody that you were a practicing heterosexual? You know, you really didn't play that one right, considering all the Betan possibilities. If only you'd spent the last few weeks dropping the right kind of hints, you could have had Mama and Da falling to their knees in thanks that you were only messing around with Mark. Though I do wonder about your taste in men."

What Martya doesn't know about my sampling of Betan possibilities, Kareen decided firmly, *won't hurt me.* "Or else they really would have locked me in the attic."

Martya waved this away. "Dr. Borgos was terrorized enough. It's really unfair to drop a normal person down in Vorkosigan House with the Chance Brothers and expect him to just cope."

"Chance Brothers?" Ekaterin inquired.

Kareen, who had heard the jibe before, gave it the bare grimace it deserved.

"Um," Martya had the good grace to look embarrassed. "It was a joke that was going around. Ivan passed it on to me." When Ekaterin continued to look blankly at her, she added reluctantly. "You know— Slim and Fat."

"Oh." Ekaterin didn't laugh, though she smiled briefly; she looked as though she was digesting this tidbit, and wasn't sure if she liked the aftertaste.

"You think Enrique is normal?" said Kareen to her sister, wrinkling her nose.

"Well . . . at least he's a change from the sort of Lieutenant Lord Vor-I'm-God's-Gift-to-Women we usually meet in Vorbarr Sultana. He doesn't back you into a corner and gab on endlessly about military history and ordnance. He backs you into a corner and gabs on endlessly about biology, instead. Who knows? He might be good husband material."

"Yeah, if his wife didn't mind dressing up as a butter bug to lure him to bed," said Kareen tartly. She made antennae of her fingers, and wriggled them at Martya.

Martya snickered, but said, "I think he's the sort who needs a managing wife, so he can work fourteen hours a day in his lab."

Kareen snorted. "She'd better seize control immediately. Yeah, Enrique has biotech ideas the way Zap the Cat has kittens, but it's a near-certainty that whatever profit he gets from them, he'll lose."

"Too trusting, do you think? Would people take advantage of him?"

"No, just too absorbed. It would come to the same thing in the end, though."

Ekaterin sighed, a distant look in her eyes. "I wish I could work *four* hours at a stretch without chaos erupting."

"Oh," said Martya, "but you're another. One of those people who pulls amazing things out of their ears, that is." She glanced around the tiny, serene garden. "You're wasted in domestic management. You're definitely R and D."

Ekaterin smiled crookedly. "Are you saying I don't need a husband, I need a wife? Well, at least that's a *slight* change from my sister-in-law's urgings."

"Try Beta Colony," Kareen advised, with a melancholy sigh.

The conversation grounded for a stretch upon this beguiling thought. The muted city street noises echoed over the walls and around the houses, and the slanting sunlight crept off the grass, putting the table into cool pre-evening shade.

"They really are utterly revolting bugs," Martya said after a time. "No one in their right mind will ever buy them."

Kareen hunched at this discouraging non-news. The bugs *did too* work. Bug butter was science's almost-perfect food. There *ought* to be a market for it. People were so prejudiced. . . .

A slight smile turned Martya's lip, and she added, "Though the brown and silver was just perfect. I thought Pym was going to pop."

"If only I'd known what Enrique was up to," mourned Kareen, "I could have stopped him. He'd been babbling on about his surprise, but I didn't pay enough attention—I didn't know he *could* do that to the bugs."

Ekaterin said, "I could have realized it, if I'd given it any thought. I scanned his thesis. The real secret is in the suite of microbes." At Martya's raised eyebrows, she explained, "It's the array of bioengineered microorganisms in the bugs' guts that do the real work of breaking down what the bugs eat and converting it into, well, whatever the designer chooses. Enrique has dozens of ideas for future products beyond food, including a wild application for environmental radiation cleanup that might excite . . . well. Anyway, keeping the microbe ecology balanced—tuned, Enrique calls it—is the most delicate part. The bugs are just self-assembling and self-propelled packaging around the microbe suite. Their shape is semi-arbitrary. Enrique just grabbed the most efficient functional elements from a dozen insect species, with no attention at all to the aesthetics."

"Most likely." Slowly, Kareen sat up. "Ekaterin . . . *you* do aesthetics."

Ekaterin made a throwaway gesture. "In a sense, I guess."

"Yes, you do. Your hair is always right. Your clothes always look better than anyone else's, and I don't think it's that you're spending more money on them."

Ekaterin shook her head in rueful agreement.

"You have what Lady Alys calls *unerring taste*, I think," Kareen continued, with rising energy. "I mean, look at this garden. Mark, Mark does money, and deals. Miles does strategy and tactics, and inveigling people into doing what he wants." Well, maybe not always; Ekaterin's lips tightened at the mention of his name. Kareen hurried on. "I still haven't figured out what I do. You—you do beauty. I really envy that."

Ekaterin looked touched. "Thank you, Kareen. But it really isn't anything that—"

Kareen waved away the self-deprecation. "No, listen, this is important. Do you think you could make a *pretty* butter bug? Or rather, make butter bugs pretty?"

"I'm no geneticist—"

"I don't mean that part. I mean, could you *design* alterations to the bugs so's they don't make people want to lose their lunch when they see one. For Enrique to apply."

Ekaterin sat back. Her brows sank down again, and an absorbed look grew in her eyes. "Well . . . it's obviously possible to change the bugs' colors and add surface designs. That has to be fairly trivial, judging from the speed with which Enrique produced the . . . um . . . Vorkosigan bugs. You'd have to stay away from fundamental structural modifications in the gut and mandibles and so on, but the wings and wing carapaces are already nonfunctional. Presumably they could be altered at will."

"Yes? Go on."

"Colors—you'd want to look for colors found in nature, for biological appeal. Birds, beasts, flowers . . . fire . . ."

"*Can* you think of something?"

"I can think of a dozen ideas, offhand." Her mouth curved up. "It seems too easy. Almost any change would be an improvement."

"Not just any change. Something *glorious*."

"A glorious butter bug." Her lips parted in faint delight, and her eyes glinted with genuine cheer for the first time this visit. "Now, *that's* a challenge."

"Oh, would you, could you? *Will* you? Please? I'm a shareholder, I have as much authority to hire you as Mark or Enrique. Qualitatively, anyway."

"Heavens, Kareen, you don't have to pay me—"

"*Never,*" said Kareen with passion, "ever suggest they don't have to pay you. What they pay for, they'll value. What they get for free, they'll take for granted, and then demand as a right. Hold them up for all the market will bear." She hesitated, then added anxiously, "You will take shares, though, won't you? Ma Kosti did, for the product development consultation she did for us."

"I must say, Ma Kosti made the bug butter ice cream work," Martya admitted. "And that bread spread wasn't bad either. It was all the garlic, I think. As long as you didn't think about where the stuff came from."

"So what, have you ever thought about where regular butter and ice cream come from? And meat, and liver sausage, and—"

"I can about guarantee you the beef filet the other night came from a nice, clean vat. Tante Cordelia wouldn't have it any other way at Vorkosigan House."

Kareen gestured this aside, irritably. "How long do you think it would take you, Ekaterin?" she asked.

"I don't know—a day or two, I suppose, for preliminary designs. But surely we'd have to meet with Enrique and Mark."

"I can't go to Vorkosigan House." Kareen slumped. She straightened again. "Could we meet *here*?"

Ekaterin glanced at Martya, and back to Kareen. "I can't be a party to undercutting your parents, or going behind their backs. But this is certainly legitimate business. We could all meet here if you'll get their permission."

"Maybe," said Kareen. "Maybe. If they have another day or so to calm down . . . As a last resort, you could meet with Mark and Enrique alone. But I want to be here, if I can. I know I can sell the idea to them, if only I have a chance." She stuck out her hand to Ekaterin. "Deal?"

Ekaterin, looking amused, rubbed the soil from her hand against the side of her skirt, leaned across the table, and shook on the compact. "Very well."

Martya objected, "You know Da and Mama will stick me with having to tag along, if they think Mark will be here."

"So, *you* can persuade them you're not needed. You're kind of an insult anyway, you know."

Martya stuck out a sisterly tongue at this, but shrugged a certain grudging agreement.

The sound of voices and footsteps wafted from the open kitchen window; Kareen looked up, wondering if Ekaterin's aunt and uncle had returned. And if maybe one of *them* had heard anything from Miles or Tante Cordelia or . . . But to her surprise, ducking out the door after Nikki came Armsman Pym, in full Vorkosigan House uniform, as neat and glittery as though ready for the Count's inspection. Pym was saying, "—I don't know about that, Nikki. But you know you're welcome to come play with my son Arthur at our flat, any time. He was asking after you just last night, in fact."

"Mama, Mama!" Nikki bounced to the garden table. "Look, Pym's here!"

Ekaterin's expression closed as though shutters had fallen across her face. She regarded Pym with extreme wariness. "Hello, Armsman," she said, in a tone of utter neutrality. She glanced across at her son. "Thank you, Nikki. Please go in now."

Nikki departed, with reluctant backward glances. Ekaterin waited.

Pym cleared his throat, smiled diffidently at her, and gave her a sort of half-salute. "Good evening, Madame Vorsoisson. I trust I find you well." His gaze went on to take in the Koudelka sisters; he favored them with a courteous, if curious, nod. "Hello, Miss Martya, Miss Kareen. I . . . this is unexpected." He looked as though he was riffling through revisions to some rehearsed speech.

Kareen wondered frantically if she could pretend that her prohibition from speaking with anyone from the Vorkosigan household was meant to apply only to the immediate family, and not the Armsmen as well. She smiled back with longing at Pym. Maybe *he* could talk to *her*. Her parents hadn't—couldn't—enforce their paranoid rule on anyone else, anyhow. But after his pause Pym only shook his head, and turned his attention back to Ekaterin.

Pym drew a heavy envelope from his tunic. Its thick cream paper was sealed with a stamp bearing the Vorkosigan arms—just like on the back of a butter bug—and addressed in ink in clear, square writing with only the words: *Madame Vorsoisson.* "Ma'am. Lord Vorkosigan directs me to deliver this into your hand. He says to say, he's sorry it took so long. It's on account of the drains, you see. Well, *m'lord* didn't say that, but the accident did delay things all round." He studied her face anxiously for her response to this.

Ekaterin accepted the envelope and stared at it as if it might contain explosives.

Pym stepped back, and gave her a very formal nod. When, after a moment, no one said anything, he gave her another half-salute, and said, "Didn't mean to intrude, ma'am. My apologies. I'll just be on my way now. Thank you." He turned on his heel.

"Pym!" His name, breaking from Kareen's lips, was almost a shriek; Pym jerked, and swung back. "Don't you dare just go off like that! What's *happening* over there?"

"Isn't that breaking your word?" asked Martya, with clinical detachment.

"Fine! Fine! *You* ask him, then!"

"Oh, very well." With a beleaguered sigh, Martya turned to Pym. "So tell me, Pym, what did happen to the drains?"

"I don't care about the drains!" Kareen cried. "I care about Mark! And my shares."

"So? Mama and Da say *you* aren't allowed to talk to anyone from Vorkosigan House, so you're out of luck. *I* want to know about the drains."

Pym's brows rose as he took this in, and his eyes glinted briefly. A sort of pious innocence informed his voice. "I'm most sorry to hear that, Miss Kareen. I trust the Commodore will see his way clear to lift our quarantine very soon. Now, *m'lord* told *me* I was not to hang about and distress Madame Vorsoisson with any ham-handed attempts at making things up to her, nor pester her by offering to wait for a reply, nor annoy her by watching her read his note. Very nearly his exact words, those. He never ordered me not to talk with you young ladies, however, not anticipating that you would be here."

"Ah," said Martya, in a voice dripping with, in Kareen's view, unsavory delight. "So you can talk to me and Kareen, but not to Ekaterin. And Kareen can talk to Ekaterin and me—"

"Not that I'd want to talk to you," Kareen muttered.

"—but not to you. That makes me the only person here who can talk to everybody. How . . . nice. *Do* tell me about the drains, dear Pym. Don't tell me they backed up again."

Ekaterin slipped the envelope into the inside pocket of her bolero, leaned her elbow on her chair arm and her chin on her hand, and sat listening with her dark eyebrows crinkling.

Pym nodded. "I'm afraid so, Miss Martya. Late last night, Dr. Borgos—" Pym's lips compressed at the name "—being in a great hurry to return to the search for his missing queen, took two days' harvest of bug butter—about forty or fifty kilos, we estimated later—which was starting to overflow the hutches on account of Miss Kareen not being there to take care of things properly, and flushed it all down the laboratory drain. Where it encountered some chemical conditions which caused it to . . . set. Like soft plaster. Entirely blocking the main drain, which, in a household with over fifty people in it—all the Viceroy and Vicereine's staff having arrived yesterday, and my fellow Armsmen and their families—caused a pretty immediate and pressing crisis."

Martya had the bad taste to giggle. Pym merely looked prim.

"Lord Auditor Vorkosigan," Pym went on, with a bare glance under his eyelashes at Ekaterin, "being of previous rich military experience with drains, he informed us, responded at once and without hesitation to his mother's piteous plea, and drafted and led a picked strike-force to the subbasement to deal with the dilemma. Which was me and Armsman Roic, in the event."

"Your courage and, um, utility, astound me," Martya intoned, staring at him with increasing fascination.

Pym shrugged humbly. "The necessity of wading knee-deep in bug butter, tree root bits, and, er, all the other things that go into drains, could not be honorably refused when following a leader who had to wade, um, knee-deeper. Being as how m'lord knew exactly what he was doing, it didn't actually take us very long, and there was much rejoicing in the household. But I was made later than intended for bringing Madame Vorsoisson her letter on account of everyone getting a slow start, this morning."

"What happened to Dr. Borgos?" asked Martya, as Kareen gritted her teeth, clenched her hands, and bounced in her chair.

"My suggestion that he be tied upside-down to the subbasement wall while the, um, *liquid* level rose being most unfairly rejected, I believe the Countess had a little talk with him, afterwards, about what kinds of materials could and could not be safely committed to Vorkosigan House's drains." Pym heaved a sigh. "Milady is quite too gentle and kindly."

The story having apparently finally wound to its conclusion, Kareen punched Martya on the shoulder and hissed, "Ask him how is *Mark*."

A little silence stretched, while Pym waited benignly for his translator, and Kareen reflected that it probably *would* take someone with a sense of humor as arcane as Pym's to get along so well with Miles as an employer. At last, Martya broke down and said ungraciously, "So, how's the fat one?"

"*Lord Mark*," Pym replied with faint emphasis, "having narrowly escaped injury in an attempt to consume—" his mouth paused, open, while he changed course in mid-sentence, "though quite visibly depressed by the unfortunate turn of events night before last, has been kept busy in assisting Dr. Borgos in his bug recovery."

Kareen decoded "visibly depressed" without difficulty. *Gorge has got out. Probably Howl, as well.* Oh, hell, and Mark had been doing so well in keeping the Black Gang subordinated. . . .

Pym went on smoothly, "I think I may speak for the entire Vorkosigan household when I say that we all wish Miss Kareen may return as soon as possible and restore order. Lacking information on the events in the Commodore's family, Lord Mark has been uncertain how to proceed, but that should be remedied now." His eyelid shivered in a ghost of a wink at Kareen. Ah yes, Pym was former ImpSec and proud of it; thinking sideways in two directions simultaneously was no mystery to him. Throwing her arms around his boots and screaming, *Help, help! Tell Tante Cordelia I'm being held prisoner by insane parents!* would be entirely redundant, she realized with satisfaction. Intelligence was about to flow.

"Also," Pym added in the same bland tone, "the piles of bug butter tubs lining the basement hall are beginning to be a problem. They toppled on a maid yesterday. The young lady was very upset."

Even the silently listening Ekaterin's eyes widened at this image. Martya snickered outright. Kareen suppressed a growl.

Martya glanced sideways at Ekaterin, and added somewhat daringly, "And so how's the skinny one?"

Pym hesitated, followed her glance, and finally replied, "I'm afraid the drain crisis brightened his life only temporarily."

He sketched a bow at all three ladies, leaving them to construe the stygian blackness of a soul that could find fifty kilos of bug butter in the main drain an *improvement* in his gloomy world. "Miss Martya, Miss Kareen, I hope we may see all the Koudelkas at Vorkosigan

House again soon. Madame Vorsoisson, allow me to excuse myself, and apologize for any discomfort I may have inadvertently caused you. Speaking only for my own house, and Arthur, may I ask if Nikki may still be permitted to visit us?"

"Yes, of course," said Ekaterin faintly.

"Good evening, then." He touched his forehead amiably, and trod off to let himself out the garden gate in the narrow space between the houses.

Martya shook her head in amazement. "Where *do* the Vorkosigans find their *people*?"

Kareen shrugged. "I suppose they get the cream of the Empire."

"So do a lot of high Vor, but they don't get a *Pym*. Or a Ma Kosti. Or a—"

"I heard Pym came personally recommended by Simon Illyan, when he was head of ImpSec," said Kareen.

"Oh, I see. They *cheat*. That accounts for it."

Ekaterin's hand strayed to touch her bolero, beneath which that fascinating cream envelope lay hidden, but to Kareen's intense disappointment, she didn't take it out and break it open. She doubtless wouldn't read it in front of her uninvited guests. It was, therefore, time to shove off.

Kareen got to her feet. "Ekaterin, thank you so much. You've been more help to me than anybody—" *in my own family*, she managed to bite back. There was no point in deliberately ticking off Martya, when she'd allowed this grudging and partial allegiance against the parental opposition. "And I'm deadly serious about the bug redesign. Call me as soon as you have something ready."

"I'll have something tomorrow, I promise." Ekaterin walked the sisters to the gate, and closed it behind them.

At the end of the block, they were more or less ambushed by Pym, who waited leaning against the parked armored groundcar.

"Did she read it?" he asked anxiously.

Kareen nudged Martya.

"Not in front of *us*, Pym," said Martya, rolling her eyes.

"Huh. Damn." Pym stared up the block at the tile front of Lord Auditor Vorthys's house, half concealed in the trees. "I was hoping— damn."

"How *is* Miles, really?" asked Martya, following his glance and then cocking her head.

Pym absently scratched the back of his neck. "Well, he's over the vomiting and moaning part. Now he's taken to wandering around the house muttering to himself, when there's nothing to distract him. Starved for action, *I'd* say. The way he took to the drain problem was right frightening. From my point of view, you understand."

Kareen did. After all, wherever Miles bolted off to, Pym would be compelled to follow. No wonder all Miles's household watched his courtship with bated breath. She pictured the conversations belowstairs: *For God's sake, can't somebody please get the little git laid, before he drives us all as crazy as he is?* Well, no, most of Miles's people were sufficiently under his spell, they probably wouldn't put it in quite such harsh terms. But she bet it came to about that.

Pym abandoned his futile surveillance of Madame Vorsoisson's house and offered the sisters a ride; Martya, possibly looking ahead to parental cross-examination later, politely declined for them both. Pym drove off. Trailed by her personal snitch, Kareen departed in the opposite direction.

Ekaterin returned slowly to the garden table, and sat again. She pulled the envelope from her left inner pocket, and turned it over, staring at it. The cream-colored paper had impressive weight and density. The back flap was indented in the pattern of the Vorkosigans' seal, pressed deeply and a little off-center into the thick paper. Not machine embossed; some hand had put it there. *His* hand. A thumb-smear of reddish pigment filled the grooves and brought out the pattern, in the highest of high Vor styles, more formal than a wax seal. She raised the envelope to her nose, but if there was any scent of him lingering from his touch, it was too faint to be certain of.

She sighed in anticipated exhaustion, and carefully opened it. Like the address, the sheet inside was handwritten.

Dear Madame Vorsoisson, it began. *I am sorry.*

This is the eleventh draft of this letter. They've all started with those three words, even the horrible version in rhyme, so I guess they stay.

Her mind hiccuped to a stop. For a moment, all she could wonder was who emptied his wastebasket, and if they could be bribed. Pym, probably, and likely not. She shook the vision from her head, and read on.

You once asked me never to lie to you. All right, so. I'll tell you the truth now even if it isn't the best or cleverest thing, and not abject enough either.

I tried to be the thief of you, to ambush and take prisoner what I thought I could never earn or be given. You were not a ship to be hijacked, but I couldn't think of any other plan but subterfuge and surprise. Though not as much of a surprise as what happened at dinner. The revolution started prematurely because the idiot conspirator blew up his secret ammo dump and lit the sky with his intentions. Sometimes those accidents end in new nations, but more often they end badly, in hangings and beheadings. And people running into the night. I can't be sorry I asked you to marry me, because that was the one true part in all the smoke and rubble, but I'm sick as hell I asked you so badly.

Even though I'd kept my counsel from you, I should at least have done you the courtesy to keep it from others as well, till you'd had the year of grace and rest you'd asked for. But I became terrified you'd choose another first.

What *other* did he imagine her choosing, for God's sake? She'd wanted no one. Vormoncrief was impossible. Byerly Vorrutyer didn't even pretend to be serious. Enrique Borgos? *Eep.* Major Zamori, well, Zamori seemed kindly enough. But dull.

She wondered when *not dull* had become her prime criterion for mate selection. About ten minutes after she'd first met Miles Vorkosigan, perhaps? Damn the man, for ruining her taste. And judgment. And . . . and . . .

She read on.

So I used the garden as a ploy to get near to you. I deliberately and consciously shaped your heart's desire into a trap. For this I am more than sorry. I am ashamed.

You'd earned every chance to grow. I'd like to pretend I didn't see it would be a conflict of interest for me to be the one to give you some of those chances, but that would be another lie. But it made me crazy to watch you constrained to tiny steps, when you could be outrunning time. There is only a brief moment of apogee to do that, in most lives.

I love you. But I lust after and covet so much more than your body. I wanted to possess the power of your eyes, the way they see form and beauty that isn't even there yet and draw it up out of nothing into the solid world. I wanted to own the honor of your heart, unbowed in the vilest horrors of those bleak hours on Komarr. I wanted your courage and your will, your caution and serenity. I wanted, I suppose, your soul, and that was too much to want.

She put the letter down, shaken. After a few deep breaths, she took it up again.

I wanted to give you a victory. But by their essential nature triumphs can't be given. They must be taken, and the worse the odds and the fiercer the resistance, the greater the honor. Victories can't be gifts.

But gifts can be victories, can't they. It's what you said. The garden could have been your gift, a dowry of talent, skill, and vision.

I know it's too late now, but I just wanted to say, it would have been a victory most worthy of our House.

Yours to command,

Miles Vorkosigan.

Ekaterin rested her forehead in her hand, and closed her eyes. She regained control of her breathing again in a few gulps.

She sat up again, and reread the letter in the fading light. Twice. It neither demanded nor requested nor seemed to anticipate reply. Good, because she doubted she could string two coherent clauses together just now. What did he expect her to make of this? Every sentence that didn't start with *I* seemed to begin with *But*. It wasn't just honest, it was *naked*.

With the back of her dirty hand, she swiped the water from her eyes across her hot cheeks to cool and evaporate. She turned over the envelope and stared again at the seal. In the Time of Isolation, such incised seals had been smeared with blood, to signify a lord's most personal protestation of loyalty. Subsequently, soft pigment sticks had been invented for rubbing over the indentations, in a palette of colors of various fashionable meanings. Wine red and purple had been popular for love letters, pink and blue for announcements of births, black for notifications of deaths. This seal-rubbing was the very most conservative and traditional color, red-brown.

The reason for that, Ekaterin realized with a blurred blink, was that it *was* blood. Conscious melodrama on Miles's part, or unthinking routine? She had not the slightest doubt that he was perfectly capable of melodrama. In fact, she was beginning to suspect he reveled in it, when he got the chance. But the horrible conviction grew on her, staring at the smear and imagining him pricking his thumb and applying it, that for him it had been as natural and original as breathing. She bet he even owned one of those daggers with the seal concealed in the hilt for the purpose, which the high lords had used to wear. One could buy imitation reproductions of them in antique and souvenir shops, with soft and blunted metal blades because nobody ever actually nicked themselves anymore to testify in blood. Genuine seal daggers with provenance from the Time of Isolation, on the rare occasions when they appeared on the market, were bid up to tens and hundreds of thousands of marks.

Miles probably used his for a letter opener, or to clean under his fingernails.

And when and how had he ever hijacked a ship? She was unreasonably certain he hadn't plucked that comparison out of the air.

A helpless puff of a laugh escaped her lips. If she ever saw him again, she would say, *People who've been in Covert Ops shouldn't write letters while high on fast-penta.*

Though if he really was suffering a virulent outbreak of truthfulness, what about that part that started, *I love you*? She turned the letter over, and read that bit again. Four times. The tense, square, distinctive letters seemed to waver before her eyes.

Something was missing, though, she realized as she read the letter through one more time. Confession was there in plenty, but nowhere was any plea for forgiveness, absolution, penance, or any begging to call or see her again. No entreaty that she respond in any way. It was very strange, that stopping-short. What did it mean? If this was some sort of odd ImpSec code, well, she didn't own the cipher.

Maybe he didn't ask for forgiveness because he didn't expect it was possible to receive it. That seemed a cold, dry place to be left standing. . . . Or was he just too bleakly arrogant to beg? Pride, or despair? Which? Though she supposed it could be both—*On sale now,* her mind supplied, *this week only, two sins for the price of one!* That . . . that sounded very *Miles,* somehow.

She thought back over her old, bitter domestic arguments with Tien. How she had hated that awful dance between break and rejoining, how many times she had short-circuited it. If you were going to forgive each other eventually, why not do it now and save days of stomach-churning tension? Straight from sin to forgiveness, without going through any of the middle steps of repentance and restitution. . . . Just go on, just do it. But they hadn't gone on, much. They'd always seemed to circle back to the start-point again. Maybe that was why the chaos had always seemed to replay in an endless loop. Maybe they hadn't learned enough, when they'd left out the hard middle parts.

When you'd made a real mistake, how did you continue? How to go on rightly from the bad place where you found yourself, on and not back again? Because there was never really any going back. Time erased the path behind your heels.

Anyway, she didn't want to go back. Didn't want to know less, didn't want to be smaller. She didn't wish these words unsaid—her hand clutched the letter spasmodically to her chest, then carefully flattened out the creases against the tabletop. She just wanted the pain to stop.

The next time she saw him, did she have to answer his disastrous question? Or at least, know what the answer was? Was there another way to say *I forgive you* short of *Yes, forever,* some third place to stand? She desperately wanted a third place to stand right now.

I can't answer this right away. I just can't.

Butter bugs. She could do butter bugs, anyway—

The sound of her aunt's voice, calling her name, shattered the spinning circle of Ekaterin's thoughts. Her uncle and aunt must be back from their dinner out. Hastily, she stuffed the letter back in its envelope and hid it again in her bolero, and scrubbed her hands over her eyes. She tried to fit an expression, any expression, onto her face. They all felt like masks.

"Coming, Aunt Vorthys," she called, and rose to collect her trowel, carry the weeds to the compost, and go into the house.

Chapter Twelve

The door-chime to his apartment rang as Ivan was alternating between slurping his first cup of coffee of the morning and fastening his uniform shirtsleeves. Company, at this hour? His brows rose in puzzlement and some curiosity, and he trod to the entryway to answer its summons.

He was yawning behind his hand as the door slid back to reveal Byerly Vorrutyer, and so he was too slow to hit the Close pad again before By got his leg through. The safety sensor, alas, brought the door to a halt rather than crushing By's foot. Ivan was briefly sorry the door was edged with rounded rubber instead of, say, a honed razor-steel flange.

"Good morning, Ivan," drawled By through the shoe-wide gap.

"What the hell are you doing up so early?" Ivan asked suspiciously.

"So late," said By, with a small smile.

Well, that made a little more sense. Upon closer examination, By was looking a bit seedy, with a beard shadow and red-rimmed eyes. Ivan said firmly, "I don't want to hear any more about your cousin Dono. Go away."

"Actually, this is about your cousin Miles."

Ivan eyed his ceremonial dress sword, sitting nearby in an umbrella canister made from an old-fashioned artillery shell. He wondered if driving it down on By's shod foot hard enough to make him recoil would allow getting the door shut and locked again. But the canister was just out of reach from the doorway. "I don't want to hear anything about my cousin Miles, either."

"It's something I judge he needs to know."

"Fine. You go tell him, then."

"I . . . would really rather not, all things considered."

Ivan's finely tuned shit-detectors began to blink red, in some corner of his brain usually not active at this hour. "Oh? What things?"

"Oh, you know . . . delicacy . . . consideration . . . family feeling . . ."

Ivan made a rude noise through his lips.

" . . . the fact that he controls a valuable vote in the Council of Counts . . ." By went on serenely.

"It's my Uncle Aral's vote Dono is after," Ivan pointed out. "Technically. He arrived back in Vorbarr Sultana four nights ago. Go hustle him." *If you dare.*

By bared his teeth in a pained smile. "Yes, Dono told me all about the Viceroy's grand entrance, and the assorted grand exits. I don't know how you managed to escape the wreckage unscathed."

"Had Armsman Roic let me out the back door," said Ivan shortly.

"Ah, I see. Very prudent, no doubt. But in any case, Count Vorkosigan has made it quite well known that he leaves his proxy to his son's discretion in nine votes out of ten."

"That's his business. Not mine."

"*Do* you have any more of that coffee?" By eyed the cup in his hand longingly.

"No," Ivan lied.

"Then perhaps you would be so kind as to make me some more. Come, Ivan, I appeal to your common humanity. It's been a very long and tedious night."

"I'm sure you can find someplace open in Vorbarr Sultana to sell you coffee. On your way home." Maybe he wouldn't leave the sword in its scabbard . . .

By sighed, and leaned against the doorframe, crossing his arms as if for a lengthy chat. His foot stayed planted. "What *have* you heard from your cousin the Lord Auditor in the last few days?"

"Nothing."

"And what do you think about that?"

"When Miles decides what I should think, I'm sure he'll tell me. He always does."

By's lip curled up, but he tamped it straight again. "Have you tried to talk to him?"

"Do I look that stupid? You heard about the party. The man crashed and burned. He'll be impossible for days. My Aunt Cordelia can hold his head under water this time, thanks."

By raised his brows, perhaps taking this last remark for an amusing metaphor. "Now, now. Miles's little *faux pas* wasn't irredeemable, according to Dono, whom I take to be a shrewder judge of women than we are." By's face sobered, and his eyes grew oddly hooded. "But it's about to become so, if nothing is done."

Ivan hesitated. "What do you mean?"

"Coffee, Ivan. And what I have to pass on to you is not, most definitely not, for the public hallway."

I'm going to regret this. Grudgingly, Ivan hit the Door-open pad and stood aside.

Ivan handed By coffee and let him sit on his sofa. Probably a strategic error. If By sipped slowly enough, he could spin out this visit indefinitely. "I'm on my way to work, mind," Ivan said, lowering himself into the one comfortable chair, across from the sofa.

By took a grateful sip. "I'll make it fast. Only my sense of Vorish duty keeps me from my bed even now."

In the interests of speed and efficiency, Ivan let this one pass. He gestured for By to proceed, preferably succinctly.

"I went to a little private dinner with Alexi Vormoncrief last night," By began.

"How exciting for you," growled Ivan.

By waved his fingers. "It proved to have moments of interest. It was at Vormoncrief House, hosted by Alexi's uncle Count Boriz. One of those little behind-the-scenes love-fests that give *party* politics its name, you know. It seems my complacent cousin Richars heard about Lord Dono's return at last, and hurried up to town to investigate the truth of the rumors. What he found alarmed him sufficiently to, ah, begin to exert himself on behalf of his vote-bag in the upcoming decision in the Council of Counts. As Count Boriz influences a significant block of Conservative Party votes in the Council, Richars, nothing if not efficient, started his campaign with him."

"Get to the point, By," sighed Ivan. "What has all this to do with my cousin Miles? It's got nothing to do with *me*; serving officers are officially discouraged from playing politics, you know."

"Oh, yes, I'm quite aware. Also present, incidentally, were Boriz's son-in-law Sigur Vorbretten, and Count Tomas Vormuir, who apparently had a little run-in with your cousin in his Auditorial capacity recently."

"The lunatic with the baby factory that Miles shut down? Yeah, I heard about that."

"I knew Vormuir slightly, before this. Lady Donna used to go target-shooting with his Countess, in happier times. Quite the gossips, those girls. At any rate, as expected, Richars opened his campaign with the soup, and by the time the salad was served had settled upon a trade with Count Boriz: a vote for Richars in exchange for allegiance to the Conservatives. This left the rest of the dinner, from entrée to dessert through the wine, free to drift onto other topics. Count Vormuir expanded much upon his dissatisfaction with his Imperial Audit, which rather brought your cousin, as it were, onto the table."

Ivan blinked. "Wait a minute. What were you doing hanging out with Richars? I thought you were on the other side in this little war."

"Richars thinks I'm spying on Dono for him."

"And are you?" If Byerly was playing both ends against the middle in this, Ivan cordially hoped he'd get both hands burned.

A sphinxlike smile lifted By's lips. "Mm, shall we say, I tell him what he needs to know. Richars is quite proud of his cunning, for planting me in Dono's camp."

"Doesn't he know about you getting the Lord Guardian of the Speaker's Circle to block him from taking possession of Vorrutyer House?"

"In a word, no. I managed to stay behind the curtain on that one."

Ivan rubbed his temples, wondering which of his cousins By was actually lying to. It wasn't his imagination; talking with the man *was* giving him a headache. He hoped By had a hangover. "Go on. Speed it up."

"Some standard Conservative bitching was exchanged about the costs of the proposed Komarran solar mirror repairs. Let the Komarrans pay for it, they broke it, didn't they, and so on as usual."

"They will be paying for it. Don't they know how much of our tax revenues are based in Komarran trade?"

"You surprise me, Ivan. I didn't know you paid attention to things like that."

"I don't," Ivan denied hastily. "It's common knowledge."

"Discussion of the Komarran incident brought up, again, our favorite little Lord Auditor, and dear Alexi was moved to unburden himself of his personal grievance. It seems the beautiful Widow Vorsoisson bounced his suit. After much trouble and expense on his part, too. All those fees to the Baba, you know."

"Oh." Ivan brightened. "Good for her." She was refusing everybody. Miles's domestic disaster was provably *not Ivan's fault,* yes!

"Sigur Vorbretten, of all people, next offered up a garbled version of Miles's recent dinner party, complete with a vivid description of Madame Vorsoisson storming out in the middle of it after Miles's calamitous public proposal of marriage." By tilted his head. "Even taking Dono's version of the dialogue over Sigur's, whatever did possess the man, anyway? I always thought Miles more reliably suave."

"Panic," said Ivan. "I believe. I was at the other end of the table." He brooded briefly. "It can happen to the best of us." He frowned. "How the hell did Sigur get hold of the story? *I* sure haven't been passing it out. Has Lord Dono been blabbing?"

"Only to me, I trust. But Ivan, there were nineteen people at that party. Plus the Armsmen and servants. It's all over town, and growing more dramatic and delicious with each reiteration, I'm sure."

Ivan could just picture it. Ivan could just picture it coming to Miles's ears, and the smoke pouring back out of them. He winced deeply. "Miles . . . Miles will be homicidal."

"Funny you should say that." By took another sip of coffee, and regarded Ivan very blandly. "Putting together Miles's investigation on Komarr, Administrator Vorsoisson's death in the middle of it, Miles's subsequent proposition of his widow, and her theatrical—in Sigur's version, though Dono claims she was quite dignified, under the circumstances—public rejection of it, plus five Conservative Vor politicians with long-time grudges against Aral Vorkosigan and all his works, *and* several bottles of fine Vormoncrief District wine, a Theory was born. And evolved rapidly, in a sort of punctuated equilibrium, to a full-grown Slander even as I watched. It was just fascinating."

"Oh, shit," whispered Ivan.

By gave him a sharp look. "You anticipate me? Goodness, Ivan. What unexpected depths. You can imagine the conversation; I had to sit through it. Alexi piping about the damned mutant daring to court the Vor lady. Vormuir opining it was bloody convenient, say what, the husband killed in some supposed-accident in the middle of Vorkosigan's case. Sigur saying, But there weren't any charges, Count Boriz eyeing him like the pitiful waif he is and rumbling, There wouldn't be—the Vorkosigans have had ImpSec under their thumb for thirty years, the only question is whether was it collusion between the wife and Vorkosigan? Alexi leaping to the defense of his lady-love—the man just *does not* take a hint—and declaring her innocent, unsuspecting till Vorkosigan's crude proposal finally tipped his hand. Her storming out was Proof! Proof!—actually, he said it three times, but he was pretty drunk by then—that she, at least, now realized Miles had cleverly made away with her beloved spouse to clear his way to her, and she ought to know, she was there. And he bet she would be willing to reconsider his own proposal now! Since Alexi is a known twit, his seniors were not altogether convinced by his arguments, but willing to give the widow the benefit of the doubt for the sake of family solidarity. And so on."

"Good God, By. Couldn't you stop them?"

"I attempted to inject sanity to the limit available to me without, as you military types say, blowing my cover. They were far too entranced with their creation to pay me much heed."

"If they bring that murder charge against Miles, he'll wipe the floor with them all. I guarantee he will *not* suffer those fools gladly."

By shrugged. "Not that Boriz Vormoncrief wouldn't be delighted to see an indictment laid against Aral Vorkosigan's son, but as I pointed out to them, they haven't enough proof for that, and for—whatever—reason, aren't likely to get any, either. No. A *charge* can be disproved. A charge can be defended against. A charge proved false can draw legal retaliation. There won't be a charge."

Ivan was less sure. The mere hint of the idea had surely put the wind up Miles.

"But a wink," By went on, "a whisper, a snicker, a joke, a deliciously horrific anecdote . . . who can get a grip on such vapor? It would be like trying to fight fog."

"You think the Conservatives will embark on a smear campaign using this?" said Ivan slowly, chilled.

"I think . . . that if Lord Auditor Vorkosigan wishes to exert any kind of damage control, he needs to mobilize his resources. Five swaggering tongues are sleeping it off this morning. By tonight, they'll be flapping again. I would not presume to suggest strategies to My Lord Auditor. He's a big boy now. But as a, shall we say, courtesy, I present him the advantage of early intelligence. What he does with it is up to him."

"Isn't this more a matter for ImpSec?"

"Oh, ImpSec." By waved a dismissive hand. "I'm sure they'll be on top of it. But—*is* it a matter for ImpSec, y'see? Vapor, Ivan. Vapor."

This is slit your throat before reading stuff, and no horseshit, Miles had said, in a voice of terrifying conviction. Ivan shrugged, carefully. "How would I know?"

By's little smile didn't shift, but his eyes mocked. "How, indeed."

Ivan glanced at the time. Ye gods. "I have to report to work now, or my mother will bitch," he said hastily.

"Yes, Lady Alys is doubtless at the Residence waiting for you already." Taking the hint for a change, Byerly rose. "I don't suppose you can use your influence upon her to get *me* issued a wedding invitation?"

"I have no influence," said Ivan, edging By towards the door. "If Lord Dono is Count Dono by then, maybe you can get him to take you along."

By acknowledged this with a wave, and strolled off down the corridor, yawning. Ivan stood for a moment after the door hissed shut, rubbing his forehead. He pictured himself presenting By's news to Miles, assuming his distraught cousin had sobered up by now. He pictured himself ducking for cover. Better yet, he pictured himself deserting it all, possibly for the life of a licensed male prostitute at Beta's Orb. Betan male prostitutes did have female customers, yes? Miles had been there, and told him not-quite-all about it. Fat Mark and Kareen had even been there. But *he'd* never even once made it to the Orb, dammit. Life was unfair, that was what.

He slouched to his comconsole, and punched in Miles's private code. But all he stirred up was the answering program, a new one, all very official announcing that the supplicant had reached *Lord Auditor Vorkosigan*, whoop-te-do. Except he hadn't. Ivan left a message for his cousin to call him on urgent private business, and cut the com.

Miles probably wasn't even awake yet. Ivan dutifully promised his conscience he'd try again later today, and if that still didn't draw a response, drag himself over to Vorkosigan House to see Miles tonight. Maybe. He sighed, and shoved off to don the tunic of his undress greens, and head out for the Imperial Residence and the day's tasks.

Mark rang the chime on the Vorthys's door, shifted from foot to foot, and gritted his teeth in anxiety. Enrique, let out of Vorkosigan House for the occasion, stared around in fascination. Tall, thin, and twitchy, the ectomorphic Escobaran made Mark feel more like a squat toad than ever. He should have given more thought to the ludicrous picture they presented when together . . . ah. Ekaterin opened the door to them, and smiled welcome.

"Lord Mark, Enrique. Do come in." She gestured them out of the afternoon glare into a cool tiled entry hall.

"Thank you," said Mark fervently. "Thank you so much for this, Madame Vorsoisson—Ekaterin—for setting this up. Thank you. Thank you. You don't know how much this means to me."

"Goodness, don't thank me. It was Kareen's idea."

"Is she here?" Mark swiveled his head in search of her.

"Yes, she and Martya were just a few minutes ahead of you both. This way . . ." Ekaterin led them to the right, into a book-crammed study.

Kareen and her sister sat in spindly chairs ranged around a comconsole. Kareen was beautiful and tight-lipped, her fists clenched in her lap. She looked up as he entered, and her smile twisted bleakly upward. Mark surged forward, stopped, stammered her name inaudibly, and seized her rising hands. They exchanged a hard grip.

"I'm allowed to talk to you now," Kareen told him, with an irritated toss of her head, "but only about business. I don't know what they're so paranoid about. If I wanted to elope, all I'd have to do is step out the door and walk six blocks."

"I, I . . . I'd better not say anything, then." Reluctantly, Mark released her hands, and backed off a step. His eyes drank her in like water. She looked tired and tense, but otherwise all right.

"Are *you* all right?" Her gaze searched him in turn.

"Yeah, sure. For now." He returned her a wan smile, and looked vaguely at Martya. "Hi, Martya. What are you doing here?"

"I'm the duenna," she told him, with a grimace quite as annoyed as her sister's. "It's the same principle as putting a guard on the picket line after the horses are stolen. Now, if they'd sent me along to Beta Colony, *that* might have been of some use. To me, at least."

Enrique folded himself into the chair next to Martya, and said in an aggrieved tone, "Did *you* know Lord Mark's mother was a *Betan Survey captain?*"

"Tante Cordelia?" Martya shrugged. "Sure."

"A *Betan Astronomical Survey captain.* And nobody even thought to mention it! A *Survey captain.* And nobody even *told* me."

Martya stared at him. "Is it important?"

"Is it important. Is it important! Holy saints, you people!"

"It was thirty years ago, Enrique," Mark put in wearily. He'd been listening to variations on this rant for two days. The Countess had acquired another worshipper in Enrique. His conversion had doubtless helped save his life from all his coreligionists in the household, after the incident with the drains in the nighttime.

Enrique clasped his hands together between his knees, and gazed up soulfully into the air. "I gave her my dissertation to read."

Kareen, her eyes widening, asked, "Did she understand it?"

"Of *course* she did. She was a *Betan Survey commander*, for God's sake! Do you have any idea how those people are chosen, what they do? If I'd completed my postgraduate work with honors, instead of all that stupid misunderstanding with the arrest, I could have hoped, only hoped, to put in an application, and even then I wouldn't have had a prayer of beating out all the Betan candidates, if it weren't for their off-worlder quotas holding open some places specifically for non-Betans." Enrique was breathless with the passion of this speech. "She said she would recommend my work to the attention of the Viceroy. And she said my sonnet was very ingenious. I composed a sestina in her honor in my head while I was catching bugs, but I haven't had time to get it down yet. Survey captain!"

"It's . . . not what Tante Cordelia is most famous for, on Barrayar," Martya offered after a moment.

"The woman is wasted here. *All* the women are wasted here." Enrique subsided grumpily. Martya turned half-around, and gave him an odd raised-brows look.

"How's the bug roundup going?" Kareen asked him anxiously.

"One hundred twelve accounted for. The queen is still missing." Enrique rubbed the side of his nose in reminded worry.

Ekaterin put in, "Thank you, Enrique, for sending me the butter bug vid model so promptly yesterday. It speeded up my design experiments vastly."

Enrique smiled at her. "My pleasure."

"Well. Perhaps I ought to move along to my presentations," said Ekaterin. "It won't take long, and then we can discuss them."

Mark lowered his short bulk into the last spindly chair, and stared mournfully across the gap at Kareen. Ekaterin sat in the comconsole chair, and keyed up the first vid. It was a full-color three-dimensional representation of a butter bug, blown up to a quarter of a meter long. Everyone but Enrique and Ekaterin recoiled.

"Here, of course, is our basic utility butter bug," Ekaterin began. "Now, I've only run up four modifications so far, because Lord Mark indicated time was of the essence, but I can certainly make more. Here's the first and easiest."

The shit-brown-and-pus-white bug vanished, to be replaced with a much classier model. This bug's legs and body were patent-leather black, as shiny as a palace guardsman's boots. A thin white racing stripe ran along the edges of the now-elongated black wing carapaces, which hid the pale pulsing abdomen from view. "Ooh," said Mark, surprised and impressed. How could such small changes have made such a large difference? "Yeah!"

"Now here's something a little brighter."

The second bug also had patent-black legs and body parts, but now the carapaces were more rounded, like fans. A rainbow progression of colors succeeded each other in curved stripes, from purple in the center through blue-and-green-and-yellow-and-orange to red on the edge.

Martya sat up. "Oh, now *that's* better. That's actually *pretty.*"

"I don't think this next one will quite be practical," Ekaterin went on, "but I wanted to play with the range of possibilities."

At first glance, Mark took it for a rose bud bursting into bloom. Now the bug's body parts were a matte leaf-green faintly edged with a subtle red. The carapaces looked like flower petals, in a delicate pale yellow blushing with pink in multiple layers; the abdomen too was a matching yellow, blending with the flower atop and receding from the eye's notice. The spurs and angles of the bug's legs were exaggerated into little blunt thorns.

"Oh, oh," said Kareen, her eyes widening. "I want that one! I vote for that one!"

Enrique looked quite stunned, his mouth slightly open. "Goodness. Yes, that could be done . . ."

"This design might possibly work for—I suppose you'd call them— the farmed or captive bugs," said Ekaterin. "I think the carapace petals might be a little too delicate and awkward for the free-range bugs that were expected to forage for their own food. They might get torn up and damaged. But I was thinking, as I was working with these, that you might have more than one design, later. Different packages, perhaps, for different microbial synthesis suites."

"Certainly," said Enrique. "Certainly."

"Last one," said Ekaterin, and keyed the vid.

This bug's legs and body parts were a deep, glimmering blue. The carapace halves flared and then swept back in a teardrop shape. Their center was a brilliant yellow, shading immediately to a deep red-orange, then to light flame blue, then dark flame blue edged with flickering iridescence. The abdomen, barely visible, was a rich dark red. The creature looked like a flame, like a torch in the dusk, like a jewel cast from a crown. Four people leaned forward so far they nearly fell off their chairs. Martya's hand reached out. Ekaterin smiled demurely.

"Wow, wow, wow," husked Kareen. "Now *that* is a *glorious* bug!"

"I believe that was what you ordered, yes," murmured Ekaterin.

She touched a vid control, and the static bug came to life momentarily. It flicked its carapace, and a luminous lace of wing flashed out, like a spray of red sparks from a fire. "If Enrique can figure out how to make the wings bio-fluoresce at the right wavelength, they could twinkle in the dark. A group of them might be quite spectacular."

Enrique leaned forward, staring avidly. "Now *there's* an idea. They'd be a *lot* easier to catch in dim locations that way . . . There would be a measurable bio-energy cost, though, which would come out of butter production."

Mark tried to imagine an array of these glorious bugs, gleaming and flashing and twinkling in the twilight. It made his mind melt. "Think of it as their advertising budget."

"Which one should we use?" asked Kareen. "I really liked the one that looked like a flower . . ."

"Take a vote, I guess," said Mark. He wondered if he could persuade anyone else to go for the slick black model. A veritable assassin-bug, that one had looked. "A shareholder's vote," he added prudently.

"We've hired a consultant for aesthetics," Enrique pointed out. "Perhaps we should take her advice." He looked over to Ekaterin.

Ekaterin opened her hands back to him. "The aesthetics were all I could supply. I could only guess at how technically feasible they were, on the bio-genetic level. There may be a trade-off between visual impact, and the time needed to develop it."

"You made some good guesses." Enrique hitched his chair over to the comconsole, and ran through the series of bug vids again, his expression going absent.

"Time is important," Kareen said. "Time is money, time is . . . time is everything. Our first goal has to be to get some saleable product launched, to start cycling in capital to get the basic business up, running, and growing. Then play with the refinements."

"And get it out of Vorkosigan House's basement," muttered Mark. "Maybe . . . maybe the black one would be quickest?"

Kareen shook her head, and Martya said, "No, Mark." Ekaterin sat back in a posture of studied neutrality.

Enrique stopped at the glorious bug, and sighed dreamily. "This one," he stated. One corner of Ekaterin's mouth twitched up, and back down. Her order of presentation hadn't been random, Mark decided.

Kareen glanced up. "Faster than the flower-bug, d'you think?"

"Yes," said Enrique.

"Second the motion."

"Are you sure you don't like that black one?" said Mark plaintively.

"You're outvoted, Mark," Kareen told him.

"Can't be, I own fifty-one percent . . . oh." With the distribution of shares to Kareen and to Miles's cook, he'd actually slipped below his automatic majority. He intended to buy them back out, later . . .

"The glorious bug it is," said Kareen. She added, "Ekaterin said she'd be willing to be paid in shares, same as Ma Kosti."

"It wasn't that hard," Ekaterin began.

"Hush," Kareen told her firmly. "We're not paying you for hard. We're paying you for good. Standard creative consultant fee. Pony up, Mark."

With some reluctance—not that the workwoman was unworthy of her hire, but merely covert regret for the additional smidge of control slipping through his fingers—Mark went to the comconsole and made out a receipt of shares paid for services rendered. He had Enrique and Kareen countersign it, sent off a copy to Tsipis's office in Hassadar, and formally presented it to Ekaterin.

She smiled a little bemusedly, thanked him, and set the flimsy aside. Well, if she took it for play-money, at least she hadn't supplied play-work. Like Miles, maybe she was one of those people who was incapable of any speeds but *off* and *flat-out*. All things done well for the glory of God, as the Countess put it. Mark glanced again at the glorious bug, which Enrique was now making cycle through its wing-flash some more. Yeah.

"I suppose," said Mark with a last longing look at Kareen, "we'd better be going." Time-the-essence and all that. "The bug hunt has stopped everything in its tracks. R and D is at a standstill . . . we're barely maintaining the bugs we have."

"Think of it as cleaning up your industrial spill," Martya advised unsympathetically. "Before it crawls away."

"Your parents let Kareen come here today. Do you think they'd at least let her come back to work?"

Kareen grimaced hopelessly.

Martya screwed up her mouth, and shook her head. "They're coming down some, but not that fast. Mama doesn't say much, but Da . . . Da has always taken a lot of pride in being a good Da, you see. The Betan Orb and, well, you, Mark, just weren't in his Barrayaran Da's instruction manual. Maybe he's been in the military too long. Although truth to tell, he's barely handling *Delia's* engagement without going all twitchy, and she *is* playing by all the old rules. As far as he knows."

Kareen raised an inquiring eyebrow at this, but Martya did not elaborate.

Martya glanced aside to the comconsole, where the glorious bug sparked and gleamed under Enrique's enraptured gaze. "On the other hand—the guard-parents haven't forbidden *me* to go over to Vorkosigan House."

"Martya . . ." Kareen breathed. "Oh, could you? *Would* you?"

"Eh, maybe." She glanced under her lashes at Mark. "I was thinking maybe I could stand to get into some of this share-action myself."

Mark's brows rose. Martya? Practical Martya? To take over the bug hunt and send Enrique back to his genetic codes, without sestinas? Martya to maintain the lab, to deal with supplies and suppliers, to not flush bug butter down the sink? So what if she looked on him as a sort of oversized repulsive fat butter bug that her sister had inexplicably taken for a pet. He had not the least doubt Martya could make the brains run on time. . . . "Enrique?"

"Hm?" Enrique murmured, not looking up.

Mark got his attention by reaching over and switching off the vid, and explained Martya's offer.

"Oh, yes, that would be lovely," the Escobaran agreed sunnily. He smiled hopefully at Martya.

The deal was struck, though Kareen looked as if she might be having second thoughts about sharing shares with her sister. Martya electing to return to Vorkosigan House with them on the spot, Mark and Enrique rose to make their farewells.

"Are you going to be all right?" Mark asked Kareen quietly, while Ekaterin was busy getting her bug designs downloaded for Enrique to carry off.

She nodded. "Yeah. You?"

"I'm hanging on. How long will it take, d'you suppose? Till this mess gets resolved?"

"It's resolved already." Her expression was disturbingly fey. "I'm done arguing, though I'm not sure they realize it yet. I've had it. While I'm still living in my parents' house, I'll continue to hold myself honor-bound to obey their rules, however ludicrous. The moment I've figured out how to be somewhere else without compromising my long-range goals, I'll walk away. Forever, if need be." Her mouth was grim and determined. "I don't expect to be there much longer."

"Oh," said Mark. He wasn't exactly sure what she meant, or meant to do, but it sounded . . . ominous. It terrified him to think that he might be the cause of her losing her family. It had taken him a lifetime, and dire effort, to win such a place of his own. The Commodore's clan had looked to be such a golden refuge, to him . . . "It's . . . a lonely place to be. On the outside like that."

She shrugged. "So be it."

The business meeting broke up. Last chance . . . They were in the tiled hallway, with Ekaterin ushering them out, before Mark worked up the courage to blurt to her, "Are there any messages I can take for you? To Vorkosigan House, I mean?" He was absolutely certain he would be ambushed by his brother on his return, given the way Miles had briefed him on his departure.

Renewed wariness closed down the expression on Ekaterin's face. She looked away from him. Her hand touched her bolero, over her heart; Mark detected a faint crackle of expensive paper beneath the soft fabric. He wondered if it would have a salutary humbling effect on Miles to learn where his literary effort was being stored, or whether it would just make him annoyingly elated.

"Tell him," she said at last, and no need to specify which *him*, "I accept his apology. But I can't answer his question."

Mark felt he had a brotherly duty to put in a good word for Miles, but the woman's painful reserve unnerved him. He finally mumbled diffidently, "He cares a lot, you know."

This wrenched a short little nod from her, and a brief, bleak smile. "Yes. I know. Thank you, Mark." That seemed to close the subject.

Kareen turned right at the sidewalk, while the rest of them turned left to head back to where the borrowed Armsman waited with the borrowed groundcar. Mark walked backwards a moment, watching her retreat. She strode on, head down, and didn't look back.

Miles, who had left the door of his suite open for the purpose, heard Mark returning in the late afternoon. He nipped out into the hall, and leaned over the balcony with a predatory stare down into the black-and-white paved entry foyer. All he could tell at a glance was that Mark looked overheated, an inescapable result of wearing that much black and fat in this weather.

Miles said urgently, "Did you see her?"

Mark stared up at him, his brows rising in unwelcome irony. He clearly sorted through a couple of tempting responses before deciding on a simple and prudent, "Yes."

Miles's hands gripped the woodwork. "What did she say? Could you tell if she'd read my letter?"

"As you may recall, you explicitly threatened me with death if I dared ask her if she'd read your letter, or otherwise broached the subject in any way."

Impatiently, Miles waved this off. "*Directly*. You know I meant not to ask *directly*. I just wondered if you could tell . . . anything."

"If I could tell what a woman was thinking just by looking at her, would I look like *this*?" Mark made a sweeping gesture at his face, and glowered.

"How the hell would I know? I can't tell what you're thinking just because you look surly. You usually look surly." *Last time, it was indigestion.* Although in Mark's case, stomach upset tended to be disturbingly connected with his other difficult emotional states.

Belatedly, Miles remembered to ask, "So . . . how *is* Kareen? Is she all right?"

Mark grimaced. "Sort of. Yes. No. Maybe."

"Oh." After a moment Miles added, "Ouch. Sorry."

Mark shrugged. He stared up at Miles, now pressed to the uprights, and shook his head in exasperated pity. "In fact, Ekaterin did give me a message for you."

Miles almost lurched over the balcony. "What, *what*?"

"She said to tell you she accepts your apology. Congratulations, dear brother; you appear to have won the thousand-meter crawl. She must have awarded you extra points for style, is all I can say."

"Yes! Yes!" Miles pounded his fist on the rail. "What else? Did she say anything else?"

"What else d'you expect?"

"I don't know. Anything. *Yes, you may call on me*, or *No, never darken my doorstep again*, or *something*. A clue, Mark!"

"Search me. You're going to have to go fish for your own clues."

"Can I? I mean, she didn't actually *say* I was not to bother her again?"

"She said, she couldn't answer your question. Chew on it, crypto-man. I have my own troubles." Shaking his head, Mark passed out of sight, heading for the back of the house and the lift tube.

Miles withdrew into his chambers, and flung himself down in the big chair in the bay window overlooking the back garden. So, hope staggered upright again, like a newly revived cryo-corpse dizzied and squinting in the light. But not, Miles decided firmly, cryo-amnesiac. Not this time. He lived, therefore he learned.

I can't answer your question did not sound like *No* to him. It didn't sound like *Yes* either, of course. It sounded like . . . one more last chance. Through a miracle of grace, it seemed he was to be permitted to begin again. Scrape it all back to Square One and start over, right.

So, how to approach her? *No more poetry, methinks. I was not born under a rhyming planet.* Judging from yesterday's effort, which he had prudently removed from his wastebasket and burned this morning along with all the other awkward drafts, any verse flowing from his pen was likely to be ghastly. Worse: if by some chance he managed something good, she'd likely want more, and then where would he be? He pictured Ekaterin, in some future incarnation, crying angrily *You're not the poet I married!* No more false pretences. Scam just wouldn't do for the long haul.

Voices drifted up from the entry hall. Pym was admitting a visitor. It wasn't anyone Miles recognized at this muffled distance; male, so it was likely a caller upon his father. Miles dismissed it from his attention, and settled back down.

She accepts your apology. She accepts your apology. Life, hope, and all good things opened up before him.

The unacknowledged panic which had gripped his throat for weeks seemed to ease, as he stared out into the sunny scene below. Now that the secret urgency driving him was gone, maybe he could even slow down enough to make of himself something so plain and quiet as her friend. What would *she* like . . . ?

Maybe he would ask her to go for a walk with him, somewhere pleasant. Possibly not in a garden, quite yet, all things considered. A wood, a beach . . . when talk lagged, there would be diversions for the eye. Not that he expected to run short of words. When he could speak truth, and was no longer constrained to concealment and lies, the possibilities opened up startlingly. There was so much more to say . . . Pym cleared his throat from the doorway. Miles swiveled his head.

"Lord Richars Vorrutyer is here to see you, Lord Vorkosigan," Pym announced.

"That's Lord Vorrutyer, if you please, Pym," Richars corrected him.

"Your cousin, m'lord." Pym, with a bland nod, ushered Richars into Miles's sitting room. Richars, perfectly alive to the nuance, shot a suspicious look at the Armsman as he entered.

Miles hadn't seen Richars for a year or so, but he hadn't altered much; he was looking maybe a little older, what with the advance of his waistline and the retreat of his hairline. He was wearing a piped and epauletted suit in blue and gray, reminiscent of the Vorrutyer House colors. More appropriate for day-wear than the imposing formality of the actual uniform, it nonetheless managed to suggest, without overtly claiming a right to, the garb of a Count's heir. Richars still looked permanently peeved: no change there.

Richars stared around General Piotr's old chambers, frowning.

"You have a sudden need of an Imperial Auditor, Richars?" Miles prodded gently, not best pleased with the intrusion. He wanted to be composing his next note to Ekaterin, not dealing with a Vorrutyer. Any Vorrutyer.

"What? No, certainly not!" Richars looked indignant, then blinked at Miles as though just now reminded of his new status. "I didn't come to see you at all. I came to see your father about his upcoming vote in Council on that lunatic suit of Lady Donna's." Richars shook his head. "He refused to see me. Sent me on to you."

Miles raised his brows at Pym. Pym intoned, "The Count and Countess, having heavy social obligations tonight, are resting this afternoon, m'lord."

He'd seen his parents at lunch; they hadn't seemed a bit tired. But his father had told him last night that he meant to take Gregor's wedding as a vacation from his duties as Viceroy, not a renewal of his duties as Count, carry on boy, you're doing fine. His mother had endorsed this plan emphatically. "I am still my father's voting deputy, yes, Richars."

"I had thought, because he was back in town, he'd take over again. Ah, well." Richars studied Miles dubiously, shrugged, and advanced toward the bay window.

All mine, eh? "Um, do sit down." Miles gestured to the chair opposite him, across the low table. "Thank you, Pym, that will be all."

Pym nodded, and withdrew. Miles did not suggest refreshments, or any other impediment to speeding Richars through his pitch, whatever it was going to be. Richars certainly hadn't dropped in for the pleasure of his company, not that his company was worth much just now. *Ekaterin, Ekaterin, Ekaterin . . .*

Richars settled himself, and offered in what was evidently meant as sympathy, "I passed your fat clone in the hallway. He must be a great trial to you all. Can't you do anything about him?"

It was hard to tell from this if Richars found Mark's obesity or his existence more offensive; on the other hand, Richars too was presently struggling with a relative in an embarrassing choice of body. But Miles was also reminded why, if he did not exactly go out of his way to avoid his Vorrutyer cousin-not-removed-far-enough, he did not seek his company. "Yes, well, he's *our* trial. What do you want, Richars?"

Richars sat back, shaking the distraction of Mark from his head. "I came to speak to Count Vorkosigan about . . . although come to think of it—I understand you've actually *met* Lady Donna since she returned from Beta Colony?"

"Do you mean Lord Dono? Yes. Ivan . . . introduced us. Haven't you seen, ah, your cousin yet?"

"Not yet." Richars smiled thinly. "I don't know who she imagines she's fooling. Just not the real thing, our Donna."

Inspired to a touch of malice, Miles let his brows climb. "Well, now, that depends entirely on what you define as *the real thing*, doesn't it? They do good work on Beta Colony. She went to a reputable clinic. I'm not as familiar with the details as, perhaps, Ivan, but I don't doubt the transformation was complete and real, biologically speaking. And no one can deny Dono is true Vor, and a Count's legitimate eldest surviving child. Two out of three, and for the rest, well, times change."

"Good God, Vorkosigan, you're not *serious*." Richars sat upright, and compressed his lips in disgust. "Nine generations of Vorrutyer service to the Imperium, to come to *this*? This tasteless joke?"

Miles shrugged. "That's for the Council of Counts to decide, evidently."

"It's absurd. Donna *cannot* inherit. Look at the consequences. One of the first duties of a Count is to sire his heir. What woman in her right mind would ever marry her?"

"There's someone for everyone, they say." A hopeful thought. Yes, and if even Richars had managed matrimony, how hard could it be? "And heir-production isn't exactly the only job requirement. Many Counts have failed to spawn their own replacements, for one reason or another. Look at poor Pierre, for example."

Richars shot him an annoyed, wary look, which Miles elected not to notice. Miles went on, "Dono seemed to be making a pretty good impression on the ladies when I saw him."

"That's just the damned women sticking together, Vorkosigan." Richars hesitated, looking struck. "You say *Ivan* brought her?"

"Yes." Just exactly how Dono had strong-armed Ivan into this was still unclear to Miles, but he felt no impulse to share his speculations with Richars.

"He used to screw her, you know. So did half the men in Vorbarr Sultana."

"I'd heard . . . something." *Go away, Richars. I don't want to deal with your smarmy notion of wit right now.*

"I wonder if he still . . . well! I'd never have thought Ivan Vorpatril climbed into that side of the bunk, but live and learn!"

"Um, Richars . . . you have a consistency problem, here," Miles felt compelled to point out. "You cannot logically imply my cousin Ivan is a homosexual for screwing Dono, not that I think he is doing so, unless you simultaneously grant Dono is actually male. In which case, his suit for the Vorrutyer Countship holds."

"I think," said Richars primly after a moment, "your cousin Ivan may be a very confused young man."

"Not about that, he's not," Miles sighed.

"This is irrelevant." Richars impatiently brushed away the question of Ivan's sexuality, of whatever mode.

"I must agree."

"Look, Miles." Richars tented his hands in a gesture of reason. "I know you Vorkosigans have backed the Progressives since Piotr's days ended, just as we Vorrutyers have always been staunch Conservatives. But this prank of Donna's attacks the basis of Vor power itself. If we Vor do not stand together on certain core issues, the time will come when all Vor will find ourselves with nothing left to stand *upon*. I assume I can count on your vote."

"I hadn't really given the suit much thought yet."

"Well, think about it now. It's coming up very soon."

All right, all right, granted, the fact that Dono amused Miles considerably more than Richars did was not, in and of itself, qualification for a Countship. He was going to have to step back and evaluate this. Miles sighed, and tried to force himself to attend more seriously to Richars's presentation.

Richars probed, "Are there any matters you are pursuing in Council at the moment, especially?"

Richars was angling for a vote-trade, or more properly, a trade in vote-futures, since, unlike Miles's, his vote was vapor right now. Miles thought it over. "Not at present. I have a personal interest in the Komarran solar mirror repair, since I think it will be a good investment for the Imperium, but Gregor seems to have his majority well in hand on that one." *In other words, you don't have anything I need, Richars. Not even in theory.* But he added after a moment's further reflection, "By-the-by, what do you think of René Vorbretten's dilemma?"

Richars shrugged. "Unfortunate. Not René's fault, I suppose, the poor sod, but what's to be done?"

"Reconfirm René in his own right?" Miles suggested mildly.

"Impossible," said Richars with conviction. "He's *Cetagandan*."

"I am trying to think by what possible criteria anyone could sanely describe René Vorbretten as a Cetagandan," said Miles.

"Blood," said Richars without hesitation. "Fortunately, there is an untainted Vorbretten line of descent to draw on to take his place. I imagine Sigur will grow into René's Countship well enough in time."

"Have you promised Sigur your vote?"

Richars cleared his throat. "Since you mention it, yes."

Therefore, Richars now possessed the promise of Count Vormoncrief's support. Nothing to be done for René with that tight little circle. Miles merely smiled.

"This delay in my confirmation has been maddening," Richars went on after a moment. "Three months wasted, while the Vorrutyer's District drifts without a hand on the controls, and Donna prances around having her sick little joke."

"Mm, that sort of surgery is neither trivial nor painless." If there was one techno-torture on which Miles was an expert, it was modern medicine. "In a strange sense, Dono killed Donna for this chance. I think he's deathly serious. And having sacrificed so much for it, I imagine he's likely to value the prize."

"You're not—" Richars looked taken aback. "You're surely not thinking of voting *for* her, are you? You can't imagine your father endorsing that!"

"Plainly, if I do, he does. I am his Voice."

"Your grandfather," Richars looked around the sitting room, "would spin in his grave!"

Miles's lips drew back on a humorless smile. "I don't know, Richars. Lord Dono makes an excellent first impression. He may be received everywhere the first time for curiosity, but I can well imagine him being invited back on his own merits."

"Is that why you received her at Vorkosigan House, for curiosity? I must say, you didn't help the Vorrutyers with that. Pierre was strange—did he ever show you his collection of hats lined with gold foil?—and his sister's no improvement. The woman should be clapped in an attic for this whole appalling escapade."

"You should get over your prejudices and meet Lord Dono." *You can leave any time now, in fact.* "He quite charmed Lady Alys."

"Lady Alys holds no vote in Council." Richars gave Miles a sharp frown. "Did he—*she*—charm you?"

Miles shrugged, compelled to honesty. "I wouldn't go that far. He wasn't my chief concern that night."

"Yes," said Richars grumpily, "I heard all about *your* problem."

What? Abruptly, Miles found that Richars had finally riveted his full, undivided attention. "And what problem would that be?" he inquired softly.

Richar's lip turned up in a sour smile. "Sometimes, you remind me of my cousin By. He's very practiced at the suave pose, but he's not nearly as slick as he pretends to be. I'd have thought you'd have had the tactical wits to seal the exits before springing a trap like that." He conceded after a moment, "Though I do think the better of Alexi's widow for standing up to you."

"Alexi's widow?" breathed Miles. "I didn't know Alexi was married, let alone deceased. Who's the lucky lady?"

Richars gave him a don't-be-stupid look. His smile grew odder, as it penetrated that he'd drawn Miles out of his irritating indifference at last. "It was just a *leetle* obvious, don't you think, My Lord Auditor? Just a *leetle* obvious?" He leaned back in his chair, squinting through narrowed eyes.

"I'm afraid you've lost me," said Miles, in an extremely neutral tone. As automatically as breathing, Miles's face, posture, gestures slid into Security mode, unrevealing, unobtrusive.

"Your Administrator Vorsoisson's so-convenient death? Alexi thinks the widow hadn't guessed earlier how—and why—her husband died. But judging from her flaming exit from your proposal-party, all of Vorbarr Sultana figures that she knows now."

Miles kept his expression to no more than a faint, slight smile. "If you are talking about Madame Vorsoisson's late husband Tien, he died in a breath mask accident." He did not add *I was there*. It didn't sound . . . helpful.

"Breath mask, eh? Easy enough to arrange. I can think of three or four ways to do it without even exerting myself."

"Motivation alone does not a murder make. Or . . . since you're so quick at this—what *did* happen the night Pierre's fiancée was killed?"

Richars's chin rose. "*I* was investigated and cleared. *You* haven't been. Now, I don't know if the talk about you is true, nor do I greatly care. But I doubt you'd care for the ordeal either way."

"No." Miles's smile remained fixed. "Enjoyed your part in that inquest, did you?"

"No," said Richars plainly. "Little officious guard bastards crawling all over my personal affairs, none of which were any of their damned business . . . drooling all over myself on fast-penta . . . The proles love having a Vor in their sights, don't you know. They'd piss all over themselves for a shot at someone of *your* rank. But you're likely safe, in the Council up there above us all. It would take a brave fool to lay the charge there, and what would he gain? No win for anyone."

"No." Such a charge would be quashed, for reasons of which Richars knew nothing—and Miles and Ekaterin would have to endure the scurrilous speculation that would follow that quashing. No win at all.

"Except possibly for young Alexi and the widow Vorsoisson. On the other hand . . ." Richars eyed Miles in growing conjecture, "There's a visible benefit to you if someone *doesn't* lay such a charge. I see a possible win-win scenario here."

"Do you."

"Come on, Vorkosigan. We're both as Old Vor as it's possible to be. It's stupid of us to be brangling when we should both be on the same side. Our interests march together. It's a tradition. Don't pretend your father and grandfather weren't top party horse-traders."

"My grandfather . . . learned his political science from the Cetagandans. Mad Emperor Yuri offered him postgraduate instruction after that. My grandfather schooled my father." *And both of them schooled me. This is the only warning you will receive, Richars.* "By the time I knew Piotr, Vorbarr Sultana party politics were just an amusing pastime to him, to entertain him in his old age."

"Well, there you are, then. I believe we understand each other pretty well."

"Let's just see. Do I gather you are offering not to lay a murder charge against me, if I vote for you over Dono in the Council?"

"Those both seem like good things to me."

"What if someone else makes such an accusation?"

"First they'd have to care, then they'd have to dare. Not all that likely, eh?"

"It's hard to say. *All of Vorbarr Sultana* seems a suddenly enlarged audience to my quiet family dinner. For example, where did you encounter this . . . fabrication?"

"At a quiet family dinner." Richars smirked, obviously satisfied at Miles's dismay.

And what route had the information traveled? Ye gods, *was* there a security rupture behind Richars's mouthings? The potential implications ranged far beyond a District inheritance fight. ImpSec was going to have a hell of a time tracking this.

All of Vorbarr Sultana. Ohshitohshitohshit.

Miles sat back, looked up to meet Richars's eyes directly, and smiled. "You know, Richars, I'm glad you came to see me. Before we had this little talk, I had actually been undecided how I was going to vote on the matter of the Vorrutyer's District."

Richars looked pleased, watching him fold so neatly. "I was sure we could see eye to eye."

The attempted bribery or blackmail of an Imperial Auditor was treason. The attempted bribery or blackmail of a District Count during wrestling for votes was more in the nature of normal business practice; the Counts traditionally expected their fellows to defend themselves in that game, or be thought too stupid to live. Richars had come to see Miles in his Voting Deputy hat, not his Imperial Auditor hat. Switching hats, and the rules of the game, on him in midstream seemed unfair. *Besides, I want the pleasure of destroying him myself.* Whatever ImpSec found in addition would be ImpSec's affair. And ImpSec had no sense of humor. Did Richars have any idea what kind of lever he was trying to pull? Miles manufactured a smile.

Richars smiled back, and rose. "Well. I have other men to see this afternoon. Thank you, Lord Vorkosigan, for your support." He stuck out his hand. Miles took it without hesitation, shook it firmly, and smiled. He smiled him to the door of his suite when Pym arrived to escort him out, and smiled while the booted feet made their way down the stairs, and smiled until he heard the front doors close.

The smile transmuted to pure snarl. He stormed around the room three times looking for something that wasn't an antique too valuable to break, found nothing of that description, and settled for whipping his grandfather's seal dagger from its sheath and hurling it quivering into the doorframe to his bedroom. The satisfying vibrant hum faded all too quickly. In a few minutes, he regained control of his breathing and swearing, and schooled his face back to bland. Cold, maybe, but very bland.

He went into his study and sat at his comconsole. He brushed aside a repeat of this morning's message from Ivan to call him marked *urgent,* and coded up the secured line. A little to his surprise, he was put through to ImpSec Chief General Guy Allegre on the first try.

"Good afternoon, my Lord Auditor," Allegre said. "How may I serve you?"

Roasted, apparently. "Good afternoon, Guy." Miles hesitated, his stomach tightening in distaste for the task ahead. No help for it. "An unpleasant development stemming from the Komarr case—" no need to specify *which* Komarr case—"has just been brought to my attention. It appears purely personal, but it may have security ramifications. It seems I am being accused in the court of capital gossip of having a direct hand in the death of that idiot Tien Vorsoisson. The imputed motive being to woo his widow." Miles swallowed. "The second half is unfortunately true. I have been," *how to put this,* "attempting to court her. Not terribly . . . well, perhaps."

Allegre raised his brows. "Indeed. Something just crossed my desk on that."

Argh! What, for God's sake? "Really? That was quick." *Or else it really is all over town.* Yeah, it stood to reason Miles might not be the first to know.

"Anything connected with that case is red-flagged for my immediate attention."

Miles waited a moment, but Allegre didn't volunteer anything more. "Well, here's my bit for you. Richars Vorrutyer has just offered to nobly refrain from laying a murder charge against me for Vorsoisson's death, in exchange for my vote in the Council of Counts confirming him as Count Vorrutyer."

"Mm. And how did you respond to this?"

"Shook his hand and sent him off thinking he had me."

"And does he?"

"Hell, no. I'm going to vote for Dono and squash Richars like the roach he is. But I would very much like to know whether this is a leak, or an independent fabrication. It makes an enormous difference in my moves."

"For what it's worth, our ImpSec informant's report didn't pinpoint anything in the rumor that looks like a leak. No key details that aren't public knowledge, for example. I have a picked analyst following up just that question now."

"Good. Thank you."

"Miles . . ." Allegre pressed his lips thoughtfully together. "I have no doubt you find this galling. But I trust your response will not draw any more attention to the Komarr matter than necessary."

"If it's a leak, it's your call. If it's pure slander . . ." *What the hell am I going to do about it?*

"If I may ask, what do you plan to do next?"

"Immediately? Call Madame Vorsoisson, and let her know what's coming down." The anticipation made him cold and sick. He could scarcely imagine anything farther from the simple affection he'd ached to give her than this nauseating news. "This concerns—this damages—her as much as it does me."

"Hm." Allegre rubbed his chin. "To avoid muddying already murky waters, I would *request* you put that off until my analyst has had a chance to evaluate her place in all this."

"Her place? Her place is innocent victim!"

"I don't disagree," Allegre said soothingly. "I'm not so much concerned with disloyalty as with possible carelessness."

ImpSec had never been happy to have Ekaterin, an oath-free civilian not under their control in any way, standing in the heart of the hottest secret of the year, or maybe the century. Despite the fact that she'd personally hand-delivered it to them, the ingrates. "She is not careless. She is in fact extremely careful."

"In your observation."

"In my professional observation."

Allegre gave him a placating nod. "Yes, m'lord. We would be pleased to prove that. You don't, after all, want ImpSec to be . . . confused."

Miles blew out his breath in dry appreciation of this last dead-pan remark. "Yeah, yeah," he conceded.

"I'll have my analyst call you with clearance just as soon as possible," Allegre promised.

Miles's fist clenched in frustration, and unfolded reluctantly. Ekaterin didn't go about much; it *might* be several days before this came to her ears from other sources. "Very well. Keep me informed."

"Will do, my lord."

Miles cut the com.

The queasy realization was dawning on him that, in his reflexive fear for the secrets behind the disasters on Komarr, he'd handled Richars Vorrutyer exactly backwards. *Ten years of ImpSec habits, argh.* Miles judged Richars a bully, not a psychotic. If Miles had stood up to him instantly, he might have folded, backed down, shied from deliberately pissing off a potential vote.

Well, it was way too late to go running after him now and try to replay the conversation. Miles's vote against Richars would demonstrate the futility of trying to blackmail a Vorkosigan.

And leave each other permanent enemies in Council . . . Would calling his bluff force Richars to make good his threat or be forsworn? *Shit, he'll have to.*

In Ekaterin's eyes, Miles had barely climbed out of the last hole he'd dug. He wanted to be thrown together with her, but not, dear God, at a murder trial for the death of her late husband, however aborted. She was just starting to leave the nightmare of her marriage behind her. A formal charge and its aftermath, regardless of the ultimate verdict, must drag her back through its traumas in the most hideous imaginable manner, plunge her into a maelstrom of stress, distress, humiliation, and exhaustion. A power struggle in the Council of Counts was not a garden in which love was like to bloom.

Of course, the entire ghastly vision could be neatly short-circuited if Richars lost his bid for the Vorrutyer Countship.

But Dono hasn't got a chance.

Miles gritted his teeth. *He does now.*

A second later, he tapped in another code, and waited impatiently.

"Hello, Dono," Miles purred, as a face formed over the vid plate. The somber, if musty, splendor of one of Vorrutyer House's salons receded dimly in the background. But the figure wavering into focus wasn't Dono; it was Olivia Koudelka, who grinned cheerfully at him. She had a smudge of dust on her cheek, and three rolled-up parchments under her arm. "Oh—Olivia. Excuse me. Is, um, Lord Dono there?"

"Sure, Miles. He's in conference with his lawyer. I'll get him." She bounced out of range of the pickup; he could hear her voice calling *Hey, Dono! Guess who's on the com!* in the distance.

In a moment, Dono's bearded face popped up; he cocked an inquiring eyebrow at his caller. "Good afternoon, Lord Vorkosigan. What can I do for you?"

"Hello, Lord Dono. It has just occurred to me that, for one reason and another, we never finished our conversation the other night. I wanted to let you know, in case there was any doubt, that your bid for the Vorrutyer Countship has my full support, and the vote of my District."

"Why, thank you, Lord Vorkosigan. I'm very pleased to hear that." Dono hesitated. "Though . . . a little surprised. You gave me the impression you preferred to remain above all this in-fighting."

"Preferred, yes. But I've just had a visit from your cousin Richars. He managed to bring me down to his level in astonishingly short order."

Dono pursed his lips, then tried not to smile too broadly. "Richars does have that effect on people sometimes."

"If I may, I'd like to schedule a meeting with you and René Vorbretten. Here at Vorkosigan House, or where you will. I think a little mutual strategizing could be very beneficial to you both."

"I'd be delighted to have your counsel, Lord Vorkosigan. When?"

A few minutes of schedule comparison and shifting, and a side-call to René at Vorbretten House, resulted in a meeting set for the day after tomorrow. Miles could have been happy with tonight, or instantly, but had to admit this gave him time to study the problem in more rational detail. He bid a tightly cordial good-bye to both his, he trusted, future colleagues.

He reached for the next code on his comconsole; then his hand hesitated and fell back. He'd hardly known how to begin again *before* this mine had blown up in his face. He could say nothing to Ekaterin now. If he called her to try to talk of other things, ordinary kindly trivial things, while knowing this and not speaking it, he'd be lying to her again. Hugely.

But what the hell was he going to say when Allegre *had* cleared him?

He rose and began to pace his chambers.

Ekaterin's requested year of mourning would have served for more than the healing of her own soul. At a year's distance, memory of Tien's mysterious death would have been softened in the public mind; his widow might have gracefully rejoined society without comment, and been gracefully courted by a man she'd known a decent interval. But no. On fire with impatience, sick with dread of losing his chance with her, he'd had to push and push, till he'd pushed it right over the edge.

Yes, and if he hadn't babbled his intentions all over town, Illyan would never have been confused and blurted out his disastrous small-talk, and the highly-misinterpretable incident at the dinner party would never have occurred. *I want a time machine, so's I can go back and shoot myself.*

He had to admit, the whole extended scenario lent itself beautifully to political disinformation. In his covert ops days, he'd fallen with chortles of joy on lesser slips by his enemies. If he were ambushing himself, he'd regard it as a godsend.

You did ambush yourself, you idiot.

If he'd only kept his mouth shut, he might have gotten away clean with that elaborate half-lie about the garden, too. Ekaterin would still be lucratively employed, and—he stopped, and contemplated this thought with extremely mixed emotions. *Cross-ball.* Would a certain miserable period of his youth have been a shade less miserable if he'd never learned of that benign deceit? *Would you rather feel a fool, or be one?* He knew the answer he'd give for himself; was he to grant Ekaterin any less respect?

You did. Fool.

In any case, the accusation seemed to have fallen on him alone. If Richars spoke truth, hah, the back-splash had missed her altogether. *And if you don't go after her again, it will stay that way.*

He stumbled to his chair, and sat heavily. How long would he have to stay away from her, for this delicious whisper to be forgotten? A year? Years and years? Forever?

Dammit, the only crime he'd committed was to fall in love with a brave and beautiful lady. Was that so wrong? He'd wanted to give her the world, or at least, as much of it as was his to give. How had so much good intention turned into this . . . *tangle*?

He heard Pym down in the foyer, and voices again. He heard a single pair of boots climbing the stairs, and gathered himself to tell Pym that he was Not At Home to any more visitors this afternoon. But it wasn't Pym who popped breezily through the door to his suite, but Ivan. Miles groaned.

"Hi, coz," said Ivan cheerily. "God, you still looked wrecked."

"You're behind the times, Ivan. I'm wrecked all over again."

"Oh?" Ivan looked at him inquiringly, but Miles waved it away. Ivan shrugged. "So, what's on? Wine, beer? Ma Kosti snacks?"

Miles pointed to the recently-restocked credenza by the wall. "Help yourself."

Ivan poured himself wine, and asked, "What are you having?"

Let's not start that again. "Nothing. Thanks."

"Eh, suit yourself." Ivan wandered back over to the bay window, swirling his drink in his glass. "You didn't pick up my comconsole messages, earlier?"

"Oh, yeah, I saw them. Sorry. It's been a busy day." Miles scowled. "I'm afraid I'm not much company right now. I've just been blindsided by Richars Vorrutyer, of all people. I'm still digesting it."

"Ah. Hm." Ivan glanced at the door, and took a gulp of wine. He cleared his throat. "If it was about the murder rumor, well, if you'd answer your damned messages, you wouldn't *get* blindsided. I tried."

Miles stared up at him, appalled. "Good God, not you *too*? Does everybody in bloody Vorbarr Sultana know about this goddamn crap?"

Ivan shrugged. "I don't know about everybody. M'mother hasn't mentioned it yet, but she might think it was too crude to take notice of. Byerly Vorrutyer passed it on to me to pass on to you. At dawn, note. He adores gossip like this. Just too excited to keep it to himself, I guess, unless he's stirring things up for his own amusement. Or else he's playing some kind of sneaky underhanded game. I can't even begin to guess which side he's on."

Miles massaged his forehead with the heels of his hands. "Gah."

"Anyway, the point is, *it wasn't me who started this*. You grasp?"

"Yeah." Miles sighed. "I suppose. Do me a favor, and quash it when you encounter it, eh?"

"As if anyone would believe me? Everybody knows I've been your donkey since forever. It's not like I was an eyewitness anyway. I don't know any more than anyone else." He asserted after a moment's thought, "Less."

Miles considered the alternatives. Death? Death would be much more peaceful, and he wouldn't have this pounding headache. But there was always the risk some misguided person would revive him again, in worse shape than ever. Besides, he had to live at least long enough to cast his vote against Richars. He studied his cousin thoughtfully. "Ivan . . ."

"It wasn't my fault," Ivan recited promptly, "it's not my job, you can't make me, and if you want any of my time you'll have to wrestle m'mother for it. *If* you dare." He nodded satisfaction at this clincher.

Miles sat back, and regarded Ivan for a long moment. "You're right," he said at last. "I have abused your loyalty too many times. I'm sorry. Never mind."

Ivan, caught with a mouthful of wine, stared at him in shock, his brows drawing down. He finally managed to swallow. "What do you mean, *never mind?*"

"I mean, never mind. There's no reason to draw you into this ugly mess, and every reason not to." Miles doubted there'd be much honor for Ivan to win in his vicinity this time, not even the sort that sparked so briefly before being buried forever in ImpSec files. Besides, he couldn't think offhand of anything Ivan could do for him.

"No *need?* Never *mind?* What are you up to?"

"Nothing, I'm afraid. You can't help me on this one. Thanks for offering, though," Miles added conscientiously.

"I didn't offer anything," Ivan pointed out. His eyes narrowed. "You're up to something."

"Not up. Just down." Down to nothing but the certainty that the next weeks were going to be unpleasant in ways he'd never experienced before. "Thank you, Ivan. I'm sure you can find your own way out."

"Well . . ." Ivan tilted up his glass, drained it, and set it down on the table. "Yeah, sure. Call me if you . . . need anything."

Ivan trod out, with a disgruntled backward look over his shoulder. Miles heard his indignant mutter, fading down the stairs: "No *need.* Never *mind.* Who the hell does he think he is . . . ?"

Miles smiled crookedly, and slumped in his seat. He had a great deal to do. He was just too tired to move.

Ekaterin. . . .

Her name seemed to stream through his fingers, as impossible to hold as smoke whipped away by the wind.

Chapter Thirteen

Ekaterin sat in the midmorning sun at the table in her aunt's back garden, and tried to rank the list of short-term jobs she'd pulled off the comconsole by location and pay. Nothing close by seemed to have anything to do with botany. Her stylus wandered to the margin of the flimsy and doodled yet another idea for a pretty butter bug, then went on to sketch a revision for her aunt's garden involving the use of more raised beds for easy maintenance. The very early stages of congestive heart failure which had been slowing Aunt Vorthys down were due to be cured this fall when she received her scheduled transplant; on the other hand, she would likely return thereafter to her full teaching load. A container-garden of all native Barrayaran species . . . no. Ekaterin returned her attention firmly to the job list.

Aunt Vorthys had been bustling in and out of the house; Ekaterin therefore didn't look up till her aunt said, in a decidedly odd tone, "Ekaterin, you have a visitor."

Ekaterin glanced up, and stifled a flinch of shock. Captain Simon Illyan stood at her aunt's elbow. All right, so, she'd sat next to him through practically a whole dinner, but that had been at Vorkosigan House, where anything seemed possible. Towering legends weren't supposed to rise up and stand casually in one's own garden in the broad morning as though some passing person—probably Miles— had dropped a dragon's tooth in the grass.

Not that Captain Illyan *towered*, exactly. He was much shorter and slighter than she'd pictured him. He'd seldom appeared in news vids. He wore a modest civilian suit of the sort any Vor with conservative tastes might choose for a morning or business call. He smiled diffidently at her, and waved her back to her seat as she started to scramble up. "No, no, please, Madame Vorsoisson . . ."

"Won't . . . you sit down?" Ekaterin managed, sinking back.

"Thank you." He pulled out a chair and seated himself a little stiffly, as if not altogether comfortable. Maybe he bore old scars like Miles's. "I wondered if I might have a private word with you. Madame Vorthys seems to think it would be all right."

Her aunt's nod confirmed this. "But Ekaterin, dear, I was just about to leave for class. Do you wish me to stay a little?"

"That won't be necessary," Ekaterin said faintly. "What's Nikki up to?"

"Playing on my comconsole, just at present."

"That's fine."

Aunt Vorthys nodded, and went back into the house.

Illyan cleared his throat, and began, "I've no wish to intrude on your privacy or time, Madame Vorsoisson, but I did want to apologize to you for embarrassing you the other night. I feel much at fault, and I'm very much afraid I might have . . . done some damage I didn't intend."

She frowned suspiciously, and her right hand fingered the braid on the left edge of her bolero. "Did Miles send you?"

"Ah . . . no. I'm an ambassador entirely without portfolio. This is on my own recognizance. If I hadn't made that foolish remark . . . I did not altogether understand the delicacy of the situation."

Ekaterin sighed bitter agreement. "I think you and I must have been the only two people in the room so poorly informed."

"I was afraid I'd been told and forgotten, but it appears I just wasn't on the need-to-know list. I'm not quite used to that yet." A tinge of anxiety flickered in his eyes, giving lie to his smile.

"It was not your fault at all, sir. Somebody . . . overshot his own calculations."

"Hm." Illyan's lips twisted in sympathy with her expression. He traced a finger over the tabletop in a crosshatch pattern. "You know—speaking of ambassadors—I began by thinking I ought to come to you and put in a good word for Miles in the romance department. I figured I owed it to him, for having put my foot down in the middle of things that way. But the more I thought about it, the more I realized I have truly no idea what kind of a husband he would make. I hardly dare recommend him to you. He was a terrible subordinate."

Her brows flew up in surprise. "I'd thought his ImpSec career was successful."

Illyan shrugged. "His ImpSec *missions* were consistently successful, frequently beyond my wildest dreams. Or nightmares. . . . He seemed to regard any order worth obeying as worth exceeding. If I could have installed one control device on him, it would have been a rheostat. Power him *down* a turn or two . . . maybe I could have made him last longer." Illyan gazed thoughtfully out over the garden, but Ekaterin didn't think the garden was what he was seeing, in his mind's eye. "Do you know all those old folk tales where the count tries to get rid of his only daughter's unsuitable suitor by giving him three impossible tasks?"

"Yes . . ."

"Don't ever try that with Miles. Just . . . don't."

She tried to rub the involuntary smile from her lips, and failed. His answering smile seemed to lighten his eyes.

"I will say," he went on more confidently, "I've never found him a slow learner. If you were to give him a second chance, well . . . he might surprise you."

"Pleasantly?" she asked dryly.

It was his turn to fail to suppress a smile. "Not necessarily." He looked away from her again, and his smile faded from wry to pensive. "I've had many subordinates over the years who've turned in impeccable careers. Perfection takes no risks with itself, you see. Miles was many things, but never perfect. It was a privilege and a terror to command him, and I'm thankful and amazed we both got out alive. Ultimately . . . his career ran aground in disaster. But before it ended, he changed worlds."

She didn't think Illyan meant that for a figure of speech. He glanced back at her, and made a little palm-open motion with his hands in his lap, as if apologizing for having once held worlds there.

"Do you take him for a great man?" Ekaterin asked Illyan seriously. *And does it take one to know one?* "Like his father and grandfather?"

"I think he is a great man . . . in an entirely different way than his father and grandfather. Though I've often been afraid he'd break his heart trying to be them."

Illyan's words reminded her strangely of her Uncle Vorthys's evaluation of Miles, back when they'd first met on Komarr. So if a genius thought Miles was a genius, and a great man thought he was a great man . . . maybe she ought to get him vetted by a *really good* husband.

Voices carried faintly from the house through the open windows into the back garden, too muffled to make out the words. One was a low-pitched male rumble. The other was Nikki's. It didn't sound like the comconsole or the vid. Was Uncle Vorthys home already? Ekaterin had thought he would be out till dinnertime.

"I will say," Illyan went on, waving a thoughtful finger in the air, "he did always have the most remarkable knack for picking personnel. Either picking or making; I was never quite sure which. If he said someone was the person for the job, they proved to be so. One way or another. If he thinks you'd be a fine Lady Vorkosigan, he's undoubtedly right. Although," his tone grew slightly morose, "if you do throw in your lot with him, I can personally guarantee you'll never be in control of what happens next again. Not that one ever is, really."

Ekaterin nodded wry agreement. "When I was twenty, I chose my life. It wasn't this one."

Illyan laughed painfully. "Oh, twenty. God. Yes. When I took oath at twenty to Emperor Ezar, I had my military career all sketched out. Ship duty, eh, and ship captain by thirty, and admiral by fifty, and retirement at sixty, a twice-twenty-years man. I did allow for being killed, of course. All very neat. My life began to diverge from the plan the following day, when I was assigned to ImpSec instead. And diverged again, when I found myself promoted to chief of ImpSec in the middle of a war I'd never foreseen, serving a boy emperor who hadn't even existed a decade earlier. My life has been one long chain of surprises. A year ago, I could not have even imagined myself today. Or dreamed myself happy. Of course, Lady Alys . . ." His face softened at the mention of her name, and he paused, an odd smile playing on his lips. "Lately, I have come to believe that the principal difference between heaven and hell is the company you keep there."

Could one judge a man by his company? Could she judge Miles that way? Ivan was charming and funny, Lady Alys fine and formidable, Illyan, despite his sinister history, strangely kind. Miles's clone brother Mark, for all his bitter bite, seemed a brother in truth. Kareen Koudelka was pure delight. The Vorbrettens, the rest of the Koudelka clan, Duv Galeni, Tsipis, Ma Kosti, Pym, even Enrique . . . Miles seemed to collect friends of wit and distinction and extraordinary ability around himself as casually and unselfconsciously as a comet trailed its banner of light.

Looking back, she realized how very few friends Tien had ever made. He'd despised his coworkers, scorned his scattered relations. She'd told herself that he hadn't the knack for socializing, or was just too busy. Once past his school days, Tien had never made a new good friend. She'd come to share his isolation; *alone together* was a perfect summation of their marriage.

"I think you are very right, sir."

From the house, Nikki's voice rose suddenly in volume and pitch, yanking her maternal ear: "No! No!" Was he defying his uncle over something? Ekaterin raised her head, listening, and frowned uneasily.

"Um . . . excuse me." She flashed a brief smile at Illyan. "I think I'd better go check something out. I'll be right back . . ."

Illyan nodded understanding, and politely pretended to fix his attention on the surrounding garden.

Ekaterin entered the kitchen, her eyes slow to adjust from the glare outside, and quietly rounded the corner through the dining room to the parlor. She stopped in the archway in surprise. The voice she'd heard was not her uncle's; it was Alexi Vormoncrief's.

Nikki was sitting scrunched up in Uncle Vorthys's big chair in the corner. Vormoncrief loomed over him, his face tense, his hands anxiously crooked.

"Back to these bandages you saw on Lord Vorkosigan's wrists the day after your father was killed," Vormoncrief was saying, in an urgent voice. "What kind were they? How big?"

"I dunno." Nikki gave a trapped shrug. "They were just bandages."

"What kind of wounds did they conceal, though?"

"Dunno."

"Well, sharp slashes? Burns, blisters, like from a plasma arc? Can you remember seeing them later?"

Nikki shrugged again, his face stiff. "I dunno. They were raggedy, all the way around, I guess. He still has the red marks." His voice was constricted, on the verge of tears.

An arrested look crossed Vormoncrief's face. "Hadn't noticed that. He's very careful to wear long sleeves, isn't he? In high summer, huh. But did he have any other marks, on his face perhaps? Bruises, scratches, maybe a black eye?"

"Dunno . . ."

"Are you *sure*?"

"Lieutenant Vormoncrief!" Ekaterin interrupted this sharply. Vormoncrief jerked upright, and lurched around. Nikki looked up, his lips parting in relief. "What are you *doing*?"

"Ah! Ekaterin, Madame Vorsoisson. I came to see you." He waved vaguely around the book-lined parlor.

"Then why didn't you come out to where I was?"

"I seized the chance to talk to Nikki, and I'm very glad I did."

"Mama," Nikki gulped from his chair-barricade, "he says Lord Vorkosigan killed Da!"

"*What?*" Ekaterin stared at Vormoncrief, for a moment almost too stunned to breathe.

Vormoncrief gestured helplessly, and gave her an earnest look. "The secret is out. The truth is known."

"What truth? By *whom*?"

"It's being whispered all over town, not that anyone dares—or cares—to do anything about it. Gossips and cowards, the lot of them. But the picture's getting plainer. Two men went out into the Komarran wilderness. One returned, and with some pretty strange injuries, apparently. *Accident with a breath mask*, indeed. But I realized at once that you couldn't have suspected foul play, till Vorkosigan dropped his guard and proposed to you at his dinner. No wonder you ran out crying."

Ekaterin opened her mouth. Nightmare memories flashed. *Your accusation is physically impossible, Alexi; I know. I found them, out in that wilderness, alive and dead both.* A cascade of security considerations poured through her head. It was a direct chain of very few links from the details of Tien's death to the persons and objects that no one dared mention. "It was not like that at all." That sounded weaker than she'd intended. . . .

"I'll wager Vorkosigan was never questioned under fast-penta. Am I right?"

"He's ex-ImpSec. I doubt he could be."

"How convenient." Vormoncrief grimaced ironically.

"*I* was questioned under fast-penta."

"They cleared you of complicity, yes! I was sure of it!"

"*What* . . . complicity?" The words caught in her throat. The embarrassing details of the relentless interrogation under the truth drug she'd endured on Komarr after Tien's death boiled up in her memory. Vormoncrief was late with his lurid accusation. ImpSec had thought of that scenario before Tien's body was cold. "Yes, I was asked all the questions you'd expect a conscientious investigator to ask a close relative in a mysterious death." *And more.* "So?"

"*Mysterious* death, yes, you suspected something even then, I knew it!" With a wave of his hand, he overrode her hasty attempt to interject an *accidental* in place of that ill-chosen *mysterious.* "Believe me, I understand your hideous dilemma perfectly. You don't dare accuse the all-powerful Vorkosigan, the mutie lord." Vormoncrief scowled at the name. "God knows what retaliation he could inflict on you. But Ekaterin, I have powerful relatives too! I came to offer you—and Nikki—my protection. Take my hand—trust me—" he opened his arms, reaching for her "—and together, I swear we can bring this little monster to justice!"

Ekaterin sputtered, momentarily beyond words, and looked around frantically for a weapon. The only one that suggested itself was the fireplace poker, but whether to whap it on his skull or jam it up his ass . . . ? Nikki was crying openly now, thin strained sobs, and Vormoncrief stood between them. She began to dodge around him; ill-advisedly, Vormoncrief tried to wrap her lovingly in his arms.

"Ow!" he cried, as the heel of her hand crunched into his nose, with all the strength of her arm behind it. It didn't drive his nasal bone up into his brain and kill him on the spot the way the books said—she hadn't really thought it would—but at least his nose began to swell and bleed. He grabbed both her wrists before she could muster aim and power for a second try. He was forced to hold them tight, and apart, as she struggled against his grip.

Her sputtering found words at last, shrieked at the top of her voice: "*Let go of me, you blithering twit!*"

He stared at her in astonishment. Just as she gathered her balance to find out if that knee-to-the-groin thing worked any better than that blow-to-the-nose one, Illyan's voice interrupted from the archway behind her, deadly dry.

"The lady asked you to unhand her, Lieutenant. She shouldn't have to ask twice. Or . . . once."

Vormoncrief looked up, and his eyes widened with belated recognition of the former ImpSec chief. His hands sprang open, his fingers wriggling a little as if to shake off their guilt. His lips moved on one or two tries at speech, before his mouth at last made it into motion. "Captain Illyan! Sir!" His hand began to salute, the realization penetrated that Illyan wore civvies, and the gesture was converted on the fly to a tender exploration of his bunged and dripping nose. Vormoncrief stared at the blood smear on his hand in surprise.

Ekaterin swerved around him to slide into her uncle's armchair and gather up the sniffling Nikki, hugging him tight. He was trembling. She buried her nose in his clean boy-hair, then glared furiously over her shoulder. "How dare you come in here uninvited and interrogate my son without my permission! How dare you harass and frighten him like this! How dare you!"

"A very good question, Lieutenant," said Illyan. His eyes were hard and cold and not kindly at all. "Would you care to answer it for both of our curiosities?"

"You see, you see, sir, I, I, I . . ."

"What *I* saw," said Illyan, in that same arctic voice, "was that you entered the home of an Imperial Auditor, uninvited and unannounced, while the Auditor was not present, and offered physical violence to a member of his family." A beat, while the dismayed Alexi clutched his nose as if trying to hide the evidence. "Who is your commanding officer, Lieutenant Vormoncrief?"

"But she hit—" Vormoncrief swallowed; he abandoned his nose and came to attention, his face faintly green. "Colonel Ushakov, sir. Ops."

In a supremely sinister gesture, Illyan pulled an audiofiler from his belt, and murmured this information into it, together with Alexi's full name, the date, time, and location. Illyan returned the audiofiler to its clip with a tiny snap, loud in the silence.

"Colonel Ushakov will be hearing from General Allegre. *You* are dismissed, Lieutenant."

Cowed, Vormoncrief retreated, walking backwards. His hand rose toward Ekaterin and Nikki in one last, futile gesture. "Ekaterin, please, let me help you . . ."

"You *lie*," she snarled, still gripping Nikki. "You lie *vilely*. Don't you *ever* come back here!"

Alexi's sincere, if daunted, confusion was more infuriating than his anger or defiance would have been. Did the man not understand a word she'd said? Still looking stunned, he made it to the entry hall, and let himself out. She set her teeth, listening to his bootsteps fade down the front walk.

Illyan remained leaning against the archway, his arms folded, watching her curiously.

"How long were you standing there?" she asked him, when her breath had slowed a bit.

"I came in on the part about the fast-penta interrogation. All those key words—ImpSec, complicity . . . Vorkosigan. My apologies for eavesdropping. Old habits die hard." His smile came back, though it regained its warmth rather slowly.

"Well . . . thank you for getting rid of him. Military discipline is a wonderful thing."

"Yes. I wonder how long it will take him to realize I don't command him, or anyone else? Ah, well. So, just what was the obnoxious Alexi blithering about?"

Ekaterin shook her head, and turned to Nikki. "Nikki, love, what happened? How long was that man here?"

Nikki sniffed, but he was no longer trembling as badly. "He came to the door right after Aunt Vorthys left. He asked me all kinds of questions about when Lord Vorkosigan and Uncle Vorthys stayed with us on Komarr."

Illyan, his hands in his pockets, strolled nearer. "Can you remember some of them?"

Nikki's face screwed up. "Was Lord Vorkosigan alone with Mama much—how would I know? If they were alone, I wouldn't 'a *been* there! What did I see Lord Vorkosigan do. Eat dinner, mostly. I told him about the aircar ride . . . he asked me all about breath masks." He swallowed, and looked wildly at Ekaterin, his hand clenching on her arm. "He said Lord Vorkosigan did something to Da's breath mask! Mama, is it *true*?"

"No, Nikki." Her own grip around him tightened in turn. "That wasn't possible. I found them, and I know." The physical evidence was plain, but how much could she say to him without violating security? The fact that Lord Vorkosigan had been chained to a rail by the wrists and unable to do anything to anyone's breath mask including his own led immediately to the question of who had chained him there and why. The fact that there were a myriad of things about that nightmare night Nikki didn't know led immediately to the question of how much more he hadn't been told, why Mama, how Mama, what Mama, why, why, why . . .

"They made it up," she said fiercely. "They made it all up, only because Lord Vorkosigan asked me at his party to marry him, and I turned him down."

"Huh?" Nikki wriggled around and stared at her in astonishment. "He *did*? Wow! But you'd be a Countess! All that money and stuff!" He hesitated. "You said *no*? Why?" His brow wrinkled. "Is that when you quit your job too? Why were you so mad at him? What *did* he lie to you about?" Doubt rose in his eyes; she could feel him tense again. She wanted to scream.

"It was nothing to do with Da," she said firmly. "This—what Alexi told you—is just a slander against Lord Vorkosigan."

"What's a *slander*?"

"It's when somebody spreads lies about somebody, lies that damage their honor." In the Time of Isolation, you could have fought a duel with the two swords over something like this, if you'd been a man. The rationale of dueling made sudden sense to her, for the first time in her life. She was ready to kill someone right now, but for the problem of where to aim. *It's being whispered all over town . . .*

"But . . ." Nikki's face was taut, puzzled. "If Lord Vorkosigan was with Da, why didn't he help him? In school on Komarr, they taught us how to share breath masks in an emergency . . ."

She could watch it in his face, as the questions began to twine. Nikki needed facts, truth to combat his frightened imaginings. But the State secrets were not hers to dispense.

Back on Komarr, she and Miles had agreed between them that if Nikki's curiosity became too much for Ekaterin to deal with, she would bring him to Lord Auditor Vorkosigan, to be told from his Imperial authority that security issues prevented discussing Tien's death until he was older. She had never imagined that the subject would take *this* form, that the Authority would himself be accused of Nikki's father's murder. Their neat solution suddenly . . . wasn't. Her stomach knotted. *I have to talk to Miles.*

"Well, now," Illyan murmured. "Here's an ugly little bit of politicking. . . . Remarkably ill-timed."

"Is this the first you've heard of this? How long has this been going around?"

Illyan frowned. "It's news to me. Lady Alys usually keeps me apprised of all the interesting conversations circulating in the capital. Last night, she had to give a reception for Laisa at the Residence, so my intelligence is a day behind . . . internal evidence suggests this has to have blown up since Miles's dinner party."

Ekaterin's horrified glance rose to his face. "Has *Miles* heard about this yet, do you think?"

"Ah . . . perhaps not. Who would tell him?"

"It's all my fault. If I hadn't gone charging out of Vorkosigan House in a huff . . ." Ekaterin bottled the remainder of this thought, as sudden distress thinned Illyan's mouth; yes, he imagined he held a link in this causal chain too.

"I need to go talk with some people," said Illyan.

"I need to go talk with Miles. I need to go talk with Miles *right now.*"

A calculating look flashed across Illyan's face, to be succeeded by his normal bland politeness. "I happen to have a car and driver waiting. May I offer you a lift, Madame Vorsoisson?"

But where to park poor Nikki? Aunt Vorthys wouldn't be back for a couple of hours. Ekaterin could not have him present for this—oh, what the hell, it was Vorkosigan House. There were half a dozen people she could send him off to be with—Ma Kosti, Pym, even Enrique. *Eep*—she'd forgot, the Count and Countess were home now. All right, *five* dozen people. After another moment of frenzied hesitation, she said, "*Yes.*"

She got shoes on Nikki, left a message for her aunt, locked up, and followed Illyan to his car. Nikki was pale, and growing quieter and quieter.

The drive was short. As they turned into Vorkosigan House's street, Ekaterin realized she didn't even know if Miles would be there. She should have called him on the comconsole, but Illyan had been so prompt with his offer. . . . They passed the bare, baking Barrayaran garden, sloping down from the sidewalk. On the far side of the desert expanse, a small, lone figure sat on the curving edge of a raised bed of dirt.

"Wait, stop!"

Illyan followed her glance, and signaled his driver. Ekaterin had the canopy popped and was climbing out almost before the vehicle had sighed to the pavement.

"Is there anything else I can do for you, Madame Vorsoisson?" Illyan called after her, as she stood aside to let Nikki exit.

She leaned back toward him to breathe venomously, "Yes. *Hang* Vormoncrief."

He offered her a sincere salute. "I shall do my humble best, madame."

His groundcar pulled away as, Nikki in tow, she turned to step over the low chain blocking foot traffic from the site, and strode down into the garden.

Soil was a living part of a garden, a complex ecosystem of microorganisms, but this soil was going to be dead in the sun and gone in the rains if no one got its proper ground cover installed . . . Miles, she saw as she drew nearer, was sitting next to the only plant in this whole blighted expanse, the little skellytum rootling. It was hard to say which of them looked more desperate and forlorn. An empty pitcher sat on the wall next to his knee, and he stared in worry at the rootling and the spreading stain of water on the soil around it. He glanced up at the sound of their approaching steps. His lips parted; the most appalling thrilled look passed over his face, to be suppressed almost instantly and replaced by an expression of wary courtesy.

"Madame Vorsoisson," he managed. "What are you uh, doing . . . um, welcome. Welcome. Hello, Nikki . . ."

She couldn't help it; the first words out of her mouth were nothing she'd rehearsed in the groundcar, but rather, "You haven't been pouring water *over* the barrel, have you?"

He glanced at it, and back to her. "Ah . . . shouldn't I?"

"Only around the roots. Didn't you read the instructions?"

He glanced guiltily again at the plant, as if expecting to find a tag he'd overlooked. "What instructions?"

"The ones I sent you, the appendix—oh, never mind." She pressed her fingers to her temples, clutching for coherence in her seething brain.

His sleeves were rolled up in the heat; the ragged red scars ringing his wrists were plainly visible in the bright sunlight, as were the fine pale lines of the much older surgical scars running up his arms. Nikki stared at them in worry. Miles's gaze finally tore itself from her general *hereness*, and took in her agitated state.

His voice went flatter. "I gather gardening isn't what you came about."

"No." This was going to be hard—or maybe not. *He knows. And he didn't tell me.* "Have you heard about this . . . this monstrous accusation going around?"

"Yesterday," he answered bluntly.

"Why didn't you *warn* me?"

"General Allegre asked me to wait on ImpSec's security evaluation. If this . . . ugly rumor has security implications, I am not free to act purely on my own behalf. If not . . . it's still a difficult business. An accusation, I could fight. This is something subtler." He glanced around. "However, since it's now come to you perforce, his request is moot, and I shall consider myself relieved of it. I think perhaps we'd better continue this inside."

She contemplated the desolate space, open to the sky and the city. "Yes."

"If you will?" He gestured toward Vorkosigan House, but made no move to touch her. Ekaterin took Nikki by the hand, and they accompanied him silently up the path and around through the guarded front gate.

He led them up to "his" floor, back to the cheerful sunny room in which he'd fed her that memorable luncheon. When they reached the Yellow Parlor, he seated her and Nikki on the delicate primrose sofa and himself on a straight chair across from them. There were lines of tension around his mouth she hadn't seen since Komarr. He leaned forward with his hands clasped between his knees and asked her, "How and when did it come to you?"

She gave a, to her ears, barely coherent account of Vormoncrief's intrusion, corroborated by occasional elaborations from Nikki. Miles listened gravely to Nikki's stammering recital, attending to him with a serious respect which seemed to steady the boy despite the horrifying nature of the subject. Although he did have to suck a smile back off his lips when Nikki got to a vivid description of how Vormoncrief acquired his bloody nose—"And he got it all over his uniform, too!" Ekaterin blinked, taken aback to find herself receiving exactly the same look of pleased masculine admiration from both parties.

But the moment of enthusiasm passed.

Miles rubbed his forehead. "If it were up to my judgment, I'd answer several of Nikki's questions here and now. My judgment is unfortunately suspect. *Conflict of interest* doesn't even begin to cover my position in this." He sighed softly, and leaned back on the hard chair in an unconvincing simulation of ease. "The first thing I would like to point out is that at the moment, all the onus is on me. The backsplash of this sewage appears to have missed you. I'd like to see it stay that way. If we . . . don't see each other, no one will have pretext to target you with further slander."

"But that would make you look worse," said Ekaterin. "It would make it look as if I believed Alexi's lies."

"The alternative would make it look as if we had somehow colluded in Tien's death. I don't see how to win this one. I do see how to cut the damage in half."

Ekaterin frowned deeply. *And leave you standing there to be pelted with this garbage all alone?* After a moment she said, "Your proposed solution is unacceptable. Find another."

His eyes rose searchingly to her face. "As you wish . . ."

"What are you talking about?" Nikki demanded, his brows drawn down in confusion.

"Ah." Miles touched his lips, and regarded the boy. "The reason, it seems, that my political opponents have accused me of sabotaging your da's breath mask, is that I want to court your mother."

Nikki's nose wrinkled, as he worked through this. "Did you really ask her to marry you?"

"Well, yes. In a pretty clumsy way. I did." Was he actually reddening? He spared her a quick glance, but she didn't know what he saw in her face. Or what he made of it. "But now I'm afraid that if she and I continue to go around together, people will say we must have plotted together against your da. She's afraid that if we don't continue to go around together, people will say that proves she thinks I did—I'm sorry if this distresses you—murder him. It's called, damned if you do, damned if you don't."

"Damn them all," said Ekaterin harshly. "I don't care what any of those ignorant idiots think, or say, or do. *People* can go choke on their vile gossip." Her hands clenched in her lap. "I do care what Nikki thinks." *Rot* Vormoncrief.

Vorkosigan raised an eyebrow at her. "And you think this version wouldn't come around to him too, the way the first one did?"

She looked away from him. Nikki was scrunching up again, glancing uncertainly from adult to adult. This was not, Ekaterin decided, the moment to tell him to keep his feet off the good furniture.

"Right," Miles breathed. "All right, then." He gave her a ghost of a nod. She was shaken by a weird inner vision of a knight drawing down his visor before facing the tilt. He studied Nikki a moment, and moistened his lips. "So—what *do* you think of it all so far, Nikki?"

"Dunno." Nikki, so briefly voluble, was drawing in again, not good.

"I don't mean facts. No one has given you enough facts yet for you to make much of. Try feelings. Worries. For example, are you afraid of me?"

"Naw," Nikki muttered, wrapping his arms around his knees and staring down at his shoes rubbing on the fine yellow silk upholstery.

"Are you afraid it might be true?"

"It could not be," said Ekaterin fiercely. "It was physically impossible."

Nikki looked up. "But he was in ImpSec, Mama! ImpSec agents can do anything, and make it look like anything!"

"Thank you for that . . . vote of confidence, Nikki," said Miles gravely. "I think. In fact, Ekaterin, Nikki's right. I can imagine several plausible scenarios that could have resulted in the physical evidence you saw."

"Name one," she said scornfully.

"Most simply, I might have had an unknown accomplice." Rather horribly, his fingers made a tiny twisting gesture, as of someone venting a bound man's oxygen supply. Nikki of course missed both the gesture and the reference. "It elaborates from there. If I can generate them, so can others, and I'm sure some won't hesitate to share their bright ideas with you."

"You foresaw this?" she asked, a little numb.

"Ten years in ImpSec does things to your brain. Some of them aren't very nice."

The tidal wave of anger that had hurled her here was receding, leaving her standing on a very bare shore indeed. She had not intended to talk so frankly in front of Nikki. But Vormoncrief had destroyed any chance of continuing to protect him by ignorance. Maybe Miles was right. They were going to have to deal with this. All three of them were going to have to deal, and go on dealing, ready or not, old enough or not.

"Shuffling facts only takes you so far anyway. Sooner or later, you come down to bare trust. Or mistrust." He turned to Nikki, his eyes unreadable. "Here's the truth. Nikki, I did not murder your father. He went out-dome with a breath mask with nearly empty reservoirs, which he did not check, and then got caught outside too long. I made two bad mistakes that prevented me from being able to save him. I don't feel very good about that, but I can't fix it now. The only thing I can do to make up for it is to take care of—" He stopped abruptly, and eyed Ekaterin with extreme wariness. "To see that his family is taken care of, and doesn't lack for any need."

She eyed him back. His family had been Tien's least concern, judging by his performance while he was alive, or else he would not have left her destitute, himself secretly dishonored, and Nikki untreated for a serious genetic disease. Yet Tien's larger failures, time bombs though they'd been for Nikki's future, had seldom impinged on the young boy. In a pensive moment during the funeral she had asked Nikki what one of his happy memories of his da was. He'd remembered Tien taking them for a wonderful week at the seaside. Ekaterin, recalling that the monorail tickets and reservations for that holiday had been slipped to her as a charity by her brother Hugo, had kept silent. Even from the grave, she thought bitterly, Tien's personal chaos still reached out to disrupt her grasp for peace. Maybe Vorkosigan's bid to shoulder responsibility was not a bad thing for Nikki to hear.

Nikki's lips were tight, and his eyes a little blurry, as he digested Miles's blunt words. "But," he began, and stalled.

"You must be starting to think of a lot of questions," Miles said in a tone of mild encouragement. "What are some of them? Or even just one or two of them?"

Nikki looked down, then up. "But—but—why didn't he check his breath mask?" He hesitated, then went on in a rush, "Why couldn't you share yours? What were your two mistakes? What did you lie to Mama about that got her so mad? Why *couldn't* you save him? How *did* your wrists get all chewed up?" Nikki took a deep breath, gave Miles an utterly daunted look, and almost wailed, "Am I supposed to kill you like Captain Vortalon?"

Miles had been following this spate with close attention, but at this last he looked taken aback. "Excuse me. Who?"

Ekaterin, flummoxed, supplied in an undervoice, "Captain Vortalon is Nikki's favorite holovid hero. He's a jump pilot who has galactic adventures with Prince Xav, smuggling arms to the Resistance during the Cetagandan invasion. There was a whole long sequence about him chasing down some collaborators who'd ambushed his da—Lord Vortalon—and avenging his death on them one by one."

"I somehow missed that one. Must have been off-world. You let him watch all that violence, at his tender age?" Miles's eyes were suddenly alight.

Ekaterin set her teeth. "It was *supposed* to be educational, on account of the historical accuracy of the background."

"When I was Nikki's age, my obsession was Lord Vorthalia the Bold, Legendary Hero from the Time of Isolation." His reminiscent voice took on a rather fruity narrator's cadence, delivering this last. "That started with a holovid too, come to think of it, though before I was done I was persuading my gran'da to take me to look up original Imperial archives. Turned out Vorthalia wasn't as legendary as all that, though his real adventures weren't all so heroic. I think I could still sing all nine verses of the song that went with—"

"Please don't," she growled.

"Well, it could have been worse. I'm glad you didn't let him watch *Hamlet.*"

"What's Hamlet?" asked Nikki instantly. He was starting to uncoil a little.

"Another great revenge drama on the same theme, except this one is an ancient stage play from Old Earth. Prince Hamlet comes home from college—by the way, how old was your Captain Vortalon?"

"Old," said Nikki. "Twenty."

"Ah, well, there you go. Nobody expects you to carry out a really good revenge till you're at least old enough to shave. You have several years yet before you have to worry about it."

Ekaterin started to cry *Lord Vorkosigan!* in outraged protest to this line of black humor, till she saw that Nikki looked noticeably relieved. Where was Miles going with this? She held her tongue, and nearly her breath, and let him run on.

"So in the play, Prince Hamlet comes home for his father's funeral, to find that his mother has married his uncle."

Nikki's eyes widened. "She married her *brother*?"

"No, no! It's not *that* racy a play. His other uncle, his da's brother."

"Oh. That's all right, then."

"You'd think so, but Hamlet gets a tip-off that his old man was murdered by the uncle. Unfortunately, he can't tell if his informant is telling truth or lies. So he spends the next five acts blundering around getting nearly the whole cast killed while he dithers."

"That was stupid," said Nikki scornfully, uncoiling altogether. "Why didn't he just use fast-penta?"

"Hadn't been invented yet, alas. Or it would have been a much shorter play."

"Oh." Nikki frowned thoughtfully at Miles. "Can *you* use fast-penta? Lieutenant Vormoncrief . . . said you couldn't. And that it was *very convenient.*" Nikki precisely mimicked Vormoncrief's sneer in these last two words.

"On myself, you mean? Ah, no. I have a screwy response to it that renders it unreliable. Which was very handy in my ImpSec days, but isn't so good right now. In fact, it's damned *in*convenient. But I wouldn't be allowed to be publicly questioned and cleared about your da's death even if it did work, because of certain security issues involved. Nor privately, in front of you alone, for the same reason."

Nikki was silent for a little, then said abruptly, "Lieutenant Vormoncrief called you *the mutie lord.*"

"A lot of people do. Not to my face."

"He doesn't know I'm a mutie too. So was my da. Doesn't it make you mad when they call you that?"

"When I was your age, it bothered me a lot. It doesn't seem very relevant anymore. Now that there's good gene cleaning available, I wouldn't pass on any problems to my children even if I were a dozen times more damaged." His lips twisted, and he carefully didn't look at Ekaterin. "Assuming I can ever persuade some daring woman to marry me."

"Lieutenant Vormoncrief wouldn't want us . . . wouldn't want Mama if he knew I was a mutie, I bet."

"In that case, I urge you to tell him right away," Vorkosigan shot back, deadpan.

Mirabile, this won a brief, sly grin from Nikki.

Was this the trick of it? Secrets so dire as to be unspeakable, thoughts so frightening as to make clear young voices mute, kicked out into the open with blunt ironic humor. And suddenly the dire didn't loom so darkly any more, and fear shrank, and anyone could say anything. And the unbearable seemed a little easier to lift.

"Nikki, the security issues I mentioned make it impossible to tell you everything."

"Yeah, I know." Nikki hunched again. "It's 'cause I'm nine."

"Nine, nineteen, or ninety wouldn't matter on this one. But I do think it's possible to tell you a good deal more than you know now. I'd like to have you talk to a man who does have authority to decide how many details are proper and safe for you to hear. He also lost a father under tragic circumstances at an early age, so he's been where you stand now. If you're willing, I'll set up an appointment."

Who did he mean? One of the high-ranking ImpSec men, it had to be. But judging from her own unpleasant brushes with ImpSec on Komarr, Ekaterin couldn't imagine any of them voluntarily parting with directions to the Great Square, let alone this.

"All right . . ." said Nikki slowly.

"Good." A little gleam of relief flickered in Miles's eyes, and faded again. "In the meanwhile . . . I expect this slander may come round to you again. Maybe from an adult, maybe from someone your own age who overhears the adults talking about it. The story will likely get garbled and changed around in a lot of strange ways. Do you know how you are going to deal with it?"

Nikki looked briefly fierce. He made a swipe with his fist. "Punch 'em in the nose?"

Ekaterin winced in guilt; Miles caught her cringe.

"I would hope for a more mature and reasoned response from you," Vorkosigan intoned piously to Nikki, one eye on her. Drat the man for making her laugh at a moment like this! Possibly it had been too long since anyone had punched *him* in the nose? Satisfaction twitched his lip at her choke.

He went on more seriously, "May I suggest instead you simply tell whoever it may be that the story isn't true, and refuse to discuss it further. If they persist, tell them they have to talk with your mother, or your uncle or aunt Vorthys. If they still persist, go *get* your mother or uncle or aunt. You don't need me to tell you this is some pretty ugly stuff, here. No thinking, honorable adult should be dragging you into it, but unfortunately all that means is that you're likely to find yourself badgered by unthinking adults."

Nikki nodded slowly. "Like Lieutenant Vormoncrief." Ekaterin could almost see the relief afforded Nikki by being presented with this conceptual slot into which to tuck his late tormentor. *United against a common enemy.*

"To put it as politely as possible, yes."

Nikki fell into a digestive silence. After letting him mull a little, Miles suggested they all repair to the kitchen for a fortifying snack, adding that the box of new kittens had just been moved to what was becoming its traditional place next to the stove. The depth of his strategy was revealed when, after Ma Kosti plied both Nikki and Ekaterin with food-rewards that would produce positive conditioning in rocks, the cook took the boy to the other end of the long room, leaving Miles and Ekaterin an almost-private moment.

Ekaterin, sitting on the stool next to Miles's, leaned her elbows on the counter and stared down the kitchen. Over by the stove, Ma Kosti and the fascinated Nikki were kneeling over the box of furry mewing bundles. "Who is this man you think Nikki should see?" she asked quietly.

"Let me make sure first he'll be willing to do what we need, and can make the time available," Miles answered cautiously. "You and Nikki will go in together, of course."

"I understand, but . . . I was thinking, Nikki tends to withdraw around strangers. Make sure this fellow grasps that just because Nikki goes monosyllabic doesn't mean he's not desperately curious."

"I'll make sure he understands."

"Does he have much experience with children?"

"Not as far as I know." Miles gave her a rueful smile. "But perhaps he'll be grateful for the practice."

"Under the circumstances, I find that unlikely."

"Under the circumstances, I'm afraid you're right. But I trust his judgment."

The myriad other questions which lay between them had to wait, as Nikki came bouncing back with the news that all newborn kittens' eyes were blue. The near-hysteria which had crumpled his face when they'd first arrived was erased. This kitchen made a fair barometer of his internal state; pleasantly distracted by food and pets, he was clearly much calmer. That he now could *be* so diverted was telling, Ekaterin judged. *I was right to come to Miles. How did Illyan know?*

Ekaterin let Nikki burble on till he ran down, then said, "We should go. My aunt will be wondering what happened to us." The hasty note she'd penned had told where they'd gone, but not why; Ekaterin had been far too upset at the time to even try to include the details. She looked forward without pleasure to explaining this whole hideous mess to her uncle and aunt, but at least they knew the truth, and could be counted upon to share her outrage.

"Pym can drive you," Miles offered immediately.

He made no attempt to trap her here this time, she noted with dark amusement. Not a slow learner, indeed?

Promising to call her when he'd cleared Nikki's interview, Miles handed them personally into the rear compartment of the groundcar, and watched them out the gates. Nikki was quiet on this trip, too, but the silence was much less fraught now.

After a little, he gave her an odd, appraising look. "Mama . . . did you turn Lord Vorkosigan down 'cause he's a mutie?"

"No," she replied at once, and firmly. His brows bent. If he didn't get a more explicit answer, he would likely make up his own, she realized with an inward sigh. "You see, when he hired me to make his garden, it wasn't because he wanted a garden, or thought I was good at the work. He just thought it would give him a chance to see me a lot."

"Well," said Nikki, "that makes sense. I mean, it did, didn't it?"

She managed not to glower at him. Her work meant nothing to him—what did? If you could say anything to anyone . . . "Would you like it, if somebody promised to help you become a jump pilot, and you worked your heart out studying, and then it turned out they were tricking you into doing something else?"

"Oh." The light glimmered, dimly.

"I was angry because he'd tried to manipulate me, and my situation, in a way I found invasive and offensive." After a short, reflective pause, she added helplessly, "It seems to be his *style*." Was it a style she could learn to live with? Or was it a style he could bloody well learn not to try on her? Live, or learn? *Can we have some of both?*

"So . . . d'you like him? Or not?"

Like was surely not an adequate word for this hash of delight and anger and longing, this profound respect laced with profound irritation, all floating on a dark pool of old pain. The past and the future, at war in her head. "I don't know. Some of the time I do, yes, very much."

Another long pause. "Are you *in love* with him?"

What Nikki knew of adult love, he'd mostly garnered off the holovid. Part of her mind readily translated this question as code for, *Which way are you going to jump, and what will happen to me?* And yet . . . he could not share or even imagine the complexity of her romantic hopes and fears, but he certainly knew how such stories were supposed to Come Out Right.

"I don't know. Some of the time. I think."

He favored her with his Big People Are Crazy look. In all, she could only agree.

Chapter Fourteen

Miles had obtained copies of archives from the Council of Counts covering all the contested succession debates from the last two centuries. Together with a stack of gleanings from Vorkosigan House's own document room, they spread themselves over two tables and a desk in the library. He was deeply engrossed in a hundred-and-fifty-year-old account of the fourth Count Vorlakial's family tragedy when Armsman Jankowski appeared at the door from the anteroom and announced, "Commodore Galeni, m'lord."

Miles looked up in surprise. "Thank you, Jankowski." The Armsman gave him an acknowledging nod, and withdrew, closing the double doors discreetly behind himself.

Galeni trod across the great library, and regarded the scattering of papers, parchments, and flimsies with an ex-historian's alert eye. "Cramming, are you?" he inquired.

"Yes. Now, you had that doctorate in Barrayaran history. Do any really interesting District succession squabbles spring to your memory?"

"Lord Midnight the horse," Galeni replied at once. "Who always voted 'neigh.'"

"Got that one already." Miles waved at the pile on the far end of the inlaid table. "What brings you here, Duv?"

"Official ImpSec business. Your requested analyst's report, My Lord Auditor, regarding certain rumors about Madame Vorsoisson's late husband."

Miles scowled, reminded. "ImpSec is late off the mark. This would have done a lot more good yesterday. Not a hell of a lot of point to order *me* to back off, and then let Ekaterin and Nikki be subjected to that surprise harassment—in her own home, good God—by that idiot Vormoncrief."

"Yes. Illyan told Allegre. Allegre told me. I wish *I* had someone to tell . . . I was still pulling in informants' reports and cross-checks as of midnight last night, thank you very much, my lord. I wasn't able to calculate anything like a decent reliability score till late yesterday."

"Oh. Oh, no, Allegre didn't put you on this . . . slander matter personally, did he? Sit, sit." Miles waved Galeni to a chair, which the Komarran pulled up around the corner of the table from Miles.

"Of course he did. I was an eyewitness to your ghastly dinner party, which seems to have launched the whole thing, and more to the point, I'm already in the need-to-know pool regarding the Komarr case." Galeni seated himself with a tired grunt; his eye automatically began to scan the documents sideways. "There was no way Allegre would add another man to that pool if he could possibly avoid it."

"Mm, makes sense, I guess. But I'd hardly think you'd have *time*."

"I didn't," said Galeni bitterly. "I've been putting in an extra half shift after dinner nearly every day since I was promoted to head of Komarran Affairs. *This* came out of my sleep cycle. I'm considering abandoning meals and just hanging a food tube over my desk, which I could suck on now and then."

"I'd think Delia would put her foot down, after a while."

"Yes, and that's another thing," Galeni added, in an aggravated tone.

Miles waited a beat, but Duv did not elaborate. Well, and did he really need to? Miles sighed. "Sorry," he offered.

"Yes, well. From ImpSec's point of view, I have excellent news. No evidence has yet surfaced indicating any leak of the classified matters surrounding Tien Vorsoisson's death. No names, no hints of . . . technical activities, not even rumors of financial chicanery. There continues to be a complete and most welcome absence of Komarran conspirators of any stripe from any of the several scenarios of your murder of Vorsoisson."

"*Several* scenarios—! How many versions are circulating—no, don't tell me. It would just raise my blood pressure to no good purpose." Miles gritted his teeth. "So, what, am I supposed to have made away with Vorsoisson—a man twice my size—through some devilish ex-ImpSec trick?"

"Perhaps. In the one version concocted so far where you were not pictured as acting alone, the only henchmen posited were vile and corrupt ImpSec personnel. In your pay."

"This could only have been imagined by someone who never had to fill out one of Illyan's arcane expenditure-and/or-income reports," Miles growled.

Galeni shrugged amused agreement.

"And were there—no, let me tell you," Miles said. "There were no leaks traced from the Vorthys's household."

"None," Galeni conceded.

Miles grumbled a few satisfied swear words under his breath. He knew he hadn't misestimated Ekaterin. "Do me a personal favor and be sure to highlight that fact in the copy of this you send up to Allegre, eh?"

Galeni opened his hand in a carefully noncommittal gesture.

Miles blew out his breath, slowly. No leaks, no treasons: just idle malice and circumstance. And a touch of theoretical blackmail. Upsetting to himself, to his parents when it came to them, as it soon must, upsetting to the Vorthyses, to Nikki, to Ekaterin. They had *dared* to upset Ekaterin with this . . . He carefully ignored his simmering fury. Rage had no place in this. Calculation and implacable action did.

"So what, if anything, is ImpSec planning to do about it all?" Miles asked at last.

"At present, as little as possible. It's not as though we don't have enough other tasks on our plate. We will, of course, continue to monitor all data for any key items that might lead public attention back to where we don't want it. It's a poor second choice to no attention at all, but this murder scenario does us one favor. For anyone who refuses to accept Tien Vorsoisson's death as a mere accident, it presents a plausible cover story, which entirely accounts for no further investigation being permitted."

"Oh, entirely," snarled Miles. *I see where this is going.* He sat back, and folded his arms mulishly. "Does this mean I'm on my own?"

"Ah . . ." said Galeni. He drew it out for a rather long time. Eventually, he ran out of *ah* and was forced to speak. "Not exactly."

Miles bared his set teeth, and waited for Galeni, who waited for him.

Miles broke first. "Dammit, Duv, am I supposed to just stand here and eat this shit raw?"

"Come on, Miles, you've done coverups before. I thought you covert ops fellows lived and breathed this sort of thing."

"Never in my own sandbox. Never where I had to live in it. My Dendarii missions were hit and run. We always left the stink far behind."

Galeni's shrug lacked sympathy. "I must also point out, these are first results. Just because there are no leaks yet doesn't mean none will be . . . siphoned out into the open later on."

Miles exhaled slowly. "All right. Tell Allegre he has his goat. Baaah." He added after a moment, "But I draw the line at pretending to guilt. It was a breath mask accident. Period."

Galeni waved a hand in acceptance of this. "ImpSec won't complain."

It was *good*, Miles reminded himself, that there was no security rupture in the Komarr case. But this also killed his faint, unvoiced hope that he could leave Richars and his cronies to the untender mercies of ImpSec to be disposed of. "As long as this is all gas, so be it. But you can let Allegre know, that if it goes to a formal murder charge against me in the Council . . ." *Then what?*

Galeni's eyes narrowed. "Do you have reason to think someone will charge you there? Who?"

"Richars Vorrutyer. I have a sort of . . . personal promise from him."

"He can't, though. Not unless he gets a member to lay it for him."

"He can if he beats out Lord Dono and is confirmed Count Vorrutyer." *And my colleagues are like to choke on Lord Dono.*

"Miles . . . ImpSec *can't* release the evidence surrounding Vorsoisson's death. Not even to the Council of Counts."

By the look on Galeni's face, Miles read that as *Especially* not to the Council of Counts. Knowing that erratic body, he sympathized. "Yes. I know."

Galeni said uneasily, "What are you planning to do?"

Miles had more compelling reasons than the strain on ImpSec's nerves to wish to sidestep this whole scenario. Two of them, mother and son. If he worked it right, none of this looming juridical mess need ever touch Ekaterin and her Nikki. "Nothing more—nor less— than my job. A little politicking. Barrayaran style."

Galeni eyed him dubiously. "Well . . . if you really intend to project innocence, you need to do a more convincing job. You . . . *twitch*."

Miles . . . twitched. "There's guilt and there's guilt. I am not guilty of willful murder. I am guilty of screwing up. Now, I'm not alone— this one took a full committee. Headed by that fool Vorsoisson himself. If only he'd—dammit, every time you step off the downside shuttle into a Komarran dome they sit you down and make you watch that vid on breath mask procedures. He'd been living there nearly a year. He'd been *told*." He fell silent a moment. "Not that I didn't know better than to go out-dome without informing *my* contacts."

"As it happens, no one is accusing you of negligence."

Miles's mouth twisted bitterly. "They flatter me, Duv. They flatter me."

"I can't help you with that one," said Galeni. "I have enough unquiet ghosts of my own."

"Check." Miles sighed.

Galeni regarded him for a long moment, then said abruptly, "About your clone."

"Brother."

"Yes, him. Do you know . . . do you understand . . . what the devil does he *intend*, with respect to Kareen Koudelka?"

"Is this ImpSec asking, or Duv Galeni?"

"Duv Galeni." Galeni paused for a rather longer time. "After the . . . ambiguous favor he did me when we first encountered each other on Earth, I was content to see him survive and escape. I wasn't even too shocked when I learned he'd popped up here, nor—now I've met your mother—that your family took him in. I'd even reconciled myself to the likelihood that we would meet, from time to time." His level voice cracked a trifle. "I wasn't expecting him to mutate into my brother-in-law!"

Miles sat back, his brows rising in partial sympathy. He refrained from doing anything so rude as, say, cackling. "I would point out, that in an exceedingly weird sense, you are related already. He's your foster brother. Your father had him made; by some interpretations of the galactic laws on clones, that makes him Mark's father too."

"This concept makes my head spin. Painfully." He stared at Miles in sudden consternation. "Mark doesn't think of *himself* as my foster brother, does he?"

"I have not so far directed his attention to that legal wrinkle. But think, Duv, how much *easier* it will be if you only have to explain him as your brother-in-law. I mean, lots of people have embarrassing in-laws; it's one of life's lotteries. You'll have all their sympathy."

Galeni gave him a look of Very Limited Amusement.

"He'll be Uncle Mark," Miles pointed out with a slow, unholy smile. "You'll be Uncle Duv. I suppose, by some loose extension, I'll be Uncle Miles. And here I never thought I'd be anybody's uncle—an only child and all that."

Come to think of it . . . if Ekaterin ever accepted him, Miles would become an instant uncle, acquiring *three* brothers-in-law simultaneously, all with attached wives, and a pack of nieces and nephews already in place. Not to mention the father-in-law and the stepmother-in-law. He wondered if any of them would be embarrassing. Or—a new and unnerving thought—if *he* was going to be the appalling brother-in-law . . .

"*Do* you think they'll marry?" asked Galeni seriously.

"I . . . am not certain what cultural format their bonding will ultimately take. I am certain you could not pry Mark away from Kareen with a crowbar. And while Kareen has good reasons to take it slowly, I don't think any of the Koudelkas know *how* to betray a trust."

That won a little eyebrow-flick from Galeni, and the slight mellowing that any reminder of Delia invariably produced in him.

"I'm afraid you're going to have to resign yourself to Mark as a permanent fixture," Miles concluded.

"Eh," said Galeni. It was hard to tell if this sound represented resignation, or stomach cramp. In any case, he climbed to his feet and took his leave.

Mark, entering the black-and-white tiled entry foyer from the back hallway to the lift tubes, encountered his mother descending the front staircase.

"Oh, Mark," Countess Vorkosigan said, in a just-the-man-I-want-to-see voice. Obediently, he paused and waited for her. She eyed his neat attire, his favorite black suit modified by what he trusted was an unthreatening dark green shirt. "Are you on your way out?"

"Shortly. I was just about to hunt up Pym and ask him to assign me an Armsman-driver. I have an interview set up with a friend of Lord Vorsmythe's, a food service fellow who's promised to explain

Barrayar's distribution system to me. He may be a future customer—I thought it might look well to arrive in the groundcar, all Vorkosiganly."

"Very likely."

Her further comment was interrupted by two half-grown boys rounding the corner: Pym's son Arthur, carrying a smelly fiber-tipped stick, and Jankowski's boy Denys, lugging an optimistically large jar. They clattered up the stairs past her with a breathless greeting of, "Hello, milady!"

She wheeled to watch them pass, her eyebrows rising in amusement. "New recruits for science?" she asked Mark as they thumped out of sight, giggling.

"For enterprise. Martya had a flash of genius. She put a bounty on escaped butter bugs, and set all the Armsmen's spare children to rounding them up. A mark apiece, and a ten-mark bonus for the queen. Enrique is back to work splicing genes full-time, the lab is caught up again, and *I* can return my attention to financial planning. We're getting bugs back at the rate of two or three an hour; it should be all over by tomorrow or the next day. At least, none of the children seem yet to have hit on the idea of sneaking into the lab and freeing Vorkosigan bugs, to renew their economic resource. I may devise a lock for that hutch."

The Countess laughed. "Come now, Lord Mark, you insult their honor. These are our *Armsmen's* offspring."

"*I* would have thought of that, at their age."

"If it weren't their liege-lord's bugs, they might have." She smiled, but her smile faded. "Speaking of insults . . . I wanted to ask you if you'd heard any of this vile talk going around about Miles and his Madame Vorsoisson."

"I've been head-down in the lab for the last several days. Miles doesn't come back there much, for some reason. What vile talk?"

She narrowed her eyes, slipped her hand through his arm, and strolled with him toward the antechamber to the library. "Illyan and Alys took me aside at the Vorinnis's dinner party last night, and gave me an earful. I'm extremely glad they got to me first. I was then cornered by two other people in the course of the evening and given garbled alternate versions . . . actually, one of them was trolling for confirmation. The other appeared to hope I'd pass it on to Aral, as he didn't dare repeat it to his face, the spineless little snipe. It seems rumors have begun to circulate through the capital that Miles somehow made away with Ekaterin's late husband while on Komarr."

"Well," said Mark reasonably, "you know more about that than I do. Did he?"

Her eyebrows went up. "Do you care?"

"Not especially. From everything I've been able to gather—between the lines, mostly, Ekaterin doesn't talk about him much—Tien Vorsoisson was a pretty complete waste of food, water, oxygen, and time."

"Has Miles said anything to you that . . . that leaves you in doubt about Vorsoisson's death?" she asked, seating herself beside the huge antique mirror gracing the side wall.

"Well, no," Mark admitted, taking a chair across from her. "Though I gather he fancies himself guilty of some carelessness. I think it would have been a much more interesting romance if he *had* assassinated the lout for her."

She sighed, looking bemused. "Sometimes, Mark, despite all your Betan therapist has done, I'm afraid your Jacksonian upbringing still leaks out."

He shrugged, unrepentantly. "Sorry."

"I am moved by your insincerity. Just don't repeat those no doubt honest sentiments in front of Nikki."

"I may be Jacksonian, ma'am, but I'm not a complete loss."

She nodded, evidently reassured. She began to speak again, but was interrupted by the double doors to the library swinging wide, and Miles escorting Commodore Duv Galeni out through the anteroom.

Seeing them, the Commodore paused to give the Countess a civil good-day. The greeting he gave to Mark was just as civil, but much warier, as though Mark had lately erupted in a hideous skin disease but Galeni was too polite to comment on it. Mark returned the greeting in kind.

Galeni did not linger. Miles saw his visitor out the front door, and retraced his steps toward the library.

"Miles!" said the Countess, rising and following him in with an expression of sudden concentration. Mark trailed in after them, uncertain if she'd finished with him or not. She cornered Miles against one of the sofas flanking the fireplace. "I understand from Pym that your Madame Vorsoisson was here yesterday, while Aral and I were out. She was *here*, and I *missed* her!"

"It was not exactly a social call," Miles said. Trapped, he gave up and sat down. "And I could hardly have delayed her departure till you and Father returned at midnight."

"Reasonable enough," his mother said, completing her capture by plunking down on the matching sofa across from him. Gingerly, Mark seated himself next to her. "But when *are* we to be permitted to meet her?"

He eyed her warily. "Not . . . just now. If you don't mind. Things are in a rather delicate, um, situation between us just at the moment."

"Delicate," echoed the Countess. "Isn't that a distinct improvement over a life in ruins with vomiting?"

A brief hopeful look glimmered in his eye, but he shook his head. "Just now, it's pretty hard to say."

"I quite understand. But only because Simon and Alys explained it to us last night. Might I ask why we had to hear about this nasty slander from them, and not from you?"

"Oh. Sorry." He sketched her an apologetic bow. "I only first heard about it day before yesterday myself. We've been running on separate tracks the past few days, what with your social whirl."

"You've been sitting on this for two days? I should have wondered at your sudden fascination with Chaos Colony during our last two meals together."

"Well, I *was* interested in hearing about your life on Sergyar. But more critically, I was waiting on the ImpSec analysis."

The Countess glanced toward the door Commodore Galeni had lately exited. "Ah," she said, in a tone of enlightenment. "Hence Duv."

"Hence Duv." Miles nodded. "If there had been a security leak involved, well, it would have been a whole different matter."

"And there was not?"

"Apparently not. It seems to be an entirely politically motivated fiction, made up out of altogether circumstantial . . . circumstances. By a small group of Conservative Counts and their hangers-on whom I have lately offended. And vice versa. I've decided to deal with it . . . politically." His face set in a grim look. "In my own way. In fact, Dono Vorrutyer and René Vorbretten will be here shortly to consult."

"Ah. Allies. Good." Her eyes narrowed in satisfaction.

He shrugged. "That's what politics is about, in part. Or so I take it."

"That's your department now. I leave you to it, and it to you. But what about you and your Ekaterin? Are you two going to be able to weather this?"

His expression grew distant. "We three. Don't leave out Nikki. I don't know yet."

"I've been thinking," said the Countess, watching him closely, "that I should invite Ekaterin and Kareen to tea. Just us ladies."

A look of alarm, if not outright panic, crossed Miles's face. "I . . . I . . . not yet. Just . . . not yet."

"No?" said the Countess, in a tone of disappointment. "When, then?"

"Her parents wouldn't let Kareen come, would they?" Mark put in. "I mean . . . I thought they'd cut the connection." A thirty-year friendship, destroyed by him. *Good work, Mark. What shall we do for an encore? Accidentally burn down Vorkosigan House?* At least that would get rid of the butter bug infestation. . . .

"Kou and Drou?" said the Countess. "Well, of *course* they've been avoiding me! I'm sure they don't dare look me in the eye, after that performance the night we came back."

Mark wasn't sure what to make of that, though Miles snorted wryly.

"I miss her," said Mark, his hand clenching helplessly along his trouser seam. "I *need* her. We're supposed to start presenting bug butter products to potential major accounts in a few days. I was counting on having Kareen along. I . . . I can't do sales very well. I've tried. The people I pitch to all seem to end up huddled on the far end of the room with lots of furniture between us. And Martya is too . . . forthright. But Kareen is brilliant. She could sell anything to anyone. Especially Barrayaran men. They sort of lie down and roll over, waving their paws in the air and wagging their tails—it's just amazing. And, and . . . I can stay calm, when she's with me, no matter how much other people irritate me. Oh, I want her *back* . . ." These last words escaped him in a muffled wail.

Miles looked at his mother, and at Mark, and shook his head in bemused exasperation. "You're not making proper use of your Barrayaran resources, Mark. Here you have, in-house, the most high-powered potential Baba on the planet, and you haven't even brought her into play!"

"But . . . what could she do? Under the circumstances?"

"To Kou and Drou? I hate to think." Miles rubbed his chin. "Butter, meet laser-beam. Laser-beam, butter. Oops."

His mother smiled, but then crossed her arms and stared thoughtfully around the great library.

"But, ma'am . . ." Mark stammered, "could you? *Would* you? I didn't presume to ask, after all the things . . . people said to one another that night, but I'm getting desperate." *Desperately* desperate.

"I didn't presume to intrude, without a direct invitation," the Countess told him. She waited, favoring him with a bright, expectant smile.

Mark thought it over. His mouth shaped the unfamiliar word twice, for practice, before he licked his lips, took a breath, and launched it into unsupported air. "*Help . . . ?*"

"Why, *gladly*, Mark!" Her smile sharpened. "I think what we need to do is to sit down together, the five of us—you and me and Kareen and Kou and Drou—right here, oh, yes, right *here* in this library, and talk it all over."

The vision filled him with inchoate terror, but he grasped his knees and nodded. "Yes. That is—you'll talk, right?"

"It will be just fine," she assured him.

"But how will you even get them to come here?"

"I think you can confidently leave that to me."

Mark glanced at his brother, who was smiling dryly. *He* did not look in the least dubious of her statement.

Armsman Pym appeared at the library door. "Sorry to interrupt, m'lady. M'lord, Count Vorbretten is arriving."

"Ah, good." Miles jumped to his feet, and hastened around to the long table, where he began gathering up stacks of flimsies, papers, and notes. "Bring him straight up to my suite, and tell Ma Kosti to start things rolling."

Mark seized the opportunity. "Oh, Pym, I'm going to need the car and a driver in about," he glanced at his chrono, "ten minutes."

"I'll see to it, m'lord."

Pym set off about his duties; Miles, a determined look on his face and a pile of documentation under his arm, charged out after his Armsman.

Mark looked doubtfully at the Countess.

"Run along to your meeting," she told him comfortably. "Stop up to my study when you get back, and tell me all about it."

She actually sounded interested. "Do you think you might like to invest?" he offered in a burst of optimism.

"We'll talk about it." She smiled at him with genuine pleasure, surely one of the few people in the universe to do so. Secretly heartened, he took himself off in Miles's wake.

The ImpSec gate guard passed Ivan through to Vorkosigan House's grounds, then returned to his kiosk at a beep from his comm link. Ivan had to step aside while the iron gates swung wide and the gleaming armored groundcar lumbered out into the street. A brief hope flared in Ivan's breast that he had missed Miles, but the blurred shape that waved at him through the half-mirroring of the rear canopy was much too round. It was Mark who was off somewhere. When Pym ushered him into Miles's suite, Ivan found his leaner cousin sitting by the bay window with Count René Vorbretten.

"Oh, sorry," said Ivan. "Didn't know you were enga—occupied."

But it was too late to back out; Miles, turning toward him in surprise, controlled a wince, sighed, and waved him to enter. "Hello, Ivan. What brings you here?"

"M'mother sent me with this note. Why she couldn't just call you on the comconsole I don't know, but I wasn't going to argue with a chance to escape." Ivan proffered the heavy envelope, Residence stationery sealed with Lady Alys's personal crest.

"Escape?" asked René, looking amused. "It sounded to me as though you have one of the cushiest jobs of any officer in Vorbarr Sultana this season."

"Hah," said Ivan darkly. "You want it? It's like working in an office with an entire boatload of mothers-in-law-to-be with pre-wedding nerves, every one of them a flaming control freak. I don't know where Mama *found* that many Vor dragons. You usually only meet them one at a time, surrounded by an entire family to terrorize. Having them all in a bunch teamed up together is just *wrong*." He pulled up a chair between Miles and René, and sat down in a pointedly temporary posture. "My chain of command is built upside down; there are twenty-three commanders, and only one enlisted. Me. I want to go back to Ops, where my officers don't preface every insane demand with a menacing trill of, '*Ivan*, dear, won't you be a *sweetheart* and—' What I wouldn't give to hear a nice, deep, straightforward masculine bellow of '*Vorpatril!*' . . . From someone other than Countess Vorinnis, that is."

Miles, grinning, started to open the envelope, but then paused and listened to the sound of more persons being admitted into the hall by Pym. "Ah," he said. "Good. Right on time."

To Ivan's dismay, the visitors Pym next gated into his lord's chambers were Lord Dono and Byerly Vorrutyer, and Armsman Szabo. All of them greeted Ivan with repulsive cheer; Lord Dono shook Count René's hand with firm cordiality, and seated himself around the low table from Miles. By draped himself over the back of Dono's armchair and looked on. Szabo took a straight chair like Ivan's a little back from the principals and folded his arms.

"Excuse me," said Miles, and finished opening the envelope. He pulled out Lady Alys's note, glanced down it, and smiled. "So, gentlemen. My aunt Alys writes: *Dear Miles,* the usual elegant courtesies, and then—*Tell your friends Countess Vorsmythe reports René may be sure of her husband's vote. Dono will need a little more push there, but the topic of his future as a straight Progressive Party voter may bear fruit. Lady Mary Vorville also reports comfortable tidings to René due to some fondly remembered military connection between his late father and her father Count Vorville. I had thought it indelicate to lobby Countess Vorpinski regarding a vote for Lord Dono, but she surprised me by her quite enthusiastic approval of Lady Donna's transformation.*"

Lord Dono muffled a laugh, and Miles paused to raise an inquiring eyebrow.

"Count—then Lord—Vorpinski and I were quite good friends for a little while," Dono explained, with a small smirk. "After your time, Ivan; I believe you were off to Earth for that stint of embassy duty."

To Ivan's relief, Miles did not ask for further details, but merely nodded understanding and read on, his voice picking up the precise cadences of Lady Alys's diction. "*A personal visit by Dono to the Countess, to assure her of the reality of the change and the unlikelihood*—unlikelihood is underscored—*of its reversal in the event of Lord Dono obtaining his Countship, may do some good in that quarter.*

"*Lady Vortugalov reports not much hope for either René or Dono from her father-in-law. However,*—hah, get this—*she has shifted the birthdate of the Count's first grandson two days forward, so it just happens to coincide with the day the votes are scheduled, and has invited the Count to be present when the replicator is opened. Lord Vortugalov of course will also be there. Lady Vortugalov also mentions the Count's voting deputy's wife pines for a wedding invitation. I shall release one of the spares to Lady VorT. to pass along at her discretion. The Count's alternate will not vote against his lord's wishes, but it may chance he will be very late to that morning's session, or even miss it altogether. This is not a plus for you, but may prove an unexpected minus for Richars and Sigur."*

René and Dono were starting to scribble notes.

"Old Vorhalas has a deal of personal sympathy for René, but will not vote against Conservative Party interests in the matter. Since Vorhalas's rigid honesty is matched by his other rigid habits of mind, I'm afraid Dono's case is quite hopeless there.

"Vortaine is also hopeless; save your energy. However, I am reliably informed his lawsuit over his District's boundary waters with his neighbor Count Vorvolynkin continues unresolved, with undiminished acrimony, to the mortification of both families. I would not normally consider it possible to detach Count Vorvolynkin from the Conservatives, but a whisper in his ear from his daughter-in-law Lady Louisa, upon whom he dotes, that votes for Dono and René would seriously annoy, underscored, *his adversary has borne startling results. You may reliably add him to your accounting."*

"Now, *that's* an unexpected boon," said René happily, scribbling harder.

Miles turned the page over and read on, *"Simon has described to me the appalling behavior of,* well, that's not pertinent, hum de hum, heh, *extremely poor taste,* underscored, thank you Aunt Alys, here we go, *Finally, my dear Countess Vorinnis has assured me that the vote of Vorinnis's District may also be counted upon for both your friends. Your Loving Aunt Alys.*

"P.S. There is no excuse for this to be done in a scrambling way at the last minute. This Office wishes the prompt settlement of the confusion, so that invitations may be issued to the proper persons in a punctual and graceful manner. In the interest of a timely resolution to these matters, feel free to set Ivan to any little task upon which you may find him useful."

"What?" said Ivan. "You made that up! Let me see . . ." With an unpleasant smirk, Miles tilted the paper toward Ivan, who leaned over his shoulder to read the postscript. It was his mother's impeccable handwriting, all right. Damn.

"Richars Vorrutyer sat right there," said Miles, pointing to René's chair, "and informed me that Lady Alys held no vote in Council. The fact that she has spent more years in the Vorbarr Sultana political scene than all of us here put together seemed to escape him. Too bad." His smile broadened.

He turned to look half over his shoulder as Pym re-entered the sitting room trundling a tea cart. "Ah. May I offer you gentlemen some refreshments?"

Ivan perked up, but to his disappointment, the tea cart held tea. Well, and coffee, and a tray of Ma Kosti delectables resembling a decorative food-mosaic. "Wine?" he suggested hopefully to his cousin, as Pym began to pour. "Beer, even?"

"At this hour?" said René.

"For me, it's been a long day already," Ivan assured him. "Really."

Pym handed him a cup of coffee. "This will buck you up, m'lord."

Ivan took it reluctantly.

"When my grandfather held political conferences in these chambers, I could always tell if he was scheming with allies, or negotiating with adversaries," Miles informed them all. "When he was working with friends, he served coffee and tea and the like, and everyone was expected to stay on his toes. When he was working over the other sort, there was always a startling abundance of alcoholic beverages of every description. He always began with the good stuff, too. Later in the session the quality would drop, but by that time his visitors were in no shape to discriminate. I always snuck in when his man brought the wine cart, because if I stayed quiet enough, people were less likely to notice me and run me out."

Ivan pulled his straight chair closer to the tray of snacks. By took a chair equally strategically positioned on the other side of the cart. The other guests accepted cups from Pym and sipped. Miles smoothed a hand-scribbled agenda out on his knee.

"Item the first," he began. "René, Dono, has the Lord Guardian of the Speaker's Circle set the time and order in which the votes on your two suits go down?"

"Back to back," replied René. "Mine is first. I confess, I was grateful to know I'd be getting it over with as soon as possible."

"That's perfect, but not for the reason you think," Miles replied. "René, when your suit is called, you should yield the Circle to Lord Dono. Who, when his vote is over, should yield it back to you. You see why, of course?"

"Oh. Yes," said René. "Sorry, Miles, I wasn't thinking."

"Not . . . entirely," said Lord Dono.

Miles ticked the alternatives off on his fingers. "If you are made Count Vorrutyer, Dono, you may then immediately turn around and cast the vote of the Vorrutyer's District for René, thus increasing his vote bag by one. But if René goes first, the seat of the Vorrutyer's District will still be empty and will only cast a blank tally. And if René subsequently loses—by, let us say, one vote—you would also lose the Vorbretten vote on your round."

"Ah," said Dono, in a tone of enlightenment. "And you expect our opponents will also be making this calculation? Hence the value of the last-minute switch."

"Just so," said Miles.

"Will they anticipate the alteration?" asked Dono anxiously.

"They are not, as far as I know, quite aware of your alliance," By replied, with a slightly mocking semibow.

Ivan frowned at him. "And how long till they are? How do we know you won't just pipeline everything you see here to Richars?"

"He won't," said Dono.

"Yeah? *You* may be sure which side By's on, but *I'm* not."

By smirked. "Let us hope Richars shares your confusion."

Ivan shook his head, and snabbled a flaky shrimp puff which seemed to melt in his mouth, and chased it with coffee.

Miles reached under his chair and pulled out a stack of large transparent flimsies. He peeled off the top two, and handed one each to Dono and René across the low table. "I've always wanted to try this," he said happily. "I pulled these out of the attic last night. They were one of my grandfather's old tactical aids; I believe he had the trick from his father. I suppose I could devise a comconsole program to do the same thing. They're seating plans of the Council chamber."

Lord Dono held one up to the light. Two rows of blank squares arced in a semicircle across the page. Dono said, "The seats aren't labeled."

"If you need to use this, you're supposed to know," Miles explained. He thumbed off an extra and handed it across. "Take it home, fill it out, and memorize it, eh?"

"Excellent," said Dono.

"Theory is, you use 'em to compare two related close votes. Color code each District's desk—say, red for no, green for yes, blank for unknown or undecided—and put one atop the other." Miles dropped a handful of bright flow pens onto the table. "Where you end up with two reds or two greens, ignore that Count. You've either no need, or no leverage. Where you have blanks, a blank and a color, or a red and a green, look to those men as the ones to concentrate your lobbying on."

"Ah," said René, taking up two pens, leaning over the table, and starting to color. "How elegantly simple. I always tried to do this in my head."

"Once you start talking maybe three or five related votes, times sixty men, nobody's head can hold it all."

Dono, lips pursed thoughtfully, filled out some dozen or so squares, then moved around next to René to crib the rest of the names versus locations. René, Ivan noticed, colored very meticulously, neatly filling each square. Dono scribbled bold, quick splashes. When they'd finished, they laid the two flimsies a little askew atop one another.

"My word," said Dono. "They do just jump out at you, don't they?"

Their voices fell to murmurs, as they began to develop their list of men to go tag-team. Ivan brushed shrimp puff crumbs off his uniform trousers. Byerly bestirred himself to gently suggest one or two slight corrections to the distribution of marks and blanks, based upon impressions he'd, oh quite casually to be sure, garnered during his sojourns in Richars's company.

Ivan craned his neck, counting up greens and double-greens. "You're not there yet," he said. "Regardless of how few votes Richars and Sigur obtain, no matter how many of their supporters get diverted that day, you each have to have a positive majority of thirty-one votes, or you don't get your Districts."

"We're working on it, Ivan," said Miles.

From his sparkling eye and dangerously cheerful expression, Ivan recognized his cousin in full forward momentum mode. Miles was reveling in this. Ivan wondered if Illyan and Gregor would ever rue the day they'd dragged him off his beloved galactic covert ops and stuck him home. Scratch that—*how soon* they would rue the day.

To Ivan's dismay, his cousin's thumb descended forcefully on a pair of blank squares Ivan had hoped he would overlook.

"Count Vorpatril," said Miles. "Ah, ha." He smiled up at Ivan.

"Why are you looking at me?" asked Ivan. "It's not as though Falco Vorpatril and I are drinking buddies. In fact, the last time I saw the old man he told me I was a hopeless floater, and the despair of my mother, himself, and all other geezer-class Vorpatrils. Well, he didn't say *geezer-class*, he said *right-thinking*. Comes to the same thing."

"Oh, Falco is tolerably amused by you," Miles ruthlessly contradicted Ivan's personal experience. "More to the point, you'll have no trouble getting Dono in to see him. And while you're there, you can both put in good words for René."

I knew it would come to this, sooner or later. "I'd have had to swallow chaff enough if I'd presented Lady Donna to him as a fiancée. He's never had the time of day for Vorrutyers generally. Presenting Lord Dono to him as a future colleague . . ." Ivan shuddered, and stared at the bearded man, who stared back with a peculiar lift to his lip.

"Fiancée, Ivan?" inquired Dono. "I didn't know you cared."

"Well, and I've missed my chance now, haven't I?" Ivan said grumpily.

"Yes, now and any time these past five years while I was cooling my heels down in the District. I was there. Where were you?" Dono dismissed Ivan's plaint with a jerk of his chin; the tiny flash of bitterness in his brown eyes made Ivan squirm inside. Dono saw his discomfort, and smiled slowly, and rather evilly. "Indeed, Ivan, clearly this entire episode is *all your fault*, for being so slow off the mark."

Ivan flinched. *Dammit, that woman—man—person, knows me too bloody well . . .*

"Anyway," Dono went on, "since the choice is between Richars and me, Falco's stuck with a Vorrutyer whatever the case. The only question is which one."

"And I'm sure you can point out all the disadvantages of Richars," Miles interposed smoothly.

"Somebody else can. Not me," said Ivan. "Serving officers are not supposed to involve themselves with party politics anyway, so there." He folded his arms and stood, or at any rate, sat, precariously on his dignity.

Miles tapped Ivan's mother's letter. "But you have a lawful order from your assigned superior. In writing, no less."

"Miles, if you don't burn that damned letter after this meeting, you're out of your mind! It's so hot I'm surprised it hasn't burst into flame all on its own!" Hand-written, hand-delivered, no copy electronic or otherwise anywhere—the destroy-after-reading directive was inherent.

Miles's teeth bared in a small smile. "Teaching me my business, Ivan?"

Ivan glowered. "I flat refuse to go a step farther in this. I told Dono that taking him to your dinner party was the last favor I'd do for him, and I'm standing on my word."

Miles eyed him. Ivan shifted uneasily. He hoped Miles wouldn't think to call the Residence for a reiteration. Standing up to his mother seemed safer in absentia than in person. He fixed a surly look on his face, hunkered in his chair, and waited—somewhat curiously—for whatever creative blackmail or bribery or strong-arm tactic Miles would next evolve to twist him to his will. Escorting Dono to Falco Vorpatril was going to be so damned *embarrassing*. He was planning just how to present himself to Falco as a thoroughly disinterested bystander, when Miles said, "Very well. Moving right along—"

"I said no!" Ivan cried desperately.

Miles glanced up at him in faint surprise. "I heard you. Very well: you're off the hook. I shall ask nothing further of you. You can relax."

Ivan sat back in profound relief.

Not, he assured himself, profound disappointment. And most *certainly* not profound alarm. *But . . . but . . . but . . . the obnoxious little git* needs *me, to pull his nuts out of the fire . . .*

"Moving right along now," Miles continued, "we come to the subject of dirty tricks."

Ivan stared at him in horror. *Ten years as Illyan's top agent in ImpSec coverts ops . . .* "Don't do it, Miles!"

"Don't do what?" Miles inquired mildly.

"Whatever you're thinking of. Just don't. I don't want anything to do with it."

"What I was *about* to say," said Miles, giving him an extremely dry look, "was that *we*, being on the side of truth and justice, need not stoop to such chicanery as, say, bribery, assassination or milder forms of physical diversion, or—heh!—blackmail. Besides, those sorts of things tend to . . . backfire." His eye glinted. "We do need to keep a sharp lookout for any such moves on the part of our adversaries. Beginning with the obvious—put everyone's full duty roster of Armsmen on high-alert status, make sure your vehicles are guarded from tampering *and* that you have alternate modes and routes for reaching Vorhartung Castle the morning of the vote. Also, detach whatever trusted and resourceful men you can spare to be certain that nothing untoward happens to impede the arrival of your supporters."

"If we're not stooping, what do you call that shell game with the Vortugalovs and the uterine replicator?" Ivan demanded indignantly.

"A piece of wholly unexpected good fortune. None of us *here* had anything to do with it," Miles replied tranquilly.

"So it's not a dirty trick if it's untraceable?"

"Correct, Ivan. You learn fast. Grandfather would have been . . . surprised."

Lord Dono looked very thoughtful at this, leaning back and gently stroking his beard. His faint smile gave Ivan chills.

"Byerly." Miles looked across to the other Vorrutyer, who was nibbling gently on a canapé and either listening or dozing, depending on what those half-closed eyes signified. By opened his eyes fully, and smiled. Miles went on, "Have you overheard anything we ought to know on this last head from Richars or the Vormoncrief party?"

"So far, they appear to have limited themselves to ordinary canvassing. I believe they have not yet realized you're closing on them."

René Vorbretten regarded By doubtfully. "Are we? Not by my tally. And when and if they do realize—and I'll bet Boriz Vormoncrief will catch on to it eventually—how d'you think they'll jump?"

By held out his hand, and tilted it back and forth in a balancing gesture. "Count Vormoncrief is a staid old stick. However things fall out, he'll live to vote another day. And another, and another. He's far from indifferent to Sigur's fate, but I don't think he'll cross the line for him. Richars . . . well, this vote is everything to Richars, now, isn't it? He started out in a fury at being forced to exert himself for it at all. Richars is a loose cannon, getting looser." This image did not appear to disturb By; in fact, he seemed to draw some private pleasure from it.

"Well, keep us informed if anything changes in that quarter," said Miles.

Byerly made a little salute of spreading his hand over his heart. "I live to serve."

Miles raised his eyes and gave By a penetrating look; Ivan wondered if this sardonic cooption of the old ImpSec tag-line perhaps did not sit too well with one who'd laid down so much blood and bone in Imperial service. He cringed in anticipation of the exchange if Miles sought to censure By for this minor witticism, but to Ivan's relief Miles let it pass. After a few more minutes spent apportioning target Counts, the meeting broke up.

Chapter Fifteen

Ekaterin waited on the sidewalk, holding Nikki's hand, while Uncle Vorthys hugged his wife good-bye and his chauffeur loaded his valise into the back of his groundcar. Uncle Vorthys would be going straight from this upcoming morning meeting to the shuttleport and an Imperial fast courier to Komarr, there to deal with what he'd described to Ekaterin as *a few technical matters*. The trip was the culmination, she supposed, of the long hours he'd been spending lately closeted at the Imperial Science Institute; in any case, it hadn't seemed to take the Professora by surprise.

Ekaterin reflected on Miles's penchant for understatement. She'd felt ready to faint, last night, when Uncle Vorthys had sat her and Nikki down and informed them *who* Miles's "man with authority" was, the fellow he thought could talk with understanding to Nikki because he too had lost a father young. Emperor-to-be Gregor had been not yet five years old when the gallant Crown Prince Serg had been blown to bits in Escobar orbit during the retreat from that ill-advised military adventure. In all, she was glad no one had told her till the audience was confirmed, or she would have worked herself into an even worse state of nerves. She was uncomfortably aware that her hand gripping Nikki's was a little too moist, a little too chill. He would take his cue from the adults; she *must* appear calm, for his sake.

They all piled into the rear compartment at last, waved to the Professora, and pulled away. Her eye was becoming more educated, Ekaterin decided. The first time she'd ridden in the courtesy car that the Imperium provided her uncle on permanent loan, she hadn't known to interpret its odd smooth handling as a cue to its level of armoring, nor the attentive young driver as ImpSec to the bone. For all her uncle's deceptive failure to deck himself out in high Vor mode, he moved in the same rarefied circles Miles inhabited with equal ease—Miles because he'd lived there all his life, her uncle because his engineer's eye gauged men by other criteria.

Uncle Vorthys smiled fondly down at Nikki, and patted him on the hand. "Don't look so scared, Nikki," he rumbled comfortably. "Gregor is a good fellow. You'll be fine, and we'll be with you."

Nikki nodded dubiously. It was his black suit that made him look so pale, Ekaterin told herself. His only really good suit; he'd last worn it at his father's funeral, a piece of unpleasant irony Ekaterin schooled herself to ignore. She'd drawn the line at donning her own funeral dress. Her everyday black-and-gray outfit was getting a trifle shabby, but it would have to do. At least it was clean and pressed. Her hair was pulled back with neat severity, braided into a knot at the back of her neck. She touched the lump of the little Barrayar pendant, hidden beneath her high-necked black blouse, for secret reassurance.

"Don't you look so scared either," Uncle Vorthys added to her.

She smiled wanly.

It was a short drive from the University district to the Imperial Residence. The guards scanned them and passed them smoothly through the high iron gates. The Residence was a vast stone building several times the size of Vorkosigan House, four stories high and built, over a couple of centuries and radical changes of architectural styles, in the form of a somewhat irregular hollow square. They drew up under a secondary portico on the east end.

Some sort of high household officer in Vorbarra livery met them, and guided them down two very long and echoing corridors to the north wing. Nikki and Ekaterin both stared around, Nikki openly, Ekaterin covertly. Uncle Vorthys seemed indifferent to the museum-quality décor; he'd trod this corridor dozens of times to deliver his personal reports to the ruler of three worlds. Miles had lived here till he was six, he'd said. Had he been oppressed by the somber weight of this history, or had he regarded it all as his personal play set? *One guess.*

The liveried man ushered them into a sleekly-appointed office the size of most of one floor of the Professor's house. On the near end, a half-familiar figure leaned against a huge comconsole desk, his arms folded. Emperor Gregor Vorbarra was grave, lean, dark, good-looking in a narrow-faced, cerebral fashion. The holovid did not flatter him, Ekaterin decided instantly. He wore a dark blue suit, with only the barest hint of military decoration in the thin side-piping on the trousers and the high-necked tunic. Miles stood across from him dressed in his usual impeccable gray, rendered somewhat less impeccable by his feet-apart posture and his hands stuffed in his trouser pockets. He broke off in midsentence; his eyes rose anxiously to Ekaterin's face as she entered, and his lips parted. He gave his fellow Auditor a jerky little encouraging nod.

The Professor did not need the cue. "Sire, may I present my niece, Madame Ekaterin Vorsoisson, and her son, Nikolai Vorsoisson."

Ekaterin was spared an awkward attempt at a curtsey when Gregor stepped forward, took her hand, and shook it firmly, as though she were one of the equals he was first among. "Madame, I am honored." He turned to Nikki, and shook his hand in turn. "Welcome, Nikki. I'm sorry our first meeting should be occasioned by such a difficult matter, but I trust it will be followed by many happier ones." His tone was neither stiff nor patronizing, but perfectly straightforward. Nikki managed an adult handshake, and only goggled a little.

Ekaterin had met a few powerful men before; they had mostly looked through her, or past her, or at her with the sort of vague aesthetic appreciation she'd bestowed on the knickknacks in the corridor outside. Gregor looked her directly in the eye as if he saw all the way through to the back of her skull. It was at once unnervingly uncomfortable and strangely heartening. He gestured them all toward a square arrangement of leather-covered couches and armchairs at the far end of the room, and said softly, "Won't you please be seated?"

The tall windows overlooked a garden of descending terraces, brilliant with full summer growth. Ekaterin sank down with her back to it, Nikki beside her; the cool northern light fell on their Imperial host's face, as he took an armchair opposite them. Uncle Vorthys sat between; Miles pulled up a straight chair and sat a little apart from them all. He appeared arms crossed and at his ease. She wasn't quite sure how she came to read him as tense and nervous and miserable. And masked. A glass mask . . .

Gregor leaned forward. "Lord Vorkosigan asked me to meet with you, Nikki, because of the unpleasant rumors which have sprung up surrounding your father's death. Under the circumstances, your mother and your great-uncle agreed it was needful."

"Mind you," Uncle Vorthys put in, "I wouldn't have chosen to drag the poor little fellow further into it if it weren't for those gabbling fools."

Gregor nodded understanding. "Before I begin, some caveats— words of warning. You may not be aware of it, Nikki, but in your uncle's household you have been living under a certain degree of security monitoring. At his request, it is usually as limited and unobtrusive as possible. It's only gone to a higher and more visible level twice in the last three years, during some unusually difficult cases of his."

"Aunt Vorthys showed us the outside vid pickups," Nikki offered tentatively.

"Those are part of it," Uncle Vorthys said. The least part, according to the thorough briefing a polite ImpSec officer in plainclothes had given Ekaterin the day after she and Nikki had moved in.

"All the comconsoles are also either secured or monitored," Gregor elaborated. "Both his vehicles are kept in guarded locations. Any unauthorized intruder should bring down an ImpSec response in under two minutes."

Nikki's eyes widened.

"One wonders how Vormoncrief got in," Ekaterin couldn't help darkly muttering.

Gregor smiled apologetically. "Your uncle doesn't choose to have ImpSec shake down his every casual visitor. And Vormoncrief was on the Known list due to his previous visits." He looked again at Nikki. "But if we continue this conversation today, you will perforce step over an invisible line, from a lower level of security monitoring to a rather higher one. While you live in your uncle's household, or if . . . you should ever go to live in Lord Vorkosigan's household, you wouldn't notice the difference. But any extensive travel on Barrayar will have to be cleared with a certain security officer, and your potential off-planet travel restricted. The list of schools you may attend will become suddenly much shorter, more exclusive, and, I'm sorry, more expensive. On the bright side, you won't have to worry much about encounters with casual criminals. On the dark side, any," he spared a nod for Ekaterin, "*hypothetical* kidnappers who did get through would have to be assumed to be highly professional and extremely dangerous."

Ekaterin caught her breath. "Miles didn't mention that part."

"I daresay Miles didn't even think about it. He's lived under exactly this sort of security screen most of his life. Does a fish think about water?"

Ekaterin darted a glance at Miles. He had a very odd look on his face, as though he'd just bounced off a force wall he hadn't known was there.

"Off-planet travel." Nikki seized on the one item in this intimidating list of importance to him. "But . . . I want to be a jump pilot."

"By the time you are old enough to study for a jump pilot, I expect the situation will have changed," said Gregor. "This applies mainly to the next few years. Do you still want to go on?"

He hadn't asked her. He'd asked Nikki. She held her breath, resisting the urge to prompt him.

Nikki licked his lips. "Yes," he said. "I want to know."

"Second warning," said Gregor. "You will not walk out of here with fewer questions than you have now. You will just trade one set for another. Everything I tell you will be true, but it will not be complete. And when I come to the end, you will be at the absolute limit of what you may presently know, both for your own safety and that of the Imperium. Do you still want to go on?"

Nikki nodded dumbly. He was transfixed by this intense man. So was Ekaterin.

"Third and last. Our Vor duties come upon us at a too-early age, sometimes. What I am about to tell you will impose a burden of silence upon you that would be hard for an adult to bear." He glanced at Miles and Ekaterin, and at Uncle Vorthys. "Though you will have your mother and aunt and uncle to share it with. But for what may be the first time, you must give your name's word in all seriousness. Can you?"

"Yes," Nikki whispered.

"Say it."

"I swear by my word as Vorsoisson . . ." Nikki hesitated, searching Gregor's face anxiously.

"To hold this conversation in confidence."

"To hold this conversation in confidence."

"Very well." Gregor sat back, apparently fully satisfied. "I'm going to make this as plain as possible. When Lord Vorkosigan went out-dome with your father that night to the experiment station, they surprised some thieves. And vice versa. Both your father and Lord Vorkosigan were hit with stunner fire. The thieves fled, leaving both men chained by the wrists to a railing on the outside of the station. Neither of them were strong enough to break the chains, though both tried."

Nikki sneaked a look at Miles, half the size of Tien, little bigger than Nikki himself. Ekaterin thought she could see the wheels turning in his head. If his father, so much bigger and stronger, had been unable to free himself, could Miles be blamed for likewise failing?

"The thieves did not mean for your father to die. They didn't know his breath-mask reservoirs were low. Nobody did. That was confirmed by fast-penta interrogation later. The technical name for this sort of accidental killing is not murder, but manslaughter, by the way."

Nikki was pale, but not yet on the verge of tears. He ventured, "And Lord Vorkosigan . . . couldn't share his mask because he was tied up . . . ?"

"We were about a meter apart," said Miles in a flat tone. "Neither of us could reach the other." He spread his hands a certain distance out to the sides. At the motion, his sleeves pulled back from his wrists; the ropy pink scars where the chains had cut to the bone edged into view. Could Nikki see that he'd nearly ripped his hands off, trying, Ekaterin wondered bleakly? Self-consciously, Miles pulled his cuffs back down, and put his hands on his knees.

"Now for the hard part," said Gregor, gathering Nikki back in by eye. It had to feel to Nikki as though they were the only two people in the universe.

He's going to go on? No—no, stop there . . . She wasn't sure what apprehension showed in her face, but Gregor spared it an acknowledging nod.

"This is the part your mother would never tell you. The *reason* your da took Lord Vorkosigan out to the station was because your da had let himself be bribed by the thieves. But he had changed his mind, and wanted Lord Vorkosigan to declare him an Imperial Witness. The thieves were angry at this betrayal. They chained him to the rail in that cruel way to punish his attempt to retrieve his honor. They left a data disc with documentation of his involvement taped to his back for his rescuers to find, to be certain of disgracing him, and then called your mama to come get him. But—not knowing about the low reservoirs—they called her too late."

Now Nikki was looking stunned and small. *Oh, poor son. I would not have tarnished Tien's honor in your eyes; surely in your eyes is where all our honor is kept. . . .*

"Due to further facts about the thieves that no one can discuss with you, all of this is a State secret. As far as the rest of the world knows, your da and Lord Vorkosigan went out alone, met no one, became separated while on foot in the dark, and Lord Vorkosigan found your da too late. If anyone thinks Lord Vorkosigan had something to do with your da's death, we are not going to argue with them. You may state that it's not true and that you don't wish to discuss it. But don't let yourself be drawn into disputes."

"But . . ." said Nikki, "but that's not fair!"

"It's hard," said Gregor, "but it's necessary. Fair has nothing to do with it. To spare you the hardest part, your mama and uncle and Lord Vorkosigan told you the cover story, and not the real one. I can't say they were wrong to do so."

His eye and Miles's caught each other in a steady gaze; Miles's eyebrows inched up in a quizzical look, to which Gregor returned a tiny ironic nod. The Emperor's lips thinned in something that was not quite a smile.

"All the thieves are in Imperial custody, in a top-security prison. None of them will be leaving soon. All the justice that could be done, has been done; there's nothing left to finish there. If your father had lived, he would be in prison now too. Death wipes out all debts of honor. In my eyes, he has redeemed his crime and his name. He cannot do more."

It was all much, much tougher than anything Ekaterin had pictured, had dared to imagine Gregor or anyone forcing Nikki to confront. Uncle Vorthys looked very grim, and even Miles looked daunted.

No: this *was* the softened version. Tien had not been trying to retrieve his honor; he'd merely learned that his crime had been discovered and was scrambling to evade the consequences. But if Nikki were to cry out, *I don't care about honor! I want my da back!* could she say he was wrong? A little of that cry flickered in his eyes, she imagined.

Nikki looked across at Miles. "What *were* your two mistakes?"

He replied steadily, with what effort Ekaterin could not guess, "First, I failed to inform my security backup when I left the dome. When Tien took me out to the station we were both anticipating a cooperative confession, not a hostile confrontation. Then, when we surprised the . . . thieves, I was a second too slow drawing my own stunner. They fired first. A diplomatic hesitation. A second's delay. The greatest regrets are the tiniest."

"I want to see your wrists."

Miles pushed back his cuffs, and held out his hands, palm down and then palm up, for Nikki's close inspection.

Nikki's brow wrinkled. "Was your breath mask running out too?"

"No. Mine was fine. I'd checked it when I'd put it on."

"Oh." Nikki sat back, looking extremely subdued and pensive.

Everyone waited. After a minute, Gregor asked gently, "Do you have any more questions at this time?"

Mutely, Nikki shook his head.

Frowning thoughtfully, Gregor glanced at his chrono and rose, with a hand-down gesture that kept everyone else from popping to their feet. He strode to his desk, rummaged in a drawer, and returned to his seat. Leaning across the table he held out a code-card to Nikki. "Here, Nikki. This is for you to keep. Don't lose it."

The card had no markings at all. Nikki turned it over curiously, and looked his inquiry at Gregor.

"This card will code you in to my personal comconsole channel. A very few friends and relatives of mine have this access. When you put it in the read-slot of your comconsole, a man will appear and identify you and, if I am available, pass you through to the comconsole nearest to me. You don't have to tell him anything about your business. If you think of more questions later—as you may, I gave you a lot to absorb in a very short time—or if you simply need someone to talk to about this matter, you may use it to call me."

"Oh," said Nikki. Gingerly, after turning it over again, he tucked the card into his tunic's breast pocket.

By the slight easing of Gregor's posture, and of Uncle Vorthys's, Ekaterin concluded the audience was over. She shifted, preparing to catch the cue to rise, but then Miles lifted a hand—did he always seize the last word?

"Gregor—while I appreciate your gesture of confidence in refusing my resignation—"

Uncle Vorthys's brows shot up. "Surely you didn't offer to resign your Auditorship over this miserable gibble-gabble, Miles!"

Miles shrugged. "I thought it was traditional for an Imperial Auditor not only to be honest, but to appear so. Moral authority and all that."

"Not always," said Gregor mildly. "I inherited a couple of damned shifty old sticks from my grandfather Ezar. And for all that he's called Dorca the Just, I believe my great-grandfather's main criterion for his Auditors was their ability to convincingly terrorize a pretty tough crew of liegemen. Can you imagine the nerve it would have taken one of Dorca's Voices to stand up to, say, Count Pierre Le Sanguinaire?"

Miles smiled at this vision. "Given the enthusiastic awe with which my grandfather recalled old Pierre . . . the mind boggles."

"If public confidence in your worth as an Auditor is that damaged, my Counts and Ministers will have to indict you themselves. Without my assistance."

"Unlikely," growled Uncle Vorthys. "It's a smarmy business, my boy, but I doubt it will come to that pass."

Miles looked less certain.

"You've now danced through all the proper forms," said Gregor. "Leave it, Miles."

Miles nodded what seemed to Ekaterin reluctant, if relieved, acceptance. "Thank you, Sire. But I wanted to add, I was also thinking of the personal ramifications. Which are going to get worse before they bottom out and die away. Are you quite sure you want me standing on your wedding circle, while this uproar persists?"

Gregor gave him a direct, and slightly pained, look. "You will not escape your social duty that easily. If General Alys does not request I remove you, there you will stand."

"I wasn't trying to escape—! . . . anything." He ran down a trifle, in the face of Gregor's grim amusement.

"Delegation is a wonderful thing, in my line of work. You may let it be known that anyone who objects to the presence of my foster-brother in my wedding circle may take their complaints to Lady

Alys, and suggest whatever major last-minute dislocations in her arrangements they . . . dare."

Miles could not quite keep the malicious smile off his lips, though he tried valiantly. Fairly valiantly. Some. "I would pay money to watch." His smile faded again. "But it's going to keep coming up as long as—"

"Miles." Gregor's raised hand interrupted him. His eyes were alight with something between amusement and exasperation. "You have, in-house, possibly the greatest living source of Barrayaran political expertise in this century. Your father's been dealing with uglier Party in-fighting than this, with and without weapons, since before you were born. Go tell *him* your troubles. Tell him I said to give you that lecture on honor versus reputation he gave me that time. In fact . . . tell him I request and require it." His hand-wave, as he rose from his armchair, put an emphatic end to the topic. Everyone rustled to their feet.

"Lord Auditor Vorthys, a word before you depart. Madame Vorsoisson—" he took Ekaterin's hand again "—we'll talk more when I am less pressed for time. Security concerns have deferred public recognition, but I hope you realize you've earned a personal account of honor with the Imperium of great depth, which you may draw upon at need and at will."

Ekaterin blinked, startled almost to protest. Surely it was for Miles's sake that Gregor had wedged open this slice of his schedule? But this was all the oblique reference to the *further* events on Komarr they dared to make in front of Nikki. She managed a short nod, and a murmur of thanks for the Imperial time and concern. Nikki, modeling himself a little awkwardly upon her, did likewise.

Uncle Vorthys bid her and Nikki good-bye, and lingered for whatever word his Imperial master wanted before he took ship. Miles escorted them into the corridor, where he told the waiting liveried man, "I'll see them out, Gerard. Call for Madame Vorsoisson's car, please."

They began the long walk around the building. Ekaterin glanced back over her shoulder toward the Emperor's private office.

"That was . . . that was more than I'd expected." She looked down at Nikki, walking between them. His face was set, but not crumpled. "Stronger." *Harsher.*

"Yes," said Miles. "Be careful what you ask for. . . . There are special reasons I trust Gregor's judgment in this above anyone else's.

But . . . I think perhaps I'm not the only fish who doesn't think about water. Gregor is routinely expected to endure daily pressures that would drive, well, me, to drink, madness, or downright lethal irritability. In return, he overestimates us, and we . . . scramble not to disappoint him."

"*He* told me the truth," said Nikki. He marched on in silence for a moment more. "I'm glad."

Ekaterin held her peace, satisfied.

Miles found his father in the library.

Count Vorkosigan was seated on one of the sofas flanking the fireplace, perusing a hand-reader. By his semiformal garb, a dark green tunic and trousers reminiscent of the uniforms he'd worn most of his life, Miles deduced he was on his way out soon, doubtless to one of the many official meals the Viceroy and Vicereine seemed obliged to munch their way through before Gregor's wedding. Miles was reminded of the intimidating list of engagements that Lady Alys had handed him, coming up soon. But whether he dared try to mitigate their social and culinary rigors by having Ekaterin accompany him was now a very dubious question.

Miles flung himself onto the sofa opposite his father; the Count looked up and regarded him with cautious interest.

"Hello. You look a trifle wrung."

"Yes. I've just come from one of the more difficult interviews of my Auditorial career." Miles rubbed the back of his neck, still achingly tense. The Count lifted politely inquiring eyebrows. Miles continued, "I asked Gregor to straighten out Nikki Vorsoisson on this slander mess to the limit he judged wise. He set the limit a lot further out than Ekaterin or I would have."

The Count sat back, and laid his reader aside. "Do you feel he compromised security?"

"No, actually," Miles admitted. "Any enemy snatching Nikki for questioning would already know more than he does. They could empty him out in ten minutes on fast-penta, and no harm done. Maybe they'd even bring him back. Or not . . . He's no more a security risk than before. And no more nor less *at* risk, as a lever on Ekaterin." *Or on me.* "The real conspiracy was very closely held even among the principals. That's not the problem."

"And the problem is—?"

Miles leaned his elbows on his knees, and stared at his dim distorted reflections in the toes of his half-boots. "I thought, because of Crown Prince Serg, Gregor would know how—or whether— someone ought to be apprised that his da was a criminal. If you can call Prince Serg that, for his secret vices."

"I can," breathed the Count. "Criminal, and halfway to raving mad, by the time of his death." Then-Admiral Vorkosigan had been an eyewitness to the Escobaran invasion disaster on the highest levels, Miles reflected. He sat up; his father looked him full in the face, and smiled somberly. "That Escobaran ship's lucky shot was the best piece of political good fortune ever to befall Barrayar. In hindsight, though, I regret that we handled Gregor so poorly on the matter. I take it that he did better?"

"I think he handled Nikki . . . well. At any rate, Nikki won't experience that sort of late shock to his world. Of course, compared to Serg, Tien wasn't much worse than foolish and venal. But it was hard to watch. No nine-year-old should have to deal with something this vile, this close to his heart. What will it make him?"

"Eventually . . . ten," the Count said. "You do what you have to do. You grow or go under. You have to believe he will grow."

Miles drummed his fingers on the sofa's padded arm. "Gregor's subtlety is still dawning on me. By admitting Tien's peculation, he's pulled Nikki to the inside with us. Nikki too now has a vested interest in maintaining the cover story, to protect his late da's reputation. Strange. Which is what brings me to you, by the way. Gregor asks—requests and requires, no less!—you give me the lecture you gave him on honor versus reputation. It must have been memorable."

The Count's brow wrinkled. "Lecture? Oh. Yes." He smiled briefly. "So that stuck in his mind, good. You wonder sometimes, with young people, if anything you say goes in, or if you're just throwing your words on the wind."

Miles stirred uncomfortably, wondering if any of that last remark was to his address. All right, *how much* of that remark. "Mm?" he prompted.

"I wouldn't have called it a lecture. Just a useful distinction, to clarify thought." He spread his hand, palm up, in a gesture of balance. "Reputation is what other people know about you. Honor is what you know about yourself."

"Hm."

"The friction tends to arise when the two are not the same. In the matter of Vorsoisson's death, how do you stand with yourself?"

How does he strike to the center in one cut like that? "I'm not sure. Do impure thoughts count?"

"No," said the Count firmly. "Only acts of will."

"What about acts of ineptitude?"

"A gray area, and don't tell me you haven't lived in that twilight before."

"Most of my life, sir. Not that I haven't leaped up into the blinding light of competence now and then. It's sustaining the altitude that defeats me."

The Count raised his brows, and smiled crookedly, but charitably refrained from agreeing. "So. Then it seems to me your immediate problems lie more in the realm of reputation."

Miles sighed. "I feel like I'm being gnawed all over by rats. Little corrosive rats, flicking away too fast for me to turn and whap them on the head."

The Count studied his fingernails. "It could be worse. There is no more hollow feeling than to stand with your honor shattered at your feet while soaring public reputation wraps you in rewards. *That's* soul-destroying. The other way around is merely very, very irritating."

"Very," said Miles bitterly.

"Heh. All right. Can I offer you some consoling reflections?"

"Please do, sir."

"First, this too shall pass. Despite the undoubted charms of sex, murder, conspiracy, and more sex, people will eventually grow bored with the tale, and some other poor fellow will make some other ghastly public mistake, and their attention will go haring off after the new game."

"*What* sex?" Miles muttered in exasperation. "There hasn't *been* any sex. Dammit. Or this would all seem a great deal more worthwhile. I haven't even gotten to *kiss* the woman yet!"

The Count's lips twitched. "My condolences. Secondly, given this accusation, no charge against you that's *less* exciting will ruffle anyone's sensibilities in the future. The near future, anyway."

"Oh, great. Does this mean I'm free to run riot from now on, as long as I stop short of premeditated murder?"

"You'd be amazed." A little of the humor died in the Count's eyes, at what memory Miles could not guess, but then his lips tweaked up again. "Third, there is no thought control—or I'd certainly have put it to use before this. Trying to shape, or respond to, what every idiot on the street believes—on the basis of little logic and less information—would only serve to drive you mad."

"Some people's opinions do matter."

"Yes, sometimes. Have you identified whose, in this case?"

"Ekaterin's. Nikki's. Gregor's." Miles hesitated. "That's all."

"What, your poor aging parents aren't on that short list?"

"I should be sorry to lose your good opinion," said Miles slowly. "But in this case, you're not the ones . . . I'm not sure how to put this. To use Mother's terminology—you are not the ones sinned against. So your forgiveness is moot."

"Hm," said the Count, rubbing his lips and regarding Miles with cool approval. "Interesting. Well. For your fourth consoling thought, I would point out that in *this* venue," a wave of his finger took in Vorbarr Sultana, and by extension Barrayar, "acquiring a reputation as a slick and dangerous man, who would kill without compunction to obtain and protect his own, is not *all* bad. In fact, you might even find it useful."

"Useful! Have you found the name of *the Butcher of Komarr* a handy prop, then, sir?" Miles said indignantly.

His father's eyes narrowed, partly in grim amusement, partly in appreciation. "I've found it a mixed . . . damnation. But yes, I have used the weight of that reputation, from time to time, to lean on certain susceptible men. Why not, I paid for it. Simon says he's experienced the same phenomenon. After inheriting ImpSec from Negri the Great, he claimed all he had to do in order to unnerve his opponents was stand there and keep his mouth shut."

"I worked with Simon. He damned well *was* unnerving. And it wasn't just because of his memory chip, *or* Negri's lingering ghost." Miles shook his head. Only his father could, with perfect sincerity, regard Simon Illyan as an ordinary, everyday sort of subordinate. "Anyway, people may have seen Simon as sinister, but never as corrupt. He wouldn't have been half as scary if he hadn't been able to convincingly project that implacable indifference to, well, any human appetite." He paused in contemplation of his former commander-and-mentor's quelling management style. "But dammit, if . . . if my enemies won't allow me minimal moral sense, I wish they'd at least give me credit for competence in my vices! If I were going to murder someone, I'd have done a much smoother job than that hideous mess. No one would even guess a murder had occurred, ha!"

"I believe you," soothed the Count. He cocked his head in sudden curiosity. "Ah . . . have you ever?"

Miles burrowed back into the sofa, and scratched his cheek. "There was one mission for Illyan . . . I don't want to talk about it. It was close, unpleasant work, but we brought it off." His eyes fixed broodingly on the carpet.

"Really. I had asked him not to use you for assassinations."

"Why? Afraid I'd pick up bad habits? Anyway, it was a lot more complicated than a simple assassination."

"It generally is."

Miles stared away for a minute into the middle distance. "So what you're telling me boils down to the same thing Galeni said. I have to stand here and eat this, and smile."

"No," said his father, "you don't have to smile. But if you're really asking for advice from my accumulated experience, I'm saying, Guard your honor. Let your reputation fall where it will. And outlive the bastards."

Miles's gaze flicked up curiously to his father's face. He'd never known him when his hair wasn't gray; it was nearly all white now. "I know you've been up and down over the years. The first time your reputation took serious damage—how did you get through it?"

"Oh, the first time . . . that was a long time ago." The Count leaned forward, and tapped his thumbnail pensively on his lips. "It suddenly occurs to me, that among observers above a certain age—the few survivors of that generation—the dim memory of that episode may not be helping your cause. Like father, like son?" The Count regarded him with a concerned frown. "*That's* certainly a consequence I could never have foreseen. You see . . . after the suicide of my first wife, I was widely rumored to have killed her. For infidelity."

Miles blinked. He'd heard disjointed bits of this old tale, but not that last wrinkle. "And, um . . . was she? Unfaithful?"

"Oh, yes. We had a grotesque blowup about it. I was hurt, confused—which emerged as a sort of awkward, self-conscious rage—and severely handicapped by my cultural conditioning. A point in my life when I could definitely have used a Betan therapist, instead of the bad Barrayaran advice we got from . . . never mind. I didn't know—couldn't imagine such alternatives existed. It was a darker, older time. Men still dueled, you know, though it was illegal by then."

"But did you . . . um, you didn't really, um . . ."

"Murder her? No. Or only with words." It was the Count's turn to look away, his eyes narrowing. "Though I was never one hundred percent sure your grandfather hadn't. He'd arranged the marriage; I know he felt responsible."

Miles's brows rose, as he considered this. "Remembering Gran'da, that does seem faintly and horribly possible. Did you ever ask him?"

"No." The Count sighed. "What, after all, would I have done if he'd said yes?"

Aral Vorkosigan had been what, twenty-two at the time? Over half a century ago. *He was far younger then than I am now. Hell, he was just a kid.* Dizzily, Miles's world seemed to spin slowly around and click into some new and tilted axis, with altered perspectives. "So . . . how did you survive?"

"I had the luck of fools and madmen, I believe. I was certainly both. *I* didn't give a damn. Vile gossip? I would prove it an understatement, and give them twice the tale to chew upon. I think I stunned them into silence. Picture a suicidal loon with nothing to lose, staggering around in a drunken, hostile haze. Armed. Eventually, I got as sick of myself as everyone else must have been of me by that time, and pulled out of it."

That anguished boy was gone now, leaving this grave old man to sit in merciful judgment upon him. It did explain why, old-Barrayaran though he was in parts, his father had never so much as breathed the suggestion of an arranged marriage to Miles as a solution to his romantic difficulties, nor murmured the least criticism of his few affairs. Miles jerked up his chin, and favored his father with a tilted smile. "Your strategy does not appeal to me, sir. Drink makes me sick. I'm not feeling a bit suicidal. And I have *everything* to lose."

"I wasn't recommending it," the Count said mildly. He sat back. "Later—much later—when I also had too much to lose, I had acquired your mother. Her good opinion was the only one I needed."

"Yes? And what if it had been her good opinion that had been at risk? How would you have stood then?" *Ekaterin . . .*

"On my hands and knees, belike." The Count shook his head, and smiled slowly. "So, ah . . . when *are* we going to be permitted to meet this woman who has had such an invigorating effect on you? Her and her Nikki. Perhaps you might invite them to dinner here soon?"

Miles cringed. "Not . . . not another dinner. Not soon."

"My glimpse of her was so frustratingly brief. What little I could see was very attractive, I thought. Not too thin. She squished well, bouncing off me." Count Vorkosigan grinned briefly, at this memory. Miles's father shared an archaic Barrayaran ideal of feminine beauty that included the capacity to survive minor famines; Miles admitted a susceptibility to that style himself. "Reasonably athletic, too. Clearly, she could outrun you. I would therefore suggest blandishments, rather than direct pursuit, next time."

"I've been *trying*," sighed Miles.

The Count regarded his son, half amused, half serious. "This parade of females of yours is very confusing to your mother and me, you know. We can't tell whether we're supposed to start bonding to them, or not."

"*What* parade?" said Miles indignantly. "I brought home *one* galactic girlfriend. *One.* It wasn't my fault things didn't work out."

"Plus the several, um, extraordinary ladies decorating Illyan's reports who didn't make it this far."

Miles thought he could feel his eyes cross. "But how could he—Illyan never knew—he never told you about—no. Don't tell me. I don't want to know. But I swear the next time I see him—" He glowered at the Count, who was laughing at him with a perfectly straight face. "I suppose Simon won't remember. Or he'll pretend he doesn't. Damned convenient, that optional amnesia he's developed." He added, "Anyway, I've mentioned all the important ones to Ekaterin already, so there."

"Oh? Were you confessing, or bragging?"

"Clearing the decks. Honesty . . . is the only way, with her."

"Honesty is the only way with anyone, when you'll be so close as to be living inside each other's skins. So . . . *is* this Ekaterin another passing fancy?" The Count hesitated, his eyes crinkling. "Or is she the one who *will* love my son forever and fiercely—hold his household and estates with integrity—stand beside him through danger, and dearth, and death—and guide my grandchildren's hands when they light my funeral offering?"

Miles paused in momentary admiration of his father's ability to *deliver* lines like that. It put him in mind of the way a combat drop shuttle delivered pinpoint incendiaries. "That would be . . . that would be Column B, sir. All of the above." He swallowed. "I hope. If I don't fumble it again."

"So when do we get to *meet* her?" the Count repeated reasonably.

"Things are still very unsettled." Miles climbed to his feet, sensing that his moment to retreat with dignity was slipping away rapidly. "I'll let you know."

But the Count did not pursue his erratic line of humor. Instead he looked at his son with eyes gone serious, though still warm. "I am glad she came to you when you were old enough to know your own mind."

Miles favored him with an analyst's salute, a vague wave of two fingers in the general vicinity of his forehead. "So am I, sir."

Chapter Sixteen

Ekaterin sat at her aunt's comconsole, attempting to compose a résumé that would conceal her lack of experience from the supervisor of an urban plant nursery that supplied the city's public gardens. She was not, drat it, going to name *Lord Auditor Vorkosigan* as a reference. Aunt Vorthys had left for her morning class, and Nikki for an outing with Arthur Pym under the aegis of Arthur's elder sister; when the door chime's second ring tore her attention from her task, Ekaterin was abruptly aware that she was alone in the house. Would enemy agents bent on kidnapping come to the front door? Miles would know. She pictured Pym, at Vorkosigan House, frostily informing the intruders that they would have to go round back to the *spies'* entrance . . . which would be sprinkled with appropriate high-tech caltrops, no doubt. Controlling her new paranoia, she rose and went to the front hall.

To her relief and delight, instead of Cetagandan infiltrators, her brother Hugo Vorvayne stood on the front stoop, along with a pleasant-featured fellow she recognized after an uncertain blink as Vassily Vorsoisson, Tien's closest cousin. She had seen him exactly once before in her life, at Tien's funeral, where they had met long enough for him to officially sign over Nikki's guardianship to her. Lieutenant Vorsoisson held a post in traffic control at the big military shuttleport in Vorbretten's District; when she'd first and last seen him, he'd worn Service dress greens as suited the somber formality of the occasion, but today he'd changed to more casual civvies.

"Hugo, Vassily! This is a surprise—come in, come in!" She gestured them both into the Professora's front parlor. Vassily gave her a polite, acknowledging nod, and refused an offer of tea or coffee, they'd had some at the monorail station, thank you. Hugo gave her hands a brief squeeze, and smiled at her in a worried way before taking a seat. He was in his mid-forties; the combination of his desk work in the Imperial Bureau of Mines and his wife Rosalie's care was broadening him a trifle. On him, it looked wonderfully solid and reassuring. But alarm tightened Ekaterin's throat at the tension in his face. "Is everything all right?"

"*We're* all fine," he said with peculiar emphasis.

A chill flushed through her. "Da—?"

"Yes, yes, he's fine too." Impatiently, he gestured away her anxiety. "The only member of the family who seems to be a source of concern at the moment is you, Kat."

Ekaterin stared at him, baffled. "Me? I'm all right." She sank down into her uncle's big chair in the corner. Vassily pulled up one of the spindly chairs, and perched a little awkwardly upon it.

Hugo conveyed greetings from the family, Rosalie and Edie and the boys, then looked around vaguely and asked, "Are Uncle and Aunt Vorthys here?"

"No, neither one. Aunt will be back from class in a while, though."

Hugo frowned. "I was hoping we could see Uncle Vorthys, really. When will he be back?"

"Oh, he's gone to Komarr. To clear up some last technical bits about the solar mirror disaster, you know. He doesn't expect to be back till just before Gregor's wedding."

"Whose wedding?" said Vassily.

Gah, now Miles had *her* doing it. She was *not* on a first-name basis with Grego—with the Emperor, she was *not*. "Emperor Gregor's wedding. As an Imperial Auditor, Uncle Vorthys will of course attend."

Vassily's lips formed a little O of enlightenment, *that* Gregor.

"No chance of any of us getting near it, I suppose," Hugo sighed. "Of course, *I* have no interest in such things, but Rosalie and her lady friends have all gone quite silly over it." After a short hesitation, he added inconsistently, "Is it true that the Horse Guards will parade in squads of all the uniforms they've worn through history, from the Time of Isolation through Ezar's day?"

"Yes," said Ekaterin. "And there will be massive fireworks displays over the river *every* night." A faintly envious look crept into Hugo's eyes at this news.

Vassily cleared his throat, and asked, "Is Nikki here?"

"No . . . he went out with a friend to see the pole-barge regatta on the river this morning. They have it every year; it commemorates the relief of the city by Vlad Vorbarra's forces during the Ten-Years' War. I understand they're doing a bang-up job of it this summer—new costumes, and a reenactment of the assault on the Old Star Bridge. The boys were very excited." She did not add that they expected to have an especially fine view from the balconies of Vorbretten House, courtesy of a Vorbretten Armsman friend of Pym's.

Vassily stirred uncomfortably. "Perhaps it's just as well. Madame Vorsoisson—Ekaterin—we actually came down here today for a particular reason, a very serious matter. I should like to talk with you frankly."

"That's . . . generally best, when one is going to talk," Ekaterin responded. She glanced in query at Hugo.

"Vassily came to me . . ." Hugo began, and trailed off. "Well, *you* explain it, Vassily."

Vassily leaned forward with his hands clasped between his knees and said heavily, "You see, it's this. I received a most disturbing communication from an informant here in Vorbarr Sultana about what has been happening—what has recently come to light—some very disturbing information about you, my late cousin, and Lord Auditor Vorkosigan."

"Oh," she said flatly. So, the circuit of the Old Walls, what remained of them, did not limit the slander to the capital; the slime-trail even stretched to provincial District towns. She had somehow thought this vicious game an exclusively High Vor pastime. She sat back and frowned.

"Because it seemed to concern both our families very nearly—and, of course, because something of this peculiar nature must be cross-checked—I brought it to Hugo, for his advice, hoping that he could allay my fears. The corroborations your sister-in-law Rosalie supplied served to increase them instead."

Corroborations of what? She could probably make a few shrewd guesses, but she declined to lead the witnesses. "I don't understand."

"I was told," Vassily stopped to lick his lips nervously, "it's become common knowledge among his high Vor set that Lord Auditor Vorkosigan was responsible for sabotaging Tien's breath mask, the night he died on Komarr."

She could demolish this quickly enough. "You are told lies. That story was made up by a nasty little cabal of Lord Vorkosigan's political enemies, who wished to embarrass him during some District inheritance in-fighting presently going on here in the Council of Counts. Tien sabotaged himself; he was always careless about cleaning and checking his equipment. It's just whispering. No such actual charge has been made."

"Well, how could it be?" said Vassily reasonably. But her confidence that she'd brought him swiftly to his senses died as he went on, "As it was explained to me, any charge would have to be laid in the Council, before and by his peers. His father may be retired to Sergyar, but you may be sure his Centrist coalition remains powerful enough to suppress any such move."

"I would hope so." It might be suppressed, oh yes, but not for the reason Vassily thought. Lips thinning, she stared coldly at him.

Hugo put in anxiously, "But you see, Ekaterin, the same person informed Vassily that Lord Vorkosigan attempted to force you to accept a proposal of marriage from him."

She sighed in exasperation. "Force? No, certainly not."

"Ah." Hugo brightened.

"He did ask me to marry him. Very . . . awkwardly."

"My God, that was really *true*?" Hugo looked momentarily stunned. He sounded a deal more appalled at this than at the murder charge—doubly unflattering, Ekaterin decided. "You refused, of course!"

She touched the left side of her bolero, tracing the now not-so-stiff shape of the paper she kept folded there. Miles's letter was not the sort of thing she cared to leave lying around for anyone to pick up and read, and besides . . . she wanted to reread it herself now and then. From time to time. Six or twelve times a day . . . "Not exactly."

Hugo's brow wrinkled. "What do you mean by *not exactly*? I thought that was a yes-or-no sort of question."

"It's . . . difficult to explain." She hesitated. Detailing in front of Tien's closest cousin how a decade of Tien's private chaos had worn out her soul was just not on her list, she decided. "And rather personal."

Vassily offered helpfully, "The letter said that you seemed confused and distraught."

Ekaterin's eyes narrowed. "Just what busybody did you have this—*communication*—from, anyway?"

Vassily replied, "A friend of yours—he claimed—who is gravely concerned for your safety."

A friend? The Professora was her friend. Kareen, Mark . . . Miles, but he would hardly traduce himself, now . . . Enrique? *Tsipis*? "I cannot imagine any friend of mine doing or saying any such thing."

Hugo's frown of worry deepened. "The letter also said Lord Vorkosigan has been putting all sorts of pressure on you. That he has some strange hold on your mind."

No. Only on my heart, I think. Her mind was perfectly clear. It was the rest of her that seemed to be in rebellion. "He's a very attractive man," she admitted.

Hugo exchanged a baffled look with Vassily. Both men had met Miles at Tien's funeral; of course, Miles had been very closed and formal there, and still grayly fatigued from his case. They'd had no opportunity to see what he was like when he opened up—the elusive smile, the bright, particular eyes, the wit and the words and the passion . . . the confounded look on his face when confronted by Vorkosigan liveried butter bugs . . . she smiled helplessly in memory.

"Kat," said Hugo in a disconcerted tone, "the man's a mutie. He barely comes up to your shoulder. He's *distinctly* hunched—I don't know why that wasn't surgically corrected. He's just *odd*."

"Oh, he's had dozens of surgeries. His original damage was far, far more severe. You can still see these faint old scars running all over his body from the corrections."

Hugo stared at her. "*All* over his body?"

"Um. I assume so. As much of it as I've seen, anyway." She stopped her tongue barely short of adding, *The top half*. A perfectly unnecessary vision of Miles entirely naked, gift-wrapped in sheets and blankets in bed, and her with him, slowly exploring his intricacies all the way down, distracted her imagination momentarily. She blinked it away, hoping her eyes weren't crossing. "You have to concede, he has a good face. His eyes are . . . very alive."

"His head's too big."

"No, his body's just a little undersized for it." How had she ended up arguing Miles's anatomy with Hugo, anyway? He wasn't some spavined horse she was considering purchasing against veterinary advice, drat it. "Anyway, this is none of it our business."

"It is if he—if you—" Hugo sucked his lip. "Kat . . . if you're under some kind of threat, or blackmail or some strange thing, you don't stand alone. I know we can get help. You may have abandoned your family, but we haven't abandoned you."

More's the pity. "Thank you for that estimate of my character," she said tartly. "And do you imagine our Uncle *Lord Auditor* Vorthys is incapable of protecting me, if it should come to that? And Aunt Vorthys, too?"

Vassily said uneasily, "I'm sure your uncle and aunt are very kind—after all, they took you and Nikki in—but I'm given to understand they are both rather unworldly intellectuals. Possibly they do not understand the dangers. My informant says they haven't been guarding you at all. They've permitted you to go where you will, when you will, in a completely unregulated fashion, and come in contact with all sorts of dubious persons."

Their *unworldly* aunt was one of Barrayar's foremost experts on every gory detail of the political history of the Time of Isolation, spoke and read four languages flawlessly, could sift through documentation with an eye worthy of an ImpSec analyst—a line of work several of her former graduate students were now in—and had thirty years of experience dealing with young people and their self-inflicted troubles. And as for Uncle Vorthys—"Engineering failure analysis does not strike me as an especially unworldly discipline. Not when it includes expertise on sabotage." She inhaled, preparing to enlarge on this.

Vassily's lips tightened. "The capital has a reputation as an unsavory milieu. Too many wealthy, powerful men—and their women—with too few restraints on their appetites and vices. That's a dangerous world for a young boy to be exposed to, especially through his mother's . . . love affairs." Ekaterin was still mentally sputtering over this one when Vassily's voice dropped to a tone of hushed horror, and he added, "I've even heard—they say—that there's a high Vor lord here in Vorbarr Sultana who used to be a *woman*, who had her brain transplanted to a *man's body.*"

Ekaterin blinked. "Oh. Yes, that would be Lord Dono Vorrutyer. I've met him. It wasn't a brain transplant—ick! what a horrid misrepresentation—it was just a perfectly ordinary Betan body mod."

Both men boggled at her. "You *encountered* this creature?" said Hugo. "Where?"

"Um . . . Vorkosigan House. Actually. Dono seemed a very bright fellow. I think he'll do very well for Vorrutyer's District, if the Council grants him his late brother's Countship." She added after a moment of bitter consideration, "All things considered, I quite hope he gets it. *That* would give Richars and his slandering cronies one in the eye!"

Hugo, who had absorbed this exchange with growing dismay, put in, "I have to agree with Vassily, I'm a little uneasy myself about having you down here in the capital. The family so wishes to see you *safe*, Kat. I grant you're no girl anymore. You should have your own household, watched over by a steady husband who can be trusted to guard your welfare *and* Nikki's."

You could get your wish. Yet . . . she had stood up to armed terrorists, and survived. And *won*. Her definition of *safe* was . . . not so very narrow as that, anymore.

"A man of your own class," Hugo went on persuasively. "Someone who's right for you."

I think I've found him. He comes with a house where I don't hit the walls each time I stretch, either. Not even if I stretched out forever. She cocked her head. "Just what do you think my class is, Hugo?"

He looked nonplused. "*Our* class. Solid, honest, loyal Vor. On the women's side, modest, proper, upright. . . ."

She was suddenly on fire with a desire to be immodest, improper, and above all . . . not upright. Quite gloriously horizontal, in fact. It occurred to her that a certain disparity of height would be immaterial, when one—or two—were lying down . . . "You think I should have a house?"

"Yes, certainly."

"Not a planet?"

Hugo looked taken aback. "What? Of course not!"

"You know, Hugo, I never realized it before, but your vision lacks . . . scope." *Miles* thought she should have a planet. She paused, and a slow smile stole over her lips. After all, *his* mother had one. It was all in what you were used to, she supposed. No point in saying this aloud; they wouldn't get the joke.

And how had her big brother, admired and generous if more than a little distant due to their disparity of age, grown so small-minded of late? No . . . *Hugo* hadn't changed. The logical conclusion shook her.

Hugo said, "Damn, Kat. I thought that part of the letter was twaddle at first, but this mutie lord *has* turned your head around in some strange way."

"And if it's true . . . he has frightening allies," said Vassily. "The letter claimed that Vorkosigan had Simon Illyan himself riding point for him, herding you into his trap." His lips twisted dubiously. "That was the part that most made me wonder if I was being made a game of, to tell you the truth."

"I've met Simon," Ekaterin conceded. "I found him rather . . . sweet."

A dazed silence greeted this declaration.

She added a little awkwardly, "Of course, I understand he's relaxed quite a lot since his medical retirement from ImpSec. One can see that would be a great burden off his mind." Belatedly, the internal evidence slotted into place. "Wait a minute—*who* did you say sent you this hash of hearsay and lies?"

"It was in the strictest confidence," said Vassily warily.

"It was that blithering idiot Alexi Vormoncrief, wasn't it? Ah!" The light dawned, furiously, like the glare from an atomic fireball. But screaming, swearing, and throwing things would be counterproductive. She gripped the chair arms, so that the men could not see her hands shake. "Vassily, Hugo should have told you—I turned down a proposal of marriage from Alexi. It seems he's found a way to revenge his outraged vanity." *Vile twit!*

"Kat," said Hugo slowly, "I did consider that interpretation. I grant you the fellow's a trifle, um, idealistic, and if you've taken against him I won't try to argue his suit—though he seemed perfectly unobjectionable to me—but I saw his letter. I judged it quite sincerely concerned for you. A little over the top, yes, but what do you expect from a man in love?"

"Alexi Vormoncrief is not in love with me. He can't see far enough past the end of his own Vor nose to even know who or what I am. If you stuffed my clothes with straw and put a wig on top, he'd scarcely notice the change. He's just going through the motions supplied by his cultural programming." Well, all right, and his more fundamental biological programming, and he wasn't the only one suffering from that, now was he? She would concede Alexi a ration of sincere sex drive, but she was certain its object was arbitrary. Her hand strayed to her bolero, over her heart, and Miles's memorized words echoed, cutting through the uproar between her ears: *I wanted to possess the power of your eyes . . .*

Vassily waved an impatient hand. "All this is beside the point, for me if not for your brother. You're not a dowered maiden anymore, for your father to hoard up with his other treasures. I, however, have a clear family duty to see to Nikki's safety, if I have reason to believe it is threatened."

Ekaterin froze.

Vassily had granted her custody of Nikki with his word. He could take it back again as easily. It was she who'd have to take suit to court—*his* District court—not only to prove herself worthy, but also to prove him unworthy and unfit to have charge of the child. Vassily was no convicted criminal, nor habitual drunkard, nor spendthrift nor berserker; he was just a bachelor officer, a conscientious, duty-minded orbital traffic controller, an ordinary honest man. She hadn't a prayer of winning against him. If only Nikki had been her daughter, those rights would be reversed. . . .

"You would find a nine-year-old boy an awkward burden on a military base, I should think," she said neutrally at last.

Vassily looked startled. "Well, I hope it won't come to *that*. In the worst scenario, I'd planned to leave him with his Grandmother Vorsoisson, until things were straightened out."

Ekaterin held her teeth together for a moment, then said, "Nikki is of course welcome to visit Tien's mother any time she invites him. At the funeral she gave me to understand she was too unwell to receive visitors this summer." She moistened her lips. "Please define the term *worst scenario* for me. And just what exactly do you mean by *straightened out*?"

"Well," Vassily shrugged apologetically, "coming down here and finding you actually betrothed to the man who murdered Nikki's father would have been pretty bad, don't you agree?"

Had he been prepared to take Nikki away this very day, in that case? "I told you. Tien's death was accidental, and that accusation is pure slander." His disregard of her words reminded her horribly of Tien, for a moment; was obliviousness a Vorsoisson family trait? Despite the danger of offending him, she glowered. "Do you think I'm lying, or do you think I'm just stupid?" She fought for control of her breathing. She had faced far more frightening men than the earnest, misguided, Vassily Vorsoisson. *But never one who could cost me Nikki with a word.* She stood on the edge of a deep, dark pit. If she fell now, the struggle to get out again would be as filthy and painful as anything she could imagine. Vassily must *not* be pushed into taking Nikki. *Trying to take Nikki.* And she could stop him— how? She was legally overmatched before she even began. *So don't begin.*

She chose her words with utmost caution. "So what do you mean by straightened out?"

Hugo and Vassily looked at each other uncertainly. Vassily ventured, "I beg your pardon?"

"I cannot know if I have toed your line unless you show me where you've drawn it."

Hugo protested, "That's not very kindly put, Kat. We have your interests at heart."

"You don't even know what my interests are." Not true, Vassily had his thumb right down on the most mortal one. Nikki. *Eat rage, woman.* She had used to be expert at swallowing herself, during her marriage. Somehow she'd lost the taste for it.

Vassily groped, "Well . . . I'd certainly wish to be assured Nikki was not being exposed to persons of undesirable character."

She granted him a thin smile. "No problem. I shall be more than happy to entirely avoid Alexi Vormoncrief in the future."

He gave her a pained look. "I was referring to Lord Vorkosigan. And his political and personal set. At least—at least until this very dark cloud is cleared from his reputation. After all, the man is accused of *murdering* my *cousin.*"

Vassily's outrage was dutiful clan loyalty, not personal grief, Ekaterin reminded herself. If he and Tien had met more than three times in their lives it was news to her. "Excuse me," she said steadily. "If Miles is not to be charged—and I can't think he will be, on this— how may he be cleared, in your view? What has to happen?"

Vassily appeared momentarily baffled.

Hugo put in tentatively, "I don't want *you* exposed to corruption, either, Kat."

"You know, Hugo, it's the strangest thing," Ekaterin said genially to him, "but somehow Lord Vorkosigan has overlooked sending me invitations to *any* of his orgies. I'm quite put out. Do you suppose it's not the orgy season in Vorbarr Sultana yet?" She bit back further words. Sarcasm was not a luxury she—or Nikki—could afford.

Hugo rewarded this sally with a flat-lipped frown. He and Vassily gave one another a long look, each so obviously trying to divest the dirty work onto his companion that Ekaterin would have laughed, if it hadn't been so painful. Vassily finally muttered weakly, "She's *your* sister . . ."

Hugo took a breath. He was a Vorvayne; he knew his duty, by God. *All us Vorvaynes know our duty. And we'll keep on doing it till we die. No matter how stupid or painful or counterproductive it is, yes! After all, look at me. I kept oath for eleven years to Tien. . . .*

"Ekaterin, I think the burden falls on me to say this. Till this murder rumor business is settled, I'm flat requesting you not to encourage or, or see this Miles Vorkosigan fellow again. Or I will have to agree Vassily is completely justified in removing Nikki from the situation."

Removing Nikki from his mother and her paramour, you mean. Nikki had lost one parent this year, and lost all his friends in the move back to Barrayar. He was just starting to find the city he'd been dropped into less strange, to begin to unfold in tentative new friendships, to lose that wooden caution that had marred his smile for a while. She imagined him ripped away again, denied the chance to see her—for it would come down to that, wouldn't it? it was she, not the capital, Vassily suspected of corruption—plopped down in the third strange place in a year among unknown adults who regarded him not as a child to be delighted in, but as a duty to be discharged . . . no. No.

"Excuse me. I am willing to cooperate. I just haven't been able to compel either of you to say what I'm supposed to be cooperating with. I perfectly see what you are worried about, but *how* is it *to be settled*? Define *settled*. If it's till Miles's enemies stop saying nasty things about him, it could be a long wait. His line of work routinely pits him against the powerful. And he's not the sort to back down from any counterattack."

Hugo said, a bit more feebly, "Avoid him for a time, anyway."

"A time. Good. Now we're getting somewhere. How long exactly?"

"I . . . can hardly say."

"A week?"

Vassily, sounding a bit offended, put in, "Certainly more than that!"

"A month?"

Hugo rolled his hands in a frustrated gesture. "*I* don't know, Kat! Till you forget these odd notions you have about him, I suppose."

"Ah. Till the end of time. Hm. I can't quite decide if that's specific enough, or not. I think not." She took a breath, and said reluctantly, because it was such a long time and yet likely to sound so plausible to them, "To the end of my mourning year?"

Vassily said, "At the very minimum!"

"Very well." Her eyes narrowed, and she smiled, because smiling would do more good than howling. "I shall take you at your name's word, Vassily Vorsoisson."

"I, I, uh . . ." said Vassily, unexpectedly cornered. "Well . . . something should be settled by then. Surely."

I gave up too much, too soon. I should have tried for Winterfair. She added in sudden afterthought, "I reserve the right to tell him—and tell him why—myself, however. In person."

"Is that wise, Kat?" asked Hugo. "Better to call him on the comconsole."

"Anything less would be cowardly."

"Can't you send him a note?"

"*Absolutely* not. Not with this . . . news." What a vile return *that* would be, for Miles's own declaration sealed in his heart's blood.

At her defiant stare, Hugo weakened. "One visit, then. A brief one."

Vassily shrugged reluctant acquiescence.

An uncomfortable silence fell, after this. Ekaterin realized she ought to invite the pair of them to lunch, except that she didn't feel like inviting them to continue breathing. Yes, and she should exert herself to charm and soothe Vassily. She rubbed her temples, which were throbbing. When Vassily made a feeble motion toward escape from the Professora's parlor by mumbling about *things to do*, she did not impede them.

She locked the front door on their retreating forms, and returned to curl up in her uncle's chair, unable to decide whether to go lie down, or pace, or weed. Anyway, the garden was still stripped of weeds from her last upset about Miles. It would be an hour yet before Aunt Vorthys returned from her class, and Ekaterin could pour out her fury and panic into her ear. Or her lap.

To Hugo's credit, she reflected, he hadn't seemed enticed by the promise of a Countess's place for his little sister at any price, nor had he suggested that was the prize that motivated her. Vorvaynes were above that sort of material ambition.

Once, she had bought Nikki a rather expensive robopet, which he'd played with for a few days and then neglected. It had been forgotten on a shelf until, attempting to clean, she'd tried to give it away. Nikki's sudden frantic protests and heartbroken carryings-on had shaken the roof.

The parallel was embarrassing. Was Miles a toy she hadn't wanted till they'd tried to take him from her? Deep down in her chest, someone was screaming and sobbing. *You're not in charge here. I'm the adult, dammit.* Yet Nikki had kept his robopet . . .

She would deliver the bad news about Vassily's interdict to Miles's face. But not yet, oh, not quite yet. Because unless this smear upon his reputation was suddenly and spectacularly *settled*, that might be her last look at him for a very long time.

Kareen watched her father sink into the soft upholstery of the groundcar that Tante Cordelia had sent for them, and hitch around restlessly, placing his swordstick first on his lap and then at his side. Somehow, she didn't think his discomfort was all from his old war wounds.

"We're going to regret this, I know we are," he said querulously to Mama, for about the sixth time, as she settled in beside him. The rear canopy closed over the three of them, blocking the bright afternoon sun, and the groundcar started up smoothly and quietly. "Once that woman gets her hands on us, you know she'll have our heads turned inside out in ten minutes, and we'll be sitting there nodding away like fools, agreeing with every insane thing she says."

Oh, I hope so, I hope so! Kareen clamped her lips shut, and sat very still. She wasn't safe yet. The Commodore could still order Tante Cordelia's driver to turn the car around and take them back home.

"Now, Kou," said Mama, "we can't go on like this. Cordelia's right. It's time things were arranged more sensibly."

"Ah! There's that word—*sensible.* One of her favorites. I feel like I already have a plasma arc targeter spot right *there*." He pointed to the middle of his chest, as though a red dot wavered across his green uniform.

"It's been very uncomfortable," said Mama, "and I for one am getting tired of it. *I* want to see our old friends, and hear all about Sergyar. We can't stop all our lives over this."

Yeah, just mine. Kareen's teeth clenched a little harder.

"Well, *I* do not want that fat little weird clone—" he hesitated, judging by the ripple of his lips editing his word choice at least twice "—making up to my daughter. Explain to me why he needs two years of Betan therapy if he isn't half mad, eh? Eh?"

Don't say it, girl, don't say it. She gnawed on her knuckles instead. Fortunately, the drive was very short.

Armsman Pym met them at the door to Vorkosigan House. He favored her father with one of those formal nods that evoked a salute. "Good afternoon Commodore, Madame Koudelka. Welcome, Miss Kareen. Milady will receive you in the library. This way, please . . ." Kareen could almost swear, as he turned to escort them, that his eyelid shivered at her in a wink, but he was playing the Bland Servitor to the hilt today, and he gave her no more clues.

Pym ushered them through the double doors, and announced them with formality. He withdrew discreetly but with a—knowing Pym—deliberate air of abandoning them to a deserved fate.

In the library, part of the furniture had been rearranged. Tante Cordelia waited in a large wing chair perhaps accidentally reminiscent of a throne. At her right and left hands, two smaller armchairs faced one another. Mark sat in one of them, wearing his best black suit, shaved and slick as he'd been for Miles's ill-fated party. He popped to his feet and stood at a sort of awkward attention as the Koudelkas entered, clearly unable to decide whether it would be worse to nod cordially or do nothing. He compromised by standing there looking stuffed.

Across from Tante Cordelia, an entirely new piece of furniture had been placed. Well, *new* was a misnomer; it was an elderly, shabby couch which had lived for at least the past fifteen years up in one of Vorkosigan House's attics. Kareen remembered it dimly from the old hide-and-seek days. Last she'd seen it, it had been piled high with dusty boxes.

"Ah, and there you all are," said Tante Cordelia cheerfully. She waved at the second armchair. "Kareen, why don't you sit right here." Kareen scooted in as directed, clutching the arms. Mark seated himself again on the edge of his own chair, and watched her anxiously. Tante Cordelia's index finger rose like a target seeker, and pointed first to Kareen's parents, then to the old sofa. "Kou and Drou, you sit down—*there.*"

Both of them stared with inexplicable dismay at the harmless piece of old furniture.

"Oh," breathed the Commodore. "Oh, Cordelia, this is fighting dirty . . ." He started to swing around and head for the exit, but was brought up short by his wife's hand closing like a vise on his arm.

The Countess's gaze sharpened. In a voice Kareen had rarely heard her use before, she repeated, "*Sit. Down.*" It wasn't even her Countess Vorkosigan voice; it was something older, firmer, even more appallingly confident. It was her old Ship Captain's voice, Kareen realized; and her parents had both lived under military authority for decades.

Her parents sank as though folded.

"There." The Countess sat back with a satisfied smile on her lips.

A long silence followed. Kareen could hear the old-fashioned mechanical clock ticking on the wall in the antechamber next door. Mark gave her a beseeching stare, *Do you know what the hell is going on here?* She returned it in kind, *No, don't you?*

Her father rearranged the position of his swordstick three times, dropped it on the carpet, and finally scooted it back toward himself with the heel of his boot and left it there. She could see the muscle jump in his jaw as he gritted his teeth. Her mother crossed and uncrossed her legs, frowned, stared down the room out the glass doors, and then back at her hands twisting in her lap. They looked like nothing so much as two guilty teenagers caught . . . hm. Like two guilty teenagers caught screwing on the living room couch, actually. Clues seemed to float soundlessly down like feathers, in Kareen's mind, falling all around. *You don't suppose . . .*

"But Cordelia," Mama burst out suddenly, for all the world as though continuing aloud a conversation just now going on telepathically, "we want our children to do *better* than we did. To *not* make the same mistakes!"

Ooh. Ooh. Oooh! Check, and did she ever want the story behind this one . . . ! Her father had underestimated the Countess, Kareen realized. That hadn't taken any more than *three* minutes.

"Well, Drou," said Tante Cordelia reasonably, "it seems to me that you have your wish. Kareen has most certainly done better. Her choices and actions have been considered and rational in every way. And as far as I can tell, she hasn't made any mistakes at all."

Her father shook a finger at Mark, and sputtered, "That . . . *that* is a mistake."

Mark hunched, and wrapped his arms protectively around his belly. The Countess frowned faintly; the Commodore's jaw tightened.

The Countess said coolly, "We'll discuss Mark presently. Right now, allow me to draw your attention to how intelligent and informed your daughter is. Granted, she had not your disadvantage of trying to construct her life in the emotional isolation and chaos of a civil war. You both bought her a better, brighter chance than that, and I doubt you're sorry for it."

The Commodore shrugged grudging agreement. Mama sighed in something like negative nostalgia, not longing for the remembered past but relief at having escaped it.

"Just to pick one example not at random," the Countess went on, "Kareen, didn't you obtain your contraceptive implant before you began physical experimentation?"

Tante Cordelia was so bloody Betan . . . she just belted out things like that in casual conversation. Kareen and her chin rose to the challenge. "Of course," she said steadily. "And I had my hymen cut and did the programmed learning course the clinic gave on related anatomy and physiology issues, and Gran-tante Naismith bought me my first pair of earrings, and we went out for dessert."

Da rubbed his reddening face. Mama looked . . . envious.

"And I daresay," Tante Cordelia went on, "you wouldn't describe your first steps into claiming your adult sexuality as a mad secret scramble in the dark, full of confusion, fear and pain, either?"

Mama's negative-nostalgia look deepened. So did Mark's.

"Of course not!" Kareen drew the line at discussing *those* details with Mama and Da, although she was dying for a comfortable gossip with Tante Cordelia about it all. She'd been too shy to start with an actual *man*, so she'd hired a hermaphrodite Licensed Practical Sexuality Therapist whom Mark's counselor had recommended. The L.P.S.T. had explained to her kindly that hermaphrodites were extremely popular with young persons taking the introductory practical course for just that reason. It had all worked out *really really* well. Mark, anxiously hovering by his comconsole for her post-coital report, had been so pleased for her. Of course, his introduction to his own sexuality had included such ghastly trauma and tortures, it was only natural he be worried sick. She smiled reassuringly at him now. "If that's Barrayar, I'll take Beta!"

Tante Cordelia said thoughtfully, "It's not entirely that simple. Both societies seek to solve the same fundamental problem—to assure that all children arriving will be cared for. Betans make the choice to do it directly, technologically, by mandating a biochemical padlock on everyone's gonads. Sexual behavior seems open at the price of absolute social control on its reproductive consequences. Has it never crossed your mind to wonder how that is enforced? It should. Now, Beta *can* control one's ovaries; Barrayar, especially during the Time of Isolation, was forced to try to control the entire woman attached to them. Throw in Barrayar's need to increase its population to survive, at least as pressing as Beta's to limit its to the same end, and your *peculiar* gender-biased inheritance laws, and, well, here we all are."

"Scrambling in the dark," growled Kareen. "No *thank* you."

"We should never have sent her there. With *him*," Da grumbled.

Tante Cordelia observed, "Kareen was committed to her student year on Beta before she ever met Mark. Who knows? If Mark hadn't been there to, ah, insulate her, she might have met a nice Betan and stayed with him."

"Or it," Kareen murmured. "Or her."

Da's lips tightened.

"These trips can be more one-way than you expect. I haven't seen my own mother face-to-face more than three times in the last thirty years. At least if she sticks with Mark, you may be certain Kareen will return to Barrayar frequently."

Mama appeared very struck by this. She eyed Mark in new speculation. He essayed a hopeful, helpful smile.

Da said, "I want Kareen to be safe. Well. Happy. Financially secure. Is that so wrong?"

Tante Cordelia's lips twisted up with sympathy. "Safe? Well? That's what I wanted for my boys, too. Didn't always get it, but here we are anyway. As for happiness . . . I don't think you can *give* that to anyone, if they don't have it in them. However, it's certainly possible to give *un*-happiness—as you are finding."

Da's frown deepened in a somewhat surly manner, quelling Kareen's impulse to loudly cheer on this line of reasoning. Better let the Baba handle this . . .

The Countess continued, "As for that last . . . hm. Has anyone discussed Mark's financial status with you? Kareen, or Mark . . . or Aral?"

Da shook his head. "I thought he was broke. I assumed the family made him an allowance, like any other Vor scion. And that he ran through it—like any other Vor scion."

"I'm not *broke*," Mark objected strenuously. "It's a temporary cash-flow problem. When I budgeted for this period, I wasn't expecting to be starting up a new business in the middle of it."

"In other words, you're broke," said Da.

"Actually," Tante Cordelia said, "Mark is completely self-supporting. He made his first million on Jackson's Whole."

Da opened his mouth, but then shut it again. He gave his hostess a disbelieving stare. Kareen hoped it would not occur to him to inquire closely into Mark's method for winning this fortune.

"Mark has invested it in an interesting variety of more and less speculative enterprises," Tante Cordelia went on kindly. "The family *backs* him—I've just bought some shares in his butter bug scheme myself—and we'll always be here for emergencies, but Mark doesn't need an allowance."

Mark looked both grateful and awed to be so maternally defended, as if . . . well . . . just so. As if no one had ever done so before.

"If he's so rich, why is he paying my daughter in IOUs?" demanded Da. "Why can't he just draw something out?"

"Before the end of the period?" said Mark, in a voice of real abhorrence. "And lose all that *interest*?"

"And they're not IOUs," said Kareen. "They're shares!"

"Mark doesn't need money," said Tante Cordelia. "He needs what he knows money can't buy. Happiness, for example."

Mark, puzzled but pliable, offered, "So . . . do they want me to pay for Kareen? Like a dowry? How much? I *will*—"

"No, you twit!" cried Kareen in horror. "This isn't Jackson's Whole—you can't buy and sell *people*. Anyway, dowries were what the girl's family gave the fellow, not the other way around."

"That seems very wrong," said Mark, lowering his brows and pinching his chin. "Backwards. Are you sure?"

"Yes."

"I don't care if the boy has a million marks," Da began, sturdily and, Kareen suspected, not quite truthfully.

"Betan dollars," Tante Cordelia corrected absently. "Jacksonians do insist on hard currencies."

"The galactic exchange rates on the Barrayaran Imperial mark have been improving steadily since the War of the Hegen Hub," Mark started to explain. He'd written a paper on the subject last term; Kareen had helped proofread it. He could probably talk for a couple of hours about it. Fortunately, Tante Cordelia's raised finger staunched this threatened flow of nervous erudition.

Da and Mama appeared lost in a brief calculation of their own.

"All right," Da began again, a little less sturdily. "I don't care if the boy has *four* million marks. I care about Kareen."

Tante Cordelia tented her fingers thoughtfully. "So what is it that you want from Mark, Kou? Do you wish him to offer to marry Kareen?"

"Er," said Da, caught out. What he *wanted*, near as Kareen could tell, was for Mark to be carried off by predators, possibly even along with his four million marks in nonliquid investments, but he could hardly say so to Mark's mother.

"Yes, of course I'll offer, if she wants," Mark said. "I just didn't think she wanted to, yet. Did you?"

"No," said Kareen firmly. "Not . . . not yet, anyway. It's like I've just started to find myself, to figure out who I really am, to grow. I don't want to *stop*."

Tante Cordelia's brows rose. "Is that how you see marriage? As the end and abolition of yourself?"

Kareen realized belatedly that her remark might be construed as a slur on certain parties here present. "It is for some people. Why else do all the stories *end* when the Count's daughter gets married? Hasn't that ever struck you as a bit sinister? I mean, have you ever read a folk tale where the Princess's mother gets to do anything but die young? I've never been able to figure out if that's supposed to be a warning, or an instruction."

Tante Cordelia pressed her finger to her lips to hide a smile, but Mama looked rather worried.

"You grow in different ways, afterward," Mama said tentatively. "Not like a fairy tale. Happily ever after doesn't cover it."

Da's brows drew down; he said, in an odd, suddenly uncertain voice, "*I* thought we were doing all right . . ."

Mama patted his hand reassuringly. "Of course, love."

Mark said valiantly, "If Kareen wants me to marry her, I will. If she doesn't, I won't. If she wants me to go away, I'll go—" This last was accompanied by a covertly terrified glance her way.

"No!" cried Kareen.

"If she wants me to walk downtown backwards on my hands, I'll try. Whatever she wants," Mark finished up.

The thoughtful expression on Mama's face suggested that at least she liked his attitude. . . . "Is it that you wish to just be betrothed?" she asked Kareen.

"That's almost the same as marriage, here," said Kareen. "You give these oaths."

"You take those oaths seriously, I gather?" said Tante Cordelia, with a flick of her eyebrow toward the occupants of the mystery couch.

"Of *course*."

"I think it's down to you, Kareen," said Tante Cordelia with a small smile. "What do you want?"

Mark's hands clenched on his knees. Mama sat breathless. Da looked as if he was still worrying about the implications of that happily-ever-after remark.

This was Tante Cordelia. That wasn't a rhetorical question. Kareen sat silent, struggling for truth in confusion. Nothing less or else than truth would do. Yet where were the words for it? What she wanted was simply not a traditional Barrayaran option . . . ah. Yes. She sat up, and looked Tante Cordelia, and then Mama and Da, and then Mark in the eye.

"Not a betrothal. What I want . . . what *I* want—is an *option* on Mark."

Mark sat up, brightening. Now she was speaking a language they both understood.

"*That's* not Betan," said Mama, sounding confused.

"This isn't some weird Jacksonian practice, is it?" Da demanded suspiciously.

"No. It's a new Kareen custom. I just now made it up. But it fits." Her chin lifted.

Tante Cordelia's lips twitched up in amusement. "Hm. Interesting. Well. Speaking as Mark's, ah, agent in the matter, I would point out that a good option is not infinitely open-ended, nor all one-way. They have time limits. Renewal clauses. Compensation."

"Mutual," Mark broke in breathlessly. "Mutual option!"

"That would appear to cover the problem of compensation, yes. What about time limits?"

"I want a year," said Kareen. "To next Midsummer. I want at least a year, to see what we can do. I don't want anything from anybody," she glared at her parents, "but to *back off!*"

Mark nodded eagerly. "Agreed, agreed!"

Da jerked his thumb at Mark. "He'd agree to anything!"

"No," said Tante Cordelia judiciously. "I think you'll find he won't agree to anything that would make Kareen unhappy. Or smaller. Or unsafe."

Da's frown took on a serious edge. "Is that so? And what about her safety *from* him? All that Betan therapy wasn't for no reason!"

"Indeed not," agreed Tante Cordelia. Her nod acknowledged that seriousness. "But I believe it has been effective—Mark?"

"Yes, ma'am!" He sat there trying desperately to look Cured. He couldn't quite bring it off, but the effort was clearly sincere.

The Countess added quietly, "Mark is as much a veteran of our wars as any Barrayaran I know, Kou. He was conscripted earlier, is all. In his own strange and lonely way, he fought as hard, and risked as much. And lost as much. Surely you can grant him as much time to heal as you needed?"

The Commodore looked away, his face grown still.

"Kou, I wouldn't have encouraged this relationship if I thought it was unsafe for either of our children."

He looked back. "You? I know you! You trust beyond reason."

She met his eyes steadily. "Yes. It's how I get results beyond hope. As you may recall."

He pursed his lips, unhappily, and toed his swordstick a little. He had no reply for this one. But a funny little smile turned Mama's mouth, as she watched him.

"Well," said Tante Cordelia cheerfully into the lengthening silence, "I do believe we've achieved a meeting of the minds. Kareen to have an option upon Mark, and vice versa, until next Midsummer, when perhaps we should all meet again and evaluate the results, and consider negotiating an extension."

"What, are we supposed to just stand back while those two just— carry on?" cried Da, in a last fading attempt at indignation.

"Yes. Both to have the same freedom of action that, ah, you two," she nodded at Kareen's parents, "had at the same phase of your lives. I admit, carrying on was made easier for you, Kou, by the fact that all your fiancée's relatives lived in other towns."

"I remember you were terrified of my brothers," Mama recalled, the funny little smile spreading a bit. Mark's eyes widened thoughtfully.

Kareen marveled at this inexplicable bit of history; her Droushnakovi uncles all had hearts of butter, in her experience. Da set his teeth, except that when he looked at Mama his eyes softened.

"Agreed," said Kareen firmly.

"Agreed," echoed Mark at once.

"Agreed," said Tante Cordelia, and raised her brows at the couple on the couch.

Mama said, "Agreed." That quizzical, quirky smile in her eyes, she waited for Da.

He gave her a long, appalled, *You, too?!* stare. "You've gone over to their side!"

"Yes, I believe so. Won't you join us?" Her smile broadened further. "I know we don't have Sergeant Bothari to knock you on the jaw and help kidnap you along against your better judgment this time. But it would've been dreadfully unlucky for us to have tried to go collect the Pretender's head without you." Her grip on his hand tightened.

After a long moment, Da turned from her and frowned fiercely at Mark. "You understand, if you hurt her, I'll hunt you down myself!"

Mark nodded anxiously.

"Your codicil is accepted," murmured Tante Cordelia, her eyes alight.

"Agreed, then!" Da snapped. He sat back grumpily, with a See-what-I-do-for-you-people look on his face. But he didn't let go of Mama's hand.

Mark was staring at Kareen with a smothered elation. She could almost picture the entire Black Gang, jumping up and down in the back of his head, cheering, and Lord Mark hushing them lest they draw attention to themselves.

Kareen took a breath, for courage, dipped her hand into her bolero pocket, and drew out her Betan earrings, the pair that declaimed her implant and her adult status. With a little push, she slipped one into each earlobe. It was not, she thought, a declaration of independence, for she still lived in a web of dependencies. It was more of a declaration of Kareen. *I am who I am. Now, let's see how much I can do.*

Chapter Seventeen

Armsman Pym, a little out of breath, admitted Ekaterin to the front hall of Vorkosigan House. He tugged his tunic's high collar into adjustment, and smiled his usual welcome.

"Good afternoon, Pym," Ekaterin said. She was satisfied that she was able to keep any tremor out of her voice. "I need to see Lord Vorkosigan."

"Yes, ma'am."

That *Yes, milady!* in this hall the night of the dinner party had been a revealing slip of his tongue, Ekaterin realized belatedly. She hadn't noticed it at the time.

Pym keyed his wrist com. "M'lord? Where are you?"

A faint thump sounded from the com link, and Miles's muted voice: "North wing attic. Why?"

"Madame Vorsoisson is here to see you."

"I'll be right down—no, wait." A brief pause. "Bring her up. She'll like to see this, I bet."

"Yes, m'lord." Pym gestured toward the back entry. "This way." As she followed him to the lift tube, he added, "Little Nikki not with you today, ma'am?"

"No." Her heart failed her at the prospect of explaining why. She left it at that.

They exited the tube at the fifth level, a floor she hadn't penetrated on that first, memorable tour. She followed him down an uncarpeted hallway and through a pair of double doors into an enormous low-ceilinged room that extended from one side of the wing to the other. Roof beams hand-sawn from great trees crossed it overhead, with yellowing plaster between. Utilitarian lighting fixtures hung from them along a pair of center aisles created by the high-piled stowage.

Part of it was normal attic detritus: shabby furniture and lamps rejected even from the servants' quarters, picture frames that had lost their contents, spotted mirrors, wrapped squares and rectangles that might be some of the paintings, rolled tapestries. Still older oil lamps and candelabras. Mysterious crates and cartons and cracking leather-bound cases and scarred wooden trunks with long-dead people's initials burned in below their latches.

From there it grew more remarkable. A bundle of rusty cavalry javelins with wrinkled, faded brown-and-silver pennons wrapped about them wedged up against a hand-sawn post. Racks of faded Armsmen's uniforms bunched tightly together, brown and silver. Quantities of horse gear: saddles and bridles and harnesses with rusty bells, with unraveling tassels, with tarnished silver facings, with clacking beads all battered with their bright paint flaking off; hand-embroidered hangings and saddle blankets, with the Vorkosigans' VK and variations of their crest elaborated in thread. Dozens of swords and daggers, thrust randomly into barrels like steel bouquets.

Miles, in shirtsleeves, sat in the debris in the middle of one aisle about two-thirds of the way down the long room, surrounded by three open trunks and several half-sorted piles of papers and flimsies. One of the trunks, apparently just unlocked, was full to the brim with a miscellaneous cache of obsolete energy weapons, their power cartridges, Ekaterin trusted, long gone. A second, smaller case seemed to be the source of some of the papers. He glanced up and gave her an exhilarated grin.

"I told you the attics were something to see. Thank you, Pym."

Pym nodded and withdrew, giving his lord what Ekaterin's eye was now able to decode as a little good-luck salute.

"You weren't exaggerating," Ekaterin agreed. What kind of stuffed bird *was* that, hung upside down in the corner, glaring down at them through malignant glass eyes?

"The one time I had Duv Galeni up here, he nearly had a gibbering fit. He reverted right in front of my eyes back into Doctor

Professor Galeni, and raved at me for hours—days—about the fact that we haven't cataloged all this junk. He's still on about it, if I make the mistake of reminding him. I should have thought that my father installing that climate-controlled document room would have been enough." He waved her to a seat on a long polished walnut chest.

She sat, and smiled mutely at him. She should tell him her bad news, and leave. But he was so clearly in an expansive mood, she hated to derail him. When had his voice become a caress upon her ears? Let him babble on just a little longer . . .

"Anyway, what I ran across that I thought might interest you—" His hand started for a lump covered with a heavy white cloth, then wavered over the trunk of weapons. "Actually, *this* is pretty interesting, too, though it might be more in Nikki's line. Does he appreciate the grotesque? I'd have thought it a fabulous find when I was his age. I don't know how I missed it—oh, of course, Gran'da would have held the keys." He held up a coarse brown cloth bag, and poked a little dubiously into its contents. "I *believe* this is a sack of Cetagandan scalps. Want to see?"

"See, maybe. Touch, no."

Obligingly, he held it open for her inspection. The dried yellowing parchmentlike scraps with bits of hair clinging, or in some cases, falling off, indeed looked like human scalps to her. "Eeuw," she said appreciatively. "Did your grandfather take them himself?"

"Mm, possibly, though it seems rather a lot for one man, even General Piotr. I think it's more likely they were collected and brought to him as trophies by his guerillas. All fine, but then what could he do with 'em? Can't throw 'em away, they're *presents*."

"What are you going to do with them?"

He shrugged, and laid the bag back in the trunk. "If Gregor needed to send a subtle diplomatic insult to the Cetagandan Empire, which he doesn't just now, I suppose we could return them with elaborate apologies. Can't think of any other use offhand."

He shut the trunk, sorted through a variety of mechanical keys in the little pile at his knee, and locked it again. He rose to his knees, upended a crate in front of her, hoisted the shrouded object onto it, and pulled back the covering for her inspection.

It was a beautiful old saddle, similar to the old-fashioned cavalry style but more lightly built, for a lady. Its dark leather was elaborately carved and stamped in leaf, fern and flower patterns. The green velvet of its padded and stitched seat was worn half-bald, dried and split, the stuffing peeking out. Maple and olive leaves, carved and delicately tinted in the leather, surrounded a V flanked by a smaller B and K all closed in an oval. More embroidery, its colors surprisingly bright, echoed the botanical pattern in a blanket pad.

"There *ought* to be a matching bridle, but I haven't found it yet," Miles said, his fingers tracing over the initials. "It's one of my paternal grandmother's saddles. General Piotr's wife, Princess-and-Countess Olivia Vorbarra Vorkosigan. She obviously used this one quite a bit. My mother could never be persuaded to take up riding— I never was able to figure out why not—and it wasn't one of my father's passions. So it was left to Gran'da to try to teach me to keep the tradition alive. But I didn't have time to keep it up once I was an adult. Didn't you say you ride?"

"Not since I was a child. My great-aunt kept a pony for me— though I suspect it was as much for the manure for her garden. My parents had no room in town. He was a fat, ill-tempered beast, but I adored him." Ekaterin smiled in memory. "Saddles were a bit optional."

"I was thinking, maybe we could get this repaired and reconditioned, and put it back into use."

"Use? Surely that belongs in a museum! Hand-made—absolutely unique—historically significant—I can't even imagine what it would fetch at auction!"

"Ah—I had this same argument with Duv. It wasn't just hand-made, it was custom-made, especially for the Princess. Probably a gift from my grandfather. Imagine the fellow, not just a worker but an artist, selecting the leather, piecing and stitching and carving. I picture him hand-rubbing in the oil, thinking of *his* work used by his Countess, envied and admired by her friends, being part of this— this whole work of art that was her life." His finger traced the leaves around the initials.

Her guess of its value kept ratcheting up in time to his words. "For heaven's sake get it appraised first!"

"Why? To loan to a museum? Don't need to set a price on my grandmother for that. To sell to some collector to hoard like money? Let him hoard money, that's all that sort wants anyway. The only collector who'd be worthy of it would be someone who was personally obsessed with the Princess-and-Countess, one of those men who fall hopelessly in love across time. No. I owe it to its maker to put it to its *proper* use, the use he intended."

The weary straitened housewife in her—Tien's pinchmark spouse—was horrified. The secret soul of her rang like a bell in resonance to Miles's words. Yes. That was how it should be. This saddle belonged under a fine lady, not under a glass cover. Gardens were meant to be seen, smelled, walked through, grubbed in. A hundred objective measurements didn't sum the worth of a garden; only the delight of its users did that. Only the use made it *mean* something. How had Miles learned that? *For this alone I could love you . . .*

"Now." He grinned in response to her smile, and drew breath. "God knows I need to start doing something for exercise, or all this culinary diplomacy I do nowadays will defeat Mark's attempt to differentiate himself from me. There are several parks here in town with hacking paths. But it's not much fun to ride by myself. Think you'd be willing to keep me company?" He blinked a trifle ingenuously.

"I would love to," she said honestly, "but I can't." She could see in his eyes a dozen counterarguments springing up, ready to charge into the breach. She held up a hand to stop him bursting into speech. She must bring this little self-indulgent ration of pretend-happiness to a close, before her will broke. Her forced agreement with Vassily only permitted her a taste of Miles, not a meal. Not a banquet . . . Back to harsh reality. "Something new has come up. Yesterday, Vassily Vorsoisson and my brother Hugo came to see me. Set on, apparently, by a nasty letter from Alexi Vormoncrief."

Tersely, she detailed their visit. Miles sat back on his heels, his face setting, listening closely. For once, he didn't interrupt.

"You set them straight?" he said slowly, when she paused for breath.

"I *tried*. It was infuriating to watch them just . . . dismiss my word, in favor of all those sordid insinuations from that fool Alexi, of all men. Hugo was genuinely worried about me, I suppose, but Vassily is all wound up in this misconstrued family duty and some inflated ideas about the depraved decadence of the capital."

"Ah," said Miles thinly. "A romantic, I see."

"Miles, they were ready to take Nikki away right then! And I have no legal way to fight for custody. Even if I took Vassily to the Vorbretten District magistrate's court, I couldn't prove him grossly unfit—he's not. He's just grossly gullible. But I thought—too late, last night—about Nikki's security classification. Would ImpSec do something to stop Vassily?"

Miles frowned, his brows drawing down. "Possibly . . . not. It's not as if he wanted to take Nikki off-world. ImpSec could have no objection to Nikki going to live on a military base—in fact, they'd probably consider it a better safe-zone than your uncle's or Vorkosigan House either one. More anonymous. I can't think they'd be too keen about a lawsuit drawing more public attention to the Komarran affair, either."

"Would they quash it? In whose favor?"

He hissed thoughtfully through his teeth. "Yours, if I asked them to, but it would be just like them to do so in a way that provides maximum support to the cover story—which is how they've classified this murder-slander in their little one-track minds this week. I hardly dare touch it; I'd only make things worse. I wonder if somebody . . . I wonder if somebody anticipated that?"

"I know Alexi's pulling Vassily's strings. Do you think someone's pulling Alexi's strings, trying to bait you into making some ruinous public move?" That would make *her* the last link in a chain by which his hidden enemy sought to yank Miles into an untenable position. A chilling realization. But only if she—and Miles—did what that enemy anticipated.

"I . . . hm. Possibly." His frown deepened. "Better by far that your uncle straighten things out, anyway, privately, inside the family. Is he still due back from Komarr before the wedding?"

"Yes, but that's only if his so-called *few little technical matters* don't get more complicated than he anticipates."

Miles grimaced in sympathetic understanding. "No guarantees then, right." He paused. "Vorbretten's District, eh? If push came to shove, I could quietly call in a favor from René Vorbretten, and have him, ah, arrange things. You could jump over the magistrate's court and take it to him on direct appeal. I wouldn't have to involve ImpSec or appear in the matter at all. That wouldn't work if Sigur holds Countship of the Vorbretten's District by then, though."

"I don't want push to come to shove. I don't want Nikki troubled more at all. It's been ghastly enough for him." She sat tight and trembling, whether with fear or anger or a venomous combination she could hardly say.

Miles scrambled up off his heels, and came round and sat rather tentatively next to her on the walnut chest, and gave her a searching

look. "One way or another, we can make it come round right in the
end. In two days, both these District inheritance votes come due in
the Council of Counts. Once the vote's over, the political motivation
to stir up trouble with this accusation against me evaporates, and the
whole thing will start to fade." That would have sounded very
comfortable, if he hadn't added, "I hope."

"I shouldn't have suggested putting you in quarantine till my
mourning year was over. I should have tried Vassily on Winterfair
first. I thought of that too late. But I can't risk Nikki, I just can't. Not
when we've come so far, survived so much."

"Sh, now. I think your instincts are right. My grandfather had an
old cavalry saying: 'You should get over heavy ground as lightly as
you can.' We'll just lie low for a little while here so as not to rile poor
Vassily. And when your uncle gets back, he'll straighten the fellow
out." He glanced up at her, sideways. "Or, of course, you could
simply not see me for a year, eh?"

"I should dislike that exceedingly," she admitted.

"Ah." One corner of his mouth curled up. After a little pause, he
said, "Well, we can't have that, then."

"But Miles, I gave my word. I didn't want to, but I did."

"Stampeded into it. A tactical retreat is not a bad response to a
surprise assault, you know. First you survive. Then you choose your
own ground. *Then* you counterattack."

Somehow, not her doing, his thigh lay by hers, not quite touching
but warm and solid even through two layers of cloth, gray and black.
She couldn't exactly lay her head on his shoulder for comfort, but
she might sneak her arm around his waist, and lean her cheek on the
top of his head. It would be a pleasant sensation, easing to the heart.
I shouldn't do that.

Yes, I should. Now and always . . . No.

Miles sighed. "Bitten by my reputation. Here I thought the only
opinions that mattered were yours, Nikki's, and Gregor's. I forgot
Vassily's."

"So did I."

"My da gave me this definition: he told me reputation was what
other people knew about you, but honor was what you knew about
yourself."

"Was that what Gregor meant, when he told you to talk to him?
Your da sounds wise. I'd like to meet him."

"He wants to meet you, too. Of course, he immediately followed this up by asking me how I stood with myself. He has this . . . this *eye*."

"I think . . . I know what he means." She might curl her fingers around his hand, lying loosely on his thigh so close to hers. Surely it would lie warm and reassuring in her palm . . . *You've betrayed yourself before, in starvation for touch. Don't.* "The day Tien died, I went from being the kind of person who made, and kept, a life-oath, to one who broke it in two and walked away. My oath had mattered the world to me, or at least . . . I'd traded the world for it. I still don't know if I was forsworn for nothing or not. I don't suppose Tien would have gone charging out in that stupid way that night if I hadn't shocked him by telling him I was leaving." She fell silent for a little. The room was very still. The thick old stone walls kept out the city noises. "I am not who I was. I can't go back. I don't quite like who I have become. Yet I still . . . stand. But I hardly know how to go on from here. No one ever gave me a map for this road."

"Ah," said Miles. "Ah. That one." His voice was not in the least puzzled; he spoke in a tone of firm recognition.

"Towards the end, my oath was the only piece of me left that hadn't been ground down. When I tried to talk about this to Aunt Vorthys, she tried to reassure me that it was all right because everyone else thought Tien was an ass. *You* see . . . it has nothing to do with Tien, saint or monster. It was me, and my word."

He shrugged. "What's hard to see about that? It's blazingly obvious to *me*."

She turned her head, and looked down at his face, which looked up at her in patient curiosity. Yes, he perfectly understood—yet did not seek to comfort her by dismissing her distress, or trying to convince her it didn't matter. The sensation was like opening the door to what she'd thought was a closet, and stepping through into another country, rolling out before her widening eyes. *Oh.*

"In my experience," he said, "the trouble with oaths of the form, *death before dishonor*, is that eventually, given enough time and abrasion, they separate the world into just two sorts of people: the dead, and the forsworn. It's a survivor's problem, this one."

"Yes," she agreed quietly. *He knows. He knows it all, right down to that bitter muck of regret at the bottom of the soul's well. How does he know?*

"Death before dishonor. Well, at least no one can complain I got them out of order . . . You know . . ." He started to look away, but then looked back, to hold her eye directly. His face was a little pale. "I wasn't exactly medically discharged from ImpSec. Illyan fired me. For falsifying a report about my seizures."

"Oh," she said. "I didn't know that."

"I know you didn't. I don't exactly go round advertising the fact, for pretty obvious reasons. I was trying so hard to hang on to my career—Admiral Naismith was everything to me, life and honor and most of my identity by then—I broke it instead. Not that I didn't set myself up for it. Admiral Naismith began as a lie, one I redeemed by making him come true later. And it worked really well, for a while; the little Admiral brought me everything I ever thought I wanted. After a while I began to think all sins could be redeemed like that. Lie now, fix it later. Same as I tried to do with you. Even love is not as strong as habit, eh?"

Now she did dare to tighten her arm around him. No reason for them both to starve. . . . For a moment, he went as breathless as a man laying food before a wild animal, trying to coax it to his hand. Abashed, she drew back.

She inhaled, and ventured, "Habits. Yes. I feel as if I'm half-crippled with old reflexes." *Old scars of mind.* "Tien . . . seems never more than a thought away from me. Will his death ever fade, do you suppose?"

Now he didn't look at her. Didn't dare? "I can't answer for you. My own ghosts just seem to ride along, mostly unconsulted, always there. Their density gradually thins, or I grow used to them." He stared around the attic, blew out his breath, and added elliptically, "Did I ever tell you how I came to kill my grandfather? The great general who survived it all, Cetagandans, Mad Yuri, everything this century could throw at him?"

She declined to be baited into whatever shocked response he thought this dramatic statement deserved, but merely raised her brows.

"I disappointed him to death, eh, the day I blew my Academy entrance exams, and lost my first chance at a military career. He died that night."

"Of course," she said dryly, "you were the cause. It couldn't possibly have had anything to do with his being nearly a hundred years old."

"Yeah, sure, I know." Miles shrugged, and gave her a sharp look up from under his dark brows. "The same way you know Tien's death was an accident."

"Miles," she said, after a long, thoughtful pause, "are you trying to one-up my dead?"

Taken aback, his lips began to form an indignant denial, which weakened to an, "Oh." He gently thumped his forehead on her shoulder as if beating his head against a wall. When he spoke again, his ragging tone did not quite muffle real anguish. "How *can* you stand me? I can't even stand me!"

I think that was the true confession. We are surely come to the end of one another. "Sh. Sh."

Now he did take her hand, his fingers tightening around it as warmly as any embrace. She did not jerk back in startlement, though an odd shiver ran through her. *Isn't starving yourself a betrayal too, self against self?*

"To use Kareen's Betan psychology terminology," she said a little breathlessly, "I have this Thing about oaths. When you became an Imperial Auditor, you took oath again. Even though you were forsworn once. How could you bear to?"

"Oh," he said, looking around a little vaguely. "What, when they issued you your honor, didn't they give you the model with the reset button? Mine's right here." He pointed to the general vicinity of his navel.

She couldn't help it; her black laughter pealed out, echoing off the beams. Something inside her, wrapped tight to the breaking-point, loosened at that laugh. When he made her laugh like that, it was like light and air let in upon wounds too dark and painful to touch, and so a chance at healing. "Is that what that's for? I never knew."

He smiled, recapturing her hand. "A very wise woman once told me—you just go on. I've never encountered any good advice that didn't boil down to that, in the end. Not even my father's."

I want to be with you always, so you can make me laugh myself well. He stared down at her palm in his as though he wanted to kiss it. He was close enough that she could feel their every breath, matching rhythms. The silence lengthened. She had come to give him up, not get into a necking session . . . if this went on, she'd end up kissing him. The scent of him filled her nose, her mouth, seemed rushed by her blood to every cell of her body. Intimacy of the flesh seemed easy, after the far more terrifying intimacy of the mind.

Finally, with enormous effort, she sat up straight. With perhaps equal effort, he released her hand. Her heart was thumping as though she'd been running. Trying for an ordinary voice, she said, "Then your considered opinion is, we should wait for my uncle to take on Vassily. Do you really think this nonsense is meant as a trap?"

"It has that smell. I can't quite tell yet how many levels down the stench is coming from. It *might* only be Alexi trying to cut me out."

"But then one considers who Alexi's friends are. I see." She attempted a brisk tone. "So, are you going to nail Richars and the Vormoncrief party, in the Council day after tomorrow?"

"Ah," he said. "There's something I need to tell you about that." He looked away, tapped his lips, looked back. He was still smiling, but his eyes had gone serious, almost bleak. "I believe I've made a strategic error. You, ah, know Richars Vorrutyer seized on this slander as a lever to try and force a vote from me?"

She said hesitantly, "I'd gathered something of a sort was going on, behind the scenes. I didn't realize it was quite so overt."

"Crude. Actually." He grimaced. "Since blackmail wasn't a behavior I wished to reward, my answer was to put all my clout, such as it is, behind Dono."

"Good!"

He smiled briefly, but shook his head. "Richars and I now stand at an impasse. If he wins the Countship, my open opposition almost forces him to go on to make his threat good. At that point, he'll have the right and the power. He won't move immediately—I expect it will take him some weeks to collect allies and marshal resources. And if he has any tactical wits, he'll wait till after Gregor's wedding. But you see what comes next."

Her stomach tightened. She could see all too well, but . . . "*Can* he get rid of you by charging you with Tien's murder? I thought any such charge would be quashed."

"Well, if wiser heads can't talk Richars out of it . . . the practicalities become peculiar. In fact, the more I think about it, the messier it looks." He spread his fingers on his gray-trousered knee, and counted down the list. "Assassination is out." By his grimace, that was meant as a joke. Almost. "Gregor wouldn't authorize it for anything less than overt treason, and Richars is embarrassingly loyal to the Imperium. For all I know, he really *does* believe I murdered Tien, which makes him an honest man, of sorts. Taking Richars quietly aside and telling him the truth about Komarr is right out. I'd expect a lot of maneuvering around the lack of evidence, and a verdict of Not Proven. Well, ImpSec might manufacture some evidence, but I'm getting pretty queasy wondering what kind. Neither my reputation nor yours will be their top priority. And you're bound to be sucked into it at some point, and I . . . won't be in control of all that happens."

She found her teeth were pressed together. She ran her tongue over her lips, to loosen the taut muscles of her jaw. "Endurance used to be my specialty. In the old days."

"I was hoping to bring you some new days."

She scarcely knew what to say to this, so merely shrugged.

"There is another choice. Another way I can divert this . . . sewer."

"Oh?"

"I can fold. Stop campaigning. Cast the Vorkosigan's District vote as an abstention . . . no, that likely wouldn't be enough to repair the damages. Cast it for Richars, then. Publicly back down."

She drew in her breath. *No!* "Has Gregor asked you to do this? Or ImpSec?"

"No. Not yet, anyway. But I was wondering if . . . you would wish it so."

She looked away from him, for three long breaths. When she looked back, she said levelly, "I think we'd both have to use that reset button of yours, after that."

He took this in with almost no change of expression, but for a weird little quirk at the corner of his mouth. "Dono doesn't have enough votes."

"As long as he has yours . . . I should be satisfied."

"As long as you understand what's likely coming down."

"I understand."

He vented a long, covert exhalation.

Was there nothing she could do to help his cause? Well, Miles's hidden enemies wouldn't be jerking so many strings if they didn't want to produce some ill-considered motions. Stillness, then, and silence—not of the prey that cowered, but of the hunter who waited. She regarded Miles searchingly. His face was its usual cheerful mask, but nerve-stretched underneath . . . "Just out of curiosity, when was the last time you used your seizure stimulator?"

He didn't quite meet her eye. "It's . . . been a while. I've been too busy. You know it knocks me on my ass for a day."

"As opposed to falling on your ass in the Council chamber on the day of reckoning? No. I believe you have a couple of votes to cast. You use it tonight. Promise me!"

"Yes, ma'am," he said humbly. From the odd little gleam in his eye, he was not so crushed as his briefly hang-dog look suggested. "I promise."

Promises. "I have to go."

He rose without argument. "I'll walk you out." They strolled arm in arm, picking their way down the aisle through the hazards of discarded history. "How did you get here?"

"Autocab."

"Can I have Pym give you a lift home?"

"Sure."

In the end, he rode with her, in the back of the vast old armored groundcar. They talked only of little things, as if they had all the time in the world. The drive was short. They did not touch each other, when he let her off. The car pulled away. The silvered canopy hid . . . everything.

Ivan's smile muscles were giving out. Vorhartung Castle was brilliantly appointed tonight for the Council of Counts' reception for the newly arrived Komarran delegation to Gregor's wedding, which the Komarrans persisted in calling Laisa's wedding. Lights and flowers decorated the main entry hall, the grand staircase to the Council Chamber gallery, and the great salon where dinner had been held. The party did dual duty, also celebrating the augmented solar mirror array voted by, or rammed through, depending on one's political view, the Council last week. It was an Imperial bride-gift of truly planetary scope.

The feast had been followed by speeches and a holovid presentation displaying plans not only for the mirror array, vital to Komarr's ongoing terraforming, but unveiling designs for a new jump-point station to be built by a joint Barrayaran-Komarran consortium including Toscane Industries and Vorsmythe Ltd. His mother had assigned Ivan a Komarran heiress to squire about this intimate little soiree of five hundred persons; alas that she was sixty-plus years old, married, and the empress-to-be's aunt.

Unintimidated by her high Vor surroundings, this cheerful gray-haired lady was serene in her possession of a large chunk of Toscane Industries, a couple of thousand Komarran planetary voting shares, and an unmarried granddaughter upon whom she plainly doted. Ivan, admiring the vid pix, agreed that the girl was charming, beautiful, and clearly vastly intelligent. But since she was also only seven years old, she'd been left at home. After dutifully conducting Aunt Anna and her immediate hangers-on about the castle and pointing out its most salient architectural and historical features, Ivan managed to wedge the whole party back into the crowd of Komarrans around Gregor and Laisa, and plotted his escape. As Aunt Anna, in a voice raised to pierce the hubbub, informed Ivan's mother that he was a *very cute boy*, he faded backwards through the mob, angling toward the servitors stationed by the side walls handing out after-dinner drinks.

He almost bounced off a young couple making their way down the side aisle, who were looking at each other instead of where they were going. Lord William Vortashpula, Count Vortashpula's heir, had lately announced his engagement to Lady Cassia Vorgorov. Cassie was in wonderful looks: eyes bright, face becomingly flushed, low-cut gown—dammit, *had* she done something to augment her bustline, or had she simply matured a bit over the past couple of years? Ivan was still trying to decide when she caught his gaze; she tossed her head, making the flowers wound in her smooth brown hair bounce, smirked, gripped her fiancé's arm more tightly, and stalked past him. Lord Vortashpula twittered a brief distracted greeting to Ivan before he was towed off.

"Pretty girl," said a gruff voice at Ivan's elbow, making him flinch. Ivan turned to find his cousin-several-times-removed Count Falco Vorpatril watching him from under fiercely bushy gray eyebrows. "Too bad you missed your chance with her, Ivan. Dumped you for a better berth, did she?"

"I was not *dumped* by Cassie Vorgorov," said Ivan a little hotly. "I was never even courting her."

Falco's deep chuckle was unpleasantly disbelieving. "Your mother told me Cassie had quite a crush on you, at one time. She seems to have recovered nicely. Cassie, not your mother, poor woman. Although Lady Alys seems to have got over all her disappointments in your ill-fated love matches, too." He glanced across the room toward the group around the Emperor, where Illyan attended upon Lady Alys with his usual quiet panache.

"None of my love matches were ill-fated, sir," said Ivan stiffly. "They were all brought to mutually agreeable conclusions. I *choose* to play the field."

Falco merely smiled. Ivan, disdaining to be baited further, made a polite bow to the aged but upright Count Vorhalas, who had come up to his old colleague Falco. Falco was either a progressive Conservative, or a conservative Progressive, a notorious fence-sitter courted by both sides. Vorhalas had been key man in the Conservative opposition to the Vorkosigan-led Centrist machine for as long as Ivan could remember. He was not a Party leader, but his reputation for iron integrity made him the man to whom all others looked to set the standard.

Ivan's cousin Miles came strolling down the aisle just then, smiling slightly, his hands in the pockets of his brown-and-silver Vorkosigan House uniform. Ivan tensed to duck out of the line of fire, should Miles be looking for volunteers for whatever ungodly scheme he might be pursuing at the moment, but Miles merely gave him a half-salute. He murmured greetings to the two Counts, and gave Vorhalas a respectful nod, which, after a moment, the old man returned.

"Where away, Vorkosigan?" Falco inquired easily. "Are you going to that reception at Vorsmythe House after this?"

"No, the rest of the team will be covering that one. I'll be joining Gregor's party." He hesitated, then smiled invitingly. "Unless, perhaps, you two gentlemen would be willing to reconsider Lord Dono's suit, and would like to go somewhere and discuss it?"

Vorhalas just shook his head, but Falco grunted a laugh. "Give over, Miles, do. That one's hopeless. God knows you've been giving it your all—at least, I know *I've* tripped over you everywhere I've been for the past week—but I'm afraid the Progressives are going to have to be satisfied with this soletta gift victory."

Miles glanced around at the dwindling crowd, and gave a judicious shrug. He'd done a good bit of tearing around on Gregor's behalf to bring this vote off, Ivan knew, in addition to his intense campaigning for Dono and René. Little wonder he looked drained. "We have all done a good turn for our future, here. I think this mirror augmentation will be bearing fruit for the Imperium long before the terraforming is complete."

"Mm," said Vorhalas neutrally. His had been an abstaining vote on the mirror matter, but Gregor's majority had made it of no moment.

"I wish Ekaterin might have been here tonight to see this," Miles added wistfully.

"Yeah, why didn't you bring her?" asked Ivan. He didn't understand Miles's strategy on this one; he thought the beleaguered couple would be far better served openly defying public opinion, and so forcing it to bend around them, than cravenly bowing to it. Bravado would be much more Miles's style, too.

"We'll see. After tomorrow." He added under his breath, "I wish the damn vote was over."

Ivan grinned, and lowered his tone in response. "What, and you so Betan? Half-Betan. I thought you approved of democracy, Miles. Don't you like it after all?"

Miles smiled thinly, and declined to be baited. He bade his seniors a cordial good-night, and walked off a bit stiffly.

"Aral's boy doesn't look well," Vorhalas observed, staring after him.

"Well, he did have that medical discharge from the Service," Falco allowed. "It was a wonder he was able to serve as long as he did. I suppose his old troubles caught up with him."

This was true, Ivan reflected, but not in the sense Falco meant. Vorhalas looked a bit grim, possibly thinking about Miles's prenatal soltoxin damage, and the painful Vorhalas family history that went with it. Ivan, taking pity on the old man, put in, "No, sir. He was injured on duty." In fact, that gray skin tone and hampered motion strongly suggested Miles had undergone one of his seizures lately.

Count Vorhalas frowned thoughtfully at him. "So, Ivan. You know him about as well as anyone. What do you make of this ugly tale going around about him and that Vorsoisson woman's late husband?"

"I think it is a complete fabrication, sir."

"Alys says the same," Falco noted. "I'd say she's in a position to know the truth if anyone is."

"That, I grant you." Vorhalas glanced at the Emperor's entourage, across the glittering and crowded salon. "I also think she is entirely loyal to the Vorkosigans, and would lie without hesitation to protect their interests."

"You are half right, sir," said Ivan testily. "She is entirely loyal."

Vorhalas made a placating gesture. "Don't bite me, boy. I suppose we'll never really know. One learns to live with such uncertainties, as one grows older."

Ivan choked back an irritable reply. Count Vorhalas's was the sixth such more or less oblique inquiry into his cousin's affairs Ivan had endured tonight. If Miles was putting up with *half* this, it was no wonder he looked exhausted. Although, Ivan reflected morosely, it was probable that very few men dared asked him such questions to his face—which meant that Ivan was drawing *all* the fire meant for Miles. Typical, just typical.

Falco said to Vorhalas, "If you're not going on to Vorsmythe's, why don't you come back with me to Vorpatril House? Where we can at least drink sitting down. I've been meaning to have a quiet talk with you about that watershed project."

"Thank you, Falco. That sounds considerably more restful. Nothing like the prospect of vast sums of money changing hands to generate rather wearing excitement among our colleagues."

From which Ivan concluded that the industries in Vorhalas's District had largely missed the boat on this new Komarran economic opportunity. The glazed numbness creeping over him had nothing to do with too much to drink; in fact, it suggested he'd had far too little. He was about to continue his trip to the bar when an even better diversion crossed his vision.

Olivia Koudelka. She was wearing a white-and-beige lace confection that somehow emphasized her blond shyness. And she was *alone*. At least temporarily.

"Ah. Excuse me, gentlemen. I see a friend in need." Ivan escaped the grayhairs, and bore down on his quarry, a smile lighting his face and his brain going into overdrive. Gentle Olivia had always been eclipsed on Ivan's scanner by her older and bolder sisters Delia and Martya. But Delia had chosen Duv Galeni, and Martya had bounced Ivan's suit in no uncertain terms. Maybe . . . maybe he'd stopped working his way down the Koudelka family tree a tad too soon.

"Good evening, Olivia. What a pretty frock." Yes, women spent so much time on their clothes, it was always a good opening move to notice the effort. "Enjoying yourself?"

"Oh, hi, Ivan. Yes, certainly."

"I didn't see you earlier. Mama put me to work buttering up Komarrans."

"We were rather late arriving. This is our fourth stop this evening."

We? "The rest of your family here? I saw Delia with Duv, of course. They're caught over there in that cluster around Gregor."

"Are they? Oh, good. We'll have to say hi before we go."

"What are you doing after this?"

"Going on to that squeeze at Vorsmythe House. It's potentially extremely valuable."

While Ivan was trying to decode this last cryptic remark, Olivia looked up, her gaze caught by someone. Her lips parted and her eyes lit, reminding Ivan for a dizzy moment of Cassie Vorgorov. Alarmed, he followed the line of her glance. But there was no one in it except Lord Dono Vorrutyer, apparently just parting company with his/her old friend Countess Vormuir. The Countess, svelte in a red dress that strikingly complemented Dono's sober black, patted Dono on the arm, laughed, and strolled away. Countess Vormuir was still estranged from her husband, as far as Ivan knew; he wondered what kind of time Dono might be making with her. The concept made his brain cramp.

"Vorsmythe House, eh?" said Ivan. "Maybe I'll go along. I can about guarantee they'll be trotting out the *good* wine, for this. How are you getting there?"

"Groundcar. Would you like a lift?"

Perfect. "Why, yes, thank you. I would." He'd ridden here with his mother and Illyan, from his point of view to avoid risking his speedster's enamel in the parking cram, from hers so that she could be sure he'd show up for duty as ordered. He hadn't anticipated that the absence of his own car would prove a tactical aid. He smiled brilliantly down upon Olivia.

Dono strode over to them, smiling in a peculiarly satisfied manner that put Ivan disquietingly in mind of the lost Lady Donna. Dono was not a person with whom Ivan cared to be quite so publicly paired. Perhaps he could keep Olivia's hellos brief, and then whisk her off.

"Things look like they're breaking up," said Dono to Olivia. He gave Ivan a nod of greeting. "Shall I call Szabo to bring round the car?"

"We ought to see Delia and Duv first. Then we can go. Oh, I offered Ivan a ride along with us to Vorsmythe's. I think there'll be room."

"Certainly." Dono smiled cheerful welcome.

"Did she take the packet?" Olivia asked Dono, with a glance up at the flash of red now vanishing into the crowd.

Dono's smile broadened briefly to a remarkably evil grin. "Yep."

While Ivan was still trying, and failing, to calculate how to get rid of the person providing the transportation, Byerly Vorrutyer made his way around some tables and descended upon them. Damn. Worse and worse.

"Ah, Dono," By greeted his cousin. "Are you still planning on Vorsmythe's for your last stop of the night?"

"Yes. Do you need a ride too?"

"Not from here to there. I have other arrangements. I'd appreciate if you could drop me home after, though."

"Of course."

"What a long talk you had with Countess Vormuir, out there on the balcony. Chewing over old times, were you?"

"Oh, yes." Dono smiled vaguely. "This and that, you know."

By gave him a penetrating look, but Dono declined to elaborate. By asked, "Did you manage to get in to see Count Vorpinski this afternoon?"

"Yes, finally, and a couple of others too. Vortaine was no help, but at least with Olivia along he was forced to stay polite. Vorfolse, Vorhalas, and Vorpatril all declined to hear my pitch, unfortunately." Dono shot Ivan a somewhat ambiguous look from under his black brows. "Well, I'm not sure about Vorfolse. No one answered the door; he might really have not been home. It was hard to tell."

"So how's the vote tally doing?" By asked.

"Close, By. Closer than I'd ever dared to dream, to tell you the truth. The uncertainty is now making me quite sick to my stomach."

"You'll get through it. Ah . . . close on which side?" By inquired.

"The wrong one. Unfortunately. Well . . ." Dono sighed, "it will have been a great try."

Olivia said sturdily, "You're going to make history." Dono pressed her hand to his arm, and smiled gratefully at her.

Byerly shrugged, which by his standards qualified as a consoling gesture. "Who knows what might happen to turn things around?"

"Between now and tomorrow morning? Not much, I'm afraid. The die is pretty much cast."

"Chin up. There're still a couple of hours to work on the men at Vorsmythe House. Just stay sharp. I'll help. See you over there. . . ."

And so Ivan found himself not with a private opportunity to make time with Olivia, but rather, trapped with her, Dono, Szabo, and two other Vorrutyer Armsmen in the back of the late Count Pierre's official car. Pierre's was one of the few vehicles Ivan had ever encountered that could beat Miles's Regency relic for both fusty luxury and a paranoid armoring that made its best progress a sort of lumbering wallow. Not that it wasn't *comfortable*; Ivan had slept in space station hostel rooms that were smaller than this rear compartment. But Olivia had somehow ended up seated between Dono and Szabo, while Ivan shared body heat with a couple of Armsmen.

They were two-thirds of the way to Vorsmythe House when Dono, who had been staring out the canopy with little vertical lines scored between his brows, suddenly leaned forward and spoke into the intercom to his driver. "Joris, swing around by Count Vorfolse's again. We'll give him one more try."

The car lumbered around the next corner, and began to backtrack. In a couple of minutes, the apartment building containing Vorfolse's flat loomed into view.

The Vorfolse family had a remarkable record for picking the losers in every Barrayaran war of the last century, including choosing to collaborate with the Cetagandans and backing the wrong side in Vordarian's Pretendership. The somewhat morose present heir, oppressed by his ancestors' many defeats, eked out his life in the capital by renting the drafty old Vorfolse clan mansion to an enterprising prole with grandiose ambitions, and living entirely off the proceeds. Instead of the permitted squad of twenty, he kept only a single Armsman, an equally depressed and rather elderly fellow who doubled as every servant the Count had. Still, Vorfolse's apprehensive refusal to align himself with any faction or party or project, no matter how benign it appeared, at least meant he wasn't an automatic *yes* for Richars. And a vote was a vote, Ivan supposed, no matter how eccentric.

A narrow, multilevel parking garage attached to the building provided spaces for the prole residents to house their vehicles, at a stiff surcharge Ivan had no doubt. Parking space in the capital was normally leased by the square meter. Joris oozed Pierre's groundcar into the meager clearances, then suffered a check when he discovered all the ground-floor visitor parking to be taken.

Ivan, planning to stay in the comfy car with Olivia, revised his plan when Olivia jumped out to accompany Dono. Dono left Joris waiting for a space to open up, and, flanked by Olivia and his security outriders, strode out through the street-level pedestrian access and around toward the apartment building's front entrance.

Torn between curiosity and caution, Ivan trailed along. With a short gesture, Szabo left one of his men to take station by the outer door, and the second by the lift tube exit on the third floor, so that by the time they arrived at Vorfolse's flat they were a not-too-intimidating party of four.

A discreet brass tag was screwed a little crookedly to the door above the apartment's number; it read *Vorfolse House* in a script that was meant to be imposing, but, in context, succeeded mainly in being rather pathetic. Ivan was reminded of his Aunt Cordelia's frequent assertion that governments were mental constructs. Lord Dono touched the chime-pad.

After a couple of minutes, a querulous voice issued from the intercom. The little square of its vid viewer stayed blank. "What do you want?"

Dono glanced at Szabo, and whispered, "That Vorfolse?"

"Sounds like," Szabo murmured back. "It's not quavery enough to be his old Armsman."

"Good evening, Count Vorfolse," Dono said smoothly into the com. "I'm Lord Dono Vorrutyer." He gestured at his companions. "I believe you know Ivan Vorpatril, and my senior Armsman, Szabo. Miss Olivia Koudelka. I stopped by to talk to you about tomorrow's vote on my District's Countship."

"It's too late," said the voice.

Szabo rolled his eyes.

"I have no wish to disturb your rest," Dono pressed on.

"Good. Go away."

Dono sighed. "Certainly, sir. But before we depart, may I at least be permitted to know how you intend to vote on the issue tomorrow?"

"I don't care which Vorrutyer gets the District. The whole family's deranged. A plague on both your parties."

Dono took a breath, and kept smiling. "Yes, sir, but consider the consequences. If you abstain, and the vote falls short of a decision, it will simply have to be done over again. And over and over, until a majority is finally reached. I would also point out that you would find my cousin Richars a most unrestful colleague—short-tempered, and much given to factionalism and strife."

Such a long silence issued from the intercom, Ivan began to wonder if Vorfolse had gone off to bed.

Olivia leaned into the scan pickup to say brightly, "Count Vorfolse, sir, if you vote for Lord Dono, you won't regret it. He'll give diligent service to both the Vorrutyer's District and to the Imperium."

The voice replied after a moment, "Eh, you're one of Commodore Koudelka's girls, aren't you? Does Aral Vorkosigan support this nonsense, then?"

"Lord Miles Vorkosigan, who is acting as his father's voting deputy, supports me fully," Dono returned.

"Unrestful. Eh! *There's* unrestful for you."

"No doubt," said Dono agreeably. "I have noticed that myself. But how do you intend to vote?"

Another pause. "I don't know. I'll think about it."

"Thank you, sir." Dono motioned them all to decamp; his little retinue followed him back toward the lift tubes.

"That wasn't too conclusive," said Ivan.

"Do you have any idea how positive *I'll think about it* seems, in light of some of the responses I've gotten?" said Dono ruefully. "Compared to certain of his colleagues, Count Vorfolse is a fountain of liberality." They collected the Armsman, and descended the lift tube. Dono added as they reached the ground foyer, "You have to give Vorfolse credit for integrity. There are a number of dubious ways he could be stripping his District of funds to support a more opulent lifestyle here, but he doesn't choose 'em."

"Huh," said Szabo. "If *I* were one of his liege people, I'd damn well *encourage* him to steal something. It would be better than this miserable miserly farce. It's just not proper Vor. It's not good *show*."

They exited the building with Szabo in the lead, Dono and Olivia somehow walking side by side, and Ivan following, trailed by the two other Armsmen. As they passed through the pedestrian entry to the dim garage, Szabo stopped short and said, "Where the hell's the car?" He lifted his wrist comm to his lips. "Joris?"

Olivia said uneasily, "If somebody else had come in, he'd have had to take the car all the way up, back down, and around the block to let them past. No room to turn *that* car in here."

"Not without—" Szabo began. He was interrupted by a quiet buzz, seemingly out of nowhere, a sound familiar enough to Ivan's ears. Szabo fell like a tree.

"Stunner tag!" bellowed Ivan, and jumped behind the nearest pillar to his right. He looked around for Olivia, but she had dodged the other way, with Dono. Two more well-aimed stunner shots took out the other two Armsmen as they broke right and left, though one got off a wild shot with his own weapon before he went down.

Ivan, crouching between the pillar and a dilapidated groundcar, cursed his unarmed state and tried to see where the shots had come from. Pillars, cars, inadequate lighting, shadows . . . further up the ramp, a dim shape flitted from the shadow of a pier and vanished among the tightly packed vehicles.

Stunner combat rules were simple. Drop everything that moved, and sort them out later, hoping that no one harbored a bad heart condition. Dono's unconscious Armsman could supply Ivan with a stunner, if he could reach it without getting himself zapped. . . .

A voice from up the ramp whispered hoarsely, "Which way did he go?"

"Down toward the entry. Goff'll get him. Drop that damned officer as soon as you get a clear shot."

At least three assailants, then. Assume one more. At *least* one more. Cursing the tight clearances, Ivan retreated backward on his hands and knees from his stunner-bolt-stopping pillar and tried to work his way between the row of cars and the wall, edging toward the entry again. If he could make it out onto the street—

This had to be a snatch. If it had been an assassination, their attackers would have picked a much deadlier weapon, and the whole party would be well-mixed hamburger on the walls by now. In a slice of vision between two cars, away down the descending ramp to his left, a white shape moved: Olivia's party dress. A meaty thunk came from behind a pillar there, followed by a nauseating noise like a pumpkin hitting concrete. "Good one!" Dono's voice jerked out.

Olivia's mother, Ivan reminded himself, had been the boy-Emperor's *personal* bodyguard. He tried to imagine the cozy mother-daughter instruction rituals in the Koudelka household. He was pretty sure they hadn't been limited to baking cakes together.

A black-clad shape darted.

"There he goes! Get him! No, no—he's supposed to stay *conscious!*"

Running footsteps, scuffling and breathing, a thunk, a strangled yelp—praying everyone's attention would be diverted, Ivan dove for the Armsman's stunner, snatched it up, and ducked again for cover. From the ascending ramp to the right came the *whuff* of a vehicle backing rapidly and illegally down toward them. Ivan risked a peek over a car. The back doors of the battered lift van swung wildly open, as it jerked to a halt at the curve. Two men hustled Dono toward it. Dono was open-mouthed, stumbling, a look of astonished agony on his face.

"Where's Goff?" barked the driver, swinging out to look at his two comrades and their prize. "Goff!" he shouted.

"Where's the girl?" asked one of them.

The other said, "Never mind the girl. Here, help me bend him back. We'll do the job, dump him, and get out of here before she can run for help. Malka, circle around and get that big officer. He wasn't supposed to be in this picture." They pulled Dono into the van—no, only half into the van. One man pulled a bottle from his pocket, flipped off its cap, and placed it ready-to-hand on the edge of the van floor. What the hell . . . ? *This isn't a kidnapping.*

"Goff?" the man detailed to hunt down Ivan called uncertainly into the shadows, as he crouched and skittered past the cars.

The, under the circumstances, *extremely* unpleasant hum of a vibra knife sounded from the hand of the man bending over Dono. Risking everything, Ivan popped to his feet and fired.

He scored a direct hit on the fellow seeking Goff; the man spasmed, fell, and failed to move thereafter. Dono's men carried *heavy* stunners, and not without cause, apparently. Ivan only managed to wing one of the others. They both abandoned Dono and dashed behind the van. Dono fell to the pavement, and curled up around himself; with all this stunner fire flashing around, probably no worse a move than trying to run for it, but Ivan had a gruesome vision of what would happen if the van backed up.

From further up the ramp, on the far side of the van, two more stunner bolts snapped out in quick succession.

Silence.

After a moment, Ivan called cautiously, "Olivia?"

She responded from higher up the ramp in a breathless sort of little-girl voice, "Ivan? Dono?"

Dono spasmed on the pavement, and vented a moan.

Warily, Ivan stood up and started for the van. After a couple of seconds, probably to see if he would draw any more fire, Olivia rose from her cover and ran lightly down the ramp to join him.

"Where'd you get the stunner?" he inquired, as she popped around the vehicle's side. She was barefoot, and her party dress was tucked up around her hips.

"Goff." Somewhat absently, she jerked her skirts back down with her free hand. "Dono! Oh, no!" She jammed the stunner into her cleavage and knelt by the black-clad man. She raised a hand covered, sickeningly, with blood.

"Only," gasped Dono, "a cut on my leg. He missed. Oh, God! Ow, ow!"

"You're bleeding all over the place. Lie still, love!" Olivia commanded. She looked around a little frantically, jumped up and peered into the dark cavernous emptiness of the van's freight compartment, then determinedly ripped off the beige lace overskirt of her party dress. More quick ripping sounds, as she hastily fashioned a pad and some strips. She began to bind the pad tightly to the long shallow slash along Dono's thigh, to staunch the bleeding.

Ivan circled the van, collected Olivia's two victims, and dragged them back to deposit in a heap where he could keep an eye on them. Olivia now had Dono half sitting up, his head cradled between her breasts as she anxiously stroked his dark hair. Dono was pale and shaking, his breathing disrupted.

"Take a punch in the solar plexus, did you?" Ivan inquired.

"No. Further down," Dono wheezed. "Ivan . . . do you remember, whenever one of you fellows got kicked in the nuts and went over, doing sports or whatever, how I laughed? I'm sorry. I never knew. I'm *sorry* . . ."

"Sh," Olivia soothed him.

Ivan knelt down for a closer look. Olivia's first aid was doing its job; the beige lace was soaked with bright gore, but the bleeding had definitely slowed. Dono wasn't going to exsanguinate here. His assailant had sliced Dono's trousers open; the vibra-knife lay abandoned on the pavement nearby. Ivan rose, and examined the bottle. His head jerked back at the sharp scent of liquid bandage. He considered offering it to Olivia for Dono, but there was no telling what nasty additives it might be spiked with. Carefully, he recapped it, and stared around at the scene. "It seems," he said shakily, "someone was aiming to reverse your Betan surgery, Dono. Disqualify you just before the vote."

"I'd figured that out, yeah," Dono mumbled.

"Without anesthetic. I think the liquid bandage was to stop the bleeding, after. To be sure you'd live through it."

Olivia cried out in revolted horror. "That's *awful*!"

"That's," Dono sighed, "Richars, in all probability. I didn't think he'd go this far. . . ."

"That's—" said Ivan, and stopped. He scowled at the vibra knife, and stirred it with the toe of his boot. "Now, I'm not saying I approve of what you did, Dono, or of what you're trying to do. But that's just *wrong*."

Dono's hands wandered protectively to his groin. "Hell," he said in a faint voice. "I hadn't even got to try it *out* yet. I was saving myself. For once in my life, I wanted to be a virgin on my wedding night . . ."

"Can you stand up?"

"Are you joking?"

"No." Ivan glanced around uneasily. "Where'd you leave Goff, Olivia?"

She pointed. "Over by that third pillar."

"Right." Ivan went to collect him, seriously wondering where Pierre's car had gone. The thug Goff was still unconscious too, although of a subtly more disturbing limpness than the stunner victims. It was the greenish skin tone, Ivan decided, and the weird spongy lump on his head. He paused along the route, in dragging Goff to join the others, to check Szabo's wrist comm for Joris. No answer, though Szabo's pulse seemed to be bumping along all right.

Dono was stirring, but still not ready to stand. Ivan frowned, stared around, then jogged up the ramp.

Just around the next curve, Ivan found Pierre's groundcar sitting skewed a little sideways across the concrete. Ivan didn't know by what trick they'd lured Joris out of it, but the young Armsman lay in a stunned heap in front of the car. Ivan sighed, and dragged him around to dump in the rear compartment, and backed the car carefully down to the van.

Dono's color was coming back, and he was now sitting up only a little bent over.

"We have to get Dono medical attention," Olivia told Ivan anxiously.

"Yep. We're going to need all kinds of drugs," Ivan agreed. "Synergine for some," he craned his neck toward Szabo, who twitched and moaned but didn't quite claw back to consciousness, "fast-penta for others." He frowned at the heap of thugs. "You recognize any of these goons, Dono?"

Dono squinted. "Never seen 'em in my life."

"Hirelings, I suppose. Contracted through who knows how many middlemen. Could be days before the municipal guard, or ImpSec if they take an interest, get to the bottom of it all."

"The vote," sighed Dono, "will be over by then."

I don't want anything to do with this. This isn't my job. It's not my fault. But really, this was a political precedent *nobody* was going to favor. This was damned *offensive*. This was just . . . really *wrong*.

"Olivia," Ivan said abruptly, "can you drive Dono's car?"

"I think so . . ."

"Good. Help me get the troops loaded up."

With Olivia's assistance, Ivan managed to get the three stunned Vorrutyer Armsmen laid into the rear compartment with the unfortunate Joris, and the disarmed thugs hoisted rather less carefully into the back of their own van. He locked the doors firmly from the outside, and took charge of the vibra knife, the armload of illegal stunners, and the bottle of liquid bandage. Tenderly, Olivia helped Dono limp over to his car, and settled him into the front seat with his leg out. Ivan, watching the pair, blond head bent over dark, sighed deeply, and shook his head.

"Where to?" called Olivia, punching controls to lower the canopies.

Ivan swung up into the van's cab, and shouted over his shoulder, "Vorpatril House!"

Chapter Eighteen

The great Chamber of the Council of Counts had a hushed, cool air, despite the bright dapple of colored light falling through the stained glass windows high in the east wall onto the oak flooring. Miles had thought he was early, but he spotted René at the Vorbretten's District desk, arrived even before him. Miles laid out his flimsies and checklists on his own desk in the front row, and circled around the benches to René's place, second row right.

René looked trim enough in his Vorbretten House uniform of dark green piped with bittersweet orange, but his face was wan.

"Well," said Miles, feigning cheer for the sake of his colleague's morale. "This is it, then."

René managed a thin smile. "It's too close. We're not going to make it, Miles." He tapped a finger nervously on his checklist, twin to the one on Miles's desk.

Miles put a brown-booted foot up on René's bench, leaned forward with a deliberately casual air, and glanced at his papers. "It's tighter than I'd hoped it would be," he admitted. "Don't take our precount as a done deal, though. You never know who's going to change his mind at the last second and bolt."

"Unfortunately, that cuts both ways," René pointed out ruefully.

Miles shrugged, not disagreeing. He would plan for a hell of a lot more redundancy in future votes, he decided. *Democracy, faugh.* He felt a twinge of his old familiar adrenaline-pumped prebattle nerves, without the promised catharsis of being able to shoot at someone later if things went really badly. On the other hand, he was unlikely to be shot *at* here, either. *Count your blessings.*

"Did you make any more progress last night, after you went off with Gregor?" René asked him.

"I think so. I was up till two in the morning, pretending to drink and arguing with Henri Vorvolk's friends. I believe I nailed Vorgarin for you after all. Dono . . . was a harder sell. How did things go last night at Vorsmythe's? Were you and Dono able to make your list of last-minutes contacts?"

"I did," said René, "but I never saw Dono. He didn't show."

Miles frowned. "Oh? I'd understood he was going on to the party. I figured between the two of you, you'd have it in hand."

"You couldn't be in two places at once." René hesitated. "Dono's cousin Byerly was hunting all over for him. He finally went off to look for him, and didn't come back."

"Huh." If . . . no, dammit. If Dono had been, say, assassinated in the night, the chamber would be abuzz with the news by now. The Vorbarr Sultana Armsmen's grapevine would have passed it on, ImpSec would have called, something. Miles would have to have heard. Wouldn't he?

"Tatya's here." René sighed. "She said she couldn't stand to wait at home, not knowing . . . if it was still going to *be* home by tonight."

"It will be all right."

Miles walked out onto the floor of the chamber and gazed up at the in-curving crescent of the gallery, with its ornately carved wooden balustrade. The gallery was beginning to fill also, with interested Vor relatives and other people with the right or the pull to gain admittance. Tatya Vorbretten was there, hiding in the back row, looking even more wan than René, supported by one of René's sisters. Miles gave her an optimistic thumb's-up he was by no means feeling.

More men filtered into the chamber. Boriz Vormoncrief's crowd arrived, including young Sigur Vorbretten, who exchanged a polite, wary nod with his cousin René. Sigur did not attempt to stake a claim to René's bench, but sat close under his father-in-law's protective wing. Sigur was neutrally dressed in conservative day-wear, not quite daring a Vorbretten House uniform. He looked nervous, which would have cheered Miles up more if he hadn't known it was Sigur's habitual look. Miles went to his desk and assuaged his own nerves by checking off arrivals.

René wandered over. "Where *is* Dono? I can't hand off the circle to him as planned if he's late."

"Don't panic. The Conservatives will drag their feet for all of us, trying to delay things till they have all their men in. Some of whom won't be coming. I'll stand up and gabble if I have to, but meanwhile, let *them* filibuster."

"Right," said René, and returned to his seat. He laced his hands on top of his desk as if to keep them from twitching.

Blast it, Dono had twenty good Armsmen of his own. He *couldn't* have gone missing with no one to notice. A potential Count should be able to find his way to the Chamber on his own. He shouldn't need Miles to take him by the hand and lead him in. Lady Donna was famous for being fashionably late, and making dramatic entrances; Miles thought she should have dumped those habits with the rest of her baggage back on Beta Colony. He drummed his fingers on his desk, turned a little away from René's line of sight, and tapped his wrist com.

"Pym?" he murmured into it.

"Yes, m'lord?" Pym replied promptly from his station out in the parking area, guarding Miles's groundcar and, no doubt, chatting with all his opposite number Armsmen doing the same duty. Well, not quite all: Count Vorfolse always arrived alone by autocab. Except that he hadn't, yet.

"I want you to call Vorrutyer House for me and find out if Lord Dono is on his way. If there's anything holding him up, take care of it, and speed him along. All due assistance, eh? Then report back to me."

"Understood, m'lord." The tiny activation light winked out.

Richars Vorrutyer marched into the chamber, looking pugnacious in a neat Vorrutyer House uniform that already claimed his status as a Count. He arranged his notes on the Vorrutyer's District desk in the second row center, looked around the chamber, and sauntered over to Miles. The blue-and-gray fit him well enough, but, as he approached Miles's desk, Miles saw to his secret delight that the side seams showed signs of having been let out recently. Just how many years had Richars kept it hanging in his closet, awaiting this moment? Miles greeted him with a slight smile, concealing rage.

"They say," Richars growled to him in an undervoice, not concealing rage quite so well, Miles fancied, "that an honest politician is one who stays bought. It seems you don't qualify, Vorkosigan."

"You should choose your enemies more wisely," Miles breathed back.

Richars grunted. "So should you. I don't bluff. As you'll find out before this day is over." He stalked away to confer with the group of men now clustered around Vormoncrief's desk.

Miles controlled his irritation. At least they had Richars worried; he wouldn't be going out of his way to be such an ass otherwise. Where the hell was *Dono*? Miles made doodles of mercenary hand weapons in the margin of his check-list, and reflected on just how much he didn't want Richars Vorrutyer sitting back there in his blind spot for the next forty years.

The chamber was filling now, getting warmer and noisier, coming alive. Miles rose and made a circuit of the room, checking in with his Progressive allies, pausing to add a few urgent words in support of René and Dono to men he still had listed as undecided. Gregor arrived, with a minute to spare, entering from the little door to his private conference chamber in back of his dais. He took his traditional seat on his plain military camp stool, facing all his Counts, and exchanged a nod with the Lord Guardian of the Speaker's Circle. Miles broke off his last conversation, and slid onto his own bench. At the precise hour, the Lord Guardian called the room to order.

Still no sign of Dono, dammit! But the other team was short of men, too. As Miles had predicted to René, a string of Conservative Party Counts called in their two-minute speaking rights, and began handing the Circle off to one another, with lots of long, paper-shuffling pauses between speakers. All the Counts, experienced in this drill, checked chronos, counted heads, and settled in comfortably. Gregor watched impassively, allowing no sign of impatience or, indeed, any other emotion to show on his cool, narrow face.

Miles bit his lip, as his heartbeat intensified. Very like a battle, yes, this moment of commitment. Whatever he'd left undone, it was too late to fix it now. *Go. Go. Go.*

✧   ✧   ✧

A rush of anxiety clogged Ekaterin's throat when she answered the door chime and discovered Vassily and Hugo waiting on her aunt's porch. It was followed by a rush of anger at them both for so destroying her former pleasure in seeing her family. She kept herself, barely, from leaping into a gabble of protests that she *had too* followed their rules. *At least wait till you're accused.* She controlled her exploding emotions, and said uninvitingly, "Yes? What do you two want now?"

They looked at each other. Hugo said, "May we come in?"

"Why?"

Vassily's hands clenched; he rubbed one damp-looking palm on his trouser seam. He had chosen his lieutenant's uniform today. "It's extremely urgent."

Vassily was wearing his nervous, Help-I-Am-In-The-Corrupt-Capital look again. Ekaterin was strongly tempted to shut the door on them both, leaving Vassily to be killed and eaten by whatever cannibals he imagined populated Vorbarr Sultana's alleyways—or drawing rooms. But Hugo added, "Please, Ekaterin. It really is most urgent."

Grudgingly, she gave way, and motioned them into her aunt's parlor.

They did not sit. "Is Nikki here?" Vassily asked at once.

"Yes. Why?"

"I want you to get him ready to travel immediately. I want to get him out of the capital as soon as possible."

"*What?*" Ekaterin almost shrieked. "Why? *Now* what lies have you been swallowing down whole? I *have not* seen or spoken with Lord Vorkosigan except for one short visit day before yesterday to tell him I was exiled. And you agreed to that! Hugo is my witness!"

Vassily waved his hands. "It's not that. I have a new and even more disturbing piece of information."

"If it's from the same source, you're a bigger fool than I thought possible, Vassily Vorsoisson."

"I checked it by calling Lord Richars himself. I've learned a lot more about this volatile situation in the last two days. As soon as Richars Vorrutyer is voted into the Countship of the Vorrutyer's District this morning, he intends to lay a murder charge in the Council of Counts against Lord Auditor Vorkosigan for the death of my cousin. At that point, I believe the blood will hit the walls."

Ekaterin's stomach knotted. "Oh, no! The fool . . . !"

Aunt Vorthys, attracted by the raised voices, rounded the corner from the kitchen in time to hear this. Nikki, trailing her, muted his enthusiastic cry of *Uncle Hugo!* at the sight of the adults' strained faces.

"Why, hello, Hugo," said Aunt Vorthys. She added uncertainly, "And, um . . . Vassily Vorsoisson, yes?" Ekaterin had given her and Nikki only the barest outline of their previous visit; Nikki had been indignant and a little frightened. Aunt Vorthys had endorsed Miles's opinion that it would be best to wait for Uncle Vorthys's return to attempt to adjust the misunderstanding.

Hugo gave her a respectful nod of greeting, and continued heavily, "I have to agree with Ekaterin, but it only supports Vassily's worries. I can't imagine what has possessed Vorrutyer to make such a move while Aral Vorkosigan *himself* is in town. You'd think he'd at least have the sense wait till the Viceroy returned to Sergyar before attacking his heir."

"Aral Vorkosigan!" cried Ekaterin. "Do you really think *Gregor* will blithely accept this assault on one of his chosen Voices? Not to mention look forgivingly on someone trying to start a huge public scandal two weeks before his wedding . . . ! Richars isn't a fool, he's *mad*." Or acting in some kind of blind panic, but what did Richars have to be panicked about?

"For all I know, he is mad," said Vassily. "He's a Vorrutyer, after all. If this comes down to the sort of internecine street fighting among the high Vor we've seen in the past, no one in the capital is safe. And especially no one they've managed to draw into their orbits. I want to have Nikki well on his way before that vote comes down. The monorail lines could be cut, you know. They were during the Pretendership." He gestured to Aunt Vorthys for confirmation of this fact.

"Well, that's true," she admitted. "But even the open warfare of the Pretendership didn't lay waste to the whole of the capital. The fighting was quite focused, all in all."

"But there *was* fighting around the University," he flashed back.

"Some, yes."

"Did you see it?" asked Nikki, his interest immediately diverted.

"We only located it so as to go round, dear," she told him.

Vassily added a little grudgingly, "You are welcome to accompany us too, Ekaterin—and you too, of course, Madame Vorthys—or better still, take refuge with your brother." He gestured at Hugo. "It's possible, given that it's widely known you've drawn Lord Vorkosigan's attention, that you could become a target yourself."

"And hasn't it crossed your mind yet that you are being aimed by Miles's enemies at just that target? That you've let yourself be manipulated, used as their tool?" Ekaterin took a deep, calming breath. "Has it occurred to either of you that Richars Vorrutyer may *not* be voted the Countship? That it could go to Lord Dono instead?"

"That crazy woman?" said Vassily in astonishment. "Impossible!"

"Neither crazy nor a woman," said Ekaterin. "And if he becomes Count Vorrutyer, this entire exercise of yours comes to nothing."

"Not a chance I propose to bet my life—or Nikki's—on, madame," said Vassily stiffly. "If you choose to stay here and bear the risks, well, I shall not argue with you. I have an absolute obligation to protect Nikki, however."

"So do I," said Ekaterin levelly.

"But Mama," said Nikki, clearly trying to unravel this rapid debate, "Lord Vorkosigan *didn't* murder Da."

Vassily bent slightly, and gave him a pained, sympathetic smile. "But how do you know, Nikki?" he asked gently. "How does anyone know? That's the trouble."

Nikki closed his lips abruptly, and stared uncertainly at Ekaterin. She realized that he didn't know just how private his private interview with the Emperor was supposed to remain—and neither did she.

She had to admit, Vassily's anxiety was contagious. Hugo had clearly taken a fever of it. And while it had been a long time since strife among the Counts had seriously threatened the stability of the Imperium, that wouldn't make you any less dead if you had the bad luck to be caught in a cross-fire before Imperial troops arrived to shut it down. "Vassily, this close to Gregor's wedding, the capital is crawling with Security. Anyone—of any rank—who made the least move toward public disorder at the moment would find himself slapped down so fast he wouldn't know what hit him. Your fears are . . . exaggerated." She'd wanted to say, *groundless.* But what if Richars did win his Countship, and its concomitant right to lay criminal charges against his new peers in the Council?

Vassily shook his head. "Lord Vorkosigan has made a dangerous enemy."

"Lord Vorkosigan *is* a dangerous enemy!" She bit her tongue, too late.

Vassily stared at her a moment, shook his head, and turned to Nikki. "Nikki, get your things. I'm taking you away."

Nikki looked at Ekaterin. "Mama?" he said uncertainly.

What was it Miles had said about being ambushed by your habits? Time and again, she'd yielded to Tien's wishes over matters pertaining to Nikki, even when she'd disagreed with him, because he was Nikki's father, because he had a right, but most of all because to force Nikki to choose between his two parents seemed a cruelty little short of ripping him apart. Nikki had always been off-limits as a pawn in their conflicts. That Nikki had been Tien's hostage in the peculiar gender bias of Barrayar's custody laws had been a secondary consideration, though it was a wall she'd felt press against her back more than once.

But dammit, she'd never taken an oath of honor to Vassily Vorsoisson. He didn't hold half of Nikki's heart. What if, instead of player and pawn, she and Nikki were suddenly allies, beleaguered equals? What then was possible?

She folded her arms and said nothing.

Vassily reached for Nikki's hand. Nikki dodged around Ekaterin, and cried, "Mama, I don't have to go, do I? I was supposed to go to Arthur's tonight! I don't want to go with Vassily!" His voice was edged with sharp distress.

Vassily inhaled, and attempted to recover his balance and his dignity. "Madame, control your child!"

She stared at him for a long moment. "Why, Vassily," she said at last, her voice silky, "I thought you were revoking my authority over Nikki. You certainly don't seem to trust my judgment for his safety and well-being. How shall *I* control him, then?"

Aunt Vorthys, catching the nuance, winced; Hugo, father of three, also got it. She had just given Nikki tacit permission to go to his limit. Bachelor Vassily missed the curve.

Aunt Vorthys began faintly, "Vassily, do you really think this is wise—"

Vassily held out a hand, more sternly. "Nikki. Come along. We must catch the eleven-oh-five train out of North Gate Station!"

Nikki put his hands behind his back, and said valiantly, "No."

Vassily said in a tone of final warning, "If I have to pick you up and carry you, I will!"

Nikki returned breathlessly, "I'll scream. I'll tell everybody you're kidnapping me. I'll tell them you're *not* my father. And it'll all be true!"

Hugo looked increasingly alarmed. "For God's sake, don't drive the boy into hysterics, Vassily. They can keep it up for *hours*. And everybody stares at you as if you were the reincarnation of Pierre Le Sanguinaire. Little old ladies come up and threaten you—"

"Like this one," Aunt Vorthys interrupted. "Gentlemen, let me dissuade you—"

The harassed and reddening Vassily made another grab, but Nikki was quicker, dodging around the Professora this time. "I'll tell them you're kidnapping me for '*moral purposes*'!" he declaimed from behind this ample barrier.

Vassily asked Hugo in a shocked voice, "How does he know about that sort of thing?"

Hugo waved this away. "He probably just heard the phrase. Children repeat things like that, you know."

Vassily clearly didn't. A poor memory, perhaps?

"Nikki, look," said Hugo, in a voice of reason, bending a little to peer at the boy in his refuge behind the seething Professora. "If you don't want to go with Vassily, suppose you come and visit me and Aunt Rosalie, and Edie and the boys, for a little while instead?"

Nikki hesitated. So did Ekaterin. This ploy might have been made to work, with another push, but Vassily took advantage of the momentary distraction to make another grab at Nikki's arm.

"Ha! Got you!"

"Ow! Ow! Ow!" screamed Nikki.

Perhaps it was because Vassily didn't have the trained parental ear that could instantly distinguish between real pain and noise for effect, but when Ekaterin started grimly forward, he flinched back, his grip unconsciously loosening. Nikki broke away, and ran for the hall stairs.

"I'm not going!" Nikki yelled over his shoulder, scrambling up the stairs. "I'm not, I won't! You can't make me. Mama doesn't *want* me to go!" At the top he whirled to fling frantically back, as Vassily, baited into chasing him, reached the bottom, "You'll be sorry you made my mama unhappy!"

Hugo, ten years older and vastly more experienced, shook his head in exasperation and followed more slowly. Aunt Vorthys, looking very distressed and a little gray, brought up the rear. From above, a door slammed.

Ekaterin arrived, her heart hammering, in the upper hallway as Vassily bent over the door to her uncle's study and rattled the knob.

"Nikki! Open this door! Unlock it at once, do you hear me?" Vassily turned to look beseechingly at Ekaterin. "Do something!"

Ekaterin leaned her back against the opposite wall, folded her arms again, and smiled slowly. "I only know one man who was ever able to talk Nikki out of a locked room. And he isn't here."

"Order him out!"

"If you are indeed insisting on taking custody of him, Vassily, this is your problem," Ekaterin told him coolly. She let *The first of many* stand implied.

Hugo, stumping breathlessly up the stairs, offered, "Eventually, they do calm down and come out. Sooner if there's no food in there."

"Nikki," said Aunt Vorthys distantly, "knows where the Professor hides his cookies."

Vassily stood up, and stared at the heavy wood and old iron hardware. "We could break it down, I suppose," he said hesitantly.

"Not in *my* house, Vassily Vorsoisson!" Aunt Vorthys said.

Vassily gestured at Ekaterin. "Fetch me a screwdriver, then!"

She didn't move. "Find it yourself." She didn't add, *you blundering nitwit* aloud, quite, but it seemed to be understood.

Vassily flushed angrily, but bent again. "What's he doing in there? I hear voices."

Hugo bent too. "He's using the comconsole, I think."

Aunt Vorthys glanced briefly down the hallway toward her bedroom door. From which there was a door to the bath, from which there was another door into the Professor's study. Well, if Aunt Vorthys wasn't going to point out this alternate and unguarded route to the two men now pressing their ears to the door, why should Ekaterin?

"I hear two voices. Who in the world could he be calling on the comconsole?" asked Vassily, in a dismissive tone that didn't invite an answer.

Suddenly, Ekaterin thought she knew. Her breath caught. "Oh," she said faintly, "*dear.*" Aunt Vorthys stared at her.

For a hysterical moment, Ekaterin considered dashing around and diving through the alternate doors, to shut down the comconsole before it was too late. But the echo of a laughing voice drifted through her mind . . . *Let's see what happens.*

Yes. Let's.

One of Boriz Vormoncrief's allied Counts droned on in the Speaker's Circle. Miles wondered how much longer these delaying tactics could continue. Gregor was starting to look mighty bored.

The Emperor's personal Armsman appeared from the little conference chamber, mounted the dais, and murmured something into his master's ear. Gregor looked briefly surprised, returned a few words, and motioned the man off. He made a small gesture to the Lord Guardian of the Speaker's Circle, who trod over to him. Miles tensed, expecting Gregor was about to call a halt to the filibuster and command the voting to begin, but instead the Lord Guardian merely nodded, and returned to his bench. Gregor rose, and ducked through the door behind the dais. The speaking Count glanced aside at this motion, hesitated, then carried on. It might not be significant, Miles told himself; even Emperors had to go to the bathroom now and then.

Miles seized the moment to key his wristcom again. "Pym? What's up with Dono?"

"Just got a confirmation from Vorrutyer House," Pym returned after a moment. "Dono's on his way. Captain Vorpatril is escorting him."

"Only *now*?"

"He apparently only arrived home less than an hour ago."

"What was he doing all night?" Surely Dono hadn't picked the night before the vote to go tomcatting with Ivan—on the other hand, maybe he'd wanted to prove something. . . . "Never mind. Just be sure he gets here all right."

"We're on it, m'lord."

Gregor indeed returned in about the amount of time it would have taken him to take a leak. He settled back in his seat without interfering with the Speaker's Circle, but he cast an odd, exasperated, faintly bemused glance in Miles's direction. Miles sat up and stared back, but Gregor gave him no further clue, returning instead to his usual impassive expression that could conceal anything from terminal boredom to fury.

Miles would not give his adversaries the satisfaction of seeing him bite his nails. The Conservatives were going to run out of speakers very soon, unless more of their men arrived. Miles did another head count, or rather, survey of empty desks. The turnout was high today, for this important vote. Vortugalov and his deputy remained absent, as Lady Alys had promised. Also missing, more inexplicably, were Vorhalas, Vorpatril, Vorfolse, and Vormuir. Since three and possibly all four of these were votes secured and counted on by the Conservative faction, this was no loss. He began doodling a winding garland of knives, swords, and small explosions down the other margin of his flimsy, and waited some more.

" . . . one hundred eighty-nine, one-hundred-ninety, one-hundred ninety-one," Enrique counted, in a tone of great satisfaction.

Kareen paused in her task at the laboratory comconsole, and leaned around the display to watch the Escobaran scientist. Assisted by Martya, he was finishing the final inventory of recovered Vorkosigan liveried butter bugs, simultaneously reintroducing them into their newly cleaned stainless steel hutch propped open on the lab bench.

"Only nine individuals still missing," Enrique went on happily. "Less than five percent attrition; an acceptable loss for an accident of this unfortunate nature, I think. As long as I have *you*, my darling."

He turned to Martya, and reached past her to lift the jar containing the queen Vorkosigan butter bug, which had been brought in only last night by Armsman Jankowski's triumphant younger daughter. He tipped the jar and coaxed the bug out onto his waiting palm. The queen had grown some two centimeters longer during the rigors of her escape, according to Enrique's measurements, and now filled his hand and hung out over the sides. He held her up to his face, and made encouraging little kissing noises at her, and stroked her stubby wing carapaces with his fingertip. She clung on tightly with her claws, drawing blood, and hissed back at him.

"They make that noise when they're happy," Enrique informed Martya, in response to her doubtful stare.

"Oh," said Martya.

"Would you like to pet her?" He held out the giant bug invitingly.

"Well . . . why not?" Martya, too, attempted the experiment, and was rewarded by another hiss, as the bug arched her back. Martya smiled crookedly.

Privately, Kareen thought any man whose idea of a good time was to feed, pet, and care for a creature that mainly responded to his worship with hostile noises was going to get along great with Martya. Enrique, after a few more heartening chirps, tipped the queen into the steel hutch to be swarmed over, groomed, cosseted, and fed by her worker-progeny.

Kareen vented a mellow sigh, and returned her attention to deciphering Mark's scrawled notes on the cost-price analysis of their top five proposed food products. *Naming* them all was going to be a challenge. Mark's ideas tended to the bland, and there was no point in asking Miles, whose embittered suggestions all ran to things like *Vomit Vanilla* and *Cockroach Crunch.*

Vorkosigan House was very quiet this morning. Any Armsmen that Miles hadn't borrowed had gone off with the Viceroy and Vicereine to some fancy political breakfast being held in honor of the Empress-to-be. Most of the staff had been granted the morning off. Mark had seized the opportunity—and Ma Kosti, who was becoming their permanent product development consultant—and left to look at a small dairy packaging plant in operation. Tsipis had found a similar packager in Hassadar that was moving to a larger location, and had drawn Mark's attention to their abandoned facility as a possible venue for the pilot plant for bug butter products.

Kareen's morning commute to work had been short. Last night, she'd claimed her first sleepover at Vorkosigan House. To her secret joy, she and Mark had been treated neither as children nor criminals nor idiots, but with the same respect as any other pair of adults. They'd closed Mark's bedroom door on what was no one's business but their own. Mark had gone off to his tasks whistling this morning—off-key, as he apparently shared his progenitor-brother's total lack of musical talent. Kareen hummed under her breath rather more melodically.

She broke off at a tentative knock on the laboratory doorframe. One of the maidservants stood there, looking worried. In general, Vorkosigan House's service staff avoided the laboratory corridor. Some were afraid of the butter bugs. More were afraid of the teetering stacks of one-liter bug butter tubs, now lining the hallway to over head-height on both sides. All had learned that to venture down here invited being dragged into the laboratory to taste test new bug butter products. This last hazard had certainly cut down on the noise and interruptions. This young lady, as Kareen recalled, shared all three aversions.

"Miss Koudelka, Miss Koudelka . . . Dr. Borgos, you have visitors."

The maid stepped aside to admit two men to the laboratory. One was thin, and the other was . . . big. They both wore travel-rumpled suits in what Kareen recognized from life with Enrique as the Escobaran style. The thin man, youngish-middle-aged or young with middle-aged mannerisms, it was hard to tell, clutched a folder stuffed with flimsies. The big one merely hulked.

The thin man stepped forward, and addressed Enrique. "Are you Dr. Enrique Borgos?"

Enrique perked up at the Escobaran accent, a breath of home no doubt after his long, lonely exile among Barrayarans. "Yes?"

The thin man flung up his free hand in a gesture of rejoicing. "At last!"

Enrique smiled with shy eagerness. "Oh, you have heard of my work? Are you, by chance . . . investors?"

"Hardly." The thin man grinned fiercely. "I am Parole Officer Oscar Gustioz—this is my assistant, Sergeant Muno. Dr. Borgos—" Officer Gustioz placed a formal hand upon Enrique's shoulder, "you are under arrest by order of the Cortes Planetaris de Escobar for fraud, grand theft, failure to appear in court, and forfeiture of posted bond."

"But," sputtered Enrique, "this is Barrayar! You can't arrest me here!"

"Oh, yes I can," said Officer Gustioz grimly. He flopped down the file folder on the lab stool Martya had just vacated, and flipped it open. "I have here, in order, the official arrest order from the Cortes," he began to turn over flimsies, all stamped and creased and scrawled upon, "the preliminary consent for extradition from the Barrayaran Embassy on Escobar, with the three intermediate applications, approved, the final consent from the Imperial Office here in Vorbarr Sultana, the preliminary and final orders from the Vorbarra District Count's office, *eighteen* separate permissions to transport a prisoner from the Barrayaran Imperial jump-point stations between here and home, and last but not least, the clearance from the Vorbarr Sultana Municipal Guard, signed by Lord Vorbohn himself. It took me over a month to fight my way through all this bureaucratic obstruction, and I am not spending another *hour* on this benighted world. You may pack one bag, Dr. Borgos."

"But," cried Kareen, "but Mark *paid* Enrique's bail! We bought him—he's *ours* now!"

"Forfeiture of bond does not erase criminal charges, Miss," the Escobaran officer informed her stiffly. "It adds to them."

"But—why arrest Enrique and not Mark?" asked Martya, puzzling through all this. She stared down at the stack of flimsies.

"Don't make suggestions," Kareen huffed at her under her breath.

"If you are referring to the dangerous lunatic known as Lord Mark Pierre Vorkosigan, Miss, I tried. Believe me, I tried. I spent a week and a half trying to get the documentation. He carries a Class III Diplomatic Immunity that covers him for nearly everything short of outright murder. In addition, I found I had only to pronounce his last name correctly to produce the most damn-all stone wall obtuseness from every Barrayaran clerk, secretary, embassy officer and bureaucrat I encountered. For a while, I thought I was going mad. At last, I became reconciled to my despair."

"The medications helped, too, I thought, sir," Muno observed amiably. Gustioz glowered at him.

"But *you* are not escaping me," Gustioz continued to Enrique. "One bag. Now."

"You can't just barge in here and take him away, with no warning or anything!" Kareen protested.

"Do you have any idea the effort and attention I had to expend to assure that he was *not* warned?" said Gustioz.

"But we *need* Enrique! He's *everything* to our new company! He's our entire research and development department. Without Enrique, there will never be any Barrayaran-vegetation-eating butter bugs!"

Without Enrique, they would have no nascent bug butter industry—her shares would be worth nothing. All her summer's work, all Mark's frantic organizational efforts, would be flushed down the drain. No profits—no income—no adult independence— no hot slippery fun sex with Mark—nothing but debts, and dishonor, and a bunch of smug family members all lining up to say *I told you so* . . . "You can't take him!"

"On the contrary, miss," said Officer Gustioz, gathering up his stack of flimsies, "I can and I will."

"But what will happen to Enrique on Escobar?" asked Martya.

"Trial," said Gustioz in a voice of ghoulish satisfaction, "followed by jail, I devoutly pray. For a long, long time. I hope they append court costs. The comptroller is going to scream when I turn in my travel vouchers. It will be like a vacation, my supervisor said. You'll be back in two weeks, she said. I haven't seen my wife and family in two months . . ."

"But that's utterly wasteful," said Martya indignantly. "Why shut him up in a box on Escobar, when he could be doing humanity some real good *here*?" She was calculating the rapidly dwindling value of her shares too, Kareen guessed.

"That is between Dr. Borgos and his irate creditors," Gustioz told her. "I'm just doing my job. Finally."

Enrique looked terribly distressed. "But who will take care of all my poor little girls? You don't understand!"

Gustioz hesitated, and said in a disturbed tone, "There was no reference to any dependents in my orders." He stared in confusion at Kareen and Martya.

Martya said, "How did you get in here, anyway? How did you get past the ImpSec gate guard?"

Gustioz brandished his rumpled folder. "Page by page. It took forty minutes."

"He insisted on checking every one," Sergeant Muno explained.

Martya said urgently to the maid, "Where's Pym?"

"Gone with Lord Vorkosigan, miss."

"Jankowski?"

"Him, too."

"Anyone?"

"All the rest are gone with m'lord and m'lady."

"Damn! What about Roic?"

"He's sleeping, Miss."

"Fetch him down here."

"He won't like being waked up off-duty, miss . . ." the maid said nervously.

"Fetch him!"

Reluctantly, the maid started to drag herself out.

"Muno," said Gustioz, who'd watched this by-play with growing unease, "now." He gestured at Enrique.

"Yes, sir." Muno gripped Enrique by the elbow.

Martya grabbed Enrique's other arm. "No! Wait! You can't take him!"

Gustioz frowned at the retreating maid. "Let's go, Muno."

Muno pulled. Martya pulled back. Enrique cried, "Ow!" Kareen grabbed the first weaponlike object that came to her hand, a metal meter stick, and circled in. Gustioz tucked his folder of flimsies up under his arm and reached to detach Martya.

"Hurry!" Kareen screeched at the maid, and tried to trip Muno by thrusting the meter stick between his knees. The whole mob was circling around the stretching Enrique as the pivot-point, and she succeeded. Muno released Enrique, who fell toward Martya and Gustioz. In a wild attempt to regain his balance, Muno's hand came down hard on the corner of the bug hutch peeping over the lab bench.

The stainless steel box flipped into the air. One-hundred-ninety-two astonished brown-and-silver butter bugs were launched in a vast chittering madly fluttering trajectory out over the lab. Since butter bugs had the aerodynamic capacity of tiny bricks, they rained down upon the struggling humans, and crunch-squished underfoot. The hutch clanged to the floor, along with Muno. Gustioz, attempting to shield himself from this unexpected air assault, lost his grip on his folder; colorfully-stamped documents joined butter bugs in fluttering flight. Enrique howled like a man possessed. Muno just screamed, frantically batted bugs off himself, and tried to climb up on the lab stool.

"Now see what you've done!" Kareen yelled at the Escobaran officers. "Vandalism! Assault! Destruction of property! Destruction of a *Vor lord's* property, on Barrayar itself! Are you in trouble now!"

"Ack!" cried Enrique, trying to stand on tiptoe to reduce the carnage below. "My girls! My poor girls! Watch where you put your *feet*, you mindless murderers!"

The queen, who due to her weight had had a shorter trajectory, scuttled away under the lab bench.

"What are those horrible things?" yipped Muno, from his perch on the teetering stool.

"Poison bugs," Martya informed him venomously. "New Barrayaran secret weapon. Everywhere they touch you, your flesh will swell up, turn black, and fall off." She made a valiant attempt to introduce a chittering bug down Muno's trousers or collar, but he fended her off.

"They are not!" Enrique denied indignantly, from tiptoe.

Gustioz was down on the floor furiously gathering up flimsies and trying not to touch or be touched by the scattering butter bugs. When he rose, his face was scarlet. "Sergeant!" he bellowed. "Get down from there! Seize the prisoner! We leave *at once*."

Muno, overcoming his startlement and a little sheepish to be discovered in high retreat by his comrade, stepped carefully off the stool and grabbed Enrique in a more professional come-along style. He bundled Enrique out the lab door as Gustioz scooped up the last of his flimsies and jammed them back any-which-way into his folder.

"What about my one bag?" wailed Enrique, as Muno began to march him down the hall.

"I will buy you a damned toothbrush at the shuttleport," panted Gustioz, scrambling after. "And a change of underwear. I will buy them from my own pocket. Anything, but out, out!"

Kareen and her sister both hit the door at once, and had to sort themselves out. They stumbled into the corridor as their future biotech fortune was dragged away down it, still protesting that butter bugs were harmless and beneficial symbiotes. "We can't let him get away!" cried Martya.

A stack of bug butter tubs tumbled over on Kareen as she regained her balance, thumping off her head and shoulders and thudding to the floor. "Ow!" She caught a couple of the kilogram-plus cartons, and stared after the retreating men. She zeroed in on the back of Gustioz's head, hoisted a tub in her right hand, and drew back. Martya, fending off cascading tubs from the other wall, stared at her with widening eyes, nodded understanding, and took a similar grip on a missile of her own.

"Ready," gasped Kareen, "Aim—"

Chapter Nineteen

It didn't take ImpSec less than two minutes to arrive at Lord Auditor Vorthys's residence; it took them almost four minutes. Ekaterin, who'd heard the front door open, wondered if it would be considered rude of her to point this out to the stern-featured young captain who mounted the stairs, followed by a husky and humorless-looking sergeant. No matter: Vassily, watched by an increasingly irritated Hugo, was still calling blandishments and imprecations in vain through the locked door. A long silence had fallen in the room beyond.

Both men turned and stared in shock at these new arrivals. "Who did he *call*?" muttered Vassily.

The ImpSec officer ignored them both, and turned to give a polite salute to Aunt Vorthys, whose eyes widened only briefly. "Madame Professora Vorthys." He extended his nod to Ekaterin. "Madame Vorsoisson. Please forgive this intrusion. I was informed there was an altercation here. My Imperial master requests and requires me to detain all present."

"I believe I understand, Captain, ah, Sphaleros, isn't it?" said Aunt Vorthys faintly.

"Yes, ma'am." He ducked his head at her, and turned to Hugo and Vassily. "Identify yourselves, please."

Hugo found his voice first. "My name is Hugo Vorvayne. I'm this lady's elder brother." He gestured at Ekaterin.

Vassily came automatically to attention, his gaze riveted to the ImpSec Horus eyes on the captain's collar. "Lieutenant Vassily Vorsoisson. Presently assigned to OrbTrafCon, Fort Kithera River. I am Nikki Vorsoisson's guardian. Captain, I'm very sorry, but I'm afraid you've had some sort of false alarm."

Hugo put in uneasily, "It was very wrong of him, I'm sure, but it was only a nine-year-old boy, sir, who was upset about a domestic matter. Not a real emergency. We'll make him apologize."

"That's not my affair, sir. I have my orders." He turned to the door, pulled a small slip of flimsy from his sleeve, glanced at a hastily scrawled note thereupon, tucked it away, and rapped smartly on the wood. "Master Nikolai Vorsoisson?"

Nikki's voice returned, "Who is it?"

"Ground-Captain Sphaleros, ImpSec. You are requested to accompany me."

The lock scraped; the door swung open. Nikki, looking both triumphant and terrified, stared up at the officer, and down at the lethal weapons holstered at his hip. "Yessir," he croaked.

"Please come this way." He gestured down the stairs; the sergeant stepped aside.

Vassily almost wailed, "Why am I being arrested? I haven't done anything wrong!"

"You are not being arrested, sir," the ground-captain explained patiently. "You are being detained for questioning." He turned to Aunt Vorthys and added, "*You*, of course, are not detained, ma'am. But my Imperial Master earnestly invites you to accompany your niece."

Aunt Vorthys touched her lips, her eyes alight with curiosity. "I believe I shall, Captain. Thank you."

The captain nodded sharply to the sergeant, who hastened to offer Aunt Vorthys his arm down the stairs. Nikki slipped around Vassily, and grabbed Ekaterin's hand in a painfully tight grip.

"But," said Hugo, "but, but, *why*?"

"I was not told why, sir," said the captain, in a tone devoid of either apology or concern. He unbent just enough to add, "You'll have to ask when you get there, I suppose."

Ekaterin and Nikki followed Aunt Vorthys and the sergeant; Hugo and Vassily perforce joined the parade. At the bottom of the stairs Ekaterin glanced down at Nikki's bare feet and yipped, "Shoes! Nikki, where are your shoes?" A brief delay followed while she galloped rapidly around the downstairs and found one under her aunt's comconsole and the other by the kitchen door. Ekaterin clutched them both in her hand as they exited the front door.

A large, unmarked, shiny black aircar sat impressively wedged into a narrow area on the sidewalk, one corner crushing a small bed of marigolds, the other barely missing a sycamore tree. The sergeant helped both ladies and Nikki to seats in the rear compartment, and stood aside to oversee Hugo and Vassily climb in. The captain joined them. The sergeant slid into the front compartment with the driver, and the vehicle lurched abruptly into the air, scattering a few leaves and twigs and bark shreds from the sycamore. The car spun away at high speed at an altitude reserved for emergency vehicles, passing a lot closer to the tops of buildings than Ekaterin was used to flying.

Before Vassily had overcome his hyperventilation enough to even form the question, *Where are you taking us?*, and just as Ekaterin managed to get Nikki's feet stuffed into his shoes and the catch-strips firmly fastened, they arrived over Vorhartung Castle. The gardens around it were colorful and luxuriant with high summer growth; the river gleamed and burbled in the steep valley below. Counts' banners, indicating the Council was in session, snapped in bright rows on the battlements. Ekaterin found herself searching eagerly over Nikki's head for a brown-and-silver flag. Heavens, there it was, the silver leaf-and-mountain pattern shimmering in the sun. The parking lots and circles were all jammed. Armsmen in half a hundred different District liveries, brilliant as great birds, sat or leaned chatting among their vehicles. The ImpSec aircar came down neatly in a large, miraculously open space right by a side door.

A familiar middle-aged man in Gregor Vorbarra's own livery stood waiting. A tech waved a security scanner over each of them, even Nikki. With the captain bringing up the rear, the liveried man whisked them through two narrow corridors and past a number of guards whose arms and armor owed nothing to history and everything to technology. He ushered them into a small paneled room containing a holovid-conference table, a comconsole, a coffee machine, and very little else.

The liveried man circled the table, directing the visitors to stand behind chairs: "You, sir, you, sir, you young sir, you ma'am." He held out a chair only for Aunt Vorthys, murmuring, "If you would be pleased to sit, Madame Professora Vorthys." He glanced over his arrangements, nodded satisfaction, and ducked out a smaller door in the other wall.

"Where *are* we?" Ekaterin whispered to her aunt.

"I've never actually been in this room before, but I *believe* we are directly behind the Emperor's dais in the Counts' Chamber," she whispered back.

"He *said*," Nikki mumbled in a faintly guilty tone, "that this all sounded too complicated for him to sort out over the comconsole."

"*Who* said that, Nikki?" asked Hugo nervously.

Ekaterin glanced past him as the smaller door opened again. Emperor Gregor, also wearing his own Vorbarra House livery today, stepped through, smiled gravely at her, and nodded at Nikki. "Pray do not get up, Professora," he added in a soft voice, as she made to rise. Vassily and Hugo, both looking utterly pole-axed, came to military attention. He added aside, "Thank you, Captain Sphaleros. You may return to your duty station now."

The captain saluted and withdrew. Ekaterin wondered if he would ever find out why this bizarre transport duty had fallen upon him, or if the day's events would forever be a mystery to him.

Gregor's liveried man, who had followed him in, held out the chair at the head of the table for his master, who remarked, "Please be seated," to his guests as he sank down.

"My apologies," Gregor addressed them generally, "for your rather abrupt translocation, but I really can't absent myself from these proceedings just now. They may stop dragging their feet out there at any moment. I hope." He tented his hands on the table before him. "Now, if someone will please explain to me why Nikki thought he was being kidnapped against his mother's will?"

"Entirely against my will," Ekaterin stated, for the record.

Gregor raised his brows at Vassily. Vassily appeared paralyzed. Gregor added encouragingly, "Succinctly, if you please, Lieutenant."

His military discipline rescued Vassily from his stasis. "Yes, Sire," he stammered out. "I was told—Lieutenant Alexi Vormoncrief called me early this morning to tell me that if Lord Richars Vorrutyer obtained his Countship today, he was going to lay a charge of murder in Council against Lord Miles Vorkosigan for the death of my cousin Tien. Alexi said—Alexi feared that some considerable disruption in the capital would follow. I was afraid for Nikki's safety, and came to remove him to a safer location till things . . . things settled down."

Gregor tapped his lips. "And was this your own idea, or did Alexi suggest it?"

"I . . ." Vassily hesitated, and frowned. "Actually, Alexi did suggest it."

"I see." Gregor glanced up at his liveried man, standing waiting by the wall, and said in a crisper tone, "Gerard, take a note. This is the third time this month that the busy Lieutenant Vormoncrief has come to my negative attention in matters touching political concerns. Remind Us to find him a post somewhere in the Empire where he may be less busy."

"Yes, Sire," murmured Gerard. He didn't write anything down, but Ekaterin doubted he needed to. It didn't take a memory chip to remember the things that Gregor said; you just *did*.

"Lieutenant Vorsoisson," said Gregor briskly, "I'm afraid that gossip and rumor are staples of the capital scene. Sorting truth from lies supplies full-time and steady work for a surprising number of my ImpSec personnel. I believe they do it well. My ImpSec analysts are of the professional opinion that the slander against Lord Vorkosigan grew not from the events on Komarr—of which I am fully apprised—but was a later invention of a group of, hm, disaffected is too strong a term, disgruntled men sharing a certain political agenda that they believed would be served by his embarrassment."

Gregor let Vassily and Hugo digest this for a moment, and continued, "Your panic is premature. Even *I* don't know which way today's vote is going to fall out. But you may rest assured, Lieutenant, that my hand is held in protection over your relatives. No harm will be permitted to befall the members of Lord Auditor Vorthys's household. Your concern is laudable but not necessary." His voice grew a shade cooler. "Your gullibility is less laudable. Correct it, please."

"Yes, Sire," squeaked Vassily. He was bug-eyed by now. Nikki grinned shyly at Gregor. Gregor acknowledged him with nothing so broad as a wink, merely a slight widening of his eyes. Nikki hunkered down in satisfaction in his chair.

Ekaterin jumped as a knock sounded from the door to the hallway. The liveried man went to answer it. After a low conversation, he stepped aside to admit another ImpSec officer, this time a major in undress greens. Gregor looked up, and gestured him to his side. The man glanced around at Gregor's odd guests, and bent to murmur in the Emperor's ear.

"All right," said Gregor, and "All right," and then, "It's about time. Good. Bring him directly here." The officer nodded and hurried back out.

Gregor smiled around at them all. The Professora smiled back sunnily, and Ekaterin shyly. Hugo smiled too, helplessly, but he looked dazed. Gregor did have that effect on people meeting him for the first time, Ekaterin was reminded.

"I'm afraid," said Gregor, "that I am about to be rather busy for a time. Nikki, I assure you that no one is going to carry you off from your mother today." His eyes flicked to Ekaterin as he said this, and he added a tiny nod just for her. "I should be pleased to hear your further concerns after this Council session. Armsman Gerard will find you places to watch from the gallery; Nikki may find it educational." Ekaterin wasn't sure if this was an invitation or a command, but it was certainly irresistible. He turned a hand palm up. They all scrambled to their feet, except for Aunt Vorthys who was decorously assisted by the Armsman. Gerard gestured them courteously toward the door.

Gregor leaned over and added in a lower voice to Vassily, just before he turned to go, "Madame Vorsoisson has my full trust, Lieutenant; I recommend you give her yours."

Vassily managed something that sounded like *urkSire!* They shuffled out into the hallway. Hugo could not have stared at his sister in greater astonishment if she'd sprouted a second head.

Partway down the narrow hall, they had to go single file as they met the major coming back. Ekaterin was startled to see he was escorting a desperately strung-out looking Byerly Vorrutyer. By was unshaven, and his expensive-looking evening garb rumpled and stained. His eyes were puffy and bloodshot, but his brows quirked with recognition as he passed her, and he managed an ironic little half-bow at her, his hand spread over his heart, without breaking stride.

Hugo's head turned, and he stared at By's lanky, retreating form. "You know that odd fellow?" he asked.

"One of my suitors," Ekaterin replied instantly, deciding to turn the opportunity to good account. "Byerly Vorrutyer. Cousin to both Dono *and* Richars. Impoverished, imprudent, and impervious to put-downs, but very witty . . . if you care for a certain nasty type of humor."

Leaving Hugo to unravel the hint that there might be worse hazards to befall an unprotected widow than the regard of a certain undersized Count's heir, she followed the Armsman into what was evidently a private lift-tube. It carried the party to the second floor and another narrow hallway, which ended in a discreet door to the gallery. An ImpSec guard stood by it; another occupied a matching cross-fire position at the back of the gallery's far side.

The gallery overlooking the Council chamber was about three-quarters full, rumbling with low-voiced conversations among the well-dressed women and the men in green Service uniforms or neat suits. Ekaterin felt suddenly shabby and conspicuous in her mourning black, particularly when Gregor's Armsman cleared spaces in the center of the front row for them by politely, but without explanation, requesting five young gentlemen there to shift. None offered a protest to a man in *that* livery. She smiled apologetically at them as they filed out past her; they regarded her curiously in turn. She placed Nikki securely between herself and Aunt Vorthys. Hugo and Vassily sat on her right.

"Have you ever been here before?" Vassily whispered, staring around as wide-eyed as Nikki was.

"No," said Ekaterin.

"I was here once on a school tour, years ago," confessed Hugo. "The Council wasn't in session, of course."

Only Aunt Vorthys appeared undaunted by their surroundings, but then, she'd visited Vorhartung Castle's archives fairly frequently in her capacity as a historian even before Uncle Vorthys had been appointed an Imperial Auditor.

Eagerly, Ekaterin scanned the Council floor, spread out below her like a stage. In full session, the scene was colorful in the extreme, with all the Counts in the most elegant versions of their House liveries. She searched the rainbow-cacophony for a small figure in a uniform of, by comparison with some, subdued and tasteful brown and silver . . . there! Miles was just getting up from his desk, in the front row on the curve to Ekaterin's right. She gripped the balcony rail, her lips parting, but he did not look up.

It was unthinkable to call out to him, even though no one occupied the Speaker's Circle just now; interjections from the gallery were not permitted while the Council was in session, nor were anyone but the Counts and whatever witnesses they might call allowed onto the floor. Miles moved easily among his powerful colleagues, walking over to René Vorbretten's desk for some conference. However tricky it had been for Aral Vorkosigan to thrust his damaged heir into this assembly, all those years ago, they'd evidently grown used to him by now. Change *was* possible.

René, glancing up at the gallery, saw her first, and drew Miles's attention upward. Miles's face lifted toward her, and his eyes widened in a mixture of delight, confusion, and, as he took in Hugo and Vassily, concern. Ekaterin dared a reassuring wave, just a little spread of her open hand in front of her chest, quickly refolded in her lap. Miles returned her the odd lazy salute that he used to convey an astonishing array of editorial comment; in this case, a wary irony atop a deep respect. His gaze swept on to meet Aunt Vorthys's; his brows rose in hopeful inquiry, and he gave her a nod of greeting, which she returned. His lips turned up.

Richars Vorrutyer, talking to a Count in the front row of desks, saw Miles's salute of greeting and followed it up to the gallery. Richars was already wearing the blue-and-gray garb of his House, a Count's full livery, taking a lot for granted, Ekaterin thought with sharp disapproval. After a moment, recognition dawned in his eyes, and he frowned malevolently up at her. She frowned back coldly at this coauthor, at the very least, of her current crisis. *I know your type. I'm not afraid of you.*

Gregor had not yet returned to his dais from his private conference room; what were he and Byerly talking about back there? Dono, she realized as her eye inventoried the men below, was not here yet. That energetic figure would stand out in any crowd, even this one. Was there a secret reason for Richars's obnoxious confidence?

But just as a knot of alarm began to grow in her chest, dozens of faces below swiveled around toward the doors to the chamber. Directly beneath her, a party of men walked out onto the council floor. Even from this angle of view, she recognized the bearded Lord Dono. He wore a blue-and-gray Vorrutyer House cadet's uniform, near-twin to the one Richars wore, but more nicely calculated, its fittings and decorations those of a Count's heir. Disturbingly, Lord Dono was limping, moving stiffly as though in some lingering pain. To her surprise, Ivan Vorpatril strode in with them. She was less certain of the other four men, though she recognized some of their liveries.

"Aunt Vorthys!" she whispered. "Who are all the Counts with Dono?"

Aunt Vorthys was sitting up with a surprised and puzzled look on her face. "The one with the mane of white hair in the blue and gold is Falco Vorpatril. The younger one is Vorfolse, that very odd fellow from the South Coast, you know. The elderly gentleman with the cane is, good heavens, Count Vorhalas himself. The other one is Count Vorkalloner. Next to Vorhalas, he's considered the stiffest old stick in the Conservative Party. I expect they are the votes everyone was waiting for. Things ought to start to move now."

Ekaterin searched for Miles's response. His relief at the appearance of Lord Dono plainly warred with dismay at the arrival of Richars's most powerful supporters, in force. Ivan Vorpatril detached himself from the group and sauntered over to René's desk, the most peculiar smirk on his face. Ekaterin sat back, her heart thumping anxiously, trying desperately to decode the interplay below even though only a few words of the low-voiced buzz around the desks floated up intelligibly to her ear.

Ivan took a moment to savor the look of complete crogglement on his cousin the Imperial-Auditor-I'm-In-Charge-Here's face. *Yes, I bet you're having trouble figuring this one out.* He ought, he supposed, to feel guilty for not taking a moment in the frantic runnings-around early this morning to give Miles a quick comconsole call and let him know what was coming down, but really, it had been too late by then for Miles to make a difference anyway. For a few seconds more, Ivan was one step ahead of Miles in his own game. *Enjoy.* René Vorbretten was looking equally confused, however, and Ivan had no score to settle with him. Enough.

Miles looked up at his cousin with an expression of mixed delight and fury. "Ivan you idi—" he began.

"*Don't* . . . say it." Ivan raised a hand to cut him off before his rant was fairly launched. "I just saved your ass, again. And what thanks do I get, again? None. Nothing but abuse and scorn. My humble lot in life."

"Pym reported you were bringing in Dono. For which I do thank you," said Miles through set teeth. "But what the hell did you bring *them* for?" He jerked his head at the four Conservative Counts, now filing across the chamber toward Boriz Vormoncrief's desk.

"Watch," murmured Ivan.

As Count Vorhalas came even with Richars's desk, Richars sat up and smiled at him. "About time, sir! Am I glad to see you!"

Richars smile faded as Vorhalas walked past him without so much as turning his head in Richars's direction; Richars might have been invisible, for all the note Vorhalas took of this greeting. Vorkalloner, following close on the heels of his senior, at least gave Richars a frown, recognition of sorts.

Ivan held his breath in happy anticipation.

Richars tried again, as the snowy-haired Falco Vorpatril stumped by. "Glad you made it, sir . . . ?"

Falco stopped, and stared coldly down at him. In a voice which, while pitched low, penetrated perfectly well to the far ends of the floor, Falco said, "Not for long, you won't be. There is an unwritten rule among us, Richars; if you attempt any ploy on the far side of ethical, you'd damned well better be good enough at your game not to get caught. You're not good enough." With a snort, he followed his fellows.

Vorfolse, passing last, hissed furiously at Richars, "How dare you try to draw me into your schemes by using *my* premises to mount your attack? I'll see you taken apart for this." He marched on after Falco, distancing himself from Richars in every way.

Miles's eyes were wide, his lips parted in growing appreciation. "Busy night, was it, Ivan?" he breathed, taking in Dono's limp.

"You would not believe."

"Try me."

In a rapid undervoice, Ivan filled in both Miles and the startled René. "The short version is, a gang of paid thugs tried to reverse Dono's Betan surgery with a vibra knife. Jumped us coming out of Vorfolse's place. They had a nice plan for taking out Dono's Armsmen, but Olivia Koudelka and I weren't on their list. We took them instead, and I delivered them and the evidence to Falco and old Vorhalas, and let them take it from there. No one, of course, bothered to inform Richars; we left him in a news blackout. Richars may wish he had that vibra knife to use on his own throat before today is done."

Miles pursed his lips. "Proof? Richars has to have worked through multiple layers of middlemen for something like this. If he really had practice on Pierre's fiancée, he's damned sly. Laying the trail to his door won't be easy."

René added more urgently, "How fast can we get our hands on evidence?"

"It would have been weeks, but Richars's stirrup-man has turned Imperial Witness." Ivan inhaled, at the top of his triumph.

Miles tilted his head. "Richars's stirrup-man?"

"Byerly Vorrutyer. He apparently helped Richars set it all up. But things went wrong. Richars's hired goons were tailing Dono, supposed to jump him when he arrived at Vorsmythe House, but they saw what they thought was a better opportunity at Vorfolse's. By was having foaming fits when he finally caught up with me, just before dawn. Didn't know where all his pawns had gone, poor hysterical mastermind. *I'd* captured 'em. First time I've ever seen By Vorrutyer at a loss for words." Ivan grinned in satisfaction. "Then ImpSec arrived and took him away."

"How . . . unexpected. That's not how I'd placed Byerly in this game at all." Miles's brow furrowed.

"I thought you were too damned trusting. There was something about By that didn't add up for me from the beginning, but I just couldn't put my finger on it—"

Vorhalas and his cronies were now clustered around Boriz Vormoncrief's desk. Vorfolse seemed to be the most emphatic, gesturing angrily, with occasional glances over his shoulder at Richars, who was watching the scene with alarm. Vormoncrief's jaw set, and he frowned deeply. He shook his head twice. Young Sigur looked horrified; unconsciously, his hands closed protectively in his lap and his legs squeezed closed.

All the *sotto voce* debates ended when Emperor Gregor stepped out of the small doorway behind the dais, and mounted it to take his seat again. He motioned to the Lord Guardian of the Speaker's Circle, who hurried over to him. They conferred briefly. The Lord Guardian's gaze swept the room; he walked over to Ivan.

"Lord Vorpatril." He nodded politely. "Time to clear the floor. Gregor's about to call the vote. Unless you are to be called as a witness, you must take a seat in the gallery now."

"Right-ho," Ivan said genially. Miles exchanged a thumb's-up with René, and hurried back to his desk; Ivan turned for the door.

Ivan walked slowly past the Vorrutyer's District desk, where Dono was saying cheerfully to Richars, "Move over, sport. Your thugs missed, last night. Lord Vorbohn's municipal guardsmen will be waiting for you by the door with open arms when this vote is over."

With extreme reluctance, Richars shifted to the far end of the bench. Dono plopped down and crossed his booted legs—at the ankles, Ivan noted—and spread his elbows comfortably.

Richars snarled under his breath, "So you may wish. But Vorbohn will have no jurisdiction over me when I take the Countship. And Vorkosigan's party will be so convulsed over *his* crimes, they'll have no chance to throw stones at me."

"Stones, Richars, darling?" Dono purred back. "You should be so lucky. I foresee a landslide—with you under it."

Leaving the Vorrutyer family reunion behind, Ivan made for the double doors, which the guards opened for him. A job well done, by God. He glanced over his shoulder as he reached them, to find Gregor staring at him. The Emperor favored him with a faint smile, and the barest hint of a nod.

It didn't make him feel gratified. It made him feel *naked*. Too late, he recalled Miles's dictum that the reward for a job well done was usually a harder job. For a moment, in the hall beyond the chamber, he considered an impulse to turn right for the exit to the gardens instead of left for the stairs to the gallery. But he wouldn't miss this denouement for worlds. He climbed the stairs.

"Fire!" cried Kareen.

Two bug butter tubs sailed in high trajectories down the hallway. Kareen expected them to go *thud* on their targets, like rocks only a little more resilient. But all the tubs on the tops of the stacks were Mark's new bargain supply, bought *on sale* somewhere. The cheaper, thinner plastic didn't have the structural integrity of the earlier tubs. They didn't hit like rocks; they hit like grenades.

Upon impact with Muno's shoulders and the back of Gustioz's head, the rupturing tubs spewed bug butter on the walls, ceiling, floor, and incidentally the targets. Since the second barrage was already in the air before the first one landed, the surprised Escobarans turned around just in time to take the next bug butter bombs full in the chest. Muno's reflexes were quick enough to fend off a third tub, which burst on the floor, kneecapping the entire party with white, dripping bug butter.

Martya, wildly excited, was now keening in a sort of berserker howl, firing more tubs down the corridor as fast as she could grab them. The tubs didn't all rupture; some hit with quite satisfying thunks. Muno, swearing, batted down a couple more, but was baited into releasing Enrique long enough to snatch a couple of tubs from the stacks on their end of the corridor and heave them back at the Koudelka sisters. Martya ducked the tub aimed at her; the second exploded at Kareen's feet. Muno's attempt to lay down a covering fire for his party's retreat backfired when Enrique dropped to his knees and scrambled away down the hall toward his screaming Valkyriesque protectors.

"Back in the lab," cried Kareen, "and lock the door! We can call for help from there!"

The door at the far end of the corridor, beyond the Escobaran invaders, banged open. Kareen's heart lifted, momentarily, as Armsman Roic staggered through. Reinforcements! Roic was fetchingly attired in boots, briefs, and a stunner holster on backwards. "What t' hell—?" he began, but was interrupted as a last unfortunate round of friendly fire, launched unaimed by Martya, burst on his chest.

"Oh, sorry!" she called through cupped hands.

"What the *hell* is going on down here?" Roic bellowed, scrabbling for his stunner on the wrong side of his holster with hands slippery from their coating of bug butter. "You woke me up! 'S the *third time* somebody's woke me up this morning! I'd *just got to sleep.* 'Swore I'd *kill* the next sonuvabitch who woke me up—!"

Kareen and Martya clung together for a moment of pure aesthetic appreciation of the height, the breadth of shoulder, the bass reverberation, the generous serving of athletic young male Roic presented; Martya sighed. The Escobarans, naturally, had no idea who this giant naked screaming barbarian was who'd appeared between them and the only exit route they knew. They retreated a few steps backward.

Kareen cried urgently, "Roic, they're trying to kidnap Enrique!"

"Yeah? Good." Roic squinted blearily at her. "Make sure they pack all his devil bugs along with him . . ."

The panicked Gustioz tried to lunge past Roic toward the door, but caromed off him instead. They both slipped in the bug butter and went down in an arcing flurry of highly official documentation. Roic's trained, if sleep-deprived, reflexes cut in, and he attempted to pin his accidental assailant to the floor, not easy given that they were both now coated with quantities of lubricant. The faithful Muno, in a crouching scramble, braved another barrage of bug butter tubs to grab again for Enrique, making contact with a flailing arm trying to bat him away. They both skidded and went down on the treacherous footing. But Muno got a good grip on one of Enrique's ankles, and began sliding him back up the corridor.

"You can't stop us!" panted Gustioz, half under Roic. "I have a proper warrant!"

"Mister, I don't *want* to stop you!" yelled Roic.

Kareen and Martya dove to grab Enrique's arms, and pulled in the other direction. Since nobody had any traction, the contest was momentarily inconclusive. Kareen risked letting go of an arm, and hopped around Enrique to place a well-aimed kick to Muno's wrist; he howled and recoiled. The two women and the scientist scrambled over each other and back through the laboratory door. Martya got it jammed shut and locked just before Muno's shoulder banged into it from the other side.

"Comconsole!" she gasped over her shoulder to her sister. "Call Lord Mark! Call *somebody!*"

Kareen knuckled bug butter from her eyes, dove for the station chair, and began tapping in Mark's personal code.

Miles twisted his head around and watched, hopelessly out of earshot, as Ivan arrived in the front row of the gallery and ruthlessly evicted an unfortunate ensign. The younger officer, outranked and outweighed, reluctantly gave up his prime spot and went off searching for standing room in the back. Ivan slid in beside Professora Vorthys and Ekaterin. A low-voiced conversation ensued; from Ivan's expansive gestures and self-satisfied smirk, Miles guessed he was favoring the ladies with an account of his last night's heroic adventures.

Dammit, if I had been there, I could have saved Lord Dono just as well . . . Or maybe not.

Miles had recognized Ekaterin's brother Hugo and Vassily Vorsoisson, flanking her on the other side, from their brief encounter at Tien's funeral. Had they arrived in town to harass Ekaterin about Nikki again? Now, listening to Ivan, they looked thoroughly taken aback. Ekaterin said something fierce. Ivan laughed uneasily, then turned around to wave at Olivia Koudelka, just taking a seat in the back row. It wasn't fair for someone who'd been up all night to look that fresh. She'd changed clothes, from last night's party dress into a loose silk suit featuring fashionable Komarran-style trousers. Judging from her wave and smile, at least she hadn't been injured in the fight. Nikki asked an excited question, which the Professora answered; she stared down coolly and without approval at the back of Richars Vorrutyer's head.

What the devil was Ekaterin's whole family doing up there with her? How had she persuaded Hugo and Vassily to cooperate with this visit? And what hand did Gregor have in it? Miles swore he'd seen a Vorbarra Armsman, turning away after escorting them to their seats. . . . On the floor of the Council, the Lord Guardian of the Speaker's Circle banged the butt of a cavalry spear bearing the Vorbarra pennon onto the wooden plaque set in the floor for that purpose. The *clack-clack* echoed through the chamber. No time now to dash up to the gallery and find out what was going on. Miles tore his attention from Ekaterin, and prepared to tend to business. The business that would decide if they were both to be plunged into dream or nightmare. . . . The Lord Guardian called out, "My Imperial Master recognizes Count Vormoncrief. Come forward and make your petition, my lord."

Count Boriz Vormoncrief stood up, patted his son-in-law on the shoulder, and strode forward to take his place in the Speaker's Circle under the colorful windows, facing the semi-circle of his fellow Counts. He made a short, formal plea for the recognition of Sigur as the rightful heir to the Vorbretten's District, with reference to René's gene scan evidence, already circulated among his colleagues well before this vote. He made no comment on Richars's case, waiting in the queue. A shift from alliance to distancing, yes by God! Richars's face, as he listened, was set and stolid. Boriz stood down.

The Lord Guardian banged the spear butt again. "My Imperial Master recognizes Count Vorbretten. Come forward and claim your right of rebuttal to this petition, my lord."

René stood up at his desk. "My Lord Guardian, I yield the Circle temporarily to Lord Dono Vorrutyer." He sat again.

A little murmur of commentary rose from the floor. Everyone followed the swap and its logic; to Miles's deep and concealed satisfaction, Richars seemed taken by surprise. Dono stood, limped forward into the Speaker's Circle, and turned to confront the assembled Counts of Barrayar. A brief white grin flashed in his beard. Miles followed his glance up into the gallery just in time to see Olivia standing on her seat and making a sweeping thumb's-up gesture.

"Sire, My Lord Guardian, my lords." Dono moistened his lips, and launched into the formal wording of his petition for the Countship of the Vorrutyer's District. He reminded all present that they had received certified copies of his complete medical report and the witnessed affidavits to his new gender. Briefly, he reiterated his arguments of right by male primogeniture, Count's Choice, and his prior experience assisting his late brother Pierre in the administration of the Vorrutyer's District.

Lord Dono stood legs apart, hands clasped behind the small of his back in an assertive stance, and raised his chin. "As some of you know by now, last night someone attempted to take this decision from you. To decide the future of Barrayar not in this Council Chamber, but in the back streets. I was attacked; luckily, I escaped serious injury. My assailants are now in the hands of Lord Vorbohn's guard, and a witness has given evidence sufficient for the arrest of my cousin Richars for suspicion of conspiracy to commit this mutilation. Vorbohn's men await him outside. Richars will depart this chamber either into their arresting arms, or placed by you above their jurisdiction—in which case, judgment of the crime *will* fall upon you later.

"Government by thugs in the Bloody Centuries gave Barrayar many colorful historical incidents, suitable for high drama. I don't think it's a drama we wish to return to in real life. I stand before you ready and willing to serve my Emperor, the Imperium, my District, and its people. I also stand for the rule of law." He gave a grave nod toward Count Vorhalas, who nodded back. "Gentlemen, over to you." Dono stood down.

Years ago—before Miles was born—one of Count Vorhalas's sons had been executed for dueling. The Count had chosen not to raise his banner in rebellion over it, and had made it clear ever since that he expected like loyalty to the law from his peers. It was a kind of moral suasion with sharp teeth; *nobody* dared oppose Vorhalas on ethical issues. If the Conservative Party had a backbone that kept it standing upright, it was old Vorhalas. And Dono, it appeared, had just put Vorhalas in his back pocket. Or Richars had put him there for him . . . Miles hissed through his teeth in suppressed excitement. *Good pitch, Dono, good, good. Superb.*

The Lord Guardian banged his spear again, and called Richars up for his answer to Dono's petition. Richars looked shaken and angry. He strode forward to take his place in the Speaker's Circle with his lips already moving. He turned to face the chamber, took a deep breath, and launched into the formal preambles of his rebuttal.

Miles's attention was diverted by some rustling up in the gallery: more latecomers arriving. He glanced up, and his eyes widened to see his mother and father, in the row directly behind Ekaterin and the Professora, murmuring a negotiation for seats together and apologies and thanks to a startled Vor couple who instantly made way for the Viceroy and Vicereine. They'd evidently got away from their breakfast meeting in time to attend this vote, and were still formally dressed, Count Aral in the same brown-and-silver House uniform Miles wore, the Countess in a fancy embroidered beige ensemble, her red-roan hair in elaborate braids wreathing her head. Ivan craned around, looked surprised, nodded a greeting, and muttered something under his breath. The Professora, intent on hearing Richars's words, shushed him. Ekaterin hadn't looked behind her; she gripped the balcony rail and stared intently down at Richars as though willing him to pop an artery in the speech centers of his brain. But he droned on, coming to the summation of his arguments.

"That I have always been Pierre's heir is inherent in his lack of acknowledgement of any other in that place. I grant there was no love lost between us, which I always considered unfortunate, but as many of you have reason to know, Pierre was a, ah, *difficult* personality. But even he realized he could have no other successor but me.

"Dono is a sick joke of Lady Donna's, which we here have tolerated for too long. She is the very essence of the sort of galactic corruption," his glance, and his hand, flicked to mutie-Miles, as though to suggest his enemy's body was an outward and visible form of an inward and invisible poison, "against which we must fight, yes, I say fight, and I say it boldly and aloud, for our native purity. She is a breathing threat to our wives, daughters, sisters. She is an incitement to rebellion against our deepest and most fundamental order. She is an insult to the honor of the Imperium. I beg you will finish her strutting charade with the finality it deserves."

Richars glanced around, anxiously seeking signs of approval from his dauntingly impassive listeners, and continued, "With respect to

Lady Donna's feeble threat to bring her claimed attack—which might in fact have come from any quarter sufficiently outraged by her posturing—onto the floor of this chamber for judgment. I say, bring it on. And who would be her stalking horse, to lay the case before you, in that event?" He made a broad gesture at Miles, sitting at his desk with his booted feet out and listening with as little expression as he could maintain. "One who stands accused of far worse crimes himself, even up to premeditated murder."

Richars was rattled; he was trying to set off his smokescreen *way* too early. It was a smoke Miles choked on all the same. *Damn you, Richars.* He could not let this pass unchallenged here, not for an instant.

"A point of order, my Lord Guardian." Not changing his posture, Miles pitched his drawl to carry across the chamber. "I am not accused; I am slandered. There is an unsubtle legal distinction between the two."

"It will be an ironic day when *you* try to lay down a criminal accusation here," Richars parried, stung, Miles hoped, by the implied threat of countersuit.

Count Vorhalas called out from his place in the back row, "In the event, Sire, my Lord Guardian, my lords, having viewed the evidence and listened to the preliminary interrogations, I should be pleased to lay the charge against Lord Richars myself."

The Lord Guardian frowned, and tapped his spear suggestively. Historically, permitting men to start speaking out of turn had quickly led to shouting matches, fist fights, and, in prior eras when weapons scanners hadn't been available, famous melees and duels to the death. But Emperor Gregor, listening with very little expression himself, made no move to intervene.

Richars was growing yet more off balance; Miles could see it in his reddening face and heavy breathing. To Miles's shock, he gestured up at Ekaterin. "It's a bold villain who can stand unashamed while his victim's own wife looks down at him—though I suppose she could hardly look up at him, eh?"

Faces turned toward the pale black-clad woman in the gallery. She looked chilled and frightened, jerked out of her safe observer's invisibility by Richars's unwelcome attention. Beside her, Nikki stiffened. Miles sat upright; it was all he could do to keep himself from launching himself across the chamber at Richars's throat and attempting to throttle him on the spot. That wouldn't work anyway.

He was compelled to other means of combat, slower, but, he swore, more effective in the end. How dare Richars turn on *Ekaterin* in this public venue, invade her most private concerns, attempt to manipulate her most intimate relationships just to serve his power-grab?

Miles's anticipated nightmare of defense was here, now. Already he would be forced to turn his attention not just to truth but to appearances, to check every word out his mouth for its effect on the listeners who could become his future judges. Richars had put himself one-down through his botched attack on Dono; could he scramble back up over Miles's and Ekaterin's bodies? It seemed he was about to try.

Ekaterin's face was utterly still, but white around the lips. Some prudent back part of Miles's brain couldn't help making a note of what she looked like when she was *really* angry, for future reference. "You are mistaken, Lord Richars," she snapped down at him. "Not your first mistake, apparently."

"Am I?" Richars shot back. "Why else, then, did you flee in horror from his public proposal, if not your belated realization of his hand in your late husband's death?"

"That's no business of yours!"

"One wonders what pressures he has brought to bear since to gain your compliance . . ." His smarmy sneer invited the listeners to imagine the worst.

"Only if one is a damned fool!"

"Proof is where you find it, madame."

"That's your idea of proof?" Ekaterin snarled. "Fine. Your legal theory is easily demolished—"

The Lord Guardian banged his spear. "Interjections from the gallery are *not* permitted," he began, staring up at her.

Behind Ekaterin, the Viceroy of Sergyar stared down at the Lord Guardian, tapped his index finger suggestively against the side of his nose, and made a small two-fingered sweeping gesture taking in Richars below: *No; let him hang himself.* Ivan, glancing over his shoulder, grinned abruptly and swiveled back. The Lord Guardian's eyes flicked to Gregor, whose face bore only the faintest smile and little other cue. The Lord Guardian continued more weakly, "But direct questions from the Speaker's Circle may be answered."

Richars's questions had been more rhetorical, for effect, than direct, Miles judged. Assuming Ekaterin would be safely silenced by her position in the gallery, he hadn't expected to have to deal with direct answers. The look on Richars's face made Miles think of a man tormenting a leopardess suddenly discovering that the creature had no leash. Which way would she pounce? Miles held his breath.

Ekaterin leaned forward, gripping the railing with her knuckles going pale. "Let's finish this. Lord Vorkosigan!"

Miles jerked in his seat, taken by surprise. "Madame?" He made a little half-bow gesture. "Yours to command . . ."

"Good. Will you marry me?"

A kind of roaring, like the sea, filled Miles's head; for a moment, there were only two people in this chamber, not two hundred. If this was a ploy to impress his colleagues with his innocence, would it work? *Who cares? Seize the moment! Seize the woman! Don't let her get away again!* One side of his lip curled up, then the other; then a broad grin took over his face. He tilted toward her. "Why, *yes,* madame. Certainly. Now?"

She looked a little taken aback at the vision this perhaps conjured of his abandoning the chamber instantly, to take her up on her offer this very hour, before she could change her mind. Well, he was ready if she was. . . . She waved him down. "We'll discuss that later. Settle this business."

"My pleasure." He grinned fiercely at Richars, who was now gaping like a fish. Then he just grinned. *Two hundred witnesses. She can't back out now. . . .*

"So much for *that* line of reasoning, Lord Richars," Ekaterin finished. She sat back with a hand-dusting gesture, and added, by no means under her breath, "*Twit.*"

Emperor Gregor looked decidedly amused. Nikki, beside Ekaterin, was jittering with enthusiasm, mumbling something that looked like *go-go-mama.* The gallery had broken into half-choked titters. Ivan just rubbed his mouth with the back of his hand, though his eyes were narrowed with laughter. He glanced again behind Ekaterin, where the Vicereine looked as though she was choking, and the Viceroy turned a bark of laughter into a discreet cough. In a sudden flush of self-consciousness, Ekaterin shrank in her seat, hardly daring even to look at her brother Hugo or Vassily. She looked down at Miles, though, and her lips softened with a helpless smile.

Miles grinned back like a loon; Richars's blackest glare in his direction slid off him as though deflected by a force field. Gregor made a brief gesture to the Lord Guardian to move things along.

Richars had entirely lost the thread of his argument by now, as well as the momentum, center stage, and the sympathy of his audience. Anyone's attention that wasn't fixed on Ekaterin was aimed at Miles, with an amusement grown impatient with Richars's ugly drama. Richars finished weakly and incoherently, and left the Circle.

The Lord Guardian called the voice vote to begin. Gregor, who fell early in the roll as Count Vorbarra, voted *Pass* rather than an abstention, reserving the right to cast his ballot at the end, should a deciding vote be required, an Imperial privilege he didn't often invoke. Miles started to track the vote, but by the time the roll came around to him, had taken to jotting repeated iterations of *Lady Ekaterin Nile Vorkosigan* intertwined with *Lord Miles Naismith Vorkosigan* in his fanciest handwriting down the margins of his flimsy. René Vorbretten, grinning, had to prompt him to the correct response, which got another muffled laugh from the gallery.

No matter: Miles could tell when the magic majority of thirty-one had passed by the rustling that grew on floor and gallery, as others keeping the tally concluded that Dono was in. Richars was left with a poor showing of some dozen votes, as several of his counted-upon Conservative supporters called abstentions in the wake of Count Vorhalas's sturdy vote for Lord Dono. Dono's final total was thirty-two, not exactly an overwhelming victory, but with a vote to spare above the minimum for binding decision. Gregor, with obvious satisfaction, cast the Vorbarra vote as an abstention, affecting the outcome not at all.

A stunned-looking Richars climbed to his feet at the Vorrutyer's District desk, and cried desperately, "Sire, I appeal this decision!" Really, he had no other choice; tying the case up for another round was the only move that could now save him from the municipal guard lying patiently in wait for him outside the chamber.

"Lord Richars," Gregor responded formally, "I decline to hear your appeal. My Counts have spoken; their decision stands." He nodded to the Lord Guardian, who had the chamber's sergeants-at-arms swiftly escort Richars out the doors to his waiting fate before he could recover from his shock sufficiently to burst into futile protests or physical resistance. Miles's teeth clenched in savage contentment. *Cross me, will you, Richars? You're done.*

Well . . . really, Richars had done himself, when he'd struck at Dono in the middle of the night and missed. Thanks were due to Ivan, to Olivia, and, in a backhanded way Miles supposed, to Richars's secret supporter Byerly. With friends like By, who needed enemies? And yet . . . there was something about Ivan's version of last night's events that just didn't add up right. *Later. If an Imperial Auditor can't get to the bottom of that one, no one can.* He'd start by interrogating Byerly, now presumably safely in custody of ImpSec. Or better still, maybe with . . . Miles's eyes narrowed, but he had to give over the line of thought as Dono rose again to his feet.

Count Dono Vorrutyer entered the Speaker's Circle to give calm thanks to his new colleagues, and to formally return the speaker's right to René Vorbretten. With a small, very satisfied smile, he returned to the Vorrutyer's District desk and took sole and undisputed possession. Miles was trying very hard not to crank his head over his shoulder and stare up into the gallery, but he did keep stealing little glances up Ekaterin's way. So it was he caught the moment when his mother finally leaned forward between Ekaterin and Nikki to convey her first greetings of the morning.

Ekaterin swiveled, and turned pale. Both her future parents-in-law smiled at her in perfect delight, and exchanged, Miles trusted, suitably enthusiastic welcomes.

The Professora turned too, and made some exclamation of surprise; she, however, followed it up by a handshake with the Vicereine exhibiting all the air of some secret sisterhood revealed. Miles was slightly unnerved by the older ladies' attitude of cheerful maternal conspiracy. Had intelligence been flowing in a hidden channel between their two households all this time? *What has my mother been saying about me?* He thought about trying to debrief the Vicereine later. Then he thought better of the idea.

Viceroy Vorkosigan too extended his hand, somewhat awkwardly, over Ekaterin's shoulder, and gripped her hand warmly. He glanced down past her at Miles, smiled, and made some comment that Miles was just as glad he couldn't hear. Ekaterin rose gracefully to the challenge, naturally, and introduced her brother and a nicely stunned-looking Vassily all round. Miles made the instant decision that if Vassily tried to give Ekaterin any more trouble about Nikki, Miles would throw him ruthlessly and without compunction to the Vicereine for a dose of Betan therapy that would make his head spin.

The riveting pantomime was alas interrupted when René Vorbretten rose to take his place in the Speaker's Circle. The occupants of the gallery turned their attention back to the floor of the Council. With Ekaterin's warm eyes upon him, Miles sat up and tried to look busy and effective, or at least attentive. He was sure he didn't fool his father, who knew damned well that at this point in a normal Council vote it was all over but the posturing.

René made a valiant attempt to pull his speech together, not easy after the previous rousing events. He stood by his record of ten years' faithful service in his Countship, and his grandfather's before him, and drew his colleagues' attention to his late father's military career and death in battle in the War of the Hegen Hub. He made a dignified plea for his reconfirmation, and stood down, his smile strained.

Again, the Lord Guardian called the roll, and again, Gregor passed rather than abstaining. This time, Miles managed to follow the tally. In a firm voice, Count Dono cast his very first vote ever in the name of the Vorrutyer's District.

Sigur did better than Richars's debacle, but not quite good enough; René's count hit thirty-one at almost the very end of the call. There it stood. Gregor abstained, having a deliberately null effect on the outcome. Count Vormoncrief rather perfunctorily called his appeal, and to no one's wonder, Gregor declined to hear it. Vormoncrief and a surprisingly relieved-looking Sigur rose to a much better showing in defeat than Richars had, going up to shake René's hand. René took the Circle again to briefly thank his colleagues, and returned it to the Lord Guardian. The Lord Guardian tapped his spear on the plank, and declared the session closed. Chamber and gallery broke into a swirl of motion and noise.

Miles restrained himself from leaping across tables and chairs and over the backs of his crowd of colleagues to get up to the gallery only because the family party there rose themselves, and began to make their way up the stairs toward the back doors. Surely his mother and father could be relied upon to pilot Ekaterin down here to him? He found himself trapped anyway in a crowd of Counts offering him a barrage of congratulations, comments, and jokes. He barely heard, processing them all with an automatic *Thank you . . . thank you,* occasionally entirely at odds with what had actually been said to him.

At last, he heard his father call his name. Miles's head snapped around; such was the Viceroy's aura that the crowd seemed to melt away between them. Ekaterin peered shyly into the mob of uniformed men from between her formidable outriders. Miles strode over to her, and gripped her hands painfully hard, searching her face, *Is it true, is it real?*

She grinned back, idiotically, beautifully, *Yes, oh, yes.*

"You want a leg up?" Ivan offered him.

"Shut up, Ivan," Miles said over his shoulder. He glanced around at the nearest bench. "D'you mind?" he whispered to her.

"I believe it is customary . . ."

His grin broadened, and he jumped up on it, wrapped her in his arms, and gave her a blatantly possessive kiss. She embraced him back, just as hard, shaking a little.

"Mine to me. Yes," she whispered fiercely in his ear.

He hopped back down, but did not release her hand.

Nikki, almost eye to eye with him, stared at Miles measuringly. "You *are* going to make my mama *happy*, aren't you?"

"I'll surely try, Nikki." He returned Nikki a serious nod, with all his heart. Gravely, Nikki nodded back, as if to say, *It's a deal.*

Olivia, Tatya, and René's sister arrived, fighting their way through the departing crowd, to pounce on René and Dono. Panting in their wake came a man in Count's livery of carmine and green. He stopped short and stared around the chamber in dismay, and moaned, "Too late!"

"Who's that?" Ekaterin whispered to Miles.

"Count Vormuir. He seems to have missed the session."

Count Vormuir staggered off toward his desk on the far side of the chamber. Count Dono watched him go by with a little smile.

Ivan drifted up to Dono, and said in an undervoice, "All right, I have to know. How'd you sidetrack Vormuir?"

"I? I had nothing to do with it. However, if you must know, I believe he spent the morning having a reconciliation with his Countess."

"All morning? At his age?"

"Well, she had some assistance from a nice little Betan aphrodisiac. I believe it can extend a man's attention span for *hours*. No nasty side effects, either. Now you're getting older, Ivan, you might wish to check it out."

"Got any more?"

"Not I. Talk with Helga Vormuir."

Miles turned to Hugo and Vassily, his smile stiffening just a shade. Ekaterin gripped his hand harder, and he returned a reassuring squeeze. "Good morning, gentlemen. I'm glad you could make this historic Council session. Would you be pleased to join us all for lunch at Vorkosigan House? I feel sure we have some matters to discuss more privately."

Vassily seemed well on his way to permanently stunned, but he managed a nod and a mumbled *thank you*. Hugo eyed the grip between Miles and Ekaterin, and his lips twisted up in a bemused acquiescence. "Perhaps that would be a good idea, Lord Vorkosigan. Seeing as how we are to, um, become related. I believe that betrothal had enough witnesses to be binding. . . ."

Miles tucked Ekaterin's hand in his arm, and pulled her close. "So I trust."

The Lord Guardian of the Speaker's Circle made his way over to their group. "Miles. Gregor wishes to see you, and this lady, before you go." He gave Ekaterin a smiling nod. "He said something about a task in your Auditor's capacity . . ."

"Ah." Not loosening his grip on her hand, Miles towed Ekaterin through the thinning crowd to the dais, where Gregor was dealing with several men who were seizing the moment to present concerns to his Imperial attention. He fended them off and turned to Miles and Ekaterin, stepping down over the dais.

"Madame Vorsoisson." He nodded to her. "Do you think you will require any further assistance in dealing with your, er, domestic trouble?"

She smiled gratefully at him. "No, Sire. I think Miles and I can handle it from here, now that the unfortunate political aspect has been removed."

"I had that impression. Congratulations to you both." His mouth was solemn, but his eyes danced. "Ah." He beckoned to a secretary, who drew an official-looking document, two pages of calligraphy all stamped and sealed, from an envelope. "Here, Miles . . . I see Vormuir finally made it. I'll let you hand this off to him."

Miles glanced over the pages, and grinned. "As discussed. My pleasure, Sire."

Gregor flashed a rare smile at them both, and escaped his courtiers by ducking back through his private door.

Miles reordered the pages, and sauntered over to Vormuir's desk.

"Something for you, Count. My Imperial Master has considered your petition for the confirmation of your guardianship of all your lovely daughters. It is herewith granted."

"Ha!" said Vormuir triumphantly, fairly snatching the documents from Miles. "What did I say! Even the Imperial lawyers had to knuckle under to ties of blood, eh? Good! Good!"

"Enjoy." Miles smiled, and drew Ekaterin rapidly away.

"But Miles," she whispered, "does that mean Vormuir wins? He gets to carry on that dreadful child-assembly-line of his?"

"Under certain conditions. Step along—we really want to be out of the chamber before he gets to page two . . ."

Miles gestured his lunch guests out into the great hall, murmuring rapid instructions into his wristcom to have Pym bring up the car. The Viceroy and Vicereine excused themselves, saying they would be along later after they had a short chat with Gregor.

All paused, startled, as from the chamber, a voice echoed in a sudden howl of anguish.

"Dowries! *Dowries!* A hundred and eighteen *dowries* . . ."

"Roic," said Mark ominously, "why are these trespassers still *alive*?"

"We can't go round just shooting casual visitors, m'lord," Roic attempted to excuse himself.

"Why not?"

"This isn't the Time of Isolation! Besides, m'lord," Roic nodded toward the bedraggled Escobarans, "they do seem to have a proper warrant."

The smaller Escobaran, who'd said his name was Parole Officer Gustioz, held up a wad of sticky flimsies as evidence, and shook it meaningfully, spattering a few last white drops. Mark stepped back, and carefully flicked the stray spot from the front of his good black suit. All three men appeared to have been recently dipped headfirst into a vat of yogurt. Studying Roic, Mark was put dimly in mind of the legend of Achilles, except that his bug butter marinade seemed to extend to both heels.

"We'll see." If they had hurt Kareen . . . Mark turned, and knocked on the locked laboratory door. "Kareen? Martya? Are you all right in there?"

"Mark? Is that you?" Martya's voice came back though the door. "At last!"

Mark studied the dents in the wood, and frowned, narrow-eyed, at the two Escobarans. Gustioz recoiled slightly, and Muno inhaled and tensed. Scraping noises, as of large objects being dragged back from the entryway, emanated from the lab. After another moment, the lock tweetled, and the door stuck, then was yanked open. Martya poked her head through. "Thank heavens!"

Anxiously, Mark pressed past her to find Kareen. She almost fell into his offered embrace, then they both thought better of it. Though not as well-coated as the men, her hair, vest, shirt and trousers were liberally splattered with bug butter. She bent, carefully, to greet him with a reassuring kiss instead. "Did they hurt you, love?" Mark demanded.

"No," she said a bit breathlessly. "We're all right. But Mark, they're trying to take Enrique away! The whole business will go down the toilet without him!"

Enrique, very disheveled and gummy, nodded frightened confirmation.

"Sh, sh. I'll straighten things out." Somehow . . .

She ran a hand through her hair, half her blond curls standing wildly upright from the bug butter mousse, her chest rising and falling with her breathing. Mark had spent most of the morning finding the most remarkably obscene associations triggered in his mind by dairy packaging equipment. He'd kept his mind on his task only by promising himself an afternoon nap, not alone, when he'd got home. He'd had it all planned out. The romantic scenario hadn't included Escobarans. Dammit, if *he* had Kareen and a dozen tubs of bug butter, he would find more interesting things to do than rub it in her hair. . . . And so he did, and so he might, but first he had to get rid of these bloody unwelcome Escobaran skip-tracers.

He walked back out into the corridor, and said to them, "Well, you can't take him. In the first place, I paid his bail."

"Lord Vorkosigan—" began the irate Gustioz.

"Lord Mark," Mark corrected instantly.

"Whatever. The Escobaran Cortes does not, as you seem to think, engage itself in the slave trade. However it's done on this benighted planet, on Escobar a bond is a guarantee of court appearance, not some kind of human meat market transaction."

"It is where I come from," Mark muttered.

"He's Jacksonian," Martya explained. "Not Barrayaran. Don't be alarmed. He's getting over it, mostly."

Possession was nine-tenths of . . . something. Until he was certain he could get Enrique back, Mark was loath to let him out of his sight. There had to be some way to legally block this extradition. *Miles* would likely know, but . . . Miles had made no secret of how he felt about butter bugs. Not a good choice of advisors. But the Countess had bought shares . . . "Mother!" said Mark. "Yes. I want you to at least wait till my mother gets home and can talk to you."

"The Vicereine is a very famous lady," said Gustioz warily, "and I would be honored to be presented to her, some other time. We have an orbital shuttle to catch."

"They go every hour. You can get the next one." Mark just bet the Escobarans would prefer not to encounter the Viceroy and Vicereine. And how long had they been watching Vorkosigan House, to seize this unpopulated moment to make their snatch?

Somehow—probably because Gustioz and Muno were good at their job—Mark found that the whole conversation was moving gently and inexorably down the hallway. They left a sort of slime trail behind them, as if a herd of monstrous snails were migrating through Vorkosigan House. "I must certainly examine your documentation."

"My documentation is entirely in order," Gustioz declared, clutching what looked like a giant spit-wad of flimsies to his glutinous chest as he began to climb the stairs. "And in any case, it has nothing whatever to do with *you!*"

"The hell it doesn't. I posted Dr. Borgos's bond; I have to have some legal interest. I paid for it!"

They reached the dining room; Muno had somehow wrapped a ham hand around Enrique's upper arm. Martya, frowning at him, took preemptive possession of the scientist's other arm. Enrique's look of alarm doubled.

The argument continued, at rising volume, through several antechambers. In the black-and-white tiled entry hall, Mark dug in his heels. He nipped around in front of the pack and stood between Enrique and the door, spread-legged and bulldoggish, and snarled, "If you've been after Enrique for two bloody months, Gustioz, another half hour can make no difference to you. You *will* wait!"

"If you dare to impede me in the legal discharge of my duties, I will find some way to charge you, I guarantee it!" Gustioz snarled back. "I don't care who you're related to!"

"You start a brawl in Vorkosigan House, and you'll damned well find it matters very much who I'm related to!"

"You tell him, Mark!" Kareen cried.

Enrique and Martya added their voices to the uproar. Muno took a tighter grip on his prisoner, and eyed Roic warily, but Kareen and Martya more warily. As long as the reddening Gustioz was still bellowing, Mark reasoned, he had him blocked; when he took a deep breath and switched to forward motion, it would then descend to the physical, and then Mark was not at all sure who would be in control anymore. Somewhere in the back of Mark's head, Killer whined and scratched like an impatient wolf.

Gustioz took a deep breath, but suddenly stopped yelling. Mark tensed, dizzy with the loss of center/self/safety as the *Other* started to surge forward.

Everybody else stopped yammering, too. In fact, the noise died away as though someone had cut the power line. A breath of warm summer air stirred the hairs on the back of Mark's neck as the double doors, behind him, swung wide. He wheeled.

Framed in the doorway, a large party of persons paused in astonishment. Miles, resplendent in full Vorkosigan House livery, stood in the center with Ekaterin Vorsoisson on his arm. Nikki and Professora Vorthys flanked the couple on one side. On the other, two men Mark didn't know, one in lieutenant's undress greens and the other a stoutish fellow in civvies, goggled at the butter-beslimed arguers. Pym stared over Miles's head.

"Who is that?" whispered Gustioz uneasily. And there just wasn't any question which *who* he referred to.

Kareen snapped back under her breath, "Lord Miles Vorkosigan. *Imperial Auditor* Lord Vorkosigan! Now you've done it!"

Miles's gaze traveled slowly over the assembled multitude: Mark, Kareen and Martya, the stranger-Escobarans, Enrique—he winced a little—and up and down the considerable length of Armsman Roic. After a long, long moment, Miles's teeth unclenched.

"Armsman Roic, you appear to be out of uniform."

Roic stood to attention, and swallowed. "I'm . . . I was off-duty. M'lord."

Miles stepped forward; Mark wished to hell he knew how Miles did it, but Gustioz and Muno automatically braced too. Muno didn't let go of Enrique, though.

Miles gestured at Mark. "This is my brother, Lord Mark. And Kareen Koudelka, and her sister Martya. Dr. Enrique Borgos, from Escobar, my brother's, um, houseguest." He indicated the group of people who'd trailed him in. "Lieutenant Vassily Vorsiosson. Hugo Vorvayne," he nodded at the stoutish man, "Ekaterin's *brother*." His emphasis supplied the undertext, *This had better not be the sort of screwup it looks like.* Kareen winced.

"Everyone else, you know. I'm afraid I haven't met these other two gentlemen. Are your visitors, by chance, on their way out, Mark?" Miles suggested gently.

The dam broke; half a dozen people simultaneously began to explain, complain, excuse, plea, demand, accuse, and defend. Miles listened for a couple of minutes—Mark was uncomfortably reminded of how appallingly smoothly his progenitor-brother handled the multitracking inputs of a combat command helmet— then, at last, flung up a hand. Miraculously, he got silence, barring a few trailing words from Martya.

"Let me see if I have this straight," he murmured. "You two gentlemen," he nodded at the slowly drying Escobarans, "wish to take Dr. Borgos away and lock him up? Forever?"

Mark cringed at the hopeful tone in Miles's voice.

"Not forever," Parole Officer Gustioz admitted regretfully. "But certainly for a good long time." He paused, and held out his wad of flimsies. "I have all the proper orders and warrants, sir!"

"Ah," said Miles, eyeing the sticky jumble. "Indeed." He hesitated. "You will, of course, permit me to examine them."

He excused himself to the mob of people who'd accompanied him, gave a squeeze to Ekaterin's hand—wait a minute, hadn't they been not talking to each other? Miles had walked around all day yesterday in a dark cloud of negative energy like a black hole in motion; just looking at him had given Mark a headache. Now, beneath that heavy layer of irony, he frigging *glowed*. What the hell was happening here? Kareen, too, eyed the pair with growing surmise.

Mark abandoned this puzzle temporarily as Miles beckoned Gustioz to a side table beneath a mirror. He plucked the flower arrangement from it and handed it off to Roic, who scrambled to receive it, and had Gustioz lay down his extradition documents in a pile.

Slowly, and Mark had not the least doubt Miles was using every theatrical trick to buy time to think, he leafed gingerly through them. The entire audience in the entry hall watched him in utter silence, as if enspelled. He carefully touched the documents only with his fingertips, with an occasional glance up at Gustioz that had the Escobaran squirming in very short order. Every once in a while he had to pick up a couple of flimsies and gently peel them apart. "Mm-hm," he said, and "Mm-hm," and "All eighteen, yes, very good."

He came to the end, and stood thoughtfully a moment, his fingers just touching the pile, not releasing them back to the hovering Gustioz. He glanced up questioningly under his eyebrows at Ekaterin. She gazed rather anxiously back at him, and smiled wryly.

"Mark," he said slowly. "You did pay Ekaterin for her design work in shares, not cash, as I understand?"

"Yes," said Mark. "And Ma Kosti too," he hastened to point out.

"And me!" Kareen put in.

"And me!" added Martya.

"The company's been a little cash-strapped," Mark offered cautiously.

"Ma Kosti too. Hm. Oh, dear." Miles stared off into space a moment, then turned and smiled at Gustioz.

"Parole Officer Gustioz."

Gustioz stood upright, as if to attention.

"All the documents you have here do indeed appear to be legal and in order."

Miles picked the stack up between thumb and forefinger, and returned them to the officer's grasp. Gustioz accepted them, smiled, and inhaled.

"However," Miles continued, "you are missing one jurisdiction. Quite a critical one: the Imp Sec gate guard should not have let you in here without it. Well, the boys are soldiers, not lawyers; I don't think the poor corporal should be reprimanded. I will have to tell General Allegre to make sure it's part of their briefing in future, though."

Gustioz stared at him in horror and disbelief. "I have permissions from the Empire—the planetary local space—the Vorbarra District—and the City of Vorbarr Sultana. What other jurisdiction *is* there?"

"Vorkosigan House is the official residence of the Count of the Vorkosigan's District," Miles explained to him in a kindly tone. "As such, its grounds are considered Vorkosigan District soil, very like an embassy's. To take this man *from Vorkosigan House*, in the city of

Vorbarr Sultana, in the Vorbarra District, on Barrayar, in the Imperium, you need all those," he waved at the tacky pile, "and also an extradition authorization, an order in the Count's Voice—just like this one you have here for the Vorbarra's District—from the Vorkosigan's District."

Gustioz was trembling. "And where," he said hoarsely, "can I find the nearest Vorkosigan's District Count's Voice?"

"The nearest?" said Miles cheerily. "Why, that would be me."

The Parole Officer stared at him for a long moment. He swallowed. "Very good, sir," he said humbly, his voice cracking. "May I please have an order of extradition for Dr. Enrique Borgos from, the, the Count's Voice?"

Miles looked across at Mark. Mark stared back, his lips twisting. *You son of a bitch, you're enjoying every second of this. . . .*

Miles vented a long, rather regretful sigh—the entire audience swayed with it—and said briskly, "No. Your application is denied. Pym, please escort these gentlemen off my premises, then inform Ma Kosti that we will be sitting, um," his gaze swept the entry hall, "ten for lunch, as soon as possible. Fortunately, she likes a challenge. Armsman Roic . . ." He stared at the young man, still clutching the flowers, who stared back in pitiful panic. Miles just shook his head, "Go get a *bath*."

Pym, tall, sternly middle-aged, and in full uniform, advanced intimidatingly upon the Escobarans, who broke before him, and weakly let themselves be cowed out the doors.

"He'll have to leave this house sometime, dammit!" Gustioz shouted over his shoulder. "He can't hole up in here forever!"

"We'll fly him down to the District in the Count's official aircar," Miles called back in cheery codicil.

Gustoiz's inarticulate cry was cut off by the doors swinging shut.

"The butter bug project is really very fascinating," said Ekaterin brightly to the two men who'd come in with her and Miles. "You should see the lab."

Kareen signaled a frantic negative. "Not now, Ekaterin!"

Miles passed a grimly warning eye over Mark, and gestured his party in the opposite direction. "In the meantime, perhaps you would enjoy seeing Vorkosigan House's library. Professora, would you be so kind as to point out some of its interesting historical aspects to Hugo and Vassily, while I take care of a few things? Go with your aunt, Nikki. Thank you so much . . ." He held onto

Ekaterin's hand, keeping her by him, as the rest of the party shuffled off.

"Lord Vorkosigan," cried Enrique, his voice quavering with relief, "I don't know how I can ever repay you!"

Miles held up a hand, dryly, to cut him off in midlaunch. "I'll think of something."

Martya, a little more alive to Miles's nuances than Enrique, smiled acerbically and took the Escobaran by the hand. "Come on, Enrique. I think maybe we'd better start working off your debt of gratitude by going down and cleaning up the lab, don't you?"

"Oh! Yes, of course . . ." Firmly, she hauled him off. His voice drifted back, "Do you think he'll like the butter bugs *Ekaterin* designed . . . ?"

Ekaterin smiled down fondly at Miles. "Well played, love."

"Yes," said Mark gruffly. He found himself staring at his boots. "I know how you feel about this whole project. Um . . . thanks, eh?"

Miles reddened slightly. "Well . . . I couldn't risk offending my cook, y'know. She seems to have adopted the man. It's the enthusiastic way he eats my food, I suppose."

Mark's brows lowered in sudden suspicion. "*Is* it true that a Count's Residence is legally a part of his District? Or did you just make that up on the spot?"

Miles grinned briefly. "Look it up. Now if you two will excuse us, I think I'd better go spend some time calming the fears of my in-laws-to-be. It's been a trying morning for them. As a personal favor, dear brother, could you *please* refrain from springing any more crises upon me, just for the rest of today?"

"In-laws-to . . . ?" Kareen's lips parted in thrilled delight. "Oh, Ekaterin, good! Miles, you—you rat! When did this happen?"

Miles grinned, a real grin this time, not playing to the house. "She asked me, and I said yes." He glanced up more slyly at Ekaterin, and went on, "I had to set her a good example, after all. You see, Ekaterin, that's how a proposal *should* be answered—forthright, decisive, and above all, positive!"

"I'll keep it in mind," she told him. She was poker-faced, but her eyes were laughing as he led her off toward the library.

Kareen, watching them go, sighed in romantic satisfaction, and leaned into Mark. All right, so this stuff was contagious. This was a problem? Screw the black suit. He slipped an arm around her waist.

Kareen ran a hand through her hair. "I want a shower."

"You can use mine," Mark offered instantly. "I'll scrub your back . . ."

"You can rub everything," she promised him. "I think I pulled some muscles in the tug-of-Enrique."

By damn, he might salvage this afternoon yet. Smiling fondly, he turned with her toward the staircase.

At their feet, the queen Vorkosigan-liveried butter bug scuttled out of a shadow and waddled quickly across the black-and-white tiles. Kareen yipped, and Mark dove after the huge bug. He skidded to a halt on his stomach under the side table by the wall just in time to see the silver flash of her rear end slide out of sight between the baseboard and a loose paving stone. "God *damn* but those things can flatten out! Maybe we ought to get Enrique to make them, like, taller or something." Dusting his jacket, he climbed back to his feet. "She went into the wall." Back to her nest in the walls somewhere, he feared.

Kareen peered doubtfully under the table. "Should we tell Miles?"

"No," said Mark decisively, and took her hand to mount the stairs.

Epilogue

From Miles's point of view, the two weeks to the Imperial wedding sped past, though he suspected that Gregor and Laisa were running on a skewed relativistic time-distortion in which time went slower but one aged faster. He manufactured appropriate sympathetic noises whenever he encountered Gregor, agreeing that this social ordeal was a terrible burden, but, truly, one that everyone must bear, a commonality of the human condition, chin up, soldier on. Inside his own head, a continuous counterpoint ran in little popping bubbles, *Look! I'm engaged! Isn't she pretty?* She *asked* me. *She's smart, too. She's going to marry* me. *Mine, mine, all mine. I'm engaged! To be married! To this woman!* an effervescence that emerged, he trusted, only as a cool, suave smile.

He did arrange to dine over at the Vorthys's three times, and have Ekaterin and Nikki to meals at Vorkosigan House twice, before the wedding week hit and all his meals—even breakfasts, good God— were bespoken. Still, his timetable was not as onerous as Gregor's and Laisa's, which Lady Alys and ImpSec between them had laid out in one-minute increments. Miles invited Ekaterin to accompany him to all his social obligations. She raised her brows at him, and accepted a sensible and dignified three. It was only later that Kareen pointed out that there were limits to the number of times a lady wanted to be seen in the same dress, a problem which, had he but realized it existed, he would gladly have set out to solve. It was perhaps just as well. He wanted Ekaterin to share his pleasure, not his exhaustion.

The cloud of amused congratulation that surrounded them for their spectacular betrothal was marred only once, at a dinner in honor of the Vorbarr Sultana Fire Watch which had included handing out awards for men exhibiting notable bravery or quick thinking in the past year. Exiting with Ekaterin on his arm, Miles found the door half blocked by the somewhat drunken Lord Vormurtos, one of Richars's defeated supporters. The room had mostly emptied by that time, with only a few earnestly chatting groups of people left. Already the servers were moving in to clean up. Vormurtos leaned on the frame with his arms crossed, and failed to move aside.

At Miles's polite, "Excuse us, please," Vormurtos pursed his lips in exaggerated irony.

"Why not? Everyone else has. It seems if you are Vorkosigan enough, you can even get away with murder."

Ekaterin stiffened unhappily. Miles hesitated a fractional moment, considering responses: explanation, outrage, protest? Argument in a hallway with a half-potted fool? No. *I am Aral Vorkosigan's son, after all.* Instead, he stared up unblinkingly, and breathed, "So if you truly believe that, *why are you standing in my way?*"

Vormurtos's inebriated sneer drained away, to be replaced by a belated wariness. With an effort at insouciance that he did not quite bring off, he unfolded himself, and opened his hand to wave the couple past. When Miles bared his teeth in an edged smile, he backed up an extra and involuntary step. Miles shifted Ekaterin to his other side and strode past without looking back.

Ekaterin glanced over her shoulder once, as they made their way down the corridor. In a tone of dispassionate observation, she murmured, "He's melted. You know, your sense of humor is going to get you into deep trouble someday."

"Belike," Miles sighed.

The Emperor's wedding, Miles decided, was very like a combat drop mission, except that, wonderfully, *he* wasn't in command. It was Lady Alys's and Colonel Lord Vortala the Younger's turn for nervous breakdowns. Miles got to be a grunt. All he had to do was keep smiling and follow orders, and eventually it would all be over.

It was fortunate that it was a Midsummer event, because the only site large enough for all the circles of witnesses (barring the stunningly ugly municipal stadium) was the former parade ground, now a grassy sward, just to the south of the Residence. The ballroom was the backup venue in the event of rain, in Miles's view a terrorist plan that courted death by overheating and oxygen deprivation for most of the government of the Imperium. To match the blizzard that had made the Winterfair betrothal so memorable, they ought to have had summer tornadoes, but to everyone's relief the day dawned fair.

The morning began with yet another formal breakfast, this time with Gregor and his groom's party at the Residence. Gregor looked a little frayed, but determined.

"How are you holding up?" Miles asked him in an undervoice.

"I'll make it through dinner," Gregor assured him. "Then we drown our pursuers in a lake of wine and escape."

Even Miles didn't know what refuge Gregor and Laisa had chosen for their wedding night, whether one of the several Vorbarra properties or the country estate of a friend or maybe aboard a battle cruiser in orbit. He *was* sure there wasn't going to be any sort of unscheduled Imperial shivaree. Gregor had chosen all his most frighteningly humorless ImpSec personnel to guard his getaway.

Miles returned to Vorkosigan House to change into his very best House uniform, ornamented with a careful selection of his old military decorations that he otherwise never wore. Ekaterin would be watching him from the third circle of witnesses, in company with her uncle and aunt and the rest of his Imperial Auditor colleagues. He likely wouldn't see her till the vows were over, a thought that gave him a taste of what Gregor's anxiety must be.

The Residence's grounds were filling when he arrived back. He joined his father, Gregor, Drou and Kou, Count Henri Vorvolk and his wife, and the rest of the first circle in their assigned staging area, one of the Residence's public rooms. The Vicereine was off somewhere in support of Lady Alys. Both women and Ivan arrived with moments to spare. As the light of the summer evening gilded the air, Gregor's horse, a gloriously glossy black beast in gleaming cavalry regalia, was led to the west entrance. A Vorbarra Armsman followed with an equally lovely white mare fitted out for Laisa. Gregor mounted, looking in his parade red-and-blues both impressively Imperial and endearingly nervous. Surrounded by his party on foot, he proceeded decorously across the grounds through an aisle of people to the former barracks, now remodeled as guest quarters, where the Komarran delegation was housed.

It was then Miles's job to pound on the door and demand in formal phrases that the bride be brought forth. He was watched by a bevy of giggling Komarran women from the wide-flung flower-decked windows overhead. He stepped back as Laisa and her parents emerged. The bride's dress, he noted in the certainty that there would be a quiz later, included a white silk jacket with fascinating glittery stuff over various other layers, a heavy white silk split skirt and white leather boots, and a headdress with garlands of flowers all cascading down. Several tensely smiling Vorbarra Armsmen made sure the whole ensemble got loaded without incident aboard the notably placid mare—Miles suspected equine tranquilizers. Gregor shifted his horse around to lean across and grip Laisa's hand briefly; they smiled at each other in mutual amazement. Laisa's father, a short, round Komarran oligarch who had never been near a horse in his life before he'd had to practice for this, valiantly took the lead line, and the cavalcade wound its stately way back through the aisles of well-wishers to the south lawn.

The marriage pattern was laid on the ground in little ridges of colored groats, hundreds of kilos of them altogether, Miles had been given to understand. The small central circle awaited the couple, surrounded by a six-pointed star for the principal witnesses, and a series of concentric rings for guests. First close family and friends—then Counts and their Countesses—then high government officials, military officers, and Imperial Auditors—then diplomatic delegations; after that, people packed to the limit of the Residence's walls, and more in the street beyond. The cavalcade split, bride and groom dismounting and entering the circle each from opposite sides. The horses were led away, and Laisa's female Second and Miles were handed the official bags of groats to pour upon the ground and close the couple in, which they managed to do without either dropping the bags, or getting too many groats down their respective footwear.

Miles took his place upon his assigned star point, his parents and Laisa's parents on either hand, Laisa's Komarran female friend and Second opposite. Since *he* didn't have to remember Gregor's lines for him, he occupied the time as the couple repeated their promises—in four languages—by studying the pleasure on the Viceroy and Vicereine's faces. He didn't think he'd ever seen his father cry in public before. All right, so some of it was the sloppy sentiment overflowing everywhere today, but some of it had to be tears of sheer political relief. That was why he had to rub water from *his* eyes, certainly. Damned effective public theater, this ceremony. . . .

Swallowing, Miles stepped forward to kick the groats aside and open the circle to let the married couple out. He seized his privilege and position to be the first to grab Gregor's hand in congratulations, and to stand on tiptoe to kiss the bride's flushed cheek. And then, by damn, it was party time, he was done and off the hook, and he could go and hunt for Ekaterin in all this mob. He made his way past people scooping up handfuls of groats and tucking them away for souvenirs, craning his neck for a glimpse of an elegant woman in a gray silk gown.

Kareen gripped Mark's arm and sighed in satisfaction. The maple ambrosia was a *hit*.

It was rather clever, Kareen thought, how Gregor had shared out the astronomical cost of his wedding reception among his Counts. Each District had been invited to contribute an outdoor kiosk, scattered about the Residence grounds, to offer whatever local food and drink (vetted, of course, by Lady Alys and ImpSec) they'd cared to display to the strolling guests. The effect was a little like a District Fair, or rather, a Fair of Districts, but the competition had certainly brought out the best of Barrayar. The Vorkosigan's District kiosk had a prime location, at the northwest corner of the Residence just at the top of a path that went down into the sunken gardens. Count Aral had donated a thousand liters of his District wine, a traditional and very popular choice.

And at a side table next to the wine bar, Lord Mark Vorkosigan and MPVK Enterprises offered to the guests—tah dah!—their first food product. Ma Kosti and Enrique, wearing Staff badges, directed a team of Vorkosigan House servitors scooping out generous portions of maple ambrosia to the high Vor as fast as they could hand them across the table. At the end of the table, framed by flowers, a wire cage exhibited a couple of dozen bright new Glorious Bugs, glowing in blue-red-gold, together with a brief explanation, rewritten by Kareen to remove both Enrique's technicalities and Mark's blatant commercialism, of how they made their ambrosia. All right, so none of the renamed bug butter being distributed had actually been made by the new bugs, but that was a mere packaging detail.

Miles and Ekaterin came strolling through the crowd, along with Ivan. Miles spotted Kareen's eager wave, and angled toward them. Miles was wearing that same blitzed, deliriously pleased look he'd been sporting for two weeks; Ekaterin, at this her first Imperial Residence party, looked a trifle awed. Kareen darted aside and grabbed a cup of ambrosia, and brandished it as the trio came up.

"Ekaterin, they love the Glorious Bugs! At least half a dozen women have tried to steal them to wear as hair ornaments with their flowers—Enrique had to lock down the cage before we lost any more. He said, they are supposed to be a *demonstration*, not *free samples.*"

Ekaterin laughed. "I'm glad I was able to cure your customer resistance!"

"Oh, my, yes. And with a debut at the Emperor's wedding, everyone will want it! Here, have you had the maple ambrosia yet? Miles?"

"I've tried it before, thank you," said Miles neutrally.

"Ivan! You've got to taste this!"

Ivan's lips twisted dubiously, but with amiable grace he lifted the spoon to his mouth. His expression changed. "Wow, what did you lace this with? It's got a notable kick to it." He resisted Kareen's attempt to wrest back the cup.

"Maple mead," said Kareen happily. "It was Ma Kosti's inspiration. It really works!"

Ivan swallowed, and paused. "Maple mead? The most disgusting, gut-destroying, guerilla attack-beverage ever brewed by man?"

"It's an acquired taste," murmured Miles.

Ivan took another bite. "Combined with the most revolting food product ever invented . . . How did she make it come out like *this*?" He scraped up the last of the soft golden paste, and eyed the cup as though considering licking it out with his tongue. "Impressively efficient, that. Get fed *and* drunk simultaneously . . . no wonder they're lining up!"

Mark, smiling smugly, broke in. "I just had a nice little private chat with Lord Vorsmythe. Without going into the details, I can say that our startup money shortage looks to be solved one way or another. Ekaterin! I am now in a position to redeem the shares I gave you for the bug design. What would you say to an offer of twice their face value back?"

Ekaterin looked thrilled. "That's wonderful, Mark! And so timely. That's more than I ever expected—"

"What you say," Kareen broke in firmly, "is, *no, thank you.* You hang on to those shares, Ekaterin! What you do if you need cash is set them as collateral against a loan. Then, next year when the stock has split I don't know how many times, sell *some* of the shares, pay back the loan, and keep the rest as a growth investment. By the time Nikki's ready, you might well be able to put him through jump-pilot school with it."

"You don't *have* to do it that way—" Mark began.

"That's what I'm doing with mine. It's going to pay my way back to Beta Colony!" She wasn't going to have to beg so much as a tenth-mark from her parents, news they'd found a little more surprising than was quite flattering. They'd then tried to press the offer of a living allowance on her, just to regain their balance, Kareen thought, or possibly the upper hand. She'd taken enormous pleasure in sweetly refusing. "I told Ma Kosti not to sell, either."

Ekaterin's eyes crinkled. "I see, Kareen. In that case . . . thank you, Lord Mark. I will think about your offer for a little while."

Foiled, Mark grumbled under his breath, but, with his brother's sardonic eye upon him, didn't continue his attempted hustle.

Kareen flitted back happily to the serving table, where Ma Kosti was just hoisting up another five-liter tub of maple ambrosia and breaking the seal.

"How are we doing?" Kareen asked.

"They're going to clean us out in another hour, at this rate," the cook reported. She was wearing a lace apron over her very best dress. A large and exquisite fresh orchid necklace, which she'd said Miles had given her, fought for space on her breast with her Staff badge. There was more than one way to get in to the Emperor's wedding, by golly. . . .

"The maple mead bug butter was a great idea of yours for soothing down Miles about this," Kareen told her. "He's one of the few people I know who actually *drinks* the stuff."

"Oh, that wasn't *my* idea, Kareen lovie," Ma Kosti told her. "It was Lord Vorkosigan's. He owns the meadery, you know. . . . He's got an eye to channeling more money to all those poor people back in the Dendarii Mountains, I think."

Kareen's grin broadened. "I *see*." She stole a glance at Miles, standing benignly with his lady on his arm and feigning indifference to his clone-brother's project.

In the gathering dusk, little colored lights began to gleam all through the Residence's garden and grounds, fair and festive. In their cage, the Glorious Bugs began to flip their wing carapaces and twinkle back as if in answer.

Mark watched Kareen, all blonde and ivory and raspberry gauzy and entirely edible, returning from their bug butter table, and sighed in pleasure. His hands, stuffed in his pockets, encountered the gritty grains she had insisted he store there for her when the wedding circle had broken up. He shook them from his fingers, and held out his hand to her, asking, "What are we supposed to do with all these groats, Kareen? Plant them or something?"

"Oh, no," she said, as he pulled her in close. "They're just for remembrance. Most people will put them up in little sachets, and try to press them on their grandchildren someday. *I was at the Old Emperor's wedding, I was.*"

"It's miracle grain, you know," Miles put in. "It multiplies. By tomorrow—or later tonight—people will be selling little bags of supposedly-wedding groats to the gullible all over Vorbarr Sultana. Tons and tons."

"Really." Mark considered this. "You know, you could actually do that legitimately, with a little ingenuity. Take your handful of wedding groats, mix 'em with a bushel of filler-groats, repackage 'em . . . the customer would still get *genuine* Imperial wedding groats, in a sense, but they'd go a lot farther . . ."

"Kareen," said Miles, "do me a favor. Check his pockets before he gets out of here tonight, and confiscate any groats you find."

"I wasn't saying *I* was going to!" said Mark indignantly. Miles grinned at him, and he realized he'd just been Scored On. He smiled back sheepishly, too elated by it all tonight to sustain any emotion downwards of *mellow*.

Kareen glanced up, and Mark followed her gaze to see the Commodore in his parade red-and-blues, and Madame Koudelka in something green and flowing like the Queen of Summer, making their way toward them. The Commodore swung his swordstick jauntily enough, but he had a curiously introspective look on his face. Kareen broke away to cadge more ambrosia samples to press on them.

"How are you two holding up?" Miles greeted the couple.

The Commodore replied abstractedly, "I'm a little, um. A little . . . um . . ."

Miles cocked an eyebrow. "A little um?"

"Olivia," said Madame Koudelka, "has just announced her engagement."

"I thought this was awfully contagious," said Miles, grinning slyly up at Ekaterin.

Ekaterin returned him a melting smile, then said to the Koudelkas, "Congratulations. Who's the lucky fellow?"

"That's . . . um . . . the part it's going to take some getting used to," the Commodore sighed.

Madame Koudelka said, "Count Dono Vorrutyer."

Kareen arrived back with an armload of ambrosia cups in time to hear this; she bounced and squealed delight. Mark glanced aside at Ivan, who merely shook his head and reached for another ambrosia. Of all the party, his was the one voice that didn't break into some murmur of surprise. He looked glum, yes. Surprised, no.

Miles, after a brief digestive pause, said, "I always did think one of your girls would catch a Count."

"Yes," said the Commodore, "but . . ."

"I'm quite certain Dono will know how to make her happy," Ekaterin offered.

"Um."

"She wants a big wedding," said Madame Koudelka.

"So does Delia," said the Commodore. "I left them arm wrestling over who gets the earlier date. And the first shot at my poor budget." He stared around at the Residence grounds, and all the increasingly happy revelers. As it was still early in the evening, they were almost all still vertical. "This is giving them both grandiose ideas."

In a rapt voice, Miles said, "Ooh. I *must* talk to Duv."

Commodore Koudelka edged closer to Mark, and lowered his voice. "Mark, I, ah . . . feel I owe you an apology. Didn't mean to be so stiff-necked about it all."

"That's all right, sir," said Mark, surprised and touched.

The Commodore added, "So, you're going back to Beta in the fall—good. No need to be in a rush to settle things at your age, after all."

"That's what we thought, sir." Mark hesitated. "I know I'm not very good at family yet. But I mean to learn how."

The Commodore gave him a little nod, and a crooked smile. "You're doing fine, son. Just keep on."

Kareen's hand squeezed his. Mark cleared his suddenly inexplicably tight throat, and considered the novel thought that not only could you have a family, you might even have more than one. A wealth of relations . . . "Thank you, sir. I'll try."

Olivia and Dono themselves rounded the corner of the Residence then, arm in arm, Olivia in her favorite primrose yellow, Dono soberly splendid in his Vorrutyer House blue and gray. The dark-haired Dono was actually a little shorter than his intended bride, Mark noticed for the first time. All the Koudelka girls ran to tall. But the force of Dono's personality was such that one hardly noticed the height differential.

They arrived at the group, explaining that they'd been told by five separate people to go try the maple ambrosia before it was gone. They lingered, while Kareen collected another armload of samples, to accept congratulations from all assembled. Even Ivan rose to this social duty.

When Kareen returned, Olivia told her, "I was just talking to Tatya Vorbretten. She was so happy—she and René have started their little boy! The blastocyst just got transferred to the uterine replicator this morning. All healthy so far."

Kareen, her mother, Olivia, and Dono all put their heads together, and that end of the conversation became appallingly obstetrical for a short time. Ivan backed away.

"It's getting worse and worse," he confided to Mark in a hollow voice. "I used to only lose old girlfriends to matrimony one at a time. Now they're going in *pairs.*"

Mark shrugged. "Can't help you, old fellow. But if you want my advice—"

"*You're* giving *me* advice on how to run my love life?" Ivan interjected indignantly.

"You get what you give. Even I figured that one out, eventually." Mark grinned up at him.

Ivan growled, and made to slope off, but then paused to stare, startled, as Count Dono hailed his cousin Byerly Vorrutyer, just passing by on the walk leading to the Residence. "What's *he* doing here?" Ivan muttered.

Dono and Olivia excused themselves and left, presumably to share their announcement with this new quarry. Ivan, after a short silence, handed his empty cup to Kareen and trailed after them.

The Commodore, scraping the last of his ambrosia out of his cup with the little spoon provided, stared glumly after Olivia clinging joyfully to her new fiancé. "Countess Olivia Vorrutyer," he muttered under his breath, obviously trying to get both his mouth and his mind around the novel concept. "My son-in-law, the Count . . . dammit, the fellow's almost old enough to be Olivia's father himself."

"Mother, surely," murmured Mark.

The Commodore gave him an acerbic look. "You understand," he added after a moment, "just on principles of propinquity, I always figured my girls would go for the bright young officers. I expected I'd end up owning the general staff, in my old age. Though there is Duv, I suppose, for consolation. Not young either, but bright enough to be downright scary. Well, maybe *Martya* will find us a future general."

At the bug butter table, Martya in a mint-green gown had stopped by to check on the success of the operation, but stayed to help dish out ambrosia. She and Enrique bent together to lift another tub, and the Escobaran laughed heartily at something she said. When Mark and Kareen returned to Beta Colony, they had agreed Martya would take over as business manager, going down to the District to oversee the startup of the operations. Mark suspected she would end up with a controlling share of the company, eventually. No matter. This was only his first essay in entrepreneurship. *I can make more.* Enrique would bury himself in his development laboratory. He and Martya would both, no doubt, learn a lot, working together. Propinquity . . .

Mark tested the idea on the tip of his tongue, *And this is my brother-in-law, Dr. Enrique Borgos . . .* Mark moved so as to place the Commodore's back to the table, where Enrique was regarding Martya with open admiration and spilling a lot of ambrosia on his fingers. Gawky young intellectual types were noted for aging well, Kareen had told him. So if one Koudelka had chosen the military, and another the political, and another the economic, it would complete the set for one to select the scientific . . . It wasn't just the general staff Kou looked to own in his old age, it was the world. Charitably, Mark decided to keep this observation to himself.

If he was doing well enough by Winterfair, maybe he'd give Kou and Drou a week's all-expenses-paid trip to the Orb, just to encourage the Commodore's heartening trend toward social liberality. That it would also allow them to travel out to Beta Colony and see Kareen would be an irresistible bribe, he rather thought. . . .

Ivan stood and watched as Dono finished his cordial conversation with his cousin By. Dono and Olivia then entered the Residence through the wide-flung glass doors from which light spilled onto the stone-paved promenade. Byerly collected a glass of wine from a passing servitor's tray, sipped, and went to lean pensively on the balustrade overlooking the descending garden paths.

Ivan joined him. "Hello, Byerly," he said affably. "Why aren't you in jail?"

By looked around, and smiled. "Why, Ivan. I'm turned Imperial Witness, don't you know. My secret testimony has put dear Richars into cold storage. All is forgiven."

"Dono forgave what *you* tried?"

"It was Richars's idea, not mine. He's always fancied himself a man of action. It didn't take much encouragement at all to lure him past the point of no return."

Ivan smiled tightly, and took Byerly by the arm. "Let's take a little walk."

"Where to?" asked By uneasily.

"Someplace more private."

The first private place they came to down the path, a stone bench in a bush-shrouded nook, was occupied by a couple. As it happened, the young fellow was a Vorish ensign Ivan knew from Ops HQ. It took him about fifteen captainly seconds to evict the pair. Byerly watched with feigned admiration. "Such a man of authority you're turning into these days, Ivan."

"Sit down, By. And cut the horseshit. If you can."

Smiling, but with watchful eyes, By seated himself comfortably, and crossed his legs. Ivan positioned himself between By and the exit.

"Why are you *here*, By? Gregor invite you?"

"Dono got me in."

"Good of him. Unbelievably good. I—for example—don't believe it for a second."

By shrugged. "S'true."

"What was *really* going on the night Dono was jumped?"

"Goodness, Ivan. Your persistence begins to remind me horribly of your short cousin."

"You've lied and you're lying, but I can't tell about *what*. You make my head hurt. I'm about to share the sensation."

"Now, now . . ." By's eyes glinted in the colored lights, though his face was half shadowed. "It's really quite simple. I told Dono that I was an *agent provocateur*. Granted, I helped set up the attack. What I neglected to mention—to Richars—was that I'd also engaged a squad of municipal guardsmen to provide a timely interruption. To be followed, in the script, by Dono staggering into Vorsmythe House, very shaken up, in front of half the Council of Counts. A grand public spectacle guaranteed to cinch a substantial sympathy vote."

"You convinced Dono of this?"

"Yes. Fortunately, I *was* able to offer up the guardsmen as witnesses to my good intentions. Aren't I clever?" By smirked.

"So—I reflect—is Dono. Did he set this up with you, to trip Richars?"

"No. In fact. I meant it to be a surprise, although not quite as much of a surprise as, ah, it turned out. I wished to be certain Dono's response was absolutely convincing. The attack had to actually start—and be witnessed—to incriminate Richars, and eliminate the 'I was only joking' defense. It would not have had the proper tone at all if Richars himself had been merely—and provably—the victim of an entrapment by his political rival."

"I'll swear you weren't faking being distraught as hell that night when you caught up with me."

"Oh, I was. A most painful memory. All my beautiful choreography was just ruined. Though, thanks to you and Olivia, the outcome was saved. I should be grateful to you, I suppose. My life would be . . . most uncomfortable right now if those nasty brutal thugs had succeeded."

Just exactly how uncomfortable, By? Ivan paused for a moment, then inquired softly, "Did Gregor order this?"

"Are you having romantic visions of plausible deniability, Ivan? Goodness me. No. I went to some trouble to keep ImpSec out of the affair. This impending wedding made them all so distressingly rigid. They would, boringly, have wanted to arrest the conspirators immediately. Not *nearly* as politically effective."

If By was lying . . . Ivan didn't want to know. "You play games like that with the big boys, you'd better make damn sure you win, Miles says. Rule One. And there is no Rule Two."

Byerly sighed. "So he pointed out to me."

Ivan hesitated. "*Miles* talked to you about this?"

"Ten days ago. Has anyone ever explained the meaning of the term *déjà vu* to you, Ivan?"

"Reprimanded you, did he?"

"I have my own sources for mere reprimand. It was worse. He . . . he *critiqued* me." Byerly shuddered, delicately. "From a covert ops standpoint, don't you know. An experience I trust I may never repeat." He sipped his wine.

Ivan was almost lured into sympathetic agreement. But not quite. He pursed his lips. "So, By . . . who's your blind drop?"

By blinked at him. "My what?"

"Every deep cover informer has a blind drop. It wouldn't do for you to be seen tripping in and out of ImpSec HQ by the very men you might, perhaps, be ratting on tomorrow. How long have you had this job, By?"

"What job?"

Ivan sat silent, and frowned. Humorlessly.

By sighed. "About eight years."

Ivan raised a brow. "Domestic Affairs . . . counterintelligence . . . civilian contract employee . . . what's your rating? IS-6?"

By's lip twitched. "IS-8."

"Ooh. Very good."

"Well, I am. Of course, it *was* IS-9. I'm sure it will be again, someday. I'll just have to be boring and follow the rules for a while. For example, I will have to report this conversation."

"Feel free." Finally, it all added up, in neat columns with no messy remainders. So, Byerly Vorrutyer was one of Illyan's dirty angels . . . one of Allegre's, now, Ivan supposed. Doing a little personal moonlighting on the side, it appeared. By must certainly have received a reprimand over all his sleight-of-hand on Dono's behalf. But his career would survive. If Byerly was a bit of a loose screw, just as certainly, down in the bowels of ImpSec HQ, there was a very bright man with a screwdriver. A Galeni-caliber officer, if ImpSec was lucky enough. He might even drop in to visit Ivan, after this. The acquaintance was bound to prove interesting. Best of all, Byerly Vorrutyer was *his* problem. Ivan smiled relief, and rose.

Byerly stretched, picked up his half-empty wineglass, and prepared to accompany Ivan back up the path.

Ivan's brain kept picking at the scenario, despite his stern order to it to stop now. A glass of wine of his own ought to do the trick. But he couldn't help asking again, "So who *is* your blind drop? It ought to be someone I know, dammit."

"Why, Ivan. I'd think you'd have enough clues to figure it out for yourself by now."

"Well . . . it has to be someone in the high Vor social milieu, because that's clearly your specialty. Someone you encounter frequently, but not a constant companion. Someone who also has daily contact with ImpSec, but in an unremarkable way. Someone no one would notice. An unobserved channel, a disregarded conduit. Hidden in plain sight. Who?"

They reached the top of the path. By smiled. "*That* would be telling." He drifted away. Ivan wheeled to catch a servitor with a tray of wineglasses. He turned back to watch By, doing an excellent imitation of a half-drunk town clown not least because he *was* a half-drunk town clown, pause to give one of his little By-bows to Lady Alys and Simon Illyan, just exiting the Residence together for a breath of air on the promenade. Lady Alys returned him a cool nod.

Ivan choked on his wine.

Miles had been hauled away to pose with the rest of the wedding party for vids. Ekaterin tried not to be too nervous, left in Kareen and Mark's good company, but she felt a twinge of relief when she saw Miles again making his way down the steps from the Residence's north promenade toward her. The Imperial Residence was vast and old and beautiful and intimidating and crammed with history, and she doubted she'd ever emulate the way Miles seemed to pop in and out of side doors as though he owned the place. And yet . . . moving in this amazing space was easier this time, and she had no doubt would be still easier the next visit. Either the world was not so huge and frightening a place as she'd once been led to believe, or else . . . she was not so small and helpless as she'd once been encouraged to imagine herself. If power was an illusion, wasn't weakness necessarily one also?

Miles was grinning. As he took her hand and gripped it to his arm again, he vented a sinister chuckle.

"That is the most *villainous* laugh, love . . ."

"It's too good, it's just too good. I had to find you and share it at once." He led her a little away from the Vorkosigans' wine kiosk, crowded with revelers, around some trees to where a wide brick path climbed up out of Old Emperor Ezar's north garden. "I just found out what Alexi Vormoncrief's new posting is."

"I hope it's the ninth circle of hell!" she said vengefully. "That nitwit very nearly succeeded in having *Nikki* taken from me."

"Just as good. Almost the same thing, actually. He's been sent to Kyril Island. I was hoping they'd make him weather officer, but he's only the new laundry officer. Well, one can't have everything." He rocked on his heels with incomprehensible glee.

Ekaterin frowned in doubt. "That hardly seems punishment enough . . ."

"You don't understand. Kyril Island—they call it Camp Permafrost—is the worst military post in the Empire. Winter training base. It's an arctic island, five hundred kilometers from anywhere and anyone, including the nearest women. You can't even swim to escape, because the water would freeze you in minutes. The bogs will eat you alive. Blizzards. Freezing fog. Winds that can blow away groundcars. Cold, dark, drunken, deadly . . . I spent an eternity there, a few months once. The trainees, they come and go, but the *permanent* staff is stuck. Oh. Oh. Justice is *good*. . . ."

Impressed by his evident enthusiasm, she said, "Is it really that bad?"

"Yes, oh, yes. Ha! I'll have to send him a case of good brandy, in honor of the Emperor's wedding, just to start him off right. Or—no, better. I'll send him a case of *bad* brandy. After a while, no one there can tell the difference anyway."

Accepting his assurances for the present and future discomfort of her recent nemesis, she sauntered contentedly with him along the edge of the sunken garden. All the principal guests, including Miles, would be called in for the formal dinner soon, and they would be separated for a time, he to the high table to sit between Empress Laisa and her Komarran Second, she to join Lord Auditor Vorthys and her aunt again. There would be tedious speeches, but Miles laid firm plans for reconnecting with her right after dessert.

"So what do you think?" he asked, staring speculatively around at the party, which seemed to be gaining momentum in the dusk. "Would you like a big wedding?"

She now recognized the incipient theatrical gleam in his eye. But Countess Cordelia had primed her on how to handle this one. She swept her lashes down. "It just wouldn't feel appropriate in my mourning year. But if you didn't mind waiting till next spring, it could be as large as you like."

"Ah," he said, "ah. Fall is a nice time for weddings, too . . ."

"A quiet family wedding in the fall? I would like that."

He would find some way to make it memorable, she had no fear. And, she suspected, it might be better not to leave him time for over-planning.

"Maybe in the garden at Vorkosigan Surleau?" he said. "You haven't seen that yet. Or else the garden at Vorkosigan House." He eyed her sidelong.

"Certainly," she said amiably. "Outdoor weddings are going to be the rage for the next few years. Lord and Lady Vorkosigan will be all in the mode."

He grinned at that. His—her—*their*—Barrayaran garden would still be a bit bare by fall. But full of sprouts and hope and life waiting underground for the spring rains.

They both paused, and Ekaterin stared in fascination at the Cetagandan diplomatic delegation just climbing the brick steps that wound up from the reflecting pools. The regular ambassador and his tall and glamorous wife were accompanied not only by the haut governor of Rho Ceta, Barrayar's nearest neighbor planet of the empire, but also by an actual haut woman from the Imperial capital. Despite the fact that haut ladies were said never to travel, she had been sent as the personal delegate of Emperor the haut Fletchir Giaja and his Empresses. She was escorted by a ghem-general of the highest rank. No one knew what she looked like, as she traveled always in a personal force bubble, tonight tinted an iridescent rose color for festivity. The ghem-general, tall and distinguished, wore the formal blood-red uniform of the Cetagandan emperor's personal guard, which ought to have clashed horribly with the bubble, but didn't.

The ambassador glanced at Miles, waved polite greeting, and said something to the ghem-general, who nodded. To Ekaterin's surprise, the ghem-general and the pink bubble left their party and strolled/floated over to them.

"Ghem-general Benin," said Miles, suddenly on-stage in his most flowing Imperial Auditor's style. His eyes were alight with curiosity and, oddly, pleasure. He swept a sincere bow at the bubble. "And haut Pel. So good to see you—so to speak—once more. I hope your unaccustomed travel has not proved too wearing?"

"Indeed not, Lord Auditor Vorkosigan. I have found it quite stimulating." Her voice came from a transmitter in her bubble. To Ekaterin's astonishment, her bubble grew almost transparent for a moment. Seated in her float chair behind the pearly sheen, a tall blonde woman of uncertain age in a flowing rose-pink gown appeared momentarily. She was staggeringly beautiful, but something about her ironic smile did not suggest youth. The concealing screen clouded up once more.

"We are honored by your presence, haut Pel," Miles said formally, while Ekaterin blinked, feeling temporarily blinded. And suddenly horribly dowdy. But all the admiration in Miles's eyes burned for her, not for the pink vision. "May I introduce my fiancée, Madame Ekaterin Nile Vorvayne Vorsoisson."

The distinguished officer murmured polite greetings. He then turned his thoughtful gaze upon Miles, and touched his lips in an oddly ceremonious gesture before speaking.

"My Imperial Master the haut Fletchir Giaja had asked me, in the event that I should encounter you, Lord Vorkosigan, to extend his *personal* condolences for the death of your close friend, Admiral Naismith."

Miles paused, his smile for a moment a little frozen. "Indeed. His death was a great blow to me."

"My Imperial Master adds that he *trusts* that he will remain deceased."

Miles glanced up at the tall Benin, his eyes suddenly sparkling. "Tell your Imperial Master from me—I *trust* his resurrection will not be required."

The ghem-general smiled austerely, and favored Miles with an inclination of his head. "I shall convey your words exactly, my lord." He nodded cordially at them both, and he and the pink bubble drifted back to their delegation.

Ekaterin, still awed by the blonde, murmured to Miles, "What was *that* all about?"

Miles sucked on his lower lip. "Not news, I'm afraid, though I'll pass it on to General Allegre. Benin just confirms something Illyan had suspected over a year ago. My covert ops identity was come to the end of its usefulness, at least as far as its being a secret from the Cetagandans was concerned. Well, Admiral Naismith and his various clones, real and imagined, kept 'em confused for longer than I'd have believed possible."

He gave a short nod, not dissatisfied, she thought, despite his little flash of regret. He took a firmer grip on her.

Regret . . . And what if she and Miles had met at twenty, instead of she and Tien? It had been possible; she'd been a student at the Vorbarra District University, he'd been a newly minted officer in and out of the capital. If their paths had crossed, might she have won a less bitter life?

No. We were two other people, then. Traveling in different directions: their intersection must have been brief, and indifferent, and unknowing. And she could not unwish Nikki, or all that she had learned, not even realizing she was learning, during her dark eclipse. *Roots grow deep in the dark.*

She could only have arrived here by the path she'd taken, and here, with Miles, *this* Miles, seemed a very good place to be indeed. *If I am his consolation, he is most surely mine as well.* She acknowledged her years lost, but there was nothing in that decade she needed to circle back for, not even regret; Nikki, and the learning, traveled with her. Time to move on.

"Ah," said Miles, looking up as a Residence servitor approached them, smiling. "They must be rounding up the strays for dinner. Shall we go in, milady?"

Winterfair Gifts

From Armsman Roic's wrist com the gate guard's voice reported laconically, "They're in. Gate's rocked."

"Right," Roic returned. "Dropping the house shields." He turned to the discreet security control panel beside the carved double doors of Vorkosigan House's main entry hall, pressed his palm to the read-pad, and entered a short code. The faint hum of the force shield protecting the great house faded.

Roic stared anxiously out one of the tall, narrow windows flanking the portal, ready to throw the doors wide when m'lord's groundcar pulled into the porte cochere. He glanced no less anxiously down the considerable length of his athletic body, checking his House uniform: half-boots polished to mirrors, trousers knife-creased, silver embroidery gleaming, dark brown fabric spotless.

His face heated in mortified memory of a less expected arrival in this very hall-also of Lord Vorkosigan with honored company in tow-and the unholy tableau m'lord had surprised with the Escobaran bounty hunters and the gooey debacle of the bug butter. Roic had looked an utter fool in that moment, nearly naked except for a liberal coating of sticky slime. He could still hear Lord Vorkosigan's austere, amused voice, as cutting as a razor-slash across his ears: *Armsman Roic, you're out of uniform.*

He thinks I'm an idiot. Worse, the Escobarans' invasion had been a security breach, and while he'd not, technically, been on duty—he'd been *asleep,* dammit—he'd been present in the house and therefore on call for emergencies. The mess had been in his lap, literally. M'lord had dismissed him from the scene with no more than an exasperated *Roic . . . get a bath,* somehow more keenly excoriating than any bellowed dressing-down.

Roic checked his uniform again.

The long silvery groundcar pulled up and sighed to the pavement. The front canopy rose on the driver, the senior and dauntingly competent Armsman Pym. He released the rear canopy and hurried around the car to assist m'lord and his party. The senior armsman spared a glance through the narrow window as he strode by, his eye passing coolly over Roic and scanning the hall beyond to make sure it contained no unforeseen drama this time. These were Very Important Off-World Wedding Guests, Pym had impressed upon Roic. Which Roic might have been left to deduce by m'lord going personally to the shuttleport to greet their descent from orbit—but then, Pym had walked in on the bug butter disaster, too. Since that day, his directives to Roic had tended to be couched in words of one syllable, with no contingency left to chance.

A short figure in a well-tailored gray tunic and trousers hopped out of the car first: Lord Vorkosigan, gesturing expansively at the great stone mansion, talking nonstop over his shoulder, smiling in proud welcome. As the carved doors swung wide, admitting a blast of Vorbarr Sultana winter night air and a few glittering snow crystals, Roic stood to attention and mentally matched the other people exiting the groundcar with the security list he'd been given. A tall woman held a baby bundled in blankets; a lean, smiling fellow hovered by her side. They had to be the Bothari-Jeseks. Madame Elena Bothari-Jesek was the daughter of the late, legendary Armsman Bothari; her right of entree into Vorkosigan House, where she had grown up with m'lord, was absolute, Pym had made sure Roic understood. It scarcely needed the silver circles of a jump pilot's neural leads on midforehead and temples to identify the shorter middle-aged fellow as the Betan jump pilot, Arde Mayhew—should a jump pilot look so jump-lagged? Well, m'lord's mother, Countess Vorkosigan, was Betan, too; and the pilot's blinking, shivering stance was among the most physically unthreatening Roic had ever seen. Not so the final guest. Roic's eyes widened.

The hulking figure unfolded from the groundcar and stood up, and up. Pym, who was almost as tall as Roic, did not come quite up to its shoulder. It shook out the swirling folds of a gray-and-white greatcoat of military cut and threw back its head. The light from overhead caught the face and gleamed off . . . were those *fangs* hooked over the outslung lower jaw?

Sergeant Taura was the name that went with it, by process of elimination. One of m'lord's old military buddies, Pym had given Roic to understand, and—don't be fooled by the rank—of some *particular* importance (if rather mysterious, as was everything connected with Lord Miles Vorkosigan's late career in Imperial Security). Pym was former ImpSec himself. Roic was not, as he was reminded, oh, three times a day on average.

At Lord Vorkosigan's urging, the whole party poured into the entry hall, shaking off snow-spotted garments, talking, laughing. The greatcoat was swung from those high shoulders like a billowing sail, its owner turning neatly on one foot, folding the garment ready to hand over. Roic jerked back to avoid being clipped by a heavy, mahogany-colored braid of hair as it swept past, and rocked forward to find himself face to . . . nose to . . . staring directly into an entirely unexpected cleavage. It was framed by pink silk in a plunging vee. He glanced up. The outslung jaw was smooth and beardless. The curious pale amber eyes, irises circled with sleek black lines, looked back down at him with, he instantly feared, some amusement. *Her* fang-framed smile was deeply alarming.

Pym was efficiently organizing servants and luggage.

Lord Vorkosigan's voice yanked Roic back to focus. "Roic, did the count and countess get back in from their dinner engagement yet?"

"About twenty minutes ago, m'lord. They went upstairs to their suite to change."

Lord Vorkosigan addressed the woman with the baby, who was attracting cooing maids. "My parents would skin me if 1 didn't take *you* up to them instantly. Come on. Mother's pretty eager to meet her namesake. I predict Baby Cordelia will have Countess Cordelia wrapped around her pudgy little fingers in about, oh, three and a half seconds. At the outside."

He turned and started up the curve of the great staircase, shepherding the Bothari-Jeseks and calling over his shoulder, "Roic, show Arde and Taura to their assigned rooms, make sure they have everything they want. We'll meet back in the library when you all are freshened up or whatever. Drinks and snacks will be laid on there."

So, it was a *lady* sergeant. Galactics had those; m'lord's mother had been a famous Betan officer in her day. *But this one's a bloody giant mutant lady sergeant* was a thought Roic suppressed more firmly. Such backcountry prejudices had no place in *this* household. Though, she was clearly bioengineered, had to be. He recovered himself enough to say, "May I take your bag, um . . . Sergeant?"

"Oh, all right." With a dubious look down at him, she handed him the satchel she'd had slung over one arm. The pink enamel on her fingernails did not quite camouflage their shape as claws, heavy and efficient as a leopard's. The bag's descending weight nearly jerked Roic's arm out of its socket. He managed a desperate smile and began lugging it two-handed up the staircase in m'lord's wake.

He deposited the tired-looking pilot first. Sergeant Taura's second-floor guest room was one of the renovated ones, with its own bath, around the corridor's corner from m'lord's own suite. She reached up and trailed a claw along the ceiling and smiled in evident approval of Vorkosigan House's three-meter headspace.

"So," she said, turning to Roic, "is a Winterfair wedding considered especially auspicious, in Barrayaran custom?"

"They're not so common as in summer. Mostly I think it's now because m'lord's fiancée is between semesters at university."

Her thick brows rose in surprise. "She's a student?"

"Yes. ma'am." He had a notion one addressed female sergeants as *ma'am*. Pym would have known.

"I didn't realize she was such a *young* lady."

"No, ma'am. Madame Vorsoisson's a widow—she has a little boy, Nikki—nine years old. Mad about jumpships. Do you happen t' know—does that pilot fellow like children?" Mayhew was bound to be a magnet for Nikki.

"Why . . . I don't know. I don't think Arde knows either. He hardly ever meets any in a free mercenary fleet."

He would have to watch, then, to be sure little Nikki didn't set himself up for a painful rebuff. M'lord and m'lady-to-be might not be paying their usual attention to him, under the circumstances.

Sergeant Taura circled the room, gazing with what Roic hoped was approval at its comfortable appointments, and glanced out the window at the back garden, shrouded in winter white, the snow luminous in the security lighting. "I suppose it makes sense that he'd have to wed one of his own Vor kind, in the end." Her nose wrinkled. "So, are the Vor a social class, a warrior caste, or what? I never could quite figure it out from Miles. The way he talks about them you'd half think they were a religion. Or at any rate, *his* religion."

Roic blinked in bafflement. "Well, no. And yes. All of that. The Vor are . . . well, Vor."

"Now that Barrayar has modernized, isn't a hereditary aristocracy resented by the rest of your classes?"

"But they're *our* Vor."

"Says the Barrayaran. Hmm, So, *you* can criticize them, but heaven help any outsider who dares to?"

"Yes," he said, relieved that she seemed to have grasped it despite his stumbling tongue.

"A family matter. *I* see." Her grin faded into a frown that was actually less alarming—not so much fang. Her fingers clenching the curtain inadvertently poked claws through the expensive fabric; wincing, she shook her hand free and tucked it behind her back. Her voice lowered. "So she's Vor, well and good. But does she *love* him?"

Roic heard the odd emphasis in her voice but was unclear how to interpret it. "I'm very sure of it, ma'am," he avowed loyally. M'lady-to-be's frowns, her darkening mood, were surely just prewedding nerves piled atop examination stress on the substrate of her not-so-distant bereavement.

"Of course." Her smile flicked back in a perfunctory sort of way. "Have you served Lord Vorkosigan long, Armsman Roic?"

"Since last winter, ma'am, when a space fell vacant in the Vorkosigans' armsmen's score. I was sent up on recommendation from the Hassadar Municipal Guard," he added a bit truculently, challenging her to sneer at his humble, nonmilitary origins. "A count's twenty armsmen are always from his own district, y'see."

She did not react; the Hassadar Municipal Guard evidently meant nothing to her.

He asked in return, "Did you . . . serve him very long? Out there?" In the galactic backbeyond where m'lord had acquired such exotic friends.

Her face softened, the fanged smile reappearing. "In a sense, all my life. Since my real life began, ten years ago, anyway. He is a great man." This last was delivered with unself-conscious conviction.

Well, he was a great man's *son*, certainly. Count Aral Vorkosigan was a colossus bestriding the last half century of Barrayaran history. Lord Miles had led a less public career. Which no one would tell Roic anything about, the most junior armsman not being ex-ImpSec like m'lord and most of the rest of the armsmen, eh.

Still, Roic *liked* the little lord. What with the birth injuries and all—Roic shied away from the pejorative *mutation*—she'd had a rough ride all his life despite his high blood. Hard enough for him to achieve normal things like . . . like getting married. Although, m'lord had brains enough, belike, in compensation for his stunted body. Roic just wished he didn't think his newest armsman a dolt.

"The library is to the right of the stairs as you go down, through the first room." He touched his hand to his forehead in a farewell salute, by way of paving his escape from this unnerving giant female. "The dining's to be casual tonight; you don't need t' dress." He added, as she glanced down in bewilderment at her travel-rumpled loose pink jacket and trousers, "Dress up, that is. Fancy. What you're wearing is fine."

"Oh," she replied with evident relief. "That makes more sense. Thank you."

Having made his routine security circuit of the house, Roic arrived back at the antechamber just outside the library to find the huge woman and the pilot fellow examining the array of wedding presents temporarily staged there. The growing assortment of objects had been arriving for weeks. Each had been handed in to Pym to be unwrapped and to undergo a security check, rewrapped, and as the affianced couple's time permitted, unwrapped again and displayed with its card.

"Look, here's yours, Arde," said Sergeant Taura. "And here's Elli's."

"Oh, what did she finally decide on?" asked the pilot.

"At one point she told me she was thinking of sending the bride a barbed-wire choke chain for Miles, but was afraid it might be misinterpreted."

"No . . ." Taura held up a thick fall of shimmering black stuff as long as she was tall. "It seems to be some sort of fur coat. No, wait—it's a blanket. Beautiful! You should feel this, Arde. It's incredibly soft. And warm." She held a supple fold up to the side of her head, and a delighted laugh broke from her long lips. "It's purring!"

Mayhew's eyebrows climbed halfway to his receding hairline. "Good God! *Did* she . . .? Now, *that's* a bit edgy."

Taura stared down at him in puzzled inquiry. "Edgy? Why?"

Mayhew made an uncertain gesture. "It's a live fur—a genetic construct. It looks just like one Miles once gave to *Elli*. If she's recycling his gifts, that's a pretty pointed message." He hesitated.

"Though I suppose if she bought a fresh new one for the happy couple, that's a different message."

"Ouch." Taura tilted her head to one side and frowned at the fur. "My life's too short for arcane mind games, Arde. Which is it?"

"Search me. In the dark, all cat blankets are . . . well, black, in this case. I wonder if it's intended as an editorial?"

"Well, if it is, don't you *dare* let on to the poor bride, or I swear I'll turn both your ears into doilies." She held up her clawed fingers and wriggled them. "By hand."

Judging by the pilot's brief grin, the threat was a jest, but by his little bow of compliance, not an entirely empty one. Taura observed Roic, just then, refolded the live fur into its box, and tucked her hands discreetly behind her back.

The door to the library swung open, and Lord Vorkosigan stuck his head out. "Ah, there you two are." He strolled into the antechamber. "Elena and Baz will be down in a little—she's feeding Baby Cordelia. You must be starving by now, Taura. Come on in and try the hors d'oeuvres. My cook has outdone herself."

He smiled up affectionately at the enormous sergeant.

While the top of Roic's head barely came up to her shoulder, m'lord just about faced her belt buckle. It occurred to Roic that Taura towered over himself in almost exactly the same proportions that ladies of average height towered over Lord Vorkosigan. This must be what women looked like to m'lord *all the time*.

Oh.

M'lord waved his guests through to the library but, instead of following them, shut the door and motioned Roic to his side. He looked thoughtfully up at his tallest armsman and lowered his voice.

"Tomorrow morning, I want you to drive Sergeant Taura to the Old Town. I've prevailed upon Aunt Alys to present Taura to her modiste and fix her up with a Barrayaran lady's wardrobe suitable for the upcoming bash. Figure to hold yourself at their disposal for the day."

Roic gulped. M'lord's aunt, Lady Alys Vorpatril, was in her own way more terrifying than any woman Roic had ever encountered, regardless of height. She was the acknowledged social arbiter of the high Vor in the capital, the last word in fashion, taste, and etiquette, the official hostess for Emperor Gregor *himself.* And her tongue could slice a fellow to ribbons and tie up the remains in a bowknot before they hit the ground.

"How t' *devil* did you—" Roic began, then cut himself off.

M'lord smirked. "I was very persuasive. Besides, Lady Alys relishes a challenge. With luck, she may even be able to part Taura from that shocking pink she favors. Some damned fool once told her it was a nonthreatening color, and now she uses it in the most unsuitable garments—and quantities. It's *so* wrong on her. Well, Aunt Alys will be able to handle it. If anyone asks for your opinion— not that they're likely to—vote for whatever Alys picks."

I shouldn't dare do otherwise, Roic managed not to blurt aloud. He stood to attention and tried to look as though he were listening intelligently.

Lord Vorkosigan tapped his fingers on his trouser seam, his smile fading. "I'm also relying on you to see that Taura is not, um, offered insult, or made uncomfortable, or . . . well, you know. Not that you can keep people from staring, I don't suppose. But be her outrider in any public venue, and be alert to steer her away from any problems. I wish I had time to squire her myself, but this wedding prep has gone into high gear. Not much longer now, thank God."

"How is Madame Vorsoisson holding up?" Roic inquired diffidently. He had been wondering for two days if he ought to report the crying jag to someone, but m'lady-to-be had surely not realized her muffled breakdown in one of Vorkosigan House's back corridors had included a hastily retreating witness.

Judging by m'lord's suddenly guarded expression, perhaps he knew. "She has . . . extra stresses just now. I've tried to take as much of the organizing off her shoulders as possible." His shrug was not as reassuring as it might be, Roic felt.

M'lord brightened. "Anyway, I want Sergeant Taura to have a great time on her visit to Barrayar, a fabulous Winterfair season. It's probably the only chance she'll ever have to see the place. I want her to look back on this week like, like . . . dammit, I want her to feel like Cinderella magicked off to the ball. She's earned it, God knows. Midnight tolls too damned soon."

Roic tried to wrap his mind around the concept of Lord Vorkosigan as the enormous woman's fairy godfather. "So . . . who's t' handsome prince?"

M'lord's smile went crooked; something almost like pain sounded in his indrawn breath. "Ah. Yes. That would be the central problem, now. Wouldn't it."

He dismissed Roic with his usual casual half-salute, a vague wave of his hand in the vicinity of his forehead, and joined his guests in the library.

Roic had never in his whole career as a Hassadar municipal guardsman been in a clothing store resembling that of Lady Vorpatril's modiste. Nothing betrayed its location in the Vorbarr Sultana thoroughfare but a discreet brass plaque, labeled simply ESTELLE. Cautiously, he mounted to the second floor, Sergeant Taura's massive footsteps creaking on the carpeted stairs behind him, and poked his head into a hushed chamber that might have been a Vor lady's drawing room. There was not a garment rack nor even a mannequin in sight, just a thick carpet, soft lighting, and tables and chairs that looked suitable for offering high tea at the Imperial Residence. To his relief Lady Vorpatril had arrived before them and was standing chatting with another woman in a dark dress.

The two women turned as Taura ducked her head under the lintel behind Roic and straightened up again. Roic nodded a polite greeting. He couldn't imagine what m'lord had said to his aunt, but her eyes widened only slightly, looking up at Taura. The second woman didn't quail at the fangs, claws, or height either, but when her glance swept down the pink trouser outfit, she winced.

There was a brief pause; Lady Alys shot Roic an inquiring look, and he realized it must be his job to do the announcing, as when he brought a visitor into Vorkosigan House. "Sergeant Taura, my lady," he said loudly, then stopped, hoping for more cues.

After another moment, Lady Alys abandoned further hope of him and came forward, smiling, her hands held out. "Sergeant Taura. I am Miles Vorkosigan's aunt, Alys Vorpatril. Permit me to welcome you to Barrayar. My nephew has told me something about you."

Uncertainly, Taura stuck out one huge hand, engulfing Lady Alys's slender fingers, and shook with care. "I'm afraid he hasn't told me too much about you," she said. Shyness made her voice a gruff rumble. "I don't know many aunts. I somehow thought you would be older. And . . . and not so beautiful."

Lady Vorpatril smiled, not without approval. Only a few streaks of silver in her dark coiffure and a slight softening of her skin betrayed her age to Roic's eyes; she was trim and elegant and utterly self-possessed, as always. She introduced the other woman, Madame

Somebody—not Estelle, though Roic promptly dubbed her that in his mind—apparently the senior modiste.

"I'm very happy to have a chance to visit Miles's—Lord Vorkosigan's homeworld," Taura told them. "Although, when he invited me to come for the Winterfair season, I wasn't sure if it was hunting or social, and whether I should pack weapons or dresses."

Lady Vorpatril's smile sharpened. "Dresses *are* weapons, my dear, in sufficiently skilled hands. Permit us to introduce you to the rest of our ordnance team." She gestured toward a door at the far end of the room, through which presumably lay more utilitarian workrooms, full of laser scanners and design consoles and bolts of exotic fabrics and expert seamstresses. Or magic wands, for all Roic knew.

The other woman nodded. "Do please come this way, Sergeant Taura. We have a great deal to accomplish today, Lady Alys tells me . . ."

"My lady?" Roic called in faint panic to their disappearing forms. "What should I do?"

"Wait here a few moments, Armsman," Lady Alys murmured over her shoulder to him. "I'll be back."

Taura, too, glanced back at him, just before the door eased silently closed behind her, the expression flitting over her odd features seeming for a moment almost beseeching—*Don't abandon me.*

Did he dare sit on one of the chairs? He decided not. He stood for a few moments, walked around the chamber, and finally took up a guardsman's stance, which by dint of much recent practice he could hold for an hour at a stretch, his back to one delicately decorated wall.

In a while Lady Vorpatril returned, a pile of bright pink cloth folded over her arm. She shoved it at Roic.

"Take these back to my nephew and tell him to hide them. Or better, burn them. Or anything, but do not under any circumstances allow them to fall into that young woman's hands again. Come back in about, oh, four hours. You are by far the most ornamental of Miles's armsmen, but there's no need to have you lurking about cluttering up Estelle's reception room till then. Run along."

He looked down on the top of her perfectly groomed head and wondered how she could *always* make him feel four years old, or as though he wanted to hide in a large bag. For his consolation, Roic reflected as he made his way out, she seemed to have the same effect on her nephew, who was thirty-one and ought to be immune by now.

He reported again for duty at the appointed time, only to cool his heels for another twenty minutes or so. A submodiste of some sort offered him a choice of tea or wines while he waited, which he politely declined. At last, the door opened; voices drifted through.

Taura's vibrant baritone was unmistakable. "I'm not so sure, Lady Alys. I've never worn a skirt like this in my life."

"We'll have you practice for a few minutes, sitting and standing and walking. Oh, here's Roic back, good."

Lady Alys stepped through first, folded her arms, and looked, oddly enough, at Roic.

A stunning vision in hunter green stepped through behind her.

Oh, it was still Taura, certainly, but . . . the skin that had been sallow and dull against the pink was now revealed as a glowing ivory. The green jacket fit very trimly about the waist. Above, her pale shoulders and long neck seemed to bloom from a white linen collar; below, the jacket skirt skimmed out briefly around the upper hips. A narrow skirt continued the long green fall to her firm calves. Wide linen cuffs decorated with subtle white braid made her hands look, if not small, well-proportioned. The pink nail polish was gone, replaced by a dark mahogany shade. The heavy braid hanging down her back had been transformed into a mysteriously knotted arrangement, clinging close to her head and set off with a green . . . hat? feather? anyway, a neat little accent tilted to the other side. The odd shape of her face seemed suddenly artistic and sophisticated rather than distorted.

"Ye-es," said Lady Vorpatril. "That will do." Roic closed his mouth.

With a lopsided smile, Taura stepped carefully forward.

"I am a bodyguard by trade," she said, evidently continuing a conversation with Lady Vorpatril. "How can I kick someone's teeth in wearing this?"

"A woman wearing *that* suit, my dear, will have volunteers to kick in annoying persons' teeth for her," said Lady Alys. "Is that not so, Roic?"

"If they don't trample each other in the rush," gulped Roic and turned red.

One corner of that wide mouth lifted; the golden eyes seemed to sparkle like champagne. She caught sight of a long mirror on a carved stand in one corner and walked over to it to stare somewhat uncertainly at the portion of her it reflected. "It's effective, then?"

"Downright terrifying," Roic averred.

Roic intercepted a furious glower from Lady Alys behind Taura's back. Her lips formed the words *No, you idiot!*

He shrank into cowed silence.

"Oh." Taura's fanged smile fled. "But I already terrify people. Human beings are so fragile. If you get a good grip, you can pull their heads right off. I want to *attract* . . . somebody. For a change. Maybe I should have that pink dress with the bows after all."

Lady Alys said smoothly, "We agreed that the ingenue look is for much younger girls."

"Smaller ones, you mean."

"There is more than one kind of beauty. Yours needs dignity. *I* would never deck myself in pink bows," she threw in, a little desperately it seemed to Roic.

Taura eyed her, seeming struck by this. "No . . . I suppose not."

"You will simply attract braver men."

"Oh, I know *that*." Taura shrugged. "I was just . . . hoping for a larger selection, for once." She added under her breath, "Anyway, he's taken now."

What he? Roic couldn't help wondering Some very tall admirer, now out of the picture? Larger than Roic? There weren't too many men of that description around.

Lady Alys rounded out the afternoon by guiding her new protégée to an exclusive tearoom, much frequented by high Vor matrons. This proved to be partly for the purposes of tutorial, party to refuel Taura's ferocious metabolism. While the server brought dish after dish, Lady Alys offered a brisk stream of advice on everything from gracefully exiting a groundcar in restrictive clothing to posture to table manners to the intricacies of Vor social rank. Despite her outsized scale, Taura was naturally athletic and coordinated, seeming to improve almost as Roic watched.

Drafted as practice gentleman, Roic found himself coming in for a few sharp corrections himself. He felt very conspicuous and clumsy at first, until he realized that, next to Taura, he might as well be invisible. If they drew sidelong looks from other diners, at least the comments were low voiced or far enough away that he was not compelled to take notice; besides, Taura's attention was entirely upon her mentor. Unlike Roic, she never needed the same instruction twice.

When Lady Vorpatril removed herself to consult with the head server about some fine point, Taura leaned over to whisper, "She's *very* good at this, isn't she?"

"Yes. The best."

She sat back with a smile of satisfaction. "Miles's people generally are." She regarded Roic appraisingly.

A server guided a well-dressed Vor matron shepherding a girl-child about Nikki's age past their table toward their own seating. The girl stopped short and stared at Taura. Her hand lifted, pointing in astonishment. "Mama, look at that gigantic—"

The mother captured the hand, shot an alarmed glance at them, and began some hushed admonishment about it not being polite to point. Taura essayed a big friendly smile at the girl. A mistake . . .

The girl screamed and buried her face in her mother's skirts, hands frantically clutching. The woman shot Taura a furious, frightened glower and hustled the little girl away, not toward their table but to the exit. Across the tearoom, Lady Alys's head swiveled around.

Roic looked back at Taura, then wished he hadn't. Her face froze, appalled, then crumpled in distress; she seemed about to burst into tears but caught herself with a long indrawn breath, held for a moment.

Tensed to spring—where?—Roic instead eased back helplessly in his chair. Hadn't m'lord *specifically* detailed him to prevent this sort of thing?

With a gulp, Taura brought her breathing back under control. She looked as wan as though she'd been wounded by a knife thrust. Yet what could he have done? He couldn't very well draw his stunner arid pot some Vor lady's terrified kid . . .

Lady Alys, taking in the incident, returned quickly. With a special frown at Roic, she slid back into her seat. She smoothed over the moment with some light comment, but the outing did not recover its cheerful tone; Taura kept trying to shrink down and sit smaller, a futile exercise, and whenever she began to smile, stopped and tried to hold her hand over her mouth.

Roic wished he were back patrolling Hassadar alleys.

Roic arrived with his charges back at Vorkosigan House feeling as though he'd been run through a wringer. Backward. Several times. He peered around the tower of garment boxes he carried—the rest,

Madame Estelle had assured Taura, would be delivered—and managed not to drop them getting through the carved doors. Under Lady Vorpatril's direction, he handed off the boxes to a pair of maidservants, who whisked them away.

M'lord's voice wafted from the antechamber to the library. "Is that you, Aunt Alys? We're in here."

Roic trod belatedly after the two disparate women just in time to see m'lord introduce Sergeant Taura to his fiancee, Madame Ekaterin Vorsoisson. Like, it seemed, everyone but Roic, she had apparently been warned in advance; she didn't even blink, holding out one hand to the huge galactic woman and offering her an impeccably polite welcome. M'lady-to-be looked fatigued this evening, although that might be partially the effect of the drab gray half-mourning she still wore, her dark hair drawn back in a severe knot. The garb went with the gray civilian suits m'lord favored, though, giving the effect of two players on the same team.

M'lord regarded the new green outfit with unfeigned enthusiasm. "Splendid work, Aunt Alys! I knew I could rely on you. That's a stunning look with the hair, Taura." He peered upward. "Are the fleet medicos making some new headway with the extension treatments? I don't see any gray at all, Great!"

She hesitated, then replied, "No, I just got some customized dye to match it."

"Ah." He made an apologetic motion, as if brushing away his last words. "Well, it looks lovely."

New voices sounded from the entry hall, Armsman Pym admitting a visitor.

"No need to announce me, Pym."

"He's right in there, then, sir. Lady Alys just arrived."

"Better still."

Simon Illyan (ImpSec, retired) entered upon these words, bent to kiss Lady Alys's hand, then tucked it through one arm as he straightened. She smiled fondly at him, and he snugged her in close to his side. He, too, absorbed his introduction to the towering Sergeant Taura with unruffled calm, bowing over her hand and saying, "I am so pleased to nave a chance to meet you at last, Sergeant. I hope your visit to Barrayar has been pleasant so far?"

"Yes, sir," she rumbled back, apparently controlling an impulse to salute the man only because he still held her hand. Roic didn't blame her; he was taller than Illyan too but the formidable former Chief of

Imperial Security made *him* want to salute, and he'd never even been *in* the military. "Lady Alys has been wonderful." No one, it seemed, was going to mention the unfortunate incident in the tearoom.

"I'm not surprised. Oh, Miles," Illyan continued, "I've just come from the Imperial Residence. Some good news came in when I was saying good-bye to Gregor. Lord Vorbataille was arrested this afternoon at the Vorbarr Sultana shuttleport, trying to leave the planet in disguise."

M'lord blew out his breath. "That's going to put *that* ugly little case to bed, then. Good. I was afraid it was going to drag on over Winterfair."

Illyan smiled. "I wondered if that might have had something to do with the energy with which you tackled it."

"Heh. I shall give dear Gregor the benefit of the doubt and assume he did not have my personal deadline in mind when he assigned me to it. The mess did proliferate unexpectedly."

"Case?" Sergeant Taura inquired.

"My new job as one of the nine Imperial Auditors for Emperor Gregor took an odd and unexpected turn into criminal investigation a month or so back," m'lord explained. "We found that Lord Vorbataille, who is a count's heir—like me—from one of our southern districts, had involved himself with a Jacksonian smuggling ring. Or, possibly, been suborned by it. Anyway, by the time his sins caught up with him he was up to his eyebrows in illicit traffic, hijacking, and murder. Very bad company, now wholly out of business, I'm pleased to report. Gregor is considering sending the Jacksonians home in a box, suitably frozen; let their backers decide if they are worth the expense of reviving. If everything is finally proved on Vorbataille that I think will be . . . for his father's sake, he may be allowed to suicide in his cell." M'lord grimaced. "If not, the Council of Counts will have to be persuaded to endorse a more direct redemption of the honor of the Vor. Corruption on this level can't be allowed to slop over and give us all a bad name."

"Gregor is very pleased with your work on this one," Illyan remarked.

"I'll bet. He was livid about the *Princess Olivia* hijacking, in his own understated way. An unarmed ship, all those poor dead passengers—God, what a nightmare."

Roic listened a bit wistfully to all this. He thought he might have done more this past month when m'lord was buzzing in and out on the high-profile case, but Pym hadn't assigned him to the duty. Granted, someone had to stand night guard for Vorkosigan House. Week after week . . .

"But enough of this nasty business"—m'lord caught Madame Vorsoisson's grateful glance—"let's turn to more cheerful affairs. Why don't you finish opening that next package, love?"

Madame Vorsoisson turned back to the crowded table and the task everyone's arrival had interrupted. "Here's the card. Oh. Admiral Quinn, again?"

M'lord took it, brows rising. "What, no limerick this time? How disappointing."

"Perhaps this one is to make up for—Oh, my. I imagine so. And all the way from Earth!" From a small box, she drew a short, triple strand of matched pearls and held them up to her throat. "Choker-style . . . oh, how pretty." Momentarily, she let the iridescent spheres line up upon her neck, touching the two ends of the clasp in back.

"Would you like me to fasten it?" her bridegroom offered.

"Just for a moment . . . " She bent her head, and m'lord reached up and fiddled with the catch at her nape. She walked to the mirror over the room's unlit fireplace, turning to watch the exquisite ornament catch the light, and gave m'lord a quizzical smile. "I believe they would go perfectly with what I'm wearing the day after tomorrow. Don't you think, Lady Alys?"

Lady Alys tilted her head in sartorial judgment. "Why, yes, indeed."

M'lord bowed at this endorsement by the highest authority. The look he exchanged with his bride was less decipherable to Roic, but he seemed very pleased, even relieved. Sergeant Taura, watching the byplay, frowned in unease.

Madame Vorsoisson removed the strands and laid them back in their velvet-lined box, where they glowed softly. "I believe we should let your guests freshen up before dinner, Miles."

"Oh, yes. Except I need to borrow Simon for a moment. Will you excuse us? There will be drinks in the library again when you are all ready. Someone let Arde know. Where is Arde?"

"Nikki captured him and carried him off," said Madame Vorsoisson. "I should probably go rescue the poor man."

M'lord and Illyan withdrew to the library. Lady Alys escorted Taura away, presumably for one last tutorial on Barrayaran etiquette before the impending formal dinner with Count and Countess

Vorkosigan. Taura glanced back at the bride, still frowning. Roic watched the giant woman out with some regret, distracted by the sudden speculation of what it would be like to patrol a Hassadar alley *with* her.

"M'lady—Madame Vorsoisson, that is," Roic began as she started to turn away.

"Not for much longer." She smiled, turning back.

"What's with . . . that is, how old is Sergeant Taura? Do you know?"

"Around twenty-six standard, I believe."

A little younger than Roic, actually. It felt unfair that the galactic woman should seem so much more . . . complicated. "Then why is her hair turning gray? If she's bioengineered, I wouldn't have thought they'd muff up such details."

Madame Vorsoisson made a little gesture of apology. "I believe that is a private matter for her, which is not mine to discuss."

"Oh." Roic's brow wrinkled in bafflement. "Where'd she come from? Where did m'lord meet her?"

"On one of his old covert ops missions, he tells me. He rescued her from a particularly vile bioengineering facility on the planet of Jackson's Whole. They were trying to develop a super-soldier. Having escaped enslavement, she became an especially valued colleague on his ops team." She added after a contemplative moment, "And sometime lover. Also especially valued, I understand."

Roic felt suddenly very . . . rural. Backcountry. Not up to speed on the sophisticated, galactic-tinged Vor life of the capital, "Er . . . he *told* you? And—and you're all right with that?" He wondered if meeting Sergeant Taura had rattled her more than she'd let on.

"It was before my time, Roic." Her smile crimped a little. "I actually wasn't sure if he was confessing or bragging, but now that I've seen her, I rather think he was bragging."

"But-but how would . . . I mean, she's so tall, and he's, um . . ."

Now her eyes narrowed with laughter at him, although her lips remained demure. "He didn't supply me with *that* much detail, Roic. It wouldn't have been gentlemanly."

"To you? No, I guess not."

"To her."

"Oh. Oh. Um, yeah."

"For what it's worth, I have heard him remark that a height differential matters much less when two people are lying down. I find I must agree." With a smile he *really* didn't dare try to interpret, she moved off in search of Nikki.

A scant hour later, Roic was surprised when Pym gave him a heads-up on his wrist com to bring m'lord's groundcar around. He parked it under the porte cochere and entered the black-and-white paved hall to find m'lord assisting Madame Vorsoisson on with her wraps.

"Are you sure you don't want me to go with you?" m'lord asked her anxiously. "I'd like to go with you, see you get home and in all right."

Madame Vorsoisson pressed a hand to her forehead. Her face was pale and damp, almost greenish. "No. No. Roic will get me there. Go back to your guests. They've come so far, and you'll only be getting to see them for such a short time. I'm sorry to be such a drip. Give my abject apologies to the count and countess."

"If you don't feel well, you don't feel well. Don't apologize. Do you think you're coming down with something? I could send our personal physician round."

"I don't know. I hope not, not now! It mostly seems to be a headache." She bit her lip. "I don't think I have a fever."

He reached up to touch her brow; she winced. "No, you're not hot. But you're all clammy." He hesitated, then asked more quietly, "Nerves, d'you think?"

She hesitated, too. "I don't know."

"I have all the wedding logistics under control, you know. All you have to do is show up."

Her smile was pained. "And not fall over."

He was silent a little longer this time. "You know, if you decide that you really can't go through with it, you can call a halt. Any time. Right up to the last. Hope you won't, of course. But I need you to know you could."

"What, with everyone from the emperor and the empress on down coming? I think not."

"I'd cover it, if I had to." He swallowed. "I know you said you wanted a small wedding, but 1 didn't realize you meant *tiny*. I'm sorry."

She blew out her breath in something like exasperation. "Miles, I love you dearly, but if I'm going to start throwing up, I'd really prefer to be home first."

"Oh. Yes. Roic, if you please?" He motioned to his armsman.

Roic took Madame Vorsoisson's arm, which was trembling.

"I'll send Nikki home safely with one of the armsmen after dessert, or after he wears Arde out. I'll call your house and let them know you're coming," m'lord called after her.

She waved in acknowledgment; Roic helped her into the rear compartment and closed the canopy. Her shadowed form sat bent, head clutched in her hands.

M'lord chewed on his knuckle and stared in distress as the house doors swung shut upon him.

Roic's night shift was cut short at dawn the next morning when the count's guard commander called him on his wrist com and told him to report to the front hall in running gear; one of m'lord's guests wanted to go out to take some exercise.

He arrived, shrugging on his jacket, to find Taura bending and stretching in a vigorous series of warm-ups under Pym's bemused eye. Lady Alys's modiste hadn't gotten around to providing active wear, it appeared, because the huge woman wore a plain set of well-worn ship knits, although in neutral gray rather than blinding pink. The fabric hugged the smooth curves of a lean musculature that without being bulky, gave an unmistakable impression of coiled power. The braid down her back looked cheery and sporting in this comfortable context.

"Oh, Armsman Roic, good morning," she said, started to smile, then lifted her hand to her mouth.

"You don't—" Roic motioned inarticulately. "You don't have to do that for me. I like your smile." It wasn't, he realized, altogether a polite lie. *Now that I'm getting used to it.*

Her fangs glinted. "I hope they didn't drag you out of bed. Miles said his people just used the sidewalk around this block for their running track, since it was about a kilometer. I don't think I can go astray."

Roic intercepted a Look from Pym. Roic hadn't been called out to keep m'lord's galactic guest from getting lost; he was there to deal with any altercations that might result from startled Vorbarr Sultana drivers crashing their vehicles onto the sidewalk or each other at the sight of her.

"No problem," said Roic promptly. "We usually use the ballroom for a sort of gymnasium in weather like this, but it's being all decorated for the reception. So I'm behind on my fitness training for the month. It'll be a nice change to do my laps with someone who's not so much older, um, that is, so much shorter than me." He sneaked a glance at Pym.

Pym's wintry smile promised retribution for that dig as he coded open the doors for them. "Enjoy yourselves, children."

The biting air blew away Roic's night's fatigue. He guided Taura out past the guard at the main gate and turned right along the high gray wall. After a few steps, she extended herself and began an easy lope. Within a very few minutes, Roic was regretting his cheap shot at the middle-aged Pym; Taura's long legs ate the distance. Roic kept half an eye on the early morning, traffic, fortunately still light, and concentrated the rest of his attention on not disgracing House Vorkosigan by collapsing in a gasping heap. Taura's eyes grew brilliant with exhilaration as she ran, as if her spirit expanded into her body as her body stretched out to make room.

Half a dozen laps barely winded her, but she slowed at last to a walk, perhaps out of pity for her guide. "Let's circle through the garden to cool down," Roic wheezed. Madame Vorsoisson's garden, which occupied a third of the block and was her bride-gift to m'lord, was among other things sheltered from view of the cross streets by walls and banks. They dodged around the barricades temporarily barring public access till after the wedding.

"Oh, my," said Taura as they turned down the winding walk descending between curving snow hillocks. The chilly brook, its water running black and silky between feathery fingers of ice, snaked gracefully from one corner to the other. The peach-colored dawn light glimmered off the ice on the young trees and shrubs in the blue shadows. "Why, it's beautiful. I didn't expect a garden to be so pretty in winter. What are those men doing?"

A crew was unloading some float pallets piled high with boxes of all sizes, marked FRAGILE. Another pair was going around with water hoses, misting selected branches marked with yellow tags to create yet more delicate, shimmering icicles. The shapes of the native Barrayaran vegetation grew luminous and exotic with this silver-gilding.

"They're putting out all the ice sculptures. M'lord ordered ice flowers and sculptured creatures and things to fill up the garden, since all the real plants are under the snow, pretty much. And fresh snow to be added, too, if there isn't enough." They can't put out t' real live flowers for the ceremony till the very last gasp, late tomorrow morning."

"Good grief, he's having an outdoor garden wedding in *this* weather? Is that—a Barrayaran thing, is it?"

"Um, no. Not exactly. I believe m'lord originally was shooting for fall, but Madame Vorsoisson wasn't ready yet. But he'd got his heart set on getting married in the garden, because it was hers, y'see. So he is, by damn, going to have the wedding in the garden. The idea is people will assemble in Vorkosigan House, then troop out here for the vows, then scurry back into the ballroom for the reception and the food and dancing and all." *And the frostbite and hypothermia treatments.* "It'll be all right if the weather stays clear, I guess." The backstairs commentary on the potential disasters inherent in this scenario, Roic decided to keep to himself. Vorkosigan House's, staff seemed united in their determination to make the eccentric scheme work for m'lord, anyway.

Taura's eyes glinted in the level dawn light now filtering between the buildings of the surrounding cityscape. "I can hardly wait to try out the dress Lady Alys got up for me to wear to the ceremony. Barrayaran ladies' clothes are so interesting. But complicated. In a way, I suppose they're another kind of uniform, but I don't know whether I feel like a recruit or an enemy spy in them. Well, I don't suppose the real ladies will shoot me in any case. So much to learn about how to go on—though I suppose it all seems ridiculously easy to you. You grew up with it."

"I didn't grow up with *this*." Roic waved a hand toward the imposing stone pile of Vorkosigan House rising above the high, bare trees on its grounds. "My father is just a construction hand in Hassadar—that's the Vorkosigan's District capital city, just this side of the Dendarii Mountains, a few hundred kilometers south of here. Lots of building going on there. He offered to apprentice me to the trade, but I got the chance to become a street guard, and I took it— sort of an impulse, truth to tell. I was eighteen, didn't know up from down. Sure learned a lot after that."

"What does a street guard guard? Streets?"

"Among other things. The whole city, really. You do what needs done. Sort out traffic, before or after it's a big bent pile. Deal with upset people's problems, try to keep 'em from murdering their relatives, or clean up the mess after if you can't. Trace stolen property, if you get lucky. I did a lot of night foot patrol. You learn a lot about a place on foot, up close. I learned how to handle stunners and shocksticks and big, hostile drunks. I was getting pretty good at it, I thought, after a few years."

"How did you end up here?"

"Oh . . . there was a little incident . . ." He gave an embarrassed shrug. "Some crazed loon tried to shoot up Hassadar Square at rush hour with an auto-needler. I, um, took it away from him."

Her brows went up. "With a stunner?"

"No, unfortunately, I was off duty at the time. Had to do it by hand."

"A little hard to get up close and personal with someone firing a needler."

"That was a problem, yeah."

Her lips curved up, or at least the ivory hooks lengthened.

"It seemed to make perfect sense at the moment, though later I wondered what t' hell I'd been thinking. I don't think I was thinking. At any rate, he only killed five and not fifty-five. People seemed to think it was a big deal, but I'm sure it's nothing compared to what you've seen out there."

His glance upward was meant to indicate the distant stars, though the sky was now a paling blue.

"Hey, I may be big, but I'm not needler-proof. I hate the shrieky sound when the razor-strands unwind and whiz around, even though I know in my head that those are the ones that *missed*."

"Yeah," Roic said in heartfelt agreement. "Anyways, after that there was a stupid fuss, and someone recommended me to m'lord's own armsman commander, Pym, and here I am." He glanced around the sparkling fairy garden. "I think I was a better fit in the Hassadar alleys."

"Naw, Miles always did like having big backup. Saves a lot of small-scale grief. Though the large-scale grief we still had to take as it came."

He asked after a moment, "How did you bodyguard, um, m'lord?"

"Such a funny way of thinking of him. To me, he'll always be the little admiral. Mostly, I just loomed at people. If I had to, I smiled."

"But your smile's really kind of nice," he protested, and managed not to add the *once you get used to it* out loud. He'd get the hang of this savoir faire thing yet.

"Oh, no. The *other* smile." She demonstrated, her lips wrinkling back, her jaw thrusting out. Roic had to admit, it was a much *wider* smile. And, um, *sharper.* They were just treading past a workman on the rising path; he gasped and fell backward into a snowbank. With lightning reflexes, Taura reached past Roic and caught the heavy, life-size ice sculpture of a crouching fox before it hit the pavement and shattered into shards. Roic lifted the gibbering man to his feet and dusted snow off his parka, and Taura handed back the elegant ornament with a compliment upon its artistry.

Roic managed not to choke with muffled laughter till they both had their backs to the fellow, heading away. "See what you mean. Did it ever not work?"

"Occasionally. Next step was to pick up the recalcitrant one by the neck. Since my arms were invariably longer than theirs, they'd swing like mad but couldn't connect. Very frustrating for them."

"And after that?"

She grinned. "Stunner, by preference."

"Heh. Yep."

They'd fallen unconsciously into an easy side-by-side pace, tracing loops around the garden paths. Talking shop, Roic thought. "What mass d'you lift?"

"With or without adrenaline?"

"Oh, without, say."

"Two hundred fifty kilos, with a good grip and a good angle."

He emitted a respectful whistle. "If you ever want to give up mercenary-ing, I can think of a fire fighting cadre might could welcome you. M'brother's in one, down Hassadar way. Though come to think of it, m'lord'd be a more powerful reference."

"Now, there's an idea I'd never thought of." She pursed her long lips, and her brows bent in a quizzical curve. "But, no. I expect I'll be, as you say, mercenary-ing till . . . for the rest of my life. I like seeing new planets. I like seeing this one. I could never have imagined it."

"How many have you seen?"

"I think I've lost count. 1 used to know. Dozens. How many have you—seen?"

"Just t' one," he admitted. "Though hanging around m'lord, this one keeps getting wider till I'm almost dizzy. More complicated. Does that make sense?"

She threw back her head and laughed. "That's our Miles. Admiral Quinn always said she'd follow him halfway to hell just to find out what happened next."

"Wait—this Quinn you all keep talking about is a *lady* admiral?"

"She was a lady commander when I first met her. Second-sharpest tactical brain it's ever been my privilege to know. Things may get tight, following Elli Quinn, but you know they won't get *stupid*. She didn't sleep her way to the top by a long shot, and they're half-wits who say so." She grinned briefly. "*That* was just a *perk*. Some might say his, but *I'd* say hers."

Roic's eyes crossed, trying to unravel this. "Y'mean m'lord was lovers with *her*, t-" He cut off the *too* not quite in time, and flushed. It seemed m'lord's covert ops career was even more . . . *complicated* than he'd ever imagined.

Taura cocked her head and regarded him with crinkling eyes. "That's my favorite shade of pink, Roic. You *are* a country boy, aren't you? Life's uncertain out there. Things can go down bad, fast, anytime. People learn to grab what they can, when they can. For a time. We all just get a time, in our different ways." She sighed. "Their ways diverged when he took those horrible injuries that bounced him out of ImpSec. He couldn't go back up, and she wouldn't come down here. Elli Quinn's got no one but herself to blame for any chances she threw away. Though some people are born with more chances to waste than others, I'll admit. I say, grab the ones you're issued, run with them, and don't look back."

"Something might be gaining on you?"

"I know perfectly well what's gaining on me." Her grin flashed, oddly tilted this time. "Anyway, Quinn might be more beautiful, but *I* was always taller." She gave a satisfied nod. Glancing at him, she added, "I guarantee Miles likes *your* height. It's sort of an issue with him. I know recruiting officers in three genders who would swoon for your shoulders, as well."

He hadn't the least idea how to respond to *that*. He hoped she was enjoying the pink. "M'lord thinks I'm a fool," he said glumly.

Her brows shot up. "Surely not."

"Oh, yeah. You have no idea how I screwed up."

"I've seen him forgive screwups that put *his* guts on the bloody ceiling. Literally. You'd have to go some to top that. How many people died?"

If you put it in *that* perspective . . . "No one," he admitted. "I just wished *I* could have."

She grinned in sympathy. "Ah, one of *those* kinds of screwups. Oh, c'mon, tell."

He hesitated. "Y'know those nightmares where you find yourself walking around naked in the town square, or in front of your schoolteachers, or something?"

"My nightmares tend to be a bit more exotic, but yeah?"

"So, no lie, there I was . . . Last summer, m'lord's brother Mark brought home this damned Escobaran biologist, Dr. Borgos, that he'd picked up somewheres, and put him up in the basement of Vorkosigan House. An investment scheme. The biologist made bugs. And the bugs made bug butter. Tons of it. Slimy white stuff, edible, sort of. We found out the biologist had jumped bail back on Escobar—for fraud, no surprise—when t' skip-tracers they'd sent to arrest him showed up and talked their way into Vorkosigan House. Naturally, they picked a time when almost everyone had gone out. Lord Mark and the Koudelka sisters, who were in on the bug butter scheme, got in a fight with them when they tried to carry off Borgos, and the house staff waked me up to go sort it out. All in a tearing panic wouldn't even let me grab my uniform trousers. I'd *just* got to sleep . . . Martya Koudelka claims it was friendly fire, but I dunno. I'd just about pushed the whole mess of 'em out the front door when in walks m'lord with Madame Vorsoisson and all her relatives. He'd just got engaged and wanted to make a good impression on 'em all . . . It was an unforgettable one, 1 guarantee. I was wearing briefs, boots, and about five kilos of bug butter, trying to deal wit' all these screaming, sticky maniacs . . ."

A muffled sound escaped from Taura. She had her hand over her mouth, but it wasn't helping; little squeaks still leaked out. Her eyes were alight.

"I swear it wouldn't a' been half so bad if I'd had my briefs on backwards and my stunner holster on frontways. 1 can still hear Pym's voice . . ." He mimicked the senior armsman's driest tones: " 'Your weapon is worn on the right, Armsman.' "

She laughed out loud then, and looked him up and down in somewhat unsettling appreciation. "That's a pretty amazing word picture, Roic."

Despite himself, he smiled a little. "I guess so. I dunno if m'lord's forgiven me, but I'm right sure Pym hasn't." He sighed. "If you see one of those damned vomit bugs still around, squash it on sight. Hideous bioengineered mutant things, kill 'em all before they multiply."

Her laughter stopped cold.

Roic reran his last sentence in his head and made the unpleasant discovery that one could do far worse things to oneself with words than with dubious food products, or possibly even with needlers. He hardly dared look up to see her face. He forced his eyes right.

Her face was perfectly still, perfectly pale, perfectly blank. Perfectly appalling.

I meant those devil-bugs, not you! He managed to stop that idiocy on his lips before it escaped to do even more damage, but only just. He couldn't think of any way to apologize that wouldn't make it worse.

"Ah, yes," she said at last. "Miles did warn me that Barrayarans had some pretty ugly issues about gene manipulation. I just forgot."

And I reminded you. "We're getting better," he tried.

"Good for you." She inhaled, a long breath. "Let's go in. I'm getting cold."

Roic was frozen straight through. "Um. Yeah."

They walked back to the gate in silence

Roic slept the day around, trying to force his body back onto the boring night shift cycle that by the duty roster was to be his junior armsman's fate this Winterfair. He was quite sorry to thus miss seeing m'lord take his galactic guests and a selection of his in-laws-to-be on a tour of Vorbarr Sultana. He'd have been fascinated by what the two disparate parties made of each other. Madame Vorsoisson's family, the Vorvaynes, were solid provincial Vor types of the sort Roic had always regarded as normal to the class, before he'd taken up his duties in Vorkosigan House's high Vor milieu. M'lord, well . . . m'lord wasn't standard by anybody's standard. The four Vorvayne brothers, though dutifully pleased with their widowed sister's upward social leap, plainly found m'lord an unnerving catch. Roic wished he could see what they would make of Taura. He melted into sleep with a vague scenario drifting through his reeling brain of somehow imposing his body between her and some undefined social insult. Maybe then she would see that he hadn't meant anything by his awful gaffe . . .

He woke at sunset and made a foray down to Vorkosigan House's huge kitchen, below stairs. Usually m'lord's genius cook, Ma Kosti, left delectable surprises in the staff refrigerator and was always looking for a good gossip, but tonight the pickings were slim and the personal attention nonexistent. The place was plunged into final preparations for tomorrow's great event, and Ma Kosti, driving her harried scullions before her, made it plain that anyone below the rank of count, or perhaps emperor, was very much in the way just now. Roic fueled up and retreated.

At least the kitchen did not have to deal with a formal dinner atop all the rest. M'lord, the count and countess, and all the guests were off to the Imperial Residence for the Winterfair Ball and midnight bonfire, the heart of the festivities marking solstice night and the turning of the season. When they all decamped from Vorkosigan House, Roic had the vast place to himself, but for the rumble from the kitchen and the servants rushing about completing the last-minute decorations and arrangements in the public rooms, the great dining room, and the seldom-used ballroom.

He was therefore surprised, about an hour before midnight, when the gate guard called him to code open the front door. He was even more surprised when a small car with government markings pulled up under the porte cochere and m'lord and Sergeant Taura climbed out. The car buzzed off, and its passengers entered the hall, shaking the cold air out of their outer garments and handing them off to Roic.

M'lord was dressed in the most elaborate version of the brown and silver Vorkosigan House uniform, befitting a count's heir attending upon the emperor, complete with custom-fitted polished riding boots to his knees. Taura wore a close-fitting, embroidered russet jacket, made high to the neck where a bit of lace showed, and a matching skirt sweeping to ankles clad in soft, russet-colored leather boots. A graceful spray of cream-and-rust colored orchids was wound into her braided-up hair. Roic wished he could have seen her entrance into the Imperial Winterfair Ball, and heard what the emperor and empress had said upon meeting her . . .

"No, I'm all right," Taura was saying to m'lord. "I saw the palace and the ball—they were beautiful—but I've had enough. It's just that I was up at dawn, and to tell the truth, I think I'm still a little jump-lagged. Go see to your bride. Is she still sick?"

"I wish I knew." M'lord paused on the steps, three up, and leaned on the banister to speak face-to-face with Taura, who was watching him in concern. "She wasn't sure even last week about attending the emperor's bonfire tonight, though I thought it would be a valuable distraction. She insisted she was all right when I talked to her earlier. But her aunt Helen says she's all to pieces, hiding in her room and crying. This is just not like her. I thought she was tough as anything. Oh, God, Taura. I think I've screwed up this whole wedding thing so badly . . . I rushed her into it, and now it's all coming apart. I can't imagine how bad the stress must be to make her physically ill."

"Slow down, dammit, Miles. Look. You said her first marriage was dire, yes?"

"Not bruises and black eyes bad, no. Draining the blood of your spirit out drop by drop for years bad, maybe. I only saw the very end of it. It was pretty gruesome by then."

"Words can cut worse than knives. The wounds take longer to heal, too."

She didn't look at Roic. Roic didn't look back.

"Isn't that the truth," said m'lord, who wasn't looking at either of them. "Damn! Should I go over there or not? They say it's bad luck to see the bride before the wedding. Or was that the wedding dress? I can't remember."

Taura made a face. "And you accuse *her* of having wedding heebie-jeebies! Miles, listen. You know how the recruits got precombat nerves before they went out on a mission the first time?"

"Oh, yes."

"Now. Do you remember how they got precombat nerves before they had to go out on a big drop for the *second* time?"

After a long pause, m'lord said, "Oh." Another silence. "I hadn't thought of it like that. I thought it was *me*."

"That's because you're an egotist. I only met the woman for one hour, but even I could see that you're the delight of her eyes. At least consider, for five consecutive seconds, the possibility that it might be *him*. The late Vorsoisson, whoever he was."

"Oh, he was something else, all right, I've cursed him before for the scars he left on her soul."

"I don't think you have to say anything much. Just *be* there. And be not him."

M'lord drummed his fingers on the banister. "Yes. Maybe. God. Pray God. Dammit . . ." He glanced across at Roic, ignored as if he were Vorkosigan House furniture, a rack to hold coats. A dummy. "Roic, scrape up a vehicle; meet me back here in a few minutes. I want you to drive me over to Ekaterin's aunt and uncle's house. I'm going to run up and change out of this armor-plating first, though." He ran his fingers across the elaborate silver embroidery upon his sleeve. He turned away, and his bootsteps scuffed up the stairs.

This was way too alarming. "What in t' world's going on?" Roic dared to ask Taura.

"Ekaterin's aunt called him. I gather Ekaterin lives at her house—"

"With Lord Auditor and Professora Vorthys, yes. She's been going to University from there."

"Anyway, the bride-to-be seems to be having some sort of awful nervous breakdown or something." She frowned. "Or something . . . Miles isn't sure if he should go over and sit with her or not. I think he should."

That didn't sound good. In fact, it sounded about as not-good it could be.

"Roic . . ." Taura's brows knotted. "Do you happen to know if I could find any commercial pharmaceutical laboratories open at this time of night in Vorbarr Sultana?"

"Pharmaceutical labs?" Roic repeated blankly. "Why, do you feel sick, too? I can call out the Vorkosigans' personal physician for you, or one of the medtechs who ride herd on the count and countess . . ." Would she need some kind of off-world specialist? No matter, the Vorkosigan name could access one, he was sure. Even on Bonfire Night.

"No, no, I feel fine. I was just wondering."

"Nothing much is open tonight. It's a holiday. Everyone's out to the parties and bonfires and the fireworks. Tomorrow, too. It'll be the first day of the new year here, by the Barrayaran calendar."

She smiled briefly. "It would be. A new start all round; I'll bet he liked the symbolism of that."

"I suppose hospital labs are open all night. Their emergency treatment intakes will be. Busy as hell, too. We used to bring the ones in Hassadar all kinds of customers on 'Bonfire Night"

"Hospitals, yes, of course! I should have thought of them at once."

"Why do you want one?" he asked again.

She hesitated. "I'm not sure that I do. It was just a train of thought I had earlier this evening, when that aunt-lady called Miles. Not sure I like its destination, though . . ." She turned away and swung up the stairs, taking them two at a time without effort. Roic frowned, then went off to scare up a vehicle from whatever remained in the sub-basement garage. With so many signed out to transport the household and its guests already, this might take some rapid extemporizing.

But Taura had spoken to him, almost normally. Maybe . . . maybe there were such things as second chances. If a fellow was brave enough to take them.

Lord Auditor and Professora Vorthys's home was a tall, old, colorfully tiled structure close to the District University. The street was quiet when Roic pulled the car—borrowed without notification, ultimately, from one of the armsmen off with the count at the Residence—up to the front. From a distance, mainly in the direction of the university, drifted the sharp crackle of fireworks, harmonious singing, and blurred drunken singing. A rich, heady scent of wood smoke and black powder permeated the frosty night air.

The porch light was on. The Professora, an aging, smiling, neat Vor lady who intimidated Roic only slightly less than did Lady Alys, let them in herself. Her soft round face was tense with worry.

"Did you tell her I was coming?" m'lord asked in a low tone as he shed his coat. He stared anxiously up the stairs leading from the narrow, wood-paneled hallway.

"I didn't dare."

"Helen . . . what should I do?" M'lord looked suddenly smaller, and scared, and younger and older all at the same time.

"Just go up, I think. This isn't something that's about talking, or words, or reason. I've run through all those."

He buttoned then unbuttoned the gray tunic he'd thrown on over an old white shirt, pulled down his sleeves, took a deep breath, mounted the stairs, and turned out of sight. After a minute or two, the Professora stopped picking nervously at her hands, gestured Roic to a straight chair beside a small table piled with books and flimsies and tiptoed up after him.

Roic sat in the hall and listened to the old house creak. From the sitting room, visible through one archway, a glow from a fireplace gilded the air. Through the opposite arch way, the Professora's study lay, lined with books; the light from the hall picked out an occasional bit of gold lettering on an ancient spine in the gloom. Roic wasn't bookish himself, but he liked the comfortable academic smell of this place. It occurred to him that back when he was a Hassadar guard, he'd never once gone into a house to clean up a bad scene, blood on the walls and evil smells in the air where there were books like this.

After a long time, the Professora came back down to the hall.

Roic ducked his head respectfully. "Is she sick, ma'am?"

The tired-looking woman pursed her lips and let her breath run out. "She certainly was last night. Terrible headache, so bad she was crying and almost vomiting. But she thought she was much better this morning. Or she said she was. She wanted to be better. Maybe she was trying too hard."

Roic peered anxiously up the staircase. "Would she see him?"

The tension in her face eased a little. "Yes."

"Is it going to be all right?"

"I think so, now." Her lips sought a smile. "Anyway, Miles says you are to go on home. That he expects to be a while, and that he'll call if he needs anything."

"Yes, ma'am." He rose, have her a kind of vague salute copied from m'lord's own style, and let himself out.

The night duty guard at the gate kiosk reported no entries since Roic had left. The festivities at the Imperial Residence would go on till dawn, although Roic didn't expect Vorkosigan House's attendees to stay that late, not with the grand party planned here for tomorrow afternoon and evening. He put the borrowed car away in the subbasement garage, relieved that it hadn't acquired any hard-to-explain dings in its passage back through some of the rowdier crowds between here and the university.

He made his way softly up through the mostly darkened great house. All was quiet now. The kitchen crew had at last retreated till tomorrow's onslaught. The maids and menservants had gone to roost. For all that he complained about missing the daytime excitements, Roic usually enjoyed these quiet night hours when the whole world seemed his personal property. Granted, by three hours before dawn, coffee would be a necessity little less urgent than oxygen. But by two hours before dawn, life would start trickling back, as those with early duties roused themselves and padded down to start work. He checked the security monitors in the basement HQ and started his physical rounds. Floor by floor, window and door, never in quite the same order or at quite the same hour.

As he crossed the great entry hall, a creak and a clink sounded from the half-lit antechamber to the library. He paused for a moment, frowned, and rose on his toes, moving his feet as gently as possible across the marble pavement, breathing through his open mouth for silence. His shadow wavered, passed along from dim wall sconce to dim wall sconce. He made sure it was not thrown before him as he moved to the archway. Easing up beside the door frame, he stared into the half-gloom.

Taura stood with her back to him, sorting through the gifts displayed upon the long table by the far wall. Her head bent over something in her hands. She shook out a cloth and upended a small box. The elegant triple strand of pearls slithered from their velvet backing into the cloth, which she wrapped around them. She clicked the box closed, set it back on the table, and slipped the folded cloth into a side pocket of her russet jacket.

Shock held Roic paralyzed for a moment longer. M'lord's honored guest, rifling the gifts?

But I liked her. I really liked her. Only now, in this moment of hideous revelation, did he realize just how much he'd come to . . . to *admire* her in their brief time together. Brief, but so damned awkward. She was really beautiful in her own unique way, if only you looked at her right. For a moment it had seemed as though far suns and strange adventures had beckoned to him from her gold eyes; just possibly, more intimate and exotic adventures than a shy backcountry boy from Hassadar had ever dared to imagine. If only he were a braver man. A handsome prince. Not a fool. But Cinderella was a thief, and the fairy tale was gone suddenly sour.

Sick dismay flooded him as he imagined the altercation, the shame, the wounded friendship and shattered trust that must follow this discovery—he almost turned away. He didn't know the value of the pearls, but even if it were a city's ransom he was certain m'lord would trade them in a heartbeat for the ease of spirit he'd had with his old followers.

It was no good. They'd be missed first thing tomorrow in any case. He drew a breath and touched the light pad.

Taura spun like a huge cat at the flare of the overhead lights. After a moment, she let out her breath in a huff; visibly powering down. "Oh. It's you. You startled me."

Roic moistened his lips. Could he patch up this shattered fantasy? "Put them back, Taura. Please."

She stood still, looking back at him, tawny eyes wide; a grimace crossed her odd features. She seemed to coil, tension flowing back into her long body.

"Put them back now," Roic tried again, "and I won't tell." He bore a stunner. Could he draw it in time? He'd seen how fast she moved . . .

"I can't."

He stared at her without comprehension.

"I don't *dare*." Her voice grew edgy. "Please, Roic. Let me go now, and I promise I'll bring them back again tomorrow."

Huh? What? "I . . . can't. All the gifts have to go through a security check."

"Did this?" Her hand twitched by her pocket full of spoils.

"Yes, certainly."

"What kind? What did you check it for?"

"Everything is scanned for devices and explosives. All food and drink and their containers are tested for chemicals and biologicals."

"Only the food and drink?" She straightened, eyes glinting in rapid thought. "Anyway, I wasn't stealing it."

Maybe it was the covert ops training that enabled her to stand there and utter bald-faced . . . what? Counter-factual statements? *Complicated things?* "Well . . . then what *were* you doing?"

Again, a kind of frozen misery stiffened her features. She looked down, away, into the distance. "Borrowing it," she said in a gruff voice. She glanced across at him, as if to check his reaction to this feeble statement.

But Taura wasn't feeble, not by any definition. He felt out of his depth, flailing for firm footing and not finding it. He dared to move closer, to hold out his hand. "Give them to me."

"You mustn't touch them!" Her voice went frantic. "No one must touch them."

Lies and treachery? Trust and truth? What was he seeing here? Suddenly, he wasn't sure. *Back up, guardsman.* "Why not?"

She glowered at him narrow-eyed, as if trying to see through to the back of his head. "Do you care about Miles? Or is he just your employer?"

Roic blinked in increasing confusion. He considered his armsman's oath, its high honor and weight. "A Vorkosigan armsman isn't just what I am; it's *who* I am. He's not my *employer* at all. He's my liege lord."

She made a frustrated gesture. "If you knew a secret that would hurt him to the heart—would you, could you, keep it from him even if *he* asked?"

What secret? This? That his ex-lover was a thief? It didn't seem as though that could be what she was talking about—around. *Think, man.*

"I . . . can't pass a judgment without knowledge." Knowledge. What did she know that he didn't? A million things, he was sure, He'd glimpsed some of them, dizzying vistas. But she didn't know *him,* now, did she? Not the way she evidently knew, say, m'lord. To her, he was a blank in a brown-and-silver uniform. With his mirror-polished boot stuck in his mouth, eh. He hesitated, then countered, "M'lord can requisition my life with a word. I gave him that right on my name and breath. Can you trust *me* to hold his best interests to heart?"

Stare met stare, and no one blinked

"Trust for trust," Roic breathed at last. "Trade, Taura." Slowly, not dropping her intent, searching gaze from his face, she drew the cloth from her pocket. She shook it gently, spilling the pearls back into their velvet box. She held the box out. "What do you see?"

Roic frowned. "Pearls. Pretty. White and shiny."

She shook her head. "I have a host of genetic modificaitions. Hideous bioengineered mutant or no—"

He flinched, his mouth opening and shutting.

"—among other things I can see slightly farther into the ultraviolet, and quite a bit farther into the infrared, than a normal person. *I* see dirty pearls. Strangely dirty pearls. And that's not what I usually see when I look at pearls. And then Miles's bride touched them, and an hour later was so sick she could hardly stand up."

An unpleasant tremor coursed down Roic's body. And why the devil hadn't *he* noticed that progression of events? "Yes. That's so. They'll have to be checked."

"Maybe I'm wrong. I could be wrong. Maybe I'm just being horrible and paranoid and—and jealous. If they were proved clean, that would be the end of it. But, Roic—*Quinn.* You don't have any idea how much he loved Quinn. And vice versa. I've been going half-mad all evening, ever since it all clicked in, wondering if Quinn really sent these. It would about slay him, if it were so."

"Wasn't him these are meant to slay." It seemed his liege lord's love life was as deceptively complicated as his intelligence, both camouflaged by his crippled body. Or by the assumptions people made about his crippled body, Roic considered the ambiguous message Arde Mayhew had evidently seen in the live fur blanket. *Had* this Quinn woman, the other ex-lover—and how many more of them were going to turn up at this wedding, anyway? And in what frame of mind? How many *were* there, altogether? And what t' *hell* did the little guy do to have acquired what was beginning to seem far more than his fair share, when Roic didn't even have— He cut off the gyrating digression. "Or—is this necklace lethal, or not? Could it be some nasty practical joke, to just make the bride sick on her wedding night?"

"Ekaterin barely touched them. I don't know what this horrible goo may be, but 1 wouldn't lay those pearls against my skin for Betan dollars." Her face twisted up. "I want it to not be true. Or I want it to not be Quinn!"

Her dismay, Roic was increasingly convinced, was unfeigned, a cry from her heart. "Taura, think. You know this Quinn woman. I don't. But you said she was smart. D'you think she'd be plain stupid enough to sign her own name to murder?"

Taura looked taken aback, but then shook her head in renewed doubt. "Maybe. If it were done for rage or revenge, maybe."

"What if her name was stolen by another? If she didn't send these, she deserves to be cleared. And if she did . . . she doesn't deserve anything."

What was Taura going to do? He hadn't the least doubt she could kill him with one clawed hand before he could fumble his stunner out. The box was still tightly clutched in her great hand. Her body radiated tension the way a bonfire radiated heat.

"It seems almost unimaginable," she said. "Almost. But people mad in love do the wildest things. Sometimes things they regret forever afterward. But then it's too late. That's why I wanted to sneak the pearls away and check them in secret. I was praying I'd be proved wrong." Tears stood in her eyes now.

Roic swallowed and stood straighter. "Look, I can call ImpSec. They can have those—whatever they are—on the best forensics lab bench on the planet inside half an hour. They can check the wrappings, check the origin, everything. If *another* person stole your friend Quinn's name to cloak their crime . . ." He shuddered as his imagination sketched that crime in elaborating and grotesque detail: m'lady dying at m'lord's feet in the snow while her vows were still frost in the air; m'lord's shock, disbelief, howling anguish—"Then they should be hunted down without mercy. ImpSec can do that, too."

She still stood poised in doubt, on the balls of her feet. . "They would hunt *her* down with the same . . . un-mercy. What if they got it wrong, made a mistake?"

"ImpSec is competent."

"Roic, *I'm* an ImpSec employee. I can absolutely *guarantee* you, they are *not* infallible."

He ran his gaze down the crowded table. "Look. There's that other wedding gift." He pointed to the folds of shimmering black blanket, still piled in the box. The room was so quiet he could hear the live fur's gentle rumble from here. "Why would she send two? The blanket even came with a dirty limerick, handwritten on a card." Not presently on display, true. "Madame Vorsoisson laughed out loud when m'lord read it to her."

A reluctant smile twitched Taura's mouth for a moment. "Oh, *that's* Quinn, all right."

"If *that's* truly Quinn, then this"—he pointed at the pearls—"can't be. Eh? Trust me. Trust your own judgment." Slowly, with the deepest distress in her strange gold eyes, Taura wrapped the box in the cloth and handed it to him.

Then Roic found himself facing the task, all by himself, of stirring up ImpSec Supreme headquarters in the middle of the night. He almost wanted to wait for Pym's return. But he *was* a Vorkosigan armsman: senior man present, even if merely because sole man present. It was his duty, it was his right, and time was of the essence, if only to relieve Taura's troubled mind at the earliest possible instant. She hovered, bleak and worried, as he gulped for nerve and fired up the secured comconsole in the nearby library.

A serious-looking ImpSec captain reported to the front hall in less than thirty minutes. He recorded everything, including Roic's verbal report, Taura's description of what the pearls had looked like to her, both their accounts of Madame Vorsoisson's witnessed symptoms, and a copy of Pym's original security check records. Roic tried to be straightforward, as he'd often wished witnesses would have been to him back in Hassadar, although in this version the fraught confrontation in the antechamber became merely *Sergeant Taura voiced a suspicion to me.* Well, it was *true.*

For Taura's sake, Roic made sure to mention the possibility that the pearls had not been sent by Ouinn at all and pointed out the other gift certainly known to be from her. The captain frowned and bundled up the live fur as well, and looked as though he wanted to bundle up Taura along with it. He carried off the pearls, the still-purring blanket, and all related packaging in a series of sealed and labeled plastic bags. All this chill efficiency took a bare half hour more.

"Do you want to go to bed?" Roic asked Taura when the doors closed behind the ImpSec captain. *She looks so tired.* "I have to stay up anyway. I can give you a call to your room when there's any news. If there's any news."

She shook her head. "I couldn't sleep. Maybe they'll have something soon."

"There's no telling, but I hope so."

They settled down to wait together on a sturdy-looking sofa in the antechamber opposite the one displaying the gifts. The noises of the night—odd squeaks of the house settling against the winter cold, the faint whir or hum of distant automated machinery—were very noticeable in the stillness. Taura stretched what Roic suspected were knotted shoulders, and he was briefly inspired to offer a back rub, but he wasn't sure how she'd take it. The impulse dissolved in cowardice.

"Quiet around here at night," she said after a moment.

She was speaking to him again. *Please, don't stop.* "Yeah, I sort of like it, though."

"Oh, you, too? The night watch is a philosophical kind of time. Its own world. Nothing moving out there but maybe people being born or people dying, necessity, and us."

"Eh, and the bad night people we're put on watch against."

She glanced through the archway into the great hall and beyond. "Apparently so. What an evil trick . . ." She trailed off in a grimace.

"This Quinn, you've known her a long time?"

"She was in the Dendarii mercenaries at the time I joined the fleet—'original equipment,' as she says. A good leader, a friend by many shared disasters. And victories, sometimes. Ten years adds up to some weight, even if you're not watching. Especially if you're not watching, I suppose."

He followed the thought spoken by her glance, as well as her words. "Eh, yeah. God spare me from ever facing such a puzzle. It would be as bad as having your count revolt against the emperor, I suppose. Or like finding m'lord in on some insane plot to murder Empress Laisa. Shouldn't wonder that you've been running around in circles in your head all night."

"Tighter and tighter, yes. I couldn't enjoy the emperor's party from the moment I thought of it, and I know Miles so wanted me to. And I couldn't tell him why—I'm afraid he thought I was feeling out of place. Well, I was, but it wasn't a problem, exactly. I'm usually out of place." She blinked tawny eyes gone dark and wide in the half-light. "What would you do? If you discovered or suspected such a horror?"

His lips twisted. "That's a tough one. A higher honor must underlie ours, the count says. We can't ever obey unthinkingly."

"Huh. That's what Miles says, too. Is that where he got it, from his father?"

"I shouldn't be surprised. M'lord's brother Mark says integrity is a disease, and you can only catch it from someone who has it."

A little laugh sounded in her throat. "That sounds like Mark, all right."

He considered her question with the seriousness it merited. "I'd have to turn him in, I guess. I hope I'd have the courage, anyways. Nobody would win, in the end. Least of all me."

"Oh, yeah. I can see that."

Her hand lay on the sofa fabric between them, clawed fingers tapping. He wanted to take it and squeeze it for comfort—hers, or his? But he didn't dare. *Dammit, try, can't you?*

His argument with himself was interrupted when his wrist com sounded. The gate guard reported the return of the Vorkosigan House party from the Imperial Residence. Roic coded down the house shields and stood aside as the crowd disembarked from a small fleet of groundcars. Pym was in close attendance upon the countess, smiling at something she was saying over her shoulder to him. The guests, variously cheerful, drowsy, or drunk, streamed past chatting and laughing.

"Anything to report?" Pym inquired perfunctorily. He glanced in curiosity past Roic at Taura, looming over his shoulder.

"Yes, sir. See me in private as soon as you can, please." The benign sleepy look evaporated from Pym's features.

"Oh?" He glanced back at the mob now divesting wraps and streaming up the stairs. "Right."

Low-voiced as Roic had been, the countess had caught the exchange. A wave of her finger dismissed Pym from her side. "Although, if this is of moment, Pym, I'll take a report before bed," she murmured.

"Yes, my lady."

Roic jerked his head toward the antechamber of the library, and Pym followed him and Taura through the archway. The moment the guests had cleared the next room, Roic decanted a short precis of the night's adventure, self-plagiarized from the one he'd given to the ImpSec forensics' captain. Omitting, again, the part about Taura's attempted theft. He hoped like hell that it wasn't going to turn out to be horribly pertinent later. He would submit the full account to m'lord's judgment, he decided. When the devil was m'lord going to return?

Pym grew rigid as he took in the report. "I checked that necklace myself, Roic. Scanned it clear of devices—the chemical sniffer didn't pick up anything either."

"Did you touch it?" asked Taura.

Pym's eyes narrowed in memory. "I mainly handled it by the clasp. Well . . . well, ImpSec will run it through the wringer. M'lord always claims they can use the exercise. It can't hurt. You acted correctly, Armsman Roic. You can continue about your duties now. I'll follow it up with ImpSec."

With this tepid praise, he moved off, frowning

"Is that all we get?" Taura whispered as Pym's ascending footsteps faded on the winding staircase.

Roic glanced at his chrono. "Till ImpSec reports back, I guess. It depends on how hard that dirty stuff you saw"—he didn't insult her by phrasing it as *you claimed you saw*—"is to identify."

She scrubbed tired-looking eyes with the back of her hand. "Can I, uh, can I stay with you till they call?"

"Sure."

In a moment of true inspiration, he led her down to the kitchen and introduced her to the staff refrigerator. He'd been correct; her extraordinary metabolism was in need of fuel again. Ruthlessly, he cleared out everything on the shelves and laid it in front of her. The early morning crew could fend for themselves. There was no shame here in offering up servants' food to a guest; *everyone* ate well from Ma Kosti's kitchen. He dialed up coffee for himself and tea for her, and they perched together on two stools at the counter.

Pym found them there as they were finishing eating. The senior armsman's face was so drained of blood as to be nearly green.

"Well done, Roic, Sergeant Taura," he began in a stiff voice. "Very well done. I just now spoke with ImpSec headquarters. The pearls *were* doctored—with a designer neurotoxin. ImpSec thinks it's of Jacksonian origin, but they're still cross-checking. The dose was sealed under a chemically neutral transparent lacquer that dissolves with body heat. Casual handling wouldn't release it, but if someone put the necklace on and wore it for a time . . . half an hour or so . . . "

"Enough to kill someone?" Taura's tone was tense.

"Enough to kill a bloody elephant, the lab boys say."

Pym moistened dry lips. "And I checked it myself. I bloody *passed* it." His teeth clenched. "She was going to wear them to—M'lord would have—" He choked himself off and ran a hand over his face, hard.

"Does ImpSec know who really sent them?" asked Taura.

"Not yet. But they're all over it, you can believe."

A vision of the deadly pale spheres lying on m'lady-tobe's warm throat flashed through Roic's memory. "Madame Vorsoisson touched the pearls last night—night before last, that is now," said Roic urgently. "She had them on for at least five minutes. Is she going to be all right?"

"ImpSec is dispatching a physician to Lord Auditor Vorthys's to check her—one of their toxins experts. If she'd taken in enough to kill her, she'd have died right then, so *that's* not going to happen, but I don't know what other . . . I have to go now and call m'lord there and warn him to expect a visitor. And—and tell him why. Well done, Roic. Did I say well done? Well done." Pym drew a shaken, unhappy, breath and strode back out.

Taura, her chin in her hand as she drooped over her plate, scowled after him. "Jacksonian neurotoxin, eh? That doesn't prove much. The Jacksonians will sell anything to anyone. Miles made enough enemies there in some of our old sorties—if they knew it was intended for him, they'd probably offer a deep discount."

"Yeah, I imagine tracing the source is going to take a little longer. Even for ImpSec." He hesitated. "Although, wouldn't they know him on Jackson's Whole only under his old covert ops identity? Your little admiral?"

"That cover's been well-blown for a couple of years, he tells me. Partly as a result of the mess his last mission there produced, partly from some other things. Over my head." She yawned, hugely. It was . . . impressive. She'd been up since dawn, Roic was reminded, and hadn't slept through the afternoon as he had. Stranded in what must seem to her an alien place and wrestling terrible fears. All by herself.

For the first time, he wondered if she was lonely. One of a kind, the last of her kind if he understood correctly, WIthout home or kin except for that chancy wandering mercenary fleet. And then he wondered why he hadn't noticed her essential aloneness sooner. Armsmen were supposed to be observant. *Yeah?*

"If I promise to come by and tell you if I get any news, d'you suppose you could try to sleep?"

She rubbed the back of her neck. "Would you? Then I think I could. Try, that is."

He escorted her to her door, past m'lord's dark and empty suite. When he clasped her hand briefly, she clasped back. He swallowed, for courage.

"Dirty pearls, eh?" he said, still holding her hand. "Y'know . . . I can't speak for any other Barrayarans . . . but *I* think your genetic modifications are beautiful."

Her lips curved up, he hoped not altogether bleakly. "You *are* getting better."

When she let go and turned in, a claw trailing lightly over the skin of his palm made his body shudder in involuntary, sensual surprise. He stared at the closing door and swallowed a perfectly foolish urge to call her back. Or follow her inside . . . He was still on duty, he reminded himself. The next monitors check was overdue. He forced himself to turn away.

The sky outside was shifting from the amber night of the city to a chill blue dawn when the gate guard called Roic to code down the house shields for m'lord's return. As the armsman who'd been called out to chauffeur drove the big car off to put away, Roic opened one door to admit the hunched, frowning figure. M'lord looked up to recognize Roic, and a rather ghastly smile lightened his furrowed features.

Roic had seen m'lord looking strung-out before, but never so alarmingly as this, not even after one of his bad seizures or when he'd had that spectacular hangover after the disastrous butter bug banquet. His eyes stared out from gray circles like feral animals from their dens. His skin was pale, and lines of tension mapped the anxiety across his face. His movements were simultaneously. tired and stiff, and jerky and nervous, a spinning exhaustion that could find no place of rest.

"Roic. Thank you. Bless you," m'lord began in a voice that sounded as though it were coming from the bottom of a well.

"Is m'lady-to-be all right?" Roic asked in some apprehension.

M'lord nodded. "Yes, now. She fell asleep in my arms, finally, after the ImpSec doctor left. God, Roic! I can't believe I missed the signs. Poisoning! And I fastened that death around her neck with my own hands! It's a damned metaphor for this whole thing, that's what it is. She thought it was just her. *I* thought it was just her. How little faith in herself, or me in her, to misidentify dying of poison for dying of self-doubt?"

"She's *not* dying, is she?" Roic asked again, to be sure. In this spate of dramatic angst, it was a little hard to tell. "T' bit of exposure she got isn't going to have any permanent effects, is it?"

M'lord began to pace in circles around the entry hall, while Roic followed vainly trying to take his coat. "The doctor, said not, not once the headaches pass off, which they seem to have done now. She was so relieved to find out what it really was she burst into tears. Go figure *that* one out, eh?"

"Yeah, except that—" Roic began, then bit his tongue. Except that the crying jag he'd inadvertently witnessed had occurred well before the poisoning.

"What?"

"Nothing, m'lord."

Lord Vorkosigan paused at the archway to the anitechamber. "ImpSec. We must call ImpSec to take away all those gifts and recheck them for—"

"They already came and collected them, m'lord," Roic soothed him, or tried to. "An hour ago. They say they'll try get as many as possible cleared and back before the wedding guests start arriving come midafternoon."

"Oh, Good." M'lord stood still a moment, staring into nothing, and Roic finally managed to get his coat away from him.

"M'lord . . . *you* don't think your Admiral Quinn sent that necklace, do you?"

"Oh, good heavens, no. Of course not." M'lord dismissed this fear with a startlingly casual wave of his hand. "Not her style at all. If she were ever that mad at me she'd kick me downstairs personally. Great woman, Quinn."

"Sergeant Taura was worried. I think she thought this Ouinn might a' been, um, jealous."

M'lord blinked. "Why? I mean, yes, it's almost exactly a year since Elli and I parted company, but Ekaterin had nothing to do with *that*. Didn't even meet her till a couple of months later. The timing's pure coincidence, you can assure her. Yeah, so Elli turned down the wedding invitation—she has responsibilities. She got the fleet, after all." A small sigh escaped him. His lips screwed up in further thought. "I'd sure like to know who knew enough to steal Quinn's name to smuggle that hellish package in here, though. *That's* the real puzzle. Quinn's connected to Admiral Naismith, not to Lord Vorkosigan. Which was the sticking point in the first place, but never mind now. I want ImpSec to put every available resource on to tearing *that* one apart."

"I believe they already are, m'lord."

"Oh. Good." He looked up, and his face grew, if possible, more serious. "You saved my House last night, you know. Eleven generations of Vorkosigans have narrowed down to the choke point of me, this generation, this marriage. I'd have been the last, but for that chance—no, not chance—that moment of shrewd observation."

Roic waved an embarrassed hand. "Wasn't me who spotted it, m'lord. It was Sergeant Taura. She'd have reported it herself earlier, if she hadn't been half taken in by t' bad guy's nasty camouflage with your, um, friend Admiral Quinn's name."

M'lord took, up his taut orbit of the hall again. "Bless Taura, then. A woman beyond price. Which I already knew, but anyway. I could kiss her feet, by God. I could kiss her all over!"

Roic was beginning to think that line about the barbed wire choke chain wasn't such a joke after all. All this frenetic tension was, if not precisely infectious, starting to get on what was left of his nerves. He remarked dryly, in Pymlike periods, "I was given to understand you already had, m'lord."

M'lord jerked to a halt again. "Who told you that?" Under the circumstances, Roic decided not to mention Madame Vorsoisson. "Taura."

"Eh, maybe it's the women's secret code. I don't have the key, though. You're on your own there, boy." He snorted a trifle hysterically. "But if you ever *do* win an invitation from her, beware— it's like being mugged in a dark alley by a goddess. You're not the same man after. Not to mention critical feminine, body parts on a scale you can actually *find*, and as for the fangs, there's no thrill quite like—"

"Miles," a bemused voice interrupted from overhead. Roic glanced up to see the countess, wrapped in a robe, leaning over the balcony railing and observing her son. How long had she been standing there? She was Betan; maybe m'lord's last remarks wouldn't discombobulate her as much as they did Roic. In fact, he reflected, he was certain they couldn't.

"Good morning, Mother," m'lord managed. "Some bastard tried to poison Ekaterin, did you hear? When I catch up with him, I swear I'm going to make the Dismemberment of Mad Emperor Yuri look like a house party—"

"Yes, ImpSec has kept your father and me fully apprised during the night, and I just spoke with Helen. Everything seems under control for the moment, except for persuading Pym not to throw himself off the Star Bridge in expiation. He's pretty distraught over this slipup. For pity's sake, come up and take a sleeptimer and lie down for a while."

"I don't want a pill. I have to check the garden. I have to recheck everything—"

"The garden is fine. Everything is fine. As you have just discovered in Armsman Roic here, your staff is more than competent." She started down the stairs, a distinctly steely look in her eye. "It's either a sleeptimer or a sledgehammer for you, son. I am *not* handing you off to your blameless bride in the state you're in, or the worse one it'll be if you don't get some real sleep before this afternoon. It's not fair to her."

"Nothing about this marriage is fair to her," m'lord muttered, bleak. "She was afraid it would be the nightmare of her old marriage all over again. No! It's going to be a completely *different* nightmare— much *worse*. How can I ask her to step into my line of fire if—"

"As I recall, she asked *you*. I was there, remember? Stop gibbering." The countess took his arm, and began more or less frog-marching him upstairs. Roic made a mental note of her technique for future reference. She glanced over her shoulder and gave Roic a reassuring, if rather unexpected, wink.

The brief remainder of the most memorable night shift of his career passed, to Roic's relief, without further incident of note. He dodged excited maidservants hurrying to the big day's tasks and mounted the stairs to his tiny fourth-floor bedroom thinking that m'lord wasn't the only one who should get some sleep before the afternoon's more public duties. M'lord's last, decidedly free-floating comments kept him awake for some time, though, beguiling him with visions of somewhat shocking charm. Such as he'd never dreamed of back in Hassadar. He fell asleep with his lips curling up.

A few minutes before his alarm was set to go off, Roic was awakened by Armsman Jankowski tapping at his bedroom door.

"Pym says you're to report to m'lord's suite right away. Some kind of briefing—you don't have to be in your uniform yet."

"Right."

Dress uniform, Jankowski meant, although Jankowski was already sharp in his own. Roic slipped on last night's wear and ran a comb through his hair, frowned in frustration at his beard shadow—*right away* presumably meant just that—and hurried downstairs.

Roic found m'lord in his suite's sitting room, halfway dressed in a silk shirt, the brown trousers with silver sidepiping and the silver-embroidered suspenders that went-with and slippers. He was attended by his cousin Ivan Vorpatril, resplendent in his own House's blue-and-gold uniform. As m'lord's Second and chief witness in the imminent ceremony, Lord Ivan was also playing groom's batman as well as general supporter.

One of Roic's fonder secret memories from the past weeks was of witnessing, in his role as disregarded coatrack, the great Viceroy Count Vorkosigan himself taking this handsome nephew aside and promising, in a voice so low as to be almost a whisper, to have Ivan's hide for a drumskin if he allowed his misplaced sense of fun to do *anything at all* to screw up the impending ceremony for m'lord. Ivan had been humorless as a judge all week; sidebets were being taken belowstairs for how long it would last. Remembering that deeply ominous voice, Roic had selected the longest shot in the pool—and thought himself likely to win.

Taura, also in last night's gear of skirt and lacy blouse, lounged on one of the small sofas in the bay window, apparently offering bracing advice. M'lord had evidently taken the sleeptimer, for he looked vastly better: clean, shaved, clear-eyed, and very nearly calm.

"Ekaterin's here," he told Roic, in the awed tone of a besieged garrison commander describing the unexpected relieving force. "The bride's party is using my mother's suite for their staging area. Mother's going to bring her down in a moment. She needs to be in on this."

In on what? was answered before Roic could voice the question by the entry of ImpSec chief General Allegre himself; in dress greens, escorted by the count, also already in his best House uniform. Allegre was a wedding guest in his own right, but it clearly wasn't for social reasons that he'd arrived an hour early.

The countess and Ekaterin followed on their heels, the countess graceful in something sparkling and green, m'lady-to-be still in her drab dress but with her hair already braided up and thickly entwined with tiny roses and other exquisite little scented flowers that Roic could not name. Both women looked grave, but a smile like a fugitive gleam from paradise lit Ekaterin's eyes as they met m'lord's. Roic found he had to look away from that brief intensity, feeling a clumsy intruder. He thus surprised Taura's expression: shrewdly approving, but more than a little wistful.

Ivan drew up extra chairs, and all disposed themselves around the small table near the window. Madame Vorsoisson took a seat beside m'lord, decorously but with no wasted centimeters between. He gripped her hand. Roic managed to slip in next to Taura; she smiled down at him. These chambers had once belonged to the late great General Piotr Vorkosigan, before they'd been claimed by his grandson, the rising young Lord Auditor. This spot, not the grand public rooms downstairs, was the site of more military, political, and secret conferences of historic import to Barrayar than Roic could readily imagine.

"I dropped by early to give you ImpSec's latest report in person, Miles, Madame Vorsoisson, Count, Countess." Allegre, half-leaning on a sofa arm, nodded around. He reached into his tunic and withdrew a plastic bag in which something white glimmered and gleamed. "And to return these. I had my forensics people clean them after collecting and recording the evidence. They're safe now."

Gingerly, m'lord took the pearls from his hand and set them down on the table. "And do you know yet who gets the thank-you note for this gift? I'm rather hoping to deliver it in person." Ill-concealed menace vibrated beneath his light tone.

"That has actually broken open much faster than I was expecting," said Allegre. "It was a *very* nice forgery job on the date stamps from Escobar on the outer packaging, but the inner decorative wrapping checked out under analysis as of Barrayaran origin. Once we knew which planet to look on, the item was sufficiently unique—the necklace *is* of Earth origin, by the way—we were able to trace it by jeweler's import records almost at once. It was purchased two weeks ago in Vorbarr Sultana for a large sum of cash, and the store security vids for the month hadn't been erased yet. My agent positively identified Lord Vorbataille."

M'lord hissed through his teeth. "He was on my short list, yes. No wonder he was trying so hard to get off planet."

"He was up to his eyebrows in the plan, but he wasn't its originator. Do you remember how you said to me three weeks ago that while there had to be brains behind this operation, you'd swear they weren't in Vorbataille's head?"

"Yes," said m'lord. "I had him pegged for a front man, suborned for his connections. And his yacht, of course."

"You were right. We picked up his Jacksonian crime consultant about three hours ago."

"You have him!"

"We have him. He'll keep, now." Allegre gave m'lord a grim nod. "Although he had the wit to *not* bring attention to himself by trying to get off planet, one of my analysts, who came in last night to look over the new evidence that came in with the necklace, was able to run a back-trace and cross-connect, and so identify him. Well, actually he fingered three suspects, but fast-penta cleared two of them. The source for the toxin was a fellow by the name of Luca Tarpan."

M'lord mouthed the syllables; his face screwed up. "Damn. Are you sure? I've never heard of him."

"Quite sure. He appears to have ties with the Bharapu'a syndicate on Jackson's Whole."

"Well, that would give him access to quite a lot of somewhat scrambled two-year-old information about me and Quinn, yes. Both mes, in fact. And it accounts for the superior forgery. But why such a heinous attack? It's almost *more* distubing to think that some total stranger would—Have we crossed paths before?"

Allegre shrugged. "It seems not. The preliminary interrogation suggests it was a purely professional ploy—though he clearly had no love left for you by the time you were about half done ripping open this case. Your talent for making interesting new enemies has evidently not deserted you. The plan was to create distracting chaos in your investigation just after the group made its getaway— Vorbataille was preselected to be thrown to us for a goat, it turns out—but we shut them down about eight days early. The necklace had only just been slipped into the delivery service's records and dispatched at that point."

M'lord's teeth set. "You've had Vorbataille in your hands for two days. And fast-penta didn't turn this up?"

Allegre grimaced. "I just reviewed the transcripts before I drove over here. It came very close to surfacing. But to get an answer, even—especially—under fast-penta, as useful a truth drug as it is, you must first know enough to ask the question. My interrogators were concentrating on the *Princess Olivia.* It *was* Vorbataille's yacht that was used to insert the hijacking team, by the way."

"Knew it had to be," grunted m'lord.

"We'd have caught up with this necklace scheme in a few more days on our own, I think," said Allegre,

M'lord glanced at his chrono and said rather thickly, "You'd have caught up with it in about one more hour, actually. On your own,"

Allegre tilted his head in frank acknowledgment. "Yes, unfortunately. Madame Vorsoisson"—he touched his brow in a considerably more formal gesture than the usual ImpSec salute—"on behalf of myself and my organization, I wish to offer you my most abject apologies. My Lord Auditor. Count. Countess." He looked up at Roic and Taura, sitting side by side on the sofa opposite. "Fortunately, ImpSec was not your last line of defense."

"Indeed," rumbled the count, who had seated himself on a straight chair turned backward, arms comfortably crossed over its back, listening intently but without comment till now. Countess Vorkosigan stood by his side; her hand touched his shoulder, and he caught it under his own thicker one.

Allegre said, "Illyan once told me that half the secret of House Vorkosigan's preeminence in Barrayaran history was the quality of the people it drew to its service. I'm glad to see this continues to hold true. Armsman Roic, Sergeant Taura—ImpSec salutes you with more gratitude than I can rightly express." He did so, in a sober gesture altogether free of his sporadic irony.

"Well, love,"—m'lord blew out his breath, staring down at the plastic bag—"I think that's your final warning. Travel with me and you travel into hazard. I don't want it to be so. But it's going to go on being so, as long as I serve . . . what I serve."

M'lady-to-be glanced at the countess, whose return smile was decidedly twisted. "I never imagined it would be otherwise for a Lady Vorkosigan."

I'll have these destroyed," m'lord said, reaching for the pearls.

"No," said m'lady-to-be, her eyes narrowing. "Wait."

He paused, raising his eyebrows at her.

"They were sent to me. They're *my* souvenir. I shall keep them. I'd have worn them as a courtesy to your friend." She reached past him and scooped up the bag, tossed it up and caught it again out of the air, her long fingers closing tightly around it. Her edged smile took Roic aback. "I'll wear them now as a defiance to our enemies."

M'lord's eyes blazed back at her.

The countess seized the moment—possibly, Roic thought, to cut off her son from further blithering—and tapped her chrono. "Speaking of wearing things, it's time to get dressed."

M'lord went a shade paler. "Yes, of course." He kissed m'lady-to-be's hand as she rose, looking as if he never wanted to let it go again. Countess Vorkosigan herded everyone except m'lord and his cousin into the hallway, shutting the door to the suite firmly behind her.

"He looks much better now," said Roic to her, glancing back. "I think your sleeptimer was just t' thing."

"Yes, plus the tranquilizers I had Aral give him when he went in to wake him up a while ago. The double dose seems to have been just about right." She hooked her arm through her husband's.

"Still think it should have been a triple," he murmured.

"Now, now. Calm, not comatose, is the goal for our groom." She escorted Madame Vorsoisson toward the stairs; the count went off with Allegre, taking advantage of the chance to discuss details, or perhaps drinks, in private.

Taura stared after them, her smile askew. "You know, I wasn't sure about that woman for Miles at first, but I think she'll do him very well. That Vor thing of his always baffled Elli. Ekaterin has it in her bones same as he does. God help them both."

Roic had been about to say that he thought m'lady-to-be *better* than m'lord deserved, but Taura's last remark brought him up short. "Huh. Yeah. She's true Vor, all right. It's no easy thing."

Taura started down the corridor but stopped at the corner and half-turned back to ask, "So, what are you doing after the party?"

"Night guard duty." *All bloody week,* Roic realized in dismay. And Taura only had ten days left on-planet.

"Ah."

She whisked away; Roic glanced at his chrono and gulped. The generous time he'd allotted to dress and report for wedding duty was almost gone. He ran for the stairs.

The guests were already starting to arrive, spilling from the entry hall through the succession of flower-graced public rooms, when Roic scuffed quickly down the staircase to take up his allotted place as backup to Armsman Pym, in backing up Count and Countess Vorkosigan. Some on-site guests were already in place Lady Alys Vorpatril, acting as assistant hostess and general expediter, and her benevolently absentminded escort, Simon Illyan; the Bothari-Jeseks; Mayhew, in apparent permanent tow of Nikki; an assortment of Vorvaynes who had overflowed from Lord Auditor Vorthys's packed house to Vorkosigan House guest rooms. M'lord's friend Commodore Galeni, Chief of ImpSec Komarran Affairs, and his wife were early arrivals, along with m'lord's special Progressive Party colleagues, the Vorbrettens and the Vorrutyers.

Commodore Koudelka and his spouse, known universally as Kou and Drou, arrived with their daughter Martya. Martya was standing in as Madame Vorsoisson's Second in place of m'lady-to-be's closest friend-yet another Koudelka daughter, Kareen, still at school on Beta Colony. Kareen and m'lord's brother, Lord Mark, were much missed (albeit, in remembrance of the bug butter incident, not by Roic) but the interstellar travel time had proved too tight for their schedules. Lord Mark's wedding present was a gift certificate for the bridal couple for a week at an exlusive and very expensive Betan resort, however, so perhaps m'lord and his lady would soon be visiting his brother and their friend, not to mention m'lord's Betan relatives. As gifts went, it at least had the advantage of shifting all the security challenges inherent in the trip to some *later time.*

Martya was sped upstairs by a maid detailed to that purpose. Martya's escort and Lord Mark's business partner, Dr. Borgos, was quietly taken aside by Pym for an unscheduled frisking for any surprise gift insects he might have been harboring, but this time the scientist proved clean. Martya returned unexpectedly soon, her brow wrinkled thoughtfully, and repossessed him to stroll off in search of drinks and company.

Lord Auditor and Professora Vorthys arrived with the rest of the Vorvaynes, altogether a goodly company: four brothers, three wives, ten children, and m'lady-to-be's father and stepmother, in addition to her beloved aunt and uncle. Roic glimpsed Nikki showing off Arde to his mob of awed young Vorvayne cousins, pressing the jump pilot to decant galactic war stories to this enthralled audience. Nikki didn't, Roic noted, seem to have to press very hard. The Betan pilot grew downright expansive in the warm glow of these attentions.

The Vorvayne side stood up bravely to the glittering company that was Vorkosigan House's norm—well, Lord Auditor Vorthys was notoriously oblivious to any status not backed by proven engineering expertise. But even the bride's most buoyant older brother grew subdued and thoughtful when Count Gregor and Countess Laisa Vorbarra were announced. The emperor and empress had chosen to attend the supposedly informal afternoon affair as social equals to the Vorkosigans, which saved a world of protocol hassles for everyone, not least themselves. Not in any other uniform but that of his Count's House could the emperor have publicly embraced his little foster brother Miles, who ran downstairs to greet him, nor been so sincerely embraced in return.

In all, m'lord's "little" wedding numbered one hundred twenty guests. Vorkosigan House absorbed them all.

At last, the moment arrived; the hall and antechambers became brief, crowded chaos as wraps were redonned and the guests all streamed out the gate and around the corner to the garden. The air was cold but not bitter, and thankfully windless, the sky a deepening clear blue, the slanting afternoon sun liquid gold. It turned the snowy garden into as gilded, glittering, spectacular and utterly unique a showplace as m'lord's heart could ever have desired. The flowers and ribbons were concentrated around the central place where the vows were to be, complementing the wild brilliance of the ice and snow and light.

Although Roic was fairly sure that the two realistically detailed ice rabbits humping under a discreet bush were *not* part of the decorations m'lord had ordered. They did not pass unnoticed, as the first person to observe them immediately pointed them out to everyone within earshot. Ivan Vorpatril averted his gaze from the cheerfully obscene artwork—the rabbits were grinning—a look of innocence on his face. The count's menacing glower at him was as undercut by an escaping snicker, which became a guffaw when the countess whispered something in his ear.

The groom's party took up their positions. In the center of the garden, the walkways, swept clear of snow, met at a wide circle of paving brick, with the Vorkosigan crest of mountains and maple leaves picked out in contrasting brick. In this obvious' spot, the small circle of colored groats was laid out on the ground for the oath-making couple, surrounded by a multipointed star for the principal witnesses, Another circle of groats crowned a temporary paththway of tanbark flung wide around the first two rings, providing dry footing for the rest of the guests.

Roic, wearing a sword for the first time since he'd taken his liegeman's oath, took his place in the formal lineup of armsmen making an aisle on either side of the main pathway. He looked around in worry, for Taura did not loom up among the groom's guests sorting themselves out along the outer circle. M'lord, his hand clutching his cousin Ivan's blue sleeve, gazed up at the entrance in almost painful anticipation. M'lord had, with difficulty, been talked out of hauling his horse in to town to fetch the bride from the house in the old Vor style, though Roic personally had no doubt that the placid, elderly steed would have proved much less nervous and difficult to handle than its master. So the Vorvayne party made their entrance on foot.

Lady Alys, as Coach, led the way like some silken banner carrier. The bride followed on her blinking father's arm, shimmering in a jacket and skirt of beige velvet embroidered with shining silver, her booted feet striding out fearlessly, her eyes seeking only one other face in the mob. The triple stand of pearls gracing her throat glimmered their secret message of bravado to only a few persons here. A few extraordinary persons. By his narrowed eyes and wryly pursed lips, it was clear that Emperor Gregor was one of them.

Roic's might have been the sole gaze not to linger on the bride, for following beside her stepmother, in the place of—no, *as*—the bride's Second, walked Sergeant Taura. Roic's eyes shifted, though he kept his rigid posture—yes, there was Martya Koudelka with Dr. Borgos on the outer circle, apparently demoted to the status of mere guest but not looking in the least put-out. In fact, she seemed to be watching Taura with smug approval. Taura's dress was everything that Lady Alys had. promised. Champagnecolored velvet exactly matched her eyes, which seemed to spring to a brilliant prominence in her face. The jacket sleeves and long swinging skirt were decorated on their margins with black cord shaped into winding patterns. Champagne-colored orchids coiled in her bound-back hair.

Roic thought he'd never seen anything so stunningly sophisticated in his life.

Everyone took their places. M'lord and m'lady-to-be stepped into the inner circle, hands gripping hands like two lovers drowning. The bride looked not so much radiant as incandescent; the groom looked gobsmacked. Lord Ivan and Taura were handed the two little bags of groats with which to close the circle, then stood back to their star points between Count and Countess Vorkosigan and Vorvayne and his wife. Lady Alys read out the vows, and m'lord and m'lady-to—*m'lady* repeated their responses, her voice clear, his only cracking once. The kiss was managed with remarkable grace, m'lady somehow bending her knee in a curtsylike motion so m'lord didn't have to stretch unduly. It suggested thought and practice. Lots of practice.

With immense panache, Lord Ivan then swept the groat circle wide with one booted foot, triumphantly collecting his kiss from the bride as she exited. Lord and Lady Vorkosigan passed out of the dazzling ice garden between the lines of Vorkosigan armsmen; swords, drawn and lowered at their feet, rose in salute as they passed. When Pym led the Armsmen's Shout, the sound of twenty enthusiastic male voices bounced and echoed off the garden walls and thundered to the sky. M'lord grinned over his shoulder and blushed with pleasure at this deafening endorsement.

As Seconds, Taura followed next on Lord Ivan's arm, bending her head to hear something he said, laughing. The row of armsmen remained to rigid attention while all the principals streamed past them, then formed up and marched smartly in their wake, followed by the guests, back around and into Vorkosigan House. It had all gone off *perfectly.* Pym looked as though he wanted to pass out there and then from sheer relief.

Vorkosigan House's main state dining room boasted seatting for ninety-six when both tables were brought out in parallel the overflow fit in the chamber immediately beyond, through a wide archway, so that the whole company could sit down at once essentially together. Serving was not Roic's responsibility tonight, but in his role as arbiter of emergencies and general assistant for any guest needing anything, he kept to his feet and moving. Taura was seated at the head table with the principals and the most honored guests—the *other* most honored guests. Between tall, dark, handsome Lord Ivan and tall, dark, lean Emperor Gregor, she looked *really* happy. Roic could not wish her anywhere else, but he found himself mentally erasing Ivan and replacing him with himself . . . yet Ivan and the emperor were the very pattern of debonair wit. They made Taura laugh, fangs flashing without constraint. Roic would probably just sit there in inarticulate silence and gawp at her . . .

Martya Koudelka passed him in the entryway, where he'd temporarily taken up guard stance, and smiled cheerily at him. "Hi, Roic."

He nodded. "Miss Martya."

She followed his glance to the head table. "Taura looks wonderful, doesn't she?"

"Sure does." He hesitated. "How come you're not up there?"

Her voice lowered. "I heard the story about last night from Ekaterin. She asked me if I'd mind trading. I said, *God, no.* Gets me out of having to sit there and make small talk with Ivan, for one thing." She wrinkled her nose.

"It was well thought of, of m'lady,"

She hitched up one shoulder. "It was the one honor here that was wholly hers to bestow. The Vorkosigans are amazing, but you have to admit, they do eat you up. They give you a wild ride in return, though." She stood on tiptoe and planted an unexpected kiss on Roic's cheek.

He touched the spot in surprise. "What's that for?"

"For your half of last night. For saving us all from having to live with a *really* insane Miles Vorkosigan. As long as he lasted." A brief quaver shook her flippant voice. She tossed her blond hair and bounced off.

The toasts were made with the count's very best wines, including a few historical bottles, reserved for the head table, that had been laid down before the end of the Time of Isolation. Afterward the party moved to the brilliant ballroom, seeming another garden, heady with the scent of a sudden spring. Lord and Lady Vorkosigan opened the dancing. Those who could still move after the dinner followed them onto the polished marquetry floor.

Roic found himself, all too briefly, passing by Taura as she watched the dancers sway and twirl.

"Do you dance, Roic?" she asked him.

"Can't. I'm on duty. You?"

I'm afraid I don't know any of these dances. Although, I'm sure Miles would have foisted an instructor on me if he'd thought of it."

"Actually," he admitted in a lower voice, "I don't know how either."

Her lips curled up. "Well, don't let Miles know if you want it to stay that way. He'd have you out there thumping around before you knew what hit you."

He tried not to snicker. He hardly knew what to say to this, but his parting half-salute did not betoken disagreement.

On the sixth number, m'lady danced past Roic with her eldest brother, Hugo.

"Splendid necklace, Kat. From your spouse, is it?"

No, actually. From one of his . . . business associates."

"Expensive!"

"Yes." M'lady's faint smile made the hairs stir on Roic's arms.

"I expect it to cost him everything he has."

They spun away.

Taura nailed it. She'll do for m'lord, all right. And God help their enemies.

Promptly on schedule, the aircar was brought round for the bridal couple's getaway. The night was still fairly young, but it was more than an hour's flight to Vorkosigan Surleau and the lakeside estate that was to be the honeymoon refuge. The place would be quiet this time of year, blanketed with snow and peace. Roic could not imagine two people more in need of a little peace.

The guests in residence were to be left behind under the care of the count and countess for a few days, although the galactic guests would travel down to the lake later. Among other things, Roic was given to understand, Madame Bothari-Jesek wished to visit her father's grave there with her husband and new daughter and burn a death offering.

Roic had thought Pym would be doing the flying, but to his surprise, Armsman Jankowski took the controls as the newlyweds ran the gauntlet of raucous family and friends and made it to the rear compartment.

"I've shuffled some assignments," Pym murmured to Roic as they both stood smiling in the porte cochere to watch and salute. M'lord and m'lady seemed to melt into each other's arms in an equal mix of love and exhaustion as the silvered canopy finally closed over them. "I'm taking night watch in Vorkosigan House for the next week. *You* have the week off with double holiday pay. With m'lady's own thanks."

"Oh," said Roic. He blinked. Pym had been quite frustrated by the fact that no one, from the count down, had seen fit to censure him for the slipup with the necklace. He could only conclude that Pym had given up and decided to supply his own penance. Well, if the senior armsman looked to be carrying it too far, the countess could be relied upon to step in. "Thanks!"

"You can consider yourself free from whenever Count and Countess Vorbarra leave." Pym nodded and stepped back as the aircar eased out from under the overhang and began to rise into the cold night air as if buoyed up by the yells and cheers of the well-wishers.

A splendid and prolonged burst of fireworks made the send-off a thing of beauty and a joy to Barrayaran hearts. Taura applauded and hooted, too, and, along with Arde Mayhew, joined Nikki's cohort for some added, unscheduled crackers and sparklers in the back garden. Powder smoke perfumed the air in clouds as the children ran around Taura, urging her to throw the lights *higher*. Security and an assortment of mothers might have quashed the game, except for the fact that the large bag of most remarkable incendiary goodies had been slipped to Nikki by Count Vorkosigan.

The party wound down. Sleepy, protesting children were carried past Roic to their cars or to their beds. The emperor and empress were seen out fondly by the count and countess; soon after their departure, a score of unobtrusive, efficient servants, on loan from ImpSec, vanished quietly and without fanfare. The remaining energetic young people hijacked the ballroom to dance to music more to their taste. Their tired elders sought quieter corners in the succession of public rooms in which to converse and sam, le more of the count's very best wines.

Roic found Taura sitting alone in one of the small side rooms on a sturdy-looking sofa of the style she favored, reflectively working her way through a platter of Ma Kosti's dainties on a low table before her. She looked drowsy and contented, and yet little apart from it all. As if she were a guest in her own life . . .

Roic gave her a smile, a nod, a semi-salute. He wished he'd thought to provide himself with roses or something. What could a fellow give to a woman like this? The finest chocolate, maybe, yeah, although that was redundant at the moment. Tomorrow for sure. "Um . . . have you had a good time?"

"Oh, yes. Wonderful."

She sat back and smiled almost up at him—an unusual angle of view. She looked good from this direction, too. M'lord's comment about horizontal height differentials drifted through his memory. She patted the sofa beside her; Roic glanced around, overcame his guard-stance habits, and sat down. His feet hurt, he realized.

The silence that fell was companionable, not strained, but after a time he broke it. "You like Barrayar, then?"

"It's been a great visit. Better than my best dreams."

Ten more days. Ten days was an eyeblink. Ten days was just not enough for all he had to say, to give, to do. Ten years might be a start. "You, uh, have you ever thought of staying? Here? It could be done, y'know. Find a place you would fit. Or make one." M'lord would figure out how, if anyone could. With great daring, he let his hand curl over hers on the seat between them.

Her brows rose. "I already have a place I fit."

"Yeah, but . . . forever? Your mercs seem like a chancy sort of thing to me. No solid ground under them. And nothing lasts forever, not even organizations."

"*Nobody* lives long enough to have *all* their choices."

She was silent for a moment, then added, "The people who bioengineered me to be a super-soldier didn't consider a long life span to be a necessity. Miles has a few biting remarks about that, but oh well. The fleet medics give me about a year yet."

"Oh," It took him a minute to work through this; his stomach felt suddenly tight and cold. A dozen obscure remarks from the past few days fell into place. He wished they hadn't. *No, oh, no . . . !*

"Hey, don't look so bludgeoned." Her hand curled around to clasp his in return. "The bastards have been giving me a year yet for the past four years running. I've seen other soldiers have their whole careers and die in the time the medics have been screwing around with me. I've stopped worrying about it."

He had no idea what to say to this. Screaming was right out. He shifted a bit closer to her instead.

She eyed him thoughtfully. "Some fellows, when I tell them this, get spooked and veer off. It's not contagious."

Roic swallowed hard. "I'm not running away."

"I see that." She rubbed her neck with her free hand; an orchid petal parted from her hair and caught upon her velvet-clad shoulder. "Part of me wishes the medics would get it settled. Part of me says, the hell with it. Every day is a gift. Me, I rip open the package and wolf it down on the spot."

He looked up at her in wonder. His grip tightened, as though she might be pulled from him as they sat, right now, if he didn't hold hard enough. He leaned over, reached across and picked off the fragile petal, touched it to his lips. He took a deep, scared breath. "Can you teach me how to do that?"

Her fantastic gold eyes widened. "Why, Roic! I think that's the most delicately worded proposition I've ever received. S' beautiful." An uncertain pause. "Um, that *was* a proposition, wasn't it? I'm not always sure I parlay Barrayaran."

Desperately terrified now, he blurted in what he imagined to be merc-speak, "Ma'am, yes, *ma'am!*"

This won an immense fanged smile—*not* in a version he'd ever seen before. It made him, too, want to fall over backward, though preferably not into a snowbank. He ganced around. The softly lit room was littered with abandoned plates and wineglasses, detritus of pleasure and good company. Low voices chatted idly in the next chamber. Somewhere in another room, softened by the distance, clock was chiming the hour. Roic declined to count the beats.

They floated in a bubble of fleeting time, live heat in the art of a bitter winter. He leaned forward, raised his face slid his hand around her warm neck, drew her face down to his. It wasn't hard. Their lips brushed, locked.

Several minutes later, in a shaken, hushed voice, he breathed, "*Wow.*"

Several minutes after *that,* they went upstairs, hand in hand.

Afterword

I prefer afterwords to prefaces, in most cases, because it horrifies me that anything should get between the reader and the tale, including the author. When a reader's attention has overcome every obstacle and is finally focused on the opening page of my book, it's no time to interrupt with a drone of, "And another thing . . . !" Besides, talking about a piece of fiction makes ever so much more sense after one has read it, which sums up the essential difference between a book review (before) and a critical article (after), although this afterword is more that third literary animal, a memoir.

The title of this omnibus was probably inevitable ever since I saw *Shakespeare in Love*, one of my favorite films about writers. My large and unwieldy backlist was already in process of being rounded up and herded into omnibus volumes, and it was clear these present books would someday have their turn. There was a long pause in the collecting process, however, occasioned both by my wandering off to write other things, and because the books from *Memory* onward, taken in series-internal-chronology, did not divide into packages in the neat way the prior volumes had, or not in any way that would come out even. But time and the need to re-license brought the problem back to the table. The other thing that time brought was a new and closely-related novella in the mix, of which more below.

Casting back to the late nineties, a, ye gods, decade ago now. (The calendar goes by faster these days.) My Vorkosigan series had been growing in my mind for a long time by then, and on the bookstore shelves as well. I had already explored blending several genres or styles of story within the putatively-space-opera series: gothic romance, coming-of-age, military, mystery, suspense, Golden Age engineering, and a much less common subject: coming-of-age *again*, because growing up isn't something you do once and then stop; it's a continuous-flow-process over a person's lifetime. And the tricks that worked at first may not work the next time.

This exploration led me to both *Mirror Dance* and *Memory*, two closely related tales where my main character Miles was really forced to come to grips with growing up again, and with the fact that although the questions may be the same—*what is my relationship with my work, my world, myself?*—the answers change. And in those pivotal books his answers changed hugely.

I have noticed a curious bifurcation in outcome in the way romances are written by women and written by men. The popular romances by men—*Love Story, The Bridges of Madison County,* every James Bond tale ever penned, even the film named above—end with the woman either lost or dead. And the man free to love, or at least to have sex, again. Romances (in the modern genre sense) written by women end with the couple alive, together, and in a committed and at least potentially fertile relationship, ready to turn to the work of their world. In other words, men's romances are about love and death; women's romances are about love and life.

Let me add in all fairness, that it's not just in men's romances that the adolescent self is preserved, not allowed to be destroyed even by its own growth, at the cost of slaying the Other. There are some pretty dodgy tropes on the women's side as well that I can only describe as Electra fantasies, although this type of story seems to have fallen out of favor in late years, which I take to be a good social sign. Miles had already experienced a number of men's-style romances by this point in his series, and I don't like to repeat myself. It was time to move him along into the true adulthood at last made possible by his reintegration and improving maturity. (Well . . . somewhat improving. He's *Miles*, after all.)

As an aside here, because I've already had this argument and don't want to have it again, no, I don't think it's marriage-and-children that makes the adult, although learning to meet those demands has grown many a person up, in a kind of on-the-job training. (I'm rather in that camp myself.) It's more of a common symbolic marker of the state; the point at which certain kinds of stories stop and others must take their place. There are a million other adult human activities that serve to foster individuals and the culture—teaching tops the list—but in all cases, there is a shift of focus from the self (most excruciating in adolescence) to the needs of others, from receiving nurture to giving it.

So an—at last—successful romance was the next big step in Miles's growth.

I really, really wanted to write a lighter book after *Memory*. I didn't think I could, or should, attempt two thematically "big", emotionally draining books in a row. It's like spacing pregnancies too close together; it leeches the minerals out of one's bones. But *Komarr* lay across my path to everything else; it had to be done first.

Komarr is the romantic drama, *A Civil Campaign* the romantic comedy. After all, Miles had two births, and will have two deaths, why shouldn't he have two romances? On a practical level, the split of the emotional plot of story into two halves was to solve a problem of tone. I could not have combined the material I dealt with in *Komarr* with a comedy of the goofiness I desired in the same book. It would have been too schizophrenic even for me.

With military plots knocked out of the menu by Miles's prior shift from mercenary admiral to Imperial Auditor, mystery and suspense—and romance—took up the load. Miles is sent to Komarr, a planet his father helped conquer a generation before, in the unenviable position as a hated occupier, to investigate the possible sabotage of a solar mirror designed to help terraform the planet, a very long-range project. There he meets Ekaterin, his female opposite in most ways, whose life has been as restricted as his has been adventurous. Each, it turns out, has value to offer the other, this time across boundaries of culturally-mandated gender splits. The backdrop of a cold world requiring decades of dedication to bring to fruitfulness is not accidental.

The character of Ekaterin also gave me a way to explore a lot of women's-life realities that were just not within Miles's scope. Miles is an enormously flexible character—hence my ability to put him through so many kinds of plots—but feminist theories about the codedly feminine aside, he just doesn't stretch that far. The romance allowed me to put the two halves of human experience back together, even if not in one person.

Also feeling that it would be nice to get some actual *science fiction* back into this rather organic series, I did a certain amount of research on then-current terraforming theories by the sort of folks who crunched real numbers instead of just hand-waving. A book titled, reasonably enough, *Terraforming* by Martyn J. Fogg (1995) gave me an authentic engineer's view, and allowed me a certain amount of verisimilitude in my setting. The model for Lord Auditor Vorthys, a distinguished senior professor with a lot of experience in analyzing accidents and engineering failures, I had ready-to-hand in my memories of my own father, not to mention in books filched from his shelves such as the now dimly-remembered *The Probable Cause*, a memoir by an early plane crash investigator. The wormhole physics in my plot is genuine hand-waving, however, even if—I hope—it's internally consistent. The social consequences which flow from the structure of the Nexus that the wormholes grant are perhaps more open to real-world critique.

Meanwhile, I'd been itching to write a Barrayaran Regency romance ever since I realized I'd given Barrayar a regency period. I dedicated it to four inspiring female writers. I'd read Charlotte Bronte's *Jane Eyre* fairly early on, but I only came to Georgette Heyer and Dorothy L. Sayers in my twenties, when my reading branched out, and I've only picked up Jane Austen fairly recently. Heyer remains my favorite comfort reading—*A Civil Campaign* is very much a tribute to her— though there was a period when her inherent class-ism got up my nose. Sayers' work, even more than that of C.S. Forester and Arthur Conan Doyle, is a model for the kind of wonderful character development that can only be done over a long series.

The book's title came late to it, when it was already turned in and started on the publication process. *Komarr* had spent most of its earlier drafts titled *Ekaterin*; after experimenting with many kludgy alternatives I finally gave up and just named it after its planet because I already had two other books titled that way—*Barrayar* and *Cetaganda*—and at least it would be consistent with the series. And short. Because it was set against the frenetic backdrop of Emperor Gregor's wedding, *ACC*'s early-draft title was *ImpWed*, a riff on ImpSec, Imperial Security (or, more correctly, "the Dreaded Imperial Security"), Miles's former employer and purveyor of plots. That joke wouldn't do for the bookstore shelves, however, so I approached the problem as Miles would, and tried to dragoon my friends into coming up with something better. Mike Ford passed along the very inspired suggestion *Rules of Engagement,* which seemed perfect— done!—until we discovered that Elizabeth Moon already had that title on a book of hers in Baen's pipeline, oops. Back to the drawing board. The title I finally came up with, all on my own, was a riff on Heyer's *A Civil Contract*, which both sustained the homage and had the advantage of non-duplication. At the moment, there is no other book in print by mine's name.

The tale offered many delicious levels of play, not least that of dissecting a lot of romance tropes under a true SF knife. What happens to the old dance between men, women, and DNA when new technologies explode old definitions of, well, everything? What happens to a tradition-bound society whose channels of property and power assume gender divisions and functions that new science throws into a cocked hat? Just what rude things do those butter bugs symbolize? What happens to two supposedly-immiscible genres when you put them both in a bottle and give it a good shake? What can each say about the other? Chamomile tea and blasters: give me both!

The butterbugs in *A Civil Campaign* have several sources. First, I was a biology major back in my college days, and my faculty advisor was an insect toxicologist. He raised various strains of cockroaches in his lab to test poisons and resistances. (For some reason, the animal rights people never hassled him . . .) His most interesting strain was one which, when he sprinkled roach powder in their plastic boxes, would stand up on their hind two legs with their front four legs on the sides, a behavioral adaptation. I also did a great deal of insect photography during that period.

Second were some wonderful old Robert Sheckley tales read in my youth about a pair of down-on-their-luck spacers and their misadventures with live cargo. Thirdly was the movie *Joe's Apartment*, and fourthly, at about the same time, was a trip to the Minnesota State Fair where I saw, among other things, a large apiary exhibit. I was scratching around for an idea for a short story when the notion of entrepreneur Mark's adventure in bioengineering with Dr. Borgos and his yogurt-barfing bugs first began to take shape. It quickly became apparent both that the idea could not be crammed into the length, and that it was much too good to waste on a mere short story, and so the Vorkosigan House butterbug scheme was born. Or hatched.

The butterbugs have proved very popular with the readers, generating butterbug hand puppets, at least two fan-written songs, and a great deal of speculation as to their future. (Fans have written well over a hundred songs about my stories, to date. And then there are the limericks ...)

In the book, I also explored the multitude of options of technology-meets-romance, what-happens-next? news-at-11 through the three—or rather, two-and-a-half—parallel couples who had the viewpoints, with sidelights from others. Properly speaking, the book ought to have had six viewpoints, but Donna/Dono's was missing; I think my back-brain did that on purpose. But all the subplots—Rene Vorbretten's political-genetic difficulties, Lord Vormuir and his platoon of vat-daughters, Dono's daring raid on the definition of a Countship—served the theme.

Which points up a difference in approach to genre-blending. My reading survey is still very incomplete, but I've noticed some writers from the romance side of the fence tend to drop standard emotional plots into a futuristic setting, and the world-building doesn't always go to the edge of the page. I'm more inclined to ask, "What could this future setting and its technology do to romances?" Which may be, I suppose, why my romances all come out mutants.

The very last Miles story I wrote before breaking off, or out, of the SF milieu to try my hand again at fantasy was the novella "Winterfair Gifts", set against the backdrop of Miles and Ekaterin's wedding. I came to it just after completing *Diplomatic Immunity*, violating my rule against prequels, but not by much. It had its seeds in some ideas and images I'd been kicking around earlier that did not seem to support the weight of a whole novel. But their right-sized container found them when I was approached for an anthology by its editor, Catherine Asaro. She wanted to try some cross-over blending between the usually immiscible genres of F&SF and Romance, a project that appealed to me on many levels. (Reintegration across boundaries, again.) The tale gave me a chance to follow up on Sergeant Taura, and explore the character of Roic, whose development had intrigued me in *Diplomatic Immunity*. I also had some fun with role-reversal, or at least putting some of both men's and women's romance tropes into an SF-nal blender and pushing "puree". I'm not sure if that makes me a mad scientist or just a mad cook, but I had a good time, and I can only trust my readers may do so too.

—Lois McMaster Bujold
Oct. 1, 2007